CW01203271

THE
GODS
TRILOGY

Also by Terry Pratchett

THE CARPET PEOPLE · THE DARK SIDE OF THE SUN
STRATA · TRUCKERS · DIGGERS · WINGS
ONLY YOU CAN SAVE MANKIND
JOHNNY AND THE DEAD · JOHNNY AND THE BOMB
THE UNADULTERATED CAT
(with Gray Jolliffe)

GOOD OMENS
(with Neil Gaiman)

The Discworld® Series:

THE COLOUR OF MAGIC* · THE LIGHT FANTASTIC*
EQUAL RITES* · MORT* · SORCERY · WYRD SISTERS · PYRAMIDS
GUARDS! GUARDS! · ERIC (with Josh Kirby) · MOVING PICTURES
REAPER MAN · WITCHES ABROAD · SMALL GODS · LORDS AND LADIES
MEN AT ARMS · INTERESTING TIMES · MASKERADE · FEET OF CLAY
HOGFATHER · JINGO · THE LAST CONTINENT · CARPE JUGULUM
MORT: A DISCWORLD BIG COMIC (with Graham Higgins)

THE PRATCHETT PORTFOLIO (with Paul Kidby)

THE DISCWORLD COMPANION (with Stephen Briggs)

THE STREETS OF THE ANKH-MORPORK (with Stephen Briggs)

THE DISCWORLD MAPP (with Stephen Briggs)

DEATH'S DOMAIN (with Paul Kidby)

THE DISCWORLD'S UNSEEN UNIVERSITY DIARY 1998
(with Stephen Briggs and Paul Kidby)

THE DISCWORLD'S ANKH-MORPORK CITY WATCH DIARY 1999
(with Stephen Briggs and Paul Kidby)

THE DISCWORLD ASSASSINS' GUILD DIARY 2000 (with Stephen Briggs and Paul Kidby)

* also available as Compact editions

THE
GODS
TRILOGY

Terry Pratchett

VICTOR GOLLANCZ
LONDON

First published as one volume in Great Britain 2000
by Victor Gollancz Ltd
Orion House, 5 Upper St Martin's Lane, London WC2H 9EA

Pyramids © Terry and Lyn Pratchett 1989
Small Gods © Terry and Lyn Pratchett 1992
Hogfather © Terry and Lyn Pratchett 1996

The right of Terry Pratchett to be identified as author
of this work has been asserted by him in accordance with
the Copyright, Designs and Patents Act, 1988.

Discworld® is a trade mark registered by Terry Pratchett.

Second impression 2001

A catalogue record for this book
is available from the British Library

ISBN 0 575 070366

Typeset by Deltatype Ltd, Birkenhead, Merseyside
Printed in Great Britain by
Clays Ltd, St Ives plc

All rights reserved. No part of this publication may be
reproduced or transmitted in any form or by any means,
electronic or mechanical including photocopying, recording
or any information storage or retrieval system,
without prior permission in writing from the publishers.

This book is sold subject to the condition that it shall not,
by way of trade or otherwise, be lent, resold, hired out, or
otherwise circulated without the publisher's prior consent
in any form of binding or cover other than that in which it
is published and without a similar condition including this
condition being imposed on the subsequent purchaser.

CONTENTS

Pyramids   1

Small Gods   241

Hogfather   497

PYRAMIDS

(THE BOOK OF GOING FORTH)

BOOK I

The Book of Going Forth

Nothing but stars, scattered across the blackness as though the Creator had smashed the windscreen of his car and hadn't bothered to stop to sweep up the pieces.

This is the gulf between universes, the chill deeps of space that contain nothing but the occasional random molecule, a few lost comets and ...

... but a circle of blackness shifts slightly, the eye reconsiders perspective, and what was apparently the awesome distance of interstellar wossname becomes a world under darkness, its stars the lights of what will charitably be called civilisation.

For, as the world tumbles lazily, it is revealed as the Discworld – flat, circular, and carried through space on the back of four elephants who stand on the back of Great A'tuin, the only turtle ever to feature on the Hertzsprung-Russell Diagram, a turtle ten thousand miles long, dusted with the frost of dead comets, meteor-pocked, albedo-eyed. No-one knows the reason for all this, but it is probably quantum.

Much that is weird could happen on a world on the back of a turtle like that.

It's happening already.

The stars below are campfires, out in the desert, and the lights of remote villages high in the forested mountains. Towns are smeared nebulae, cities are vast constellations; the great sprawling city of Ankh-Morpork, for example, glows like a couple of colliding galaxies.

But here, away from the great centres of population, where the Circle Sea meets the desert, there is a line of cold blue fire. Flames as chilly as the slopes of Hell roar towards the sky. Ghostly light flickers across the desert.

The pyramids in the ancient valley of the Djel are flaring their power into the night.

The energy streaming up from their paracosmic peaks may, in chapters to come, illuminate many mysteries: why tortoises hate philosophy, why too much religion is bad for goats, and what it is that handmaidens actually *do*.

It will certainly show what our ancestors would be thinking if they were alive today. People have often speculated about this. Would they approve of modern society, they ask, would they marvel at present-day achievements? And of course this misses a fundamental point. What our ancestors would really be thinking, if they were alive today, is: 'Why is it so dark in here?'

In the cool of the river valley dawn the high priest Dios opened his eyes. He didn't sleep these days. He couldn't remember when he last slept. Sleep was too close to the other thing and, anyway, he didn't seem to need it. Just lying down was enough – at least, just lying down *here*. The fatigue poisons dwindled away, like everything else. For a while.

Long enough, anyway.

He swung his legs off the slab in the little chamber. With barely a conscious prompting from his brain his right hand grasped the snake-entwined staff of office. He paused to make another mark on the wall, pulled his robe around him and stepped smartly down the sloping passage and out into the sunlight, the words of the Invocation of the New Sun already lining up in his mind. The night was forgotten, the day was ahead. There was much careful advice and guidance to be given, and Dios existed only to serve.

Dios didn't have the oddest bedroom in the world. It was just the oddest bedroom anyone has ever walked out of.

And the sun toiled across the sky.

Many people have wondered why. Some people think a giant dung beetle pushes it. As explanations go it lacks a certain technical edge, and has the added drawback that, as certain circumstances may reveal, it is possibly correct.

It reached sundown without anything particularly unpleasant happening to it[*], and its dying rays chanced to shine in through a window in the city of Ankh-Morpork and gleam off a mirror.

It was a full-length mirror. All assassins had a full-length mirror in their rooms, because it would be a terrible insult to anyone to kill them when you were badly dressed.

Teppic examined himself critically. The outfit had cost him his last penny, and was heavy on the black silk. It whispered as he moved. It was pretty good.

---

[*] Such as being buried in the sand and having eggs laid in it.

At least the headache was going. It had nearly crippled him all day; he'd been in dread of having to start the run with purple spots in front of his eyes.

He sighed and opened the black box and took out his rings and slipped them on. Another box held a set of knives of Klatchian steel, their blades darkened with lamp black. Various cunning and intricate devices were taken from velvet bags and dropped into pockets. A couple of long-bladed throwing *tlingas* were slipped into their sheaths inside his boots. A thin silk line and folding grapnel were wound around his waist, over the chain-mail shirt. A blowpipe was attached to its leather thong and dropped down his back under his cloak; Teppic pocketed a slim tin container with an assortment of darts, their tips corked and their stems braille-coded for ease of selection in the dark.

He winced, checked the blade of his rapier and slung the baldric over his right shoulder, to balance the bag of lead slingshot ammunition. As an afterthought he opened his sock drawer and took a pistol crossbow, a flask of oil, a roll of lockpicks and, after some consideration, a punch dagger, a bag of assorted caltraps and a set of brass knuckles.

Teppic picked up his hat and checked its lining for the coil of cheesewire. He placed it on his head at a jaunty angle, took a last satisfied look at himself in the mirror, turned on his heel and, very slowly, fell over.

It was high summer in Ankh-Morpork. In fact it was more than high. It was stinking.

The great river was reduced to a lava-like ooze between Ankh, the city with the better address, and Morpork on the opposite bank. Morpork was not a good address. Morpork was twinned with a tar pit. There was not a lot that could be done to make Morpork a worse place. A direct hit by a meteorite, for example, would count as gentrification.

Most of the river bed was a honeycomb crust of cracked mud. Currently the sun appeared to be a big copper gong nailed to the sky. The heat that had dried up the river fried the city by day and baked it by night, curling ancient timbers, turning the traditional slurry of the streets into a drifting, choking ochre dust.

It wasn't Ankh-Morpork's proper weather. It was by inclination a city of mists and drips, of slithers and chills. It sat panting on the crisping plains like a toad on a firebrick. And even now, around midnight, the heat was stifling, wrapping the streets like scorched velvet, searing the air and squeezing all the breath out of it.

High in the north face of the Assassins' Guildhouse there was a click as a window was pushed open.

Teppic, who had with considerable reluctance divested himself of some of the heavier of his weapons, took a deep draught of the hot, dead air.

This was *it*.

This was the *night*.

They said you had one chance in two unless you drew old Mericet as examiner, in which case you might as well cut your throat right at the start.

Teppic had Mericet for Strategy and Poison Theory every Thursday afternoon, and didn't get along with him. The dormitories buzzed with rumours about Mericet, the number of kills, the astonishing technique ... He'd broken all the records in his time. They said he'd even killed the Patrician of Ankh-Morpork. Not the present one, that is. One of the dead ones.

Maybe it would be Nivor, who was fat and jolly and liked his food and did Traps and Deadfalls on Tuesdays. Teppic was good at traps, and got on well with the master. Or it could be the Kompt de Yoyo, who did Modern Languages and Music. Teppic was gifted at neither, but the Kompt was a keen edificeer and liked boys who shared his love of dangling by one hand high above the city streets.

He stuck one leg over the sill and unhitched his line and grapnel. He hooked the gutter two floors up and slipped out of the window.

No assassin ever used the stairs.

In order to establish continuity with later events, this may be the time to point out that the greatest mathematician in the history of the Discworld was lying down and peacefully eating his supper.

It is interesting to note that, owing to this mathematician's particular species, what he was eating for his supper was his lunch.

Gongs around the Ankh-Morpork sprawl were announcing midnight when Teppic crept along the ornate parapet four storeys above Filigree Street, his heart pounding.

There was a figure outlined against the afterglow of the sunset. Teppic paused alongside a particularly repulsive gargoyle to consider his options.

Fairly solid classroom rumour said that if he inhumed his examiner before the test, that was an automatic pass. He slipped a Number Three throwing knife from its thigh sheath and hefted it thoughtfully. Of course, any attempt, any overt move which missed would attract immediate failure and loss of privileges[*].

The silhouette was absolutely still. Teppic's eyes swivelled to the maze of chimneys, gargoyles, ventilator shafts, bridges and ladders that made up the rooftop scenery of the city.

Right, he thought. That's some sort of dummy. I'm supposed to attack it and that means he's watching me from somewhere else.

Will I be able to spot him? No.

On the other hand, maybe I'm *meant* to think it's a dummy. Unless he's thought of that as well . . .

He found himself drumming his fingers on the gargoyle, and hastily pulled himself together. What is the sensible course of action at this point?

A party of revellers staggered through a pool of light in the street far below.

Teppic sheathed the knife and stood up.

'Sir,' he said, 'I am here.'

A dry voice by his ear said, rather indistinctly, 'Very well.'

Teppic stared straight ahead. Mericet appeared in front of him, wiping grey dust off his bony face. He took a length of pipe out of his mouth and tossed it aside, then pulled a clipboard out of his coat. He was bundled up even in this heat. Mericet was the kind of person who could freeze in a volcano.

'Ah,' he said, his voice broadcasting disapproval, 'Mr Teppic. Well, well.'

'A fine night, sir,' said Teppic. The examiner gave him a chilly look, suggesting that observations about the weather acquired an automatic black mark, and made a note on his clipboard.

'We'll take a few questions first,' he said.

'As you wish, sir.'

'What is the maximum permitted length of a throwing knife?' snapped Mericet.

Teppic closed his eyes. He'd spent the last week reading nothing but *The Cordat*; he could see the page now, floating tantalisingly just inside his eyelids – they never ask you lengths and weights,

---

[*] Breathing, for a start.

students had said knowingly, they expect you to bone up on the weights and lengths and throwing distances but they never –

Naked terror hotwired his brain and kicked his memory into gear. The page sprang into focus.

'"Maximum length of a throwing knife may be ten finger widths, or twelve in wet weather",' he recited. '"Throwing distance is –"'

'Name three poisons acknowledged for administration by ear.'

A breeze sprang up, but it did nothing to cool the air; it just shifted the heat about.

'Sir, wasp agaric, Achorion purple and Mustick, sir,' said Teppic promptly.

'Why not spime?' snapped Mericet, fast as a snake.

Teppic's jaw dropped open. He floundered for a while, trying to avoid the gimlet gaze a few feet away from him.

'S-sir, spime isn't a poison, sir,' he managed. 'It is an extremely rare antidote to certain snake venoms, and is obtained –' He settled down a bit, more certain of himself: all those hours idly looking through the old dictionaries had paid off – 'is obtained from the liver of the inflatable mongoose, which –'

'What is the meaning of this sign?' said Mericet.

'– is found only in the . . .' Teppic's voice trailed off. He squinted down at the complex rune on the card in Mericet's hand, and then stared straight past the examiner's ear again.

'I haven't the faintest idea, sir,' he said. Out of the corner of his ear he thought he heard the faintest intake of breath, the tiniest seed of a satisfied grunt.

'But if it were the other way up, sir,' he went on, 'it would be thiefsign for "Noisy dogs in this house".'

There was absolute silence for a moment. Then, right by his shoulder, the old assassin's voice said, 'Is the killing rope permitted to all categories?'

'Sir, the rules call for three questions, sir,' Teppic protested.

'Ah. And that is your answer, is it?'

'Sir, no, sir. It was an observation, sir. Sir, the answer you are looking for is that all categories may bear the killing rope, but only assassins of the third grade may use it as one of the three options, sir.'

'You are sure of that, are you?'

'Sir.'

'You wouldn't like to reconsider?' You could have used the examiner's voice to grease a wagon.

'Sir, no, sir.'

'Very well.' Teppic relaxed. The back of his tunic was sticking to him, chilly with sweat.

'Now, I want you to proceed at your own pace towards the Street of Book-keepers,' said Mericet evenly, 'obeying all signs and so forth. I will meet you in the room under the gong tower at the junction with Audit Alley. And – take this, if you please.'

He handed Teppic a small envelope.

Teppic handed over a receipt. Then Mericet stepped into the pool of shade beside a chimney pot, and disappeared.

So much for the ceremony.

Teppic took a few deep breaths and tipped the envelope's contents into his hand. It was a Guild bond for ten thousand Ankh-Morpork dollars, made out to 'Bearer'. It was an impressive document, surmounted with the Guild seal of the double-cross and the cloaked dagger.

Well, no going back now. He'd taken the money. Either he'd survive, in which case of course he'd traditionally donate the money to the Guild's widows and orphans fund, or it would be retrieved from his dead body. The bond looked a bit dog-eared, but he couldn't see any bloodstains on it.

He checked his knives, adjusted his swordbelt, glanced behind him, and set off at a gentle trot.

At least this was a bit of luck. The student lore said there were only half a dozen routes used during the test, and on summer nights they were alive with students tackling the roofs, towers, eaves and coils of the city. Edificing was a keen inter-house sport in its own right; it was one of the few things Teppic was sure he was good at – he'd been captain of the team that beat Scorpion House in the Wallgame finals. And this was one of the easiest courses.

He dropped lightly over the edge of the roof, landed on a ridge, ran easily across the sleeping building, jumped a narrow gap on to the tiled roof of the Young Men's Reformed-Cultists-of-the-Ichor-God-Bel-Shamharoth Association gym, jogged gently over the grey slope, swarmed up a twelve foot wall without slowing down, and vaulted on to the wide flat roof of the Temple of Blind Io.

A full, orange moon hung on the horizon. There was a real breeze up here, not much, but as refreshing as a cold shower after the stifling heat of the streets. He speeded up, enjoying the coolness on his face, and leapt accurately off the end of the roof on to the narrow plank bridge that led across Tinlid Alley.

And which someone, in defiance of all probability, had removed.

*

At times like this one's past life flashes before one's eyes . . .

His aunt had wept, rather theatrically, Teppic had thought, since the old lady was as tough as a hippo's instep. His father had looked stern and dignified, whenever he could remember to, and tried to keep his mind free of beguiling images of cliffs and fish. The servants had been lined up along the hall from the foot of the main stairway, handmaidens on one side, eunuchs and butlers on the other. The women bobbed a curtsey as he walked by, creating a rather nice sine wave effect which the greatest mathematician on the Disc, had he not at this moment been occupied by being hit with a stick and shouted at by a small man wearing what appeared to be a nightshirt, might well have appreciated.

'But,' Teppic's aunt blew her nose, 'it's *trade*, after all.'

His father patted her hand. 'Nonsense, flower of the desert,' he said, 'it is a profession, at the very least.'

'What is the difference?' she sobbed.

The old man sighed. 'The money, I understand. It will do him good to go out into the world and make friends and have a few corners knocked off, and it will keep him occupied and prevent him from getting into mischief.'

'But . . . *assassination* . . . he's so young, and he's never shown the *least* inclination . . .' She dabbed at her eyes. 'It's not from our side of the family,' she added accusingly. 'That brother-in-law of yours —'

'Uncle Vyrt,' said his father.

'Going all over the world killing people!'

'I don't believe they use that word,' said his father. 'I think they prefer words like conclude, or annul. Or inhume, I understand.'

'Inhume?'

'I think it's like exhume, O flooding of the waters, only it's *before* they bury you.'

'I think it's terrible.' She sniffed. 'But I heard from Lady Nooni that only one boy in fifteen actually passes the final exam. Perhaps we'd just better let him get it out of his system.'

King Teppicymon XXVII nodded gloomily, and went by himself to wave goodbye to his son. He was less certain than his sister about the unpleasantness of assassination; he'd been reluctantly in politics for a long time, and felt that while assassination was probably worse than debate it was certainly better than war, which some people tended to think of as the same thing only louder. And there was no doubt that young Vyrt always had plenty of money, and used to turn up at the palace with expensive gifts, exotic suntans and thrilling tales of the interesting people he'd met in foreign parts, in most cases quite briefly.

He wished Vyrt was around to advise. His majesty had also heard that only one student in fifteen actually became an assassin. He wasn't entirely certain what happened to the other fourteen, but he was pretty sure that if you were a poor student in a school for assassins they did a bit more than throw the chalk at you, and that the school dinners had an extra dimension of uncertainty.

But everyone agreed that the assassins' school offered the best all-round education in the world. A qualified assassin should be at home in any company, and able to play at least one musical instrument. Anyone inhumed by an alumnus of the Guild school could go to his rest satisfied that he had been annulled by someone of taste and discretion.

And, after all, what was there for him at home? A kingdom two miles wide and one hundred and fifty miles long, which was almost entirely underwater during the flood season, and threatened on either side by stronger neighbours who tolerated its existence only because they'd be constantly at war if it wasn't there.

Oh, Djelibeybi* had been great once, when upstarts like Tsort and Ephebe were just a bunch of nomads with their towels on their heads. All that remained of those great days was the ruinously-expensive palace, a few dusty ruins in the desert and – the pharaoh sighed – the pyramids. Always the pyramids.

His ancestors had been keen on pyramids. The pharaoh wasn't. Pyramids had bankrupted the country, drained it drier than ever the river did. The only curse they could afford to put on a tomb these days was 'Bugger Off'.

The only pyramids he felt comfortable about were the very small ones at the bottom of the garden, built every time one of the cats died.

He'd promised the boy's mother.

He missed Artela. There'd been a terrible row about taking a wife from outside the Kingdom, and some of her foreign ways had puzzled and fascinated even him. Maybe it was from her he'd got the strange dislike of pyramids; in Djelibeybi that was like disliking breathing. But he'd promised that Pteppic could go to school outside the kingdom. She'd been insistent about that. 'People never learn anything in this place,' she'd said. 'They only remember things.'

* Lit. 'Child of the Djel'.

If only she'd remembered about not swimming in the river . . .

He watched two of the servants load Teppic's trunk on to the back of the coach, and for the first time either of them could remember laid a paternal hand on his son's shoulder.

In fact he was at a loss for something to say. We've never really had time to get to know one another, he thought. There's so much I could have given him. A few bloody good hidings wouldn't have come amiss.

'Um,' he said. 'Well, my boy.'

'Yes, father?'

'This is, er, the first time you've been away from home by yourself —'

'No, father. I spent last summer with Lord Fhem-pta-hem, you remember.'

'Oh, did you?' The pharaoh recalled the palace had seemed quieter at the time. He'd put it down to the new tapestries.

'Anyway,' he said, 'you're a young man, nearly thirteen —'

'Twelve, father,' said Teppic patiently.

'Are you sure?'

'It was my birthday last month, father. You bought me a warming pan.'

'Did I? How singular. Did I say why?'

'No, father.' Teppic looked up at his father's mild, puzzled features. 'It was a very *good* warming pan,' he added reassuringly. 'I like it a lot.'

'Oh. Good. Er.' His majesty patted his son's shoulder again, in a vague way, like a man drumming his fingers on his desk while trying to think. An idea appeared to occur to him.

The servants had finished strapping the trunk on to the roof of the coach and the driver was patiently holding open the door.

'When a young man sets out in the world,' said his majesty uncertainly, 'there are, well, it's very important that he remembers . . . The point is, that it is a very big world after all, with all sorts . . . And of course, especially so in the city, where there are many additional . . .' He paused, waving one hand vaguely in the air.

Teppic took it gently.

'It's quite all right, father,' he said. 'Dios the high priest explained to me about taking regular baths, and not going blind.'

His father blinked at him.

'You're not going blind?' he said.

'Apparently not, father.'

'Oh. Well. Jolly good,' said the king. 'Jolly, jolly good. That *is* good news.'

'I think I had better be going, father. Otherwise I shall miss the tide.'

His majesty nodded, and patted his pockets.

'There was something . . .' he muttered, and then tracked it down, and slipped a small leather bag into Teppic's pocket. He tried the shoulder routine again.

'A little something,' he murmured. 'Don't tell your aunt. Oh, you can't, anyway. She's gone for a lie-down. It's all been rather too much for her.'

All that remained then was for Teppic to go and sacrifice a chicken at the statue of Khuft, the founder of Djelibeybi, so that his ancestor's guiding hand would steer his footsteps in the world. It was only a small chicken, though, and when Khuft had finished with it the king had it for lunch.

Djelibeybi really was a small, self-centred kingdom. Even its plagues were half-hearted. All self-respecting river kingdoms have vast supernatural plagues, but the best the Old Kingdom had been able to achieve in the last hundred years was the Plague of Frog[*].

That evening, when they were well outside the delta of the Djel and heading across the Circle Sea to Ankh-Morpork, Teppic remembered the bag and examined its contents. With love, but also with his normal approach to things, his father had presented him with a cork, half a tin of saddlesoap, a small bronze coin of uncertain denomination, and an extremely elderly sardine.

It is a well-known fact that when one is about to die the senses immediately become excruciatingly sharp, and it has always been believed that this is to enable their owner to detect any possible exit from his predicament other than the obvious one.

This is not true. The phenomenon is a classical example of displacement activity. The senses are desperately concentrating on anything apart from the immediate problem – which in Teppic's case consisted of a broad expanse of cobblestones some eighty feet away and closing – in the hope that it will go away.

The trouble is that it soon will.

[*] It was quite a big frog, however, and got into the air ducts and kept everyone awake for weeks.

Whatever the reason, Teppic was suddenly acutely aware of things around him. The way the moonlight glowed on the rooftops. The smell of fresh bread wafting from a nearby bakery. The whirring of a cockchafer as it barrelled past his ear, upwards. The sound of a baby crying, in the distance, and the bark of a dog. The gentle rush of the air, with particular reference to its thinness and lack of handholds ...

There had been more than seventy of them enrolling that year. The Assassins didn't have a very strenuous entrance examination; the school was easy to get into, easy to get out of (the trick was to get out *upright*). The courtyard in the centre of the Guild buildings was thronged with boys who all had two things in common – overlarge trunks, which they were sitting on, and clothes that had been selected for them to grow into, and which they were more or less sitting *in*. Some optimists had brought weapons with them, which were confiscated and sent home over the next few weeks.

Teppic watched them carefully. There were distinct advantages to being the only child of parents too preoccupied with their own affairs to worry much about him, or indeed register his existence for days at a time.

His mother, as far as he could remember, had been a pleasant woman and as self-centred as a gyroscope. She'd liked cats. She didn't just venerate them – everyone in the kingdom did *that* – but she actually liked them, too. Teppic knew that it was traditional in river kingdoms to approve of cats, but he suspected that usually the animals in question were graceful, stately creatures; his mother's cats were small, spitting, flatheaded, yellow-eyed maniacs.

His father spent a lot of time worrying about the kingdom and occasionally declaring that he was a seagull, although this was probably from general forgetfulness. Teppic had occasionally speculated about his own conception, since his parents were rarely in the same frame of reference, let alone the same state of mind.

But it had apparently happened and he was left to bring himself up on a trial and error basis, mildly hindered and occasionally enlivened by a succession of tutors. The ones hired by his father were best, especially on those days when he was flying as high as he could, and for one glorious winter Teppic had as his tutor an elderly ibis poacher who had in fact wandered into the royal gardens in search of a stray arrow.

That had been a time of wild chases with soldiers, moonlight rambles in the dead streets of the necropolis and, best of all, the introduction to the puntbow, a fearsomely complicated invention which at considerable risk to its operators could turn a slough full of innocent waterfowl into so much floating pâté.

He'd also had the run of the library, including the locked shelves – the poacher had several other skills to ensure gainful employment in inclement weather – which had given him many hours of quiet study; he was particularly attached to *The Shuttered Palace*, Translated from the Khalian by A Gentleman, with Hand-Coloured Plates for the Connoisseur in A Strictly Limited Edition. It was confusing but instructive and, when a rather fey young tutor engaged by the priests tried to introduce him to certain athletic techniques favoured by the classical Pseudopolitans, Teppic considered the suggestion for some time and then floored the youth with a hatstand.

Teppic hadn't been educated. Education had just settled on him, like dandruff.

It started to rain, in the world outside his head. Another new experience. He'd heard about it, of course, how water came down out of the sky in small bits. He just hadn't expected there to be so much of it. It never rained in Djelibeybi.

Masters moved among the boys like damp and slightly scruffy blackbirds, but he was eyeing a group of older students lolling near the pillared entrance to the school. They also wore black – different colours of black.

That was his first introduction to the tertiary colours, the colours on the far side of blackness, the colours that you get if you split blackness with an eight-sided prism. They are also almost impossible to describe in a non-magical environment, but if someone were to try they'd probably start by telling you to smoke something illegal and take a good look at a starling's wing.

The seniors were critically inspecting the new arrivals.

Teppic stared at them. Apart from the colours, their clothes were cut off the edge of the latest fashion, which was currently inclining towards wide hats, padded shoulders, narrow waists and pointed shoes and gave its followers the appearance of being very well-dressed nails.

I'm going to be like them, he told himself.

Although probably better dressed, he added.

He recalled Uncle Vyrt, sitting out on the steps overlooking the Djel on one of his brief, mysterious visits. 'Satin and leather are no good. Or jewelry of any kind. You can't have anything that will shine or squeak or clink. Stick to rough silk or velvet. The important thing is not how many people you inhume, it's how many fail to inhume *you*.'

He'd been moving at an unwise pace, which might assist now. As he arced over the emptiness of the alley he twisted in the air, thrust out his arms desperately, and felt his fingertips brush a ledge on the building opposite. It was enough to pivot him; he swung around, hit the crumbling brickwork with sufficient force to knock what remained of his breath out of him, and slid down the sheer wall . . .

'Boy!'

Teppic looked up. There was a senior assassin standing beside him, with a purple teaching sash over his robes. It was the first assassin he'd seen, apart from Vyrt. The man was pleasant enough. You could imagine him making sausages.

'Are you talking to me?' he said.

'You will stand up when you address a master,' said the rosy face.

'I will?' Teppic was fascinated. He wondered how this could be achieved. Discipline had not hitherto been a major feature in his life. Most of his tutors had been sufficiently unnerved by the sight of the king occasionally perched on top of a door that they raced through such lessons as they had and then locked themselves in their rooms.

'I will *sir*,' said the teacher. He consulted the list in his hand.

'What is your name, boy?' he continued.

'Prince Pteppic of the Old Kingdom, the Kingdom of the Sun,' said Teppic easily. 'I appreciate you are ignorant of the etiquette, but you should not call me sir, and you should touch the ground with your forehead when you address me.'

'Pateppic, is it?' said the master.

'No. *Pt*eppic.'

'Ah. Teppic,' said the master, and ticked off a name on his list. He gave Teppic a generous smile.

'Well, now, your majesty,' he said, 'I am Grunworth Nivor, your housemaster. You are in Viper House. To my certain knowledge there are at least eleven Kingdoms of the Sun on the Disc and, before the end of the week, you will present me with a short essay detailing their geographical location, political complexion, capital city or principal seat of government, and a suggested route into the bedchamber of the head of state of your choice. However, in all the world there is only one Viper House. Good morning to you, boy.'

He turned away and homed in on another cowering pupil.

'He's not a bad sort,' said a voice behind Teppic. 'Anyway, all the stuff's in the library. I'll show you if you like. I'm Chidder.'

Teppic turned. He was being addressed by a boy of about his own age and height, whose black suit – plain black, for First Years – looked as though it had been nailed on to him in bits. The youth was holding out a hand. Teppic gave it a polite glance.

'Yes?' he said.

'What's your name, kiddo?'

Teppic drew himself up. He was getting fed up with this treatment. 'Kiddo? I'll have you know the blood of pharaohs runs in my veins!'

The other boy looked at him unabashed, with his head on one side and a faint smile on his face.

'Would you like it to stay there?' he said.

The bakery was just along the alley, and a handful of the staff had stepped out into the comparative cool of the pre-dawn air for a quick smoke and a break from the desert heat of the ovens. Their chattering spiralled up to Teppic, high in the shadows, gripping a fortuitous window sill while his feet scrabbled for a purchase among the bricks.

It's not that bad, he told himself. You've tackled worse. The hubward face of the Patrician's palace last winter, for example, when all the gutters had overflowed and the walls were solid ice. This isn't much more than a 3, maybe a 3.2. You and old Chiddy used to go up walls like this rather than stroll down the street, it's just a matter of perspective.

Perspective. He glanced down, at seventy feet of infinity. Splat City, man, get a grip on yourself. On the *wall*. His right foot found a worn section of mortar, into which his toes planted themselves with barely a conscious instruction from a brain now feeling too fragile to take more than a distant interest in the proceedings.

He took a breath, tensed, and then dropped one hand to his belt, seized a dagger, and thrust it between the bricks beside him before gravity worked out what was happening. He paused, panting, waiting for gravity to lose interest in him again, and then swung his body sideways and tried the same thing a second time.

Down below one of the bakers told a suggestive joke, and brushed a speck of mortar from his ear. As his colleagues laughed Teppic stood up in the moonlight, balancing on two slivers of Klatchian steel, and gently walked his palms up the wall to the window whose sill had been his brief salvation.

It was wedged shut. A good blow would surely open it, but only at about the same moment as it sent him reeling back into empty air. Teppic sighed and, moving with the delicacy of a watchmaker, drew his diamond compasses from their pouch and dragged a slow, gentle circle on the dusty glass . . .

'You carry it yourself,' said Chidder. 'That's the rule around here.'

Teppic looked at the trunk. It was an intriguing notion.

'At home we've people who do that,' he said. 'Eunuchs and so on.'

'You should of brought one with you.'

'They don't travel well,' said Teppic. In fact he'd adamantly refused all suggestions that a small retinue should accompany him, and Dios had sulked for days. That was not how a member of the royal blood should go forth into the world, he said. Teppic had remained firm. He was pretty certain that assassins weren't expected to go about their business accompanied by handmaidens and buglers. Now, however, the idea seemed to have some merit. He gave the trunk an experimental heave, and managed to get it across his shoulders.

'Your people are pretty rich, then?' said Chidder, ambling along beside him.

Teppic thought about this. 'No, not really,' he said. 'They mainly grow melons and garlic and that kind of thing. And stand in the streets and shout "hurrah".'

'This is your parents you're talking about?' said Chidder, puzzled.

'Oh, them? No, my father's a pharaoh. My mother was a concubine, I think.'

'I thought that was some sort of vegetable.'

'I don't think so. We've never really discussed it. Anyway, she died when I was young.'

'How dreadful,' said Chidder cheerfully.

'She went for a moonlight swim in what turned out to be a crocodile.' Teppic tried politely not to be hurt at the boy's reaction.

'My father's in commerce,' said Chidder, as they passed through the archway.

'That's fascinating,' said Teppic dutifully. He felt quite broken by all these new experiences, and added, 'I've never been to Commerce, but I understand they're very fine people.'

Over the next hour or two Chidder, who ambled gently through life as though he'd already worked it all out, introduced Teppic to the various mysteries of the dormitories, the classrooms and the plumbing. He left the plumbing until last, for all sorts of reasons.

'Not *any*?' he said.

'There's buckets and things,' said Teppic vaguely, 'and lots of servants.'

'Bit old fashioned, this kingdom of yours?'

Teppic nodded. 'It's the pyramids,' he said. 'They take all the money.'

'Expensive things, I should imagine.'

'Not particularly. They're just made of stone.' Teppic sighed. 'We've got lots of stone,' he said, 'and sand. Stone and sand. We're really big on them. If you ever need any stone and sand, we're the people for you. It's fitting out the insides that is really expensive. We're still avoiding paying for grandfather's, and that wasn't very big. Just three chambers.' Teppic turned and looked out of the window; they were back in the dormitory at this point.

'The whole kingdom's in debt,' he said, quietly. 'I mean even our *debts* are in debt. That's why I'm here, really. Someone in our house needs to earn some money. A royal prince can't hang around looking ornamental any more. He's got to get out and do something useful in the community.'

Chidder leaned on the window sill.

'Couldn't you take some of the stuff out of the pyramids, then?' he said.

'Don't be silly.'

'Sorry.'

Teppic gloomily watched the figures below.

'There's a lot of people here,' he said, to change the subject. 'I didn't realise it would be so big.' He shivered. 'Or so cold,' he added.

'People drop out all the time,' said Chidder. 'Can't stand the course. The important thing is to know what's what and who's who. See that fellow over there?'

Teppic followed his pointing finger to a group of older students, who were lounging against the pillars by the entrance.

'The big one? Face like the end of your boot?'

'That's Fliemoe. Watch out for him. If he invites you for toast in his study, *don't go*.'

'And who's the little kid with the curls?' said Teppic. He pointed to a small lad receiving the attentions of a washed-out looking lady. She was licking her handkerchief and dabbing apparent smudges off his face. When she stopped that, she straightened his tie.

Chidder craned to see. 'Oh, just some new kid,' he said. 'Arthur someone. Still hanging on to his mummy, I see. He won't last long.'

'Oh, I don't know,' said Teppic. 'We do, too, and we've lasted for thousands of years.'

A disc of glass dropped into the silent building and tinkled on the floor. There was no other sound for several minutes. Then there was the faint clonk-clonk of an oil can. A shadow that had been lying naturally on the window sill, a morgue for blue-bottles, turned out to be an arm which was moving with vegetable slowness towards the window's catch.

There was a scrape of metal, and then the whole window swung out in tribological silence.

Teppic dropped over the sill and vanished into the shadow below it.

For a minute or two the dusty space was filled with the intense absence of noise caused by someone moving with extreme care. Once again there was the squirting of oil, and then a metallic whisper as the bolt of a trapdoor leading on to the roof moved gently aside.

Teppic waited for his breath to catch up with him, and in that moment heard the sound. It was down among the white noise at the edge of hearing, but there was no doubt about it. Someone was waiting just above the trapdoor, and they'd just put their hand on a piece of paper to stop it rattling in the breeze.

His own hand dropped from the bolt. He eased his way with exquisite care back across the greasy floor and felt his way along a rough wooden wall until he came to a door. This time he took no chances, but uncorked his oil can and let a silent drop fall on to the hinges.

A moment later he was through. A rat, idly patrolling the drafty passage beyond, had to stop itself from swallowing its own tongue as he floated past.

There was another doorway at the end, and a maze of musty storerooms until he found a stairway. He judged himself to be about thirty yards from the trapdoor. There hadn't been any flues that he could see. There ought to be a clear shot across the roof.

He hunkered down and pulled out his knife roll, its velvet

blackness making a darker oblong in the shadows. He selected a Number Five, not everyone's throwing knife, but worthwhile if you had the trick of it.

Shortly afterwards his head rose very carefully over the edge of the roof, one arm bent behind it but ready to uncurl in a complex interplay of forces that would combine to send a few ounces of steel gliding across the night.

Mericet was sitting by the trapdoor, looking at his clipboard. Teppic's eyes swivelled to the oblong of the plank bridge, stored meticulously against the parapet a few feet away.

He was certain he had made no noise. He'd have to swear that the examiner heard the sound of his gaze falling on him.

The old man raised his bald head.

'Thank you, Mr Teppic,' he said, 'you may proceed.'

Teppic felt the sweat of his body grow cold. He stared at the plank, and then at the examiner, and then at his knife.

'Yes, sir,' he said. This didn't seem like enough, in the circumstances. He added, 'Thank you, sir.'

He'd always remember the first night in the dormitory. It was long enough to accommodate all eighteen boys in Viper House, and draughty enough to accommodate the great outdoors. Its designer may have had comfort in mind, but only so that he could avoid it wherever possible: he had contrived a room that could actually be colder than the weather outside.

'I thought we got rooms to ourselves,' said Teppic.

Chidder, who had laid claim to the least exposed bed in the whole refrigerator, nodded at him.

'Later on,' he said. He lay back, and winced. 'Do they sharpen these springs, do you reckon?'

Teppic said nothing. The bed was in fact rather more comfortable than the one he'd slept in at home. His parents, being high born, naturally tolerated conditions for their children which would have been rejected out of hand by destitute sandflies.

He stretched out on the thin mattress and analysed the day's events. He'd been enrolled as an assassin, all right, a student assassin, for more than seven hours and they hadn't even let him lay a hand on a knife yet. Of course, tomorrow was another day . . .

Chidder leaned over.

'Where's Arthur?' he said.

Teppic looked at the bed opposite him. There was a pathetically small sack of clothing positioned neatly in its centre, but no sign of its intended occupant.

'Do you think he's run away?' he said, staring around at the shadows.

'Could be,' said Chidder. 'It happens a lot, you know. Mummy's boys, away from home for the first time –'

The door at the end of the room swung open slowly and Arthur entered, backwards, tugging a large and very reluctant billy goat. It fought him every step of the way down the aisle between the bedsteads.

The boys watched in silence for several minutes as he tethered the animal to the end of his bed, upended the sack on the blankets, and took out several black candles, a sprig of herbs, a rope of skulls, and a piece of chalk. Taking the chalk, and adopting the shiny, pink-faced expression of someone who is going to do what they know to be right no matter what, Arthur drew a double circle around his bed and then, getting down on his chubby knees, filled the space between them with as unpleasant a collection of occult symbols as Teppic had ever seen. When they were completed to his satisfaction he placed the candles at strategic points and lit them; they spluttered and gave off a smell that suggested that you really wouldn't want to know what they were made of.

He drew a short, red-handled knife from the jumble on the bed and advanced towards the goat –

A pillow hit him on the back of the head.

'Garn! Pious little bastard!'

Arthur dropped the knife and burst into tears. Chidder sat up in bed.

'That was you, Cheesewright!' he said. 'I saw you!'

Cheesewright, a skinny young man with red hair and a face that was one large freckle, glared at him.

'Well, it's too much,' he said. 'A fellow can't sleep with all this religion going on. I mean, only little kids say their prayers at bedtime these days, we're supposed to be learning to be *assassins* –'

'You can jolly well shut up, Cheesewright,' shouted Chidder. 'It'd be a better world if more people said their prayers, you know. I know I don't say mine as often as I should –'

A pillow cut him off in mid-sentence. He bounded out of bed and vaulted at the red-haired boy, fists flailing.

As the rest of the dormitory gathered around the scuffling pair Teppic slid out of bed and padded over to Arthur, who was sitting on the edge of his bed and sobbing.

He patted him uncertainly on the shoulder, on the basis that this sort of thing was supposed to reassure people.

'I shouldn't cry about it, youngster,' he said, gruffly.

'But – but all the runes have been scuffed,' said Arthur. 'It's all too late now! And that means the Great Orm will come in the night and wind out my entrails on a stick!'

'Does it?'

'And suck out my eyes, my mother said!'

'Gosh!' said Teppic, fascinated. 'Really?' He was quite glad his bed was opposite Arthur's, and would offer an unrivalled view. 'What religion would this be?'

'We're Strict Authorised Ormits,' said Arthur. He blew his nose. 'I noticed you don't pray,' he said. 'Don't you have a god?'

'Oh yes,' said Teppic hesitantly, 'no doubt about that.'

'You don't seem to want to talk to him.'

Teppic shook his head. 'I can't,' he said, 'not here. He wouldn't be able to hear, you see.'

'*My* god can hear *me* anywhere,' said Arthur fervently.

'Well, mine has difficulty if you're on the other side of the room,' said Teppic. 'It can be very embarrassing.'

'You're not an Offlian, are you?' said Arthur. Offler was a Crocodile God, and lacked ears.

'No.'

'What god *do* you worship, then?'

'Not exactly worship,' said Teppic, discomforted. 'I wouldn't say worship. I mean, he's all right. He's my father, if you must know.'

Arthur's pink-rimmed eyes widened.

'You're the son of a *god*?' he whispered.

'It's all part of being a king, where I come from,' said Teppic hurriedly. 'He doesn't have to do very much. That is, the priests do the actual running of the country. He just makes sure that the river floods every year, d'you see, and services the Great Cow of the Arch of the Sky. Well, *used* to.'

'The Great –'

'My mother,' explained Teppic. 'It's all very embarrassing.'

'Does he smite people?'

'I don't think so. He's never said.'

Arthur reached down to the end of the bed. The goat, in the confusion, had chewed through its rope and trotted out of the door, vowing to give up religion in future.

'I'm going to get into awful trouble,' he said. 'I suppose you couldn't ask your father to explain things to the Great Orm?'

'He might be able to,' said Teppic doubtfully. 'I was going to write home tomorrow anyway.'

'The Great Orm is normally to be found in one of the Nether Hells,' said Arthur, 'where he watches everything we do. Everything I do, anyway. There's only me and mother left now, and she doesn't do much that needs watching.'

'I'll be sure and tell him.'

'Do you think the Great Orm will come tonight?'

'I shouldn't think so. I'll ask my father to be sure and tell him not to.'

At the other end of the dormitory Chidder was kneeling on Cheesewright's back and knocking his head repeatedly against the wall.

'Say it again,' he commanded. 'Come on – "There's nothing wrong –"'

'"There's nothing wrong with a chap being man enough –" curse you, Chidder, you beastly –'

'I can't hear you, Cheesewright,' said Chidder.

'"Man enough to say his prayers in front of other chaps", you rotter.'

'Right. And don't you forget it.'

After lights out Teppic lay in bed and thought about religion. It was certainly a very complicated subject.

The valley of the Djel had its own private gods, gods which had nothing to do with the world outside. It had always been very proud of the fact. The gods were wise and just and regulated the lives of men with skill and foresight, there was no question about that, but there were some puzzles.

For example, he knew his father made the sun come up and the river flood and so on. That was basic, it was what the pharaohs had done ever since the time of Khuft, you couldn't go around questioning things like that. The point was, though, did he just make the sun come up in the Valley or everywhere in the world? Making the sun come up in the Valley seemed a more reasonable proposition, after all, his father wasn't getting any younger, but it was rather difficult to imagine the sun coming up everywhere else and *not* the Valley, which led to the distressing thought that the sun would come up even if his father forgot about it, which was a very likely state of affairs. He'd never seen his father do anything much about making the sun rise, he had to admit. You'd expect at least a grunt of effort round about dawn. His father never got up until after breakfast. The sun came up just the same.

He took some time to get to sleep. The bed, whatever Chidder said, was too soft, the air was too cold and, worst of all, the sky outside the high windows was too dark. At home it would have been full of flarelight from the necropolis, its silent flames eerie but somehow familiar and comforting, as though the ancestors were watching over their valley. He didn't like the darkness . . .

The following night in the dormitory one of the boys from further along the coast shyly tried to put the boy in the next bed inside a wickerwork cage he made in Craft and set fire to him, and the night after that Snoxall, who had the bed by the door and came from a little country out in the forests somewhere, painted himself green and asked for volunteers to have their intestines wound around a tree. On Thursday a small war broke out between those who worshipped the Mother Goddess in her aspect of the Moon and those who worshipped her in her aspect of a huge fat woman with enormous buttocks. After that the masters intervened and explained that religion, while a fine thing, could be taken too far.

Teppic had a suspicion that unpunctuality was unforgivable. But surely Mericet would have to be at the tower ahead of him? And he was going by the direct route. The old man couldn't possibly get there before him. Mind you, he couldn't possibly have got to the bridge in the alley first . . . He must have taken the bridge away before he met me and then he climbed up on the roof while I was climbing up the wall, Teppic told himself, without believing a word of it.

He ran along a roof ridge, senses alert for dislodged tiles or tripwires. His imagination equipped every shadow with watching figures.

The gong tower loomed ahead of him. He paused, and looked at it. He had seen it a thousand times before, and scaled it many times although it barely rated a 1.8, notwithstanding that the brass dome on top was an interesting climb. It was just a familiar landmark. That made it worse now; it bulked in front of him, a stubby menacing shape against the greyness of the sky.

He advanced more slowly now, approaching the tower obliquely across the sloping roof. It came to him that his initials were up there, on the dome, along with Chiddy's and those of hundreds of other young assassins, and that they'd carry on being up there even if he died tonight. It was sort of comforting. Only not very.

He unslung his rope and made an easy throw on to the wide

parapet that ran around the tower, just under the dome. He tested it, and heard the gentle clink as it caught.

Then he tugged it as hard as possible, bracing himself with one foot on a chimney stack.

Abruptly, and with no sound, a section of parapet slid outwards and dropped.

There was a crash as it hit the roof below and then slid down the tiles. Another pause was punctuated by a distant thump as it hit the silent street. A dog barked.

Stillness ruled the rooftops. Where Teppic had been the breeze stirred the burning air.

After several minutes he emerged from the deeper shadow of a chimney stack, smiling a strange and terrible smile.

Nothing the examiner could do could possibly be unfair. An assassin's clients were invariably rich enough to pay for extremely ingenious protection, up to and including hiring assassins of his own[*]. Mericet wasn't trying to kill him; he was merely trying to make him kill himself.

He sidled up to the base of the tower and found a drainpipe. It hadn't been coated with slipall, rather to his surprise, but his gently questing fingers did find the poisoned needles painted black and glued to the inner face of the pipe. He removed one with his tweezers and sniffed it.

Distilled *bloat*. Pretty expensive stuff, with an astonishing effect. He took a small glass phial from his belt and collected as many needles as he could find, and then put on his armoured gloves and, with the speed of a sloth, started to climb.

'Now it may well be that, as you travel across the city on your lawful occasions, you will find yourselves in opposition to fellow members, even one of the gentlemen with whom you are currently sharing a bench. And this is quite right and *what are you doing Mr Chidder no don't tell me I'm sure I wouldn't want to know see me afterwards* proper. It is open to everyone to defend themselves as best they may. There are, however, other enemies who will dog your steps and against whom you are all ill-prepared *who are they Mr Cheesewright?*'

Mericet spun round from his blackboard like a vulture who has

---

[*] It was said that life was cheap in Ankh-Morpork. This was, of course, completely wrong. Life was often very expensive; you could get *death* for free.

just heard a death-rattle and pointed the chalk at Cheesewright, who gulped.

'Thieves' Guild, sir?' he managed.

'Step out here, boy.'

There were whispered rumours in the dormitories about what Mericet had done to slovenly pupils in the past, which were always vague but horrifying. The class relaxed. Mericet usually concentrated on one victim at a time, so all they had to do now was look keen and enjoy the show. Crimson to his ears, Cheesewright got to his feet and trooped down the aisle between the desks.

The master inspected him thoughtfully.

'Well, now,' he said, 'and here we have Cheesewright, G., skulking across the quaking rooftops. See the determined ears. See the firm set of those knees.'

The class tittered dutifully. Cheesewright gave them an idiotic grin and rolled his eyes.

'But what are these sinister figures that march in step with him, hey? *Since you find this so funny, Mr Teppic, perhaps you would be so good as to tell Mr Cheesewright?*'

Teppic froze in mid-laugh.

Mericet's gaze bored into him. He's just like Dios the high priest, Teppic thought. Even *father*'s frightened of Dios.

He knew what he ought to do, and he was damned if he was going to do it. He ought to be scared.

'Ill-preparedness,' he said. 'Carelessness. Lack of concentration. Poor maintenance of tools. Oh, and over-confidence, sir.'

Mericet held his gaze for some time, but Teppic had practised on the palace cats.

Finally the teacher gave a brief smile that had absolutely nothing to do with humour, tossed the chalk in the air, caught it again, and said: 'Mr Teppic is exactly right. Especially about the over-confidence.'

There was a ledge leading to an invitingly open window. There was oil on the ledge, and Teppic invested several minutes in screwing small crampons into cracks in the stonework before advancing.

He hung easily by the window and proceeded to take a number of small metal rods from his belt. They were threaded at the ends, and after a few seconds' brisk work he had a rod about three feet long on the end of which he affixed a small mirror.

That revealed nothing in the gloom beyond the opening. He

pulled it back and tried again, this time attaching his hood into which he'd stuffed his gloves, to give the impression of a head cautiously revealing itself against the light. He was confident that it would pick up a bolt or a dart, but it remained resolutely unattacked.

He was chilly now, despite the heat of the night. Black velvet looked good, but that was about all you could say for it. The excitement and the exertion meant he was now wearing several pints of clammy water.

He advanced.

There was a thin black wire on the window sill, and a serrated blade screwed to the sash window above it. It was the work of a moment to wedge the sash with more rods and then cut the wire; the window dropped a fraction of an inch. He grinned in the darkness.

A sweep with a longer rod inside the room revealed that there was a floor, apparently free of obstructions. There was also a wire at about chest height. He drew the rod back, affixed a small hook on the end, sent it back, caught the wire, and tugged.

There came the dull smack of a crossbow bolt hitting old plaster.

A lump of clay on the end of the same rod, pushed gently across the floor, revealed several caltraps. Teppic hauled them back and inspected them with interest. They were copper. If he'd tried the magnet technique, which was the usual method, he wouldn't have found them.

He thought for a while. He had slip-on priests in his pouch. They were devilish things to prowl around a room in, but he shuffled into them anyway. (Priests were metal-reinforced overshoes. They saved your soles. This is an Assassin joke.) Mericet was a poisons man, after all. Bloat! If he tipped them with that Teppic would plate himself all over the walls. They wouldn't need to bury him, they'd just redecorate over the top.*

The rules. Mericet would have to obey the rules. He couldn't simply kill him, with no warning. He'd have to let him, by carelessness or over-confidence, kill himself.

He dropped lightly on to the floor inside the room and let his eyes adjust to the darkness. A few exploratory swings with the rods detected no more wires; there was a faint crunch underfoot as a priest crushed a caltrap.

---

* Bloat is extracted from the deep sea blowfish, *Singularis minutia gigantica*, which protects itself from enemies by inflating itself to many times its normal size. If taken by humans the effect is to make every cell in the body instantaneously try to swell some 2,000 times. This is invariably fatal, and very loud.

'In your own time, Mr Teppic.'

Mericet was standing in a corner. Teppic heard the faint scratching of his pencil as he made a note. He tried to put the man out of his mind. He tried to think.

There was a figure lying on a bed. It was entirely covered by a blanket.

This was the last bit. This was the room where everything was decided. This was the bit the successful students never told you about. The unsuccessful ones weren't around to ask.

Teppic's mind filled up with options. At a time like this, he thought, some divine guidance would be necessary. Where are you, dad?

He envied his fellow students who believed in gods that were intangible and lived a long way away on top of some mountain. A fellow could really *believe* in gods like that. But it was extremely hard to believe in a god when you saw him at breakfast every day.

He unslung his crossbow and screwed its greased sections together. It wasn't a proper weapon, but he'd run out of knives and his lips were too dry for the blowpipe.

There was a clicking from the corner. Mericet was idly tapping his teeth with his pencil.

It could be a dummy under there. How would he know? No, it had to be a real person. You heard tales. Perhaps he could try the rods –

He shook his head, raised the crossbow, and took careful aim.

'Whenever you like, Mr Teppic.'

This was it.

This was where they found out if you could kill.

This was what he had been trying to put out of his mind.

He knew he couldn't.

Octeday afternoons was Political Expediency with Lady T'malia, one of the few women to achieve high office in the Guild. In the lands around the Circle Sea it was generally agreed that one way to achieve a long life was not to have a meal with her Ladyship. The jewelry of one hand alone carried enough poison to inhume a small town. She was stunningly beautiful, but with the kind of calculated beauty that is achieved by a team of skilled artists, manicurists, plasterers, corsetiers and dressmakers and three hours' solid work every morning. When she walked there was the faint squeak of whalebone under incredible stress.

The boys were learning. As she talked they didn't watch her figure. They watched her fingers.

'And thus,' she said, 'let us consider the position before the founding of the Guild. In this city, and indeed in many places elsewhere, civilisation is nurtured and progresses by the dynamic interplay of interests among many large and powerful advantage cartels.

'In the days before the founding of the Guild the seeking of advancement among these consortia invariably resulted in regrettable disagreements which were terminated with extreme prejudice. These were extremely deleterious to the common interest of the city. Please understand that where disharmony rules, commerce flags.

'And yet, and yet.' She clasped her hands to her bosom. There was a creak like a galleon beating against a gale.

'Clearly there was a need for an extreme yet responsible means of settling irreconcilable differences,' she went on, 'and thus was laid the groundwork for the Guild. What *bliss* –' the sudden peak in her voice guiltily jerked several dozen young men out of their private reveries – 'it must have been to have been present in those early days, when men of stout moral purpose set out to forge the ultimate political *tool* short of warfare. How *fortunate* you are now, in training for a guild which demands so much in terms of manners, deportment, bearing and esoteric skills, and yet offers a power once the preserve only of the gods. Truly, the world is the mollusc of your choice . . .'

Chidder translated much of this behind the stables during the dinner break.

'I know what Terminate with Extreme Prejudice means,' said Cheesewright loftily. 'It means to inhume with an axe.'

'It bloody well doesn't,' said Chidder.

'How do you know, then?'

'My family have been in commerce for years,' said Chidder.

'Huh,' said Cheesewright. '*Commerce.*'

Chidder never went into details about what kind of commerce it was. It had something to with moving items around and supplying needs, but exactly what items and which needs was never made clear.

After hitting Cheesewright he explained carefully that Terminate with Extreme Prejudice did not simply require that the victim was inhumed, preferably in an extremely thorough way, but that his associates and employees were also intimately involved, along with the business premises, the building, and a large part of the surrounding neighbourhood, so that everyone involved would know that the man had been unwise enough to make the kind of enemies who could get very angry and indiscriminate.

'Gosh,' said Arthur.

'Oh, that's nothing,' said Chidder, 'one Hogswatchnight my grandad and his accounts department went and had a high-level business conference with the Hubside people and fifteen bodies were never found. Very bad, that sort of thing. Upsets the business community.'

'All the business community, or just that part of it floating face down in the river?' said Teppic.

'That's the point. Better it should be like this,' said Chidder, shaking his head. 'You know. *Clean*. That's why my father said I should join the Guild. I mean, you've got to get on with the business these days, you can't spend your whole time on public relations.'

The end of the crossbow trembled.

He liked everything else about the school, the climbing, the music studies, the broad education. It was the fact that you ended up killing people that had been preying on his mind. He'd never killed anyone.

That's the whole point, he told himself. This is where everyone finds out if you can, including you.

If I get it wrong now, I'm dead.

In his corner, Mericet began to hum a discouraging little tune.

There was a price the Guild paid for its licence. It saw to it that there were no careless, half-hearted or, in a manner of speaking, murderously inefficient assassins. You never met *anyone* who'd failed the test.

People did fail. You just never met them. Maybe there was one under there, maybe it was Chidder, even, or Snoxall or any one of the lads. They were all doing the run this evening. Maybe if he failed he'd be bundled under there . . .

Teppic tried to sight on the recumbent figure.

'Ahem,' coughed the examiner.

His throat was dry. Panic rose like a drunkard's supper.

His teeth wanted to chatter. His spine was freezing, his clothes a collection of damp rags. The world slowed down.

No. He wasn't going to. The sudden decision hit him like a brick in a dark alley, and was nearly as surprising. It wasn't that he hated the Guild, or even particularly disliked Mericet, but this wasn't the way to test anyone. It was just wrong.

He decided to fail. Exactly what could the old man do about it, here?

And he'd fail with flair.

He turned to face Mericet, looked peacefully into the examiner's eyes, extended his crossbow hand in some vague direction to his right, and pulled the trigger.

There was a metallic twang.

There was a click as the bolt ricocheted off a nail in the window sill. Mericet ducked as it whirred over his head. It hit a torch bracket on the wall, and went past Teppic's white face purring like a maddened cat.

There was a thud as it hit the blanket, and then silence.

'Thank you, Mr Teppic. If you could bear with me just one moment.'

The old assassin pored over his clipboard, his lips moving.

He took the pencil, which dangled from it by a bit of frayed string, and made a few marks on a piece of pink paper.

'I will not ask you to take it from my hands,' he said, 'what with one thing and another. I shall leave it on the table by the door.'

It wasn't a particularly pleasant smile: it was thin and dried-up, a smile with all the warmth long ago boiled out of it; people normally smiled like that when they had been dead for about two years under the broiling desert sun. But at least you felt he was making the effort.

Teppic hadn't moved. 'I've passed?' he said.

'That would appear to be the case.'

'But –'

'I am sure you know that we are not allowed to discuss the test with pupils. However, I can tell you that I personally do not approve of these modern flashy techniques. Good morning to you.'

And Mericet stalked out.

Teppic tottered over to the dusty table by the door and looked down, horrified, at the paper. Sheer habit made him extract a pair of tweezers from his pouch in order to pick it up.

It was genuine enough. There was the seal of the Guild on it, and the crabbed squiggle that was undoubtedly Mericet's signature; he'd seen it often enough, generally at the bottom of test papers alongside comments like *3/10. See me.*

He padded over to the figure on the bed and pulled back the blanket.

It was nearly one in the morning. Ankh-Morpork was just beginning to make a night of it.

It had been dark up above the rooftops, in the aerial world of thieves and assassins. But down below the life of the city flowed through the streets like a tide.

Teppic walked through the throng in a daze. Anyone else who tried that in the city was asking for a guided tour of the bottom of the river, but he was wearing assassin's black and the crowd just automatically opened in front of him and closed behind. Even the pickpockets kept away. You never knew what you might find. He wandered aimlessly through the gates of the Guild House and sat down on a black marble seat, with his chin on his knuckles.

The fact was that his life had come to an end. He hadn't thought about what was going to happen next. He hadn't dared to think that there was going to *be* a next.

Someone tapped him on the shoulder. As he turned, Chidder sat down beside him and wordlessly produced a slip of pink paper.

'Snap,' he said.

'You passed too?' said Teppic.

Chidder grinned. 'No problem,' he said. 'It was Nivor. No problem. He gave me a bit of trouble on the Emergency Drop, though. How about you?'

'Hmm? Oh. No.' Teppic tried to get a grip on himself. 'No trouble,' he said.

'Heard from any of the others?'

'No.'

Chidder leaned back. 'Cheesewright will make it,' he said loftily, 'and young Arthur. I don't think some of the others will. We could give them twenty minutes, what do you say?'

Teppic turned an agonised face towards him.

'Chiddy, I –'

'What?'

'When it came to it, I –'

'What about it?'

Teppic looked at the cobbles. 'Nothing,' he said.

'You're lucky – you just had a good airy run over the rooftops. I had the sewers and then up the garderobe in the Haberdashers' Tower. I had to go in and change when I got here.'

'You had a dummy, did you?' said Teppic.

'Good grief, didn't you?'

'But they let us think it was going to be real!' Teppic wailed.

'It felt real, didn't it?'

35

'Yes!'

'Well, then. And you passed. So no problem.'

'But didn't you wonder who might be under the blanket, who it was, and why –'

'I was worried that I might not do it properly,' Chidder admitted. 'But then I thought, well, it's not up to me.'

'But I –' Teppic stopped. What could he do? Go and explain? Somehow that didn't seem a terribly good idea.

His friend slapped him on the back.

'Don't worry about it!' he said. 'We've done it!'

And Chidder held up his thumb pressed against the first two fingers of his right hand, in the ancient salute of the assassins.

A thumb pressed against two fingers, and the lean figure of Dr Cruces, head tutor, looming over the startled boys.

'We do not *murder*,' he said. It was a soft voice; the doctor never raised his voice, but he had a way of giving it the pitch and spin that could make it be heard through a hurricane.

'We do not *execute*. We do not *massacre*. We never, you may be very certain, we never *torture*. We have no truck with crimes of passion or hatred or pointless gain. We do not do it for a delight in inhumation, or to feed some secret inner need, or for petty advantage, or for some cause or belief; I tell you, gentlemen, that all these reasons are in the highest degree suspect. Look into the face of a man who will kill you for a belief and your nostrils will snuff up the scent of abomination. Hear a speech declaring a holy war and, I assure you, your ears should catch the clink of evil's scales and the dragging of its monstrous tail over the purity of the language.

'No, we do it for the money.

'And, because we above all must know the value of a human life, we do it for a great deal of money.

'There can be few cleaner motives, so shorn of all pretence.

'*Nil mortifi, sine lucre*. Remember. No killing without payment.'

He paused for a moment.

'And always give a receipt,' he added.

'So it's all okay,' said Chidder. Teppic nodded gloomily. That was what was so likeable about Chidder. He had this enviable ability to avoid thinking seriously about anything he did.

A figure approached cautiously through the open gates.* The light from the torch in the porters' lodge glinted off blond curly hair.

'You two made it, then,' said Arthur, nonchalantly flourishing the slip.

Arthur had changed quite a lot in seven years. The continuing failure of the Great Orm to wreak organic revenge for lack of piety had cured him of his tendency to run everywhere with his coat over his head. His small size gave him a natural advantage in those areas of the craft involving narrow spaces. His innate aptitude for channelled violence had been revealed on the day when Fliemoe and some cronies had decided it would be fun to toss the new boys in a blanket, and picked Arthur first; ten seconds later it had taken the combined efforts of every boy in the dormitory to hold Arthur back and prise the remains of the chair from his fingers. It had transpired that he was the son of the late Johan Ludorum, one of the greatest assassins in the history of the Guild. Sons of dead assassins always got a free scholarship. Yes, it could be a caring profession at times.

There hadn't been any doubt about Arthur passing. He'd been given extra tuition and was allowed to use really complicated poisons. He was probably going to stay on for post-graduate work.

They waited until the gongs of the city struck two. Clockwork was not a precise technology in Ankh-Morpork, and many of the city's various communities had their own ideas of what constituted an hour in any case, so the chimes went on bouncing around the rooftops for five minutes.

When it was obvious that the city's consensus was in favour of it being well past two the three of them stopped looking silently at their shoes.

'Well, that's it,' said Chidder.

'Poor old Cheesewright,' said Arthur. 'It's tragic, when you think about it.'

'Yes, he owed me fourpence,' agreed Chidder. 'Come on. I've arranged something for us.'

King Teppicymon XXVII got out of bed and clapped his hands over his ears to shut out the roar of the sea. It was strong tonight.

It was always louder when he was feeling out of sorts. He needed something to distract himself. He could send for Ptraci, his

---

* The gates of the Assassins' Guild were never shut. This was said to be because Death was open for business all the time, but it was really because the hinges had rusted centuries before and no-one had got around to doing anything about it.

favourite handmaiden. She was *special*. Her singing always cheered him up. Life seemed so much brighter when she stopped.

Or there was the sunrise. That was always comforting. It was pleasant to sit wrapped in a blanket on the topmost roof of the palace, watching the mists lift from the river as the golden flood poured over the land. You got that warm, contented feeling of another job well done. Even if you didn't actually know how you'd done it ...

He got up, shuffled on his slippers, and padded out of his bedroom and down the wide corridor that led to the huge spiral stairs and the roof. A few rushlights illuminated the statues of the other local gods, painting the walls with shifting shadow pictures of things dog-headed, fish-bodied, spider-armed. He'd known them since childhood. His juvenile nightmares would have been quite formless without them.

The sea. He'd only seen it once, when he was a boy. He couldn't recall a lot about it, except the size. And the noise. And the seagulls.

They'd preyed on his mind. They seemed to have it far better worked out, seagulls. He wished he could come back as one, one day, but of course that wasn't an option if you were a pharaoh. You never came back. You didn't exactly go away, in fact.

'Well, what *is* it?' said Teppic.

'Try it,' said Chidder, 'just try it. You'll never have the chance again.'

'Seems a shame to spoil it,' said Arthur gallantly, looking down at the delicate pattern on his plate. 'What are all the little red things?'

'They're just radishes,' said Chidder dismissively. 'They're not the important part. Go on.'

Teppic reached over with the little wooden fork and skewered a paper-thin sliver of white fish. The *squishi* chef was scrutinising him with the air of one watching a toddler on his first birthday. So, he realised, was the rest of the restaurant.

He chewed it carefully. It was salty and faintly rubbery, with a hint of sewage outfall.

'Nice?' said Chidder anxiously. Several nearby diners started to clap.

'Different,' Teppic conceded, chewing. 'What is it?'

'Deep sea blowfish,' said Chidder.

'It's all right,' he said hastily as Teppic laid down his fork meaningfully, 'it's perfectly safe provided every bit of stomach, liver and digestive tract is removed, that's why it cost so much, there's no such thing as a second-best blowfish chef, it's the most expensive food in the world, people write poems about it –'

'Could be a taste explosion,' muttered Teppic, getting a grip on himself. Still, it must have been done properly, otherwise the place would now be wearing him as wallpaper. He poked carefully at the sliced roots which occupied the rest of the plate.

'What do these do to you?' he said.

'Well, unless they're prepared in exactly the right way over a six-week period they react catastrophically with your stomach acids,' said Chidder. 'Sorry. I thought we should celebrate with the most expensive meal we could afford.'

'I see. Fish and chips *for Men*,' said Teppic.

'Do they have any vinegar in this place?' said Arthur, his mouth full. 'And some mushy peas would go down a treat.'

But the wine was good. Not incredibly good, though. Not one of the great vintages. But it did explain why Teppic had gone through the whole of the day with a headache.

It had been the hangunder. His friend had bought four bottles of otherwise quite ordinary white wine. The reason it was so expensive was that the grapes it was made from hadn't actually been planted yet.*

Light moves slowly, lazily on the Disc. It's in no hurry to get anywhere. Why bother? At lightspeed, everywhere is the same place.

King Teppicymon XXVII watched the golden disc float over the edge of the world. A flight of cranes took off from the mist-covered river.

He'd been conscientious, he told himself. No-one had ever explained to him *how* one made the sun come up and the river flood and the corn grow. How could they? *He* was the god, after all. He should know. But he didn't, so he'd just gone through life hoping like hell that it would all work properly, and that seemed to have done the trick. The trouble was, though, that if it didn't work, he wouldn't know why not. A recurrent nightmare was of Dios the high priest shaking him awake one morning, only it wouldn't be a morning, of course, and of every light in the palace burning and an angry crowd muttering in the star-lit darkness outside and

---

* Counterwise wine is made from grapes belonging to that class of flora – reannuals – that grow only in excessively high magic fields. Normal plants grow after the seeds have been planted – with reannuals it's *the other way round*. Although reannual wine causes inebriation in the normal way, the action of the digestive system on its molecules causes an unusual reaction whose net effect is to thrust the ensuing hangover backwards in time, to a point some hours before the wine is drunk. Hence the saying: have a hair of the dog that's going to bite you.

everyone looking expectantly at him ...

And all he'd be able to say was, 'Sorry'.

It terrified him. How easy to imagine the ice forming on the river, the eternal frost riming the palm trees and snapping off the leaves (which would smash when they hit the frozen ground) and the birds dropping lifeless from the sky ...

Shadow swept over him. He looked up through eyes misted with tears at a grey and empty horizon, his mouth dropping open in horror.

He stood up, flinging aside the blanket, and raised both hands in supplication. But the sun had gone. He was the god, this was his job, it was the only thing he was here to do, and he had failed the people.

Now he could hear in his mind's ear the anger of the crowd, a booming roar that began to fill his ears until the rhythm became insistent and familiar, until it reached the point where it pressed in no longer but drew him out, into that salty blue desert where the sun always shone and sleek shapes wheeled across the sky.

The pharaoh raised himself on his toes, threw back his head, spread his wings. And leapt.

As he soared into the sky he was surprised to hear a thump behind him. And the sun came out from behind the clouds.

Later on, the pharaoh felt awfully embarrassed about it.

The three new assassins staggered slowly along the street, constantly on the point of falling over but never quite reaching it, trying to sing 'A Wizard's Staff Has A Knob On The End' in harmony or at least in the same key.

'Tis big an' i'ss round an' weighs three to the –' sang Chidder. 'Blast, what've I stepped in?'

'Anyone know where we are?' said Arthur.

'We – we were headed for the Guildhouse,' said Teppic, 'only must of took the wrong way, that's the river up ahead. Can smell it.'

Caution penetrated Arthur's armour of alcohol.

'Could be dangerous pep – plep – people around, this time o' night,' he hazarded.

'Yep,' said Chidder, with satisfaction, 'us. Got ticket to prove it. Got test and everything. Like to see anyone try anything with us.'

'Right,' agreed Teppic, leaning against him for support of a sort. 'We'll slit them from wossname to thingy.'

'Right!'

They lurched uncertainly out on to the Brass Bridge.

In fact there *were* dangerous people around in the pre-dawn shadows, and currently these were some twenty paces behind them.

The complex system of criminal Guilds had not actually made Ankh-Morpork a safer place, it just rationalised its dangers and put them on a regular and reliable footing. The major Guilds policed the city with more thoroughness and certainly more success than the old Watch had ever managed, and it was true that any freelance and unlicensed thief caught by the Thieves' Guild would soon find himself remanded in custody for social inquiry reports plus having his knees nailed together[*]. However, there were always a few spirits who would venture a precarious living outside the lawless, and five men of this description were closing cautiously on the trio to introduce them to this week's special offer, a cut throat plus theft and burial in the river mud of your choice.

People normally keep out of the way of assassins because of an instinctive feeling that killing people for very large sums of money is disapproved of by the gods (who generally prefer people to be killed for very small sums of money or for free) and could result in hubris, which is the judgement of the gods. The gods are great believers in justice, at least as far as it extends to humans, and have been known to dispense it so enthusiastically that people miles away are turned into a cruet.

However, assassin's black doesn't frighten everyone, and in certain sections of society there is a distinct cachet in killing an assassin. It's rather like smashing a sixer in conkers.

Broadly, therefore, the three even now lurching across the deserted planks of the Brass Bridge were dead drunk assassins and the men behind them were bent on inserting the significant comma.

Chidder wandered into one of the heraldic wooden hippopotami[†] that lined the seaward edge of the bridge, bounced off and flopped over the parapet.

'Feel sick,' he announced.

'Feel free,' said Arthur, 'that's what the river's for.'

---

[*] When the Thieves' Guild declared a General Strike in the Year of the Engaging Sloth, the actual level of crime doubled.

[†] One of the two[‡] legends about the founding of Ankh-Morpork relates that the two orphaned brothers who built the city were in fact found and suckled by a hippopotamus (lit. *orijeple*, although some historians hold that this is a mistranslation of *orejaple*, a type of glass-fronted drinks cabinet). Eight heraldic hippos line the bridge, facing out to sea. It is said that if danger ever threatens the city, they will run away.

[‡] The other legend, not normally recounted by citizens, is that at an even earlier time a group of wise men survived a flood sent by the gods by building a huge boat, and on this boat they took two of every type of animal then existing on the Disc. After some weeks the combined manure was beginning to weigh the boat low in the water so – the story runs – they tipped it over the side, and called it Ankh-Morpork.

Teppic sighed. He was attached to rivers, which he felt were designed to have water lilies on top and crocodiles underneath, and the Ankh always depressed him because if you put a water lily in it, it would dissolve. It drained the huge silty plains all the way to the Ramtop mountains, and by the time it had passed through Ankh-Morpork, pop. one million, it could only be called a liquid because it moved faster than the land around it; actually being sick in it would probably make it, on average, marginally cleaner.

He stared down at the thin trickle that oozed between the central pillars, and then raised his gaze to the grey horizon.

'Sun's coming up,' he announced.

'Don't remember eating that,' muttered Chidder.

Teppic stepped back, and a knife ripped past his nose and buried itself in the buttocks of the hippo next to him.

Five figures stepped out of the mists. The three assassins instinctively drew together.

'You come near me, you'll really regret it,' moaned Chidder, clutching his stomach. 'The cleaning bill will be *horrible*.'

'Well now, what have we here?' said the leading thief. This is the sort of thing that gets said in these circumstances.

'Thieves' Guild, are you?' said Arthur.

'No,' said the leader, 'we're the small and unrepresentative minority that gets the rest a bad name. Give us your valuables and weapons, please. This won't make any difference to the outcome, you understand. It's just that corpse robbing is unpleasant and degrading.'

'We could rush them,' said Teppic, uncertainly.

'Don't look at me,' said Arthur, 'I couldn't find my arse with an atlas.'

'You'll really be sorry when I'm sick,' said Chidder.

Teppic was aware of the throwing knives stuffed up either sleeve, and that the chances of him being able to get hold of one in time still to be alive to throw it were likely to be very small.

At times like this religious solace is very important. He turned and looked towards the sun, just as it withdrew from the cloudbanks of the dawn.

There was a tiny dot in the centre of it.

The late King Teppicymon XXVII opened his eyes.

'I was flying,' he whispered, 'I remember the feeling of wings. What am I doing here?'

He tried to stand up. There was a temporary feeling of heaviness, which suddenly dropped away so that he rose to his feet almost without any effort. He looked down to see what had caused it.

'Oh dear,' he said.

The culture of the river kingdom had a lot to say about death and what happened afterwards. In fact it had very little to say about life, regarding it as a sort of inconvenient prelude to the main event and something to be hurried through as politely as possible, and therefore the pharaoh reached the conclusion that he was dead very quickly. The sight of his mangled body on the sand below him played a major part in this.

There was a greyness about everything. The landscape had a ghostly look, as though he could walk straight through it. Of course, he thought, I probably can.

He rubbed the analogue of his hands. Well, this is it. This is where it gets interesting; this is where I start to really *live*.

Behind him a voice said, GOOD MORNING.

The king turned.

'Hallo,' he said. 'You'd be –'

DEATH, said Death.

The king looked surprised.

'I understood that Death came as a three-headed giant scarab beetle,' he said.

Death shrugged. WELL. NOW YOU KNOW.

'What's that thing in your hand?'

THIS? IT'S A SCYTHE.

'Strange-looking object, isn't it?' said the pharaoh. 'I thought Death carried the Flail of Mercy and the Reaping Hook of Justice.'

Death appeared to think about this.

WHAT IN? he said.

'Pardon?'

ARE WE STILL TALKING ABOUT A GIANT BEETLE?

'Ah. In his mandibles, I suppose. But I think he's got arms in one of the frescoes in the palace.' The king hesitated. 'Seems a bit silly, really, now I come to tell someone. I mean, a giant beetle with arms. And the head of an ibis, I seem to recall.'

Death sighed. He was not a creature of Time, and therefore past and future were all one to him, but there had been a period when he'd made an effort to appear in whatever form the client expected. This foundered because it was usually impossible to know what the client was expecting until after they were dead. And then he'd decided that, since no-one ever really expected to die anyway, he might as well please himself and he'd henceforth stuck to the familiar black-cowled robe, which was neat and very familiar and acceptable everywhere, like the best credit cards.

'Anyway,' said the pharaoh, 'I expect we'd better be going.'

WHERE TO?

'Don't *you* know?'

I AM HERE ONLY TO SEE THAT YOU DIE AT THE APPOINTED TIME. WHAT HAPPENS NEXT IS UP TO YOU.

'Well . . .' The king automatically scratched his chin. 'I suppose I have to wait until they've done all the preparations and so forth. Mummified me. And built a bloody pyramid. Um. Do I have to hang around here to wait for all that?'

I ASSUME SO. Death clicked his fingers and a magnificent white horse ceased its grazing on some of the garden greenery and trotted towards him.

'Oh. Well, I think I shall look away. They take all the squishy inside bits out first, you know.' A look of faint worry crossed his face. Things that had seemed perfectly sensible when he was alive seemed a little suspect now that he was dead.

'It's to preserve the body so that it may begin life anew in the Netherworld,' he added, in a slightly perplexed voice. 'And then they wrap you in bandages. At least *that* seems logical.'

He rubbed his nose. 'But then they put all this food and drink in the pyramid with you. Bit weird, really.'

WHERE ARE ONE'S INTERNAL ORGANS AT THIS POINT?

'That's the funny thing, isn't it? They're in a jar in the next room,' said the king, his voice edged with doubt. 'We even put a damn great model cart in dad's pyramid.'

His frown deepened. 'Solid wood, it was,' he said, half to himself, 'with gold leaf all over it. And four wooden bullocks to pull it. Then we whacked a damn great stone over the door . . .'

He tried to think, and found that it was surprisingly easy. New ideas were pouring into his mind in a cold, clear stream. They had to do with the play of light on the rocks, the deep blue of the sky, the manifold possibilities of the world that stretched away on every side of him. Now that he didn't have a body to importune him with its insistent demands the world seemed full of astonishments, but unfortunately among the first of them was the fact that much of what you thought was true now seemed as solid and reliable as marsh gas. And also that, just as he was fully equipped to enjoy the world, he was going to be buried inside a pyramid.

When you die, the first thing you lose is your life. The next thing is your illusions.

I CAN SEE YOU HAVE GOT A LOT TO THINK ABOUT, said Death, mounting up. AND NOW, IF YOU'LL EXCUSE ME –

'Hang on a moment –'

YES?

'When I ... fell, I could have sworn that I was flying.'

THAT PART OF YOU THAT WAS DIVINE DID FLY, NATURALLY. *YOU* ARE NOW FULLY MORTAL.

'Mortal?'

TAKE IT FROM ME. I KNOW ABOUT THESE THINGS.

'Oh. Look, there's quite a few questions I'd like to ask –'

THERE ALWAYS ARE. I'M SORRY. Death clapped his heels to his horse's flanks, and vanished.

The king stood there as several servants came hurrying along the palace wall, slowed down as they approached his corpse, and advanced with caution.

'Are you all right, O jewelled master of the sun?' one of them ventured.

'No, I'm not,' snapped the king, who was having some of his basic assumptions about the universe severely rattled, and that never puts anyone in a good mood. 'I'm by way of being dead just at the moment. Amazing, isn't it,' he added bitterly.

'Can you hear us, O divine bringer of the morning?' inquired the other servant, tiptoeing closer.

'I've just fallen off a hundred foot wall on to my head, what do you think?' shouted the king.

'I don't think he can hear us, Jahmet,' said the other servant.

'Listen,' said the king, whose urgency was equalled only by the servants' total inability to hear anything he was saying, 'you must find my son and tell him to forget about the pyramid business, at least until I've thought about it a bit, there are one or two points which seem a little self-contradictory about the whole afterlife arrangements, and –'

'Shall I shout?' said Jahmet.

'I don't think you can shout loud enough. I think he's dead.'

Jahmet looked down at the stiffening corpse.

'Bloody hell,' he said eventually. 'Well, that's tomorrow up the spout for a start.'

The sun, unaware that it was making its farewell performance, continued to drift smoothly above the rim of the world. And out of it, moving faster than any bird should be able to fly, a seagull bore down on Ankh-Morpork, on the Brass Bridge and eight still figures, on one staring face ...

Seagulls were common enough in Ankh. But as this one flew over the group it uttered one long, guttural scream that caused three of the thieves to drop their knives. Nothing with feathers ought to have been able to make a noise like that. It had claws in it.

The bird wheeled in a tight circle and fluttered to a perch on a convenient wooden hippo, where it glared at the group with mad red eyes.

The leading thief tore his fascinated gaze away from it just as he heard Arthur say, quite pleasantly, 'This is a no.2 throwing knife. I got ninety-six per cent for throwing knives. Which eyeball don't you need?'

The leader stared at him. As far as the other young assassins were concerned, he noticed, one was still staring fixedly at the seagull while the other was busy being noisily sick over the parapet.

'There's only one of you,' he said. 'There's five of us.'

'But soon there will only be four of you,' said Arthur.

Moving slowly, like someone in a daze, Teppic reached out his hand to the seagull. With any normal seagull this would have resulted in the loss of a thumb, but the creature hopped on to it with the smug air of the master returning to the old plantation.

It seemed to make the thieves increasingly uneasy. Arthur's smile wasn't helping either.

'That's a nice bird,' said the leader, in the inanely cheerful tones of the extremely worried. Teppic was dreamily stroking its bullet head.

'I think it would be a good idea if you went away,' said Arthur, as the bird shuffled sideways on to Teppic's wrist. Gripping with webbed feet, thrusting out its wings to maintain its balance, it should have looked clownish but instead looked full of hidden power, as though it was an eagle's secret identity. When it opened its mouth, revealing a ridiculous purple bird tongue, there was a suggestion that this seagull could do a lot more than menace a seaside tomato sandwich.

'Is it magic?' said one of the thieves, and was quickly hushed.

'We'll be going, then,' said the leader, 'sorry about the misunderstanding –'

Teppic gave him a warm, unseeing smile.

Then they all heard the insistent little noise. Six pairs of eyes swivelled around and down; Chidder's were already in position.

Below them, pouring darkly across the dehydrated mud, the Ankh was rising.

Dios, First Minister and high priest among high priests, wasn't a naturally religious man. It wasn't a desirable quality in a high priest, it affected your judgement, made you *unsound*. Start believing in things and the whole business became a farce.

Not that he had anything against belief. People needed to believe in gods, if only because it was so hard to believe in people. The gods were necessary. He just required that they stayed out of the way and let him get on with things.

Mind you, it was a blessing that he had the looks for it. If your genes saw fit to give you a tall frame, a bald head and a nose you could plough rocks with, they probably had a definite aim in mind.

He instinctively distrusted people to whom religion came easily. The naturally religious, he felt, were unstable and given to wandering in the desert and having revelations – as if the gods would lower themselves to that sort of thing. And they never got anything done. They started thinking that rituals weren't important. They started thinking that you could talk to the gods direct. Dios knew, with the kind of rigid and unbending certainty you could pivot the world on, that the gods of Djelibeybi liked ritual as much as anyone else. After all, a god who was against ritual would be like a fish who was against water.

He sat on the steps of the throne with his staff across his knees, and passed on the king's orders. The fact that they were not currently being issued by any king was not a problem. Dios had been high priest now for, well, more years than he cared to remember, he knew quite clearly what orders a sensible king would be giving, and he gave them.

Anyway, the Face of the Sun was on the throne, and that was what mattered. It was a solid gold, head-enveloping mask, to be worn by the current ruler on all public occasions; its expression, to the sacrilegious, was one of good-natured constipation. For thousands of years it had symbolised kingship in Djelibeybi. It had also made it very difficult to tell kings apart.

This was extremely symbolic as well, although no-one could remember what of.

There was a lot of that sort of thing in the Old Kingdom. The staff across his knees, for example, with its very symbolic snakes entwined symbolically around an allegorical camel prod. The people believed this gave the high priests power over the gods and the dead, but this was probably a metaphor, i.e., a lie.

Dios shifted position.

'Has the king been ushered to the Room of Going Forth?' he said.

The circle of lesser high priests nodded.

'Dil the embalmer is attending upon him at this instant, O Dios.'

'Very well. And the builder of pyramids has been instructed?'

Hoot Koomi, high priest of Khefin, the Two-Faced God of Gateways, stepped forward.

'I took the liberty of attending to that myself, O Dios,' he purred.

Dios tapped his fingers on his staff. 'Yes,' he said, 'I have no doubt that you did.'

It was widely expected by the priesthood that Koomi would be the one to succeed Dios in the event of Dios ever actually dying, although hanging around waiting for Dios to die had never seemed to be a rewarding occupation. The only dissenting opinion was that of Dios himself who, if he had any friends, would probably have confided in them certain conditions that would need to apply first, viz., blue moons, aerial pigs and he, Dios, being seen in Hell. He would probably have added that the only difference between Koomi and a sacred crocodile was the crocodile's basic honesty of purpose.

'Very well,' he said.

'If I may remind your lordship?' said Koomi. The faces of the other priests went a nice safe blank as Dios glared.

'Yes, Koomi?'

'The prince, O Dios. Has he been summoned?'

'No,' said Dios.

'Then how will he know?' said Koomi.

'He will know,' said Dios firmly.

'How will this be?'

'He will *know*. And now you are all dismissed. Go away. See to your gods!'

They scurried out, leaving Dios alone on the steps. It had been his accustomed position for so long that he'd polished a groove in the stonework, into which he fitted exactly.

Of course the prince would know. It was part of the neatness of things. But in the grooves of his mind, ground deep by the years of ritual and due observance, Dios detected a certain uneasiness. It was not at home in there. Uneasiness was something that happened to other people. He hadn't got where he was today by allowing room for doubt. Yet there was a tiny thought back there, a tiny *certainty*, that there was going to be trouble with this new king.

Well. The boy would soon learn. They all learned.

He shifted position, and winced. The aches and pains were back, and he couldn't allow that. They got in the way of his duty, and his duty was a sacred trust.

He'd have to visit the necropolis again. Tonight.

'He's not himself, you can see that.'

'Who is he, then?' said Chidder.

They splashed unsteadily down the street, not drunkenly this time, but with the awkward gait of two people trying to do the steering for three. Teppic was walking, but not in a way that gave them any confidence that his mind was having any part of it.

Around them doors were being thrown open, curses were being cursed, there was the sound of furniture being dragged up to first-floor rooms.

'Must have been a hell of a storm up in the mountains,' said Arthur. 'It doesn't usually flood like this even in the spring.'

'Maybe we should burn some feathers under his nose,' suggested Chidder.

'That bloody seagull would be favourite,' Arthur growled.

'What seagull?'

'You saw it.'

'Well, what about it?'

'You *did* see it, didn't you?' Uncertainty flickered its dark flame in Arthur's eyes. The seagull had disappeared in all the excitement.

'My attention was a bit occupied,' said Chidder diffidently. 'It must have been those mint wafers they served with the coffee. I thought they were a bit off.'

'Definitely a touch eldritch, that bird,' said Arthur. 'Look, let's put him down somewhere while I empty the water out of my boots, can we?'

There was a bakery nearby, its doors thrown open so that the trays of new loaves could cool in the early morning. They propped Teppic against the wall.

'He looks as though someone hit him on the head,' said Chidder.

'No-one did, did they?'

Arthur shook his head. Teppic's face was locked in a gentle grin.

Whatever his eyes were focused on wasn't occupying the usual set of dimensions.

'We ought to get him back to the Guild and into the san –'

He stopped. There was a peculiar rustling sound behind him. The loaves of bread were bouncing gently on their trays. One or two of them vibrated on to the floor, where they spun around like overturned beetles.

Then, their crusts cracking open like eggshells, they sprouted hundreds of green shoots.

Within a few seconds the trays were waving stands of young corn, their heads already beginning to fill out and bend over. Through them marched Chidder and Arthur, poker-faced, doing the 100-metre nonchalant walk with Teppic held rigidly between them.

'Is it him doing all this?'

'I've got a feeling that –' Arthur looked behind them, just in case any angry bakers had come out and spotted such aggressively wholemeal produce, and stopped so suddenly that the other two swung around him, like a rudder.

They looked thoughtfully at the street.

'Not something you see every day, that,' said Chidder at last.

'You mean the way there's grass and stuff growing up everywhere he puts his feet?'

'Yes.'

Their eyes met. As one, they looked down at Teppic's shoes. He was already ankle-deep in greenery, which was cracking the centuries-old cobbles in its urgency.

Without speaking a word, they gripped his elbows and lifted him into the air.

'The san,' said Arthur.

'The san,' agreed Chidder.

But they both knew, even then, that this was going to involve more than a hot poultice.

The doctor sat back.

'Fairly straightforward,' he said, thinking quickly. 'A case of *mortis portalis tackulatum* with complications.'

'What's that mean?' said Chidder.

'In layman's terms,' the doctor sniffed, 'he's as dead as a doornail.'

'What are the complications?'

The doctor looked shifty. 'He's still breathing,' he said. 'Look, his pulse is nearly humming and he's got a temperature you could fry eggs on.' He hesitated, aware that this was probably too straightforward and easily understood; medicine was a new art on the Disc, and wasn't going to get anywhere if people could understand it.

'*Pyrocerebrum ouerf culinaire*,' he said, after working it out in his head.

'Well, what can you do about it?' said Arthur.

'Nothing. He's dead. All the medical tests prove it. So, er . . . bury him, keep him nice and cool, and tell him to come and see me next week. In daylight, for preference.'

'But he's still breathing!'

'These are just reflex actions that might easily confuse the layman,' said the doctor airily.

Chidder sighed. He suspected that the Guild, who after all had an unrivalled experience of sharp knives and complex organic compounds, were much better at elementary diagnostics than were the doctors. The Guild might kill people, but at least it didn't expect them to be grateful for it.

Teppic opened his eyes.

'I must go home,' he said.

'Dead, is he?' said Chidder.

The doctor was a credit to his profession. 'It's not unusual for a corpse to make distressing noises after death,' he said valiantly, 'which can upset relatives and –'

Teppic sat bolt upright.

'Also, muscular spasms in the stiffening body can in certain circumstances –' the doctor began, but his heart wasn't in it any more. Then an idea occurred to him.

'It's a rare and mysterious ailment,' he said, 'which is going around a lot at the moment. It's caused by a – a – by something so small it can't be detected in any way whatsoever,' he finished, with a self-congratulatory smile on his face. It was a good one, he had to admit. He'd have to remember it.

'Thank you very much,' said Chidder, opening the door and ushering him through. 'Next time we're feeling really well, we'll definitely call you in.'

'It's probably a walrus,' said the doctor, as he was gently but firmly propelled out of the room. 'He's caught a walrus, there's a lot of it going –'

The door slammed shut.

Teppic swung his legs off the bed and clutched at his head.

'I've got to go home,' he repeated.

'Why?' said Arthur.

'Don't know. The kingdom wants me.'

'You seemed to be taken pretty bad there –' Arthur began. Teppic waved his hands dismissively.

'Look,' he said, 'please, I don't want anyone sensibly pointing out things. I don't want anyone telling me I should rest. None of it matters. I will be back in the kingdom as soon as possible. It's not a case of *must*, you understand. I *will*. And you can help me, Chiddy.'

'How?'

'Your father has an extremely fast vessel he uses for smuggling,' said Teppic flatly. 'He will lend it to me, in exchange for favourable consideration of future trading opportunities. If we leave inside the hour, it will do the journey in plenty of time.'

'My father is an honest trader!'

'On the contrary. Seventy per cent of his income last year was from undeclared trading in the following commodities –' Teppic's eyes stared into nothingness – 'From illegal transport of gullanes and leuchars, nine per cent. From nightrunning of untaxed –'

'Well, thirty per cent honest,' Chidder admitted, 'which is a lot more honest than most. You'd better tell me how you know. Extremely quickly.'

'I – don't know,' said Teppic. 'When I was . . . asleep, it seemed I knew everything. Everything about everything. I think my father is dead.'

'Oh,' said Chidder. 'Gosh. I'm sorry.'

'Oh, no. It's not like that. It's what he would have wanted. I think he was rather looking forward to it. In our family, death is when you really start to, you know, enjoy life. I expect he's rather enjoying it.'

In fact the pharaoh was sitting on a spare slab in the ceremonial preparation room watching his own soft bits being carefully removed from his body and put into the special canopic jars.

This is not a sight often seen by people – at least, not by people in a position to take a thoughtful interest.

He was rather upset. Although he was no longer officially inhabiting his body he was still attached to it by some sort of occult bond, and it is hard to be very happy at seeing two artisans up to the elbows in bits of you.

The jokes aren't funny, either. Not when you are, as it were, the butt.

'Look, master Dil,' said Gern, a plump, red-faced young man who the king had learned was the new apprentice, 'Look . . . right . . . watch this, watch this . . . look . . . your name in lights. Get it? Your name in lights, see?'

'Just put them in the jar, boy,' said Dil wearily. 'And while we're on the subject I didn't think much of the Gottle of Geer routine, either.'

'Sorry, master.'

'And pass me over a number three brain hook while you're up that end, will you?'

'Coming right up, master,' said Gern.

'And don't jog me. This is a fiddly bit.'

'Sure thing.'

The king craned nearer.

Gern rummaged around at his end of the job and then gave a long, low whistle.

'Will you look at the colour of this!' he said. 'You wouldn't think so, would you? Is it something they eat, master?'

Dil sighed. 'Just put it in the pot, Gern.'

'Right you are, master. Master?'

'Yes, lad?'

'Which bit's got the god in it, master?'

Dil squinted up the king's nostril, trying to concentrate.

'That gets sorted out before he comes down here,' he said patiently.

'I wondered,' said Gern, 'because there's not a jar for it, see.'

'No. There wouldn't be. It'd have to be a rather strange jar, Gern.'

Gern looked a bit disappointed. 'Oh,' he said, 'so he's just ordinary, then, is he?'

'In a strictly organic sense,' said Dil, his voice slightly muffled.

'Our mum said he was all right as a king,' said Gern. 'What do you think?'

Dil paused with a jar in his hand, and seemed to give the conversation some thought for the first time.

'Never think about it until they come down here,' he said. 'I suppose he was better than most. Nice pair of lungs. Clean kidneys. Good big sinuses, which is what I always look for in a king.' He looked down, and delivered his professional judgement. 'Pleasure to work with, really.'

'Our mum said his heart was in the right place,' said Gern. The king, hovering dismally in the corner, gave a gloomy nod. Yes, he thought. Jar three, top shelf.

Dil wiped his hands on a rag, and sighed. Possibly thirty-five years in the funeral business, which had given him a steady hand, a philosophic manner and a keen interest in vegetarianism, had also granted him powers of hearing beyond the ordinary. Because he was almost persuaded that, right beside his ear, someone else sighed too.

The king wandered sadly over to the other side of the room, and stared at the dull liquid of the preparation vat.

Funny, that. When he was alive it had all seemed so sensible, so *obvious*. Now he was dead it looked a huge waste of effort.

It was beginning to annoy him. He watched Dil and his apprentice tidy up, burn some ceremonial resins, lift him – it – up, carry it respectfully across the room and slide it gently into the oily embrace of the preservative.

Teppicymon XXVII gazed into the murky depths at his own body lying sadly on the bottom, like the last pickled gherkin in the jar.

He raised his eyes to the sacks in the corner. They were full of straw. He didn't need telling what was going to be done with it.

The boat didn't glide. It *insinuated* itself through the water, dancing across the waves on the tips of the twelve oars, spreading like an oil slick, gliding like a bird. It was matt black and shaped like a shark.

There was no drummer to beat the rhythm. The boat didn't want the weight. Anyway, he'd have needed the full kit, including snares.

Teppic sat between the lines of silent rowers, in the narrow gully that was the cargo hold. Better not to speculate what cargoes. The boat looked designed to move very small quantities of things very quickly and without anyone noticing, and he doubted whether even the Smugglers' Guild was aware of its existence. Commerce was more interesting than he thought.

They found the delta with suspicious ease – how many times had this whispering shadow slipped up the river, he wondered – and above the exotic smells from the mysterious former cargo he could detect the scents of home. Crocodile dung. Reed pollen. Waterlily blossoms. Lack of plumbing. The rank of lions and reek of hippos.

The leading oarsman tapped him gently on the shoulder and motioned him up, steadied him as he stepped overboard into a few feet of water. By the time he'd waded ashore the boat had turned and was a mere suspicion of a shadow downstream.

Because he was naturally curious, Teppic wondered where it would lie up during the day, since it had the look about it of a boat designed to travel only under cover of darkness, and decided that it'd probably lurk somewhere in the high reed marshes on the delta.

And because he was now a king, he made a mental note to have the marshes patrolled periodically from now on. A king should know things.

He stopped, ankle deep in river ooze. He had known *everything*.

Arthur had rambled on vaguely about seagulls and rivers and loaves of bread sprouting, which suggested he'd drunk too much. All Teppic could remember was waking up with a terrible sense of loss, as his memory failed to hold and leaked away its new treasures. It was like the tremendous insights that come in dreams and vanish on waking. He'd known everything, but as soon as he tried to remember what it was it poured out of his head, as from a leaky bucket.

But it had left him with a new sensation. Before, his life had been ambling along, bent by circumstance. Now it was clicking along on bright rails. Perhaps he hadn't got it in him to be an assassin, but he knew he could be a king.

His feet found solid ground. The boat had dropped him off a little way downstream of the palace and, blue in the moonlight, the pyramid flares on the far bank were filling the night with their familiar glow.

The abodes of the happy dead came in all sizes although not, of course, in all shapes. They clustered thickly nearer the city, as though the dead like company.

And even the oldest ones were all complete. No-one had borrowed any of the stones to build houses or make roads. Teppic felt obscurely proud of that. No-one had unsealed the doors and wandered around inside to see if the dead had any old treasures they weren't using any more. And every day, without fail, food was left in the little antechambers; the commissaries of the dead occupied a large part of the palace.

Sometimes the food went, sometimes it didn't. The priests, however, were very clear on this point. Regardless of whether the food was consumed or not, *it had been eaten by the dead*. Presumably they enjoyed it; they never complained, or came back for seconds.

Look after the dead, said the priests, and the dead would look after you. After all, they were in the majority.

Teppic pushed aside the reeds. He straightened his clothing, brushed some mud off his sleeve and set off for the palace.

Ahead of him, dark against the flarelight, stood the great statue of Khuft. Seven thousand years ago Khuft had led his people out of – Teppic couldn't remember, but somewhere where they hadn't liked being, probably, and for thoroughly good reasons; it was at times like this he wished he knew more history – and had prayed in the desert and the gods of the place had shown him the Old Kingdom. And he had entered, yea, and taken possession thereof, that it should ever be the dwelling place of his seed. Something like that, anyway. There were probably more yeas and a few verilys, with added milk and honey. But the sight of that great patriarchal face, that outstretched arm, that chin you could crack stones on, bold in the flarelight, told him what he already knew.

He was home, and he was never going to leave again.

The sun began to rise.

The greatest mathematician alive on the Disc, and in fact the last one in the Old Kingdom, stretched out in his stall and counted the pieces of straw in his bedding. Then he estimated the number of nails in the wall. Then he spent a few minutes proving that an automorphic resonance field has a semi-infinite number of irresolute prime ideals. After that, in order to pass the time, he ate his breakfast again.

BOOK II

The Book of the Dead

Two weeks went past. Ritual and ceremony in their due times kept the world under the sky and the stars in their courses. It was astonishing what ritual and ceremony could do.

The new king examined himself in the mirror, and frowned.

'What's it made of?' he said. 'It's rather foggy.'

'Bronze, sire. Polished bronze,' said Dios, handing him the Flail of Mercy.

'In Ankh-Morpork we had glass mirrors with silver on the back. They were very good.'

'Yes, sire. Here we have bronze, sire.'

'Do I really have to wear this gold mask?'

'The Face of the Sun, sire. Handed down through all the ages. Yes, sire. On all public occasions, sire.'

Teppic peered out through the eye slots. It was certainly a handsome face. It smiled faintly. He remembered his father visiting the nursery one day and forgetting to take it off; Teppic had screamed the place down.

'It's rather heavy.'

'It is weighted with the centuries,' said Dios, and passed over the obsidian Reaping Hook of Justice.

'Have you been a priest long, Dios?'

'Many years, sire, man and eunuch. Now –'

'Father said you were high priest even in grandad's time. You must be very old.'

'Well-preserved, sir. The gods have been kind to me,' said Dios, in the face of the evidence. 'And now, sire, if we could just hold this as well . . .'

'What is it?'

'The Honeycomb of Increase, sire. Very important.'

Teppic juggled it into position.

'I expect you've seen a lot of changes,' he said politely.

A look of pain passed over the old priest's face, but quickly, as if it was in a hurry to get away. 'No, sire,' he said smoothly, 'I have been very fortunate.'

'Oh. What's this?'

'The Sheaf of Plenty, sire. Extremely significant, very symbolic.'

'If you could just tuck it under my arm, then . . . Have you ever heard of plumbing, Dios?'

The priest snapped his fingers at one of the attendants. 'No, sire,' he said, and leaned forward. 'This is the Asp of Wisdom. I'll just tuck it in here, shall I?'

'It's like buckets, but not as, um, smelly.'

'Sounds dreadful, sire. The smell keeps bad influences away, I have always understood. This, sire, is the Gourd of the Waters of the Heavens. If we could just raise our chin . . .'

'This is all necessary, is it?' said Teppic indistinctly.

'It is traditional, sire. If we could just rearrange things a little, sire . . . here is the Three-Pronged Spear of the Waters of the Earth; I think we will be able to get *this* finger around it. We shall have to see about our marriage, sire.'

'I'm not sure we would be compatible, Dios.'

The high priest smiled with his mouth. 'Sire is pleased to jest, sire,' he said urbanely. 'However, it is essential that you marry.'

'I am afraid all the girls I know are in Ankh-Morpork,' said Teppic airily, knowing in his heart that this broad statement referred to Mrs Collar, who had been his bedder in the sixth form, and one of the serving wenches who'd taken a shine to him and always gave him extra gravy. (But . . . and his blood pounded at the memory . . . there had been the annual Assassins' Ball and, because the young assassins were trained to move freely in society and were expected to dance well, and because well-cut black silk and long legs attracted a certain type of older woman, they'd whirled the night away through baubons, galliards and slow-stepping pavonines, until the air thickened with musk and hunger. Chidder, whose simple open face and easygoing manner were a winner every time, came back to bed very late for days afterwards and tended to fall asleep during lessons . . .)

'Quite unsuitable, sire. We would require a consort well-versed in the observances. Of course, our aunt is available, sire.'

There was a clatter. Dios sighed, and motioned the attendants to pick things up.

'If we could just begin again, sire? This is the Cabbage of Vegetative Increase –'

'Sorry,' said Teppic, 'I didn't hear you say I should marry my aunt, did I?'

'You did, sire. Interfamilial marriage is a proud tradition of our lineage,' said Dios.

'But my aunt is my *aunt*!'

Dios rolled his eyes. He'd advised the late king repeatedly about the education of his son, but the man was stubborn, stubborn. Now he'd have to do it on the fly. The gods were testing him, he decided. It took decades to make a monarch, and he had weeks to do it in.

'Yes, sire,' he said patiently. 'Of course. And she is also your uncle, your cousin and your father.'

'Hold on. My father –'

The priest raised his hand soothingly. 'A technicality,' he said. 'Your great-great-grandmother once declared she is king as a matter of political expediency and I don't believe the edict is ever rescinded.'

'But she *was* a woman, though?'

Dios looked shocked. 'Oh no, sire. She is a man. She herself declared this.'

'But look, a chap's aunt –'

'Quite so, sire. I quite understand.'

'Well, thank you,' said Teppic.

'It is a great shame that we have no sisters.'

'Sisters!'

'It does not do to water the divine blood, sire. The sun might not like it. Now *this*, sire, is the Scapula of Hygiene. Where would you like it put?'

King Teppicymon XXVII was watching himself being stuffed. It was just as well he didn't feel hunger these days. Certainly he would never want to eat chicken again.

'Very nice stitching there, master.'

'Just keep your finger still, Gern.'

'My mother does stitching like that. She's got a pinny with stitching like that, has our mum,' said Gern conversationally.

'Keep it still, I said.'

'It's got all ducks and hens on it,' Gern supplied helpfully.

Dil concentrated on the job in hand. It was good workmanship, he was prepared to admit. The Guild of Embalmers and Allied Trades had awarded him medals for it.

'It must make you feel really proud,' said Gern.

'What?'

'Well, our mam says the king goes on living, sort of thing, after all this stuffing and stitching. Sort of in the Netherworld. With your stitching in him.'

And several sacks of straw and a couple of buckets of pitch, thought the shade of the king sadly. And the wrapping off Gern's lunch, although he didn't blame the lad, who'd just forgotten where he'd put it. All eternity with someone's lunch wrapping as part of your vital organs. There had been half a sausage left, too.

He'd become quite attached to Dil, and even to Gern. He seemed still to be attached to his body, too – at least, he felt uncomfortable if he wandered more than a few hundred yards away from it – and so in the course of the last couple of days he'd learned quite a lot about them.

Funny, really. He'd spent the whole of his life in the kingdom talking to a few priests and so forth. He knew objectively there had been other people around – servants and gardeners and so forth – but they figured in his life as blobs. He was at the top, and then his family, and then the priests and the nobles of course, and then there were the blobs. Damn fine blobs, of course, some of the finest blobs in the world, as loyal a collection of blobs as a king might hope to rule. But blobs, none the less.

But now he was absolutely engrossed in the daily details of Dil's shy hopes for advancement within the Guild, and the unfolding story of Gern's clumsy overtures to Glwenda, the garlic farmer's daughter who lived nearby. He listened in fascinated astonishment to the elaboration of a world as full of subtle distinctions of grade and station as the one he had so recently left; it was terrible to think that he might never know if Gern overcame her father's objections and won his intended, or if Dil's work on this job – on *him* – would allow him to aspire to the rank of Exalted Grand Ninety-Degree Variance of the Natron Lodge of the Guild of Embalmers and Allied Trades.

It was as if death was some astonishing optical device which turned even a drop of water into a complex hive of life.

He found an overpowering urge to counsel Dil on elementary politics, or apprise Gern of the benefits of washing and looking respectable. He tried it several times. They could sense him, there was no doubt about that. But they just put it down to draughts.

Now he watched Dil pad over to the big table of bandages, and come back with a thick swatch which he held reflectively against what even the king was now prepared to think of as his corpse.

'I think the linen,' he said at last. 'It's definitely his colour.'

Gern put his head on one side.

'He'd look good in the hessian,' he said. 'Or maybe the calico.'

'Not the calico. Definitely not the calico. On him it's too big.'

'He could moulder into it. With wear, you know.'

Dil snorted. 'Wear? Wear? You shouldn't talk to me about calico and wear. What happens if someone robs the tomb in a thousand years' time and him in calico, I'd like to know. He'd lurch halfway down the corridor, maybe throttle one of them, I'll grant you, but then he's coming undone, right? The elbows'll be out in no time, I'll never live it down.'

'But you'll be dead, master!'

'Dead? What's that got to do with it?' Dil riffled through the samples. 'No, it'll be the hessian. Got plenty of give in it, hessian. Good traction, too. He'll really be able to lurch up speed in the passages, if he ever needs to.'

The king sighed. He'd have preferred something lightweight in taffeta.

'And go and shut the door,' Dil added. 'It's getting breezy in here.'

'And now it's time,' said the high priest, 'for us to see our late father.' He allowed himself a quiet smile. 'I am sure he is looking forward to it,' he added.

Teppic considered this. It wasn't something *he* was looking forward to, but at least it would get everyone's mind off him marrying relatives. He reached down in what he hoped was a kingly fashion to stroke one of the palace cats. This also was not a good move. The creature sniffed it, went cross-eyed with the effort of thought, and then bit his fingers.

'Cats are sacred,' said Dios, shocked at the words Teppic uttered.

'Long-legged cats with silver fur and disdainful expressions are, maybe,' said Teppic, nursing his hand, 'I don't know about this sort. I'm sure sacred cats don't leave dead ibises under the bed. And I'm certain that sacred cats that live surrounded by endless sand don't come indoors and do it in the king's sandals, Dios.'

'All cats are cats,' said Dios, vaguely, and added, 'If we would be so gracious as to follow us.' He motioned Teppic towards a distant arch.

Teppic followed slowly. He'd been back home for what seemed like ages, and it still didn't feel right. The air was too dry. The clothes felt wrong. It was too hot. Even the buildings seemed wrong. The pillars, for one thing. Back ho – back at the Guild, pillars were graceful fluted things with little bunches of stone grapes and things around the top. Here they were massive pear-shaped lumps, where all the stone had run to the bottom.

Half a dozen servants trailed behind him, carrying the various items of regalia.

He tried to imitate Dios's walk, and found the movements coming back to him. You turned your torso *this* way, then you turned your head *this* way, and extended your arms at forty-five degrees to your body with the palms down, and then you attempted to move.

The high priest's staff raised echoes as it touched the flagstones. A blind man could have walked barefoot through the palace by tracing the time-worn dimples it had created over the years.

'I am afraid that we will find that our father has changed somewhat since we last saw him,' said Dios conversationally, as they undulated by the fresco of Queen Khaphut accepting Tribute from the Kingdoms of the World.

'Well, yes,' said Teppic, bewildered by the tone. 'He's dead, isn't he?'

'There's that, too,' said Dios, and Teppic realised that he hadn't been referring to something as trivial as the king's current physical condition.

He was lost in a horrified admiration. It wasn't that Dios was particularly cruel or uncaring, it was simply that death was a mere irritating transition in the eternal business of existence. The fact that people died was just an inconvenience, like them being out when you called.

It's a strange world, he thought. It's all busy shadows, and it never changes. And I'm part of it.

'Who's he?' he said, pointing to a particularly big fresco showing a tall man with a hat like a chimney and a beard like a rope riding a chariot over a lot of other, much smaller, people.

'His name *is* in the cartouche below,' said Dios primly.

'What?'

'The small oval, sire,' said Dios.

Teppic peered closely at the dense hieroglyphics.

'"Thin eagle, eye, wiggly line, man with a stick, bird sitting down, wiggly line",' he read. Dios winced.

'I believe we must apply ourselves more to the study of modern languages,' he said, recovering a bit. 'His name is Ptaka-ba. He is king when the Djel Empire extends from the Circle Sea to the Rim Ocean, when almost half the continent pays tribute to us.'

Teppic realised what it was about the man's speech that was strange. Dios would bend any sentence to breaking point if it meant avoiding a past tense. He pointed to another fresco.

'And her?' he said.

'She is Queen Khat-leon-ra-pta,' said Dios. 'She wins the kingdom of Howandaland by stealth. This is the time of the Second Empire.'

'But she is dead?' said Teppic.

'I understand so,' said the high priest, after the slightest of pauses. Yes. The past tense definitely bothered Dios.

'I have learned seven languages,' said Teppic, secure in the knowledge that the actual marks he had achieved in three of them would remain concealed in the ledgers of the Guild.

'Indeed, sire?'

'Oh, yes. Morporkian, Vanglemesht, Ephebe, Laotation and – several others . . .' said Teppic.

'Ah.' Dios nodded, smiled, and continued to proceed down the corridor, limping slightly but still measuring his pace like the ticking of centuries. 'The barbarian lands.'

Teppic looked at his father. The embalmers had done a good job. They were waiting for him to tell them so.

Part of him, which still lived in Ankh-Morpork, said: This is a dead body, wrapped up in bandages, surely they can't think that this will help him *get better*? In Ankh, you die and they bury you or burn you or throw you to the ravens. Here, it just means you slow down a bit and get given all the best food. It's ridiculous, how can you run a kingdom like this? They seem to think that being dead is like being deaf, you just have to speak up a bit.

But a second, older voice said: We've run a kingdom like this for seven thousand years. The humblest melon farmer has a lineage that makes kings elsewhere look like mayflies. We used to own the continent, before we sold it again to pay for pyramids. We don't even *think* about other countries less than three thousand years old. It all seems to work.

'Hallo, father,' he said.

The shade of Teppicymon XXVII, which had been watching him closely, hurried across the room.

'You're looking well!' he said. *'Good to see you! Look, this is urgent. Please pay attention, it's about death –'*

'He says he is pleased to see you,' said Dios.

'You can hear him?' said Teppic. 'I didn't hear anything.'

'The dead, naturally, speak through the priests,' said the priest. 'That is the custom, sire.'

'But he can hear me, can he?'

'Of course.'

'I've been thinking about this whole pyramid business and, look, I'm not certain about it.'

Teppic leaned closer. 'Auntie sends her love,' he said loudly. He thought about this. 'That's my aunt, not yours.' I hope, he added.

'I say? I say? Can you hear me?'

'He bids you greetings from the world beyond the veil,' said Dios.

'Well, yes, I suppose I do, but LOOK, I don't want you to go to a lot of trouble and build –'

'We're going to build you a marvellous pyramid, father. You'll really like it there. There'll be people to look after you and everything.' Teppic glanced at Dios for reassurance. 'He'll like that, won't he?'

'I don't WANT one!' screamed the king. 'There's a whole interesting eternity I haven't seen yet. I forbid you to put me in a pyramid!'

'He says that is very proper, and you are a dutiful son,' said Dios.

'Can you see me? How many fingers am I holding up? Think it's fun, do you, spending the rest of your death under a million tons of rock, watching yourself crumble to bits? Is that your idea of a good epoch?'

'It's rather draughty in here, sire,' said Dios. 'Perhaps we should get on.'

'Anyway, you can't possibly afford it!'

'And we'll put your favourite frescoes and statues in with you. You'll like that, won't you,' said Teppic desperately. 'All your bits and pieces around you.

'He will like it, won't he?' he asked Dios, as they walked back to the throne room. 'Only, I don't know, I somehow got a feeling he isn't too happy about it.'

'I assure you, sire,' said Dios, 'he can have no other desire.'

Back in the embalming room King Teppicymon XXVII tried to tap Gern on the shoulder, which had no effect. He gave up and sat down beside himself.

'Don't do it, lad,' he said bitterly. 'Never have descendants.'

And then there was the Great Pyramid itself.

Teppic's footsteps echoed on the marble tiles as he walked around the model. He wasn't sure what one was supposed to do here. But kings, he suspected, were often put in that position; there was always the good old fallback, which was known as taking an interest.

'Well, well,' he said. 'How long have you been designing pyramids?'

Ptaclusp, architect and jobbing pyramid builder to the nobility, bowed deeply.

'All my life, O light of noonday.'

'It must be fascinating,' said Teppic. Ptaclusp looked sidelong at the high priest, who nodded.

'It has its points, O fount of waters,' he ventured. He wasn't used to kings talking to him as though he was a human being. He felt obscurely that it wasn't right.

Teppic waved a hand at the model on its podium.

'Yes,' he said uncertainly. 'Well. Good. Four walls and a pointy tip. Jolly good. First class. Says it all, really.' There still seemed to be too much silence around. He plunged on.

'Good show,' he said. 'I mean, there's no doubt about it. This is . . . a . . . pyramid. And what a pyramid it is! Indeed.'

This still didn't seem enough. He sought for something else. 'People will look at it in centuries to come and they'll say, they'll say . . . that *is* a pyramid. Um.'

He coughed. 'The walls slope nicely,' he croaked.

'But,' he said.

Two pairs of eyes swivelled towards his.

'Um,' he said.

Dios raised an eyebrow.

'Sire?'

'I seem to remember once, my father said that, you know, when he died, he'd quite like to, sort of thing, be buried at sea.'

There wasn't the choke of outrage he had expected. 'He meant the delta. It's very soft ground by the delta,' said Ptaclusp. 'It'd take months to get decent footings in. Then there's your risk of sinking. And the damp. Not good, damp, inside a pyramid.'

'No,' said Teppic, sweating under Dios's gaze, 'I think what he meant was, you know, *in* the sea.'

Ptaclusp's brow furrowed. 'Tricky, that,' he said thoughtfully. 'Interesting idea. I suppose one *could* build a small one, a million tonner, and float it out on pontoons or something . . .'

'No,' said Teppic, trying not to laugh, 'I think what he meant was, buried *without* –'

'Teppicymon XXVII means that he would want to be buried without delay,' said Dios, his voice like greased silk. 'And there is no doubt that he would require to honour the very best you can build, architect.'

67

'No, I'm sure you've got it wrong,' said Teppic.

Dios's face froze. Ptaclusp's slid into the waxen expression of someone with whom it is, suddenly, nothing to do. He started to stare at the floor as if his very survival depended on his memorising it in extreme detail.

'Wrong?' said Dios.

'No offence. I'm sure you mean well,' said Teppic. 'It's just that, well, he seemed very clear about it at the time and –'

'I mean well?' said Dios, tasting each word as though it was a sour grape. Ptaclusp coughed. He had finished with the floor. Now he started on the ceiling.

Dios took a deep breath. '*Sire*,' he said, 'we have always been pyramid builders. All our kings are buried in pyramids. It is how we do things, sire. It is how things are done.'

'Yes, but –'

'It does not admit of dispute,' said Dios. 'Who could wish for anything else? Sealed with all artifice against the desecrations of Time –' now the oiled silk of his voice became armour, hard as steel, scornful as spears – 'Shielded for all Time against the insults of Change.'

Teppic glanced down at the high priest's knuckles. They were white, the bone pressing through the flesh as though in a rage to escape.

His gaze slid up the grey-clad arm to Dios's face. Ye gods, he thought, it's really true, he *does* look like they got tired of waiting for him to die and pickled him anyway. Then his eyes met those of the priest, more or less with a clang.

He felt as though his flesh was being very slowly blown off his bones. He felt that he was no more significant than a mayfly. A necessary mayfly, certainly, a mayfly that would be accorded all due respect, but still an insect with all the rights thereof. And as much free will, in the fury of that gaze, as a scrap of papyrus in a hurricane.

'The king's will is that he be interred in a pyramid,' said Dios, in the tone of voice the Creator must have used to sketch out the moon and stars.

'Er,' said Teppic.

'The finest of pyramids for the king,' said Dios.

Teppic gave up.

'Oh,' he said. 'Good. Fine. Yes. The very best, of course.'

Ptaclusp beamed with relief, produced his wax tablet with a flourish, and took a stylus from the recesses of his wig. The important thing, he knew, was to clinch the deal as soon as possible. Let things slip in a situation like this and a man could find himself with 1,500,000 tons of bespoke limestone on his hands.

'Then that will be the standard model, shall we say, O water in the desert?'

Teppic looked at Dios, who was standing and glaring at nothing now, staring the bulldogs of Entropy into submission by willpower alone.

'I think something larger,' he ventured hopelessly.

'That's the Executive,' said Ptaclusp. 'Very exclusive, O base of the eternal column. Last you a perpetuality. Also our special offer this aeon is various measurements of paracosmic significance built into the very fabric at no extra cost.'

He gave Teppic an expectant look.

'Yes. Yes. That will be fine,' said Teppic.

Dios took a deep breath. 'The king requires far more than that,' he said.

'I do?' said Teppic, doubtfully.

'Indeed, sire. It is your express wish that the greatest of monuments is erected for your father,' said Dios smoothly. This was a contest, Teppic knew, and he didn't know the rules or how to play and he was going to *lose*.

'It is? Oh. Yes. Yes. I suppose it is, really. Yes.'

'A pyramid unequalled along the Djel,' said Dios. 'That is the command of the king. It is only right and proper.'

'Yes, yes, something like that. Er. Twice the normal size,' said Teppic desperately, and had the brief satisfaction of seeing Dios look momentarily disconcerted.

'Sire?' he said.

'It is only right and proper,' said Teppic.

Dios opened his mouth to protest, saw Teppic's expression, and shut it again.

Ptaclusp scribbled busily, his adam's apple bobbing. Something like this only happened once in a business career.

'Can do you a very nice black marble facing on the outside,' he said, without looking up. 'We may have *just* enough in the quarry. O king of the celestial orbs,' he added hurriedly.

'Very good,' said Teppic.

Ptaclusp picked up a fresh tablet. 'Shall we say the capstone picked out in electrum? It's cheaper to have built in right from the start, you don't want to use just silver and then say later, I wish I'd had a –'

'Electrum, yes.'

'And the usual offices?'

'What?'

'The burial chamber, that is, and the outer chamber. I'd recommend the Memphis, very select, that comes with a matching extra large treasure room, so handy for all those little things one cannot bear to leave behind.' Ptaclusp turned the tablet over and started on the other side. 'And of course a similar suite for the Queen, I take it? O King who shall live forever.'

'Eh? Oh, yes. Yes. I suppose so,' said Teppic, glancing at Dios. 'Everything. You know.'

'Then there's mazes,' said Ptaclusp, trying to keep his voice steady. 'Very popular this era. Very important, your maze, it's no good deciding you ought to have put a maze in after the robbers have been. Maybe I'm old-fashioned, but I'd go for the Labrys every time. Like we say, they may get in all right, but they'll never get out. It costs that little bit extra, but what's money at a time like this? O master of the waters.'

Something we don't have, said a warning voice in the back of Teppic's head. He ignored it. He was in the grip of destiny.

'Yes,' he said, straightening up. 'The Labrys. Two of them.'

Ptaclusp's stylus went through his tablet.

'His 'n hers, O stone of stones,' he croaked. 'Very handy, very convenient. With selection of traps from stock? We can offer deadfalls, pitfalls, sliders, rolling balls, dropping spears, arrows –'

'Yes, yes,' said Teppic. 'We'll have them. We'll have them all. All of them.'

The architect took a deep breath.

'And of course you'll require all the usual steles, avenues, ceremonial sphinxes –' he began.

'Lots,' said Teppic. 'We leave it entirely up to you.'

Ptaclusp mopped his brow.

'Fine,' he said. 'Marvellous.' He blew his nose. 'Your father, if I may make so bold, O sower of the seed, is extremely fortunate in having such a dutiful son. I may add –'

'You may *go*,' said Dios. 'And we will expect work to start imminently.'

'Without delay, I assure you,' said Ptaclusp. 'Er.'

He seemed to be wrestling with some huge philosophical problem.

'Yes?' said Dios coldly.

'It's uh. There's the matter of uh. Which is not to say uh. Of course, oldest client, valued customer, but the fact is that uh. Absolutely no doubt about credit worthiness uh. Would not wish to suggest in any way whatsoever that uh.'

Dios gave him a stare that would have caused a sphinx to blink and look away.

'You wish to say something?' he said. 'His majesty's time is extremely limited.'

Ptaclusp worked his jaw silently, but the result was a foregone conclusion. Even gods had been reduced to sheepish mumbling in the face of Dios's face. And the carved snakes on his staff seemed to be watching him too.

'Uh. No, no. Sorry. I was just, uh, thinking aloud. I'll depart, then, shall I? Such a lot of work to be done. Uh.' He bowed low.

He was halfway to the archway before Dios added: 'Completion in three months. In time for Inundation.'*

'What?'

'You are talking to the 1,398th monarch,' said Dios icily.

Ptaclusp swallowed. 'I'm sorry,' he whispered, 'I mean, *what?*, O great king. I mean, block haulage alone will take. Uh.' The architect's lips trembled as he tried out various comments and, in his imagination, ran them full tilt into Dios's stare. 'Tsort wasn't built in a day,' he mumbled.

'We do not believe we laid the specifications for that job,' said Dios. He gave Ptaclusp a smile. In some ways it was worse than everything else. 'We will, of course,' he said, 'pay extra.'

'But you never pa –' Ptaclusp began, and then sagged.

'The penalties for not completing on time will, of course, be terrible,' said Dios. 'The usual clause.'

Ptaclusp hadn't the nerve left to argue. 'Of course,' he said, utterly defeated. 'It is an honour. Will your eminences excuse me? There are still some hours of daylight left.'

Teppic nodded.

'Thank you,' said the architect. 'May your loins be truly fruitful. Saving your presence, Lord Dios.'

They heard him running down the steps outside.

'It will be magnificent. Too big, but – magnificent,' said Dios. He looked out between the pillars at the necropolic panorama on the far bank of the Djel.

---

* Like many river valley cultures the Kingdom has no truck with such trivia as summer, springtime and winter, and bases its calendar squarely on the great heartbeat of the Djel; hence the three seasons, Seedtime, Inundation and Sog. This is logical, straightforward and practical, and only disapproved of by barbershop quartets.†

† Because you feel an idiot singing 'In the Good Old Inundation', that's why.

'Magnificent,' he repeated. He winced once more at the stab of pain in his leg. Ah. He'd have to cross the river again tonight, no doubt of it. He'd been foolish, putting it off for days. But it would be unthinkable not to be in a position to serve the kingdom properly . . .

'Something wrong, Dios?' said Teppic.

'Sire?'

'You looked a bit pale, I thought.'

A look of panic flickered over Dios's wrinkled features. He pulled himself upright.

'I assure, you, sire, I am in the best of health. The best of health, sire!'

'You don't think you've been overdoing it, do you?'

This time there was no mistaking the expression of terror.

'Overdoing what, sire?'

'You're always bustling, Dios. First one up, last one to bed. You should take it easy.'

'I exist only to serve, sire,' said Dios, firmly. 'I exist only to serve.'

Teppic joined him on the balcony. The early evening sun glowed on a man-made mountain range. This was only the central massif; the pyramids stretched from the delta all the way up to the second cataract, where the Djel disappeared into the mountains. And the pyramids occupied the best land, near the river. Even the farmers would have considered it sacrilegious to suggest anything different.

Some of the pyramids were small, and made of rough-hewn blocks that contrived to look far older than the mountains that fenced the valley from the high desert. After all, mountains had always been there. Words like 'young' and 'old' didn't apply to them. But those first pyramids had been built by human beings, little bags of thinking water held up briefly by fragile accumulations of calcium, who had cut rocks into pieces and then painfully put them back together again in a better shape. They were *old*.

Over the millennia the fashions had fluctuated. Later pyramids were smooth and sharp, or flattened and tiled with mica. Even the steepest of them, Teppic mused, wouldn't rate more than 1.0 on any edificeer's scale, although some of the stelae and temples, which flocked around the base of the pyramids like tugboats around the dreadnoughts of eternity, could be worthy of attention.

Dreadnoughts of eternity, he thought, sailing ponderously through the mists of Time with every passenger travelling first class . . .

A few stars had been let out early. Teppic looked up at them. Perhaps, he thought, there is life somewhere else. On the stars, maybe. If it's true that there are billions of universes stacked alongside one another, the thickness of a thought apart, then there must be people elsewhere.

But wherever they are, no matter how mightily they try, no matter how magnificent the effort, they surely can't manage to be as godawfully stupid as us. I mean, we work at it. We were given a spark of it to start with, but over hundreds of thousands of years we've really improved on it.

He turned to Dios, feeling that he ought to repair a little bit of the damage.

'You can feel the age radiating off them, can't you,' he said conversationally.

'Pardon, sire?'

'The pyramids, Dios. They're so old.'

Dios glanced vaguely across the river. 'Are they?' he said. 'Yes, I suppose they are.'

'Will you get one?' said Teppic.

'A pyramid?' said Dios. 'Sire, I have one already. It pleased one of your forebears to make provision for me.'

'That must have been a great honour,' said Teppic. Dios nodded graciously. The staterooms of forever were usually reserved for royalty.

'It is, of course, very small. Very plain. But it will suffice for my simple needs.'

'Will it?' said Teppic, yawning. 'That's nice. And now, if you don't mind, I think I'll turn in. It's been a long day.'

Dios bowed as though he was hinged in the middle. Teppic had noticed that Dios had at least fifty finely-tuned ways of bowing, each one conveying subtle shades of meaning. This one looked like No.3, I Am Your Humble Servant.

'And a very good day it was too, if I may say so, sire.'

Teppic was lost for words. 'You thought so?' he said.

'The cloud effects at dawn were particularly effective.'

'They were? Oh. Do I have to do anything about the sunset?'

'Your majesty is pleased to joke,' said Dios. 'Sunsets happen by themselves, sire. Haha.'

'Haha,' echoed Teppic.

Dios cracked his knuckles. 'The trick is in the sunrise,' he said.

The crumbling scrolls of Knot said that the great orange sun was eaten every evening by the sky goddess What, who saved one pip in time to grow a fresh sun for next morning. And Dios knew that this was so.

The *Book of Staying in The Pit* said that the sun was the Eye of Yay, toiling across the sky each day in His endless search for his toenails.* And Dios knew that this was so.

The secret rituals of the Smoking Mirror held that the sun was in fact a round hole in the spinning blue soap bubble of the goddess Nesh, opening into the fiery real world beyond, and the stars were the holes that the rain comes through. And Dios knew that this, also, was so.

Folk myth said the sun was a ball of fire which circled the world every day, and that the world itself was carried through the everlasting void on the back of an enormous turtle. And Dios also knew that this was so, although it gave him a bit of trouble.

And Dios knew that Net was the Supreme God, and that Fon was the Supreme God, and so were Hast, Set, Bin, Sot, Io, Dhek, and Ptooie; that Herpetine Triskeles alone ruled the world of the dead, and so did Syncope, and Silur the Catfish-Headed God, and Orexis-Nupt.

Dios was maximum high priest to a national religion that had fermented and accreted and bubbled for more than seven thousand years and never threw a god away in case it turned out to be useful. He knew that a great many mutually-contradictory things were all true. If they were not, then ritual and belief were as nothing, and if they were nothing, then the world did not exist. As a result of this sort of thinking, the priests of the Djel could give mindroom to a collection of ideas that would make even a quantum mechanic give in and hand back his toolbox.

Dios's staff knocked echoes from the stones as he limped alone in the darkness down little-frequented passages until he emerged on a small jetty. Untying the boat there, the high priest climbed in with difficulty, unshipped the oars and pushed himself out into the turbid waters of the dark Djel.

His hands and feet felt too cold. Foolish, foolish. He should have done this before.

The boat jerked slowly into midstream as full night rolled over the valley. On the far bank, in response to the ancient laws, the pyramids started to light the sky.

---

* Lit. 'Dhar-ret-kar-mon', or 'clipping of the foot'. But some scholars say that it should be 'Dar-rhet-kare-mhun', lit. 'hot-air paint stripper'.

*

Lights also burned late in the house of Ptaclusp Associates, Necropolitan Builders to the Dynasties. The father and his twin sons were hunched over the huge wax designing tray, arguing.

'It's not as if they ever *pay*,' said Ptaclusp IIa. 'I mean it's not just a case of not being able to, they don't seem to have grasped the *idea*. At least dynasties like Tsort pay up within a hundred years or so. Why didn't you –'

'We've built pyramids along the Djel for the last three thousand years,' said his father stiffly, 'and we haven't lost by it, have we? No, we haven't. Because the other kingdoms look to the Djel, they say there's a family that really knows its pyramids, connysewers, they say we'll have what they're having, if you please, with knobs on. Anyway, they're real royalty,' he added, 'not like some of the ones you get these days – here today, gone next millennium. They're half gods, too. You don't expect real royalty to pay its way. That's one of the signs of real royalty, not having any money.'

'You don't get more royal than them, then. You'd need a new word,' said IIa. '*We're* nearly royal in that case.'

'You don't understand business, my son. You think it's all bookkeeping. Well, it isn't.'

'*It's a question of mass. And the power to weight ratio.*'

They both glared at Ptaclusp IIb, who was sitting staring at the sketches. He was turning his stylus over and over in his hands, which were trembling with barely-suppressed excitement.

'We'll have to use granite for the lower slopes,' he said, talking to himself, 'the limestone wouldn't take it. Not with all the power flows. Which will be, whooeee, they'll be big. I mean we're not talking razor blades here. This thing could put an edge on a rolling pin.'

Ptaclusp rolled his eyes. He was only one generation into a dynasty and already it was trouble. One son a born accountant, the other in love with this new-fangled cosmic engineering. There hadn't been any such thing when he was a lad, there was just architecture. You drew the plans, and then got in ten thousand lads on time-and-a-half and double bubble at weekends. They just had to pile the stuff up. You didn't have to be *cosmic* about it.

Descendants! The gods had seen fit to give him one son who charged you for the amount of breath expended in saying 'Good morning', and another one who worshipped geometry and stayed up all night designing aqueducts. You scrimped and saved to send them to the best schools, and then they went and paid you back by getting educated.

'What are you talking about?' he snapped.

'The discharge alone . . .' IIb pulled his abacus towards him and rattled the pottery beads along the wires. 'Let's say we're talking twice the height of the Executive model, which gives us a mass of . . . plus additional coded dimensions of occult significance as per spec . . . we couldn't do this sort of thing even a hundred years ago, you realise, not with the primitive techniques we had then . . .' His finger became a blur.

IIa gave a snort and grabbed his own abacus.

'Limestone at two talents the ton . . .' he said. 'Wear and tear on tools . . . masonry charges . . . demurrage . . . breakages . . . oh dear, oh dear . . . on-cost . . . black marble at replacement prices . . .'

Ptaclusp sighed. Two abaci rattling in tandem the whole day long, one changing the shape of the world and the other one deploring the cost. Whatever happened to the two bits of wood and a plumbline?

The last beads clicked against the stops.

'It'd be a whole quantum leap in pyramidology,' said IIb, sitting back with a messianic grin on his face.

'It'd be a whole kwa –' IIa began.

'Quantum,' said IIb, savouring the word.

'It'd be a whole *quantum* leap in bankruptcy,' said IIa. 'They'd have to invent a new word for that too.'

'It'd be worth it as a loss leader,' said IIb.

'Sure enough. When it comes to making a loss, we'll be in the lead,' said IIa sourly.

'It'd practically glow! In millennia to come people will look at it and say "That Ptaclusp, he knew his pyramids all right".'

'They'll call it Ptaclusp's Folly, you mean!'

By now the brothers were both standing up, their noses a few inches apart.

'The trouble with you, sibling, is that you know the cost of everything and the value of nothing!'

'The trouble with *you* is – is – is that you don't!'

'Mankind must strive ever upwards!'

'Yes, on a sound financial footing, by Khuft!'

'The search for knowledge –'

'The search for probity –'

Ptaclusp left them to it and stood staring out at the yard, where, under the glow of torches, the staff were doing a feverish stocktaking.

It'd been a small business when father passed it on to him – just a yard full of blocks and various sphinxes, needles, steles and other stock items, and a thick stack of unpaid bills, most of them addressed to the palace and respectfully pointing out that our esteemed account presented nine hundred years ago appeared to have been overlooked and prompt settlement would oblige. But it had been fun in those days. There was just him, five thousand labourers, and Mrs Ptaclusp doing the books.

You had to do pyramids, dad said. All the profit was in mastabas, small family tombs, memorial needles and general jobbing necropoli, but if you didn't do pyramids, you didn't do anything. The meanest garlic farmer, looking for something neat and long lasting with maybe some green marble chippings but within a budget, wouldn't go to a man without a pyramid to his name.

So he'd done pyramids, and they'd been good ones, not like some you saw these days, with the wrong number of sides and walls you could put your foot through. And yes, somehow they'd gone from strength to strength.

To build the biggest pyramid ever . . .

In three months . . .

With terrible penalties if it wasn't done on time. Dios hadn't specified how terrible, but Ptaclusp knew his man and they probably involved crocodiles. They'd be pretty terrible, all right . . .

He stared at the flickering light on the long avenues of statues, including the one of bloody Hat the Vulture-Headed God of Unexpected Guests, bought on the offchance years ago and turned down by the client owing to not being up to snuff in the beak department and unshiftable ever since even at a discount.

The biggest pyramid ever . . .

And after you'd knocked your pipes out seeing to it that the nobility had their tickets to eternity, were you allowed to turn your expertise homeward, i.e., a bijou pyramidette for self and Mrs Ptaclusp, to ensure safe delivery into the Netherworld? Of course not. Even dad had only been allowed to have a mastaba, although it was one of the best on the river, he had to admit, that red-veined marble had been ordered all the way from Howonderland, a lot of people had asked for the same, it had been good for business, that's how dad would have liked it . . .

The biggest pyramid ever . . .

And they'd never remember who was under it.

It didn't matter if they called it Ptaclusp's Folly or Ptaclusp's Glory. They'd call it *Ptaclusp's*.

He surfaced from this pool of thought to hear his sons still arguing.

If this was his posterity, he'd take his chances with 600-ton limestone blocks. At least they were quiet.

'Shut up, the pair of you,' he said.

They stopped, and sat down, grumbling.

'I've made up my mind,' he said.

IIb doodled fitfully with his stylus. IIa strummed his abacus.

'We're going to do it,' said Ptaclusp, and strode out of the room. 'And any son who doesn't like it will be cast into the outer darkness where there is a wailing and a crashing of teeth,' he called over his shoulder.

The two brothers, left to themselves, glowered at each other.

At last IIa said, 'What does "quantum" mean, anyway?'

IIb shrugged. 'It means add another nought,' he said.

'Oh,' said IIa, 'is that all?'

All along the river valley of the Djel the pyramids were flaring silently into the night, discharging the accumulated power of the day.

Great soundless flames erupted from their capstones and danced upwards, jagged as lightning, cold as ice.

For hundreds of miles the desert glittered with the constellations of the dead, the aurora of antiquity. But along the valley of the Djel the lights ran together in one solid ribbon of fire.

It was on the floor and it had a pillow at one end. It had to be a bed.

Teppic found he was doubting it as he tossed and turned, trying to find some part of the mattress that was prepared to meet him halfway. This is stupid, he thought, I grew up on beds like this. And pillows carved out of rock. I was born in this palace, this is my heritage, I must be prepared to accept it . . .

I must order a proper bed and a feather pillow from Ankh, first thing in the morning. I, the king, have said this shall be done.

He turned over, his head hitting the pillow with a thud.

And plumbing. What a great idea that was. It was amazing what you could do with a hole in the ground.

Yes, plumbing. And bloody doors. Teppic definitely wasn't used to having several attendants waiting on his will all the time, so performing his ablutions before bed had been extremely embarrassing. And the people, too. He was definitely going to get to know the people. It was wrong, all this skulking in palaces.

And how was a fellow supposed to sleep with the sky over the river glowing like a firework?

Eventually sheer exhaustion wrestled his body into some zone between sleeping and waking, and mad images stalked across his eyeballs.

There was the shame of his ancestors when future archaeologists translated the as-yet unpainted frescoes of his reign: ' "Squiggle, constipated eagle, wiggly line, hippo's bottom, squiggle": And in the year of the Cycle of Cephnet the Sun God Teppic had Plumbing Installed and Scorned the Pillows of his Forebears.'

He dreamed of Khuft – huge, bearded, speaking in thunder and lightning, calling down the wrath of the heavens on this descendant who was betraying the noble past.

Dios floated past his vision, explaining that as a result of an edict passed several thousand years ago it was essential that he marry a cat.

Various-headed gods vied for his attention, explaining details of godhood, while in the background a distant voice tried to attract his attention and screamed something about not wanting to be buried under a load of stone. But he had no time to concentrate on this, because he saw seven fat cows and seven thin cows, one of them playing a trombone.

But that was an old dream, he dreamt that one nearly every night . . .

And then there was a man firing arrows at a tortoise . . .

And then he was walking over the desert and found a tiny pyramid, only a few inches high. A wind sprang up and blew away the sand, only now it wasn't a wind, it was the pyramid rising, sand tumbling down its gleaming sides . . .

And it grew bigger and bigger, bigger than the world, so that at last the pyramid was so big that the whole world was a speck in the centre.

And in the centre of the pyramid, something very strange happened.

And the pyramid grew smaller, taking the world with it, and vanished . . .

Of course, when you're a pharaoh, you get a very high class of obscure dream.

*

Another day dawned, courtesy of the king, who was curled up on the bed and using his rolled-up clothes as a pillow. Around the stone maze of the palace the servants of the kingdom began to wake up.

Dios's boat slid gently through the water and bumped into the jetty. Dios climbed out and hurried into the palace, bounding up the steps three at a time and rubbing his hands together at the thought of a fresh day laid out before him, every hour and ritual ticking neatly into place. So much to organise, so much to be needed for . . .

The chief sculptor and maker of mummy cases folded up his measure.

'You done a good job there, Master Dil,' he said.

Dil nodded. There was no false modesty between craftsmen.

The sculptor gave him a nudge. 'What a team, eh?' he said. 'You pickle 'em, I crate 'em.'

Dil nodded, but rather more slowly. The sculptor looked down at the wax oval in his hands.

'Can't say I think much of the death mask, mind,' he said.

Gern, who was working hard on the corner slab on one of the Queen's late cats, which he been allowed to do all by himself, looked up in horror.

'I done it very careful,' he said sulkily.

'That's the whole point,' said the sculptor.

'I know,' said Dil sadly, 'it's the nose, isn't it.'

'It was more the chin.'

'And the chin.'

'Yes.'

'Yes.'

They looked in gloomy silence at the waxen visage of the pharaoh. So did the pharaoh.

'Nothing wrong with my chin.'

'You could put a beard on it,' said Dil eventually. 'It'd cover a lot of it, would a beard.'

'There's still the nose.'

'You could take half an inch off that. And do something with the cheekbones.'

'Yes.'

'Yes.'

Gern was horrified. 'That's the face of our late king you're talking about,' he said. 'You can't do that sort of thing! Anyway, people would notice.' He hesitated. 'Wouldn't they?'

The two craftsmen eyed one another.

'Gern,' said Dil patiently, 'certainly they'll notice. But they won't say anything. They expect us to, er, *improve* matters.'

'After all,' said the chief sculptor cheerfully, 'you don't think they're going to step up and say "It's all wrong, he really had a face like a short-sighted chicken", do you?'

'Thank you very much. Thank you very much indeed, I must say.' The pharaoh went and sat by the cat. It seemed that people only had respect for the dead when they thought the dead were listening.

'I suppose,' said the apprentice, with some uncertainty, 'he did look a bit ugly compared to the frescoes.'

'That's the point, isn't it,' said Dil meaningfully.

Gern's big honest spotty face changed slowly, like a cratered landscape with clouds passing across it. It was dawning on him that this came under the heading of initiation into ancient craft secrets.

'You mean even the *painters* change the –' he began.

Dil frowned at him.

'We don't talk about it,' he said.

Gern tried to force his features into an expression of worthy seriousness.

'Oh,' he said. 'Yes. I see, master.'

The sculptor clapped him on the back.

'You're a bright lad, Gern,' he said. 'You catch on. After all, it's bad enough being ugly when you're alive. Think how terrible it would be to be ugly in the netherworld.'

King Teppicymon XXVII shook his head. We all have to look alike when we're alive, he thought, and now they make sure we're identical when we're dead. What a kingdom. He looked down and saw the soul of the late cat, which was washing itself. When he was alive he'd hated the things, but just now it seemed positively companionable. He patted it gingerly on its flat head. It purred for a moment, and then attempted to strip the flesh from his hand. It was on a definite hiding to nothing there.

He was aware with growing horror that the trio was now discussing a pyramid. *His* pyramid. It was going to be the biggest one ever. It was going to go on a highly fertile piece of sloping ground on a prime site in the necropolis. It was going to make even the biggest existing pyramid look like something a child might construct in a sand tray. It was going to be surrounded by marble gardens and granite obelisks. It was going to be the greatest memorial ever built by a son for his father.

The king groaned.

Ptaclusp groaned.

It had been *better* in his father's day. You just needed a bloody great heap of log rollers and twenty years, which was useful because it kept everyone out of trouble during Inundation, when all the fields were flooded. Now you just needed a bright lad with a piece of chalk and the right incantations.

Mind you, it was impressive, if you liked that kind of thing.

Ptaclusp IIb walked around the great stone block, tidying an equation here, highlighting a hermetic inscription there. He glanced up and gave his father a brief nod.

Ptaclusp hurried back to the king, who was standing with his retinue on the cliff overlooking the quarry, the sun gleaming off the mask. A royal visit, on top of everything else . . .

'We're ready, if it please you, O arc of the sky,' he said, breaking into a sweat, hoping against hope that . . .

Oh gods. The king was going to Put Him at his Ease again.

He looked imploringly at the high priest, who with the merest twitch of his features indicated that there was nothing he proposed to do about it. This was too much, he wasn't the only one to object to this, Dil the master embalmer had been subjected to half an hour of having to Talk about his Family only yesterday, it was wrong, people expected the king to stay in the palace, it was too . . .

The king ambled towards him in a nonchalant way designed to make the master builder feel he was among friends. Oh no, Ptaclusp thought, he's going to Remember my Name.

'I must say you've done a tremendous amount in nine weeks, it's a very good start. Er. It's Ptaclusp, isn't it?' said the king.

Ptaclusp swallowed. There was no help for it now.

'Yes, O hand upon the waters,' he said, 'O fount of –'

'I think "your majesty" or "sire" will do,' said Teppic.

Ptaclusp panicked and glanced fearfully at Dios, who winced but nodded again.

'The king wishes you to address him –' a look of pain crossed his face – 'informally. In the fashion of the barba – of foreign lands.'

'You must consider yourself a very fortunate man to have such talented and hard-working sons,' said Teppic, staring down at the busy panorama of the quarry.

'I . . . will, O . . . sire,' mumbled Ptaclusp, interpreting this as an order. Why couldn't kings order people around like in the old days? You knew where you were then, they didn't go round being charming and treating you as some sort of equal, as if *you* could make the sun rise too.

'It must be a fascinating trade,' Teppic went on.

'As your sire wishes, sire,' said Ptaclusp. 'If your majesty would just give the word –'

'And how exactly does all this *work*?'

'Your sire?' said Ptaclusp, horrified.

'You make the blocks fly, do you?'

'Yes, O sire.'

'That is very interesting. How do you do it?'

Ptaclusp nearly bit through his lip. Betray Craft secrets? He was horrified. Against all expectation, Dios came to his aid.

'By means of certain secret signs and sigils, sire,' he said, 'into the origin of which it is not wise to inquire. It is the wisdom of –' he paused – 'the moderns.'

'So much quicker than all that heaving stuff around, I expect,' said Teppic.

'It had a certain glory, sire,' said Dios. 'Now, if I may suggest . . .?'

'Oh. Yes. Press on, by all means.'

Ptaclusp wiped his forehead, and ran to the edge of the quarry. He waved a cloth.

All things are defined by names. Change the name, and you change the thing. Of course there is a lot more to it than that, but paracosmically that is what it boils down to . . .

Ptaclusp IIb tapped the stone lightly with his staff.

The air above it wavered in the heat and then, shedding a little dust, the block rose gently until it bobbed a few feet off the ground, held in check by mooring ropes.

That was all there was to it. Teppic had expected some thunder, or at least a gout of flame. But already the workers were clustering around another block, and a couple of men were towing the first block down towards the site.

'Very impressive,' he said sadly.

'Indeed, sire,' said Dios. 'And now, we must go back to the palace. It will soon be time for the Ceremony of the Third Hour.'

'Yes, yes, all right,' snapped Teppic. 'Very well done, Ptaclusp. Keep up the good work.'

Ptaclusp bowed like a seesaw in flustered excitement and confusion.

'Very good, your sire,' he said, and decided to go for the big one. 'May I show your sire the latest plans?'

'The king has approved the plans already,' said Dios. 'And, excuse me if I am mistaken, but it seems that the pyramid is well under construction.'

'Yes, yes, but,' said Ptaclusp, 'it occurred to us, this avenue here, you see, overlooking the entrance, what a place, we thought, for a statue of for instance Hat the Vulture-Headed God of Unexpected Guests at practically cost –'

Dios glanced at the sketches.

'Are those supposed to be wings?' he said.

'Not even cost, not even cost, tell you what I'll do –' said Ptaclusp desperately.

'Is that a nose?' said Dios.

'More a beak, more a beak,' said Ptaclusp. 'Look, O priest, how about –'

'I think not,' said Dios. 'No. I really think not.' He scanned the quarry for Teppic, groaned, thrust the sketches into the builder's hands and started to run.

Teppic had strolled down the path to the waiting chariots, looking wistfully at the bustle around him, and paused to watch a group of workers who were dressing a corner piece. They froze when they felt his gaze on them, and stood sheepishly watching him.

'Well, well,' said Teppic, inspecting the stone, although all he knew about stonemasonry could have been chiselled on a sand grain. 'What a splendid piece of rock.'

He turned to the nearest man, whose mouth fell open.

'You're a stonemason, are you?' he said. 'That must be a very interesting job.'

The man's eyes bulged. He dropped his chisel. 'Erk,' he said.

A hundred yards away Dios's robes flapped around his legs as he pounded down the path. He grasped the hem and galloped along, sandals flapping.

'What's your name?' said Teppic. 'Aaaargle,' said the man, terrified.

'Well, jolly good,' said Teppic, and took his unresisting hand and shook it.

'Sire!' Dios bellowed. 'No!'

And the mason spun away, holding his right hand by the wrist, fighting it, screaming ...

Teppic gripped the arms of the throne and glared at the high priest.

'But it's a gesture of fellowship, nothing more. Where I come from –'

'*Where you come from, sire, is here!*' thundered Dios.

'But, good grief, cutting it off? It's too cruel!'

Dios stepped forward. Now his voice was back to its normal oil-smooth tones.

'Cruel, sire? But it will be done with precision and care, with drugs to take away the pain. He will certainly live.'

'But *why?*'

'I did explain, sire. He cannot use the hand again without defiling it. He is a devout man and knows this very well. You see, sire, you are a *god*, sire.'

'But *you* can touch me. So can the servants!'

'I am a priest, sire,' said Dios gently. 'And the servants have special dispensation.'

Teppic bit his lip.

'This is barbaric,' he said.

Dios's features did not move.

'It will not be done,' Teppic said. 'I am the king. I forbid it to be done, do you understand?'

Dios bowed. Teppic recognised No.49, Horrified Disdain.

'Your wish will certainly be done, O fountain of all wisdom. Although, of course, the man himself may take matters into, if you will excuse me, his own hands.'

'What do you mean?' snapped Teppic.

'Sire, if his colleagues had not stopped him he would have done it himself. With a chisel, I understand.'

Teppic stared at him and thought, I am a stranger in a familiar land.

'I see,' he said eventually.

He thought a little further.

'Then the – operation is to be done with all care, and the man is to be given a pension afterwards, d'you see?'

'As you wish, sire.'

'A proper one, too.'

'Indeed, sire. A golden handshake, sire,' said Dios impassively.

85

'And perhaps we can find him some light job around the palace?'

'As a one-handed stonemason, sire?' Dios's left eyebrow arched a fraction.

'As whatever, Dios.'

'Certainly, sire. As you wish. I will undertake to see if we are currently short-handed in any department.'

Teppic glared at him. 'I *am* the king, you know,' he said sharply.

'The fact attends me with every waking hour, sire.'

'Dios?' said Teppic, as the high priest was leaving.

'Sire?'

'I ordered a feather bed from Ankh-Morpork some weeks ago. I suppose you would not know what became of it?'

Dios waved his hands in an expressive gesture.

'I gather, sire, that there is considerable pirate activity off the Khalian coast,' he said.

'Doubtless the pirates are also responsible for the non-appearance of the expert from the Guild of Plumbers and Dunnikindivers?' Teppic said sourly*.

'Yes, sire. Or possibly bandits, sire.'

'Or perhaps a giant two-headed bird swooped down and carried him off,' said Teppic.

'All things are possible, sire,' said the high priest, his face radiating politeness.

'You may go, Dios.'

'Sire. May I remind you, sire, that the emissaries from Tsort and Ephebe will be attending you at the fifth hour.'

'Yes. You may go.'

Teppic was left alone, or at least as alone as he ever was, which meant that he was all by himself except for two fan wavers, a butler, two enormous Howonder guards by the door, and a couple of handmaidens.

Oh, yes. Handmaidens. He hadn't quite come to terms with the handmaidens yet. Presumably Dios chose them, as he seemed to oversee everything in the palace, and he had shown surprisingly good taste in the matter of, for example, olive skins, bosoms and legs. The clothing these two wore would between them have covered a small saucer. And this was odd, because the net effect was to turn them into two attractive and mobile pieces of furniture,

---

* Dunnikindiver: a builder and cleaner of cesspits. A particularly busy profession in Ankh-Morpork, where the water table is generally at ground level, and one which attracts considerable respect. At least, everyone passes by on the other side of the street when a dunnikindiver walks by.

as sexless as pillars. Teppic sighed with the recollection of women in Ankh-Morpork who could be clothed from neck to ankle in brocade and still cause a classroom full of boys to blush to the roots of their hair.

He reached down for the fruit bowl. One of the girls immediately grasped his hand, moved it gently aside, and took a grape.

'Please don't peel it,' said Teppic. 'The peel's the best part. Full of nourishing vitamins and minerals. Only I don't suppose you've heard about them, have you, they've only been invented recently,' he added, mainly to himself. 'I mean, within the last seven thousand years,' he finished sourly.

So much for time flowing past, he thought glumly. It might do that everywhere else, but not here. Here it just piles up, like snow. It's as though the pyramids slow us down, like those things they used on the boat, whatd'youcallem, sea anchors. Tomorrow here is just like yesterday, warmed over.

She peeled the grape anyway, while the snowflake seconds drifted down.

At the site of the Great Pyramid the huge blocks of stone floated into place like an explosion in reverse. They were *flowing* between the quarry and the site, drifting silently across the landscape above deep rectangular shadows.

'I've got to hand it to you,' said Ptaclusp to his son, as they stood side by side in the observation tower. 'It's astonishing. One day people will wonder how we did it.'

'All that business with the log rollers and the whips is old hat,' said IIb. 'You can throw them away.' The young architect smiled, but there was a manic hint to the rictus.

It *was* astonishing. It was more astonishing than it ought to be. He kept getting the feeling that the pyramid was . . .

He shook himself mentally. He should be ashamed of that sort of thinking. You could get superstitious if you weren't careful, in this job.

It was natural for things to form a pyramid – well, a cone, anyway. He'd experimented this morning. Grain, salt, sand . . . not water, though, that'd been a mistake. But a pyramid was only a neat cone, wasn't it, a cone which had decided to be a bit tidier.

Perhaps he'd overdone it just a gnat on the paracosmic measurements?

His father slapped him on the back.

'Very well done,' he repeated. 'You know, it almost looks as though it's building itself!'

IIb yelped and bit his wrist, a childish trait that he always resorted to when he was nervous. Ptaclusp didn't notice, because at that moment one of the foremen was running to the foot of the tower, waving his ceremonial measuring rod.

Ptaclusp leaned over.

'What?' he demanded.

'I said, please to come at once, O master!'

On the pyramid itself, on the working surface about halfway up, where some of the detailed work on the inner chambers was in progress, the word 'impressive' was no longer appropriate. The word 'terrifying' seemed to fit the bill.

Blocks were stacking up in the sky overhead in a giant, slow dance, passing and re-passing, their mahouts yelling at one another and at the luckless controllers down on the pyramid top, who were trying to shout instructions above the noise.

Ptaclusp waded into the cluster of workers around the centre. Here, at least, there was silence. Dead silence.

'All right, all right,' he said. 'What's going . . . oh.'

Ptaclusp IIb peered over his father's shoulder, and stuck his wrist in his mouth.

The thing was wrinkled. It was ancient. It clearly had once been a living thing. It lay on the slab like a very obscene prune.

'It was my lunch,' said the chief plasterer. 'It was my bloody lunch. I was really looking forward to that apple.'

'But it can't start yet,' whispered IIb. 'It can't form temporal nodes yet, I mean, how does it *know* it's going to be a pyramid?'

'I put my hand down for it, and it felt just like . . . it felt pretty unpleasant,' the plasterer complained.

'And it's a negative node, too,' added IIb. 'We shouldn't be getting them at *all*.'

'Is it still there?' said Ptaclusp, and added. 'Tell me yes.'

'If more blocks have been set into position it won't be,' said his son, looking around wildly. 'As the centre of mass changes, you see, the nodes will be pulled around.'

Ptaclusp pulled the young man to one side.

'What are you telling me now?' he demanded, in a camel whisper.*

'We ought to put a cap on it,' mumbled IIb. 'Flare off the trapped time. Wouldn't be any problems then . . .'

---

* Hoarse whispers are not suitable for a desert environment.

'How can we cap it? It isn't damn well finished,' said Ptaclusp. 'What have you been and gone and done? Pyramids don't start accumulating until they're finished. Until they're *pyramids*, see? Pyramid energy, see? Named after pyramids. That's why it's called pyramid energy.'

'It must be something to do with the mass, or something,' the architect hazarded, 'and the speed of construction. The time is getting trapped in the fabric. I mean, in theory you could get small nodes during construction, but they'd be so weak you wouldn't notice; if you went and stood in one maybe you'd become a few hours older or younger or –' he began to gabble.

'I recall when we did Kheneth XIV's tomb the fresco painter said it took him two hours to do the painting in the Queen's Room, and we said it was three days and fined him,' said Ptaclusp, slowly. 'There was a lot of Guild fuss, I remember.'

'You just said that,' said IIb.

'Said what?'

'About the fresco painter. Just a moment ago.'

'No, I didn't. You couldn't have been listening,' said Ptaclusp.

'Could have sworn you did. Anyway, this is worse than that business,' said his son. 'And it's probably going to happen again.'

'We can expect more like it?'

'Yes,' said IIb. 'We shouldn't get negative nodes, but it looks as though we will. We can expect fast flows and reverse flows and probably even short loops. I'm afraid we can expect all kinds of temporal anomalies. We'd better get the men off.'

'I suppose you couldn't work out a way we could get them to work in fast time and pay them for slow time?' said Ptaclusp. 'It's just a thought. Your brother's bound to suggest it.'

'No! Keep everyone off! We'll get the blocks in and cap it first!'

'All right, all right. I was just thinking out loud. As if we didn't have enough problems . . .'

Ptaclusp waded into the cluster of workers around the centre. Here, at least, there was silence. Dead silence.

'All right, all right,' he said. 'What's going . . . oh.'

Ptaclusp IIb peered over his father's shoulder, and stuck his wrist in his mouth.

The thing was wrinkled. It was ancient. It clearly had once been a living thing. It lay on the slab like a very obscene prune.

'It was my lunch,' said the chief plasterer. 'It was my bloody lunch. I was really looking forward to that apple.'

Ptaclusp hesitated. This all seemed very familiar. He'd had this feeling before. An overwhelming sensation of *reja vu*[*].

He met the horrified gaze of his son. Together, dreading what they might see, they turned around slowly.

They saw themselves standing behind themselves, bickering over something IIb was swearing that he had already heard.

He has, too, Ptaclusp realised in dread. That's me over there. I look a lot different from the outside. And it's me over *here*, too. As well. Also.

It's a loop. Just like in the river, a tiny whirlpool, only it's in the flow of time. And I've just gone round it twice.

The other Ptaclusp looked up at him.

There was a long, agonising moment of temporal strain, a noise like a mouse blowing bubblegum, and the loop broke, and the figure faded.

'I know what's causing it,' muttered IIb indistinctly, because of his wrist. 'I know the pyramid isn't complete, but it *will* be, so the effects are sort of echoing backwards, dad, we ought to stop right now, it's too *big*, I was wrong –'

'Shut up. Can you work out where the nodes will form?' said Ptaclusp. 'And come away over here, all the lads are staring. Pull yourself together, son.'

IIb instinctively put his hand to his belt abacus.

'Well, yes, probably,' he said. 'It's just a function of mass distribution and –'

'Right,' said the builder firmly. 'Start doing it. And then get all the foremen to come and see me.'

There was a glint like mica in Ptaclusp's eye. His jaw was squared like a block of granite. Maybe it's the pyramid that's got me thinking like this, he said, I'm thinking fast, I know it.

'And get your brother up here, too,' he added.

It *is* the pyramid effect. I'm remembering an idea I'm going to have.

Best not to think too hard about that. Be practical.

He stared around at the half-completed site. The gods knew we couldn't do it in time, he said. Now we don't have to. We can take as long as we like!

'Are you all right?' said IIb. 'Dad, are you all right?'

'Was that one of your time loops?' said Ptaclusp dreamily. What an idea! No-one would ever beat them on a contract ever again,

---

[*] Lit: 'I am going to be here again.'

they'd win bonuses for completion and it didn't matter how long it took!

'No! Dad, we ought –'

'But you're sure you can work out where these loops will occur, are you?'

'Yes, I expect so, but –'

'Good.' Ptaclusp was trembling with excitement. Maybe they'd have to pay the men more, but it would be worth it, and IIa would be bound to think up some sort of scheme, finance was nearly as good as magic. The lads would have to accept it. After all, they'd complained about working with free men, they'd complained about working with Howondanians, they'd complained about working with everyone except proper paid-up Guild members. So they could hardly complain about working with themselves.

IIb stepped back, and gripped the abacus for reassurance.

'Dad,' he said cautiously, 'what are you thinking about?'

Ptaclusp beamed at him. *'Doppelgangs,'* he said.

Politics was more interesting. Teppic felt that here, at least, he could make a contribution.

Djelibeybi was old. It was respected. But it was also small and in the sword-edged sense, which was what seemed to matter these days, had no power. It wasn't always thus, as Dios told it. Once it had ruled the world by sheer force of nobility, hardly needing the standing army of twenty-five thousand men it had in those high days.

Now it wielded a more subtle power as a narrow state between the huge and thrusting empires of Tsort and Ephebe, each one both a threat and a shield. For more than a thousand years the kings along the Djel had, with extreme diplomacy, exquisite manners and the footwork of a centipede on adrenaline, kept the peace along the whole widdershins side of the continent. Merely having existed for seven thousand years can be a formidable weapon, if you use it properly.

'You mean we're neutral ground?' said Teppic.

'Tsort is a desert culture like us,' said Dios, steepling his hands. 'We have helped to shape it over the years. As for Ephebe –' He sniffed. 'They have some very strange beliefs.'

'How do you mean?'

'They believe the world is run by geometry, sire. All lines and angles and numbers. That sort of thing, sire –' Dios frowned – 'can lead to some very unsound ideas.'

'Ah,' said Teppic, resolving to learn more about unsound ideas as soon as possible. 'So we're secretly on the side of Tsort, yes?'

'No. It is important that Ephebe remains strong.'

'But we've more in common with Tsort?'

'So we allow them to believe, sire.'

'But they *are* a desert culture?'

Dios smiled. 'I am afraid they don't take pyramids seriously, sire.'

Teppic considered all this.

'So whose side are we really on?'

'Our own, sire. There is always a way. Always remember, sire, that your family was on its third dynasty before our neighbours had worked out, sire, how babies are made.'

The Tsort delegation did indeed appear to have studied Djeli culture assiduously, almost frantically. It was also clear that they hadn't begun to understand it; they'd merely borrowed as many bits as seemed useful and then put them together in subtly wrong ways. For example, to a man they employed the Three-Turning-Walk, as portrayed on friezes, and only used by the Djeli court on certain occasions. Occasional grimaces crossed their faces as their vertebrae protested.

They were also wearing the Khruspids of Morning and the bangles of Going Forth, as well as the kilt of Yet with, and no wonder even the maidens on fan duty were hiding their smiles, matching greaves![*]

Even Teppic had to cough hurriedly. But then, he thought, they don't know any better. They're like children.

And this thought was followed by another one which added, These children could wipe us off the map in one hour.

Hot on the synapses of the other two came a third thought, which said: It's only clothes, for goodness sake, you're beginning to take it all seriously.

The group from Ephebe were more sensibly dressed in white togas. They had a certain sameness about them, as if somewhere in the country there was a little press that stamped out small bald men with curly white beards.

The two parties halted before the throne, and bowed.

'Hallo,' said Teppic.

---

[*] Some translation is needed here. If a foreign ambassador to the Court of St James wore (out of a genuine desire to flatter) a bowler hat, a claymore, a Civil War breastplate, Saxon trousers and a Jacobean haircut, he'd create pretty much the same impression.

'His Greatness the King Teppicymon XXVIII, Lord of the Heavens, Charioteer of the Wagon of the Sun, Steersman of the Barque of the Sun, Guardian of the Secret Knowledge, Lord of the Horizon, Keeper of the Way, the Flail of Mercy, the High-Born One, the Never-Dying King, bids you welcome and commands you to take wine with him,' said Dios, clapping his hands for a butler.

'Oh yes,' said Teppic. 'Do sit down, won't you?'

'His Greatness the King Teppicymon XXVIII, Lord of the Heavens, Charioteer of the Wagon of the Sun, Steersman of the Barque of the Sun, Guardian of the Secret Knowledge, Lord of the Horizon, Keeper of the Way, the Flail of Mercy, the High-Born One, the Never-Dying King, commands you to be seated,' said Dios.

Teppic racked his brains for a suitable speech. He'd heard plenty in Ankh-Morpork. They were probably the same the whole world over.

'I'm sure we shall get on –'

'His Greatness the King Teppicymon XXVIII, Lord of the Heavens, Charioteer of the Wagon of the Sun, Steersman of the Barque of the Sun, Guardian of the Secret Knowledge, Lord of the Horizon, Keeper of the Way, the Flail of Mercy, the High-Born One, the Never-Dying King, bids you harken!' Dios boomed.

'– long history of friendship –'

'Harken to the wisdom of His Greatness the King Teppicymon XXVIII, Lord of the Heavens, Charioteer of the Wagon of the Sun, Steersman of the Barque of the Sun, Guardian of the Secret Knowledge, Lord of the Horizon, Keeper of the Way, the Flail of Mercy, the High-Born One, the Never-Dying King!'

The echoes died away.

'Could I have a word with you a moment, Dios?'

The high priest leaned down.

'Is all this necessary?' hissed Teppic.

Dios's aquiline features took on the wooden expression of one who is wrestling with an unfamiliar concept.

'Of course, sire. It is traditional,' he said, at last.

'I thought I was supposed to talk to these people. You know, about boundaries and trade and so on. I've been doing a lot of thinking about it and I've got several ideas. I mean, it's going to be a little difficult if you're going to keep shouting.'

Dios gave him a polite smile.

'Oh no, sire. That has all been sorted out, sire. I met with them this morning.'

'What am I supposed to do, then?'

Dios made a slight circling motion with one hand.

'Just as you wish, sire. It is normal to smile a little, and put them at their ease.'

'Is that *all?*'

'Sire could ask them whether they enjoy being diplomats, sire,' said Dios. He met Teppic's glare with eyes as expressionless as mirrors.

'I am the *king*,' Teppic hissed.

'Certainly, sire. It would not do to sully the office with mere matters of leaden state, sire. Tomorrow, sire, you will be holding supreme court. A very fit office for a monarch, sire.'

'Ah. Yes.'

It was quite complicated. Teppic listened carefully to the case, which was alleged cattle theft compounded by Djeli's onion-layered land laws. This is what it should all be about, he thought. No-one else can work out who owns the bloody ox, this is the sort of thing kings have to do. Now, let's see, five years ago, *he* sold the ox to *him*, but as it turned out –

He looked from the face of one worried farmer to the other. They were both clutching their ragged straw hats close to their chests, and both of them wore the paralysed wooden expressions of simple men who, in pursuit of their parochial disagreement, now found themselves on a marble floor in a great room with their god enthroned before their very eyes. Teppic didn't doubt that either one would cheerfully give up all rights to the wretched creature in exchange for being ten miles away.

It's a fairly mature ox, he thought, time it was slaughtered, even if it's *his* it's been fattening on his neighbour's land all these years, half each would be about right, they're really going to remember this judgement . . .

He raised the Sickle of Justice.

'His Greatness the King Teppicymon XXVIII, Lord of the Heavens, Charioteer of the Wagon of the Sun, Steersman of the Barque of the Sun, Guardian of the Secret Knowledge, Lord of the Horizon, Keeper of the Way, the Flail of Mercy, the High-Born One, the Never-Dying King, will give judgement! Cower to the justice of His Greatness the King Tep–'

Teppic cut Dios off in mid-intone.

'Having listened to both sides of the case,' he said firmly, the mask giving it a slight boom, 'and, being impressed by the argument and counter-argument, it seems to us only just that the beast in question should be slaughtered without delay and shared with all fairness between both plaintiff and defendant.'

He sat back. They'll call me Teppic the Wise, he thought. The common people go for this sort of thing.

The farmers gave him a long blank stare. Then, as if they were both mounted on turntables, they turned and looked to where Dios was sitting in his place on the steps in a group of lesser priests.

Dios stood up, smoothed his plain robe, and extended the staff.

'Harken to the interpreted wisdom of His Greatness the King Teppicymon XXVIII, Lord of the Heavens, Charioteer of the Wagon of the Sun, Steersman of the Barque of the Sun, Guardian of the Secret Knowledge, Lord of the Horizon, Keeper of the Way, the Flail of Mercy, the High-Born One, the Never-Dying King,' he said. 'It is our divine judgement that the beast in dispute is the property of Rhumusphut. It is our divine judgement that the beast be sacrificed upon the altar of the Concourse of Gods in thanks for the attention of Our Divine Self. It is our further judgement that both Rhumusphut and Ktoffle work a further three days in the fields of the King in payment for this judgement.'

Dios raised his head until he was looking along his fearsome nose right into Teppic's mask. He raised both hands.

'Mighty is the wisdom of His Greatness the King Teppicymon XXVIII, Lord of the Heavens, Charioteer of the Wagon of the Sun, Steersman of the Barque of the Sun, Guardian of the Secret Knowledge, Lord of the Horizon, Keeper of the Way, the Flail of Mercy, the High-Born One, the Never-Dying King!'

The farmers bobbed in terrified gratitude and backed out of the presence, framed between the guards.

'Dios,' said Teppic, levelly.

'Sire?'

'Just attend upon me a moment, please?'

'Sire?' repeated Dios, materialising by the throne.

'I could not help noticing, Dios, excuse me if I am wrong, a certain flourish in the translation there.'

The priest looked surprised.

'Indeed no, sire. I was most precise in relaying your decision, saving only to refine the detail in accordance with precedent and tradition.'

'How was that? The damn creature really belonged to both of them!'

'But Rhumusphut is known to be punctilious in his devotions, sire, seeking every opportunity to laud and magnify the gods, whereas Ktoffle has been known to harbour foolish thoughts.'

'What's that got to do with justice?'

'Everything, sire,' said Dios smoothly.

'But now neither of them has the ox!'

'Quite so, sire. But Ktoffle does not have it because he does not deserve it, while Rhumusphut, by his sacrifice, has ensured himself greater stature in the netherworld.'

'And you'll eat beef tonight, I suppose,' said Teppic.

It was like a blow; Teppic might as well have picked up the throne and hit the priest with it. Dios took a step backward, aghast, his eyes two brief pools of pain. When he spoke, there was a raw edge to his voice.

'I do not eat meat, sire,' he said. 'It dilutes and tarnishes the soul. May I summon the next case, sire?'

Teppic nodded. 'Very well.'

The next case was a dispute over the rent of a hundred square yards of riverside land. Teppic listened carefully. Good growing land was at a premium in Djeli, since the pyramids took up so much of it. It was a serious matter.

It was especially serious because the land's tenant was by all accounts hard-working and conscientious, while its actual owner was clearly rich and objectionable*. Unfortunately, however one chose to stack the facts, he was also in the right.

Teppic thought deeply, and then squinted at Dios. The priest nodded at him.

'It seems to me –' said Teppic, as fast as possible but not fast enough.

'Harken to the judgement of His Greatness the King Teppicymon XXVIII, Lord of the Heavens, Charioteer of the Wagon of the Sun, Steersman of the Barque of the Sun, Guardian of the Secret Knowledge, Lord of the Horizon, Keeper of the Way, the Flail of Mercy, the High-Born One, the Never-Dying King!'

'It seems to me – to *us*,' Teppic repeated, 'that, taking all matters in consideration beyond those of mere mortal artifice, the true and just outcome in this matter –' He paused. This, he thought, isn't how a god king speaks.

'The landlord has been weighed in the balance and found wanting,' he boomed through the mask's mouth slit. 'We find for the tenant.'

---

* Younger assassins, who are usually very poor, have very clear ideas about the morality of wealth until they become older assassins, who are usually very rich, when they begin to take the view that injustice has its good points.

As one man the court turned to Dios, who held a whispered consultation with the other priests and then stood up.

'Hear now the interpreted word of His Greatness the King Teppicymon XXVIII, Lord of the Heavens, Charioteer of the Wagon of the Sun, Steersman of the Barque of the Sun, Guardian of the Secret Knowledge, Lord of the Horizon, Keeper of the Way, the Flail of Mercy, the High-Born One, the Never-Dying King! Ptorne the farmer will at once pay 18 *toons* in back rent to Prince Imtebos! Prince Imtebos will at once pay 12 *toons* into the temple offerings of the gods of the river! Long live the king! Bring on the next case!'

Teppic beckoned to Dios again.

'Is there any point in me being here?' he demanded in an overheated whisper.

'Please be calm, sire. If you were not here, how would the people know that justice had been done?'

'But you twist everything I say!'

'No, sire. Sire, you give the judgement of the man. I interpret the judgement of the king.'

'I see,' said Teppic grimly. 'Well, from now on –'

There was a commotion outside the hall. Clearly there was a prisoner outside who was less than confident in the king's justice, and the king didn't blame him. He wasn't at all happy about it, either.

It turned out to be a dark-haired girl, struggling in the arms of two guards and giving them the kind of blows with fist and heel that a man would blush to give. She wasn't wearing the right kind of costume for the job, either. It would be barely adequate for lying around peeling grapes in.

She saw Teppic and, to his secret delight, flashed him a glance of pure hatred. After an afternoon of being treated like a mentally-deficient statue it was a pleasure to find someone prepared to take an interest in him.

He didn't know what she had done, but judging by the thumps she was landing on the guards it was a pretty good bet that she had done it to the very limits of her ability.

Dios bent down to the level of the mask's ear holes.

'Her name is Ptraci,' he said. 'A handmaiden of your father. She has refused to take the potion.'

'What potion?' said Teppic.

'It is customary for a dead king to take servants with him into the netherworld, sire.'

Teppic nodded gloomily. It was a jealously-guarded privilege, the only way a penniless servant could ensure immortality. He remembered grandfather's funeral, and the discreet clamour of the old man's personal servants. It had made father depressed for days.

'Yes, but it's not compulsory,' he said.

'Yes, sire. It is not compulsory.'

'Father had plenty of servants.'

'I gather she was his favourite, sire.'

'What exactly has she done wrong, then?'

Dios sighed, as one might if one were explaining things to an extremely backward child.

'She has refused to take the potion, sire.'

'Sorry. I thought you said it wasn't compulsory, Dios.'

'Yes, sire. It is not, sire. It is entirely voluntary. It is an act of free will. And she has refused it, sire.'

'Ah. One of *those* situations,' said Teppic. Djelibeybi was built on those sort of situations. Trying to understand them could drive you mad. If one of his ancestors had decreed that night was day, people would go around groping in the light.

He leaned forward.

'Step forward, young lady,' he said.

She looked at Dios.

'His Greatness the King Teppicymon XXVIII –'

'Do we have to go all through that every time?'

'Yes, sire – Lord of the Heavens, Charioteer of the Wagon of the Sun, Steersman of the Barque of the Sun, Guardian of the Secret Knowledge, Lord of the Horizon, Keeper of the Way, the Flail of Mercy, the High-Born One, the Never-Dying King, bids you declare your guilt!'

The girl shook herself out of the guards' grip and faced Teppic, trembling with terror.

'*He* told me he didn't want to be buried in a pyramid,' she said. 'He said the idea of those millions of tons of rock on top of him gave him nightmares. I don't want to die yet!'

'You refuse to gladly take the poison?' said Dios.

'Yes!'

'But, child,' said Dios, 'then the king will have you put to death anyway. Surely it is better to go honourably, to a worthy life in the netherworld?'

'I don't want to be a servant in the netherworld!'

There was a groan of horror from the assembled priests. Dios nodded.

'Then the Eater of Souls will take you,' he said. 'Sire, we look to your judgement.'

Teppic realised he was staring at the girl. There was something hauntingly familiar about her which he couldn't quite put his finger on. 'Let her go,' he said.

'His Greatness the King Teppicymon XXVIII, Lord of the Heavens, Charioteer of the Wagon of the Sun, Steersman of the Barque of the Sun, Guardian of the Secret Knowledge, Lord of the Horizon, Keeper of the Way, the Flail of Mercy, the High-Born One, the Never-Dying King, has spoken! Tomorrow at dawn you will be cast to the crocodiles of the river. Great is the wisdom of the king!'

Ptraci turned and glared at Teppic. He said nothing. He did not dare, for fear of what it might become.

She went away quietly, which was worse than sobbing or shouting.

'That is the last case, sire,' said Dios.

'I will retire to my quarters,' said Teppic coldly. 'I have much to think about.'

'Therefore I will have dinner sent in,' said the priest. 'It will be roast chicken.'

'I hate chicken.'

Dios smiled. 'No, sire. On Wednesdays the king always enjoys chicken, sire.'

The pyramids flared. The light they cast on the landscape was curiously subdued, grainy, almost grey, but over the capstone of each tomb a zigzag flame crackled towards the sky.

A faint clink of metal and stone sprang Ptraci from a fitful doze into extreme wakefulness. She stood up very carefully and crept towards the window.

Unlike proper cell windows, which should be large and airy and requiring only the removal of a few inconvenient iron bars to ensure the escape of any captives, this window was a slit six inches wide. Seven thousand years had taught the kings along the Djel that cells should be designed to keep prisoners *in*. The only way they could get out through this slit was in bits.

But there was a shadow against the pyramid light, and a voice said, 'Psst.'

She flattened herself against the wall and tried to reach up to the slit.

'Who are you?'

'I'm here to help you. Oh damn. Do they call this a window? Look, I'm lowering a rope.'

A thick silken cord, knotted at intervals, dropped past her shoulder. She stared at it for a second or two, and then kicked off her curly-toed shoes and climbed up it.

The face on the other side of the slit was half-concealed by a black hood, but she could just make out a worried expression.

'Don't despair,' it said.

'I wasn't despairing. I was trying to get some sleep.'

'Oh. Pardon me, I'm sure. I'll just go away and leave you, shall I?'

'But in the morning I shall wake up and *then* I'll despair. What are you standing on, demon?'

'Do you know what a crampon is?'

'No.'

'Well, it's two of them.'

They stared at each other in silence.

'Okay,' said the face at last. 'I'll have to go around and come in through the door. Don't go away.' And with that it vanished upwards.

Ptraci let herself slide back down to the chilly stones of the floor. Come in through the door! She wondered how it could manage that. Humans would need to open it first.

She crouched in the furthest corner of the cell, staring at the small rectangle of wood.

Long minutes went past. At one point she thought she heard a tiny noise, like a gasp.

A little later there was subtle clink of metal, so slight as to be almost beyond the range of hearing.

More time wound on to the spool of eternity and then the silence beyond the cell, which had been the silence caused by absence of sound, very slowly became the silence caused by someone making no noise.

She thought: it's right outside the door.

There was a pause in which Teppic oiled all the bolts and hinges so that, when he made the final assault, the door swished open in heart-gripping noiselessness.

'I say?' said a voice in the darkness.

Ptraci pressed herself still further into the corner.

'Look, I've come to rescue you.'

Now she could make out a blacker shadow in the flarelight. It stepped forward with rather more uncertainty than she would have expected from a demon.

'Are you coming or not?' it said. 'I've only knocked out the guards, it's not their fault, but we haven't got a lot of time.'

'I'm to be thrown to the crocodiles in the morning,' whispered Ptraci. 'The king himself decreed it.'

'He probably made a mistake.'

Ptraci's eyes widened in horrified disbelief.

'The Soul Eater will take me!' she said.

'Do you want it to?'

Ptraci hesitated.

'Well, then,' said the figure, and took her unresisting hand. He led her out of the cell, where she nearly tripped over the prone body of a guard.

'Who is in the other cells?' he said, pointing to the line of doors along the passage.

'I don't know,' said Ptraci.

'Let's find out, shall we?'

The figure touched a can to the bolts and hinges of the next door and pushed it open. The flare from the narrow window illuminated a middle-aged man, seated cross-legged on the floor.

'I'm here to rescue you,' said the demon.

The man peered up at him.

'Rescue?' he said.

'Yes. Why are you here?'

The man hung his head. 'I spoke blasphemy against the king.'

'How did you do that?'

'I dropped a rock on my foot. Now my tongue is to be torn out.'

The dark figure nodded sympathetically.

'A priest heard you, did he?' he said.

'No. I told a priest. Such words should not go unpunished,' said the man virtuously.

We're really good at it, Teppic thought. Mere animals couldn't possibly manage to act like this. You need to be a human being to be really stupid. 'I think we ought to talk about this outside,' he said. 'Why not come with me?'

The man pulled back and glared at him.

'You want me to *run* away?' he said.

'Seems a good idea, wouldn't you say?'

The man stared into his eyes, his lips moving silently. Then he appeared to reach a decision.

'Guards!' he screamed.

The shout echoed through the sleeping palace. His would-be rescuer stared at him in disbelief.

'Mad,' Teppic said. 'You're all mad.'

He stepped out of the room, grabbed Ptraci's hand, and hurried along the shadowy passages. Behind them the prisoner made the most of his tongue while he still had it and used it to scream a stream of imprecations.

'Where are you taking me?' said Ptraci, as they marched smartly around a corner and into a pillar-barred courtyard.

Teppic hesitated. He hadn't thought much beyond this point.

'Why do they bother to bolt the doors?' he demanded, eyeing the pillars. 'That's what I want to know. I'm surprised you didn't wander back to your cell while I was in there.'

'I – I don't want to die,' she said quietly.

'Don't blame you.'

'You mustn't say that! It's wrong not to want to die!'

Teppic glanced up at the roof around the courtyard and unslung his grapnel.

'I think I *ought* to go back to my cell,' said Ptraci, without actually making any move in that direction. 'It's wrong even to think of disobeying the king.'

'Oh? What happens to you, then?'

'Something bad,' she said vaguely.

'You mean, worse than being thrown to the crocodiles or having your soul taken by the Soul Eater?' said Teppic, and caught the grapnel firmly on some hidden ledge on the flat roof.

'That's an interesting point,' said Ptraci, winning the Teppic Award for clear thinking.

'Worth considering, isn't it?' Teppic tested his weight on the cord.

'What you're saying is, if the worst is going to happen to you *anyway*, you might as well not bother any more,' said Ptraci. 'If the Soul Eater is going to get you whatever you do, you might as well avoid the crocodiles, is that it?'

'You go up first,' said Teppic, 'I think someone's coming.'

'Who *are* you?'

Teppic fished in his pouch. He'd come back to Djeli an aeon ago with just the clothes he stood up in, but they were the clothes he'd stood up in throughout his exam. He balanced a Number Two throwing knife in his hand, the steel glinting in the flarelight. It was possibly the only steel in the country; it wasn't that Djelibeybi hadn't heard about iron, it was just that if copper was good enough for your great-great-great-great-grandfather, it was good enough for you.

No, the guards didn't deserve knives. They hadn't done anything wrong.

His hand closed over the little mesh bag of caltraps. These were a small model, a mere one inch per spike. Caltraps didn't kill anyone, they just slowed them down a bit. One or two of them in the sole of the foot induced extreme slowness and caution in all except the terminally enthusiastic.

He scattered a few across the mouth of the passage and ran back to the rope, hauling himself up in a few quick swings. He reached the roof just as the leading guards ran under the lintel. He waited until he heard the first curse, and then coiled up the rope and hurried after the girl.

'They'll catch us,' she said.

'I don't think so.'

'And then the king will have us thrown to the crocodiles.'

'Oh no, I don't think –' Teppic paused. It was an intriguing idea.

'He might,' he ventured. 'It's very hard to be sure about anything.'

'So what shall we do now?'

Teppic stared across the river, where the pyramids were ablaze. The Great Pyramid was still under construction, by flarelight; a swarm of blocks, dwarfed by distance, hovered near its tip. The amount of labour Ptaclusp was putting on the job was amazing.

What a flare that will give, he thought. It'll be seen all the way to Ankh.

'Horrible things, aren't they,' said Ptraci, behind him.

'Do you think so?'

'They're creepy. The old king hated them, you know. He said they nailed the Kingdom to the past.'

'Did he say why?'

'No. He just hated them. He was a nice old boy. Very kind. Not like this new one.' She blew her nose and replaced her handkerchief in its scarcely adequate space in her sequined bra.

'Er, what exactly did you have to do? As a handmaiden, I mean?' said Teppic, scanning the rooftop panorama to hide his embarrassment.

She giggled. 'You're not from around here, are you?'

'No. Not really.'

'Talk to him, mainly. Or just listen. He could really talk, but he always said no-one ever really listened to what he said.'

'Yes,' said Teppic, with feeling. 'And that was all, was it?'

She stared at him, and then giggled again. 'Oh, that? No, he was very kind. I wouldn't of minded, you understand, I had all the proper training. Bit of a disappointment, really. The women of my family have served under the kings for centuries, you know.'

'Oh yes?' he managed.

'I don't know whether you've ever seen a book, it's called *The Shuttered* –'

'– *Palace*,' said Teppic automatically.

'I thought a gentleman like you'd know about it,' said Ptraci, nudging him. 'It's a sort of textbook. Well, my great-great-grandmother posed for a lot of the pictures. Not recently,' she added, in case he hadn't fully understood, 'I mean, that would be a bit off-putting, she's been dead for twenty-five years. When she was younger. I look a lot like her, everyone says.'

'Urk,' agreed Teppic.

'She was famous. She could put her feet behind her head, you know. So can I. I've got my Grade Three.'

'Urk?'

'The old king told me once that the gods gave people a sense of humour to make up for giving them sex. I think he was a bit upset at the time.'

'Urk.' Only the whites of Teppic's eyes were showing.

'You don't say much, do you?'

The breeze of the night was blowing her perfume towards him. Ptraci used scent like a battering ram.

'We've got to find somewhere to hide you,' he said, concentrating on each word. 'Haven't you got any parents or anything?' He tried to ignore the fact that in the shadowless flarelight she appeared to glow, and didn't have much success.

'Well, my mother still works in the palace somewhere,' said Ptraci. 'But I don't think she'd be very sympathetic.'

'We've got to get you away from here,' said Teppic fervently. 'If you can hide somewhere today, I can steal some horses or a boat or something. Then you could go to Tsort or Ephebe or somewhere.'

'Foreign, you mean? I don't think I'd like that,' said Ptraci.

'Compared to the netherworld?'

'Well. Put like that, of course . . .' She took his arm. 'Why did you rescue me?'

'Er? Because being alive is better than being dead, I think.'

'I've read up to number 46, Congress of the Five Auspicious Ants,' said Ptraci. 'If you've got some yoghurt, we could –'

'No! I mean, no. Not here. Not now. There must be people looking for us, it's nearly dawn.'

'There's no need to yelp like that! I was just trying to be kind.'

'Yes. Good. Thank you.' Teppic broke away and peered desperately over a parapet into one of the palace's numerous light wells.

'This leads to the embalmers' workshops,' he said. 'There must be plenty of places to hide down here.' He unwound the cord again.

Various rooms led off the well. Teppic found one lined with benches and floored with wood shavings; a doorway led through to another room stacked with mummy cases, each one surmounted by the same golden dolly face he'd come to know and loathe. He tapped on a few, and raised the lid of the nearest.

'No-one at home,' he said. 'You can have a nice rest in here. I can leave the lid open a bit so you can get some air.'

'You can't think I'd risk that? Supposing you didn't come back!'

'I'll be back tonight,' said Teppic. 'And – and I'll see if I can drop some food and water in some time today.'

She stood on tiptoe, her ankle bangles jingling all the way down Teppic's libido. He glanced down involuntarily and saw that every toenail was painted. He remembered Cheesewright telling them behind the stables one lunch-hour that girls who painted their toenails were ... well, he couldn't quite remember now, but it had seemed pretty unbelievable at the time.

'It looks very hard,' she said.

'What?'

'If I've got to lie in it, it'll need some cushions.'

'I'll put some wood shavings in, look!' said Teppic. 'But hurry up! Please!'

'All right. But you will be back, won't you? Promise?'

'Yes, yes! I promise!'

He wedged a splinter of wood on the case to allow an airhole, heaved the lid back on and ran for it.

The ghost of the king watched him go.

The sun rose. As the golden light spilled down the fertile valley of the Djel the pyramid flares paled and became ghost dancers against the lightening sky. They were now accompanied by a noise. It had been there all the time, far too high-pitched for mortal ears, a sound now dropping down from the far ultrasonic...

KKKkkkkkkhhheeee ...

It screamed out of the sky, a thin rind of sound like a violin bow dragged across the raw surface of the brain.

kkkhheeeeeee ...

Or a wet fingernail dragged over an exposed nerve, some said. You could set your watch by it, they would have said, if anyone knew what one was.

. . . keeee . . .

It went deeper and deeper as the sunlight washed over the stones, passing through cat scream to dog growl.

. . . ee . . . ee . . . ee . . .

The flares collapsed.

. . . ops.

'A fine morning, sire. I trust you slept well?'

Teppic waved a hand at Dios, but said nothing. The barber was working through the Ceremony of Going Forth Shaven.

The barber was trembling. Until recently he had been a one-handed, unemployed stonemason. Then the terrible high priest had summoned him and ordered him to be the king's barber, but it meant you had to touch the king but it was all right because it was all sorted out by the priests and nothing more had to be chopped off. On the whole, it was better than he had thought, and a great honour to be single-handedly responsible for the king's beard, such as it was.

'You were not disturbed in any way?' said the high priest. His eyes scanned the room on a raster of suspicion; it was surprising that little lines of molten rock didn't drip off the walls.

'Verrr –'

'If you would but hold still, O never-dying one,' said the barber, in the pleading tone of voice employed by one who is assured of a guided tour of a crocodile's alimentary tract if he nicks an ear.

'You heard no strange noises, sire?' said Dios. He stepped back suddenly so that he could see behind the gilded peacock screen at the other end of the room.

'Norr.'

'Your majesty looks a little peaky this morning, sire,' said Dios. He sat down on the bench with the carved cheetahs on either end. Sitting down in the presence of the king, except on ceremonial occasions, was not something that was allowed. It did, however, mean that he could squint under Teppic's low bed.

Dios was rattled. Despite the aches and the lack of sleep, Teppic felt oddly elated. He wiped his chin.

'It's the bed,' he said. 'I think I have mentioned it. Mattresses, you know. They have feathers in them. If the concept is unfamiliar, ask the pirates of Khali. Half of them must be sleeping on goosefeather mattresses by now.'

'His majesty is pleased to joke,' said Dios.

Teppic knew he shouldn't push it any further, but he did so anyway.

'Something wrong, Dios?' he said.

'A miscreant broke into the palace last night. The girl Ptraci is missing.'

'That is very disturbing.'

'Yes, sire.'

'Probably a suitor or a swain or something.'

Dios's face was like stone. 'Possibly, sire.'

'The sacred crocodiles will be going hungry, then.' But not for long, Teppic thought. Walk to the end of any of the little jetties down by the bank, let your shadow fall on the river, and the mud-yellow water would become, by magic, mud-yellow bodies. They looked like large, sodden logs, the main difference being that logs don't open at one end and bite your legs off. The sacred crocodiles of the Djel were the kingdom's garbage disposal, river patrol and occasional morgue.

They couldn't simply be called big. If one of the huge bulls ever drifted sideways on to the current, he'd dam the river.

The barber tiptoed out. A couple of body servants tiptoed in.

'I anticipated your majesty's natural reaction, sire,' Dios continued, like the drip of water in deep limestone caverns.

'Jolly good,' said Teppic, inspecting the clothes for the day. 'What was it, exactly?'

'A detailed search of the palace, room by room.'

'Absolutely. Carry on, Dios.'

My face is perfectly open, he told himself. I haven't twitched a muscle out of place. I *know* I haven't. He can read me like a stele. I can outstare him.

'Thank you, sire.'

'I imagine they'll be miles away by now,' said Teppic. 'Whoever they were. She was only a handmaiden, wasn't she?'

'It is unthinkable that anyone could disobey your judgements! There is no-one in the kingdom that would dare to! Their souls would be forfeit! They will be hunted down, sire! Hunted down and destroyed!'

The servants cowered behind Teppic. This wasn't mere anger. This was wrath. Real, old-time, vintage wrath. And waxing? It waxed like a hatful of moons.

'Are you feeling all right, Dios?'

Dios had turned to look out across the river. The Great Pyramid was almost complete. The sight of it seemed to calm him down or, at least, stabilise him on some new mental plateau.

'Yes, sire,' he said. 'Thank you.' He breathed deeply. 'Tomorrow, sire, you are pleased to witness the capping of the pyramid. A momentous occasion. Of course, it will be some time before the interior chambers are completed.'

'Fine. Fine. And this morning, I think, I should like to visit my father.'

'I am sure the late king will be pleased to see you, sire. It is your wish that I should accompany you.'

'Oh.'

It's a fact as immutable as the Third Law of Sod that there is no such thing as a good Grand Vizier. A predilection to cackle and plot is apparently part of the job spec.

High priests tend to get put in the same category. They have to face the implied assumption that no sooner do they get the funny hat than they're issuing strange orders, e.g., princesses tied to rocks for itinerant sea monsters and throwing little babies in the sea.

This is a gross slander. Throughout the history of the Disc most high priests have been serious, pious and conscientious men who have done their best to interpret the wishes of the gods, sometimes disembowelling or flaying alive hundreds of people in a day in order to make sure they're getting it absolutely right.

King Teppicymon XXVII's casket lay in state. Crafted it was of foryphy, smaradgine, skelsa and delphinet, inlaid it was with pink jade and shode, perfumed and fumed it was with many rare resins and perfumes . . .

It looked very impressive but, the king considered, it wasn't worth dying for. He gave up and wandered across the courtyard.

A new player had entered the drama of his death.

Grinjer, the maker of models.

He'd always wondered about the models. Even a humble farmer expected to be buried with a selection of crafted livestock, which would somehow become real in the nether-world. Many a man made do with one cow like a toast rack in this world in order to afford a pedigree herd in the next. Nobles and kings got the complete set, including model carts, houses, boats and anything else too big or inconvenient to fit in the tomb. Once on the other side, they'd somehow become the genuine article.

The king frowned. When he was alive he'd known that it was true. Not doubted it for a moment . . .

Grinjer stuck his tongue out of the corner of his mouth as, with great care, he tweezered a tiny oar to a perfect 1/80th scale river trireme. Every flat surface in his corner of the workshop was stacked with midget animals and artifacts; some of his more impressive ones hung from wires on the ceiling.

The king had already ascertained from overheard conversation that Grinjer was twenty-six, couldn't find anything to stop the inexorable advance of his acne, and lived at home with his mother. Where, in the evenings, he made models. Deep in the duffel coat of his mind he hoped one day to find a nice girl who would understand the absolute importance of getting every detail right on a ceremonial six-wheeled ox cart, and who would hold his glue-pot, and always be ready with a willing thumb whenever anything needed firm pressure until the paste dried.

He was aware of trumpets and general excitement behind him. He ignored it. There always seemed to be a lot of fuss these days. In his experience it was always about trivial things. People just didn't have their priorities right. He'd been waiting two months for a few ounces of gum varneti, and it didn't seem to bother anyone. He screwed his eyeglass into a more comfortable position and slotted a minute steering oar into place.

Someone was standing next to him. Well, they could make themselves useful . . .

'Could you just put your finger here,' he said, without glancing around. 'Just for a minute, until the glue sets.'

There seemed to be a sudden drop in temperature. He looked up into a smiling golden mask. Over its shoulder Dios's face was shading, in Grinjer's expert opinion, from No.13 (Pale Flesh) to No.37 (Sunset Purple, Gloss).

'Oh,' he said.

'It's very good,' said Teppic. 'What is it?'

Grinjer blinked at him. Then he blinked at the boat.

'It's an eighty-foot Khali-fashion river trireme with fishtail spear deck and ramming prow,' he said automatically.

He got the impression that more was expected of him. He cast around for something suitable.

'It's got more than five hundred bits,' he added. 'Every plank on the deck is individually cut, look.'

'Fascinating,' said Teppic. 'Well, I won't hold you up. Carry on the good work.'

'The sail really unfurls,' said Grinjer. 'See, if you pull this thread, the –'

The mask had moved. Dios was there instead. He gave Grinjer a short glare which indicated that more would be heard about this later on, and hurried after the king. So did the ghost of Teppicymon XXVII.

Teppic's eyes swivelled behind the mask. There was the open doorway into the room of caskets. He could just make out the one containing Ptraci; the wedge of wood was still under the lid.

'Our father, however, is over here. Sire,' said Dios. He could move as silently as a ghost.

'Oh. Yes.' Teppic hesitated and then crossed to the big case on its trestles. He stared down at it for some time. The gilded face on the lid looked like every other mask.

'A very good likeness, sire,' prompted Dios.

'Ye-ess,' said Teppic. 'I suppose so. He definitely looks happier. I suppose.'

'Hallo, my boy,' said the king. He knew that no-one could hear him, but he felt happier talking to them all the same. It was better than talking to himself. He was going to have more than enough time for that.

'I think it brings out the best in him, O commander of the heavens,' said the head sculptor.

'Makes me look like a constipated wax dolly.'

Teppic cocked his head on one side.

'Yes,' he said, uncertainly. 'Yes. Er. Well done.'

He half-turned to look through the doorway again.

Dios nodded to the guards on either side of the passageway.

'If you will excuse me, sire,' he said urbanely.

'Hmm?'

'The guards will continue their search.'

'Right. Oh –'

Dios bore down on Ptraci's casket, flanked by guards. He gripped the lid, thrust it backwards, and said. 'Behold! What do we find?'

Dil and Gern joined him. They looked inside.

'Wood shavings,' said Dil.

Gern sniffed. 'They smell nice, though,' he said.

Dios's fingers drummed on the lid. Teppic had never seen him at a loss before. The man actually started tapping the sides of the case, apparently seeking any hidden panels.

He closed the lid carefully and looked blankly at Teppic, who for the first time was very glad that the mask didn't reveal his expression.

'She's not in there,' said the old king. *'She got out for a call of nature when the men went to have their breakfast.'*

She must have climbed out, Teppic told himself. So where is she now?

Dios scanned the room carefully and then, after swinging slowly backwards and forwards like a compass needle, his eyes fixed on the king's mummy case. It was big. It was roomy. There was a certain inevitability about it.

He crossed the room in a couple of strides and heaved it open.

'Don't bother to knock,' the king grumbled. *'It's not as if I'm going anywhere.'*

Teppic risked a look. The mummy of the king was quite alone.

'Are you sure you're feeling all right, Dios?' he said.

'Yes, sire. We cannot be too careful, sire. Clearly they are not here, sire.'

'You look as if you could do with a breath of fresh air,' said Teppic, upbraiding himself for doing this but doing it, nevertheless. Dios at a loss was an awe-inspiring sight, and slightly disconcerting; it made one instinctively fear for the stability of things.

'Yes, sire. Thank you, sire.'

'Have a sit down and someone will bring you a glass of water. And then we will go and inspect the pyramid.'

Dios sat down.

There was a terrible little splintering noise.

'He's sat on the boat,' said the king. *'First humorous thing I've ever seen him do.'*

The pyramid gave a new meaning to the word 'massive'. It bent the landscape around it. It seemed to Teppic that its very weight was deforming the shape of things, stretching the kingdom like a lead ball on a rubber sheet.

He knew that was a ridiculous idea. Big though the pyramid was, it was tiny compared to, say, a mountain.

But big, very big, compared to anything else. Anyway, mountains were *meant* to be big, the fabric of the universe was used to the idea. The pyramid was a made thing, and much bigger than a made thing ought to be.

It was also very cold. The black marble of its sides was shining white with frost in the roasting afternoon sun. He was foolish enough to touch it and left a layer of skin on the surface.

'It's freezing!'

'It's storing already, O breath of the river,' said Ptaclusp, who was sweating. 'It's the wossname, the boundary effect.'

'I note that you have ceased work on the burial chambers,' said Dios.

'The men . . . the temperature . . . boundary effects . . . a bit too much to risk . . .' muttered Ptaclusp. 'Er.'

Teppic looked from one to the other.

'What's the matter?' he said. 'Are there problems?'

'Er,' said Ptaclusp.

'You're way ahead of schedule. Marvellous work,' said Teppic. 'You've put a tremendous amount of labour on the job.'

'Er. Yes. Only.'

There was silence except for the distant sounds of men at work, and the faint noise of the air sizzling where it touched the pyramid.

'It's bound to be all right when we get the capstone on,' the pyramid builder managed eventually. 'Once it's flaring properly, no problem. Er.'

He indicated the electrum capstone. It was surprisingly small, only a foot or so across, and rested on a couple of trestles.

'We should be able to put it on tomorrow,' said Ptaclusp. 'Would your sire still be honouring us with the capping-out ceremony?' In his nervousness he gripped the hem of his robe and began to twist it. 'There's drinks,' he stuttered. 'And a silver trowel that you can take away with you. Everyone shouts hurrah and throws their hats in the air.'

'Certainly,' said Dios. 'It will be an honour.'

'And for us too, your sire,' said Ptaclusp loyally.

'I *meant* for you,' said the high priest. He turned to the wide courtyard between the base of the pyramid and the river, which was lined with statues and stelae commemorating King Teppicymon's mighty deeds,[*] and pointed.

---

[*] The carvers had to use quite a lot of imagination. The late king had had many fine attributes, but doing mighty deeds wasn't among them. The score was: Number of enemies ground as dust under his chariot wheels = 0. Number of thrones crushed beneath his sandalled feet = 0. Number of times world bestrode like colossus = 0. On the other hand: Reigns of terror = 0. Number of times own throne crushed beneath enemy sandals = 0. Faces of poor ground = 0.

'And you can get rid of that,' he added.

Ptaclusp gave him a look of unhappy innocence.

'That statue,' said Dios, 'is what I am referring to.'

'Oh. Ah. Well, we thought once you saw it in place, you see, in the right light, and what with Hat the Vulture-Headed God being very –'

'It goes,' said Dios.

'Right you are, your reverence,' said Ptaclusp miserably. It was, right now, the least of his problems, but on top of everything else he was beginning to think that the statue was following him around.

Dios leaned closer.

'You haven't seen a young woman anywhere on the site, have you?' he demanded.

'No women on the site, my lord,' said Ptaclusp. 'Very bad luck.'

'This one was provocatively dressed,' the high priest said.

'No, no women.'

'The palace is not far, you see. There must be many places to hide over here,' Dios continued, insistently.

Ptaclusp swallowed. He knew that, all right. Whatever had possessed him . . .

'I assure you, your reverence,' he said.

Dios gave him a scowl, and then turned to where Teppic, as it turned out, had been.

'Please ask him not to shake hands with anybody,' said the builder, as Dios hurried after the distant glint of sunlight on gold. The king still didn't seem to be able to get alongside the idea that the last thing the people wanted was a man of the people. Those workers who couldn't get out of the way in time were thrusting their hands behind their back.

Alone now, Ptaclusp fanned himself and staggered into the shade of his tent.

Where, waiting to see him, were Ptaclusp IIa, Ptaclusp IIa, Ptaclusp IIa and Ptaclusp IIa. Ptaclusp always felt uneasy in the presence of accountants, and four of them together was very bad, especially when they were all the same person. Three Ptaclusp IIbs were there as well; the other two, unless it was three by now, were out on the site.

He waved his hands in a conciliatory way.

'All right, all right,' he said. 'What are today's problems?'

One of the IIas pulled a stack of wax tablets towards him.

Expensive crusades embarked upon = 0. His life had, basically, been a no-score win.

'Have you any idea, father,' he began, employing that thin, razor-edged voice that accountants use to preface something unexpected and very expensive, 'what calculus is?'

'You tell me,' said Ptaclusp, sagging on to a stool.

'It's what I've had to invent to deal with the wages bill, father,' said another IIa.

'I thought that was algebra?' said Ptaclusp.

'We passed algebra last week,' said a third IIa. 'It's calculus now. I've had to loop myself another four times to work on it, and there's three of me working on –' he glanced at his brothers – 'quantum accountancy.'

'What's that for?' said his father wearily.

'Next week.' The leading accountant glared at the top slab. 'For example,' he said. 'You know Rthur the fresco painter?'

'What about him?'

'He – that is, *they* – have put in a bill for two years' work.'

'Oh.'

'They said they did it on Tuesday. On account of how time is fractal in nature, they said.'

'They said that?' said Ptaclusp.

'It's amazing what they pick up,' said one of the accountants, glaring at the paracosmic architects.

Ptaclusp hesitated. 'How many of them are there?'

'How should we know? We *know* there were fifty-three. Then he went critical. We've certainly seen him around a lot.' Two of the IIas sat back and steepled their fingers, always a bad sign in anyone having anything to do with money. 'The problem is,' one of them continued, 'that after the initial enthusiasm a lot of the workers looped themselves unofficially so that they could stay at home and send themselves out to work.'

'But that's ridiculous,' Ptaclusp protested weakly. 'They're not different people, they're just doing it to themselves.'

'That's never stopped anyone, father,' said IIa. 'How many men have stopped drinking themselves stupid at the age of twenty to save a stranger dying of liver failure at forty?'

There was silence while they tried to work this one out.

'A stranger –?' said Ptaclusp uncertainly.

'I mean himself, when older,' snapped IIa. 'That was philosophy,' he added.

'One of the masons beat himself up yesterday,' said one of the IIbs gloomily. 'He was fighting with himself over his wife. Now he's going mad because he doesn't know whether it's an earlier version

114

of him or someone he hasn't been yet. He's afraid he's going to creep up on him. There's worse than that, too. Dad, we're paying forty thousand people, and we're only *employing* two thousand.'

'It's going to bankrupt us, that's what you're going to say,' said Ptaclusp. 'I know. It's all my fault. I just wanted something to hand on to you, you know. I didn't expect all this. It seemed too easy to start with.'

One of the IIas cleared his throat.

'It's . . . uh . . . not *quite* as bad as all that,' he said quietly.

'What do you mean?'

The accountant laid a dozen copper coins on the table.

'Well, er,' he said. 'You see, eh, it occurred to me, since there's all this movement in time, that it's not just *people* who can be looped, and, er, look, you see these coins?'

One coin vanished.

'They're all the same coin, aren't they,' said one of his brothers.

'Well, yes,' said the IIa, very embarrassed, because interfering with the divine flow of money was alien to his personal religion. 'The same coin at five minute intervals.'

'And you're using this trick to pay the men?' said Ptaclusp dully.

'It's not a trick! I give them the money,' said IIa primly. 'What happens to it afterwards isn't my responsibility, is it?'

'I don't like any of this,' said his father.

'Don't worry. It all evens out in the end,' said one of the IIas. 'Everyone gets what's coming to them.'

'Yes. That's what I'm afraid of,' said Ptaclusp.

'It's just a way of letting your money work for you,' said another son. 'It's probably quantum.'

'Oh, good,' said Ptaclusp weakly.

'We'll get the block on tonight, don't worry,' said one of the IIbs. 'After it's flared the power off we can all settle down.'

'I told the king we'd do it tomorrow.'

The Ptaclusp IIbs went pale in unison. Despite the heat, it suddenly seemed a lot colder in the tent.

'Tonight, father,' said one of them. 'Surely you mean tonight?'

'Tomorrow,' said Ptaclusp, firmly. 'I've arranged an awning and people throwing lotus blossom. There's going to be a band. Tocsins and trumpets and tinkling cymbals. And speeches and a meat tea afterwards. That's the way we've always done it. Attracts new customers. They like to have a look round.'

'Father, you've seen the way it soaks up . . . you've seen the frost . . .'

'Let it soak. We Ptaclusps don't go around capping off pyramids as though we were finishing off a garden wall. We don't knock off like a wossname in the night. People expect a ceremony.'

'But –'

'I'm not listening. I've listened to too much of this new-fangled stuff. Tomorrow. I've had the bronze plaque made, and the velvet curtains and everything.'

One of the IIas shrugged. 'It's no good arguing with him,' he said. 'I'm from three hours ahead. I remember this meeting. We couldn't change his mind.'

'I'm from two hours ahead,' said one of his clones. 'I remember you saying that, too.'

Beyond the walls of the tent, the pyramid sizzled with accumulated time.

There is nothing mystical about the power of pyramids.

Pyramids are dams in the stream of time. Correctly shaped and orientated, with the proper paracosmic measurements correctly plumbed in, the temporal potential of the great mass of stone can be diverted to accelerate or reverse time over a very small area, in the same way that a hydraulic ram can be induced to pump water *against the flow.*

The original builders, who were of course ancients and therefore wise, knew this very well and the whole point of a correctly-built pyramid was to achieve absolute null time in the central chamber so that a dying king, tucked up there, would indeed live forever – or at least, never actually die. The time that should have passed in the chamber was stored in the bulk of the pyramid and allowed to flare off once every twenty-four hours.

After a few aeons people forgot this and thought you could achieve the same effect by a) ritual b) pickling people and c) storing their soft inner bits in jars.

This seldom works.

And so the art of pyramid tuning was lost, and all the knowledge became a handful of misunderstood rules and hazy recollections. The ancients were far too wise to build very big pyramids. They could cause very strange things, things that would make mere fluctuations in time look tiny by comparison.

By the way, contrary to popular opinion pyramids don't sharpen razor blades. They just take them back to when they weren't blunt. It's probably because of quantum.

*

Teppic lay on the strata of his bed, listening intently.

There were two guards outside the door, and another two on the balcony outside, and – he was impressed at Dios's forethought – one on the roof. He could hear them trying to make no noise.

He'd hardly been able to protest. If black-clad miscreants were getting into the palace, then the person of the king had to be protected. It was undeniable.

He slipped off the solid mattress and glided through the twilight to the statue of Bast the Cat-Headed God in the corner, twisted off the head, and pulled out his assassin's costume. He dressed quickly, cursing the lack of mirrors, and then padded across and lurked behind a pillar.

The only problem, as far as he could see, was not laughing. Being a soldier in Djelibeybi was not a high risk job. There was never a hint of internal rebellion and, since either neighbour could crush the kingdom instantly by force of arms, there was no real point in selecting keen and belligerent warriors. In fact, the last thing the priesthood wanted was enthusiastic soldiers. Enthusiastic soldiers with no fighting to do soon get bored and start thinking dangerous thoughts, like how much better they could run the country.

Instead the job attracted big, solid men, the kind of men who could stand stock still for hours at a time without getting bored, men with the build of an ox and the mental processes to match. Excellent bladder control was also desirable.

He stepped out on to the balcony.

Teppic had learned how not to move stealthily. Millions of years of being eaten by creatures that know how to move stealthily has made humanity very good at spotting stealthy movement. Nor was it enough to make no noise, because little moving patches of silence always aroused suspicion. The trick was to glide through the night with a quiet reassurance, just like the air did.

There was a guard standing just outside the room. Teppic drifted past him and climbed carefully up the wall. It had been decorated with a complex bas relief of the triumphs of past monarchs, so Teppic used his family to give him a leg up.

The breeze was blowing off the desert as he swung his legs over the parapet and walked silently across the roof, which was still hot underfoot. The air had a recently-cooked smell, tinted with spice.

It was a strange feeling, to be creeping across the roof of your own palace, trying to avoid your own guards, engaged on a mission in direct contravention of your own decree and knowing that if you were caught you would have yourself thrown to the sacred crocodiles. After all, he'd apparently already instructed that he was to be shown no mercy if he was captured.

Somehow it added an extra thrill.

There was freedom of a sort up here on the rooftops, the only kind of freedom available to a king of the valley. It occurred to Teppic that the landless peasants down on the delta had more freedom than he did, although the seditious and non-kingly side of him said, yes, freedom to catch any diseases of their choice, starve as much as they wanted, and die of whatever dreadful ague took their fancy. But freedom, of a sort.

A faint noise in the huge silence of the night drew him to the riverward edge of the roof. The Djel sprawled in the moonlight, broad and oily.

There was a boat in midstream, heading back from the far bank and the necropolis. There was no mistaking the figure at the oars. The flarelight gleamed off his bald head.

One day, Teppic thought, I'll follow him. I'll find out what it is he does over there.

If he goes over in daylight, of course.

In daylight the necropolis was merely gloomy, as though the whole universe had shut down for early-closing. He'd even explored it, wandering through streets and alleys that contrived to be still and dusty no matter what the weather was on the other, the *living* side of the water. There was always a breathless feel about it, which was probably not to be wondered at. Assassins liked the night on general principles, but the night of the necropolis was something else. Or rather, it was the same thing, but a lot more of it. Besides, it was the only city anywhere on the Disc where an assassin couldn't find employment.

He reached the light well that opened on the embalmers' courtyard and peered down. A moment later he landed lightly on the floor and slipped into the room of cases.

'Hallo, lad.'

Teppic opened the lid of the case. It was still empty.

'*She's in one of the ones at the back,*' said the king. '*Never had much of a sense of direction.*'

It was a great big palace. Teppic could barely find his way around it by daylight. He considered his chances of carrying out a search in pitch darkness.

'*It's a family trait, you know. Your grandad had to have Left and Right painted on his sandals, it was that bad. It's lucky for you that you take after your mother in that respect.*'

It was strange. She didn't talk, she chattered. She didn't seem to be able to hold a simple thought in her head for more than about ten seconds. Her brain appeared to be wired directly to her mouth, so that as soon as a thought entered her head she spoke it out loud. Compared to the ladies he had met at soirees in Ankh, who delighted in entertaining young assassins and fed them expensive delicacies and talked to them of high and delicate matters while their eyes sparkled like carborundum drills and their lips began to glisten . . . compared to them, she was as empty as a, as a, well, as an empty thing. Nevertheless, he found he desperately wanted to find her. The sheer undemandingness of her was like a drug. The memory of her bosom was quite beside the point.

'I'm glad you've come back for her,' said the king vaguely. 'She's your sister, you know. Half sister, that is. Sometimes I wish I'd married her mother, but you see she wasn't royal. Very bright woman, her mother.'

Teppic listened hard. There it was again: a faint breathing noise, only heard at all because of the deep silence of the night. He worked his way to the back of the room, listened again, and lifted the lid of a case.

Ptraci was curled up on the bottom, fast asleep with her head on her arm.

He leaned the lid carefully against the wall and touched her hair. She muttered something in her sleep, and settled into a more comfortable position.

'Er, I think you'd better wake up,' he whispered.

She changed position again and muttered something like: 'Wstflgl.'

Teppic hesitated. Neither his tutors nor Dios had prepared him for this. He knew at least seventy different ways of killing a sleeping person, but none to wake them up first.

He prodded her in what looked like the least embarrassing area of her skin. She opened her eyes.

'Oh,' she said. 'It's you.' And she yawned.

'I've come to take you away,' said Teppic. 'You've been asleep all day.'

'I heard someone talking,' she said, stretching in a fashion that made Teppic look away hurriedly. 'It was that priest, the one with the face like a bald eagle. He's really horrible.'

'He is, isn't he?' agreed Teppic, intensely relieved to hear it said.

'So I just kept quiet. And there was the king. The *new* king.'

'Oh. He was down here, was he?' said Teppic weakly. The

119

bitterness in her voice was like a Number Four stabbing knife in his heart.

'All the girls say he's really *weird*,' she added, as he helped her out of the case. 'You *can* touch me, you know. I'm not made of china.'

He steadied her arm, feeling in sore need of a cold bath and a quick run around the rooftops.

'You're an assassin, aren't you,' she went on. 'I remembered that after you'd gone. An assassin from foreign parts. All that black. Have you come to kill the king?'

'I wish I could,' said Teppic. 'He's really beginning to get on my nerves. Look, could you take your bangles off?'

'Why?'

'They make such a noise when you walk.' Even Ptraci's earrings appeared to chime the hours when she moved her head.

'I don't want to,' she said. 'I'd feel naked without them.'

'You're nearly naked *with* them,' hissed Teppic. 'Please!'

'*She can play the dulcimer*,' said the ghost of Teppicymon XXVII, apropos of nothing much. '*Not very well, mind you. She's up to page five of "Little Pieces for Tiny Fingers".*'

Teppic crept to the passage leading out of the embalming room and listened hard. Silence ruled in the palace, broken only by heavy breathing and the occasional clink behind him as Ptraci stripped herself of her jewelry. He crept back.

'Please hurry up,' he said, 'we haven't got a lot of –'

Ptraci was crying.

'Er,' said Teppic. 'Er.'

'Some of these were presents from my granny,' sniffed Ptraci. 'The old king gave me some, too. These earrings have been in my family for ever such a long time. How would you like it if you had to do it?'

'*You see, jewelry isn't just something she wears*,' said the ghost of Teppicymon XXVII. '*It's part of who she is.*' My word, he added to himself, that's probably an Insight. Why is it so much easier to think when you're dead?

'I don't wear any,' said Teppic.

'You've got all those daggers and things.'

'Well, I need them to do my job.'

'Well then.'

'Look, you don't have to leave them here, you can put them in my pouch,' he said. 'But we must be going. Please!'

'*Goodbye*,' said the ghost sadly, watching them sneak out to the courtyard. He floated back to his corpse, who wasn't the best of company.

The breeze was stronger when they reached the roof. It was hotter, too, and dry.

Across the river one or two of the older pyramids were already sending up their flares, but they were weak and looked wrong.

'I feel itchy,' said Ptraci. 'What's wrong?'

'It feels like we're in for a thunderstorm,' said Teppic, staring across the river at the Great Pyramid. Its blackness had intensified, so that it was a triangle of deeper darkness in the night. Figures were running around its base like lunatics watching their asylum burn.

'What's a thunderstorm?'

'Very hard to describe,' he said, in a preoccupied voice. 'Can you see what they're doing over there?'

Ptraci squinted across the river.

'They're very busy,' she said.

'Looks more like panic to me.'

A few more pyramids flared, but instead of roaring straight up the flames flickered and lashed backwards and forwards, driven by intangible winds.

Teppic shook himself. 'Come on,' he said. 'Let's get you away from here.'

'I said we should have capped it this evening,' shouted Ptaclusp IIb above the screaming of the pyramid. 'I can't float it up now, the turbulence up there must be terrific!'

The ice of day was boiling off the black marble, which was already warm to the touch. He stared distractedly at the capstone on its cradle and then at his brother, who was still in his nightshirt.

'Where's father?' he said.

'I sent one of us to go and wake him up,' said IIa.

'Who?'

'One of you, actually.'

'Oh.' IIb stared again at the capstone. 'It's not that heavy,' he said. 'Two of us could manhandle it up there.' He gave his brother an enquiring look.

'You must be mad. Send some of the men to do it.'

'They've all run away –'

Down river another pyramid tried to flare, spluttered, and then ejected a screaming, ragged flame that arched across the sky and grounded near the top of the Great Pyramid itself.

'It's interfering with the others now!' shouted IIb. 'Come on. We've got to flare it off, it's the only way!'

About a third of the way up the pyramid's flanks a crackling blue zigzag arced out and struck itself on a stone sphinx. The air above it boiled.

The two brothers slung the stone between them and staggered to the scaffolding, while the dust around them whirled into strange shapes.

'Can you hear something?' said IIb, as they stumbled on to the first platform.

'What, you mean the fabric of time and space being put through the wringer?' said IIa.

The architect gave his brother a look of faint admiration. It was an unusual remark for an accountant. Then his face returned to its previous look of faint terror.

'No, not that,' he said.

'Well, the sound of the very air itself being subjected to horrible tortures?'

'Not that, either,' said IIb, vaguely annoyed. 'I mean the creaking noise.'

Three more pyramids struck their discharges, which fizzled through the roiling clouds overhead and poured into the black marble above them.

'Can't hear anything like that,' said IIa.

'I think it's coming from the pyramid.'

'Well, you can put your ear against it if you like, but *I'm* not going to.'

The scaffolding swayed in the storm as they eased their way up another ladder, the heavy capstone rocking between them.

'I said we shouldn't do it,' muttered the accountant, as the stone slid gently on to his toes. 'We shouldn't have built this.'

'Just shut up and lift your end, will you?'

And so, one rocking ladder after another, the brothers Ptaclusp eased their bickering way up the flanks of the Great Pyramid, while the lesser tombs along the Djel fired one after another, and the sky streamed with lines of sizzling time.

It was around about this point that the greatest mathematician in the world, lying in cosy flatulence in his stall below the palace, stopped chewing the cud and realised that something very wrong was happening to numbers. All the numbers.

The camel looked along its nose at Teppic. Its expression made it clear that of all the riders in all the world it would least like to ride it, he was right at the top of the list. However, camels look like that at everyone. Camels have a very democratic approach to the human race. They hate every member of it, without making any distinctions for rank or creed.

This one appeared to be chewing soap.

Teppic looked distractedly down the shadowy length of the royal stables, which had once contained a hundred camels. He'd have given the world for a horse, and a moderately-sized continent for a pony. But the stables now held only a handful of rotting war chariots, relics of past glories, an elderly elephant whose presence was a bit of a mystery, and this camel. It looked an extremely inefficient animal. It was going threadbare at the knees.

'Well, this is it,' he said to Ptraci. 'I don't dare try the river during the night. I could try and get you over the border.'

'Is that saddle on right?' said Ptraci. 'It looks awfully funny.'

'It's on an awfully odd creature,' said Teppic. 'How do we climb on to it?'

'I've seen the camel drivers at work,' she replied. 'I think they just hit them very hard with a big stick.'

The camel knelt down and gave her a smug look.

Teppic shrugged, pulled open the doors to the outside world, and stared into the faces of five guards.

He backed away. They advanced. Three of them were holding the heavy Djel bows, which could propel an arrow through a door or turn a charging hippo into three tons of mobile kebab. The guards had never had to fire them at a fellow human, but looked as though they were prepared to entertain the idea.

The guard captain tapped one of the men on the shoulder, and said, 'Go and inform the high priest.'

He glared at Teppic.

'Throw down all your weapons,' he said.

'What, *all* of them?'

'Yes. All of them.'

'It might take some time,' said Teppic cautiously.

'And keep your hands where I can see them,' the captain added.

'We could be up against a real impasse here,' Teppic ventured. He looked from one guard to another. He knew a variety of methods of unarmed combat, but they all rather relied on the opponent not being about to fire an arrow straight through you as soon as you moved. But he could probably dive sideways, and once he had the cover of the camel stalls he could bide his time . . .

And that would leave Ptraci exposed. Besides, he could hardly go around fighting his own guards. That wasn't acceptable behaviour, even for a king.

There was a movement behind the guards and Dios drifted into view, as silent and inevitable as an eclipse of the moon. He was holding a lighted torch, which reflected wild highlights on his bald head.

'Ah,' he said. 'The miscreants are captured. Well done.' He nodded to the captain. 'Throw them to the crocodiles.'

'Dios?' said Teppic, as two of the guards lowered their bows and bore down on him.

'Did you speak?'

'You know who I am, man. Don't be silly.'

The high priest raised the torch.

'You have the advantage of me, boy,' he said. 'Metaphorically speaking.'

'This is not funny,' said Teppic. 'I order you to tell them who I am.'

'As you wish. This *assassin*,' said Dios, and the voice had the cut and sear of a thermic lance, 'has killed the king.'

'I *am* the king, damn it,' said Teppic. 'How could I kill myself?'

'We are not stupid,' said Dios. 'These men know the king does not skulk the palace at night, or consort with condemned criminals. All that remains for us to find out is how you disposed of the body.'

His eyes fixed on Teppic's face, and Teppic realised that the high priest was indeed, truly mad. It was the rare kind of madness caused by being yourself for so long that habits of sanity have etched themselves into the brain. I wonder how old he *really* is? he thought.

'These assassins are cunning creatures,' said Dios. 'Have a care of him.'

There was a crash beside the priest. Ptraci had tried to throw a camel prod, and missed.

When everyone looked back Teppic had vanished. The guards beside him were busy collapsing slowly to the floor, groaning.

Dios smiled.

'Take the woman,' he snapped, and the captain darted forward and grabbed Ptraci, who hadn't made any attempt to run away. Dios bent down and picked up the prod.

'There are more guards outside,' he said. 'I'm sure you will realise that. It will be in your interests to step forward.'

'Why?' said Teppic, from the shadows. He fumbled in his boot for his blowpipe.

'You will then be thrown to the sacred crocodiles, by order of the king,' said Dios.

'Something to look forward to, eh?' said Teppic, feverishly screwing bits together.

'It would certainly be preferable to many alternatives,' said Dios.

In the darkness Teppic ran his fingers over the little coded knobs on the darts. Most of the really spectacular poisons would have evaporated or dissolved into harmlessness by now, but there were a number of lesser potions designed to give their clients nothing more than a good night's sleep. An assassin might have to work his way to an inhumee past a number of alert bodyguards. It was considered impolite to inhume them as well.

'You could let us go,' said Teppic. 'I suspect that's what you want, isn't it? For me to go away and never come back? That suits me fine.'

Dios hesitated.

'You're supposed to say "And let the girl go",' he said.

'Oh, yes. And that, too,' said Teppic.

'No. I would be failing in my duty to the king,' said Dios.

'For goodness sake, Dios, you *know* I am the king!'

'No. I have a very clear picture of the king. You are not the king,' said the priest.

Teppic peered over the edge of the camel stall. The camel peered over his shoulder.

And then the *world* went mad.

All right, madder.

All the pyramids were blazing now, filling the sky with their sooty light as the brothers Ptaclusp struggled to the main working platform.

IIa collapsed on the planking, wheezing like an elderly bellows. A few feet away the sloping side was hot to the touch, and there was no doubt in his mind now that the pyramid *was* creaking, like a sailing ship in a gale. He had never paid much attention to the actual mechanics as opposed to the cost of pyramid construction, but he was pretty certain that the noise was as wrong as II and II making V.

His brother reached out to touch the stone, but drew his hand back as small sparks flashed around his fingers.

'You can feel the warmth,' he said. 'It's astonishing!'

'Why?'

'Heating up a mass like this. I mean, the sheer tonnage . . .'

'I don't like it, Two-bee,' IIa quavered. 'Let's just leave the stone here, shall we? I'm sure it'll be all right, and in the morning we can send a gang up here, they'll know exactly what –'

His words were drowned out as another flare crackled across the sky and hit the column of dancing air fifty feet above them. He grabbed part of the scaffolding.

'Sod take this,' he said. 'I'm off.'

'Hang on a minute,' said IIb. 'I mean, what *is* creaking? Stone can't creak.'

'The whole bloody scaffolding is moving, don't be daft!' He stared goggle-eyed at his brother. 'Tell me it's the scaffolding,' he pleaded.

'No, I'm certain this time. It's coming from inside.'

They stared at one another, and then at the rickety ladder leading up to the tip, or to where the tip should be.

'Come on!' said IIb. 'It can't flare off, it's trying to find ways of discharging –'

There was a sound as loud as the groaning of continents.

Teppic felt it. He felt that his skin was several sizes too small. He felt that someone was holding his ears and trying to twist his head off.

He saw the guard captain sag to his knees, fighting to get his helmet off, and he leapt the stall.

Tried to leap the stall. Everything was wrong, and he landed heavily on a floor that seemed undecided about becoming a wall. He managed to get to his feet and was pulled sideways, dancing awkwardly across the stable to keep his balance.

The stables stretched and shrank like a picture in a distorting mirror. He'd gone to see some once in Ankh, the three of them hazarding a half-coin each to visit the transient marvels of Dr Mooner's Travelling Take Your Breath Away Emporium. But you knew then that it was only twisted glass that was giving you a head like a sausage and legs like footballs. Teppic wished he could be so certain that what was happening around him would allow of such a harmless explanation. You'd probably *need* a wobbly glass mirror to make it look normal.

He ran on taffy legs towards Ptraci and the high priest as the world was expanded and squeezed around him, and was momentarily gratified to see the girl squirm in Dios's grip and fetch him a tidy thump on the ear.

He moved as though in a dream, with the distances changing as though reality was an elastic thing. Another step sent him cannoning into the pair of them. He grabbed Ptraci's arm and staggered back to the camel stall, where the creature was still cudding and watching the scene with the nearest thing a camel will ever get to mild interest, and snatched its halter.

No-one seemed to be interested in stopping them as they helped each other through the doorway and out into the mad night.

'It helps if you shut your eyes,' said Ptraci.

Teppic tried it. It worked. A stretch of courtyard that his eyes told him was a quivering rectangle whose sides twanged like bowstrings became, well, just a courtyard under his feet.

'Gosh, that was clever,' he said. 'How did you think of that?'

'I always shut my eyes when I'm frightened,' said Ptraci.

'Good plan.'

'What's *happening*?'

'I don't know. I don't want to find out. I think going away from here could be an amazingly sensible idea. How do you make a camel kneel, did you say? I've got any amount of sharp things.'

The camel, who had a very adequate grasp of human language as it applied to threats, knelt down graciously. They scrambled aboard and the landscape lurched again as the beast jacked itself back on to its feet.

The camel knew perfectly well what was happening. Three stomachs and a digestive system like an industrial distillation plant give you a lot of time for sitting and thinking.

It's not for nothing that advanced mathematics tends to be invented in hot countries. It's because of the morphic resonance of all the camels, who have that disdainful expression and famous curled lip as a natural result of an ability to do quadratic equations.

It's not generally realised that camels have a natural aptitude for advanced mathematics, particularly where they involve ballistics. This evolved as a survival trait, in the same way as a human's hand and eye co-ordination, a chameleon's camouflage, and a dolphin's renowned ability to save drowning swimmers if there's any chance that biting them in half might be observed and commented upon adversely by other humans.

The fact is that camels are far more intelligent than dolphins*. They are so much brighter that they soon realised that the most prudent thing any intelligent animal can do, if it would prefer its descendants not to spend a lot of time on a slab with electrodes clamped to their brains or sticking mines on the bottom of ships or being patronised rigid by zoologists, is to make bloody certain humans don't find out about it. So they long ago plumped for a lifestyle that, in return for a certain amount of porterage and being prodded with sticks, allowed them adequate food and grooming and the chance to spit in a human's eye and get away with it.

And this particular camel, the result of millions of years of selective evolution to produce a creature that could count the grains of sand it was walking over, and close its nostrils at will, and survive under the broiling sun for many days without water, was called You Bastard.

And he was, in fact, the greatest mathematician in the world.

You Bastard was thinking: There seems to be some growing dimensional instability here, swinging from zero to nearly forty-five degrees by the look of it. How interesting. I wonder what's causing it? Let V equal 3. Let Tau equal Chi/4. *cudcudcud* Let Kappa/y be an Evil-Smelling-Bugger† differential tensor domain with four imaginary spin co-efficients . . .

Ptraci hit him across the head with her sandal. 'Come on, get a move on!' she yelled. You Bastard thought: Therefore H to the enabling power equals V/s. *cudcudcud* Thus in hypersyllogic notation . . .

Teppic looked behind them. The strange distortions in the landscape seemed to be settling down, and Dios was . . .

Dios was striding out of the palace, and had actually managed to find several guards whose fear of disobedience overcame the terror of the mysteriously distorted world.

You Bastard stood stoically chewing . . . *cudcudcud* which gives us an interesting shortening oscillation. What would be the period of this? Let period = x. *cudcudcud* Let t = time. Let initial period . . .

Ptraci bounced up and down on his neck and kicked hard with her heels, an action which would have caused any anthropoid male to howl and bang his head against the wall.

---

* Never trust a species that grins all the time. It's up to something.

† Renowned as the greatest camel mathematician of all time, who invented a math of eight-dimensional space while lying down with his nostrils closed in a violent sandstorm.

'It won't move! Can't you hit it?'

Teppic brought his hand down as hard as he could on You Bastard's hide, raising a cloud of dust and deadening every nerve in his fingers. It was like hitting a large sack full of coathangers.

'Come *on*,' he muttered.

Dios raised a hand.

'Halt, in the name of the king!' he shouted.

An arrow thudded into You Bastard's hump.

. . . equals 6.3 recurring. Reduce. That gives us . . . *ouch* . . . 314 seconds . . .

You Bastard turned his long neck around. His great hairy eyebrows made accusing curves as his yellow eyes narrowed and took a fix on the high priest, and he put aside the interesting problem for a moment and dredged up the familiar ancient maths that his race had perfected long ago:

Let range equal forty-one feet. Let windspeed equal 2. Vector one-eight. *cud* Let glutinosity equal 7 . . .

Teppic drew a throwing knife.

Dios took a deep breath. He's going to order them to fire on us, Teppic thought. In my own name, in my own kingdom, I'm going to be shot.

. . . Angle two-five. *cud Fire.*

It was a magnificent volley. The gob of cud had commendable lift and spin and hit with a sound like, a sound like half a pound of semi-digested grass hitting someone in the face. There was nothing else it could sound like.

The silence that followed was by way of being a standing ovation.

The landscape began to distort again. This was clearly not a place to linger. You Bastard looked down at his front legs.

Let legs equal four . . .

He lumbered into a run. Camels apparently have more knees than any other creature and You Bastard ran like a steam engine, with lots of extraneous movement at right angles to the direction of motion accompanied by a thunderous barrage of digestive noises.

'Bloody stupid animal,' muttered Ptraci, as they jolted away from the palace, 'but it looks like it finally got the idea.'

. . . gauge-invariant repetition rate of 3.5/z. What's she talking about, Bloody Stupid lives over in Tsort . . .

Though they swung through the air as though jointed with bad elastic You Bastard's legs covered a lot of ground, and already they were bouncing through the sleeping packed-earth streets of the city.

'It's starting again, isn't it?' said Ptraci. 'I'm going to shut my eyes.'

Teppic nodded. The firebrick-hot houses around them were doing their slow motion mirror dance again, and the road was rising and falling in a way that solid land had no right to adopt.

'It's like the sea,' he said.

'I can't see anything,' said Ptraci firmly.

'I mean the sea. The ocean. You know. Waves.'

'I've heard about it. Is anyone chasing us?'

Teppic turned in the saddle. 'Not that I can make out,' he said. 'It looks as —'

From here he could see past the long, low bulk of the palace and across the river to the Great Pyramid itself. It was almost hidden in dark clouds, but what he could see of it was definitely wrong. He knew it had four sides, and he could see all eight of them.

It seemed to be moving in and out of focus, which he felt instinctively was a dangerous thing for several million tons of rock to do. He felt a pressing urge to be a long way away from it. Even a dumb creature like the camel seemed to have the same idea.

You Bastard was thinking: ... Delta squared. Thus, dimensional pressure k will result in a ninety-degree transformation in $Chi(16/x/pu)t$ for a K-bundle of any three invariables. Or four minutes, plus or minus ten seconds ...

The camel looked down at the great pads of his feet.

Let speed equal *gallop*.

'How did you make it do that?' said Teppic.

'I didn't! It's doing it by itself! Hang on!'

This wasn't easy. Teppic had saddled the camel but neglected the harness. Ptraci had handfuls of camel hair to hang on to. All he had was handfuls of Ptraci. No matter where he tried to put his hands, they encountered warm, yielding flesh. Nothing in his long education had prepared him for this, whereas everything in Ptraci's obviously had. Her long hair whipped his face and smelled beguilingly of rare perfume.[*]

'Are you all right?' he shouted above the wind.

'I'm hanging on with my knees!'

'That must be very hard!'

'You get special training!'

---

[*] An effect achieved by distilling the testicles of a small tree-dwelling species of bear with the vomit of a whale, and adding a handful of rose petals. Teppic probably would have felt no better for knowing this.

Camels gallop by throwing their feet as far away from them as possible and then running to keep up. Knee joints clicking like chilly castanets, You Bastard thrashed up the sloping road out of the valley and windmilled along the narrow gorge that led, under towering limestone cliffs, to the high desert beyond.

And behind them, tormented beyond measure by the inexorable tide of geometry, unable to discharge its burden of Time, the Great Pyramid screamed, lifted itself off its base and, its bulk swishing through the air as unstoppably as something completely unstoppable, ground around precisely ninety degrees and did something perverted to the fabric of time and space.

You Bastard sped along the gorge, his neck stretched out to its full extent, his mighty nostrils flaring like jet intakes.

'It's terrified!' Ptraci yelled. 'Animals always know about this sort of thing!'

'What sort of thing!'

'Forest fires and things!'

'We haven't got any trees!'

'Well, floods and – and things! They've got some strange natural instinct!'

... *Phi** 1700[u/v]. Lateral e/v. Equals a tranche of seven to twelve ...

The sound hit them. It was as silent as a dandelion clock striking midnight, but it had *pressure*. It rolled over them, suffocating as velvet, nauseating as a battered saveloy.

And was gone.

You Bastard slowed to a walk, a complicated procedure that involved precise instructions to each leg in turn.

There was a feeling of release, a sense of stress withdrawn.

You Bastard stopped. In the pre-dawn glow he'd spotted a clump of thorned syphacia bushes growing in the rocks by the track.

... angle left. x equals 37. y equals 19. z equals 43. *Bite* ...

Peace descended. There was no sound except for the eructations of the camel's digestive tract and the distant warbling of a desert owl.

Ptraci slid off her perch and landed awkwardly.

'My bottom,' she announced, to the desert in general, 'is one huge blister.'

Teppic jumped down and half-ran, half-staggered up the scree by the roadside, then jogged across the cracked limestone plateau until he could get a good look at the valley.

It wasn't there any more.

It was still dark when Dil the master embalmer woke up, his body twanging with the sensation that something was wrong. He slipped out of bed, dressed hurriedly, and pulled aside the curtain that did duty as a door.

The night was soft and velvety. Behind the chirrup of the insects there was another sound, a frying noise, a faint sizzling on the edge of hearing.

Perhaps that was what had woken him up.

The air was warm and damp. Curls of mist rose from the river, and –

The pyramids weren't flaring.

He'd grown up in this house: it had been in the family of the master embalmers for thousands of years, and he'd seen the pyramids flare so often that he didn't notice them, any more than he noticed his own breathing. But now they were dark and silent, and the silence cried out and the darkness glared.

But that wasn't the worst part. As his horrified eyes stared up at the empty sky over the necropolis they saw the stars, and what the stars were stuck to.

Dil was terrified. And then, when he had time to think about it, he was ashamed of himself. After all, he thought, it's what I've always been told is there. It stands to reason. I'm just seeing it properly for the first time.

There. Does that make me feel any better?

No.

He turned and ran down the street, sandals flapping, until he reached the house that held Gern and his numerous family. He dragged the protesting apprentice from the communal sleeping mat and pulled him into the street, turned his face to the sky and hissed. 'Tell me what you can see!'

Gern squinted.

'I can see the stars, master,' he said.

'What are they on, boy?'

Gern relaxed slightly. 'That's easy, master. Everyone knows the stars are on the body of the goddess Nept who arches herself from . . . oh, bloody hell.'

'You can see her, too?'

'Oh, mummy,' whispered Gern, and slid to his knees.

Dil nodded. He was a religious man. It was a great comfort knowing that the gods were there. It was knowing they were *here* that was the terrible part.

Because the body of a woman arched over the heavens, faintly blue, faintly shadowy in the light of the watery stars.

She was enormous, her statistics interstellar. The shadow between her galactic breasts was a dark nebula, the curve of her stomach a vast wash of glowing gas, her navel the seething, dark incandescence in which new stars were being born. She wasn't supporting the sky. She *was* the sky.

Her huge sad face, upside down on the turnwise horizon, stared directly at Dil. And Dil was realising that there are few things that so shake belief as seeing, clearly and precisely, the object of that belief. Seeing, contrary to popular wisdom, isn't believing. It's where belief stops, because it isn't needed any more.

'Oh, Sod,' moaned Gern.

Dil struck him across the arm.

'Stop that,' he said. 'And come with me.'

'Oh, master, whatever shall we do?'

Dil looked around at the sleeping city. He hadn't the faintest idea.

'We'll go to the palace,' he said firmly. 'It's probably a trick of the, of the, of the dark. Anyway, the sun will be up presently.'

He strode off, wishing he could change places with Gern and show just a hint of gibbering terror. The apprentice followed him at a sort of galloping creep.

'I can see shadows against the stars, master! Can you see them, master? Around the edge of the world, master!'

'Just mists, boy,' said Dil, resolutely keeping his eyes fixed in front of him and maintaining a dignified posture as appropriate to the Keeper of the Left Hand Door of the Natron Lodge and holder of several medals for needlework.

'There,' he said. 'See, Gern, the sun is coming up!'

They stood and watched it.

Then Gern whimpered, very quietly.

Rising up the sky, very slowly, was a great flaming ball. And it was being pushed by a dung beetle bigger than worlds.

BOOK III

The Book of the New Son

The sun rose and, because this wasn't the Old Kingdom out here, it was a mere ball of flaming gas. The purple night of the high desert evaporated under its blowlamp glare. Lizards scuttled into cracks in the rocks. You Bastard settled himself down in the sparse shadow of what was left of the syphacia bushes, peered haughtily at the landscape, and began to chew cud and calculate square roots in base seven.

Teppic and Ptraci eventually found the shade of a limestone overhang, and sat glumly staring out at the waves of heat wobbling off the rocks.

'I don't understand,' said Ptraci. 'Have you looked everywhere?'

'It's a country! It can't just bloody well fall through a hole in the ground!'

'Where is it, then?' said Ptraci evenly.

Teppic growled. The heat struck like a hammer, but he strode out over the rocks as though three hundred square miles could perhaps have been hiding under a pebble or behind a bush.

The fact was that the track dipped between the cliffs, but almost immediately rose again and continued across the dunes into what was quite clearly Tsort. He'd recognised a wind-eroded sphinx that had been set up as a boundary marker; legend said it prowled the borders in times of dire national need, although legend wasn't sure why.

He knew they had galloped into Ephebe. He should be looking across the fertile, pyramid-speckled valley of the Djel that lay between the two countries.

He'd spent an hour looking for it.

It was inexplicable. It was uncanny. It was also extremely embarrassing.

He shaded his eyes and stared around for the thousandth time at the silent, baking landscape. And moved his head. And saw Djelibeybi.

It flashed across his vision in an instant. He jerked his eyes back and saw it again, a brief flash of misty colour that vanished as soon as he concentrated on it.

Some minutes later Ptraci peered out of the shade and saw him get down on his hands and knees. When he started turning over rocks she decided it was time he should come back in out of the sun.

He shook her hand off his shoulder, and gestured impatiently.

'I've found it!' He pulled a knife from his boot and started poking at the stones.

'Where?'

'Here!'

She laid a ringed hand on his forehead.

'Oh yes,' she said. 'I see. Yes. Good. Now I think you'd better come into the shade.'

'No, I mean it! Here! Look!'

She hunkered down and stared at the rock, to humour him.

'There's a crack,' she said, doubtfully.

'Look at it, will you? You have to turn your head and sort of look out of the corner of your eye.' Teppic's dagger smacked into the crack, which was no more than a faint line on the rock.

'Well, it goes on a long way,' said Ptraci, staring along the burning pavement.

'All the way from the Second Cataract to the Delta,' said Teppic. 'Covering your eye with one hand helps. Please give it a try. Please!'

She put one hesitant hand over her eye and squinted obediently at the rock.

Eventually she said. 'It's no good, I can't – *seeee* –'

She stayed motionless for a moment and then flung herself sideways on to the rocks. Teppic stopped trying to hammer the knife into the crack and crawled over to her.

'I was right on the edge!' she wailed.

'You saw it?' he said hopefully.

She nodded and, with great care, got to her feet and backed away.

'Did your eyes feel as though they were being turned inside out?' said Teppic.

'Yes,' said Ptraci coldly. 'Can I have my bangles, please?'

'What?'

'My bangles. You put them in your pocket. I want them, please.'

Teppic shrugged, and fished in his pouch. The bangles were mostly copper, with a few bits of chipped enamel. Here and there the craftsman had tried, without much success, to do something interesting with twisted bits of wire and lumps of coloured glass. She took them and slipped them on.

'Do they have some occult significance?' he said.

'What's occult mean?' she said vaguely.

'Oh. What do you need them for, then?'

'I told you. I don't feel properly dressed without them on.'

Teppic shrugged, and went back to rocking his knife in the crack.

'Why are you doing that?' she said. He stopped and thought about it.

'I don't know,' he said. 'But you did see the valley, didn't you?'

'Yes.'

'Well, then?'

'Well what?'

Teppic rolled his eyes. 'Didn't you think it was a bit, well, odd? A whole country just more or less vanishing? It's something you don't bloody well see every day, for gods' sake!'

'How should I know? I've never been out of the valley before. I don't know what it's supposed to look like from outside. And don't swear.'

Teppic shook his head. 'I think I *will* go and lie down in the shade,' he said. 'What's left of it,' he added, for the brass light of the sun was burning away the shadows. He staggered over to the rocks and stared at her.

'The whole valley has just closed up,' he managed at last. 'All those people . . .'

'I saw cooking fires,' said Ptraci, slumping down beside him.

'It's something to do with the pyramid,' he said. 'It looked very strange just before we left. It's magic, or geometry, or one of those things. How do you think we can get back?'

'I don't want to go back. Why should I want to go back? It's the crocodiles for me. I'm not going back, not just for crocodiles.'

'Um. Perhaps I could pardon you, or something,' said Teppic.

'Oh yes,' said Ptraci, looking at her nails. 'You said you were the king, didn't you.'

'I *am* the king! That's my kingdom over –' Teppic hesitated, not knowing in which direction to point his finger – 'somewhere. I'm king of it.'

'You don't look like the king,' said Ptraci.

'Why not?'

'He had a golden mask on.'

'That was me!'

'So you ordered me thrown to the crocodiles?'

'Yes! I mean, no.' Teppic hesitated. 'I mean, the king did. I didn't. In a way. Anyway, I was the one who rescued you,' he added gallantly.

'There you are, then. Anyway, if you were the king, you'd be a god, too. You aren't acting very god-like at the moment.'

'Yes? Well. Er.' Teppic hesitated again. Ptraci's literal-mindedness meant that innocent sentences had to be carefully examined before being sent out into the world.

'I'm basically good at making the sun rise,' he said. 'I don't know how, though. And rivers. You want any rivers flooding, I'm your man. God, I mean.'

He lapsed into silence as a thought struck him.

'I wonder what's happening in there without me?' he said.

Ptraci stood up and set off down to the gorge.

'Where are you going?'

She turned. 'Well, Mr King or God or assassin, or whatever, can you make water?'

'What, here?'

'I mean to drink. There may be a river hidden in that crack or there may not, but we can't get at it, can we? So we have to go somewhere where we can. It's so simple I should think even kings could understand it.'

He hurried after her, down the scree to where You Bastard was lying with his head and neck flat on the ground, flicking his ears in the heat and idly applying You Vicious Brute's Theory of Transient Integrals to a succession of promising cissoid numbers. Ptraci kicked him irritably.

'Do you know where there is water, then?' said Teppic.

. . . e/27. Eleven miles . . .

Ptraci glared at him from kohl-ringed eyes. 'You mean *you* don't know? You were going to take me into the desert and you don't know where the water is?'

'Well, I rather expected I was going to be able to take some with me!'

'You didn't even think about it!'

'Listen, you can't talk to me like that! I'm a king!' Teppic stopped. 'You're absolutely right,' he said. 'I never thought about it. Where I come from it rains nearly every day. I'm sorry.'

Ptraci's brows furrowed. 'Who reigns nearly every day?' she said.

'No, I mean rain. You know. Very thin water coming out of the sky?'

'What a silly idea. Where *do* you come from?'

Teppic looked miserable. 'Where I come from is Ankh-Morpork. Where I started from is here.' He stared down the track. From here, if you knew what you were looking for, you could just see a faint crack running across the rocks. It climbed the cliffs on either side, a new vertical fault the thickness of a line that just happened to contain a complete river kingdom and 7,000 years of history.

He'd hated every minute of his time there. And now it had shut him out. And now, because he couldn't, he wanted to go back.

He wandered down to it and put his hand over one eye. If you jerked your head just right . . .

It flashed past his vision briefly, and was gone. He tried a few times more, and couldn't see it again.

If I hacked the rocks away? No, he thought, that's silly. It's a line. You can't get into a line. A line has no thickness. Well known fact of geometry.

He heard Ptraci come up behind him, and the next moment her hands were on his neck. For a second he wondered how she knew the Catharti Death Grip, and then her fingers were gently massaging his muscles, stresses melting under their expert caress like fat under a hot knife. He shivered as the tension relaxed.

'That's nice,' he said.

'We're trained for it. Your tendons are knotted up like ping-pong balls on a string,' said Ptraci.

Teppic gratefully subsided on to one of the boulders that littered the base of the cliff and let the rhythm of her fingers unwind the problems of the night.

'I don't know what to do,' he murmured. 'That feels *good*.'

'It's not all peeling grapes, being a handmaiden,' said Ptraci. 'The first lesson we learn is, when the master has had a long hard day it is not the best time to suggest the Congress of the Fox and the Persimmon. Who says you have to do anything?'

'I feel responsible.' Teppic shifted position like a cat.

'If you know where there is a dulcimer I could play you something soothing,' said Ptraci. 'I've got as far as "Goblins Picnic" in Book I.'

'I mean, a king shouldn't let his kingdom just vanish like that.'

'All the other girls can do chords and everything,' said Ptraci wistfully, massaging his shoulders. 'But the old king always said he'd rather hear me. He said it used to cheer him up.'

'I mean, it'll be called the Lost Kingdom,' said Teppic drowsily. 'How will I feel then, I ask you?'

'He said he liked my singing, too. Everyone else said it sounded like a flock of vultures who've just found a dead donkey.'

'I mean, king of a Lost Kingdom. It'd be dreadful. I've got to get it back.'

You Bastard slowly turned his massive head to follow the flight of an errant blowfly; deep in his brain little columns of red numbers flickered, detailing vectors and speed and elevation. The conversation of human beings seldom interested him, but it crossed his mind that the males and females always got along best when neither actually listened fully to what the other one was saying. It was much simpler with camels.

Teppic stared at the line in the rock. Geometry. That was it.

'We'll go to Ephebe,' he said. 'They know all about geometry and they have some very unsound ideas. Unsound ideas are what I could do with right now.'

'Why do you carry all these knives and things? I mean, *really*?'

'Hmm? Sorry?'

'All these knives. Why?'

Teppic thought about it. 'I suppose I don't feel properly dressed without them,' he said.

'Oh.'

Ptraci dutifully cast around for a new topic of conversation. Introducing Topics of Amusing Discourse was also part of a handmaiden's duties. She'd never been particularly good at it. The other girls had come up with an astonishing assortment: everything from the mating habits of crocodiles to speculation about life in the netherworld. She'd found it heavy going after talking about the weather.

'So,' she said. 'You've killed a lot of people, I expect?'

'Mm?'

'As an assassin, I mean. You get paid to kill people. Have you killed lots? Do you know you tense your back muscles a lot?'

'I don't think I ought to talk about it,' he said.

'I ought to know. If we've got to cross the desert together and everything. More than a hundred?'

'Good heavens, no.'

'Well, less than fifty?'

Teppic rolled over.

'Look, even the most famous assassins never killed more than thirty people in all their lives,' he said.

'Less than twenty, then?'

'Yes.'

'Less than ten?'

'I think,' said Teppic, 'it would be best to say a number between zero and ten.'

'Just so long as I know. These things are important.'

They strolled back to You Bastard. But now it was Teppic who seemed to have something on his mind.

'All this senate . . .' he said.

'Congress,' corrected Ptraci.

'You . . . er . . . more than fifty people?'

'There's a *different* name for that sort of woman,' said Ptraci, but without much rancour.

'Sorry. Less than ten?'

'Let's say,' said Ptraci, 'a number between zero and ten.'

You Bastard spat. Twenty feet away the blowfly was picked cleanly out of the air and glued to the rock behind it.

'Amazing how they do it, isn't it,' said Teppic. 'Animal instinct, I suppose.'

You Bastard gave him a haughty glare from under his sweep-the-desert eyelashes and thought:

. . . Let z=eiO. *cudcudcud* Then dz=ie[iO]dO=izdO or dO=dz/iz . . .

Ptaclusp, still in his nightshirt, wandered aimlessly among the wreckage at the foot of the pyramid.

It was humming like a turbine. Ptaclusp didn't know why, knew nothing about the vast expenditure of power that had twisted the dimensions by ninety degrees and was holding them there against terrible pressures, but at least the disturbing temporal changes seemed to have stopped. There were fewer sons around than there used to be; in truth, he could have done with finding one or two.

First he found the capstone, which had shattered, its electrum sheathing peeling away. In its descent from the pyramid it had hit the statue of Hat the Vulture-Headed God, bending it double and giving it an expression of mild surprise.

A faint groan sent him tugging at the wreckage of a tent. He tore at the heavy canvas and unearthed IIb, who blinked at him in the grey light.

'It didn't work, dad!' he moaned. 'We'd almost got it up there, and then the whole thing just sort of *twisted*!'

The builder lifted a spar off his son's legs.

'Anything broken?' he said quietly.

'Just bruised, I think.' The young architect sat up, wincing, and craned to see around.

'Where's Two-ay?' he said. 'He was higher up than me, nearly on the top –'

'I've found him,' said Ptaclusp.

Architects are not known for their attention to subtle shades of meaning, but IIb heard the lead in his father's voice.

'He's not dead, is he?' he whispered.

'I don't think so. I'm not sure. He's alive. But. He's moving – he's moving ... well, you better come and see. I think something quantum has happened to him.'

You Bastard plodded onwards at about 1.247 metres per second, working out complex conjugate co-ordinates to stave off boredom while his huge, plate-like feet crunched on the sand.

Lack of fingers was another big spur to the development of camel intellect. Human mathematical development had always been held back by everyone's instinctive tendency, when faced with something really complex in the way of triform polynomials or parametric differentials, to count fingers. Camels started from the word go by counting *numbers*.

Deserts were a great help, too. There aren't many distractions. As far as camels were concerned, the way to mighty intellectual development was to have nothing much to do and nothing to do it with.

He reached the crest of the dune, gazed with approval over the rolling sands ahead of him, and began to think in logarithms.

'What's Ephebe like?' said Ptraci.

'I've never been there. Apparently it's ruled by a Tyrant.'

'I hope we don't meet him, then.'

Teppic shook his head. 'It's not like that,' he said. 'They have a new Tyrant every five years and they do something to him first.' He hesitated. 'I think they *ee-lect* him.'

'Is that something like they do to tomcats and bulls and things?'

'Er.'

'You know. To make them stop fighting and be more peaceful.'

Teppic winced. 'To be honest, I'm not sure,' he said. 'But I don't think so. They've got something they do it with, I think it's called a mocracy, and it means everyone in the whole country can say who the new Tyrant is. One man, one –' He paused. The political history lesson seemed a very long while ago, and had introduced concepts never heard of in Djelibeybi or in Ankh-Morpork, for that matter. He had a stab at it, anyway. 'One man, one vet.'

'That's for the eelecting, then?'

He shrugged. It might be, for all he knew. 'The point is, though, that everyone can do it. They're very proud of it. Everyone has –' he hesitated again, certain now that things were amiss – 'the vet. Except for women, of course. And children. And criminals. And slaves. And stupid people. And people of foreign extraction. And people disapproved of for, er, various reasons. And lots of other people. But everyone apart from them. It's a very enlightened civilisation.'

Ptraci gave this some consideration.

'And that's a mocracy, is it?'

'They invented it in Ephebe, you know,' said Teppic, feeling obscurely that he ought to defend it.

'I bet they had trouble exporting it,' said Ptraci firmly.

The sun wasn't just a ball of flaming dung pushed across the sky by a giant beetle. It was also a boat. It depended on how you looked at it.

The light was wrong. It had a flat quality, like water left in a glass for weeks. There was no joy to it. It illuminated, but without life; like bright moonlight rather than the light of day.

But Ptaclusp was more worried about his son.

'Do you know what's wrong with him?' he said.

His other son bit his stylus miserably. His hand was hurting. He'd tried to touch his brother, and the crackling shock had taken the skin off his fingers.

'I might,' he ventured.

'Can you cure it?'

'I don't think so.'

'What *is* it, then?'

'Well, dad. When we were up on the pyramid ... well, when it couldn't flare ... you see, I'm sure it twisted around ... time, you see, is just another dimension ... um.'

Ptaclusp rolled his eyes. 'None of that architect's talk, boy,' he said. 'What's wrong with him?'

'I think he's dimensionally maladjusted, dad. Time and space has got a bit mixed up for him. That's why he's moving sideways all the time.'

Ptaclusp IIb gave his father a brave little smile.

'He *always* used to move sideways,' said Ptaclusp.

His son sighed. 'Yes, dad,' he said. 'But that was just normal. All accountants move like that. Now he's moving sideways because that's like, well, it's like Time to him.'

Ptaclusp frowned. Drifting gently sideways wasn't IIa's only problem. He was also flat. Not flat like a card, with a front, back and edge – but flat from any direction.

'Puts me exactly in mind of them people in the frescoes,' he said. 'Where's his depth, or whatever you call it?'

'I think that's in Time,' said IIb, helplessly. 'Ours, not his.'

Ptaclusp walked around his son, noting how the flatness followed him. He scratched his chin.

'So he can walk in Time, can he?' he said slowly.

'That may be possible, yes.'

'Do you think we could persuade him to stroll back a few months and tell us not to build that bloody pyramid?'

'He can't communicate, dad.'

'Not much change *there*, then.' Ptaclusp sat down on the rubble, his head in his hands. It had come to this. One son normal and stupid, one flat as a shadow. And what sort of life could the poor flat kid have? He'd go through life being used to open locks, clean the ice off windscreens, and sleeping cheaply in trouser-presses in hotel bedrooms[*]. Being able to get under doors and read books without opening them would not be much of a compensation.

IIa drifted sideways, a flat cut-out on the landscape.

'Can't we do *anything*?' he said. 'Roll him up neatly, or something?'

IIb shrugged. 'We could put something in the way. That might be a good idea. It would stop anything worse happening to him because it, er, wouldn't have time to happen in. I think.'

They pushed the bent statue of Hat the Vulture-Headed God into the flat one's path. After a minute or two his gentle sideways drift brought him up against it. There was a fat blue spark that melted part of the statue, but the movement stopped.

'Why the sparks?' said Ptaclusp.

'It's a bit like flarelight, I think.'

Ptaclusp hadn't got where he was today – no, he'd have to correct himself – hadn't got to where he had been last night without eventually seeing the advantages in the unlikeliest situations.

'He'll save on clothing,' he said slowly. 'I mean, he can just paint it on.'

'I don't think you've quite got the idea, dad,' said IIb wearily. He sat down beside his father and stared across the river to the palace.

'Something going on over there,' said Ptaclusp. 'Do you think they've noticed the pyramid?'

---

[*] This is of course a loose translation, since Ptaclusp did not know the words for 'ice', 'windscreens' or 'hotel bedrooms'; interestingly, however, *Squiggle Eagle Eagle Vase Wavyline Duck* translates directly as 'a press for barbarian leg coverings'.

'I shouldn't be surprised. It's moved around ninety degrees, after all.'

Ptaclusp looked over his shoulder, and nodded slowly.

'Funny, that,' he said. 'Bit of structural instability there.'

'Dad, it's a pyramid! We should have flared it! I *told* you! The forces involved, well, it's just too –'

A shadow fell across them. They looked around. They looked up. They looked up a bit more.

'Oh, my,' said Ptaclusp. 'It's Hat, the Vulture-Headed God . . .'

Ephebe lay beyond them, a classical poem of white marble lazing around its rock on a bay of brilliant blue –

'What's that?' said Ptraci, after studying it critically for some time.

'It's the sea,' said Teppic. 'I told you, remember. Waves and things.'

'You said it was all green and rough.'

'Sometimes it is.'

'Hmm.' The tone of voice suggested that she disapproved of the sea but, before she could explain why, they heard the sound of voices raised in anger. They were coming from behind a nearby sand dune.

There was a notice on the dune.

It said, in several languages: AXIOM TESTING STATION.

Below it, in slightly smaller writing, it added: CAUTION – UNRESOLVED POSTULATES.

As they read it, or at least as Teppic read it and Ptraci didn't, there was a twang from behind the dune, followed by a click, followed by an arrow zipping overhead. You Bastard glanced up at it briefly and then turned his head and stared fixedly at a very small area of sand.

A second later the arrow thudded into it.

Then he tested the weight on his feet and did a small calculation which revealed that two people had been subtracted from his back. Further summation indicated that they had been added to the dune.

'What did you do that for?' said Ptraci, spitting out sand.

'Someone fired at us!'

'I shouldn't think so. I mean, they didn't know we were here, did they? You needn't have pulled me off like that.'

Teppic conceded this, rather reluctantly, and eased himself

cautiously up the sliding surface of the dune. The voices were arguing again:

'Give in?'

'We simply haven't got all the parameters right.'

'I know what we haven't got all right.'

'What is that, pray?'

'We haven't got any more bloody tortoises. That's what we haven't got.'

Teppic carefully poked his head over the top of the dune.

He saw a large cleared area, surrounded by complicated ranks of markers and flags. There were one or two buildings in it, mostly consisting of cages, and several other intricate constructions he could not recognise. In the middle of it all were two men – one small, fat and florid, the other tall and willowy and with an indefinable air of authority. They were wearing sheets. Clustered around them, and not wearing very much at all, were a group of slaves. One of them was holding a bow.

Several of them were holding tortoises on sticks. They looked a bit pathetic, like tortoise lollies.

'Anyway, it's cruel,' said the tall man. 'Poor little things. They look so sad with their little legs waggling.'

'It's logically impossible for the arrow to hit them!' The fat man threw up his hands. 'It shouldn't do it! You must be giving me the wrong type of tortoise,' he added accusingly. 'We ought to try again with faster tortoises.'

'Or slower arrows?'

'Possibly, possibly.'

Teppic was aware of a faint scuffling by his chin. There was a small tortoise scurrying past him. It had several ricochet marks on its shell.

'We'll have one last try,' said the fat man. He turned to the slaves. 'You lot – go and find that tortoise.'

The little reptile gave Teppic a look of mingled pleading and hope. He stared at it, and then lifted it up carefully and tucked it behind a rock.

He slid back down the dune to Ptraci.

'There's something really weird going on over there,' he said. 'They're shooting tortoises.'

'Why?'

'Search me. They seem to think the tortoise ought to be able to run away.'

'What, from an arrow?'

'Like I said. Really weird. You stay here. I'll whistle if it's safe to follow me.'

'What will you do if it *isn't* safe?'

'Scream.'

He climbed the dune again and, after brushing as much sand as possible off his clothing, stood up and waved his cap at the little crowd. An arrow took it out of his hands.

'Oops!' said the fat man. 'Sorry!'

He scurried across the trampled sand to where Teppic was standing and staring at his stinging fingers.

'Just had it in my hand,' he panted. 'Many apologies, didn't realise it was loaded. Whatever will you think of me?'

Teppic took a deep breath.

'Xeno's the name,' gasped the fat man, before he could speak. 'Are you hurt? We did put up warning signs, I'm sure. Did you come in over the desert? You must be thirsty. Would you like a drink? Who are you? You haven't seen a tortoise up there, have you? Damned fast things, go like greased thunderbolts, there's no stopping the little buggers.'

Teppic deflated again.

'Tortoises?' he said. 'Are we talking about those, you know, stones on legs?'

'That's right, that's right,' said Xeno. 'Take your eyes off them for a second, and *vazoom!*'

'Vazoom?' said Teppic. He knew about tortoises. There were tortoises in the Old Kingdom. They could be called a lot of things – vegetarians, patient, thoughtful, even extremely diligent and persistent sex-maniacs – but never, up until now, fast. Fast was a word particularly associated with tortoises because they were not it.

'Are you sure?' he said.

'Fastest animal on the face of the disc, your common tortoise,' said Xeno, but he had the grace to look shifty. 'Logically, that is,' he added[*].

---

[*] To everyone without such a logical frame of reference the fastest animal[†] on the Disc is the extremely neurotic Ambiguous Puzuma, which moves so fast that it can actually achieve near-lightspeed in the Disc's magical field. This means that if you can see a puzuma, it isn't there. Most male puzumas die young of acute ankle failure caused by running very fast after females which aren't there and, of course, achieving suicidal mass in accordance with relativistic theory. The rest of them die of Heisenberg's Uncertainty Principle, since it is impossible for them to know who they are and where they are *at the same time*, and the see-sawing loss of concentration this engenders means that the puzuma only achieves a sense of identity when it is at rest – usually about fifty feet into the rubble of what remains of the mountain it just ran into at near light-speed. The puzuma is rumoured to be about the size of a leopard with a rather

The tall man gave Teppic a nod.

'Take no notice of him, boy,' he said. 'He's just covering himself because of the accident last week.'

'The tortoise *did* beat the hare,' said Xeno sulkily.

'The hare was *dead*, Xeno,' said the tall man patiently. 'Because you shot it.'

'I was aiming at the tortoise. You know, trying to combine two experiments, cut down on expensive research time, make full use of available –' Xeno gestured with the bow, which now had another arrow in it.

'Excuse me,' said Teppic. 'Could you put it down a minute? Me and my friend have come a long way and it would be nice not to be shot at again.'

These two seem harmless, he thought, and almost believed it.

He whistled. On cue, Ptraci came around the dune, leading You Bastard. Teppic doubted the capability of her costume to hold any pockets whatsoever, but she seemed to have been able to repair her makeup, re-kohl her eyes and put up her hair. She undulated towards the group like a snake in a skid, determined to hit the strangers with the full force of her personality. She was also holding something in her other hand.

'She's found the tortoise!' said Xeno. 'Well done!'

The reptile shot back into its shell. Ptraci glared. She didn't have much in the world except herself, and didn't like to be hailed as a mere holder of testudinoids.

The tall man sighed. 'You know, Xeno,' he said, 'I can't help thinking you've got the wrong end of the stick with this whole tortoise-and-arrow business.'

The little man glared at him.

'The trouble with you, Ibid,' he said, 'is that you think you're the biggest bloody authority on everything.'

The Gods of the Old Kingdom were awakening.

Belief is a force. It's a weak force, by comparison with gravity; when it comes to moving mountains, gravity wins every time. But it still exists, and now that the Old Kingdom was enclosed upon itself,

---

unique black and white check coat, although those specimens discovered by the Disc's sages and philosophers have inclined them to declare that in its natural state the puzuma is flat, very thin, and dead.

†The fastest *insect* is the .303 bookworm. It evolved in magical libraries, where it is necessary to eat extremely quickly to avoid being affected by the thaumic radiations. An adult .303 bookworm can eat through a shelf of books so fast that it ricochets off the wall.

floating free of the rest of the universe, drifting away from the general consensus that is dignified by the name of reality, the power of belief was making itself felt.

For seven thousand years the people of Djelibeybi had believed in their gods.

Now their gods existed. They had, as it were, the complete Set.

And the people of the Old Kingdom were learning that, for example, Vut the Dog-Headed God of the Evening looks a lot better painted on a pot than he does when all seventy feet of him, growling and stinking, is lurching down the street outside.

Dios sat in the throne room, the gold mask of the King on his knees, staring out across the sombre air. The cluster of lesser priests around the door finally plucked up the courage to approach him, in the same general frame of mind as you would approach a growling lion. No-one is more worried by the actual physical manifestation of a god than his priests; it's like having the auditors in unexpectedly.

Only Koomi stood a little aside from the others. He was thinking hard. Strange and original thoughts were crowding along rarely-trodden neural pathways, heading in unthinkable directions. He wanted to see where they led.

'O Dios,' murmured the high priest of Ket, the Ibis-Headed God of Justice. 'What is the king's command? The gods are striding the land, and they are fighting and breaking houses, O Dios. Where is the king? What would he have us do?'

'Yea,' said the high priest of Scrab, the Pusher of the Ball of the Sun. He felt something more was expected of him. 'And verily,' he added. 'Your lordship will have noticed that the sun is wobbling, because all the Gods of the Sun are fighting for it and –' he shuffled his feet – 'the blessed Scrab made a strategic withdrawal and has, er, made an unscheduled landing on the town of Hort. A number of buildings broke his fall.'

'And rightly so,' said the high priest of Thrrp, the Charioteer of the Sun. 'For, as all know, my master is the true god of the –'

His words tailed off.

Dios was trembling, his body rocking slowly back and forth. His eyes stared at nothing. His hands gripped the mask almost hard enough to leave fingerprints in the gold, and his lips soundlessly shaped the words of the Ritual of the Second Hour, which had been said at this time for thousands of years.

'I think it's the shock,' said one of the priests. 'You know, he's always been so set in his ways.'

The others hastened to show that there was at least *something* they could advise on.

'Fetch him a glass of water.'

'Put a paper bag over his head.'

'Sacrifice a chicken under his nose.'

There was a high-pitched whistling noise, the distant crump of an explosion, and a long hissing. A few tendrils of steam curled into the room.

The priests rushed to the balcony, leaving Dios in his unnerving pool of trauma, and found that the crowds around the palace were staring at the sky.

'It would appear,' said the high priest of Cephut, God of Cutlery, who felt that he could take a more relaxed view of the immediate situation, 'that Thrrp has fumbled it and has fallen to a surprise tackle from Jeht, Boatman of the Solar Orb.'

There was a distant buzzing, as of several billion bluebottles taking off in a panic, and a huge dark shape passed over the palace.

'But,' said the priest of Cephut, 'here comes Scrab again . . . yes, he's gaining height . . . Jeht hasn't seen him yet, he's progressing confidently towards the meridian . . . and here comes Sessifet, Goddess of the Afternoon! This is a surprise! What a surprise this is! A young goddess, yet to make her mark, but my word, what a lot of promise there, this is an astonishing bid, eunuchs and gentlemen, and . . . yes . . . Scrab has fumbled it! He's fumbled it! . . .'

The shadows danced and spun on the stones of the balcony.

'. . . and . . . what's this? The elder gods are, there's no other word for it, they're co-operating against these brash newcomers! But plucky young Sessifet is hanging in there, she's exploiting the weakness . . . she's in! . . . and pulling away now, pulling away, Gil and Scrab appear to be fighting, she's got a clear sky and, yes, yes . . . yes! . . . it's noon! It's noon! It's *noon!*'

Silence. The priest was aware that everyone was staring at him. Then someone said, 'Why are you shouting into that bulrush?'

'Sorry. Don't know what came over me there.'

The priestess of Sarduk, Goddess of Caves, snorted at him.

'Suppose one of them had dropped it?' she snapped.

'But . . . but . . .' He swallowed. 'It's not possible, is it? Not really? We all must have eaten something, or been out in the sun too long, or something. Because, I mean, everyone *knows* that the gods aren't . . . I mean, the sun is a big flaming ball of gas, isn't it, that goes around the whole world every day, and, and, and the gods . . . well, you know, there's a very real need in people to *believe*, don't get me wrong here –'

Koomi, even with his head buzzing with thoughts of perfidy, was quicker on the uptake than his colleagues.

'Get him, lads!' he shouted.

Four priests grabbed the luckless cutlery worshipper by his arms and legs and gave him a high-speed run across the stones to the edge of the balcony, over the parapet and into the mud-coloured waters of the Djel.

He surfaced, spluttering.

'What did you go and do that for?' he demanded. 'You all *know* I'm right. None of you really –'

The waters of the Djel opened a lazy jaw, and he vanished, just as the huge winged shape of Scrab buzzed threateningly over the palace and whirred off towards the mountains.

Koomi mopped his forehead.

'Bit of a close shave there,' he said. His colleagues nodded, staring at the fading ripples. Suddenly, Djelibeybi was no place for honest doubt. Honest doubt could get you seriously picked up and your arms and legs torn off.

'Er,' said one of them. 'Cephut's going to be a bit upset, though, isn't he?'

'All hail Cephut,' they chorused. Just in case.

'Don't see why,' grumbled an elderly priest at the back of the crowd. 'Bloody knife and fork artist.'

They grabbed him, still protesting, and hurled him into the river.

'All hail –' They paused. 'Who was he high priest of, anyway?'

'Bunu, the Goat-headed God of Goats? Wasn't he?'

'All hail Bunu, probably,' they chorused, as the sacred crocodiles homed in like submarines.

Koomi raised his hands, imploring. It is said that the hour brings forth the man. He was the kind of man that is brought forth by devious and unpleasant hours, and underneath his bald head certain conclusions were beginning to unfold, like things imprisoned for years inside stones. He wasn't yet sure what they were, but they were broadly on the subject of gods, the new age, the need for a firm hand on the helm, and possibly the inserting of Dios into the nearest crocodile. The mere thought filled him with forbidden delight.

'Brethren!' he cried.

'Excuse *me*,' said the priestess of Sarduk.

'And sistren –'

'Thank *you*.'

'– let us rejoice!' The assembled priests stood in total silence. This was a radical approach which had not hitherto occurred to them. And Koomi looked at their upturned faces and felt a thrill the like of which he had never experienced before. They were frightened out of their wits, and they were expecting him – *him* – to tell them what to do.

'Yea!' he said. 'And, indeed, verily, the hour of the gods –'

'– *and* goddesses –'

'– yes, and goddesses, is at hand. Er.'

What next? What, when you got right down to it, *was* he going to tell them to do? And then he thought: it doesn't matter. Provided I sound confident enough. Old Dios always drove them, he never tried to lead them. Without him they're wandering around like sheep.

'And, brethren – and sistren, of course – we must ask ourselves, we must ask ourselves, we, er, yes.' His voice waxed again with new confidence. 'Yes, we must ask ourselves *why* the gods are at hand. And without doubt it is because we have not been assiduous enough in our worship, we have, er, we have lusted after graven idols.'

The priests exchanged glances. Had they? How did you do it, actually?

'And, yes, and what about sacrifices? Time was when a sacrifice was a sacrifice, not some messing around with a chicken and flowers.'

This caused some coughing in the audience.

'Are we talking maidens here?' said one of the priests uncertainly.

'*Ahem*.'

'And inexperienced young men too, certainly,' he said quickly. Sarduk was one of the older goddesses, whose female worshippers got up to no good in sacred groves; the thought of her wandering around the landscape somewhere, bloody to the elbows, made the eyes water.

Koomi's heart thumped. 'Well, why not?' he said. 'Things were better then, weren't they?'

'But, er, I thought we stopped all that sort of thing. Population decline and so forth.'

There was a monstrous splash out in the river. Tzut, the Snake-Headed God of the Upper Djel, surfaced and regarded the assembled priesthood solemnly. Then Fhez, the Crocodile-Headed God of the Lower Djel, erupted beside him and made a spirited attempt at biting his head off. The two submerged in a column of spray and a minor tidal wave which slopped over the balcony.

'Ah, but maybe the population declined because we *stopped* sacrificing virgins – of both sexes, of course,' said Koomi, hurriedly. 'Have you ever thought of it like that?'

They thought of it. Then they thought of it again.

'I don't think the king would approve –' said one of the priests cautiously.

'The king?' shouted Koomi. 'Where is the king? Show me the king! Ask Dios where the king is!'

There was a thud by his feet. He looked down in horror as the gold mask bounced, and rolled towards the priests. They scattered hurriedly, like skittles.

Dios strode out into the light of the disputed sun, his face grey with fury.

'The king is dead,' he said.

Koomi swayed under the sheer pressure of anger, but rallied magnificently.

'Then his successor –' he began.

'There is *no* successor,' said Dios. He stared up at the sky. Few people can look directly at the sun, but under the venom of Dios's gaze the sun itself might have flinched and looked away. Dios's eyes sighted down that fearsome nose like twin range finders.

To the air in general he said: 'Coming here as if they own the place. *How dare they?*'

Koomi's mouth dropped open. He started to protest, and a kilowatt stare silenced him.

Koomi sought support from the crowd of priests, who were busily inspecting their nails or staring intently into the middle distance. The message was clear. He was on his own. Although, if by some chance he won the battle of wills, he'd be surrounded by people assuring him that they had been behind him all along.

'Anyway, they do own the place,' he mumbled.

'*What?*'

'They, er, they *do* own the place, Dios,' Koomi repeated. His temper gave out. 'They're the sodding *gods*, Dios!'

'They're *our* gods,' Dios hissed. 'We're not their people. They're *my* gods and they will learn to do as they are instructed!'

Koomi gave up the frontal assault. You couldn't outstare that sapphire stare, you couldn't stand the war-axe nose and, most of all, no man could be expected to dent the surface of Dios's terrifying righteousness.

'But –' he managed.

Dios waved him into silence with a trembling hand.

'They've no right!' he said. 'I did not give any orders! *They have no right!*'

'Then what are you going to *do*?' said Koomi.

Dios's hands opened and closed fitfully. He felt like a royalist might feel – a good royalist, a royalist who cut out pictures of all the Royals and stuck them in a scrapbook, a royalist who wouldn't hear a word said about them, they did such a good job and they can't answer back – if suddenly all the Royals turned up in his living room and started rearranging the furniture. He longed for the necropolis, and the cool silence among his old friends, and a quick sleep after which he'd be able to think so much more clearly . . .

Koomi's heart leapt. Dios's discomfort was a crack which, with due care and attention, could take a wedge. But you couldn't use a hammer. Head on, Dios could outfight the world.

The old man was shaking again. 'I do not presume to tell them how to run affairs in the Hereunder,' he said. 'They shall not presume to instruct me in how to run my kingdom.'

Koomi salted this treasonable statement away for further study and patted him gently on the back.

'You're right, of course,' he said. Dios's eyes swivelled.

'I am?' he said, suspiciously.

'I'm sure that, as the king's minister, you will find a way. You have our full support, O Dios.' Koomi waved an uplifted hand at the priests, who chorused wholehearted agreement. If you couldn't depend on kings and gods, you could always rely on old Dios. There wasn't one of them that wouldn't prefer the uncertain wrath of the gods to a rebuke from Dios. Dios terrified them in a very positive, human way that no supernatural entity ever could. Dios would sort it out.

'And we take no heed to these mad rumours about the king's disappearance. They are undoubtedly wild exaggerations, with no foundation,' said Koomi.

The priests nodded while, in each mind, a tiny rumour uncurled the length of its tail.

'What rumours?' said Dios out of the corner of his mouth.

'So enlighten us, master, as to the path we must now take,' said Koomi.

Dios wavered.

He did not know what to do. For him, this was a new experience. This was Change.

All he could think of, all that was pressing forward in his mind, were the words of the Ritual of the Third Hour, which he had said at this time for – how long? Too long, too long! – And he should have gone to his rest long before, but the time had never been right, there was never anyone capable, they would have been lost without him, the kingdom would founder, he would be *letting everyone down*, and so he'd crossed the river . . . he swore every time that it was the last, but it never was, not when the chill fetched his limbs, and the decades had become – longer. And now, when his kingdom needed him, the words of a Ritual had scored themselves into the pathways of his brain and bewildered all attempts at thought.

'Er,' he said.

You Bastard chewed happily. Teppic had tethered him too near a olive tree, which was getting a terminal pruning. Sometimes the camel would stop, gaze up briefly at the seagulls that circled everywhere above Ephebe city, and subject them to a short, deadly burst of olive stones.

He was turning over in his mind an interesting new concept in Thau-dimensional physics which unified time, space, magnetism, gravity and, for some reason, broccoli. Periodically he would make noises like distant quarry blasting, but which merely indicated that all stomachs were functioning perfectly.

Ptraci sat under the tree, feeding the tortoise on vine leaves.

Heat crackled off the white walls of the tavern but, Teppic thought, how different it was from the Old Kingdom. There even the heat was old; the air was musty and lifeless, it pressed like a vice, you felt it was made of boiled centuries. Here it was leavened by the breeze from the sea. It was edged with salt crystals. It carried exciting hints of wine; more than a hint in fact, because Xeno was already on his second amphora. This was the kind of place where things rolled up their sleeves and started.

'But I still don't understand about the tortoise,' he said, with some difficulty. He'd just taken his first mouthful of Ephebian wine, and it had apparently varnished the back of his throat.

''S quite simple,' said Xeno. 'Look, let's say this olive stone is the arrow and this, and this –' he cast around aimlessly – 'and this stunned seagull is the tortoise, right? Now, when you fire the arrow it goes from here to the seag – the tortoise, am I right?'

'I suppose so, but –'

'*But*, by this time, the seagu – the tortoise has moved on a bit, hasn't he? Am I right?'

'I suppose so,' said Teppic, helplessly. Xeno gave him a look of triumph.

'*So* the arrow has to go a bit further, doesn't it, to where the tortoise is now. Meanwhile the tortoise has flow – moved on, not much, I'll grant you, but it doesn't have to be much. Am I right? So the arrow has a bit further to go, but the point is that by the time it gets to where the tortoise is *now* the tortoise isn't there. So, if the tortoise keeps moving, the arrow will never hit it. It'll keep getting closer and closer but never hit it. QED.'

'Are you right?' said Teppic automatically.

'No.' said Ibid coldly. 'There's a dozen tortoise kebabs to prove him wrong. The trouble with my friend here is that he doesn't know the difference between a postulate and a metaphor of human existence. Or a hole in the ground.'

'It didn't hit it yesterday,' snapped Xeno.

'Yes, I was watching. You hardly pulled the string back. I saw you,' said Ibid.

They started to argue again.

Teppic stared into his wine mug. These men are philosophers, he thought. They had told him so. So their brains must be so big that they have room for ideas that no-one else would consider for five seconds. On the way to the tavern Xeno had explained to him, for example, why it was logically impossible to fall out of a tree.

Teppic had described the vanishing of the kingdom, but he hadn't revealed his position in it. He hadn't a lot of experience of these matters, but he had a very clear feeling that kings who hadn't got a kingdom any more were not likely to be very popular in neighbouring countries. There had been one or two like that in Ankh-Morpork – deposed royalty, who had fled their suddenly-dangerous kingdoms for Ankh's hospitable bosom carrying nothing but the clothes they stood up in and a few wagonloads of jewels. The city, of course, welcomed anyone – regardless of race, colour, class or creed – who had spending money in incredible amounts, but nevertheless the inhumation of surplus monarchs was a regular source of work for the Assassins' Guild. There was always someone back home who wanted to be certain that deposed monarchs stayed that way. It was usually a case of heir today, gone tomorrow.

'I think it got caught up in geometry,' he said, hopefully. 'I heard you were very good at geometry here,' he added, 'and perhaps you could tell me how to get back.'

'Geometry is not my forte,' said Ibid. 'As you probably know.'

'Sorry?'

'Haven't you read my *Principles of Ideal Government?*'

'I'm afraid not.'

'Or my *Discourse on Historical Inevitability?*'

'No.'

Ibid looked crestfallen. 'Oh,' he said.

'Ibid is a well-known authority on everything,' said Xeno. 'Except for geometry. And interior decorating. And elementary logic.' Ibid glared at him.

'What about you, then?' said Teppic.

Xeno drained his mug. 'I'm more into the destruct testing of axioms,' he said. 'The chap you need is Pthagonal. A very acute man with an angle.'

He was interrupted by the clatter of hooves. Several horsemen galloped with reckless speed past the tavern and on up the winding, cobbled streets of the city. They seemed very excited about something.

Ibid picked a stunned seagull out of his wine cup and laid it on the table. He was looking thoughtful.

'If the Old Kingdom has really disappeared –' he said.

'It has,' said Teppic firmly. 'It's not something you can be mistaken about, really.'

'Then that means our border is concurrent with that of Tsort,' said Ibid ponderously.

'Pardon?' said Teppic.

'There's nothing between us,' explained the philosopher. 'Oh, dear. That means we shall be forced to make war.'

'Why?'

Ibid opened his mouth, stopped, and turned to Xeno.

'Why does it mean we'll be forced to make war?' he said.

'Historical imperative,' said Xeno.

'Ah, yes. I knew it was something like that. I am afraid it is inevitable. It's a shame, but there you are.'

There was another clatter as another party of horsemen rounded the corner, heading downhill this time. They wore the high plumed helmets of Ephebian soldiery, and were shouting enthusiastically.

Ibid settled himself more comfortably on the bench and folded his hands.

'That'll be the Tyrant's men,' he said, as the troop galloped through the city gates and out on to the desert. 'He's sending them to check, you may depend upon it.'

Teppic knew about the enmity between Ephebe and Tsort, of course. The Old Kingdom had profited mightily by it, by seeing that the merchants of both sides had somewhere discreet in which to trade with one another. He drummed his fingers on the table.

'You haven't fought each other for thousands of years,' he said. 'You were tiny countries in those days. It was just a scrap. Now you're huge. People could get hurt. Doesn't that worry you?'

'It's a matter of pride,' said Ibid, but his voice was tinged with uncertainty. 'I don't think there's much choice.'

'It was that bloody wooden cow or whatever,' said Xeno. 'They've never forgiven us for it.'

'If we don't attack them, they'll attack us first,' said Ibid.

''S'right,' said Xeno. 'So we'd better retaliate before they have a chance to strike.'

The two philosophers stared uncomfortably at one another.

'On the other hand,' said Ibid, 'war makes it very difficult to think straight.'

'There is that,' Xeno agreed. 'Especially for dead people.'

There was an embarrassed silence, broken only by Ptraci's voice singing to the tortoise and the occasional squeak of stricken seagulls.

'What day is it?' said Ibid.

'Tuesday,' said Teppic.

'I think,' said Ibid, 'that it might be a good idea if you came to the symposium. We have one every Tuesday,' he added. 'All the greatest minds in Ephebe will be there. All this needs thinking about.'

He glanced at Ptraci.

'However,' he said, 'your young woman cannot attend, naturally. Females are absolutely forbidden. Their brains overheat.'

King Teppicymon XXVII opened his eyes. It's bloody dark in here, he thought.

And he realised that he could hear his own heart beating, but muffled, and some way off.

And then he remembered.

He was alive. He was alive *again*. And, this time, he was in bits.

Somehow, he'd assumed that you got assembled again once you got to the netherworld, like one of Grinjer's kits.

Get a grip on yourself, man, he thought.

It's up to you to pull yourself together.

Right, he thought. There were at least six jars. So my eyes are in one of them. Getting the lid off would be favourite, so we can see what we're at.

That's going to involve arms and legs and fingers.

This is going to be really tricky.

He reached out, tentatively, with stiff joints, and located something heavy. It felt as though it might give, so he moved his other arm into position, with a great deal of awkwardness, and pushed.

There was a distant thump, and a definite feeling of openness above him. He sat up, creaking all the way.

The sides of the ceremonial casket still hemmed him in, but to his surprise he found that one slow arm movement brushed them out of the way like paper. Must be all the pickle and stuffing, he thought. Gives you a bit of weight.

He felt his way to the edge of the slab, lowered his heavy legs to the ground and, after a pause out of habit to wheeze a bit, took the first tottering lurch of the newly undead.

It is astonishingly difficult to walk with legs full of straw when the brain doing the directing is in a pot ten feet away, but he made it as far as the wall and felt his way along it until a crash indicated that he'd reached the shelf of jars. He fumbled the lids of the first one and dipped his hand gently inside.

It must be brains, he thought manically, because semolina doesn't squidge like that. I've collected my own thoughts, haha.

He tried one or two more jars until an explosion of daylight told him he'd found the one with his eyes in. He watched his own bandaged hand reach down, growing gigantic, and scoop them up carefully.

That seems to be the important bits, he thought. The rest can wait until later. Maybe when I need to eat something, and so forth.

He turned around, and realised that he was not alone. Dil and Gern were watching him. To squeeze any further into the far corner of the room, they would have needed triangular backbones.

'Ah. Ho there, good people,' said the king, aware that his voice was a little hollow. 'I know so much about you, I'd like to shake you by the hand.' He looked down. 'Only they're rather full at the moment,' he added.

'Gkkk,' said Gern.

'You couldn't do a bit of reassembly, could you?' said the king, turning to Dil. 'Your stitches seem to be holding up nicely, by the way. Well done, that man.'

Professional pride broke through the barrier of Dil's terror.

'You're alive?' he said.

'That was the general idea, wasn't it?' said the king.

Dil nodded. Certainly it was. He'd always believed it to be true. He'd just never expected it ever actually to happen. But it had, and the first words, well, nearly the first words that had been said were in praise of his needlework. His chest swelled. No-one else in the Guild had ever been congratulated on their work by a recipient.

'There,' he said to Gern, whose shoulderblades were making a spirited attempt to dig their way through the wall. 'Hear what has been said to your master.'

The king paused. It was beginning to dawn on him that things weren't quite right here. Of *course* the netherworld was like this world, only better, and no doubt there were plenty of servants and so forth. But it seemed altogether far too much like this world. He was pretty sure that Dil and Gern shouldn't be in it yet. Anyway, he'd always understood that the common people had their own netherworld, where they would be more at ease and could mingle with their own kind and wouldn't feel awkward and socially out of place.

'I say,' he said. 'I may have missed a bit here. You're not dead, are you?'

Dil didn't answer immediately. Some of the things he'd seen so far today had made him a bit uncertain on the subject. In the end, though, he was forced to admit that he probably was alive.

'Then what's happening?' said the king.

'We don't know, O king,' said Dil. 'Really we don't. It's all come true, O fount of waters!'

'What has?'

'Everything!'

'Everything?'

'The sun, O lord. And the gods! Oh, the gods! They're everywhere, O master of heaven!'

'We come in through the back way,' said Gern, who had dropped to his knees. 'Forgive us, O lord of justice, who has come back to deliver his mighty wisdom and that. I am sorry about me and Glwenda, it was a moment of wossname, mad passion, we couldn't control ourselves. Also, it was me –'

Dil waved him into a devout silence.

'Excuse me,' he said to the king's mummy. 'But could we have a word away from the lad? Man to –'

'Corpse?' said the king, trying to make it easy for him. 'Certainly.'

They wandered over to the other side of the room.

'The fact is, O gracious king of –' Dil began, in a conspiratorial whisper.

'I think we can dispense with all that,' said the king briskly. 'The dead don't stand on ceremony. "King" will be quite sufficient.'

'The fact *is*, then – king,' said Dil, experiencing a slight thrill at this equitable treatment, 'young Gern thinks it's all his fault. I've told him over and over again that the gods wouldn't go to all this trouble just because of one growing lad with urges, if you catch my drift.' He paused, and added carefully, 'They wouldn't, would they?'

'Shouldn't think so for one minute,' said the king briskly. 'We'd never see the back of them, otherwise.'

'That's what I told him,' said Dil, immensely relieved. 'He's a good boy, sir, it's just that his mum is a bit funny about religion. We'd never see the back of them, those were my very words. I'd be very grateful if you could have a word with him, sir, you know, set his mind at rest –'

'Be happy to,' said the king graciously.

Dil sidled closer.

'The fact is, sir, these gods, sir, they aren't right. We've been watching, sir. At least, I have. I climbed on the roof. Gern didn't, he hid under the bench. They're not right, sir!'

'What's wrong with them!'

'Well, they're here, sir! That's not right, is it? I mean, not to be really here. And they're just striding around and fighting amongst themselves and shouting at people.' He looked both ways before continuing. 'Between you and me, sir,' he said, 'they don't seem too bright.'

The king nodded. 'What are the priests doing about this?' he said.

'I saw them throwing one another in the river, sir.'

The king nodded again. 'That sounds about right,' he said. 'They've come to their senses at last.'

'You know what I think, sir?' said Dil earnestly. 'Everything we believe is coming true. And I heard something else, sir. This morning, if it was this morning, you understand, because the sun's all over the place, sir, and it's not the right sort of sun, but this morning some of the soldiers tried to get out along the Ephebe road, sir, and do you know what they found?'

'What did they find?'

'The road out, sir, leads in!' Dil took a step backwards the better to illustrate the seriousness of the revelations. 'They got up into the rocks and then suddenly they were walking down the Tsort road. It all sort of curves back on itself. We're shut in, sir. Shut in with our gods.'

And I'm shut in my body, thought the king. Everything we believe is true? And what we believe isn't what we think we believe.

I mean, we *think* we believe that the gods are wise and just and powerful, but what we really believe is that they are like our father after a long day. And we think we believe the netherworld is a sort of paradise, but we really believe it's right here and you go to it in your body and I'm *in* it and I'm never going to get away. Never, ever.

'What's my son got to say about all this?' he said.

Dil coughed. It was the ominous cough. The Spanish use an upside-down question mark to tell you what you're about to hear is a question; this was the kind of cough that tells you what you're about to hear is a dirge.

'Don't know how to tell you this, sir,' he said.

'Out with it, man.'

'Sir, they say he's dead, sir. They say he killed himself and ran away.'

'Killed himself?'

'Sorry, sir.'

'And ran away afterwards?'

'On a camel, they say.'

'We lead an active afterlife in our family, don't we?' observed the king drily.

'Beg pardon, sir?'

'I mean, the two statements could be held to be mutually exclusive.'

Dil's face became a well-meaning blank.

'That is to say, they can't both be true,' supplied the king, helpfully.

'Ahem,' said Dil.

'Yes, but I'm a special case,' said the king testily. 'In this kingdom we believe you live after death only if you've been mumm –'

He stopped.

It was too horrible to think about. He thought about it, nevertheless, for some time.

Then he said, 'We must do something about it.'

Dil said, 'Your son, sir?'

'Never mind about my son, he's not dead, I'd know about it,' snapped the king. 'He can look after himself, he's my *son*. It's my ancestors I'm worried about.'

'But they're *dead* –' Dil began.

It has already been remarked that Dil had a very poor imagination. In a job like his a poor imagination was essential. But his mind's eye opened on a panorama of pyramids, stretching along the river, and his mind's ear swooped and curved through solid doors that no thief could penetrate.

And it heard the scrabbling.

And it heard the hammering.

And it heard the muffled shouting.

The king put a bandaged arm over his trembling shoulders.

'I know you're a good man with a needle, Dil,' he said. 'Tell me – how are you with a sledgehammer?'

Copolymer, the greatest storyteller in the history of the world, sat back and beamed at the greatest minds in the world, assembled at the dining table.

Teppic had added another iota to his store of new knowledge. 'Symposium' meant a knife-and-fork tea.

'Well,' said Copolymer, and launched into the story of the Tsortean Wars.

'You see, what happened was, *he'd* taken *her* back home, and her father – this wasn't the old king, this was the one before, the one with the wossname, he married some girl from over Elharib way, she had a squint, what was her name now, began with a P. Or an L. One of them letters, anyway. Her father owned an island out on the bay there, Papylos I think it was. No, I tell a lie, it was Crinix. *Anyway* the king, the other king, he raised an army and they. . . . Elenor, that was her name. She had a squint, you know. But quite attractive, they say. When I say married, I trust I do not have to spell it out for you. I mean, it was a bit unofficial. Er. Anyway, there was this wooden horse and after they'd got in . . . Did I tell you about this horse? It was a horse. I'm pretty sure it was a horse. Or maybe it was a chicken. Forget my own name next! It was wossname's idea, the one with the limp. Yes. The limp in his leg, I mean. Did I mention him? There'd been this fight. No, that was the other one, I think. Yes. Anyway, this wooden pig, damn clever idea, they made it out of thing. Tip of my tongue. Wood. But that was later, you know. The fight! Nearly forgot the fight. Yes. Damn good fight. Everyone banging on their shields and yelling. Wossname's armour shone like shining armour. Fight and a half, that fight. Between thingy, not the one with the limp, the other one, wossname, had red hair. *You* know. Tall fellow, talked with a lisp. Hold on, just remembered, he was from some other island. Not him. The other one, with the limp. Didn't want to go, he said he was mad. Of course, he *was* bloody mad, definitely. I mean, a wooden cow! Like wossname said, the king, no, not that king, the other one, he saw the goat, he said, "I fear the Ephebians, especially when they're mad enough to leave bloody great wooden livestock on the doorstep, talk about nerve, they must think we was born yesterday, set fire to it," and, of course, wossname had nipped in round the back and put everyone to the sword, talk about laugh. Did I say she had a squint? They said she was pretty, but it takes all sorts. Yes. Anyway, that's how it happened. *Now*, of course, wossname – I think he was called Melycanus, had a limp – he wanted to go home, well, you would, they'd been there for *years*, he wasn't getting any younger. That's why he dreamt up the thing about the wooden wossname. Yes. I tell a lie, Lavaelous was the one with the knee. Pretty good fight, that fight, take it from me.'

He lapsed into self-satisfied silence.

'Pretty good fight,' he mumbled and, smiling faintly, dropped off to sleep.

Teppic was aware that his own mouth was hanging open. He shut it. Along the table several of the diners were wiping their eyes.

'Magic,' said Xeno. 'Sheer magic. Every word a tassel on the canopy of Time.'

'It's the way he remembers every tiny detail. Pin-sharp,' murmured Ibid.

Teppic looked down the length of the table, and then nudged Xeno beside him. 'Who is everyone?' he said.

'Well, Ibid you already know. And Copolymer. Over there, that's Iesope, the greatest teller of fables in the world. And that's Antiphon, the greatest writer of comic plays in the world.'

'Where is Pthagonal?' said Teppic. Xeno pointed to the far end of the table, where a glum-looking, heavy-drinking man was trying to determine the angle between two bread rolls. 'I'll introduce you to him afterwards,' he said.

Teppic looked around at the bald heads and long white beards, which seemed to be a badge of office. If you had a bald head and a long white beard, they seemed to indicate, whatever lay between them must be bursting with wisdom. The only exception was Antiphon, who looked as though he was built of pork.

They are great minds, he told himself. These are men who are trying to work out how the world fits together, not by magic, not by religion, but just by inserting their brains in whatever crack they can find and trying to lever it apart.

Ibid rapped on the table for silence.

'The Tyrant has called for war on Tsort,' he said. 'Now, let us consider the place of war in the ideal republic,' he said. 'We would require –'

'Excuse me, could you just pass me the celery?' said Iesope. 'Thank you.'

'– the ideal republic, as I was saying, based on the fundamental laws that govern –'

'And the salt. It's just by your elbow.'

'– the fundamental laws, that is, which govern all men. Now, it is without doubt true that war ... could you stop that, please?'

'It's celery,' said Iesope, crunching cheerfully. 'You can't help it with celery.'

Xeno peered suspiciously at what was on his fork.

'Here, this is squid,' he said. 'I didn't ask for squid. Who ordered squid?'

'– without doubt,' repeated Ibid, raising his voice, 'without doubt, I put it to you –'

'I think this is the lamb couscous,' said Antiphon.

'Was yours the squid?'

'I asked for marida and dolmades.'

'*I* ordered the lamb. Just pass it along, will you?'

'I don't remember anyone asking for all this garlic bread,' said Xeno.

'Look, *some* of us are trying to float a philosophical concept here,' said Ibid sarcastically. 'Don't let us interrupt you, will you?'

Someone threw a breadstick at him.

Teppic looked at what was on *his* fork. Seafood was unknown in the kingdom, and what was on his fork had too many valves and suckers to be reassuring. He lifted a boiled vine leaf with extreme care, and was sure he saw something scuttle behind an olive.

Ah. Something else to remember, then. The Ephebians made wine out of anything they could put in a bucket, and ate anything that couldn't climb out of one.

He pushed the food around on his plate. Some of it pushed back.

And philosophers didn't listen to one another. And they don't stick to the point. This probably is mocracy at work.

A bread roll bounced past him. Oh, and they get over-excited.

He noticed a skinny little man sitting opposite him, chewing primly on some anonymous tentacle. Apart from Pthagonal the geometrician, who was now gloomily calculating the radius of his plate, he was the only person not speaking his mind at the top of his voice. Sometimes he'd make little notes on a piece of parchment and slip it into his toga.

Teppic leaned across. Further down the table Iesope, encouraged by occasional olive stones and bread rolls, started a long fable about a fox, a turkey, a goose and a wolf, who had a wager to see who could stay longest underwater with heavy weights tied to their feet.

'Excuse me,' said Teppic, raising his voice above the din. 'Who are you?'

The little man gave him a shy look. He had extremely large ears. In a certain light, he could have been mistaken for a very thin jug.

'I'm Endos,' he said.

'Why aren't you philosophising?'

Endos sliced a strange mollusc.

'I'm not a philosopher, actually,' he said.

'Or a humorous playwright or something?' said Teppic.

'I'm afraid not. I'm a Listener. Endos the Listener, I'm known as.'

'That's fascinating,' said Teppic automatically. 'What does that involve?'

'Listening.'

'Just listening?'

'That's what they pay me for,' said Endos. 'Sometimes I nod. Or smile. Or nod and smile at the same time. Encouragingly, you know. They like that.'

Teppic felt he was called upon to comment at this point. 'Gosh,' he said.

Endos gave him an encouraging nod, and a smile that suggested that of all the things Endos could be doing in the world right at this minute there was nothing so basically riveting as listening to Teppic. It was something about his ears. They appeared to be a vast aural black hole, begging to be filled up with words. Teppic felt an overpowering urge to tell him all about his life and hopes and dreams ...

'I bet,' he said, 'that they pay you an awful lot of money.'

Endos gave him a heartening smile.

'Have you listened to Copolymer tell his story lots of times?'

Endos nodded and smiled, although there was a faint trace of pain right behind his eyes.

'I expect,' said Teppic, 'that your ears develop protective rough surfaces after a while?'

Endos nodded. 'Do go on,' he urged.

Teppic glanced across at Pthagonal, who was moodily drawing right angles in his taramasalata.

'I'd love to stay and listen to you listening to me all day,' he said. 'But there's a man over there I'd like to see.'

'That's amazing,' said Endos, making a short note and turning his attention to a conversation further along the table. A philosopher had averred that although truth was beauty, beauty was not necessarily truth, and a fight was breaking out. Endos listened carefully[*].

Teppic wandered along the table to where Pthagonal was sitting in unrelieved misery, and currently peering suspiciously under the crust of a pie.

Teppic looked over his shoulder.

'I think I saw something moving in there,' he said.

'Ah,' said the geometrician, taking the cork out of an amphora with his teeth. 'The mysterious young man in black from the lost kingdom.'

'I was hoping you could help me find it again?' said Teppic. 'I heard that you have some very unusual ideas in Ephebe.'

'It had to happen,' said Pthagonal. He pulled a pair of dividers from the folds of his robe and measured the pie thoughtfully. 'Is it a constant, do you think? It's a depressing concept.'

'Sorry?' said Teppic.

'The diameter divides into the circumference, you know. It ought to be three times. You'd think so, wouldn't you? But does it? No. Three point one four one and lots of other figures. There's no end to the buggers. Do you know how pissed off that makes me?'

'I expect it makes you extremely pissed off,' said Teppic politely.

'Right. It tells me that the Creator used the wrong kind of circles. It's not even a proper number! I mean, three point five, you could respect. Or three point three. That'd look *right*.' He stared morosely at the pie.

'Excuse me, you said something about it had to happen?'

'What?' said Pthagonal, from the depths of his gloom. 'Pie!' he added.

'What had to happen?' Teppic prompted.

'You can't mess with geometry, friend. Pyramids? Dangerous

---

[*] The role of listeners has never been fully appreciated. However, it is well known that most people don't listen. They use the time when someone else is speaking to think of what they're going to say next. True Listeners have always been revered among oral cultures, and prized for their rarity value; bards and poets are ten a cow, but a good Listener is hard to find, or at least hard to find twice.

things. Asking for trouble. I mean,' Pthagonal reached unsteadily for his wine cup, 'how long did they think they could go on building bigger and bigger pyramids for? I mean, where did they think power comes from? I mean,' he hiccuped, 'you've been in that place, haven't you? Ever noticed how slow it all seems to be?'

'Oh, yes,' said Teppic flatly.

'That's because the time is sucked up, see? Pyramids. So they have to flare it off. Flarelight, they call it. They think it looks pretty! It's their *time* they're burning off!'

'All I know is the air feels as though it's been boiled in a sock,' said Teppic. 'And nothing actually changes, even if it doesn't stay the same.'

'Right,' said Pthagonal. 'The reason being, it's past time. They use up past time, over and over again. The pyramids take all the new time. And if you don't let the pyramids flare, the power build up'll –' he paused. 'I suppose,' he went on, 'that it'd escape along a wossname, a fracture. In space.'

'I was there before the kingdom, er, went,' said Teppic. 'I thought I saw the big pyramid move.'

'There you are then. It's probably moved the dimensions around by ninety degrees,' said Pthagonal, with the assurance of the truly drunk.

'You mean, so length is height and height is width?'

Pthagonal shook an unsteady finger.

'Nonono,' he said. 'So that length is height and height is breadth and breadth is width and width is –' he burped – 'time. S'nother dimessnon, see? Four of the bastards. Time's one of them. Ninety thingys to the other three. Degrees is what I mean. Only, only, it can't exist in *this* world like that, so the place had to sort of pop outside for a bit, see? Otherwise you'd have people getting older by walking sideways.' He looked sadly into the depths of his cup. 'And every birthday you'd age another mile,' he added.

Teppic looked at him aghast.

'That's time and space for you,' Pthagonal went on. 'You can twist them all over the place if you're not careful. Three point one four one. What sort of a number d'you call that?'

'It sounds horrible,' said Teppic.

'Damn right. Somewhere,' Pthagonal was beginning to sway on his bench, 'somewhere someone built a universe with a decent, respectable value of, of,' he peered blearily at the table, 'of pie. Not some damn number that never comes to an end, what kind of –'

'I meant, people getting older just by walking along!'

'I dunno, though. You could have a stroll back to where you were eighteen. Or wander up and see what you were going to look like when you're seventy. Travelling in width, though, that'd be the *real* trick.'

Pthagonal smiled vacantly and then, very slowly, keeled over into his dinner, some of which moved out of the way*.

Teppic became aware that the philosophic din around him had subsided a bit. He stared along the line until he spotted Ibid.

'It won't work,' said Ibid. 'The Tyrant won't listen to us. Nor will the people. Anyway —' he glanced at Antiphon — 'we're not all of one mind on the subject.'

'Damn Tsorteans need teaching a lesson,' said Antiphon sternly. 'Not room for two major powers on this continent. Damn bad sports, anyway, just because we stole their queen. Youthful high spirits, love will have its way —'

Copolymer woke up.

'You've got it wrong,' he said mildly. 'The great war, that was because they stole *our* queen. What was her name now, face that launched a thousand camels, began with an A or a T or —'

'Did they?' shouted Antiphon. 'The bastards!'

'I'm reasonably certain,' said Copolymer.

Teppic sagged, and turned to Endos the Listener. He was still eating his dinner, with the air of one who is determined to preserve his digestion.

'Endos?'

The Listener laid his knife and fork carefully on either side of his plate.

'Yes?'

'They're really all mad, aren't they?' said Teppic wearily.

'That's extremely interesting,' said Endos. 'Do go on.' He reached shyly into his toga and brought forth a scrap of parchment, which he pushed gently towards Teppic.

'What's this?'

'My bill,' said Endos. 'Five minutes Attentive Listening. Most of my gentlemen have monthly accounts, but I understand you'll be leaving in the morning?'

Teppic gave up. He wandered away from the table and into the cold garden surrounding the citadel of Ephebe. White marble statues of ancient Ephebians doing heroic things with no clothes on protruded through the greenery and, here and there, there were

---

* He was wrong. Nature abhors dimensional abnormalities, and seals them neatly away so that they don't upset people. Nature, in fact, abhors a lot of things, including vacuums, ships called the *Marie Celeste*, and the chuck keys for electric drills.

statues of Ephebian gods. It was hard to tell the difference. Teppic knew that Dios had hard words to say about the Ephebians for having gods that looked just like people. If the gods looked just like everyone else, he used to say, how would people know how to treat them?

Teppic had rather liked the idea. According to legend the Ephebians' gods *were* just like humans, except that they used their godhood to get up to things humans didn't have the nerve to do. A favourite trick of Ephebian gods, he recalled, was turning into some animal in order to gain the favours of highly-placed Ephebian women. And one of them had reputedly turned himself into a golden shower in pursuit of his intended. All this raised interesting questions about everyday night life in sophisticated Ephebe.

He found Ptraci sitting on the grass under a poplar tree, feeding the tortoise. He gave it a suspicious look, in case it was a god trying it on. It did not look like a god. If it was a god, it was putting on an incredibly good act.

She was feeding it a lettuce leaf.

'Dear little ptortoise,' she said, and then looked up. 'Oh, it's you,' she said flatly.

'You didn't miss much,' said Teppic, sagging on to the grass. 'They're a bunch of maniacs. When I left they were smashing the plates.'

'That's ptraditional at the end of an Ephebian meal,' said Ptraci.

Teppic thought about this. 'Why not before?' he said.

'And then they probably dance to the sound of the bourzuki,' Ptraci added. 'I think it's a sort of dog.'

Teppic sat with his head in his hands.

'I must say you speak Ephebian well,' he said.

'Pthank you.'

'Just a trace of an accent, though.'

'Languages is part of the ptraining,' she said. 'And my grandmother told me that a ptrace of foreign accent is more fascinating.'

'We learned the same thing,' said Teppic. 'An assassin should always be slightly foreign, no matter where he is. I'm *good* at that part,' he added bitterly.

She began to massage his neck.

'I went down to the harbour,' she said. 'There's those things like big rafts, you know, camels of the sea –'

'Ships,' said Teppic.

'And they go everywhere. We could go anywhere we want. The world is our pthing with pearls in it, if we like.'

Teppic told her about Pthagonal's theory. She didn't seem surprised.

'Like an old pond where no new water comes in,' she observed. 'So everyone goes round and round in the same old puddle. All the ptime you live has been lived already. It must be like other people's bathwater.'

'I'm going to go back.'

Her fingers stopped their skilled kneading of his muscles.

'We could go anywhere,' she repeated. 'We've got ptrades, we could sell that camel. You could show me that Ankh-Morpork place. It sounds interesting.'

Teppic wondered what effect Ankh-Morpork would have on the girl. Then he wondered what effect she would have on the city. She was definitely – flowering. Back in the Old Kingdom she'd never apparently had any original thoughts beyond the choice of the next grape to peel, but since she was outside she seemed to have changed. Her jaw hadn't changed, it was still quite small and, he had to admit, very pretty. But somehow it was more noticeable. She used to look at the ground when she spoke to him. She still didn't always look at him when she spoke to him, but now it was because she was thinking about something else.

He found he kept wanting to say, politely, without stressing it in any way, just as a very gentle reminder, that he was king. But he had a feeling that she'd say she hadn't heard, and would he please repeat it, and if she looked at him he'd never be able to say it twice.

'You could go,' he said. 'You'd get on well. I could give you a few names and addresses.'

'And what would you do?'

'I dread to think what's going on back home,' said Teppic. 'I ought to do something.'

'You can't. Why ptry? Even if you didn't want to be an assassin there's lots of pthings you could do. And you said the man said it's not a place people could get into any more. I hate pyramids.'

'Surely there's people there you care about?'

Ptraci shrugged. 'If they're dead there's nothing I can do about it,' she said. 'And if they're alive, there's nothing I can do about it. So I shan't.'

Teppic stared at her in a species of horrified admiration. It was a beautiful summary of things as they were. He just couldn't bring himself to think that way. His body had been away for seven years but his blood had been in the kingdom for a thousand times longer. Certainly he'd wanted to *leave* it behind, but that was the whole point. It would have been there. Even if he'd avoided it for the rest of his life, it would have still been a sort of anchor.

'I feel so wretched about it,' he repeated. 'I'm sorry. That's all there is to it. Even to go back for five minutes, just to say, well, that I'm not coming back. That'd be enough. It's probably all my fault.'

'But there isn't a way back! You'll just hang around sadly, like those deposed kings you ptold me about. You know, with pthreadbare cloaks and always begging for their food in a high-class way. There's nothing more useless than a king without a kingdom, you said. Just think about it.'

They wandered through the sunset streets of the city, and towards the harbour. All streets in the city led towards the harbour.

Someone was just putting a torch to the lighthouse, which was one of the More Than Seven Wonders of the World and had been built to a design by Pthagonal using the Golden Rule and the Five Aesthetic Principles. Unfortunately it had then been built in the wrong place because putting it in the right place would have spoiled the look of the harbour, but it was generally agreed by mariners to be a very beautiful lighthouse and something to look at while they were waiting to be towed off the rocks.

The harbour below it was thronged with ships. Teppic and Ptraci picked their way past crates and bundles until they reached the long curved guard wall, harbour calm on one side, choppy with waves on the other. Above them the lighthouse flared and sparked.

Those boats would be going to places he'd only ever heard of, he knew. The Ephebians were great traders. He could go back to Ankh and get his diploma, and then the world would indeed be the mollusc of his choice and he had any amount of knives to open it with.

Ptraci put her hand in his.

And there'd be none of this marrying relatives business. The months in Djelibeybi already seemed like a dream, one of those circular dreams that you never quite seem able to shake off and which make insomnia an attractive prospect. Whereas here was a future, unrolling in front of him like a carpet.

What a chap needed at a time like this was a sign, some sort of book of instructions. The trouble with life was that you didn't get a chance to practise before doing it for real. You only –

'Good grief? It's Teppic, isn't it?'

The voice was addressing him from ankle height. A head appeared over the stone of the jetty, quickly followed by its body. An extremely richly dressed body, one on which no expense had been spared in the way of gems, furs, silks and laces, provided that all of them, every single one, was black.

It was Chidder.

'What's it doing now?' said Ptaclusp.

His son poked his head cautiously over the ruins of a pillar and watched Hat, the Vulture-Headed God.

'It's sniffing around,' he said. 'I think it likes the statue. Honestly, dad, why did you have to go and buy a thing like that?'

'It was in a job lot,' said Ptaclusp. 'Anyway, I thought it would be a popular line.'

'With who?'

'Well, *he* likes it.'

Ptaclusp IIb risked another squint at the angular monstrosity that was still hopping around the ruins.

'Tell him he can have it if he goes away,' he suggested. 'Tell him he can have it at cost.'

Ptaclusp winced. 'At a *discount*,' he said. 'A special cut rate for our supernatural customers.'

He stared up at the sky. From their hiding place in the ruins of the construction camp, with the Great Pyramid still humming like a powerhouse behind them, they'd had an excellent view of the arrival of the gods. At first he'd viewed them with a certain amount of equanimity. Gods would be good customers, they always wanted temples and statues, he could deal directly, cut out the middle man.

And then it had occurred to him that a god, when he was unhappy about the product, as it might be, maybe the plasterwork wasn't exactly as per spec, or perhaps a corner of the temple was a bit low on account of unexpected quicksand, a god didn't just come around demanding in a loud voice to see the manager. No. A god knew exactly where you were, and got to the point. Also, gods were notoriously bad payers. So were humans, of course, but they didn't actually expect you to die before they settled the account.

His gaze turned to his other son, a painted silhouette against the statue, his mouth a frozen O of astonishment, and Ptaclusp reached a decision.

'I've just about had it with pyramids,' he said. 'Remind me, lad. If we ever get out of here, no more pyramids. We've got set in our ways. Time to branch out, I reckon.'

'That's what I've been telling you for *ages*, dad!' said IIb. 'I've told you, a couple of decent aqueducts will make a tremendous –'

'Yes, yes, I remember,' said Ptaclusp. 'Yes. Aqueducts. All those arches and things. Fine. Only I can't remember where you said you have to put the coffin in.'

'*Dad!*'

'Don't mind me, lad. I think I'm going mad.'

I couldn't have seen a mummy and two men over there, carrying sledgehammers . . .

It was, indeed, Chidder.

And Chidder had a boat.

Teppic knew that further along the coast the Seriph of Al-Khali lived in the fabulous palace of the Rhoxie, which was said to have been built in one night by a genie and was famed in myth and legend for its splendour*. The *Unnamed* was the Rhoxie afloat, but more so. Its designer had a gilt complex, and had tried every trick with gold paint, curly pillars and expensive drapes to make it look less like a ship and more like a boudoir that had collided with a highly suspicious type of theatre.

In fact, you needed an assassin's eye for hidden detail to notice how innocently the gaudiness concealed the sleekness of the hull and the fact, even when you added the cabin space and the holds together, that there still seemed to be a lot of capacity unaccounted for. The water around what Ptraci called the pointed end was strangely rippled, but it would be totally ridiculous to suspect such an obvious merchantman of having a concealed ramming spike underwater, or that a mere five minutes' work with an axe would turn this wallowing alcazar into something that could run away from nearly everything else afloat and make the few that *could* catch up seriously regret it.

'Very impressive,' said Teppic.

'It's all show, really,' said Chidder.

'Yes. I can see that.'

'I mean, we're poor traders.'

Teppic nodded. 'The usual phrase is "poor *but honest* traders",' he said.

Chidder smiled a merchant's smile. 'Oh, I think we'll stick on "poor" at the moment. How the hell are you, anyway? Last we heard you were going off to be king of some place no-one's ever heard of. And who is this *lovely* young lady?'

'Her na –' Teppic began.

---

* It was, therefore, colloquially known as the Djinn palace.

'Ptraci,' said Ptraci.

'She's a han –' Teppic began.

'She must surely be a royal princess,' said Chidder smoothly. 'And it would give me the greatest pleasure if she, if indeed *both* of you, would dine with me tonight. Humble sailor's fare, I'm afraid, but we muddle along, we muddle along.'

'Not Ephebian, is it?' said Teppic.

'Ship's biscuit, salt beef, that sort of thing,' said Chidder, without taking his eyes off Ptraci. They hadn't left her since she came on board.

Then he laughed. It was the old familiar Chidder laugh, not exactly without humour, but clearly well under the control of its owner's higher brain centres.

'What an astonishing coincidence,' he said. 'And us due to sail at dawn, too. Can I offer you a change of clothing? You both look somewhat, er, travel-stained.'

'Rough sailor clothing, I expect,' said Teppic, 'As befits a humble merchant, correct me if I'm wrong?'

In fact Teppic was shown to a small cabin as exquisitely and carefully furnished as a jewelled egg, where there was laid upon the bed as fine an assortment of clothing as could be found anywhere on the Circle Sea. True, it all appeared second-hand, but carefully laundered and expertly stitched so that the sword cuts hardly showed at all. He gazed thoughtfully at the hooks on the wall, and the faint patching on the wood which hinted that various things had once been hung there and hastily removed.

He stepped out into the narrow corridor, and met Ptraci. She'd chosen a red court dress such as had been the fashion in Ankh-Morpork ten years previously, with puffed sleeves and vast concealed underpinnings and ruffs the size of millstones.

Teppic learned something new, which was that attractive women dressed in a few strips of gauze and a few yards of silk *can* actually look far more desirable when fully clad from neck to ankle. She gave an experimental twirl.

'There are any amount of things like this in there,' she said. 'Is this how women dress in Ankh-Morpork? It's like wearing a house. It doesn't half make you sweaty.'

'Look, about Chidder,' said Teppic urgently. 'I mean, he's a good fellow and everything, but –'

'He's very kind, isn't he,' she agreed.

'Well. Yes. He is,' Teppic admitted, hopelessly. 'He's an old friend.'

'That's nice.'

One of the crew materialised at the end of the corridor and bowed them into the state cabin, his air of old retainership marred only by the criss-cross pattern of scars on his head and some tattoos that made the pictures in *The Shuttered Palace* look like illustrations in a DIY shelving manual. The things he could make them do by flexing his biceps could keep entire dockside taverns fascinated for hours, and he was not aware that the worst moment of his entire life was only a few minutes away.

'This is all very pleasant,' said Chidder, pouring some wine. He nodded at the tattooed man. 'You may serve the soup, Alfonz,' he added.

'Look, Chiddy, you're not a pirate, are you?' said Teppic, desperately.

'Is that what's been worrying you?' Chidder grinned his lazy grin.

It wasn't everything that Teppic had been worrying about, but it had been jockeying for top position. He nodded.

'No, we're not. We just prefer to, er, avoid paperwork wherever possible. You know? We don't like people to have all the worry of having to know everything we do.'

'Only there's all the clothes –'

'Ah. We get *attacked* by pirates a fair amount. That's why father had the *Unnamed* built. It always surprises them. And the whole thing is morally sound. We get their ship, their booty, and any prisoners they may have get rescued and given a ride home at competitive rates.'

'What do you do with the pirates?'

Chidder glanced at Alfonz.

'That depends on future employment prospects,' he said. 'Father always says that a man down on his luck should be offered a helping hand. On terms, that is. How's the king business?'

Teppic told him. Chidder listened intently, swilling the wine around in his glass.

'So that's it,' he said at last. 'We heard there was going to be a war. That's why we're sailing tonight.'

'I don't blame you,' said Teppic.

'No, I mean to get the trade organised. With both sides, naturally, because we're strictly impartial. The weapons produced on this continent are really quite shocking. Downright dangerous. You should come with us, too. You're a very valuable person.'

'Never felt more valueless than right now,' said Teppic despondently.

Chidder looked at him in amazement.

'But you're a king!' he said.

'Well, yes, but —'

'Of a country which technically still exists, but isn't actually reachable by mortal man?'

'Sadly so.'

'And you can pass laws about, well, currency and taxation, yes?'

'I suppose so, but —'

'And you don't think you're valuable? Good grief, Tep, our accountants can probably think up fifty different ways to . . . well, my hands go damp just to think about it. Father will probably ask to move our head office there, for a start.'

'Chidder, I explained. You *know* it. No-one can get in,' said Teppic.

'That doesn't matter.'

'*Doesn't matter?*'

'No, because we'll just make Ankh our main branch office and pay our taxes in wherever the place is. All we need is an official address in, I don't know, the Avenue of the Pyramids or something. Take my tip and don't give in on anything until father gives you a seat on the board. You're royal, anyway, that's always impressive . . .'

Chidder chattered on. Teppic felt his clothes growing hotter.

So this was it. You lost your kingdom, and then it was worth more because it was a tax haven, and you took a seat on the board, whatever that was, and that made it all right.

Ptraci defused the situation by grabbing Alfonz's arm as he was serving the pheasant.

'The Congress of The Friendly Dog and the Two Small Biscuits!' she exclaimed, examining the intricate tattoo. 'You hardly ever see that these days. Isn't it well done? You can even make out the yoghurt.'

Alfonz froze, and then blushed. Watching the glow spread across the great scarred head was like watching sunrise over a mountain range.

'What's the one on your other arm?'

Alfonz, who looked as though his past jobs had included being a battering ram, murmured something and, very shyly, showed her his forearm.

''S'not really suitable for ladies,' he whispered.

Ptraci brushed aside the wiry hair like a keen explorer, while Chidder stared at her with his mouth hanging open.

'Oh, I know that one,' she said dismissively. 'That's out of *130 Days of Pseudopolis*. It's physically impossible.' She let go of the arm, and turned back to her meal. After a moment she looked up at Teppic and Chidder.

'Don't mind me,' she said brightly. 'Do go on.'

'Alfonz, please go and put a proper shirt on,' said Chidder, hoarsely.

Alfonz backed away, staring at his arm.

'Er. What was I, er, saying?' said Chidder. 'Sorry. Lost the thread. Er. Have some more wine, Tep?'

Ptraci didn't just derail the train of thought, she ripped up the rails, burned the stations and melted the bridges for scrap. And so the dinner trailed off into beef pie, fresh peaches, crystallised sea urchins and desultory small talk about the good old days at the Guild. They had been three months ago. It seemed like a lifetime. Three months in the Old Kingdom *was* a lifetime.

After some time Ptraci yawned and went to her cabin, leaving the two of them alone with a fresh bottle of wine. Chidder watched her go in awed silence.

'Are there many like her back at your place?' he said.

'I don't know,' Teppic admitted. 'There could be. Usually they lie around the place peeling grapes or waving fans.'

'She's amazing. She'll take them by storm in Ankh, you know. With a figure like that and a mind like . . .' He hesitated. 'Is she . . .? I mean, are you two . . .?'

'No,' said Teppic.

'She's very attractive.'

'Yes,' said Teppic.

'A sort of cross between a temple dancer and a bandsaw.'

They took their glasses and went up on deck, where a few lights from the city paled against the brilliance of the stars. The water was flat calm, almost oily.

Teppic's head was beginning to spin slowly. The desert, the sun, two gloss coats of Ephebian retsina on his stomach lining and a bottle of wine were getting together to beat up his synapses.

'I mus' say,' he managed, leaning on the rail, 'you're doing all right for yourself.'

'It's okay,' said Chidder. 'Commerce is quite interesting. Building up markets, you know. The cut and thrust of competition in the privateering sector. You ought to come in with us, boy. It's where the future lies, my father says. Not with wizards and kings, but with enterprising people who can afford to hire them. No offence intended, you understand.'

'We're all that's left,' said Teppic to his wine glass. 'Out of the whole kingdom. Me, her, and a camel that smells like an old carpet. An ancient kingdom, lost.'

'Good job it wasn't a new one,' said Chidder. 'At least people got some wear out of it.'

'You don't know what it's like,' said Teppic. 'It's like a whole great pyramid. But upside down, you understand? All that history, all those ancestors, all the people, all funnelling down to me. Right at the bottom.'

He slumped on to a coil of rope as Chidder passed the bottle back and said, 'It makes you think, doesn't it? There's all these lost cities and kingdoms around. Like Ee, in the Great Nef. Whole countries, just gone. Just out there somewhere. Maybe people started mucking about with geometry, what do you say?'

Teppic snored.

After some moments Chidder swayed forward, dropped the empty bottle over the side – it went plunk, and for a few seconds a stream of bubbles disturbed the flat calm – and staggered off to bed.

Teppic dreamed.

And in his dream he was standing on a high place, but unsteadily, because he was balancing on the shoulders of his father and mother, and below them he could make out his grandparents, and below them his ancestors stretching away and out in a vast, all right, a vast *pyramid* of humanity whose base was lost in clouds.

He could hear the murmur of shouted orders and instructions floating up to him.

If you do nothing, we shall never have been.

'This is just a dream,' he said, and stepped out of it into a palace where a small, dark man in a loincloth was sitting on a stone bench, eating figs.

'Of course it's a dream,' he said. 'The world is the dream of the Creator. It's all dreams, different kinds of dreams. They're supposed to tell you things. Like: don't eat lobster last thing at night. Stuff like that. Have you had the one about the seven cows?'

'Yes,' said Teppic, looking around. He'd dreamed quite good architecture. 'One of them was playing a trombone.'

'It was smoking a cigar in my day. Well-known ancestral dream, that dream.'

'What does it mean?'

The little man picked a seed from between his teeth.

'Search me,' he said. 'I'd give my right arm to find out. I don't think we've met, by the way. I'm Khuft. I founded this kingdom. You dream a good fig.'

'I'm dreaming you, too?'

'Damn right. I had a vocabulary of eight hundred words, do you think I'd really be talking like this? If you're expecting a bit of helpful ancestral advice, forget it. This is a *dream*. I can't tell you anything you don't know yourself.'

'You're the *founder*?'

'That's me.'

'I . . . thought you'd be different,' said Teppic.

'How d'you mean?'

'Well . . . on the statue . . .'

Khuft waved a hand impatiently.

'That's just public relations,' he said. 'I mean, look at me. Do I look patriarchal?'

Teppic gave him a critical appraisal. 'Not in that loincloth,' he admitted. 'It's a bit, well, ragged.'

'It's got years of wear left in it,' said Khuft.

'Still, I expect it's all you could grab when you were fleeing from persecution,' said Teppic, anxious to show an understanding nature.

Khuft took another fig and gave him a lopsided look. 'How's that again?'

'You were being persecuted,' said Teppic. 'That's why you fled into the desert.'

'Oh, yes. You're right. Damn right. I was being persecuted for my beliefs.'

'That's terrible,' said Teppic.

Khuft spat. 'Damn right. I believed people wouldn't notice I'd sold them camels with plaster teeth until I was well out of town.'

It took a little while for this to sink in, but it managed it with all the aplomb of a concrete block in a quicksand.

'You're a *criminal*?' said Teppic.

'Well, criminal's a dirty word, know what I mean?' said the little ancestor. 'I'd prefer entrepreneur. I was ahead of my time, that's my trouble.'

'And you were running away?' said Teppic weakly.

'It wouldn't,' said Khuft, 'have been a good idea to hang about.'

'"And Khuft the camel herder became lost in the Desert, and there opened before him, as a Gift from the Gods, a Valley flowing with Milk and Honey",' quoted Teppic, in a hollow voice. He added, 'I used to think it must have been awfully sticky.'

'There I was, dying of thirst, all the camels kicking up a din, yelling for water, next minute – whoosh – a bloody great river valley, reed beds, hippos, the whole thing. Out of nowhere. I nearly got knocked down in the stampede.'

'No!' said Teppic. 'It wasn't like that! The gods of the valley took pity on you and showed you the way in, didn't they?' He shut up, surprised at the tones of pleading in his own voice.

Khuft sneered. 'Oh, yes? And I just happened to stumble across a hundred miles of river in the middle of the desert that everyone else had missed. Easy thing to miss, a hundred miles of river valley in the middle of a desert, isn't it? Not that I was going to look a gift camel in the mouth, you understand, I went and brought my family and the rest of the lads in soon enough. Never looked back.'

'One minute it wasn't there, the next minute it was?' said Teppic.

'Right enough. Hard to believe, isn't it.'

'No,' said Teppic. 'No. Not really.'

Khuft poked him with a wrinkled finger. 'I always reckoned it was the camels that did it,' he said. 'I always thought they sort of called it into place, like it was sort of potentially there but not quite, and it needed just that little bit of effort to make it real. Funny things, camels.'

'I know.'

'Odder than gods. Something the matter?'

'Sorry,' said Teppic, 'it's just that this is all a bit of a shock. I mean, I thought we were really royal. I mean, we're more royal than *anyone*.'

Khuft picked a fig seed from between two blackened stumps which, because they were in his mouth, probably had to be called his teeth. Then he spat.

'That's up to you,' he said, and vanished.

Teppic walked through the necropolis, the pyramids a saw-edged skyline against the night. The sky was the arched body of a woman, and the gods stood around the horizon. They didn't look like the gods that had been painted on the walls for thousands of years. They looked worse. They looked older than Time. After all, the gods hardly ever meddled in the affairs of men. But other things were proverbial for it.

'What can I do? I'm only human,' he said aloud.

Someone said, *Not all of you.*

*

Teppic awoke, to the screaming of seagulls.

Alfonz, who was wearing a long-sleeved shirt and the expression of one who never means to take it off again, ever, was helping several other men unfurl one of *Unnamed*'s sails. He looked down at Teppic in his bed of rope and gave him a nod.

They were moving. Teppic sat up, and saw the dockside of Ephebe slipping silently away in the grey morning light.

He stood up unsteadily, groaned, clutched at his head, took a run and dived over the rail.

Heme Krona, owner of the Camels-R-Us livery stable, walked slowly around You Bastard, humming. He examined the camel's knees. He gave one of its feet an experimental kick. In a swift movement that took You Bastard completely by surprise he jerked open the beast's mouth and examined his great yellow teeth, and then jumped away.

He took a plank of wood from a heap in the corner, dipped a brush in a pot of black paint, and after a moment's thought carefully wrote, ONE OWNER.

After some further consideration he added, LO! MILEAGE.

He was just brushing in GOOD RUNER when Teppic staggered in and leaned, panting, against the doorframe. Pools of water formed around his feet.

'I've come for my camel,' he said.

Krona sighed.

'Last night you said you'd be back in an hour,' he said. 'I'm going to have to charge you for a whole day's livery, right? Plus I gave him a rub down and did his feet, the full service. That'll be five *cercs*, okay emir?'

'Ah.' Teppic patted his pocket.

'Look,' he said. 'I left home in a bit of a hurry, you see. I don't seem to have any cash on me.'

'Fair enough, emir.' Krona turned back to his board. 'How do you spell YEARS WARENTY?'

'I will definitely have the money sent to you,' said Teppic.

Krona gave him the withering smile of one who has seen it all – asses with bodywork re-haired, elephants with plaster tusks, camels with false humps glued on – and knows the festering depths of the human soul when it gets down to business.

'Pull the other one, rajah,' he said. 'It has got bells on.'

Teppic fumbled in his tunic.

'I could give you this valuable knife,' he said.

Krona gave it a passing glance, and sniffed.

'Sorry, emir. No can do. No pay, no camel.'

'I could give it to you point first,' said Teppic desperately, knowing that the mere threat would get him expelled from the Guild. He was also aware that as a threat it wasn't very good. Threats weren't on the syllabus at the Guild school.

Whereas Krona had, sitting on straw bales at the back of the stables, a couple of large men who were just beginning to take an interest in the proceedings. They looked like Alfonz's older brothers.

Every vehicle depot of any description anywhere in the multiverse has them. They're never exactly grooms or mechanics or customers or staff. Their function is always unclear. They chew straws or smoke cigarettes in a surreptitious fashion. If there are such things as newspapers around, they read them, or at least look at the pictures.

They started to watch Teppic closely. One of them picked up a couple of bricks and began to toss them up and down.

'You're a young lad, I can see that,' said Krona, kindly. 'You're just starting out in life, emir. You don't want trouble.' He stepped forward.

You Bastard's huge shaggy head turned to look at him. In the depths of his brain columns of little numbers whirred upwards again.

'Look, I'm sorry, but I've got to have my camel back,' said Teppic. 'It's life and death!'

Krona waved a hand at the two extraneous men.

You Bastard kicked him. You Bastard had very concise ideas about people putting their hands in his mouth. Besides, he'd seen the bricks, and every camel knew what two bricks added up to. It was a good kick, toes well spread, powerful and deceptively slow. It picked Krona up and delivered him neatly into a steaming heap of augean stable sweepings.

Teppic ran, kicked away from the wall, grabbed You Bastard's dusty coat and landed heavily on his neck.

'I'm very sorry,' he said, to such of Krona as was visible. 'I really will have some money sent to you.'

You Bastard, at this point, was waltzing round and round in a circle. Krona's companions stayed well back as feet like plates whirred through the air.

Teppic leaned forward and hissed into one madly-waving ear.

'We're going home,' he said.

They had chosen the first pyramid at random. The king peered at the cartouche on the door.

'"Blessed is Queen Far-re-ptah",' read Dil dutifully, 'Ruler of the Skies, Lord of the Djel, Master of –'

'Grandma Pooney,' said the king. 'She'll do.' He looked at their startled faces. 'That's what I used to call her when I was a little boy. I couldn't pronounce Far-re-ptah, you see. Well, go on then. Stop gawking. Break the door down.'

Gern hefted the hammer uncertainly.

'It's a pyramid, master,' he said, appealing to Dil. 'You're not supposed to open them.'

'What do you suggest, lad? We stick a tableknife in the slot and wiggle it about?' said the king.

'Do it, Gern,' said Dil. 'It will be all right.'

Gern shrugged, spat on his hands which were, in fact, quite damp enough with the sweat of terror, and swung.

'Again,' said the king.

The great slab boomed as the hammer hit it, but it was granite, and held. A few flakes of mortar floated down, and then the echoes came back, shunting back and forth along the dead avenues of the necropolis.

'Again.'

Gern's biceps moved like turtles in grease.

This time there was an answering boom, such as might be caused by a heavy lid crashing to the ground, far away.

They stood in silence, listening to a slow shuffling noise from inside the pyramid.

'Shall I hit it again, sire?' said Gern. They both waved him into silence.

The shuffling grew closer.

Then the stone moved. It stuck once or twice, but nevertheless it moved, slowly, pivoting on one side so that a crack of dark shadow appeared. Dil could just make out a darker shape in the blackness.

'Yes?' it said.

'It's me, Grandma,' said the king.

The shadow stood motionless.

'What, young Pootle?' it said, suspiciously.

The king avoided Dil's face.

'That's right, Grandma. We've come to let you out.'

'Who're these men?' said the shadow petulantly. 'I've got nothing, young man,' she said to Gern. 'I don't keep any money in the pyramid and you can put that weapon away, it doesn't frighten me.'

'They're servants, Grandma,' said the king.

'Have they got any identification?' muttered the old lady.

'*I'm* identifying them, Grandma. We've come to let you out.'

'I was hammering *hours*,' said the late queen, emerging into the sunlight. She looked exactly like the king, except that the mummy wrappings were greyer and dusty. 'I had to go and have a lie down, come the finish. No-one cares about you when you're dead. Where're we going?'

'To let the others out,' said the king.

'Damn good idea.' The old queen lurched into step behind him.

'So this is the netherworld, is it?' she said. 'Not much of an improvement.' She elbowed Gern sharply. 'You dead too, young man?'

'No, ma'am,' said Gern, in the shaky brave tones of someone on a tightrope over the chasms of madness.

'It's not worth it. Be told.'

'Yes, ma'am.'

The king shuffled across the ancient pavings to the next pyramid.

'I know this one,' said the queen. 'It was here in my day. King Ashk-ur-men-tep. Third Empire. What's the hammer for, young man?'

'Please, ma'am, I have to hammer on the door, ma'am,' said Gern.

'You don't have to knock. He's always in.'

'My assistant means to smash the seals, ma'am,' said Dil, anxious to please.

'Who're you?' the queen demanded.

'My name is Dil, O queen. Master embalmer.'

'Oh, you are, are you? I've got some stitching wants seeing to.'

'It will be an honour and a privilege, O queen,' said Dil.

'Yes. It will,' she said, and turned creakily to Gern. 'Hammer away, young man!' she said.

Spurred by this, Gern brought the hammer round in a long, fast arc. It passed in front of Dil's nose making a noise like a partridge and smashed the seal into pieces.

What emerged, when the dust had settled, was not dressed in the height of fashion. The bandages were brown and mouldering and, Dil noticed with professional concern, already beginning to go at the elbows. When it spoke, it was like the opening of ancient caskets.

'I woket up,' it said. 'And theyre was noe light. Is thys the netherworld?'

'It would appear not,' said the queen.

'Thys is *all*?'

'Hardly worth the trouble of dying, was it?' said the queen.

The ancient king nodded, but gently, as though he was afraid his head would fall off.

'Somethyng,' he said, 'must be done.'

He turned to look at the Great Pyramid, and pointed with what had once been an arm.

'Who slepes there?' he said.

'It's mine, actually,' said Teppicymon, lurching forward. 'I don't think we've met, I haven't been interred as yet, my son built it for me. It was against my better judgment, believe me.'

'It ys a dretful thyng,' said the ancient king. 'I felt its building. Even in the sleep of deathe I felt it. It is big enough to interr the worlde.'

'I wanted to be buried at sea,' said Teppicymon. 'I hate pyramids.'

'You do not,' said Ashk-ur-men-tep.

'Excuse me, but I do,' said the king, politely.

'But you do not. What you feel nowe is myld dislike. When you have lain in one for a thousand yeares,' said the ancient one, '*then* you will begin to know the meaning of hate.'

Teppicymon shuddered.

'The sea,' he said. 'That's the place. You just dissolve away.'

They set off towards the next pyramid. Gern led the way, his face a picture, possibly one painted late at night by an artist who got his inspiration on prescription. Dil followed. He held his chest high. He'd always hoped to make his way in the world and here he was now, walking with kings.

Well. *Lurching* with kings.

It was another nice day in the high desert. It was always a nice day, if by nice you meant an air temperature like an oven and sand you could roast chestnuts on.

You Bastard ran fast, mainly to keep his feet off the ground for as long as possible. For a moment, as they staggered up the hills outside the olive-tree'd, field-patchworked oasis around Ephebe, Teppic thought he saw the *Unnamed* as a tiny speck on the azure sea. But it might have been just a gleam on a wave.

Then he was over the crest, into a world of yellow and umber. For a while scrubby trees held on against the sand, but the sand won and marched triumphantly onwards, dune after dune.

The desert was not only hot, it was quiet. There were no birds, none of the susurration of organic creatures busily being alive. At night there might have been the whine of insects, but they were deep under the sand against the scorch of day, and the yellow sky and yellow sand became a anechoic chamber in which You Bastard's breath sounded like a steam-engine.

Teppic had learned many things since he first went forth from the Old Kingdom, and he was about to learn one more. All authorities agree that when crossing the scorching desert it is a good idea to wear a hat.

You Bastard settled into the shambling trot that a prime racing camel can keep up for hours.

After a couple of miles Teppic saw a column of dust behind the next dune. Eventually they came up behind the main body of the Ephebian army, swinging along around half-a-dozen battle elephants, their helmet plumes waving in the oven breeze. They cheered on general principles as Teppic went past.

Battle elephants! Teppic groaned. Tsort went in for battle elephants, too. Battle elephants were the fashion lately. They weren't much good for anything except trampling on their own troops when they inevitably panicked, so the military minds on both sides had responded by breeding bigger elephants. Elephants were impressive.

For some reason, many of these elephants were towing great carts full of timber.

He jogged onwards as the sun wound higher and, and this was unusual, blue and purple dots began to pinwheel gently across the horizon.

Another strange thing was happening. The camel seemed to be trotting across the sky. Perhaps this had something to do with the ringing noise in his ears.

Should he stop? But then the camel might fall off . . .

It was long past noon when You Bastard staggered into the baking shade of the limestone outcrop which had once marked the edge of the valley, and collapsed very slowly into the sand. Teppic rolled off.

A detachment of Ephebians were staring across the narrow space towards a very similar number of Tsorteans on the other side. Occasionally, for the look of the thing, one of them waved a spear.

When Teppic opened his eyes it was to see the fearsome bronze masks of several Ephebian soldiers peering down at him. Their metal mouths were locked in sneers of terrible disdain. Their shining eyebrows were twisted in mortal anger.

One of them said, 'He's coming round, sarge.'

A metal face like the anger of the elements came closer, filling Teppic's vision.

'We've been out without our hat, haven't we, sonny boy,' it said, in a cheery voice that echoed oddly inside the metal. 'In a hurry to get to grips with the enemy, were we?'

The sky wheeled around Teppic, but a thought bobbed into the frying pan of his mind, seized control of his vocal chords and croaked: 'The camel!'

'You ought to be put away, treating it like that,' said the sergeant, waggling a finger at him. 'Never seen one in such a state.'

'Don't let it have a drink!' Teppic sat bolt upright, great gongs clanging and hot, heavy fireworks going off inside his skull. The helmeted heads turned towards one another.

'Gods, he must have something really terrible against camels,' said one of them. Teppic staggered upright and lurched across the sand to You Bastard, who was trying to work out the complex equation which would allow him to get to his feet. His tongue was hanging out, and he was not feeling well.

A camel in distress isn't a shy creature. It doesn't hang around in bars, nursing a solitary drink. It doesn't phone up old friends and sob at them. It doesn't mope, or write long soulful poems about Life and how dreadful it is when seen from a bedsitter. It doesn't know what angst *is*.

All a camel has got is a pair of industrial-strength lungs and a voice like a herd of donkeys being chainsawed.

Teppic advanced through the blaring. You Bastard reared his head and turned it this way and that, triangulating. His eyes rolled madly as he did the camel trick of apparently looking at Teppic with his nostrils.

He spat.

He *tried* to spit.

Teppic grabbed his halter and pulled on it.

'Come on, you bastard,' he said. 'There's water. You can *smell* it. All you have to do is work out how to get there!'

He turned to the assembled soldiers. They were staring at him with expressions of amazement, apart from those who hadn't removed their helmets and who were staring at him with expressions of metallic ferocity.

Teppic snatched a water skin from one of them, pulled out the stopper and tipped it on to the ground in front of the camel's twitching nose.

'There's a river here,' he hissed. 'You know where it is, all you've got to do is go there!'

The soldiers looked around nervously. So did several Tsorteans, who had wandered up to see what was going on.

You Bastard got to his feet, knees trembling, and started to spin around in a circle. Teppic clung on.

... let d equal 4, thought You Bastard desperately. Let a.d equal 90. Let not-d equal 45 ...

'I need a stick!' shouted Teppic, as he was whirled past the sergeant. 'They never understand anything unless you hit them with a stick, it's like punctuation to a camel!'

'Is a sword any good?'

'No!'

The sergeant hesitated, and then passed Teppic his spear.

He grabbed it point-end first, fought for balance, and then brought it smartly across the camel's flank, raising a cloud of dust and hair.

You Bastard stopped. His ears turned like radar aerials. He stared at the rock wall, rolling his eyes. Then, as Teppic grabbed a handful of hair and pulled himself up, the camel started to trot.

... Think *fractals* ...

''Ere, you're going to run straight –' the sergeant began.

There was silence. It went on for a long time.

The sergeant shifted uneasily. Then he looked across the rocks to the Tsorteans, and caught the eye of their leader. With the unspoken understanding that is shared by centurions and sergeant-majors everywhere, they walked towards one another along the length of the rocks and stopped by the barely visible crack in the cliff.

The Tsortean sergeant ran his hand over it.

'You'd think there'd be some, you know, camel hairs or something,' he said.

'Or blood,' said the Ephebian.

'I reckon it's one of them unexplainable phenomena.'

'Oh. That's all right, then.'

The two men stared at the stone for a while.

'Like a mirage,' said the Tsortean, helpfully.

'One of them things, yes.'

'I thought I heard a seagull, too.'

'Daft, isn't it. You don't get them out here.'

The Tsortean coughed politely, and stared back at his men. Then he leaned closer.

'The rest of your people will be along directly, I expect,' he said.

The Ephebian stepped a bit closer and, when he spoke, it was out of the corner of his mouth while his eyes apparently remained fully occupied by looking at the rocks.

'That's right,' he said. 'And yours too, may I ask?'

'Yes. I expect we'll have to massacre you if ours get here first.'

'Likewise, I shouldn't wonder. Still, can't be helped.'

'One of those things, really,' agreed the Tsortean.

The other man nodded. 'Funny old world, when you come to think about it.'

'You've put your finger on it, all right.' The sergeant loosened his breastplate a bit, glad to be out of the sun. 'Rations okay on your side?' he said.

'Oh, you know. Mustn't grumble.'

'Like us, really.'

''Cos if you *do* grumble, they get even worse.'

'Just like ours. Here, you haven't got any figs on your side, have you? I could just do with a fig.'

'Sorry.'

'Just thought I'd ask.'

'Got plenty of dates, if they're any good to you.'

'We're okay on dates, thanks.'

'Sorry.'

The two men stood awhile, lost in their own thoughts. Then the Ephebian put on his helmet again, and the Tsortean adjusted his belt.

'Right, then.'

'Right, then.'

They squared their shoulders, stuck out their chins, and marched away. A moment later they turned about smartly and, exchanging the merest flicker of an embarrassed grin, headed back to their own sides.

BOOK IV

The Book of 101 Things A Boy Can Do

Teppic had expected –

– what?

Possibly the splat of flesh hitting rock. Possibly, although this was on the very edge of expectation, the sight of the Old Kingdom spread out below him.

He hadn't expected chilly, damp mists.

It is now known to science that there are many more dimensions than the classical four. Scientists say that these don't normally impinge on the world because the extra dimensions are very small and curve in on themselves, and that since reality is fractal most of it is tucked inside itself. This means either that the universe is more full of wonders than we can hope to understand or, more probably, that scientists make things up as they go along.

But the multiverse is full of little dimensionettes, playstreets of creation where creatures of the imagination can romp without being knocked down by serious actuality. Sometimes, as they drift through the holes in reality, they impinge back on this universe, when they give rise to myths, legends and charges of being Drunk and Disorderly.

And it was into one of these that You Bastard, by a trivial miscalculation, had trotted.

Legend had got it nearly right. The Sphinx *did* lurk on the borders of the kingdom. The legend just hadn't been precise about what kind of borders it was talking about.

The Sphinx is an unreal creature. It exists solely because it has been imagined. It is well-known that in an infinite universe everything that can be imagined must exist somewhere, and since many of them are not things that ought to exist in a well-ordered space-time frame they get shoved into a side dimension. This may go some way to explaining the Sphinx's chronic bad temper, although any creature created with the body of a lion, bosom of a woman and wings of an eagle has a serious identity crisis and doesn't need much to make it angry.

So it had devised the Riddle.

Across various dimensions it had provided the Sphinx with considerable entertainment and innumerable meals.

This was not known to Teppic as he led You Bastard through the swirling mists, but the bones he crunched underfoot gave him enough essential detail.

A lot of people had died here. And it was reasonable to assume that the more recent ones had seen the remains of the earlier ones, and would therefore have proceeded stealthily. And that hadn't worked.

No sense in creeping along, then. Besides, some of the rocks that loomed out of the mists had a very distressing shape. This one here, for example, looked exactly like –

'Halt,' said the Sphinx.

There was no sound but the drip of the mist and the occasional sucking noise of You Bastard trying to extract moisture from the air.

'You're a sphinx,' said Teppic.

'*The* Sphinx,' corrected the Sphinx.

'Gosh. We've got any amount of statues to you at home.' Teppic looked up, and then further up. 'I thought you'd be smaller,' he added.

'Cower, mortal,' said the Sphinx. 'For thou art in the presence of the wise and the terrible.' It blinked. 'Any good, these statues?'

'They don't do you justice,' said Teppic, truthfully.

'Do you really think so? People often get the nose wrong,' said the Sphinx. 'My right profile is best, I'm told, and –' It dawned on the Sphinx that it was sidetracking itself. It coughed sternly.

'Before you can pass me, O mortal,' it said, 'you must answer my riddle.'

'Why?' said Teppic.

'What?' The Sphinx blinked at him. It hadn't been designed for this sort of thing.

'Why? Why? Because. Er. Because, hang on, yes, because I will bite your head off if you don't. Yes, I think that's it.'

'Right,' said Teppic. 'Let's hear it, then.'

The Sphinx cleared its throat with a noise like an empty lorry reversing in a quarry.

'What goes on four legs in the morning, two legs at noon, and three legs in the evening?' said the Sphinx smugly.

Teppic considered this.

'That's a tough one,' he said, eventually.

'The toughest,' said the Sphinx.

'Um.'

'You'll never get it.'

'Ah,' said Teppic.

'Could you take your clothes off while you're thinking? The threads play merry hell with my teeth.'

'There isn't some kind of animal that regrows legs that have been –'

'Entirely the wrong track,' said the Sphinx, stretching its claws.

'Oh.'

'You haven't got the faintest idea, have you?'

'I'm still thinking,' said Teppic.

'You'll never get it.'

'You're right.' Teppic stared at the claws. This isn't really a fighting animal, he told himself reassuringly, it's definitely over-endowed. Besides, its bosom will get in the way, even if its brain doesn't.

'The answer is: "A Man",' said the Sphinx. 'Now, don't put up a fight, please, it releases unpleasant chemicals into the bloodstream.'

Teppic backed away from a slashing paw. 'Hold on, hold on,' he said. 'What do you mean, a man?'

'It's easy,' said the Sphinx. 'A baby crawls in the morning, stands on both legs at noon, and at evening an old man walks with a stick. Good, isn't it?'

Teppic bit his lip. 'We're talking about *one day* here?' he said doubtfully.

There was a long, embarrassing silence.

'It's a wossname, a figure of speech,' said the Sphinx irritably, making another lunge.

'No, no, look, wait a minute,' said Teppic. 'I'd like us to be very clear about this, right? I mean, it's only fair, right?'

'Nothing wrong with the riddle,' said the Sphinx. 'Damn good riddle. Had that riddle for fifty years, sphinx and cub.' It thought about this. 'Chick,' it corrected.

'It's a good riddle,' Teppic said soothingly. 'Very deep. Very moving. The whole human condition in a nutshell. But you've got to admit, this doesn't all happen to one individual in one day, does it?'

'Well. No,' the Sphinx admitted. 'But that is self-evident from the context. An element of dramatic analogy is present in all riddles,' it added, with the air of one who had heard the phrase a long time ago and rather liked it, although not to the extent of failing to eat the originator.

'Yes, *but*,' said Teppic crouching down and brushing a clear space on the damp sand, 'is there internal consistency within the metaphor? Let's say for example that the average life expectancy is seventy years, okay?'

'Okay,' said the Sphinx, in the uncertain tones of someone who has let the salesman in and is now regretfully contemplating a future in which they are undoubtedly going to buy life insurance.

'*Right*. Good. So noon would be age 35, am I right? Now considering that most children can toddle at a year or so, the four legs reference is really unsuitable, wouldn't you agree? I mean, most of the morning is spent on two legs. According to your analogy –' he paused and did a few calculations with a convenient thighbone – 'only about twenty minutes immediately after 00.00 hours, half an hour tops, is spent on four legs. Am I right? Be fair.'

'Well –' said the Sphinx.

'By the same token you wouldn't be using a stick by six p.m. because you'd be only, er, 52,' said Teppic, scribbling furiously. 'In fact you wouldn't really be looking at any kind of walking aid until at least half past nine, I think. That's on the assumption that the entire lifespan takes place over one day which is, I believe I have already pointed out, ridiculous. I'm sorry, it's basically okay, but it doesn't work.'

'Well,' said the Sphinx, but irritably this time, 'I don't see what I can do about it. I haven't got any more. It's the only one I've ever needed.'

'You just need to alter it a bit, that's all.'

'How do you mean?'

'Just make it a bit more realistic.'

'Hmm.' The Sphinx scratched its mane with a claw.

'Okay,' it said doubtfully. 'I suppose I could ask: What is it that walks on four legs –'

'Metaphorically speaking,' said Teppic.

'Four legs, metaphorically speaking,' the Sphinx agreed, 'for about –'

'Twenty minutes, I think we agreed.'

'– okay, fine, twenty minutes in the morning, on two legs –'

'But I think calling it in "the morning" is stretching it a bit,' said Teppic. 'It's just after midnight. I mean, technically it's the morning, but in a very real sense it's still last night, what do you think?'

A look of glazed panic crossed the Sphinx's face.

'What do *you* think?' it managed.

'Let's just see where we've got to, shall we? What, metaphorically speaking, walks on four legs just after midnight, on two legs for most of the day –'

'– barring accidents,' said the Sphinx, pathetically eager to show that it was making a contribution.

'Fine, on two legs barring accidents, until at least suppertime, when it walks with three legs –'

'I've known people use two walking sticks,' said the Sphinx helpfully.

'Okay. How about: when it continues to walk on two legs or with any prosthetic aids of its choice?'

The Sphinx gave this some consideration.

'Ye – ess,' it said gravely. 'That seems to fit all eventualities.'

'Well?' said Teppic.

'Well what?' said the Sphinx.

'Well, what's the answer?'

The Sphinx gave him a stony look, and then showed its fangs. 'Oh no,' it said. 'You don't catch me out like that. You think I'm stupid? *You've* got to tell *me* the answer.'

'Oh, blow,' said Teppic.

'Thought you had me there, didn't you?' said the Sphinx.

'Sorry.'

'You thought you could get me all confused, did you?' The Sphinx grinned.

'It was worth a try,' said Teppic.

'Can't blame you. So what's the answer, then?'

Teppic scratched his nose.

'Haven't a clue,' he said. 'Unless, and this is a shot in the dark, you understand, it's: A Man.'

The Sphinx glared at him.

'You've been here before, haven't you?' it said accusingly.

'No.'

'Then someone's been talking, right?'

'Who could have talked? Has anyone ever guessed the riddle?' said Teppic.

'No!'

'Well, then. They couldn't have talked, could they?'

The Sphinx's claws scrabbled irritably on its rock.

'I suppose you'd better move along, then,' it grumbled.

'Thank you,' said Teppic.

'I'd be grateful if you didn't tell anyone, please,' added the Sphinx, coldly. 'I wouldn't like to spoil it for other people.'

Teppic scrambled up a rock and on to You Bastard.

'Don't you worry about that,' he said, spurring the camel onwards. He couldn't help noticing the way the Sphinx was moving its lips silently, as though trying to work something out.

You Bastard had gone only twenty yards or so before an enraged bellow erupted behind him. For once he forgot the etiquette that says a camel must be hit with a stick before it does anything. All four feet hit the sand and pushed.

This time he got it right.

The priests were going irrational.

It wasn't that the gods were disobeying them. The gods were *ignoring* them.

The gods always had. It took great skill to persuade a Djelibeybi god to obey you, and the priests had to be fast on their toes. For example, if you pushed a rock off a cliff, then a quick request to the gods that it should fall down was certain to be answered. In the same way, the gods ensured that the sun set and the stars came out. Any petition to the gods to see to it that palm trees grew with their roots in the ground and their leaves on top was certain to be graciously accepted. On the whole, any priest who cared about such things could ensure a high rate of success.

However, it was one thing for the gods to ignore you when they were far off and invisible, and quite another when they were strolling across the landscape. It made you feel such a fool.

'Why don't they listen?' said the high priest of Teg, the Horse-Headed god of agriculture. He was in tears. Teg had last been seen sitting in a field, pulling up corn and giggling.

The other high priests were faring no better. Rituals hallowed by time had filled the air in the palace with sweet blue smoke and cooked enough assorted livestock to feed a famine, but the gods were settling in the Old Kingdom as if they owned it, and the people therein were no more than insects.

And the crowds were still outside. Religion had ruled in the Old Kingdom for the best part of seven thousand years. Behind the eyes of every priest present was a graphic image of what would happen if the people ever thought, for one moment, that it ruled no more.

'And so, Dios,' said Koomi, 'we turn to you. What would you have us do now?'

Dios sat on the steps of the throne and stared gloomily at the floor. The gods didn't listen. He *knew* that. He knew that, of all people. But it had never mattered before. You just went through the motions and came up with an answer. It was the ritual that was important, not the gods. The gods were there to do the duties of a megaphone, because who else would people listen to?

While he fought to think clearly his hands went through the motions of the Ritual of the Seventh Hour, guided by neural instructions as rigid and unchangeable as crystals.

'You have tried everything?' he said.

'Everything that you advised, O Dios,' said Koomi. He waited until most of the priests were watching them and then, in a rather louder voice, continued: 'If the king was here, he would intercede for us.'

He caught the eye of the priestess of Sarduk. He hadn't discussed things with her; indeed, what was there to discuss? But he had an inkling that there was some fellow, sorry, feeling there. She didn't like Dios very much, but was less in awe of him than were the others.

'I told you that the king is dead,' said Dios.

'Yes, we heard you. Yet there seems to be no body, O Dios. Nevertheless, we believe what you tell us, for it is the great Dios that speaks, and we pay no heed to malicious gossip.'

The priests were silent. Malicious gossip, too? And somebody had already mentioned rumours, hadn't they? Definitely something amiss here.

'It happened many times in the past,' said the priestess, on cue. 'When a kingdom was threatened or the river did not rise, the king went to intercede with the gods. Was *sent* to intercede with the gods.'

The edge of satisfaction in her voice made it clear that it was a one-way trip.

Koomi shivered with delight and horror. Oh, yes. Those were the days. Some countries had experimented with the idea of the sacrificial king, long ago. A few years of feasting and ruling, then chop – and make way for a new administration.

'In a time of crisis, possibly any high-born minister of state would suffice,' she went on.

Dios looked up, his face mirroring the agony of his tendons.

'I *see*,' he said. 'And who would be high priest then?'

'The gods would choose,' said Koomi.

'I daresay they would,' said Dios sourly. 'I am in some doubt as to the wisdom of their choice.'

'The dead can speak to the gods in the netherworld,' said the priestess.

'But the gods are all *here*,' said Dios, fighting against the throbbing in his legs, which were insisting that, at this time, they should be walking along the central corridor en route to supervise the Rite of the Under Sky. His body cried out for the solace over the river. And once over the river, never to return . . . but he'd always said that.

'In the absence of the king the high priest performs his duties. Isn't that right, Dios?' said Koomi.

It was. It was written. You couldn't rewrite it, once it was written. He'd written it. Long ago.

Dios hung his head. This was worse than plumbing, this was worse than anything. And yet, and yet . . . to go across the river . . .

'Very well, then,' he said. 'I have one final request.'

'Yes?' Koomi's voice had timbre now, it was already a high priest's voice.

'I wish to be interred in the –' Dios began, and was cut off by a murmur from those priests who could look out across the river. All eyes turned to the distant, inky shore.

The legions of the kings of Djelibeybi were on the march.

They lurched, but they covered the ground quickly. There were platoons, battalions of them. They didn't need Gern's hammer any more.

'It's the pickle,' said the king, as they watched half-a-dozen ancestors mummyhandle a seal out of its socket. 'It toughens you up.'

Some of the more ancient were getting overenthusiastic and attacking the pyramids themselves, actually managing to shift blocks higher than they were. The king didn't blame them. How terrible to be dead, and know you were dead, and locked away in the darkness.

They're never going to get me in one of those things, he vowed.

At last they came, like a tide, to yet another pyramid. It was small, low, dark, half-concealed in drifted sand, and the blocks were hardly even masonry; they were no more than roughly squared boulders. It had clearly been built long before the Kingdom got the hang of pyramids. It was barely more than a pile.

Hacked into the doorseal, angular and deep, were the hieroglyphs of the Ur Kingdom: Khuft had me Made. The first.

Several ancestors clustered around it.

'Oh, dear,' said the king. 'This might be going too far.'

'The First,' whispered Dil. 'The First into the Kingdom. No-one here before but hippos and crocodiles. From inside that pyramid seventy centuries look out at us. Older than anything –'

'Yes, yes, all right,' said Teppicymon. 'No need to get carried away. He was a man, just like all of us.'

'"And Khuft the camel herder looked upon the valley ..."' Dil began.

'After seven thousand yeares, he wyll be wantyng to look upon yt again,' said Ashk-ur-men-tep bluntly.

'Even so,' said the king. 'It *does* seem a bit ...'

'The dead are equal,' said Ashk-ur-men-tep. 'You, younge manne. Calle hym forth.'

'Who, me?' said Gern. 'But he was the Fir –'

'Yes, we've been through all that,' said Teppicymon. 'Do it. Everyone's getting impatient. So is he, I expect.'

Gern rolled his eyes, and hefted the hammer. Just as it was about to hiss down on the seal Dil darted forward, causing Gern to dance wildly across the ground in a groin-straining effort to avoid interring the hammer in his master's head.

'It's open!' said Dil. 'Look! The seal just swings aside!'

'Youe meane he iss *oute*?'

Teppicymon tottered forward and grabbed the door of the pyramid. It moved quite easily. Then he examined the stone beneath it. Derelict and half-covered though it was, someone had taken care to keep a pathway clear to the pyramid. And the stone was quite worn away, as by the passage of many feet.

This was not, by the nature of things, the normal state of affairs for a pyramid. The whole point was that once you were in, you were in.

The mummies examined the worn entrance and creaked at one another in surprise. One of the very ancient ones, who was barely holding himself together, made a noise like a deathwatch beetle finally conquering a rotten tree.

'What'd he say?' said Teppicymon.

The mummy of Ashk-ur-men-tep translated. 'He saide yt ys Spooky,' he croaked.

The late king nodded. 'I'm going in to have a look. You two live ones, you come with me.'

Dil's face fell.

'Oh, come on, man,' snapped Teppicymon, forcing the door back. 'Look, *I'm* not frightened. Show a bit of backbone. Everyone else is.'

'But we'll need some light,' protested Dil.

The nearest mummies lurched back sharply as Gern timidly took a tinderbox out of his pocket.

'We'll need something to burn,' said Dil. The mummies shuffled further back, muttering.

'There's torches in here,' said Teppicymon, his voice slightly muffled. 'And you can keep them away from me, lad.'

It was a small pyramid, mazeless, without traps, just a stone passage leading upwards. Tremulously, expecting at any moment to see unnamed terrors leap out at them, the embalmers followed the king into a small, square chamber that smelled of sand. The roof was black with soot.

There was no sarcophagus within, no mummy case, no terror named or nameless. The centre of the floor was occupied by a raised block, with a blanket and a pillow on it.

Neither of them looked particularly old. It was almost disappointing.

Gern craned to look around.

'Quite nice, really,' he said. 'Comfy.'

'No,' said Dil.

'Hey, master king, look here,' said Gern, trotting over to one of the walls. 'Look. Someone's been scratching things. Look, all little lines all over the wall.'

'And this wall,' said the king, 'and the floor. Someone's been counting. Every ten have been crossed through, you see. Someone's been counting things. Lots of things.' He stood back.

'What things?' said Dil, looking behind him.

'Very strange,' said the king. He leaned forward. 'You can barely make out the inscriptions underneath.'

'Can you read it, king?' said Gern, showing what Dil considered to be unnecessary enthusiasm.

'No. It's one of the really ancient dialects. Can't make out a blessed hieroglyph,' said Teppicymon. 'I shouldn't think there's a single person alive today who can read it.'

'That's a shame,' said Gern.

'True enough,' said the king, and sighed. They stood in gloomy silence.

'So perhaps we could ask one of the dead ones?' said Gern.

'Er. Gern,' said Dil, backing away.

The king slapped the apprentice on the back, pitching him forward.

'Damn clever idea!' he said. 'We'll just go and get one of the real early ancestors. Oh.' He sagged. 'That's no good. No-one will be able to understand them –'

'Gern!' said Dil, his eyes growing wider.

'No, it's all right, king,' said Gern, enjoying the new-found freedom of thought, 'because, the reason being, everyone understands *someone*, all we have to do is sort them out.'

'Bright lad. Bright lad,' said the king.

'*Gern!*'

They both looked at him in astonishment.

'You all right, master?' said Gern. 'You've gone all white.'

'The t –' stuttered Dil, rigid with terror.

'The what, master?'

'The t – look at the t –'

'He ought to have a lie down,' said the king. 'I know his sort. The artistic type. Highly strung.'

Dil took a deep breath.

'*Look at the sodding torch, Gern!*' he shouted.

They looked.

Without any fuss, turning its black ashes into dry straw, the torch was burning backwards.

The Old Kingdom lay stretched out before Teppic, and it was unreal.

He looked at You Bastard, who had stuck his muzzle in a wayside spring and was making a noise like the last drop in the milkshake glass.* You Bastard looked real enough. There's nothing like a camel for looking really solid. But the landscape had an uncertain quality, as if it hadn't quite made up its mind to be there or not.

Except for the Great Pyramid. It squatted in the middle distance as real as the pin that nails a butterfly to a board. It was contriving to look extremely solid, as though it was sucking all the solidity out of the landscape into itself.

Well, he was here. Wherever here was.

How did you kill a pyramid?

And what would happen if you did?

He was working on the hypothesis that everything would snap back into place. Into the Old Kingdom's pool of recirculated time.

He watched the gods for a while, wondering what the hell they were, and how it didn't seem to matter. They looked no more real

---

* You know. The bit you can't reach with the straw.

than the land over which they strode, about incomprehensible errands of their own. The world was no more than a dream. Teppic felt incapable of surprise. If seven fat cows had wandered by, he wouldn't have given them a second glance.

He remounted You Bastard and rode him, sloshing gently, down the road. The fields on either side had a devastated look.

The sun was finally sinking; the gods of night and evening were prevailing over the daylight gods, but it had been a long struggle and, when you thought about all the things that would happen to it now – eaten by goddesses, carried on boats under the world, and so on – it was an odds-on chance that it wouldn't be seen again.

No-one was visible as he rode into the stable yard. You Bastard padded sedately to his stall and pulled delicately at a wisp of hay. He'd thought of something interesting about bivariant distributions.

Teppic patted him on the flank, raising another cloud, and walked up the wide steps that led to the palace proper. Still there were no guards, no servants. No living soul.

He slipped into his own palace like a thief in the day, and found his way to Dil's workshop. It was empty, and looked as though a robber with very peculiar tastes had recently been at work in there. The throne room smelled like a kitchen, and by the looks of it the cooks had fled in a hurry.

The gold mask of the kings of Djelibeybi, slightly buckled out of shape, had rolled into a corner. He picked it up and, on a suspicion, scratched it with one of his knives. The gold peeled away, exposing a silver-grey gleam.

He'd suspected that. There simply wasn't that much gold around. The mask felt as heavy as lead because, well, it *was* lead. He wondered if it had ever been all gold, and which ancestor had done it, and how many pyramids it had paid for. It was probably very symbolic of something or other. Perhaps not even symbolic *of* anything. Just symbolic, all by itself.

One of the sacred cats was hiding under the throne. It flattened its ears and spat at Teppic as he reached down to pat it. That much hadn't changed, at least.

Still no people. He padded across to the balcony.

And there the people were, a great silent mass, staring across the river in the fading, leaden light. As Teppic watched a flotilla of boats and ferries set out from the near bank.

We ought to have been building bridges, he thought. But we said that would be shackling the river.

He dropped lightly over the balustrade on to the packed earth and walked down to the crowd.

And the full force of its belief scythed into him.

The people of Djelibeybi might have had conflicting ideas about their gods, but their belief in their kings had been unswerving for thousands of years. To Teppic it was like walking into a vat of alcohol. He felt it pouring into him until his fingertips crackled, rising up through his body until it gushed into his brain, bringing not omnipotence but the *feeling* of omnipotence, the very strong sensation that while he didn't actually know everything, he would do soon and had done once.

It had been like this back in Ankh, when the divinity had hooked him. But that had been just a flicker. Now it had the solid power of real belief behind it.

He looked down at a rustling below him, and saw green shoots springing out of the dry sand around his feet.

Bloody hell, he thought. I really *am* a god.

This could be very embarrassing.

He shouldered his way through the press of people until he reached the riverbank and stood there in a thickening clump of corn. As the crowd caught on, those nearest fell to their knees, and a circle of reverentially collapsing people spread out from Teppic like ripples.

But I never wanted this! I just wanted to help people live more happily, with plumbing. I wanted something done about run-down inner-city areas. I just wanted to put them at their ease, and ask them how they enjoyed their lives. I thought schools might be a good idea, so they wouldn't fall down and worship someone just because he's got green feet.

And I wanted to do something about the architecture ...

As the light drained from the sky like steel going cold the pyramid was somehow even bigger than before. If you had to design something to give the very distinct impression of mass, the pyramid was It. There was a crowd of figures around it, unidentifiable in the grey light.

Teppic looked around the prostrate crowd until he saw someone in the uniform of the palace guard.

'You, man, on your feet,' he commanded.

The man gave him a look of dread, but did stagger sheepishly upright.

'What's going on here?'

'O king, who is the lord of –'

'I don't think we have time,' said Teppic. 'I know who I am, I want to know what's happening.'

'O king, we saw the dead walking! The priests have gone to talk to them.'

'The *dead* walking?'

'Yes, O king.'

'We're talking about not-alive people here, are we?'

'Yes, O king.'

'Oh. Well, thank you. That was very succinct. Not informative, but succinct. Are there any boats around?'

'The priests took them all, O king.'

Teppic could see that this was true. The jetties near the palace were usually thronged with boats, and now they were all empty. As he stared at the water it grew two eyes and a long snout, to remind him that swimming the Djel was as feasible as nailing fog to the wall.

He stared at the crowd. Every person was watching him expectantly, convinced that he would know what to do next.

He turned back to the river, extended his hands in front of him, pressed them together, and then opened them gently.

There was a damp sucking noise, and the waters of the Djel parted in front of him. There was a sigh from the crowd, but their astonishment was nothing to the surprise of a dozen or so crocodiles, who were left trying to swim in ten feet of air.

Teppic ran down the bank and over the heavy mud, dodging to avoid the tails that slashed wildly at him as the reptiles dropped heavily on to the riverbed.

The Djel loomed up as two khaki walls, so that he was running along a damp and shadowy alley. Here and there were fragments of bones, old shields, bits of spear, the ribs of boats. He leapt and jinked around the debris of centuries.

Ahead of him a big bull crocodile propelled itself dreamily out of the wall of water, flailed madly in mid-air, and flopped into the ooze. Teppic trod heavily on its snout and plunged on.

Behind him a few of the quicker citizens, seeing the dazed creatures below them, began to look for stones. The crocodiles had been undisputed masters of the river since primordial times, but if it was possible to do a little catching-up in the space of a few minutes, it was certainly worth a try.

The sound of the monsters of the river beginning the long journey to handbaghood broke out behind Teppic as he sloshed up the far bank.

*

A line of ancestors stretched across the chamber, down the dark passageway, and out into the sand. It was filled with whispers going in both directions, a dry sound, like the wind blowing through old paper.

Dil lay on the sand, with Gern flapping a cloth in his face.

'Wha' they doing?' he murmured.

'Reading the inscription,' said Gern. 'You ought to see it, master! The one doing the reading, he's practically a –'

'Yes, yes, all right,' said Dil, struggling up.

'He's more than six thousand years old! And his grandson's listening to him, and telling *his* grandson, and he's telling *his* gra –'

'Yes, yes, all –'

'"And-Khuft-too-said-Unto-the-First, What-may-We-Give-Unto-You, Who-Has-Taught-Us-the-Right-Ways",' said Teppicymon*, who was at the end of the line. '"And-the-First-Spake, and-This-He-Spake, Build-for-Me-a-Pyramid, That-I-May-Rest, and-Build-it-of-These-Dimensions, That-it-Be-Proper. And-Thus-It-Was-Done, and-the-Name-of-the-First-was . . ."'

But there was no name. It was just a babble of raised voices, arguments, ancient cursewords, spreading along the line of desiccated ancestors like a spark along a powder trail. Until it reached Teppicymon, who exploded.

The Ephebian sergeant, quietly perspiring in the shade, saw what he had been half expecting and wholly dreading. There was a column of dust on the opposite horizon.

The Tsorteans' main force was getting there first.

He stood up, nodded professionally to his counterpart across the way, and looked at the double handful of men under his command.

'I need a messenger to take, er, a message back to the city,' he said. A forest of hands shot up. The sergeant sighed, and selected young Autocue, who he knew was missing his mum.

'Run like the wind,' he said. 'Although I expect you won't need telling, will you? And then . . . and then . . .'

He stood with his lips moving silently, while the sun scoured the rocks of the hot, narrow pass and a few insects buzzed in the scrub

---

* But not immediately, of course, because messages change in the telling and some ancestors were not capable of perfect enunciation and others were trying to be helpful and supplying what they thought were lost words. The message received by Teppicymon originally began, 'Handcuffed to the bed, the aunt thirsted.'

bushes. His education hadn't included a course in Famous Last Words.

He raised his eyes in the direction of home.

'Go, tell the Ephebians –' he began.

The soldiers waited.

'What?' said Autocue after a while. 'Go and tell them what?'

The sergeant relaxed, like air being let out of a balloon.

'Go and tell them, what kept you?' he said. On the near horizon another column of dust was advancing.

This was more like it. If there was going to be a massacre, then it ought to be shared by both sides.

The city of the dead lay before Teppic. After Ankh-Morpork, which was almost its direct opposite (in Ankh, even the bedding was alive) it was probably the biggest city on the Disc; its streets were the finest, its architecture the most majestic and awe-inspiring.

In population terms the necropolis outstripped the other cities of the Old Kingdom, but its people didn't get out much and there was nothing to do on Saturday nights.

Until now.

Now it thronged.

Teppic watched from the top of a wind-etched obelisk as the grey and brown, and here and there somewhat greenish, armies of the departed passed beneath him. The kings had been democratic. After the pyramids had been emptied gangs of them had turned their attention to the lesser tombs, and now the necropolis really did have its tradesmen, its nobles and even its artisans. Not that there was, by and large, any way of telling the difference.

They were, to a corpse, heading for the Great Pyramid. It loomed like a carbuncle over the lesser, older buildings. And they all seemed very angry about something.

Teppic dropped lightly on to the wide flat roof of a mastaba, jogged to its far end, cleared the gap on to an ornamental sphinx – not without a moment's worry, but this one seemed inert enough – and from there it was but the throw of a grapnel to one of the lower storeys of a step pyramid.

The long light of the contentious sun lanced across the silent landscape as he leapt from monument to monument, zig-zagging high above the shuffling army.

Behind him shoots appeared briefly in the ancient stone, cracking it a little, and then withered and died.

This, said his blood as it tingled around his body, is what you trained for. Even Mericet couldn't mark you down for this. Speeding in the shadows above a silent city, running like a cat, finding handholds that would have perplexed a gecko – and, at the destination, a victim.

True, it was a billion tons of pyramid, and hitherto the largest client of an inhumation had been Patricio, the 23-stone Despot of Quirm.

A monumental needle recording in bas-relief the achievements of a king four thousand years ago, and which would have been more pertinent if the wind-driven sand hadn't long ago eroded his name, provided a handy ladder which needed only an expertly thrown grapnel from its top, lodging in the outstretched fingers of a forgotten monarch, to allow him a long, gentle arc on to the roof of a tomb.

Running, climbing and swinging, hastily hammering crampons in the memorials of the dead, Teppic went forth.

Pinpoints of firelight among the limestone pricked out the lines of the opposing armies. Deep and stylised though the enmity was between the two empires, they both abided by the ancient tradition that warfare wasn't undertaken at night, during harvest or when wet. It was important enough to save up for special occasions. Going at it hammer and tongs just reduced the whole thing to a farce.

In the twilight on both sides of the line came the busy sound of advanced woodwork in progress.

It's said that generals are always ready to fight the last war over again. It had been thousands of years since the last war between Tsort and Ephebe, but generals have long memories and this time they were ready for it.

On both sides of the line, wooden horses were taking shape.

'It's gone,' said Ptaclusp IIb, slithering back down the pile of rubble.

'About time, too,' said his father. 'Help me fold up your brother. You're sure it won't hurt him?'

'Well, if we do it carefully he can't move in Time, that is, width to us. So if no time can pass for him, nothing can hurt him.'

Ptaclusp thought of the old days, when pyramid building had simply consisted of piling one block on another and all you needed to remember was that you put less on top as you went up. And now it meant trying to put a crease in one of your sons.

'Right,' he said doubtfully. 'Let's be off, then.' He inched his way up the debris and poked his head over the top just as the vanguard of the dead came round the corner of the nearest minor pyramid.

His first thought was: this is it, they're coming to complain.

He'd done his best. It wasn't always easy to build to a budget. Maybe not every lintel was exactly as per drawings, perhaps the quality of the internal plasterwork wasn't always up to snuff, but . . .

They can't *all* be complaining. Not this many of them.

Ptaclusp IIb climbed up alongside him. His mouth dropped open.

'Where are they all coming from?' he said.

'You're the expert. You tell me.'

'Are they *dead*?'

Ptaclusp scrutinised some of the approaching marchers.

'If they're not, some of them are awfully ill,' he said.

'Let's make a run for it!'

'Where to? Up the pyramid?'

The Great Pyramid loomed up behind them, its throbbing filling the air. Ptaclusp stared at it.

'What's going to happen tonight?' he said.

'What?'

'Well, is it going to – do whatever it did – again?'

IIb stared at him. 'Dunno.'

'Can you find out?'

'Only by waiting. I'm not even sure what it's done *now*.'

'Are we going to like it?'

'I shouldn't think so, dad. Oh, dear.'

'What's up now?'

'Look over there.'

Heading towards the marching dead, trailing behind Koomi like a tail behind a comet, were the priests.

It was hot and dark inside the horse. It was also very crowded.

They waited, sweating.

Young Autocue stuttered: 'What'll happen now, sergeant?'

The sergeant moved a foot tentatively. The atmosphere would have induced claustrophobia in a sardine.

'Well, lad. They'll find us, see, and be so impressed they'll drag us all the way back to their city, and then when it's dark we'll leap out and put them to the sword. Or put the sword to them. One or the other. And then we'll sack the city, burn the walls and sow the ground with salt. You remember, lad, I showed you on Friday.'

'Oh.'

Moisture dripped from a score of brows. Several of the men were trying to compose a letter home, dragging styli across wax that was close to melting.

'And then what will happen, sergeant?'

'Why, lad, then we'll go home heroes.'

'Oh.'

The older soldiers sat stolidly looking at the wooden walls. Autocue shifted uneasily, still worried about something.

'My mum said to come back with my shield or on it, sergeant,' he said.

'Jolly good, lad. That's the spirit.'

'We will be all right, though. Won't we, sergeant?'

The sergeant stared into the fetid darkness.

After a while, someone started to play the harmonica.

Ptaclusp half-turned his head from the scene and a voice by his ear said, 'You're the pyramid builder, aren't you?'

Another figure had joined them in their bolthole, one who was black-clad and moved in a way that made a cat's tread sound like a one-man band.

Ptaclusp nodded, unable to speak. He had had enough shocks for one day.

'Well, switch it off. Switch it off *now*.'

IIb leaned over.

'Who're you?' he said.

'My name is Teppic.'

'What, like the king?'

'Yes. Just like the king. Now turn it off.'

'It's a pyramid! You can't turn off pyramids!' said IIb.

'Well, then, make it flare.'

'We tried that last night.' IIb pointed to the shattered capstone. 'Unroll Two-Ay, dad.'

Teppic regarded the flat brother.

'It's some sort of wall poster, is it?' he said eventually.

IIb looked down. Teppic saw the movement, and looked down also; he was ankle-deep in green sprouts.

'Sorry,' he said. 'I can't seem to shake it off.'

'It can be dreadful,' said IIb frantically. 'I know how it is, I had this verruca once, nothing would shift it.'

Teppic hunkered down by the cracked stone.

'This thing,' he said. 'What's the significance? I mean, it's coated with metal. Why?'

'There's got to be a sharp point for the flare,' said IIb.

'Is that all? This is gold, isn't it?'

'It's electrum. Gold and silver alloy. The capstone has got to be made of electrum.'

Teppic peeled back the foil.

'This isn't all metal,' he said mildly.

'Yes. Well,' said Ptaclusp. 'We found, er, that foil works just as well.'

'Couldn't you use something cheaper? Like steel?'

Ptaclusp sneered. It hadn't been a good day, sanity was a distant memory, but there were certain facts he knew for a fact.

'Wouldn't last for more than a year or two,' he said. 'What with the dew and so forth. You'd lose the point. Wouldn't last more than two or three hundred times.'

Teppic leaned his head against the pyramid. It was cold, and it hummed. He thought he could hear, under the throbbing, a faint rising tone.

The pyramid towered over him. IIb could have told him that this was because the walls sloped in at precisely 56°, and an effect known as battering made the pyramid loom even higher than it really was. He probably would have used words like perspective and virtual height as well.

The black marble was glassy smooth. The masons had done well. The cracks between each silky panel were hardly wide enough to insert a knife. But wide enough, all the same.

'How about once?' he said.

Koomi chewed his fingernails distractedly.

'Fire,' he said. 'That'd stop them. They're very inflammable. Or water. They'd probably dissolve.'

'Some of them were destroying *pyramids*,' said the high priest of Juf, the Cobra-Headed God of Papyrus.

'People always come back from the dead in such a bad temper,' said another priest.

Koomi watched the approaching army in mounting bewilderment.

'Where's Dios?' he said.

The old high priest was pushed to the front of the crowd.

'What shall I say to them?' Koomi demanded.

It would be wrong to say that Dios smiled. It wasn't an action he often felt called upon to perform. But his mouth creased at the edges and his eyes went half-hooded.

'You could tell them,' he said, 'that new times demand new men. You could tell them that it is time to make way for younger people with fresh ideas. You could tell them that they are outmoded. You could tell them all that.'

'They'll kill me!'

'Would they be that anxious for your eternal company, I wonder?'

'You're still high priest!'

'Why don't you talk to them?' said Dios. 'Don't forget to tell them that they are to be dragged kicking and screaming into the Century of the Cobra.' He handed Koomi the staff. 'Or whatever this century is called,' he added.

Koomi felt the eyes of the assembled brethren and sistren upon him. He cleared his throat, adjusted his robe, and turned to face the mummies.

They were chanting something, one word, over and over again. He couldn't quite make it out, but it seemed to have worked them up into a rage.

He raised the staff, and the carved wooden snakes looked unusually alive in the flat light.

The gods of the Disc – and here is meant the great consensus gods, who really do exist in Dunmanifestin, their semi-detached Valhalla on the world's impossibly high central mountain, where they pass the time observing the petty antics of mortal men and organising petitions about how the influx of the Ice Giants has lowered property values in the celestial regions – the gods of the Disc have always been fascinated by humanity's incredible ability to say exactly the wrong thing at the wrong time.

They're not talking here of such easy errors as 'It's perfectly safe', or 'The ones that growl a lot don't bite', but of simple little sentences which are injected into difficult situations with the same general effect as a steel bar dropped into the bearings of a 3,000 rpm, 660 megawatt steam turbine.

And connoisseurs of mankind's tendency to put his pedal extremity where his tongue should be are agreed that when the judges' envelopes are opened then Hoot Koomi's fine performance in 'Begone from this place, foul shades' will be a contender for all-time bloody stupid greeting.

The front row of ancestors halted, and were pushed forward a little by the press of those behind.

King Teppicymon XXVII, who by common consent among the other twenty-six Teppicymons was spokesman, lurched on alone and picked up the trembling Koomi by his arms.

'What did you say?' he said.

Koomi's eyes rolled. His mouth opened and shut, but his voice wisely decided not to come out.

Teppicymon pushed his bandaged face close to the priest's pointed nose.

'I remember you,' he growled. 'I've seen you oiling around the place. A bad hat, if ever I saw one. I remember thinking that.'

He glared around at the others.

'You're all priests, aren't you? Come to say sorry, have you? *Where's Dios?*'

The ancestors pressed forward, muttering. When you've been dead for hundreds of years, you're not inclined to feel generous to those people who assured you that you were going to have a lovely time. There was a scuffle in the middle of the crowd as King Psamnut-kha, who had spent five thousand years with nothing to look at but the inside of a lid, was restrained by younger colleagues.

Teppicymon switched his attention back to Koomi, who hadn't gone anywhere.

'Foul shades, was it?' he said.

'Er,' said Koomi.

'Put him down.' Dios gently took the staff from Koomi's unresisting fingers and said, 'I am Dios, the high priest. Why are you here?'

It was a perfectly calm and reasonable voice, with overtones of concerned but indubitable authority. It was a tone of voice the pharaohs of Djelibeybi had heard for thousands of years, a voice which had regulated the days, prescribed the rituals, cut the time into carefully-turned segments, interpreted the ways of gods to men. It was the sound of authority, which stirred antique memories among the ancestors and caused them to look embarrassed and shuffle their feet.

One of the younger pharaohs lurched forward.

'You bastard,' he croaked. 'You laid us out and shut us away, one by one, and you went on. People thought the name was passed on but it was always *you*. How *old* are you, Dios?'

There was no sound. No-one moved. A breeze stirred the dust a little.

Dios sighed.

'I did not mean to,' he said. 'There was so much to do. There were never enough hours in the day. Truly, I did not realise what was happening. I thought it was refreshing, nothing more. I suspected nothing, I noted the passing of the rituals, not the years.'

'Come from a long-lived family, do you?' said Teppicymon sarcastically.

Dios stared at him, his lips moving. 'Family,' he said at last, his voice softened from its normal bark. 'Family. Yes. I must have had a family, mustn't I. But, you know, I can't remember. Memory is the first thing that goes. The pyramids don't seem to preserve it, strangely.'

'This is Dios, the footnote-keeper of history?' said Teppicymon.

'Ah.' The high priest smiled. 'Memory goes from the head. But it is all around me. Every scroll and book.'

'That's the history of the kingdom, man!'

'Yes. My memory.'

The king relaxed a little. Sheer horrified fascination was unravelling the knot of fury.

'How old are you?' he said.

'I think . . . seven thousand years. But sometimes it seems much longer.'

'*Really* seven thousand years?'

'Yes,' said Dios.

'How could any man stand it?' said the king.

Dios shrugged.

'Seven thousand years is just one day at a time,' he said.

Slowly, with the occasional wince, he got down on one knee and held up his staff in shaking hands.

'O kings,' he said, 'I have always existed only to serve.'

There was a long, extremely embarrassed pause.

'We will destroy the pyramids,' said Far-re-ptah, pushing forward.

'You will destroy the kingdom,' said Dios. 'I cannot allow it.'

'*You cannot allow it?*'

'Yes. What will we be without the pyramids?' said Dios.

'Speaking for the dead,' said Far-re-ptah, 'we will be free.'

'But the kingdom will be just another small country,' said Dios, and to their horror the ancestors saw tears in his eyes. 'All that we hold dear, you will cast adrift in time. Uncertain. Without guidance. *Changeable.*'

'Then it can take its chances,' said Teppicymon. 'Stand aside, Dios.'

Dios held up his staff. The snakes around it uncoiled and hissed at the king.

'Be still,' said Dios.

Dark lightning crackled between the ancestors. Dios stared at the staff in astonishment; it had never done this before. But seven thousand years of his priests had believed, in their hearts, that the staff of Dios could rule this world and the next.

In the sudden silence there was the faint chink, high up, of a knife being wedged between two black marble slabs.

The pyramid pulsed under Teppic, and the marble was as slippery as ice. The inward slope wasn't the help he had expected.

The thing, he told himself, is not to look up or down, but straight ahead, into the marble, parcelling the impossible height into manageable sections. Just like time. That's how we survive infinity – we kill it by breaking it up into small bits.

He was aware of shouts below him, and glanced briefly over his shoulder. He was barely a third of the way up, but he could see the crowds across the river, a grey mass speckled with the pale blobs of upturned faces. Closer to, the pale army of the dead, facing the small grey group of priests, with Dios in front of them. There was some sort of argument going on.

The sun was on the horizon.

He reached up, located the next crack, found a handhold . . .

Dios spotted Ptaclusp's head peering over the debris, and sent a couple of priests to bring him back. IIb followed, his carefully-folded brother under his arm.

'What is the boy doing?' Dios demanded.

'O Dios, he said he was going to flare off the pyramid,' said Ptaclusp.

'How can he do that?'

'O lord, he says he is going to cap it off before the sun sets.'

'Is it possible?' Dios demanded, turning to the architect. IIb hesitated.

'It may be,' he said.

'And what will happen? Will we return to the world outside?'

'Well, it depends on whether the dimensional effect ratchets, as it were, and is stable in each state, or if, on the contrary, the pyramid is acting as a piece of rubber under tension –'

His voice stuttered to a halt under the intensity of Dios's stare.

'I don't know,' he admitted.

'Back to the world outside,' said Dios. 'Not our world. Our world is the Valley. Ours is a world of order. Men need order.'

He raised his staff.

'That's my son!' shouted Teppicymon. 'Don't you dare try anything! That's the king!'

The ranks of ancestors swayed, but couldn't break the spell.

'Er, Dios,' said Koomi.

Dios turned, his eyebrows raised.

'You spoke?' he said.

'Er, if it *is* the king, er, I – that is, we – think perhaps you should let him get on with it. Er, don't you think that would be a really good idea?'

Dios's staff kicked, and the priests felt the cold bands of restraint freeze their limbs.

'I gave my life for the kingdom,' said the high priest. 'I gave it over and over again. Everything it is, I created. I cannot fail it now.'

And then he saw the gods.

Teppic eased himself up another couple of feet and then gently reached down to pull a knife out of the marble. It wasn't going to work, though. Knife climbing was for those short and awkward passages, and frowned on anyway because it suggested you'd chosen a wrong route. It wasn't for this sort of thing, unless you had unlimited knives.

He glanced over his shoulder again as strange barred shadows flickered across the face of the pyramid.

From out of the sunset, where they had been engaged in their eternal squabbling, the gods were returning.

They staggered and lurched across the fields and reed beds, heading for the pyramid. Near-brainless though they were, they understood what it was. Perhaps they even understood what Teppic was trying to do. Their assorted animal faces made it hard to be certain, but it looked as though they were very angry.

*

'Are you going to control them, Dios?' said the king. 'Are you going to tell them that the world should be changeless?'

Dios stared up at the creatures jostling one another as they waded the river. There were too many teeth, too many lolling tongues. The bits of them that were human were sloughing away. A lion-headed god of justice – Put, Dios recalled the name – was using its scales as a flail to beat one of the river gods. Chefet, the Dog-Headed God of metalwork, was growling and attacking his fellows at random with his hammer; this was Chefet, Dios thought, the god that he had created to be an example to men in the art of wire and filigree and small beauty.

Yet it had worked. He'd taken a desert rabble and shown them all he could remember of the arts of civilisation and the secrets of the pyramids. He'd needed gods then.

The trouble with gods is that after enough people start believing in them, they begin to exist. And what begins to exist isn't what was originally intended.

Chefet, Chefet, thought Dios. Maker of rings, weaver of metal. Now he's out of our heads, and see how his nails grow into claws . . .

This is *not* how I imagined him.

'Stop,' he instructed. 'I order you to stop! You will obey me. I made you!'

They also lack gratitude.

King Teppicymon felt the power around him weaken as Dios turned all his attention to ecclesiastical matters. He saw the tiny shape halfway up the wall of the pyramid, saw it falter.

The rest of the ancestors saw it, too, and as one corpse they knew what to do. Dios could wait.

This was family.

Teppic heard the snap of the handle under his foot, slid a little, and hung by one hand. He'd got another knife in above him but . . . no, no good. He hadn't got the reach. For practical purposes his arms felt like short lengths of wet rope. Now, if he spreadeagled himself as he slid, he might be able to slow enough . . .

He looked down and saw the climbers coming towards him, in a tide that was tumbling *upwards*.

The ancestors rose up the face of the pyramid silently, like creepers, each new row settling into position on the shoulders of the generation beneath, while the younger ones climbed on over them.

Bony hands grabbed Teppic as the wave of edificeers broke around him, and he was half-pushed, half-pulled up the sloping wall. Voices like the creak of sarcophagi filled his ears, moaning encouragement.

'Well done, boy,' groaned a crumbling mummy, hauling him bodily on to its shoulder. 'You remind me of me when I was alive. To you, son.'

'Got him,' said the corpse above, lifting Teppic easily on one outstretched arm. 'That's a fine family spirit, lad. Best wishes from your great-great-great-great uncle, although I don't suppose you remember me. Coming *up*.'

Other ancestors were climbing on past Teppic as he rose from hand to hand. Ancient fingers with a grip like steel clutched at him, hoisting him onwards.

The pyramid grew narrower.

Down below, Ptaclusp watched thoughtfully.

'What a workforce,' he said. 'I mean, the ones at the bottom are supporting the whole weight!'

'Dad,' said IIb. 'I think we'd better run. Those gods are getting closer.'

'Do you think we could employ them?' said Ptaclusp, ignoring him. 'They're dead, they probably won't want high wages, and –'

'Dad!'

'– sort of self-build –'

'You said no more pyramids, dad. Never again, you said. Now come on!'

Teppic scrambled to the top of the pyramid, supported by the last two ancestors. One of them was his father.

'I don't think you've met your great-grandma,' he said, indicating the shorter bandaged figure, who nodded gently at Teppic. He opened his mouth.

'There's no time,' she said. 'You're doing fine.'

He glanced at the sun which, old professional that it was, chose that moment to drop below the horizon. The gods had crossed the river, their progress slowed only by their tendency to push and shove among themselves, and were lurching through the buildings of the necropolis. Several were clustered around the spot where Dios had been.

The ancestors dropped away, sliding back down the pyramid as fast as they had climbed it, leaving Teppic alone on a few square feet of rock.

A couple of stars came out.

He saw white shapes below as the ancestors hurried away on

some private errand of their own, lurching at a surprising speed towards the broad band of the river.

The gods abandoned their interest in Dios, this strange little human with the stick and the cracked voice. The nearest god, a crocodile-headed thing, jerked on to the plaza before the pyramid, squinted up at Teppic, and reached out towards him. Teppic fumbled for a knife, wondering what sort was appropriate for gods . . .

And, along the Djel, the pyramids began to flare their meagre store of hoarded time.

Priests and ancestors fled as the ground began to shake. Even the gods looked bewildered.

IIb snatched his father's arm and dragged him away.

'Come on!' he yelled into his ear. 'We can't be around here when it goes off! Otherwise you'll be put to bed on a coathanger!'

Around them several other pyramids struck their flares, thin and reedy affairs that were barely visible in the afterglow.

'Dad! I said we've got to go!'

Ptaclusp was dragged backwards across the flagstones, still staring at the hulking outline of the Great Pyramid.

'There's someone still there, look,' he said, and pointed to a figure alone on the plaza.

IIb peered into the gloom.

'It's only Dios, the high priest,' he said. 'I expect he's got some plan in mind, best not to meddle in the affairs of priests, now will you *come on*.'

The crocodile-headed god turned its snout back and forth, trying to focus on Teppic without the advantage of binocular vision. This close, its body was slightly transparent, as though someone had sketched in all the lines and got bored before it was time to do the shading. It trod on a small tomb, crushing it to powder.

A hand like a cluster of canoes with claws on hovered over Teppic. The pyramid trembled and the stone under his feet felt warm, but it resolutely forbore from any signs of wanting to flare.

The hand descended. Teppic sank on one knee and, out of desperation, raised the knife over his head in both hands.

The light glinted for a moment off the tip of the blade and *then* the Great Pyramid flared.

It did it in absolute silence to begin with, sending up a spike of eye-torturing flame that turned the whole kingdom into a criss-cross of black shadow and white light, a flame that might have turned any watchers not just into a pillar of salt but into a complete condiment set of their choice. It exploded like an unwound dandelion, silent as starlight, searing as a supernova.

Only after it had been bathing the necropolis in its impossible brilliance for several seconds did the sound come, and it was sound that winds itself up through the bones, creeps into every cell of the body, and tries with some success to turn them inside out. It was too loud to be called noise. There is sound so loud that it prevents itself from being heard, and this was that kind of sound.

Eventually it condescended to drop out of the cosmic scale and became, simply, the loudest noise anyone hearing it had ever experienced.

The noise stopped, filling the air with the dark metallic clang of sudden silence. The light went out, lancing the night with blue and purple afterimages. It was not the silence and darkness of conclusion but of pause, like the moment of equilibrium when a thrown ball runs out of acceleration but has yet to have gravity drawn to its attention and, for a brief moment, thinks that the worst is over.

This time it was heralded by a shrill whistling out of the clear sky and a swirl in the air that became a glow, became a flame, became a flare that sizzled downwards, into the pyramid, punching into the mass of black marble. Fingers of lightning crackled out and grounded on the lesser tombs around it, so that serpents of white fire burned their way from pyramid to pyramid across the necropolis and the air filled with the stink of burning stone.

In the middle of the firestorm the Great Pyramid appeared to lift up a few inches, on a beam of incandescence, and turn through ninety degrees. This was almost certainly the special type of optical illusion which can take place *even though no-one is actually looking at it*.

And then, with deceptive slowness and considerable dignity, it exploded.

It was almost too crass a word. What it did was this: it came apart ponderously into building-sized chunks which drifted gently away from one another, flying serenely out and over the necropolis. Several of them struck other pyramids, badly damaging them in a lazy, unselfconscious way, and then bounded on in silence until they ploughed to a halt behind a small mountain of rubble.

Only then did the boom come. It went on for quite a long time.

*

Grey dust rolled over the kingdom.

Ptaclusp dragged himself upright and groped ahead, gingerly, until he walked into someone. He shuddered when he thought about the kind of people he'd seen walking around lately, but thought didn't come easily because something appeared to have hit him on the head recently . . .

'Is that you, lad?' he ventured.

'Is that you, dad?'

'Yes,' said Ptaclusp.

'It's me, dad.'

'I'm *glad* it's you, son.'

'Can you see anything?'

'No. It's all mist and fog.'

'Thank the gods for that, I thought it was me.'

'It *is* you, isn't it? You said.'

'Yes, dad.'

'Is your brother all right?'

'I've got him safe in my pocket, dad.'

'Good. So long as nothing's happened to him.'

They inched forward, clambering over lumps of masonry they could barely see.

'Something exploded, dad,' said IIb, slowly. 'I think it was the pyramid.'

Ptaclusp rubbed the top of his head, where two tons of flying rock had come within a sixteenth of an inch of fitting him for one of his own pyramids. 'It was that dodgy cement we bought from Merco the Ephebian, I expect –'

'I think this was a bit worse than a moody lintel, dad,' said IIb. 'In fact, I think it was a lot worse.'

'It looked a bit wossname, a bit on the sandy side –'

'I think you should find somewhere to sit down, dad,' said IIb, as kindly as possible. 'Here's Two-Ay. Hang on to him.'

He crept on alone, climbing over a slab of what felt very suspiciously like black marble. What he wanted, he decided, was a priest. They had to be useful for something, and this seemed the sort of time one might need one. For solace, or possibly, he felt obscurely, to beat their head in with a rock.

What he found instead was someone on their hands and knees, coughing. IIb helped him – it was definitely a him, he'd been briefly afraid it might be an it – and sat him on another lump of, yes, almost certainly marble.

'Are you a priest?' he said, fumbling in the rubble.

'I'm Dil. Chief embalmer,' the figure muttered.

'Ptaclusp IIb, paracosmic archi –' IIb began and then, suspecting that architects were not going to be too popular around here for a while, quickly corrected himself. 'I'm an engineer,' he said. 'Are you all right?'

'Don't know. What happened?'

'I think the pyramid exploded,' IIb volunteered.

'Are we dead?'

'I shouldn't think so. You're walking and talking, after all.'

Dil shivered. 'That's no guideline, take it from me. What's an engineer?'

'Oh, a builder of aqueducts,' said IIb quickly. 'They're the coming thing, you know.'

Dil stood up, a little shakily.

'I,' he said, 'need a drink. Let's find the river.'

They found Teppic first.

He was clinging to a small, truncated pyramid section that had made a moderate-sized crater when it landed.

'I know him,' said IIb. 'He's the lad who was on top of the pyramid. That's ridiculous, how could he survive *that*?'

'Why's there all corn sprouting out of it, too?' wondered Dil.

'I mean, perhaps there's some kind of effect if you're right in the centre of the flare, or something,' said IIb, thinking aloud. 'A sort of calm area or something, like in the middle of a whirlpool –' He reached instinctively for his wax tablet, and then stopped himself. Man was never intended to understand things he meddled with. 'Is he dead?' he said.

'Don't look at me,' said Dil, stepping back. He'd been running through his mind the alternative occupations now open to him. Upholstery sounded attractive. At least chairs didn't get up and walk after you'd stuffed them.

IIb bent over the body.

'Look what he's got in his hand,' he said, gently bending back the fingers. 'It's a piece of melted metal. What's he got that for?'

. . . Teppic dreamed.

He saw seven fat cows and seven thin cows, and one of them was riding a bicycle.

He saw some camels, singing, and the song straightened out the wrinkles in reality.

He saw a finger write on the wall of a pyramid: *Going forth is easy. Going back requires (cont. on next wall)* . . .

He walked around the pyramid, where the finger continued: *An effort of will, because it is much harder. Thank you.*

Teppic considered this, and it occurred to him that there was one thing left to do which he had not done. He'd never known how to before, but now he could see that it was just numbers, arranged in a special way. Everything that was magical was just a way of describing the world in words it couldn't ignore.

He gave a grunt of effort.

There was a brief moment of speed.

Dil and IIb looked around as long shafts of light sparkled through the mists and dust, turning the landscape into old gold.

And the sun came up.

The sergeant cautiously opened the hatch in the horse's belly. When the expected flurry of spears did not materialise he ordered Autocue to let out the rope ladder, climbed down it, and looked across the chill morning desert.

The new recruit followed him down and stood, hopping from one sandal to another, on sand that was nearly freezing now and would be frying by lunchtime.

'There,' said the sergeant, pointing, 'see the Tsortean lines, lad?'

'Looks like a row of wooden horses to me, sergeant,' said Autocue. 'The one on the end's on rockers.'

'That'll be the officers. Huh. Those Tsorteans must think we're simple.' The sergeant stamped some life into his legs, took a few breaths of fresh air, and walked back to the ladder.

'Come on, lad,' he said.

'Why've we got to go back up there?'

The sergeant paused, his foot on a rope rung.

'Use some common, laddie. They're not going to come and take our horses if they see us hanging around outside, are they? Stands to reason.'

'You sure they're going to come, then?' said Autocue. The sergeant frowned at him.

'Look, soldier,' he said, 'anyone bloody stupid enough to think we're going to drag a lot of horses full of soldiers back to our city is certainly daft enough to drag *ours* all the way back to *theirs*. QED.'

'QED, sarge?'

'It means get back up the bloody ladder, lad.'

Autocue saluted. 'Permission to be excused first, sarge?'

'Excused what?'

'*Excused*, sarge,' said Autocue, a shade desperately. 'I mean, it's a bit cramped in the horse, sarge, if you know what I mean.'

'You're going to have to learn a bit of will power if you want to stay in the horse soldiers, boy. You know that?'

'Yes, sarge,' said Autocue miserably.

'You've got one minute.'

'Thanks, sarge.'

When the hatch closed above him Autocue sidled over to one of the horse's massive legs and put it to a use for which it wasn't originally intended.

And it was while he was staring vaguely ahead, lost in that Zen-like contemplation which occurs at moments like this, that there was a faint pop in the air and an entire river valley opened up in front of him.

It's not the sort of thing that ought to happen to a thoughtful lad. Especially one who has to wash his own uniform.

A breeze from the sea blew into the kingdom, hinting at, no, positively roaring suggestions of salt, shellfish and sun-soaked tidelines. A few rather puzzled seabirds wheeled over the necropolis, where the wind scurried among the fallen masonry and covered with sand the memorials to ancient kings, and the birds said more with a simple bowel movement than Ozymandias ever managed to say.

The wind had a cool, not unpleasant edge to it. The people out repairing the damage caused by the gods felt an urge to turn their faces towards it, as fish in a pond turn towards an influx of clear, fresh water.

No-one worked in the necropolis. Most of the pyramids had blown their upper levels clean off, and stood smoking gently like recently-extinct volcanoes. Here and there slabs of black marble littered the landscape. One of them had nearly decapitated a fine statue of Hat, the Vulture-Headed God.

The ancestors had vanished. No-one was volunteering to go and look for them.

Around midday a ship came up the Djel under full sail. It was a deceptive ship. It seemed to wallow like a fat and unprotected hippo, and it was only after watching it for some time that anyone would realise that it was also making remarkably fast progress. It dropped anchor outside the palace.

After a while, it let down a dinghy.

*

Teppic sat on the throne and watched the life of the kingdom reassemble itself, like a smashed mirror that is put together again and reflects the same old light in new and unexpected ways.

No-one was quite sure on what basis he *was* on the throne, but no-one else was at all keen on occupying it and it was a relief to hear instructions issued in a clear, confident voice. It is amazing what people will obey, if a clear and confident voice is used, and the kingdom was well used to a clear, confident voice.

Besides, giving orders stopped him thinking about things. Like, for example, what would happen next. But at least the gods had gone back to not existing again, which made it a whole lot easier to believe in them, and the grass didn't seem to be growing under his feet any more.

Maybe I can put the kingdom together again, he thought. But then what can I do with it? If only we could find Dios. He always knew what to do, that was the main thing about him.

A guard pushed his way through the milling throng of priests and nobles.

'Excuse me, your sire,' he said. 'There's a merchant to see you. He says it's urgent.'

'Not now, man. There's representatives of the Tsortean and Ephebian armies coming to see me in an hour, and there's a great deal that's got to be done first. I can't go around seeing any salesmen who happen to be passing. What's he selling, anyway?'

'Carpets, your sire.'

'*Carpets?*'

It was Chidder, grinning like half a watermelon, followed by several of the crew. He walked up the hall staring around at the frescoes and hangings. Because it was Chidder, he was probably costing them out. By the time he reached the throne he was drawing a double line under the total.

'Nice place,' he said, wrapping up thousands of years of architectural accumulation in a mere two syllables. 'You'll never guess what happened, we just happened to be sailing along the coast and suddenly there was this river. One minute cliffs, next minute river. There's a funny thing, I thought. I bet old Teppic's up there somewhere.'

'Where's Ptraci?'

'I knew you were complaining about the lack of the old home comforts, so we brought you this carpet.'

'I *said*, where's Ptraci?'

The crew moved aside, leaving a grinning Alfonz to cut the strings around the carpet and shake it out.

It uncurled swiftly across the floor in a flurry of dust balls and moths and, eventually, Ptraci, who continued rolling until her head hit Teppic's boot.

He helped her to her feet and tried to pick bits of fluff out of her hair as she swayed backwards and forwards. She ignored him and turned to Chidder, red with breathlessness and fury.

'I could have died in there!' she shouted. 'Lots of other things have, by the smell! And the *heat!*'

'You said it worked for Queen wossname, Ram-Jam-Hurrah, or whoever,' said Chidder. 'Don't blame me, at home a necklace or something is usually the thing.'

'I bet *she* had a decent carpet,' snapped Ptraci. 'Not something stuck in a bloody hold for six months.'

'You're lucky we had one at all,' said Chidder mildly. 'It was your idea.'

'Huh,' said Ptraci. She turned to Teppic. 'Hallo,' she said. 'This was meant to be a startling original surprise.'

'It worked,' said Teppic fervently. 'It really worked.'

Chidder lay on a daybed on the palace's wide veranda, while three handmaidens took turns to peel grapes for him. A pitcher of beer stood cooling in the shade. He was grinning amiably.

On a blanket nearby Alfonz lay on his stomach, feeling extremely awkward. The Mistress of the Women had found out that, in addition to the tattoos on his forearms, his back was a veritable illustrated history of exotic practices, and had brought the girls out to be educated. He winced occasionally as her pointer stabbed at items of particular interest, and stuffed his fingers firmly in his great, scarred ears to shut out the giggles.

At the far end of the veranda, given privacy by unspoken agreement, Teppic sat with Ptraci. Things were not going well.

'Everything changed,' he said. 'I'm not going to be king.'

'You *are* the king,' she said. 'You can't change things.'

'I can. I can abdicate. It's very simple. If I'm not really the king, then I can go whenever I please. If I *am* the king, then the king's word is final and I can abdicate. If we can change sex by decree, we can certainly change station. They can find a relative to do the job. I must have dozens.'

'The *job*? Anyway, you said there was only your auntie.'

Teppic frowned. Aunt Cleph-ptah-re was not, on reflection, the kind of monarch a kingdom needed if it was going to make a fresh start. She had a number of stoutly-held views on a variety of subjects, but most of them involved the flaying alive of people she disapproved of. This meant most people under the age of thirty-five, to start with.

'Well, someone else, then,' he said. 'It shouldn't be difficult, we've always seemed to have more nobles than really necessary. We'll just have to find one who has the dream about the cows.'

'Oh, the one where there's fat cows and thin cows?' said Ptraci.

'Yes. It's sort of ancestral.'

'It's a nuisance, I know that much. One of them's always grinning and playing a wimblehorn.'

'It looks like a trombone to me,' said Teppic.

'It's a ceremonial wimblehorn, if you look closely,' she said.

'Well, I expect everyone sees it a bit differently. I don't think it matters.' He sighed, and watched the *Unnamed* unloading. It seemed to have more than the expected number of feather mattresses, and several of the people wandering bemusedly down the gangplank were holding toolboxes and lengths of pipe.

'I think you're going to find it difficult,' said Ptraci. 'You can't say "All those who dream about cows please step forward". It'd give the game away.'

'I can't just hang around until someone happens to mention it, can I? Be reasonable,' he snapped. 'How many people are likely to say, hey, I had this funny dream about cows last night? Apart from you, I mean.'

They stared at one another.

'And she's my *sister*?' said Teppic.

The priests nodded. It was left to Koomi to put it into words. He'd just spent ten minutes going through the files with the Mistress of the Women.

'Her mother was, er, your late father's favourite,' he said. 'He took a great deal of interest in her upbringing, as you know, and, er, it would appear that ... yes. She may be your aunt, of course. The concubines are never very good at paperwork. But most likely your sister.'

She looked at him with tear-filled eyes.

'That doesn't make any difference, does it?' she whispered.

Teppic stared at his feet.

'Yes,' he said. 'I think it does, really.' He looked up at her. 'But you can be queen,' he added. He glared at the priests. 'Can't she,' he stated firmly.

The high priests looked at one another. Then they looked at Ptraci, who stood alone, her shoulders shaking. Small, palace trained, used to taking orders . . . They looked at Koomi.

'She would be ideal,' he said. There was a murmur of suddenly-confident agreement.

'There you are then,' said Teppic, consolingly.

She glared at him. He backed away.

'So I'll be off,' he said, 'I don't need to pack anything, it's all right.'

'Just like that?' she said. 'Is that *all*? Isn't there anything you're going to *say*?'

He hesitated, halfway to the door. You could stay, he told himself. It wouldn't work, though. It'd end up a terrible mess; you'd probably end up splitting the kingdom between you. Just because fate throws you together doesn't mean fate's got it right. Anyway, you've been forth.

'Camels are more important than pyramids,' he said slowly. 'It's something we should always remember.'

He ran for it while she was looking for something to throw.

The sun reached the peak of noon without beetles, and Koomi hovered by the throne like Hat, the Vulture-Headed God.

'It will please your majesty to confirm my succession as high priest,' he said.

'What?' Ptraci was sitting with her chin cupped in one hand. She waved the other hand at him. 'Oh. Yes. All right. Fine.'

'No trace has, alas, been found of Dios. We believe he was very close to the Great Pyramid when it . . . flared.'

Ptraci stared into space. 'You carry on,' she said. Koomi preened.

'The formal coronation will take some time to arrange,' he said, taking the golden mask. 'However, your graciousness will be pleased to wear the mask of authority now, for there is much formal business to be concluded.'

She looked at the mask.

'I'm not wearing that,' she said flatly.

Koomi smiled. 'Your majesty will be pleased to wear the mask of authority,' he said.

'No,' said Ptraci.

Koomi's smile crazed a little around the edges as he attempted to get to grips with this new concept. He was sure Dios had never had this trouble.

He got over the problem by sidling round it. Sidling had stood him in good stead all his life; he wasn't going to desert it now. He put the mask down very carefully on a stool.

'It is the First Hour,' he said. 'Your majesty will wish to conduct the Ritual of the Ibis, and then graciously grant an audience to the military commanders of the Tsortean and Ephebian armies. Both are seeking permission to cross the kingdom. Your majesty will forbid this. At the Second Hour, there will –'

Ptraci sat drumming her fingers on the arms of the throne. Then she took a deep breath. 'I'm going to have a bath,' she said.

Koomi rocked back and forth a bit.

'It is the First Hour,' he repeated, unable to think of anything else. 'Your majesty will wish to conduct –'

'Koomi?'

'Yes, O noble queen?'

'Shut up.'

'– the Ritual of the Ibis –' Koomi moaned.

'I'm sure you're capable of doing it yourself. You look like a man who does things himself, if ever I saw one,' she added sourly.

'– the commanders of the Tsortean –'

'Tell them,' Ptraci began, and then paused. 'Tell them,' she repeated, 'that they may both cross. Not one or the other, you understand? Both.'

'But –' Koomi's understanding managed at last to catch up with his ears – 'that means they'll end up on opposite sides.'

'Good. And after that you can order some camels. There's a merchant in Ephebe with a good stock. Check their teeth first. Oh, and then you can ask the captain of the *Unnamed* to come and see me. He was explaining to me what a "free port" is.'

'In your bath, O queen?' said Koomi weakly. He couldn't help noticing, now, how her voice was changing with each sentence as the veneer of upbringing burned away under the blowlamp of heredity.

'Nothing wrong with that,' she snapped. 'And see about plumbing. Apparently pipes are the thing.'

'For the asses' milk?' said Koomi, who was now totally lost in the desert*.

'Shut up, Koomi.'

---

* A less desiccated culture would have used the phrase 'at sea'.

'Yes, O queen,' said Koomi, miserably.

He'd wanted changes. It was just that he'd wanted things to stay the same, as well.

The sun dropped to the horizon, entirely unaided. For some people, it was turning out to be quite a good day.

The reddened light lit up the three male members of the Ptaclusp dynasty, as they pored over plans for –

'It's called a bridge,' said IIb.

'Is that like an aqueduct?' said Ptaclusp.

'In reverse, sort of thing,' said IIb. 'The water goes underneath, we go over the top.'

'Oh. The k– the queen won't like that,' said Ptaclusp. 'The royal family's always been against chaining the holy river with dams and weirs and suchlike.'

IIb gave a triumphant grin. 'She *suggested* it,' he said. 'And she graciously went on to say, could we see to it there's places for people to stand and drop rocks on the crocodiles.'

'She said that?'

'Large pointy rocks, she said.'

'My word,' said Ptaclusp. He turned to his other son. 'You sure you're all right?' he said.

'Feeling fine, dad,' said IIa.

'No –' Ptaclusp groped – 'headaches or anything?'

'Never felt better,' said IIa.

'Only you haven't asked about the cost,' said Ptaclusp. 'I thought perhaps you were still feeling fl – ill.'

'The queen has been pleased to ask me to have a look at the royal finances,' said IIa. 'She said priests can't add up.' His recent experiences had left him with no ill effects other than a profitable tendency to think at right angles to everyone else, and he sat wreathed in smiles while his mind constructed tariff rates, docking fees and a complex system of value added tax which would shortly give the merchant venturers of Ankh-Morpork a nasty shock.

Ptaclusp thought about all the miles of the virgin Djel, totally unbridged. And there was plenty of dressed stone around now, millions of tons of the stuff. And, you never knew, perhaps on some of those bridges there'd be room for a statue or two. He had the very thing.

He put his arms around his sons' shoulders.

'Lads,' he said proudly. 'It's looking really quantum.'

*

The setting sun also shone on Dil and Gern, although in this case it was by a roundabout route though the lightwell of the palace kitchens. They'd ended up there for no very obvious reason. It was just that it was so depressing in the embalming room, all alone.

The kitchen staff worked around them, recognising the air of impenetrable gloom that surrounded the two embalmers. It was never a very sociable job at the best of times and embalmers didn't make friends easily. Anyway, there was a coronation feast to prepare.

They sat amid the bustle, observing the future over a jug of beer.

'I expect,' said Gern, 'that Gwlenda can have a word with her dad.'

'That's it, boy,' said Dil wearily. 'There's a future there. People will always want garlic.'

'Bloody boring stuff, garlic,' said Gern, with unusual ferocity. 'And you don't get to meet people. That's what I liked about our job. Always new faces.'

'No more pyramids,' said Dil, without rancour. 'That's what she said. You've done a good job, Master Dil, she said, but I'm going to drag this country kicking and screaming into the Century of the Fruitbat.'

'Cobra,' said Gern.

'What?'

'It's the Century of the Cobra. Not the Fruitbat.'

'Whatever,' said Dil irritably. He stared miserably into his mug. That was the trouble now, he reflected. You had to start remembering what century it was.

He glared at a tray of canapes. That was the thing these days. Everyone fiddling about . . .

He picked up an olive and turned it over and over in his fingers.

'Can't say I'd feel the same about the old job, mind,' said Gern, draining the jug, 'but I bet you were proud, master – Dil, I mean. You know, when all your stitching held up like that.'

Dil, his eyes not leaving the olive, reached dreamily down to his belt and grasped one of his smaller knives for intricate jobs.

'I said, you must have felt very sorry it was all over,' said Gern.

Dil swivelled around to get more light, and breathed heavily as he concentrated.

'Still, you'll get over it,' said Gern. 'The important thing is not to let it prey on your mind –'

'Put this stone somewhere,' said Dil.

'Sorry?'

'Put this stone somewhere,' said Dil.

Gern shrugged, and took it out of his fingers.

'Right,' said Dil, his voice suddenly vibrant with purpose. 'Now pass me a piece of red pepper . . .'

And the sun shone on the delta, that little infinity of reed beds and mud banks where the Djel was laying down the silt of the continent. Wading birds bobbed for food in the green maze of stems, and billions of zig-zag midges danced over the brackish water. Here at least time had always passed, as the delta breathed twice daily the cold, fresh water of the tide.

It was coming in now, the foam-crested cusp of it trickling between the reeds.

Here and there soaked and ancient bandages unwound, wriggled for a while like incredibly old snakes and then, with the minimum of fuss, dissolved.

THIS IS MOST IRREGULAR.
We're sorry. It's not our fault.
HOW MANY OF YOU ARE THERE?
More than 1,300, I'm afraid.
VERY WELL, THEN. PLEASE FORM AN ORDERLY QUEUE.

You Bastard was regarding his empty hay rack.

It represented a sub-array in the general cluster 'hay', containing arbitrary values between zero and K.

It didn't have any hay in it. It might in fact have a negative value of hay in it, but to the hungry stomach the difference between no hay and minus-hay was not of particular interest.

It didn't matter how he worked it out, the answer was always the same. It was an equation of classical simplicity. It had a certain clean elegance which he was not, currently, in a position to admire.

You Bastard felt ill-used and hard done by. There was nothing particularly unusual about this, however, since that is the normal state of mind for a camel. He knelt patiently while Teppic packed the saddlebags.

'We'll avoid Ephebe,' Teppic said, ostensibly to the camel. 'We'll go up the end of the Circle Sea, perhaps to Quirm or over the

Ramtops. There's all sorts of places. Maybe we'll even look for a few of those lost cities, eh? I expect you'd like that.'

It's a mistake trying to cheer up camels. You may as well drop meringues into a black hole.

The door at the far end of the stable swung open. It was a priest. He looked rather flustered. The priests had been doing a lot of unaccustomed running around today.

'Er,' he began. 'Her majesty commands you not to leave the kingdom.'

He coughed.

He said, 'Is there a reply?'

Teppic considered. 'No,' he said, 'I don't think so.'

'So I shall tell her that you will be attending on her presently, shall I?' said the priest hopefully.

'No.'

'It's all very well for *you* to say,' said the priest sourly, and slunk off.

He was replaced a few minutes later by Koomi, very red in the face.

'Her majesty requests that you do not leave the kingdom,' he said.

Teppic climbed on to You Bastard's back, and tapped the camel lightly with a prod.

'She really means it,' said Koomi.

'I'm sure she does.'

'She could have you thrown to the sacred crocodiles, you know.'

'I haven't seen many of them around today. How are they?' said Teppic, and gave the camel another thump.

He rode out into the knife-edged daylight and along the packed-earth streets, which time had turned into a surface harder than stone. They were thronged with people. And every single person ignored him.

It was a marvellous feeling.

He rode gently along the road to the border and did not stop until he was up in the escarpment, the valley spreading out behind him. A hot wind off the desert rattled the syphacia bushes as he tethered You Bastard in the shade, climbed a little further up the rocks, and looked back.

The valley was old, so old that you could believe it had existed first and had watched the rest of the world form around it. Teppic lay with his head on his arms.

Of course, it had *made* itself old. It had been gently stripping itself of futures for thousands of years. Now change was hitting it like the ground hitting an egg.

Dimensions were probably more complicated than people thought. Probably so was time. Probably so were people, although people could be more predictable.

He watched the column of dust rise outside the palace and work its way through the city, across the narrow patchwork of fields, disappear for a minute in a group of palm trees near the escarpment, and reappear at the foot of the slope. Long before he could see it he knew there'd be a chariot somewhere in the cloud of sand.

He slid back down the rocks and squatted patiently by the roadside. The chariot rattled by eventually, halted some way on, turned awkwardly in the narrow space, and trundled back.

'What will you *do*?' shouted Ptraci, leaning over the rail.

Teppic bowed.

'And none of that,' she snapped.

'Don't you like being king?'

She hesitated. 'Yes,' she said. 'I do –'

'Of course you do,' said Teppic. 'It's in the blood. In the old days people would fight like tigers. Brothers against sisters, cousins against uncles. Dreadful.'

'But you don't have to go! I *need* you!'

'You've got advisers,' said Teppic mildly.

'I didn't mean that,' she snapped. 'Anyway, there's only Koomi, and he's no good.'

'You're lucky. I had Dios, and he *was* good. Koomi will be much better, you can learn a lot by not listening to what he has to say. You can go a long way with incompetent advisers. Besides, Chidder will help, I'm sure. He's full of ideas.'

She coloured. 'He advanced a few when we were on the ship.'

'There you are, then. I knew the two of you would get along like a house on fire.' Screams, flames, people running for safety . . .

'And you're going back to be an Assassin, are you?' she sneered.

'I don't think so. I've inhumed a pyramid, a pantheon and the entire old kingdom. It may be worth trying something else. By the way, you haven't been finding little green shoots springing up wherever you walk, have you?'

'No. What a stupid idea.'

Teppic relaxed. It really was all over, then. 'Don't let the grass grow under your feet, that's the important thing,' he said. 'And you haven't seen any seagulls around?'

'There's lots of them today, or didn't you notice?'

'Yes. That's good, I think.'

You Bastard watched them talk a little more, that peculiar trailing-off, desultory kind of conversation that two people of opposite sexes engage in when they have something else on their minds. It was much easier with camels, when the female merely had to check the male's methodology.

Then they kissed in a fairly chaste fashion, insofar as camels are any judge. A decision was reached.

You Bastard lost interest at this point, and decided to eat his lunch again.

IN THE BEGINNING . . .

It was peaceful in the valley. The river, its banks as yet untamed, wandered languidly through thickets of rush and papyrus. Ibises waded in the shallows; in the deeps, hippos rose and sank slowly, like pickled eggs.

The only sound in the damp silence was the occasional plop of a fish or hiss of a crocodile.

Dios lay in the mud for some time. He wasn't sure how he'd got there, or why half his robes were torn off and the other half scorched black. He dimly recalled a loud noise and a sensation of extreme speed while, at the same time, he'd been standing still. Right at this moment, he didn't want any answers. Answers implied questions, and questions never got anyone anywhere. Questions only spoiled things. The mud was cool and soothing, and he didn't need to know anything else for a while.

The sun went down. Various nocturnal prowlers wandered near to Dios, and by some animal instinct decided that he certainly wasn't going to be worth all the trouble that would accrue from biting his leg off.

The sun rose again. Herons honked. Mist unspooled between the pools, was burned up as the sky turned from blue to new bronze.

And time unrolled in glorious uneventfulness for Dios until an alien noise took the silence and did the equivalent of cutting it into small pieces with a rusty breadknife.

It was a noise, in fact, like a donkey being chainsawed. As sounds went, it was to melody what a boxful of dates is to high-performance motocross. Nevertheless, as other voices joined it, similar but different, in a variety of fractured keys and broken tones, the overall effect was curiously attractive. It had lure. It had pull. It had a strange suction.

The noise reached a plateau, one pure note made of a succession of discordances, and then, for just the fraction of a second, the voices split away, each along a vector . . .

There was a stirring of the air, a flickering of the sun.

And a dozen camels appeared over the distant hills, skinny and dusty, running towards the water. Birds erupted from the reeds. Leftover saurians slid smoothly off the sandbanks. Within a minute the shore was a mass of churned mud as the knobbly-kneed creatures jostled, nose deep in the water.

Dios sat up, and saw his staff lying in the mud. It was a little scorched, but still intact, and he noticed what somehow had never been apparent before. Before? Had there been a before? There had certainly been a dream, something like a dream . . .

Each snake had its tail in its mouth.

Down the slope after the camels, his ragged family trailing behind him, was a small brown figure waving a camel prod. He looked hot and very bewildered.

He looked, in fact, like someone in need of good advice and careful guidance.

Dios's eyes turned back to the staff. It meant something very important, he knew. He couldn't remember what, though. All he could remember was that it was very heavy, yet at the same time hard to put down. *Very* hard to put down. Better not to pick it up, he thought.

Perhaps just pick it up for a while, and go and explain about gods and why pyramids were so important. And then he could put it down afterwards, certainly.

Sighing, pulling the remnants of his robes around him to give himself dignity, using the staff to steady himself, Dios went forth.

SMALL GODS

Now consider the tortoise and the eagle.

The tortoise is a ground-living creature. It is impossible to live nearer the ground without being under it. Its horizons are a few inches away. It has about as good a turn of speed as you need to hunt down a lettuce. It has survived while the rest of evolution flowed past it by being, on the whole, no threat to anyone and too much trouble to eat.

And then there is the eagle. A creature of the air and high places, whose horizons go all the way to the edge of the world. Eyesight keen enough to spot the rustle of some small and squeaky creature half a mile away. All power, all control. Lightning death on wings. Talons and claws enough to make a meal of anything smaller than it is and at least take a hurried snack out of anything bigger.

And yet the eagle will sit for hours on the crag and survey the kingdoms of the world until it spots a distant movement and then it will focus, focus, *focus* on the small shell wobbling among the bushes down there on the desert. And it will *leap* . . .

And a minute later the tortoise finds the world dropping away from it. And it sees the world for the first time, no longer one inch from the ground but five hundred feet above it, and it thinks: what a great friend I have in the eagle.

And then the eagle lets go.

And almost always the tortoise plunges to its death. Everyone knows why the tortoise does this. Gravity is a habit that is hard to shake off. No one knows why the eagle does this. There's good eating on a tortoise but, considering the effort involved, there's much better eating on practically anything else. It's simply the delight of eagles to torment tortoises.

But of course, what the eagle does not realise is that it is participating in a very crude form of natural selection.

One day a tortoise will learn how to fly.

The story takes place in desert lands, in shades of umber and orange. When it begins and ends is more problematical, but at least one of its beginnings took place above the snowline, thousands of miles away in the mountains around the Hub.*

One of the recurring philosophical questions is:

'Does a falling tree in the forest make a sound when there is no one to hear?'

Which says something about the nature of philosophers, because there is always someone in a forest. It may only be a badger, wondering what that cracking noise was, or a squirrel a bit puzzled by all the scenery going upwards, but *someone*. At the very least, if it was deep enough in the forest, millions of small gods would have heard it.

Things just happen, one after another. They don't care who knows. But *history* ... ah, history is different. History has to be observed. Otherwise it's not history. It's just ... well, things happening one after another.

And, of course, it has to be controlled. Otherwise it might turn into anything. Because history, contrary to popular theories, *is* kings and dates and battles. And these things have to happen at the right time. This is difficult. In a chaotic universe there are too many things to go wrong. It's too easy for a general's horse to lose a shoe at the wrong time, or for someone to mishear an order, or for the carrier of the vital message to be waylaid by some men with sticks and a cash flow problem. Then there are wild stories, parasitic growths on the tree of history, trying to bend it their way.

So history has its caretakers.

They live ... well, in the nature of things they live wherever they are sent, but their *spiritual* home is in a hidden valley in the high Ramtops of the Discworld, where the books of history are kept.

These aren't books in which the events of the past are pinned like so many butterflies to a cork. These are the books from which history is derived. There are more than twenty thousand of them; each one is ten feet high, bound in lead, and the letters are so small that they have to be read with a magnifying glass.

When people say 'It is written ...' it is written *here*.

There are fewer metaphors around than people think.

Every month the abbot and two senior monks go into the cave where the books are kept. It used to be the duty of the abbot alone, but two other reliable monks were included after the unfortunate case of the 59th Abbot, who made a million dollars in small bets before his fellow monks caught up with him.

---

* Or, if you are a believer in Omnianism, the Pole.

Besides, it's dangerous to go in alone. The sheer concentratedness of History, sleeting past soundlessly out into the world, can be overwhelming. Time is a drug. Too much of it kills you.

The 493rd Abbot folded his wrinkled hands and addressed Lu-Tze, one of his most senior monks. The clear air and untroubled life of the secret valley was such that all the monks were senior; besides, when you work with Time every day, some of it tends to rub off.

'The place is Omnia,' said the abbot, 'on the Klatchian coast.'

'I remember,' said Lu-Tze. 'Young fellow called Ossory, wasn't there?'

'Things must be . . . *carefully observed*,' said the abbot. 'There are pressures. Free will, predestination . . . the power of symbols . . . turning-point . . . you know all about this.'

'Haven't been to Omnia for, oh, must be seven hundred years,' said Lu-Tze. 'Dry place. Shouldn't think there's a ton of good soil in the whole country, either.'

'Off you go, then,' said the abbot.

'I shall take my mountains,' said Lu-Tze. 'The climate will be good for them.'

And he also took his broom and his sleeping mat. The history monks don't go in for possessions. They find most things wear out in a century or two.

It took him four years to get to Omnia. He had to watch a couple of battles and an assassination on the way, otherwise they would just have been random events.

It was the Year of the Notional Serpent, or two hundred years after the Declaration of the Prophet Abbys.

Which meant that the time of the 8th Prophet was imminent.

That was the reliable thing about the Church of the Great God Om. It had very punctual prophets. You could set your calendar by them, if you had one big enough.

And, as is generally the case around the time a prophet is expected, the Church redoubled its efforts to be holy. This was very much like the bustle you get in any large concern when the auditors are expected, but tended towards taking people suspected of being less holy and putting them to death in a hundred ingenious ways. This is considered a reliable barometer of the state of one's piety in most of the really popular religions. There's a tendency to declare that there is more backsliding around than in the national toboggan championships, that heresy must be torn out root and branch, and even arm and leg and eye and tongue, and that it's time to wipe the slate clean. Blood is generally considered very efficient for this purpose.

And it came to pass that in that time the Great God Om spake unto Brutha, the Chosen One:
'Psst!'
Brutha paused in mid-hoe and stared around the Temple garden.
'Pardon?' he said.
It was a fine day early in the lesser Spring. The prayer mills spun merrily in the breeze off the mountains. Bees loafed around in the bean blossoms, but buzzed fast in order to give the impression of hard work. High above, a lone eagle circled.
Brutha shrugged, and got back to the melons.
Yea, the Great God Om spake again unto Brutha, the Chosen One:
'Psst!'
Brutha hesitated. Someone had definitely spoken to him from out of the air. Perhaps it was a demon. Novice master Brother Nhumrod was hot on the subject of demons. Impure thoughts and demons. One led to the other. Brutha was uncomfortably aware that he was probably overdue a demon.
The thing to do was to be resolute and repeat the Nine Fundamental Aphorisms.
Once more the Great God Om spake unto Brutha, the Chosen One:
'Are you deaf, boy?'
The hoe thudded on to the baking soil. Brutha spun around. There were the bees, the eagle and, at the far end of the garden, old Brother Lu-Tze dreamily forking over the dung heap. The prayer mills whirled reassuringly along the walls.
He made the sign with which the Prophet Ishkible had cast out spirits.
'Get thee behind me, demon,' he muttered.
'I *am* behind you.'
Brutha turned again, slowly. The garden was still empty.
He fled.

Many stories start long before they begin, and Brutha's story had its origins thousands of years before his birth.
There are billions of gods in the world. They swarm as thick as

herring roe. Most of them are too small to see and never get worshipped, at least by anything bigger than bacteria, who never say their prayers and don't demand much in the way of miracles.

They are the small gods – the spirits of places where two ant trails cross, the gods of microclimates down between the grass roots. And most of them stay that way.

Because what they lack is *belief*.

A handful, though, go on to greater things. Anything may trigger it. A shepherd, seeking a lost lamb, finds it among the briars and takes a minute or two to build a small cairn of stones in general thanks to whatever spirits might be around the place. Or a peculiarly shaped tree becomes associated with a cure for disease. Or someone carves a spiral on an isolated stone. Because what gods need is belief, and what humans want is gods.

Often it stops there. But sometimes it goes further. More rocks are added, more stones are raised, a temple is built on the site where the tree once stood. The god grows in strength, the belief of its worshippers raising it upwards like a thousand tons of rocket fuel. For a very few, the sky's the limit.

And, sometimes, not even that.

Brother Nhumrod was wrestling with impure thoughts in the privacy of his severe cell when he heard the fervent voice from the novitiates' dormitory.

The Brutha boy was flat on his face in front of a statue of Om in His manifestation as a thunderbolt, shaking and gabbling fragments of prayer.

There was something creepy about that boy, Nhumrod thought. It was the way he looked at you when you were talking, as if he was *listening*.

He wandered out and prodded the prone youth with the end of his cane.

'Get up, boy! What do you think you're doing in the dormitory in the middle of the day? Mmm?'

Brutha managed to spin around while still flat on the floor and grasped the priest's ankles.

'Voice! A voice! It *spoke* to me!' he wailed.

Nhumrod breathed out. Ah. This was familiar ground. Voices were right up Nhumrod's cloister. He heard them all the time.

'Get up, boy,' he said, slightly more kindly.

Brutha got to his feet.

He was, as Nhumrod had complained before, too old to be a proper novice. About ten years too old. Give me a boy up to the age of seven, Nhumrod had always said.

But Brutha was going to die a novice. When they made the rules, they'd never allowed for anything like Brutha.

His big red honest face stared up at the novice master.

'Sit down on your bed, Brutha,' said Nhumrod.

Brutha obeyed immediately. Brutha did not know the meaning of the word disobedience. It was only one of a large number of words he didn't know the meaning of.

Nhumrod sat down beside him.

'Now, Brutha,' he said, 'you know what happens to people who tell falsehoods, don't you?'

Brutha nodded, blushing.

'Very well. Now tell me about these voices.'

Brutha twisted the hem of his robe in his hands.

'It was more like one voice, master,' he said.

'– like one voice,' said Brother Nhumrod. 'And what did this voice say? Mmm?'

Brutha hesitated. Now he came to think about it, the voice hadn't *said* anything very much. It had just spoken. It was in any case hard to talk to Brother Nhumrod, who had a nervous habit of squinting at the speaker's lips and repeating the last few words they said practically as they said them. He also touched things all the time – walls, furniture, people – as if he was afraid the universe would disappear if he didn't keep hold of it. And he had so many nervous tics that they had to queue. Brother Nhumrod was perfectly normal for someone who had survived in the Citadel for fifty years.

'Well . . .' Brutha began.

Brother Nhumrod held up a skinny hand. Brutha could see the pale blue veins in it.

'And I am sure you know that there are *two* kinds of voice that are heard by the spiritual,' said the master of novices. One eyebrow began to twitch.

'Yes, master. Brother Murduck told us that,' said Brutha, meekly.

'– told us that. Yes. Sometimes, as He in His infinite wisdom sees fit, the God speaks to a chosen one and he becomes a great prophet,' said Nhumrod. 'Now, I am sure you wouldn't presume to consider yourself one of them? Mmm?'

'No, master.'

'– master. But there are *other* voices,' said Brother Nhumrod, and now his voice had a slight tremolo, 'beguiling and wheedling and persuasive voices, yes? Voices that are always waiting to catch us off our guard?'

Brutha relaxed. This was more familiar ground.

All the novices knew about *those* kinds of voices. Except that usually they talked about fairly straightforward things, like the pleasures of night-time manipulation and the general desirability of girls. Which showed that they were novices when it came to voices. Brother Nhumrod got the kind of voices that were, by comparison, a full oratorio. Some of the bolder novices liked to get Brother Nhumrod talking on the subject of voices. He was an education, they said. Especially when little bits of white spit appeared at the corners of his mouth.

Brutha listened.

Brother Nhumrod was the novice master, but he wasn't *the* novice master. He was only master of the group that included Brutha. There were others. Possibly someone in the Citadel knew how many there were. There was someone somewhere whose job it was to know *everything*.

The Citadel occupied the whole of the heart of the city of Kom, in the lands between the deserts of Klatch and the plains and jungles of Howondaland. It extended for miles, its temples, churches, schools, dormitories, gardens and towers growing into and around one another in a way that suggested a million termites all trying to build their mounds at the same time.

When the sun rose the reflection of the doors of the central Temple blazed like fire. They were bronze, and a hundred feet tall. On them, in letters of gold set in lead, were the Commandments. There were five hundred and twelve so far, and doubtless the next prophet would add his share.

The sun's reflected glow shone down and across the tens of thousands of the strong-in-faith who laboured below for the greater glory of the Great God Om.

Probably no one *did* know how many of them there were. Some things have a way of going critical. Certainly there was only one Cenobiarch, the Superior Iam. That was certain. And six Archpriests. And thirty lesser Iams. And hundreds of bishops, deacons, subdeacons and priests. And novices like rats in a grain store. And craftsmen, and bull breeders, and torturers, and Vestigial Virgins . . .

No matter what your skills, there was a place for you in the Citadel.

And if your skill lay in asking the wrong kinds of questions or losing the righteous kind of wars, the place might just be the furnaces of purity, or the Quisition's pits of justice.

A place for everyone. And everyone in their place.

The sun beat down on the temple garden.

The Great God Om tried to stay in the shade of a melon vine. He was probably safe here, here inside these walls and with the prayer towers all around, but you couldn't be too careful. He'd been lucky once, but it was asking too much to expect to be lucky again.

The trouble with being a god is that you've got no one to pray to.

He crawled forward purposefully towards the old man shovelling muck until, after much exertion, he judged himself to be within earshot.

He spake thusly: 'Hey, you!'

There was no answer. There was not even any suggestion that anything had been heard.

Om lost his temper and turned Lu-Tze into a lowly worm in the deepest cesspit of hell, and then got even more angry when the old man went on peacefully shovelling.

'The devils of infinity fill your living bones with sulphur!' he screamed.

This did not make a great deal of difference.

'Deaf old bugger,' muttered the Great God Om.

Or perhaps there was someone who *did* know all there was to be known about the Citadel. There's always someone who collects knowledge, not because of a love of the stuff but in the same way that a magpie collects glitter or a caddis fly collects little bits of twigs and rock. And there's always someone who has to do all those things that need to be done but which other people would rather not do or, even, acknowledge existed.

The third thing the people noticed about Vorbis was his height. He was well over six feet tall, but stick-thin, like a normal proportioned person modelled in clay by a child and then rolled out.

The second thing that people noticed about Vorbis was his eyes.

His ancestors had come from one of the deep desert tribes that had evolved the peculiar trait of having dark eyes – not just dark of pupil, but almost black of eyeball. It made it very hard to tell where he was looking. It was as if he had sunglasses on under his skin.

But the first thing they noticed was his skull.

Deacon Vorbis was bald by design. Most of the Church's ministers, as soon as they were ordained, cultivated long hair and beards that you could lose a goat in. But Vorbis shaved all over. He gleamed. And lack of hair seemed to add to his power. He didn't menace. He never threatened. He just gave everyone the feeling that his personal space radiated several metres from his body, and that anyone approaching Vorbis was intruding on something important. Superiors fifty years his senior felt apologetic about interrupting whatever it was he was thinking about.

It was almost impossible to know what he was thinking about and no one ever asked. The most obvious reason for this was that Vorbis was the head of the Quisition, whose job it was to do all those things that needed to be done and which other people would rather not do.

You do not ask people like that what they are thinking about in case they turn around very slowly and say 'You'.

The highest post that could be held in the Quisition was that of deacon, a rule instituted hundreds of years ago to prevent this branch of the Church becoming too big for its boots.* But with a mind like his, everyone said, he could easily be an archpriest by now, or even an Iam.

Vorbis didn't worry about that kind of trivia. Vorbis knew his destiny. Hadn't the God himself told him?

'There,' said Brother Nhumrod, patting Brutha on the shoulder. 'I'm sure you will see things clearer now.'

Brutha felt that a specific reply was expected.

'Yes, master,' he said. 'I'm sure I shall.'

'– shall. It is your holy duty to resist the voices at all times,' said Nhumrod, still patting.

'Yes, master. I will. Especially if they tell me to do any of the things you mentioned.'

'– mentioned. Good. Good. And if you hear them again, what will you do? Mmm?'

---

* Which were of the one-size-fits-all, tighten-the-screws variety.

'Come and tell you,' said Brutha, dutifully.

'– tell you. Good. Good. That's what I like to hear,' said Nhumrod. 'That's what I tell all my boys. Remember that I'm always here to deal with any little problems that may be bothering you.'

'Yes, master. Shall I go back to the garden now?'

'– now. I think so. I think so. And no more voices, d'you hear?' Nhumrod waved a finger of his non-patting hand. A cheek puckered.

'Yes, master.'

'What were you doing in the garden?'

'Hoeing the melons, master,' said Brutha.

'Melons? Ah. Melons,' said Nhumrod slowly. 'Melons. Melons. Well, that goes some way towards explaining things, of course.'

An eyelid flickered madly.

It wasn't just the Great God that spoke to Vorbis, in the confines of his head. *Everyone* spoke to an exquisitor, sooner or later. It was just a matter of stamina.

Vorbis didn't often go down to watch the inquisitors at work these days. Exquisitors didn't have to. He sent down instructions, he received reports. But special circumstances merited his special attention.

It has to be said . . . there was little to laugh at in the cellar of the Quisition. Not if you had a normal sense of humour. There were no jolly little signs saying: You Don't Have To Be Pitilessly Sadistic To Work Here But It Helps!!!

But there were things to suggest to a thinking man that the Creator of mankind had a very oblique sense of fun indeed, and to breed in his heart a rage to storm the gates of heaven.

The mugs, for example. The inquisitors stopped work twice a day for coffee. Their mugs, which each man had brought from home, were grouped around the kettle on the hearth of the central furnace which incidentally heated the irons and knives.

They had legends on them like A Present From the Holy Grotto of Ossory, or To The World's Greatest Daddy. Most of them were chipped, and no two of them were the same.

And there were the postcards on the wall. It was traditional that, when an inquisitor went on holiday, he'd send back a crudely coloured woodcut of the local view with some suitably jolly and risqué message on the back. And there was the pinned-up tearful letter from Inquisitor First Class Ishmale 'Pop' Quoom, thanking all the lads for collecting no fewer than seventy-eight *obols* for his retirement present and the lovely bunch of flowers for Mrs Quoom, indicating that he'd always remember his days in No. 3 pit, and was looking forward to coming in and helping out any time they were short-handed.

And it all meant this: that there are hardly any excesses of the most crazed psychopath that cannot easily be duplicated by a normal, kindly family man who just comes in to work every day and has a job to do.

Vorbis loved knowing that. A man who knew that, knew everything he needed to know about people.

Currently he was sitting alongside the bench on which lay what was still, technically, the trembling body of Brother Sasho, formerly his secretary.

He looked up at the duty inquisitor, who nodded. Vorbis leaned over the chained secretary.

'What were their names?' he repeated.

'. . . don't know . . .'

'I know you gave them copies of my correspondence, Sasho. They are treacherous heretics who will spend eternity in the hells. Will you join them?'

'. . . don't know names . . .'

'I trusted you, Sasho. You spied on me. You betrayed the Church.'

'. . . no names . . .'

'Truth is surcease from pain, Sasho. Tell me.'

'. . . truth . . .'

Vorbis sighed. And then he saw one of Sasho's fingers curling and uncurling under the manacles. Beckoning.

'Yes?'

He leaned closer over the body.

Sasho opened his one remaining eye.

'. . . truth . . .'

'Yes?'

'. . . The Turtle Moves . . .'

Vorbis sat back, his expression unchanged. His expression seldom changed unless he wanted it to. The inquisitor watched him in terror.

'I see,' said Vorbis. He stood up, and nodded at the inquisitor.

'How long has he been down here?'

'Two days, lord.'

'And you can keep him alive for –?'

'Perhaps two days more, lord.'

'Do so. Do so. It is, after all,' said Vorbis, 'our duty to preserve life for as long as possible. Is it not?'

The inquisitor gave him the nervous smile of one in the presence of a superior whose merest word could see him manacled on a bench.

'Er . . . yes, lord.'

'Heresy and lies everywhere,' Vorbis sighed. 'And now I shall have to find another secretary. It is too vexing.'

After twenty minutes Brutha relaxed. The siren voices of sensuous evil seemed to have gone away.

He got on with the melons. He felt capable of understanding melons. Melons seemed a lot more comprehensible than most things.

'Hey, you!'

Brutha straightened up.

'I do not hear you, oh foul succubus,' he said.

'Oh yes you do, boy. Now, what I want you to do is –'

'I've got my fingers in my ears!'

'Suits you. Suits you. Makes you look like a vase. Now –'

'I'm humming a tune! I'm humming a tune!'

Brother Preptil, the master of the music, had described Brutha's voice as putting him in mind of a disappointed vulture arriving too late at the dead donkey. Choral singing was compulsory for novitiates, but after much petitioning by Brother Preptil a special dispensation had been made for Brutha. The sight of his big round face screwed up in the effort to please was bad enough, but what was worse was listening to his voice, which was certainly powerful and full of intent conviction, swinging backwards and forwards across the tune without ever quite hitting it.

He got Extra Melons instead.

Up in the prayer towers a flock of crows took off in a hurry.

After a full chorus of *He is Trampling the Unrighteous with Hooves of Hot Iron* Brutha unplugged his ears and risked a quick listen.

Apart from the distant protests of the crows, there was silence.

It worked. Put your trust in the God, they said. And he always had. As far back as he could remember.

He picked up his hoe and turned back, in relief, to the vines.

The hoe's blade was about to hit the ground when Brutha saw the tortoise.

It was small and basically yellow and covered with dust. Its shell was badly chipped. It had one beady eye – the other had fallen to one of the thousands of dangers that attend any slow-moving creature which lives an inch from the ground.

He looked around. The gardens were well inside the temple complex, and surrounded by high walls.

'How did you get in here, little creature?' he said. 'Did you fly?'

The tortoise stared monoptically at him. Brutha felt a bit homesick. There had been plenty of tortoises in the sandy hills back home.

'I could give you some lettuce,' said Brutha. 'But I don't think tortoises are allowed in the gardens. Aren't you vermin?'

The tortoise continued to stare. Practically nothing can stare like a tortoise.

Brutha felt obliged to do something.

'There's grapes,' he said. 'Probably it's not sinful to give you one grape. How would you like a grape, little tortoise?'

'How would you like to be an abomination in the nethermost pit of chaos?' said the tortoise.

The crows, who had fled to the outer walls, took off again to a rendering of *The Way of the Infidel Is A Nest Of Thorns*.

Brutha opened his eyes and took his fingers out of his ears again.

The tortoise said, 'I'm still here.'

Brutha hesitated. It dawned on him, very slowly, that demons and succubi didn't turn up looking like small old tortoises. There wouldn't be much point. Even Brother Nhumrod would have to agree that when it came to rampant eroticism, you could do a lot better than a one-eyed tortoise.

'I didn't know tortoises could talk,' he said.

'They can't,' said the tortoise. 'Read my lips.'

Brutha looked closer.

'You haven't got lips,' he said.

'No, nor proper vocal chords,' agreed the tortoise. 'I'm doing it straight into your head, do you understand?'

'Gosh!'

'You *do* understand, don't you?'

'No.'

The tortoise rolled its eye.

'I should have known. Well, it doesn't matter. I don't have to waste time on gardeners. Go and fetch the top man, right now.'

'Top man?' said Brutha. He put his hand to his mouth. 'You don't mean ... Brother Nhumrod?'

'Who's he?' said the tortoise.

'The master of the novices!'

'Oh, *Me*!' said the tortoise. 'No,' it went on, in a singsong imitation of Brutha's voice, 'I don't mean the master of the novices. I mean the High Priest or whatever he calls himself. I suppose there *is* one?'

Brutha nodded blankly.

'High Priest, right?' said the tortoise. 'High. Priest. High Priest.'

Brutha nodded again. He knew there was a High Priest. It was just that, while he could just about encompass the hierarchical structure between his own self and Brother Nhumrod, he was unable to give serious consideration to any kind of link between Brutha the novice and the Cenobiarch. He was theoretically aware that there was one, that there was a huge canonical structure with the High Priest at the top and Brutha very firmly at the bottom, but he viewed it in the same way as an amoeba might view the chain of evolution all the way between itself and, for example, a chartered accountant. It was missing links all the way to the top.

'I can't go asking the –' Brutha hesitated. Even the *thought* of talking to the Cenobiarch frightened him into silence. 'I can't ask *anyone* to ask the High Cenobiarch to come and talk to a *tortoise*!'

'Turn into a mud leech and wither in the fires of retribution!' screamed the tortoise.

'There's no need to curse,' said Brutha.

The tortoise bounced up and down furiously.

'That wasn't a curse! That was an order! I am the Great God Om!'

Brutha blinked.

Then he said, 'No you're not. I've seen the Great God Om,' he waved a hand making the shape of the holy horns, conscientiously, 'and he isn't tortoise-shaped. He comes as an eagle, or a lion, or a mighty bull. There's a statue in the Great Temple. It's seven cubits high. It's got bronze on it and everything. It's trampling infidels. You can't trample infidels when you're a tortoise. I mean, all you could do is give them a meaningful look. It's got horns of real gold. Where I used to live there was a statue one cubit high in the next village and that was a bull too. So that's how I know you're not the Great God' – holy horns – 'Om.'

The tortoise subsided.

'How many talking tortoises have you met?' it said sarcastically.

'I don't know,' said Brutha.

'What d'you mean, you don't know?'

'Well, they might all talk,' said Brutha conscientiously, demonstrating the very personal kind of logic that got him Extra Melons. 'They just might not say anything when I'm there.'

'I am the Great God Om,' said the tortoise, in a menacing and unavoidably low voice, 'and before very long you are going to be a very unfortunate priest. Go and get him.'

'Novice,' said Brutha.

'What?'

'Novice, not priest. They won't let me –'

'Get him!'

'But I don't think the Cenobiarch ever comes into our vegetable garden,' said Brutha. 'I don't think he even knows what a melon *is*.'

'I'm not bothered about that,' said the tortoise. 'Fetch him now, or there will be a shaking of the earth, the moon will be as blood, agues and boils will afflict mankind and divers ills will befall. I really mean it,' it added.

'I'll see what I can do,' said Brutha, backing away.

'And I'm being very reasonable, in the circumstances!' the tortoise shouted after him.

'You don't sing badly, mind you!' it added, as an afterthought.

'I've heard worse!' as Brutha's grubby robe disappeared through the gateway.

'Puts me in mind of that time there was the affliction of plague in Pseudopolis,' it said quietly, as the footsteps faded. 'What a wailing and a gnashing of teeth was there, all right.' It sighed. 'Great days. Great days!'

Many feel they are called to the priesthood, but what they really hear is an inner voice saying, 'It's indoor work with no heavy lifting, do you want to be a ploughman like your father?'

Whereas Brutha didn't just believe. He really Believed. That sort of thing is usually embarrassing when it happens in a God-fearing family, but all Brutha had was his grandmother, and she Believed too. She believed like iron believes in metal. She was the kind of woman every priest dreads in a congregation, the one who knows all the chants, all the sermons. In the Omnian Church women were allowed in the temple only on sufferance, and had to keep absolutely silent and well covered-up in their own section behind the pulpit in case the sight of one half of the human race caused the male members of the congregation to hear voices not unakin to those that plagued Brother Nhumrod through every sleeping and waking hour. The problem was that Brutha's grandmother had the kind of personality that can project itself through a lead sheet and a bitter piety with the strength of a diamond-bit auger.

If she had been born a man, Omnianism would have found its 8th Prophet rather earlier than expected. As it was, she organised the temple-cleaning, statue-polishing and stoning-of-suspected-adulteresses rotas with a terrible efficiency.

So Brutha grew up in the sure and certain knowledge of the Great God Om. Brutha grew up *knowing* that Om's eyes were on him all the time, especially in places like the privy, and that demons assailed him on all sides and were only kept at bay by the strength of his belief and the weight of grandmother's cane, which was kept behind the door on those rare occasions when it was not being used. He could recite every verse in all seven Books of the Prophets, and every single Precept. He knew all the Laws and the Songs. Especially the Laws.

The Omnians were a God-fearing people.

They had a great deal to fear.

Vorbis's room was in the upper Citadel, which was unusual for a mere deacon. He hadn't asked for it. He seldom had to ask for anything. Destiny has a way of marking her own.

He also got visited by some of the most powerful men in the Church's hierarchy.

Not, of course, the six Archpriests or the Cenobiarch himself. They weren't that important. They were merely at the top. The people who really run organisations are usually found several levels down, where it's still possible to get things done.

People liked to be friends with Vorbis, mainly because of the aforesaid mental field which suggested to them, in the subtlest of ways, that they didn't want to be his enemy.

Two of them were sitting down with him now. They were General Iam Fri'it, who whatever the official records might suggest was the man who ran most of the Divine Legion, and Bishop Drunah, secretary to the Congress of Iams. People might not think that was much of a position of power, but then they'd never been minutes secretary to a meeting of slightly deaf old men.

Neither man was in fact there. They were not talking to Vorbis. It was one of *those* kinds of meeting. Lots of people didn't talk to Vorbis, and went out of their way not have meetings with him. Some of the abbots from the distant monasteries had recently been summoned to the Citadel, travelling secretly for up to a week across tortuous terrain, just so they definitely wouldn't join the shadowy figures visiting Vorbis's room. In the last few months, Vorbis had apparently had about as many visitors as the Man in the Iron Mask.

Nor were they talking. But if they *had* been there, and if they *had* been having a conversation, it would have gone like this:

'And now,' said Vorbis, 'the matter of Ephebe.'

Bishop Drunah shrugged.*

'Of no consequence, they say. No threat.'

The two men looked at Vorbis, a man who never raised his voice. It was very hard to tell what Vorbis was thinking, often even after he had told you.

'Really? Is this what we've come to?' he said. 'No *threat*? After what they did to poor Brother Murduck? The insults to Om? This must not pass. What is proposed to be done?'

'No more fighting,' said Fri'it. 'They fight like madmen. No. We've lost too many already.'

'They have strong gods,' said Drunah.

'They have better bows,' said Fri'it.

'There is no God but Om,' said Vorbis. 'What the Ephebians believe they worship are nothing but djinns and demons. If it can be called worship. Have you seen this?'

He pushed forward a scroll of paper.

'What is it?' said Fri'it cautiously.

'A lie. A history that does not exist and never existed ... the ... the things ...' Vorbis hesitated, trying to remember a word that had long since fallen into disuse, '... like the ... tales told to children, who are too young ... words for people to say ... the ...'

'Oh. A play,' said Fri'it. Vorbis's gaze nailed him to the wall.

'You know of these things?'

'I – when I travelled in Klatch once –' Fri'it stuttered. He visibly pulled himself together. He had commanded one hundred thousand men in battle. He didn't deserve this.

He found he didn't dare look at Vorbis's expression.

'They dance dances,' he said limply. 'On their holy days. The women have bells on their ... And sing songs. All about the early days of the worlds, when the gods –'

He faded. 'It was disgusting,' he said. He clicked his knuckles, a habit of his whenever he was worried.

---

* Or would have done. If he had been there. But he wasn't. So he couldn't.

'*This* one has their gods in it,' said Vorbis. '*Men* in *masks*. Can you believe that? They have a god of *wine*. A drunken old man! And people say Ephebe is no threat! And this –'

He tossed another, thicker scroll on to the table.

'*This* is far worse. For while they worship false gods in error, their error is in their choice of gods, not in their worship. But this –'

Drunah gave it a cautious examination.

'I believe there are other copies, even in the Citadel,' said Vorbis. 'This one belonged to Sasho. I believe you recommended him to my service, Fri'it?'

'He always struck me as an intelligent and keen young man,' said the general.

'But disloyal,' said Vorbis, 'and now receiving his just reward. It is only to be regretted that he has not been induced to give us the names of his fellow heretics.'

Fri'it fought against the sudden rush of relief. His eyes met those of Vorbis.

Drunah broke the silence.

'*De Chelonian Mobile*,' he said aloud. '"The Turtle Moves". What does that mean?'

'Even telling you could put your soul at risk of a thousand years in hell,' said Vorbis. His eyes had not left Fri'it, who was now staring fixedly at the wall.

'I think it is a risk we might carefully take,' said Drunah.

Vorbis shrugged. 'The writer claims that the world . . . travels through the void on the back of four huge elephants,' he said.

Drunah's mouth dropped open.

'On the back?' he said.

'It is claimed,' said Vorbis, still watching Fri'it.

'What do they stand on?'

'The writer says they stand on the shell of an enormous turtle,' said Vorbis.

Drunah grinned nervously.

'And what does that stand on?' he said.

'I see no point in speculating as to what it stands on,' snapped Vorbis, 'since it does not exist!'

'Of course, of course,' said Drunah quickly. 'It was only idle curiosity.'

'Most curiosity is,' said Vorbis. 'It leads the mind into speculative ways. Yet the man who wrote this walks around free, in Ephebe, *now*.'

Drunah glanced at the scroll.

'He says here he went on a ship that sailed to an island on the edge and he looked over and –'

'Lies,' said Vorbis evenly. 'And it would make no difference even if they were not lies. Truth lies within, not without. In the words of the Great God Om, as delivered through his chosen prophets. Our eyes may deceive us, but our God never will.'

'But –'

Vorbis looked at Fri'it. The general was sweating.

'Yes?' he said.

'Well ... Ephebe. A place where madmen have mad ideas. Everyone knows that. Maybe the wisest course is leave them to stew in their folly?'

Vorbis shook his head. 'Unfortunately, wild and unstable ideas have a disturbing tendency to move around and take hold.'

Fri'it had to admit that this was true. He knew from experience that true and obvious ideas, such as the ineffable wisdom and judgement of the Great God Om, seemed so obscure to many people that you actually had to kill them before they saw the error of their ways, whereas dangerous and nebulous and wrong-headed notions often had such an attraction for some people that they would – he rubbed a scar thoughtfully – hide up in the mountains and throw rocks at you until you starved them out. They'd prefer to die rather than see sense. Fri'it had seen sense at an early age. He'd seen it was sense not to die.

'What do you propose?' he said.

'The Council want to parley with Ephebe,' said Drunah. 'You know I have to organise a deputation to leave tomorrow.'

'How many soldiers?' said Vorbis.

'A bodyguard only. We have been guaranteed safe passage, after all,' said Fri'it.

'*We have been guaranteed safe passage,*' said Vorbis. It sounded like a lengthy curse. 'And once inside . . . ?'

Fri'it wanted to say: I've spoken to the commander of the Ephebian garrison, and I think he is a man of honour, although of course he is indeed a despicable infidel and lower than the worms. But it was not the kind of thing he felt it wise to say to Vorbis.

He substituted: 'We shall be on our guard.'

'Can we surprise them?'

Fri'it hesitated. 'We?' he said.

'I shall lead the party,' said Vorbis. There was the briefest exchange of glances between himself and the secretary. 'I . . . would like to be away from the Citadel for a while. A change of air.

Besides, we should not let the Ephebians think they merit the attentions of a superior member of the Church. I was just musing as to the possibilities, should we be provoked –'

Fri'it's nervous click was like a whip-crack.

'We have given them our word –'

'There is no truce with unbelievers,' said Vorbis.

'But there are practical considerations,' said Fri'it, as sharply as he dared. 'The palace of Ephebe is a labyrinth. I know. There are traps. No one gets in without a guide.'

'How does the guide get in?' said Vorbis.

'I assume he guides himself,' said the general.

'In my experience there is always another way,' said Vorbis. 'Into everything, there is always another way. Which the God will show in his own good time, we can be assured of that.'

'Certainly matters would be easier if there was a lack of stability in Ephebe,' said Drunah. 'It does indeed harbour certain ... elements.'

'And it will be the gateway to the whole of the Turnwise coast,' said Vorbis.

'Well –'

'The Djel, and then Tsort,' said Vorbis.

Drunah tried to avoid seeing Fri'it's expression.

'It is our duty,' said Vorbis. 'Our holy duty. We must not forget poor Brother Murduck. He was unarmed and alone.'

Brutha's huge sandals flipflopped obediently along the stone-flagged corridor towards Brother Nhumrod's barren cell.

He tried composing messages in his head. Master, there's a tortoise who says – Master, this tortoise wants – Master, guess what, I heard from this tortoise in the melons that –

Brutha would never have dared to think of himself as a prophet, but he had a shrewd idea of the outcome of any interview that began in this way.

Many people assumed that Brutha was an idiot. He looked like one, from his round open face to his splay-feet and knock-ankles. He also had the habit of moving his lips while he thought deeply, as if he was rehearsing every sentence. And this was because that was what he was doing. Thinking was not something that came easily to Brutha. Most people think automatically, thought dancing through their brains like static electricity across a cloud. At least, that's how it seemed to him. Whereas he had to construct thoughts a bit at a time, like someone building a wall. A short lifetime of being laughed at for having a body like a barrel and feet that gave the impression that they were about to set out in opposite directions had given him a strong tendency to think very carefully about anything he said.

Brother Nhumrod was prostrate on the floor in front of a statue of Om Trampling the Ungodly, with his fingers in his ears. The voices were troubling him again.

Brutha coughed. He coughed again.

Brother Nhumrod raised his head.

'Brother Nhumrod?' said Brutha.

'What?'

'Er . . . Brother Nhumrod?'

'What?'

Brother Nhumrod unplugged his ears.

'Yes?' he said testily.

'Um. There's something you ought to see. In the. In the garden. Brother Nhumrod?'

The master of novices sat up. Brutha's face was a glowing picture of concern.

'What do you mean?' Brother Nhumrod said.

'In the garden. It's hard to explain. Um. I found out . . . where the voices were coming from, Brother Nhumrod. And you did say to be sure and tell you.'

The old priest gave Brutha a sharp look. But if ever there was a person without guile or any kind of subtlety, it was Brutha.

Fear is strange soil. Mainly it grows obedience like corn, which grows in rows and makes weeding easy. But sometimes it grows the potatoes of defiance, which flourish underground.

The Citadel had a lot of underground. There were the pits and tunnels of the Quisition. There were cellars and sewers, forgotten rooms, dead ends, spaces behind ancient walls, even natural caves in the bedrock itself.

This was such a cave. Smoke from the fire in the middle of the floor found its way out through a crack in the roof and, eventually, into the maze of uncountable chimneys and light-wells above.

There were a dozen figures in the dancing shadows. They wore rough hoods over nondescript clothes – crude things made of rags, nothing that couldn't easily be burned after the meeting so that the wandering fingers of the Quisition would find nothing incriminating. Something about the way most of them moved suggested men who were used to carrying weapons. Here and there, clues. A stance. The turn of a word.

On one wall of the cave there was a drawing. It was vaguely oval, with three little extensions at the top – the middle one slightly the largest of the three – and three at the bottom, the middle one of these slightly longer and more pointed. A child's drawing of a turtle.

'Of course he'll go to Ephebe,' said a mask. 'He won't dare not to. He'll have to dam the river of truth, at its source.'

'We must bail out what we can, then,' said another mask.

'We must kill Vorbis!'

'Not in Ephebe. When that happens, it must happen here. So that people will *know*. When we're strong enough.'

'Will we ever be strong enough?' said a mask. Its owner clicked his knuckles nervously.

'Even the peasants know there's something wrong. You can't stop the truth. Dam the river of truth? Then there are leaks of great force. Didn't we find out about Murduck? Hah! *Killed in Ephebe*, Vorbis said.'

'One of us must go to Ephebe and save the Master. If he really exists.'

'He exists. His name is on the book.'

'Didactylos. A strange name. It means Two-Fingered, you know.'

'They must honour him in Ephebe.'

'Bring him back here, if possible. And the Book.'

One of the masks seemed hesitant. His knuckles clicked again.

'But will people rally behind . . . a book? People need more than a book. They're peasants. They can't read.'

'But they can listen!'

'Even so . . . they need to be shown . . . they need a symbol . . .'

'We have one!'

Instinctively, every masked figure turned to look at the drawing on the wall, indistinct in the firelight but graven on their minds. They were looking at the truth, which can often impress.

'The Turtle Moves!'

'The Turtle Moves!'

'The Turtle Moves!'

The leader nodded.

'And now,' he said, 'we will draw lots . . .'

*

The Great God Om waxed wroth, or at least made a spirited attempt. There is a limit to the amount of wroth that can be waxed one inch from the ground, but he was right up against it.

He silently cursed a beetle, which is like pouring water onto a pond. It didn't seem to make any difference, anyway. The beetle plodded away.

He cursed a melon unto the eighth generation, but nothing happened. He tried a plague of boils. The melon just sat there, ripening slightly.

Just because he was temporarily embarrassed, the whole world thought it could take advantage. Well, when Om got back to his rightful shape and power, he told himself, Steps would be Taken. The tribes of Beetles and Melons would wish they'd never been created. And something really horrible would happen to all eagles. And . . . and there would be a holy commandment involving the planting of more lettuces . . .

By the time the big boy arrived back with the waxy-skinned man, the Great God Om was in no mood for pleasantries. Besides, from a tortoise-eye viewpoint even the most handsome human is only a pair of feet, a distant pointy head and, somewhere up there, the wrong end of a pair of nostrils.

'What's this?' he snarled.

'This is Brother Nhumrod,' said Brutha. 'Master of the novices. He is very important.'

'Didn't I tell you not to bring me some fat old pederast!' shouted the voice in his head. 'Your eyeballs will be spitted on shafts of fire for this!'

Brutha knelt down.

'I can't go to the High Priest,' he said, as patiently as possible. 'Novices aren't even allowed in the Great Temple except on special occasions. I'd be Taught the Error of My Ways by the Quisition if I was caught. It's the Law.'

'Stupid fool!' the tortoise shouted.

Nhumrod decided that it was time to speak.

'Novice Brutha,' he said, 'for what reason are you talking to a small tortoise?'

'Because –' Brutha paused. 'Because it's talking to me . . . isn't it?'

Brother Nhumrod looked down at the small, one-eyed head poking out of the shell.

He was, by and large, a kindly man. Sometimes demons and devils did put disquieting thoughts in his head, but he saw to it that they stayed there and he did not in any literal sense deserve to be called what the tortoise called him which, in fact, if he had heard it, he would have thought was something to do with feet. And he was well aware that it was possible to hear voices attributed to demons and, sometimes, gods. Tortoises was a new one. Tortoises made him feel worried about Brutha, whom he'd always thought of as an amiable lump who did, without any sort of complaint, anything asked of him. Of course, many novices volunteered for cleaning out the cesspits and bull cages, out of a strange belief that holiness and piety had something to do with being up to your knees in dirt. Brutha never volunteered, but if he was told to do something he did it, not out of any desire to impress, but simply because he'd been told. And now he was talking to tortoises.

'I think I have to tell you, Brutha,' he said, 'that it is not talking.'

'You can't hear it?'

'I cannot hear it, Brutha.'

'It told me it was . . .' Brutha hesitated. 'It told me it was the Great God.'

He flinched. Grandmother would have hit him with something heavy now.

'Ah. Well, you see, Brutha,' said Brother Nhumrod, twitching gently, 'this sort of thing is not unknown among young men recently Called to the Church. I daresay you heard the voice of the Great God when you were Called, didn't you? Mmm?'

Metaphor was lost on Brutha. He remembered hearing the voice of his grandmother. He hadn't been Called so much as Sent. But he nodded anyway.

'And in your . . . enthusiasm, it's only natural that you should think you hear the Great God talking to you,' Nhumrod went on.

The tortoise bounced up and down.

'Smite you with thunderbolts!' it screamed.

'I find healthy exercise is the thing,' said Nhumrod. 'And plenty of cold water.'

'Writhe on the spikes of damnation!'

Nhumrod reached down and picked up the tortoise, turning it over. Its legs waggled angrily.

'How did it get here, mmm?'

'I don't know, Brother Nhumrod,' said Brutha dutifully.

'Your hand to wither and drop off!' screamed the voice in his head.

'There's very good eating on one of these, you know,' said the master of novices. He saw the expression on Brutha's face.

'Look at it like this,' he said. 'Would the Great God Om' – holy horns – '*ever* manifest Himself in such a lowly creature as this? A bull, yes, of course, an eagle, certainly, and I think on one occasion a swan . . . but a *tortoise*?'

'Your sexual organs to sprout wings and fly away!'

'After all,' Nhumrod went on, oblivious to the secret chorus in Brutha's head, 'what kind of miracles could a tortoise do? Mmm?'

'Your ankles to be crushed in the jaws of giants!'

'Turn lettuce into gold, perhaps?' said Brother Nhumrod, in the jovial tones of those blessed with no sense of humour. 'Crush ants underfoot? Ahaha.'

'Haha,' said Brutha dutifully.

'I shall take it along to the kitchen, out of your way,' said the master of novices. 'They make *ex*cellent soup. And then you'll hear no more voices, depend upon it. Fire cures all Follies, yes?'

'*Soup?*'

'Er . . .' said Brutha.

'Your intestines to be wound around a tree until you are sorry!'

Nhumrod looked around the garden. It seemed to be full of melons and pumpkins and cucumbers. He shuddered.

'Lots of cold water, that's the thing,' he said. 'Lots and lots.' He focused on Brutha again. 'Mmm?'

He wandered off towards the kitchens.

The Great God Om was upside down in a basket in one of the kitchens, half-buried under a bunch of herbs and some carrots.

An upturned tortoise will try to right itself firstly by sticking out its neck to its fullest extent and trying to use its head as a lever. If this doesn't work it will wave its legs frantically, in case this will rock it upright.

An upturned tortoise is the ninth most pathetic thing in the entire multiverse.

An upturned tortoise *who knows what's going to happen to it next* is, well, at least up there at number four.

The quickest way to kill a tortoise for the pot is to plunge it into boiling water.

Kitchens and storerooms and craftsmen's workshops belonging to the Church's civilian population honeycombed the Citadel.[*] This was only one of them, a smoky-ceilinged cellar whose focal point was an arched fireplace. Flames roared up the flue. Turnspit dogs

---

[*] It takes forty men with their feet on the ground to keep one man with his head in the air.

trotted in their treadmills. Cleavers rose and fell on the chopping blocks.

Off to one side of the huge hearth, among various other blackened cauldrons, a small pot of water was already beginning to seethe.

'The worms of revenge to eat your blackened nostrils!' screamed Om, twitching his legs violently. The basket rocked.

A hairy hand reached in and removed the herbs.

'Hawks to peck your liver!'

A hand reached in again and took the carrots.

'Afflict you with a thousand cuts!'

A hand reached in and took the Great God Om.

'The cannibal fungi of –!'

'Shut up!' hissed Brutha, shoving the tortoise under his robe.

He sidled towards the door, unnoticed in the general culinary chaos.

One of the cooks looked at him and raised an eyebrow.

'Just got to take this back,' Brutha burbled, bringing out the tortoise and waving it helpfully. 'Deacon's orders.'

The cook scowled, and then shrugged. Novices were regarded by one and all as the lowest form of life, but orders from the hierarchy were to be obeyed without question, unless the questioner wanted to find himself faced with more important questions like whether or not it is possible to go to heaven after being roasted alive.

When they were out in the courtyard Brutha leaned against the wall and breathed out.

'Your eyeballs to –!' the tortoise began.

'One more word,' said Brutha, 'and it's back in the basket.'

The tortoise fell silent.

'As it is, I shall probably get into trouble for missing Comparative Religion with Brother Whelk,' said Brutha. 'But the Great God has seen fit to make the poor man shortsighted and he probably won't notice I'm not there, only if he does I shall have to say what I've done because telling lies to a Brother is a sin and the Great God will send me to hell for a million years.'

'In this one case I could be merciful,' said the tortoise. 'No more than a thousand years at the outside.'

'My grandmother told me I shall go to hell when I die anyway,' said Brutha, ignoring this. 'Being alive is sinful. It stands to reason, because you have to sin every day when you're alive.'

He looked down at the tortoise.

'I know you're not the Great God Om' – holy horns – 'because if I was to touch the Great God Om' – holy horns – 'my hands would burn away. The Great God would never become a tortoise, like Brother Nhumrod said. But it says in the Book of the Prophet Cena that when he was wandering in the desert the spirits of the ground and the air spoke unto him, so I wondered if you were one of those.'

The tortoise gave him a one-eyed stare for a while. Then it said: 'Tall fellow? Full beard? Eyes wobbling all over the place?'

'What?' said Brutha.

'I think I recall him,' said the tortoise. 'Eyes wobbled when he talked. And he talked all the time. To himself. Walked into rocks a lot.'

'He wandered in the wilderness for three months,' said Brutha.

'That explains it, then,' said the tortoise. 'There's not a lot to eat there that isn't mushrooms.'

'Perhaps you *are* a demon,' said Brutha. 'The Septateuch forbids us to have discourse with demons. Yet in resisting demons, says the Prophet Fruni, we may grow strong in faith –'

'Your teeth to abscess with red-hot heat!'

'Pardon?'

'I swear to *me* that I am the Great God Om, greatest of gods!'

Brutha tapped the tortoise on the shell.

'Let me show you something, demon.'

He could feel his faith growing, if he listened hard.

This wasn't the greatest statue of Om, but it was the closest. It was down in the pit level reserved for prisoners and heretics. And it was made of iron plates riveted together.

The pits were deserted except for a couple of novices pushing a rough cart in the distance.

'It's a big bull,' said the tortoise.

'The very likeness of the Great God Om in one of his worldly incarnations!' said Brutha proudly. 'And you say you're *him*?'

'I haven't been well lately,' said the tortoise.

Its scrawny neck stretched out further.

'There's a door on its back,' it said. 'Why's there a door on its back?'

'So that the sinful can be put in,' said Brutha.

'Why's there another one in its belly?'

'So the purified ashes can be let out,' said Brutha. 'And the smoke issues forth from the nostrils, as a sign to the ungodly.'

The tortoise craned its neck round at the rows of barred doors. It looked up at the soot-encrusted walls. It looked down at the now empty fire trench under the iron bull. It reached a conclusion. It blinked its one eye.

'People?' it said eventually. 'You roast *people* in it?'

'There!' said Brutha triumphantly. 'And thus you prove you are not the Great God! *He* would know that of course we do not burn people in there. Burn people in there? That would be unheard of!'

'Ah,' said the tortoise. 'Then what –?'

'It is for the destruction of heretical materials and other such rubbish,' said Brutha.

'Very sensible,' said the tortoise.

'*Sinners* and *criminals* are purified by fire in the Quisition's pits or sometimes in front of the Great Temple,' said Brutha. 'The Great God would know that.'

'I think I must have forgotten,' said the tortoise quietly.

'The Great God Om' – holy horns – 'would know that He Himself said unto the Prophet Wallspur –' Brutha coughed and assumed the creased-eyebrow squint that meant serious thought was being undertaken. '"Let the holy fire destroy utterly the unbeliever." That's verse sixty-five.'

'Did I say that?'

'In the Year of the Lenient Vegetable the Bishop Kreeblephor converted a demon by the power of reason alone,' said Brutha. 'It actually joined the Church and became a subdeacon. Or so it is said.'

'*Fighting* I don't mind,' the tortoise began.

'Your lying tongue cannot tempt me, reptile,' said Brutha. 'For I am strong in my faith!'

The tortoise grunted with effort.

'Smite you with thunderbolts!'

A small, a very small black cloud appeared over Brutha's head and a small, a very small bolt of lightning lightly singed an eyebrow.

It was about the same strength as the spark off a cat's fur in hot dry weather.

'Ouch!'

'*Now* do you believe me?' said the tortoise.

There was a bit of breeze on the roof of the Citadel. It also offered a good view of the high desert.

Fri'it and Drunah waited for a while to get their breath back.

Then Fri'it said, 'Are we safe up here?'

Drunah looked up. An eagle circled over the dry hills. He found himself wondering how good an eagle's hearing was. It certainly was good at something. Was it hearing? It could hear a creature half a mile below in the silence of the desert. What the hells – it couldn't talk as well, could it?

'Probably,' he said.

'Can I trust you?' said Fri'it.

'Can I trust *you*?'

Fri'it drummed his fingers on the parapet.

'Uh,' he said.

And that was the problem. It was the problem of all really secret societies. They were *secret*. How many members did the Turtle Movement have? No one knew, exactly. What was the name of the man beside you? Two other members knew, because they would have introduced him, but who were they behind these masks? Because knowledge was dangerous. If you knew, the inquisitions could wind it slowly out of you. So you made sure you didn't know. This made conversation much easier during cell meetings, and impossible outside of them.

It was the problem of all tentative conspirators throughout history: how to conspire without actually uttering words to an untrusted possible fellow-conspirator which, if reported, would point the accusing red-hot poker of guilt.

The little beads of sweat on Drunah's forehead, despite the warm breeze, suggested that the secretary was agonising along the same lines. But it didn't *prove* it. And for Fri'it, not dying had become a habit.

He clicked his knuckles nervously.

'A holy war,' he said. That was safe enough. The sentence included no verbal clue to what Fri'it thought about the prospect. He hadn't said, 'Ye god, not a damn holy war, is the man insane? Some idiot missionary gets himself killed, some man writes some gibberish about the shape of the world, and we have to go to war?' If pressed, and indeed stretched and broken, he could always claim that his meaning had been 'At last! A not-to-be-missed opportunity to die gloriously for Om, the one true God, who shall Trample the Unrighteous with Hooves of Iron!' It wouldn't make a lot of difference, evidence never did once you were in the deep levels where accusation had the status of proof, but at least it might leave one or two inquisitors feeling that they might just have been wrong.

'Of course, the Church has been far less militant in the last century or so,' said Drunah, looking out over the desert. 'Much taken up with the mundane problems of the empire.'

A statement. Not a crack in it where you could insert a bone-disjointer.

'There was the crusade against the Hodgsonites,' said Fri'it distantly. 'And the Subjugation of the Melchiorites. And the Resolving of the false prophet Zeb. And the Correction of the Ashelians, and the Shriving of the –'

'But all that was just politics,' said Drunah.

'Hmm. Yes. Of course, you are right.'

'And, of course, no one could possibly doubt the wisdom of a war to further the worship and glory of the Great God.'

'No. None could doubt it,' said Fri'it, who had walked across many a battlefield the day after a glorious victory, when you had ample opportunity to see what winning meant. The Omnians forbade the use of all drugs. At times like that the prohibition bit hard, when you dared not go to sleep for fear of your dreams.

'Did not the Great God declare, through the Prophet Abbys, that there is no greater and more honourable sacrifice than one's own life for the God?'

'Indeed he did,' said Fri'it. He couldn't help recalling that Abbys had been a bishop in the Citadel for fifty years before the Great God had Chosen him. Screaming enemies had never come at him with a sword. He'd never looked into the eyes of someone who wished him dead – no, of course he had, all the time, because of course the Church had its politics – but at least they hadn't been holding the means to that end in their hands at the time.

'To die gloriously for one's faith is a noble thing,' Drunah intoned, as if reading the words off an internal notice-board.

'So the prophets tell us,' said Fri'it, miserably.

The Great God moved in mysterious ways, he knew. Undoubtedly He chose His prophets, but it seemed as if He had to be helped. Perhaps He was too busy to choose for Himself. There seemed to be a lot more meetings, a lot more nodding, a lot more exchanging of glances even during the services in the Great Temple.

Certainly there was a glow about young Vorbis – how easy it was to slip from one thought to the other. There was a man touched by destiny. A tiny part of Fri'it, the part that had lived for much of its life in tents, and been shot at quite a lot, and had been in the middle of mêlées where you could just as easily be killed by an ally as an enemy, added: or at least by something. It was a part of him that was due to spend all the eternities in all the hells, but it had already had a lot of practice.

'You know I travelled a lot when I was much younger?' he said.

'I have often heard you talk most interestingly of your travels in heathen lands,' said Drunah politely. 'Often bells are mentioned.'

'Did I ever tell you about the Brown Islands?'

'Out beyond the end of the world,' said Drunah. 'I remember. Where bread grows on trees and young women find little white balls in oysters. They dive for them, you said, while wearing not a stitc–'

'Something else I remember,' said Fri'it. It was a lonely memory, out here with nothing but scrubland under a purple sky. 'The sea is strong there. There are big waves, much bigger than the ones in the Circle Sea, you understand, and the men paddle out beyond them to fish. On strange planks of wood. And when they wish to return to shore, they wait for a wave, and then . . . they stand up, on the wave, and it carries them all the way to the beach.'

'I like the story about the young swimming women best,' said Drunah.

'Sometimes there are very big waves,' said Fri'it, ignoring him. 'Nothing would stop them. But if you ride them, you do not drown. This is something I learned.'

Drunah caught the glint in his eye.

'Ah,' he said, nodding. 'How wonderful of the Great God to put such instructive examples in our path.'

'The trick is to judge the strength of the wave,' said Fri'it. 'And ride it.'

'What happens to those who don't?'

'They drown. Often. Some of the waves are very big.'

'Such is often the nature of waves, I understand.'

The eagle was still circling. If it had understood anything, then it wasn't showing it.

'Useful facts to bear in mind,' said Drunah, with sudden brightness. 'If ever one should find oneself in heathen parts.'

'Indeed.'

From prayer towers up and down the contours of the Citadel the deacons chanted the duties of the hour.

Brutha should have been in class. But the tutor priests weren't too strict with him. After all, he had arrived word-perfect in every Book of the Septateuch and knew all the prayers and hymns off by heart, thanks to grandmother. They probably assumed he was being useful. Usefully doing something no one else wanted to do.

He hoed the bean rows for the look of the thing. The Great God Om, although currently the small god Om, ate a lettuce leaf.

All my life, Brutha thought, I've known that the Great God Om – he made the holy horns sign in a fairly half-hearted way – was a . . . a . . . great big beard in the sky, or sometimes, when He comes down into the world, as a huge bull or a lion or . . . something big, anyway. Something you could look up to.

Somehow a tortoise isn't the same. I'm trying hard . . . but it isn't the same. And hearing him talk about the SeptArchs as if they were just . . . just some mad old men . . . it's like a dream . . .

In the rain-forests of Brutha's subconscious the butterfly of doubt emerged and flapped an experimental wing, all unaware of what chaos theory has to say about this sort of thing . . .

'I feel a lot better now,' said the tortoise. 'Better than I have for months.'

'Months?' said Brutha. 'How long have you been . . . ill?'

The tortoise put its foot on a leaf.

'What day is it?' it said.

'Tenth of Grune,' said Brutha.

'Yes? What year?'

'Er . . . Notional Serpent . . . what do you mean, what *year*?'

'Then . . . three years,' said the tortoise. 'This is good lettuce. And it's *me* saying it. You don't get lettuce up in the hills. A bit of plantain, a thorn bush or two. Let there be another leaf.'

Brutha pulled one off the nearest plant. And lo, he thought, there was another leaf.

'And you were going to be a bull?' he said.

'Opened my eyes . . . my eye . . . and I was a tortoise.'

'Why?'

'How should I know? I don't know!' lied the tortoise.

'But you . . . you're omnicognisant,' said Brutha.

'That doesn't mean I know everything.'

Brutha bit his lip. 'Um. Yes. It does.'

'You sure?'

'Yes.'

'Thought that was omnipotent.'

'No. That means you're all-powerful. And you *are*. That's what it says in the Book of Ossory. He was one of the Great Prophets, you know. I hope,' Brutha added.

'Who told him I was omnipotent?'

'You did.'

'No I didn't.'

'Well, he *said* you did.'

'Don't even remember anyone called Ossory,' the tortoise muttered.

'You spoke to him in the desert,' said Brutha. 'You must remember. He was eight feet tall? With a very long beard? And a huge staff? And the glow of the holy horns shining out of his head?' He hesitated. But he'd seen the statues and the holy icons. They couldn't be wrong.

'Never met anyone like that,' said the small god Om.

'Maybe he was a bit shorter,' Brutha conceded.

'Ossory. Ossory,' said the tortoise. 'No . . . no . . . can't say I –'

'He said that you spoke unto him from out of a pillar of flame,' said Brutha.

'Oh, *that* Ossory,' said the tortoise. 'Pillar of flame. Yes.'

'And you dictated to him the Book of Ossory,' said Brutha. 'Which contains the Directions, the Gateways, the Abjurations and the Precepts. One hundred and ninety-three chapters.'

'I don't think I did all that,' said Om doubtfully. 'I'm sure I would have remembered one hundred and ninety-three chapters.'

'What *did* you say to him, then?'

'As far as I can remember it was "Hey, see what I can do!"' said the tortoise.

Brutha stared at it. It looked embarrassed, insofar as that's possible for a tortoise.

'Even gods like to relax,' it said.

'Hundreds of thousands of people live their lives by the Abjurations and the Precepts!' Brutha snarled.

'Well? I'm not stopping them,' said Om.

'If you didn't dictate them, who did?'

'Don't ask *me*. *I'm* not omnicognisant!'

Brutha was shaking with anger.

'And the Prophet Abbys? I suppose someone just *happened* to give him the Codicils, did they?'

'It wasn't me –'

'They're written on slabs of lead ten feet tall!'

'Oh, well, it *must* have been me, yes? I always have a ton of lead slabs around in case I meet someone in the desert, yes?'

'What! If you didn't give them to him, who did?'

'I don't know. Why should I know? I can't be everywhere at once!'

'You're omnipresent!'

'What says so?'

'The Prophet Hashimi!'

'Never met the man!'

'Oh? Oh? So I suppose you didn't give him the Book of Creation, then?'

'What Book of Creation?'

'You mean you don't know?'

'No!'

'Then who gave it to him?'

'I don't know! Perhaps he wrote it himself!'

Brutha put his hand over his mouth in horror.

'Thaff blafhngf!'

'What?'

Brutha removed his hand.

'I said, that's blasphemy!'

'Blasphemy? How can I blaspheme? I'm a god!'

'I don't believe you!'

'Hah! Want another thunderbolt?'

'You call that a thunderbolt?'

Brutha was red in the face, and shaking. The tortoise hung its head sadly.

'All right. All right. Not much of one, I admit,' it said. 'If I was better, you'd have been just a pair of sandals with smoke coming out.' It looked wretched. 'I don't understand it. This sort of thing has never happened to me before. I intended to be a great big roaring white bull for a week and ended up a tortoise for three years. Why? *I* don't know, and I'm supposed to know everything. According to these prophets of yours who say they've met me, anyway. You know, no one even heard me? I tried talking to goatherds and stuff, and they never took any notice! I was beginning to think I was a tortoise dreaming about being a god. That's how bad it was getting.'

'Perhaps you are,' said Brutha.

'Your legs to swell to tree-trunks!' snapped the tortoise.

'But – but,' said Brutha, 'you're saying the prophets were . . . just men who wrote things down!'

'That's what they *were*!'

'Yes, but it wasn't from you!'

'Some of it was, perhaps,' said the tortoise. 'I've . . . forgotten so much, the past few years.'

'But if you've been down here as a tortoise, who's been listening to the prayers? Who has been accepting the sacrifices? Who has been judging the dead?'

'I don't know,' said the tortoise. 'Who did it before?'

'You did!'

'Did I?'

Brutha stuck his fingers in his ears and opened up with the third verse of *Lo, the infidels flee the wrath of Om*.

After a couple of minutes the tortoise stuck its head out from under its shell.

'So,' it said, 'before unbelievers get burned alive . . . do you sing to them first?'

'No!'

'Ah. A merciful death. Can I say something?'

'If you try to tempt my faith one more time –'

The tortoise paused. Om searched his fading memory. Then he scratched in the dust with a claw.

'I . . . remember a day . . . summer day . . . you were . . . thirteen . . .'

The dry little voice droned on. Brutha's mouth formed a slowly widening O.

Finally he said, 'How did you know that?'

'You believe the Great God Om watches everything you do, don't you?'

'You're a tortoise, you couldn't have –'

'When you were almost fourteen, and your grandmother had beaten you for stealing cream from the stillroom, which in fact you had not done, she locked you in your room and you said, "I wish you were –"'

There will be a sign, thought Vorbis. There was always a sign, for the man who watched for them. A wise man always put himself in the path of the God.

He strolled through the Citadel. He always made a point of taking a daily walk through some of the lower levels, although of course always at a different time, and via a different route. Insofar as Vorbis got any pleasure in life, at least in any way that could be recognised by a normal human being, it was in seeing the faces of humble members of the clergy as they rounded a corner and found themselves face-to-chin with Deacon Vorbis of the Quisition. There was always that little intake of breath that indicated a guilty conscience. Vorbis liked to see properly guilty consciences. That was what consciences were for. Guilt was the grease in which the wheels of the authority turned.

He rounded a corner and saw, scratched crudely on the wall opposite, a rough oval with four crude legs and even cruder head and tail.

He smiled. There seemed to be more of them lately. Let heresy fester, let it come to the surface like a boil. Vorbis knew how to wield the lance.

But the second or two of reflection had made him walk past a turning and, instead, he stepped out into the sunshine.

He was momentarily lost, for all his knowledge of the byways of the church. This was one of the walled gardens. Around a fine stand of tall decorative Klatchian corn, bean vines raised red and white blossoms towards the sun; in between the bean rows, melons baked gently on the dusty soil. In the normal way, Vorbis would have noted and approved of this efficient use of space, but in the normal way he wouldn't have encountered a plump young novice, rolling back and forth in the dust with his fingers in his ears.

Vorbis stared down at him. Then he prodded Brutha with his sandal.

'What ails you, my son?'

Brutha opened his eyes.

There weren't many superior members of the hierarchy he could recognise. Even the Cenobiarch was a distant blob in the crowd. But everyone recognised Vorbis the exquisitor. Something about him projected itself on your conscience within a few days of your arrival at the Citadel. The God was merely to be feared in the perfunctory ways of habit, but Vorbis was *dreaded*.

Brutha fainted.

'How very strange,' said Vorbis.

A hissing noise made him look round.

There was a small tortoise near his foot. As he glared it tried to back away, and all the time it was staring at him and hissing like a kettle.

He picked it up and examined it carefully, turning it over and over in his hands. Then he looked around the walled garden until he found a spot in full sunshine, and put the reptile down, on its back. After a moment's thought he took a couple of pebbles from one of the vegetable beds and wedged them under the shell so that the creature's movement wouldn't tip it over.

Vorbis believed that no opportunity to acquire esoteric knowledge should ever be lost, and made a mental note to come back again in a few hours to see how it was getting on, if work permitted.

Then he turned his attention to Brutha.

There was a hell for blasphemers. There was a hell for the disputers of rightful authority. There were a number of hells for liars. There was probably a hell for little boys who wished their grandmothers were dead. There were more than enough hells to go around.

This was the definition of eternity; it was the space of time devised by the Great God Om to ensure that everyone got the punishment that was due to them.

The Omnians had a great many hells.

Currently, Brutha was going through all of them.

Brother Nhumrod and Brother Vorbis looked down at him, tossing and turning on his bed like a beached whale.

'It's the sun,' said Nhumrod, almost calm now after the initial shock of having the exquisitor come looking for him. 'The poor lad works all day in that garden. It was bound to happen.'

'Have you tried beating him?' said Brother Vorbis.

'I'm sorry to say that beating young Brutha is like trying to flog a mattress,' said Nhumrod. 'He says "ow!" but I think it's only because he wants to show willing. Very willing lad, Brutha. He's the one I told you about.'

'He doesn't *look* very sharp,' said Vorbis.

'He's not,' said Nhumrod.

Vorbis nodded approvingly. Undue intelligence in a novice was a mixed blessing. Sometimes it could be channelled for the greater glory of Om, but often it caused ... well, it did not cause trouble, because Vorbis knew exactly what to do with misapplied intelligence, but it did cause unnecessary work.

'And yet you tell me his tutors speak so highly of him,' he said.

Nhumrod shrugged.

'He is very obedient,' he said. 'And ... well, there's his memory.'

'What about his memory?'

'There's so much of it,' said Nhumrod.

'He has got a good memory?'

'Good is the wrong word. It's superb. He's word-perfect on the entire Sept-'

'Hmm?' said Vorbis.

Nhumrod caught the deacon's eye.

'As perfect, that is, as anything may be in this most imperfect world,' he muttered.

'A devoutly read young man,' said Vorbis.

'Er,' said Nhumrod, 'no. He can't read. Or write.'

'Ah. A *lazy* boy.'

The deacon was not a man who dwelt in grey areas. Nhumrod's mouth opened and shut silently as he sought for the proper words.

'No,' he said. 'He tries. We're sure he tries. He just does not seem to be able to make the . . . he cannot fathom the link between the sounds and the letters.'

'You have beaten him for that, at least?'

'It seems to have little effect, deacon.'

'How, then, has he become such a capable pupil?'

'He listens,' said Nhumrod.

No one listened quite like Brutha, he reflected. It made it very hard to teach him. It was like – it was like being in a great big cave. All your words just vanished into the unfillable depths of Brutha's head. The sheer concentrated absorption could reduce unwary tutors to stuttering silence, as every word they uttered whirled away into Brutha's ears.

'He listens to everything,' said Nhumrod. 'And he watches everything. He takes it all in.'

Vorbis stared down at Brutha.

'And I've never heard him say an unkind word,' said Nhumrod. 'The other novices make fun of him, sometimes. Call him The Big Dumb Ox. You know the sort of thing?'

Vorbis's gaze took in Brutha's ham-sized hands and tree-trunk legs. He appeared to be thinking deeply.

'Cannot read and write,' said Vorbis. 'But extremely loyal, you say?'

'Loyal and devout,' said Nhumrod.

'And a good memory,' Vorbis murmured.

'It's more than that,' said Nhumrod. 'It's not like memory at all.'

Vorbis appeared to reach a decision.

'Send him to see me when he is recovered,' he said.

Nhumrod looked panicky.

'I merely wish to talk to him,' said Vorbis. 'I may have a use for him.'

'Yes, lord?'

'For, I suspect, the Great God Om moves in mysterious ways.'

High above. No sound but the hiss of wind in feathers.

The eagle stood on the breeze, looking down at the toy buildings of the Citadel.

It had dropped it somewhere, and now it couldn't find it. Somewhere down there, in that little patch of green.

Bees buzzed in the bean blossoms. And the sun beat down on the upturned shell of Om.

There is also a hell for tortoises.

He was too tired to waggle his legs now. That was all you could do, waggle your legs. And stick your head out as far as it would go and wave it about in the hope that you could lever yourself over.

You died if you had no believers, and that was what a small god generally worried about. But you also died if you *died*.

In the part of his mind not occupied with thoughts of heat, he could feel Brutha's terror and bewilderment. He shouldn't have done that to the boy. Of course he hadn't been watching him. What god did that? Who cared what people *did*? Belief was the thing. He'd just picked the memory out of the boy's mind, to impress, like a conjuror removing an egg from someone's ear.

I'm on my back, and getting hotter, and I'm going to *die* . . .

And yet . . . and yet . . . that bloody eagle had dropped him on a compost heap. Some kind of clown, that eagle. A whole place built of rocks on a rock in a rocky place, and he landed on the one thing that'd break his fall without breaking him as well. And really close to a believer.

Odd, that. Made you wonder if it wasn't some kind of divine providence, except that you *were* divine providence . . . and on your back, getting hotter, preparing to *die* . . .

That man who'd turned him over. That expression on that mild face. He'd remember that. That expression, not of cruelty, but of some different level of being. That expression of terrible *peace* . . .

A shadow crossed the sun. Om squinted up into the face of Lu-Tze, who gazed at him with gentle, upside-down compassion. And then turned him the right way up. And then picked up his broom and wandered off, without a second glance.

Om sagged, catching his breath. And then brightened up.

Someone up there likes me, he thought. And it's Me.

*

Sergeant Simony waited until he was back in his own quarters before he unfolded his own scrap of paper.

He was not at all surprised to find it marked with a small drawing of a turtle. He was the lucky one.

He'd lived for a moment like this. Someone had to bring back the writer of the Truth, to be a symbol for the movement. It had to be him. The only shame was that he couldn't kill Vorbis.

But that had to happen where it could be seen.

One day. In front of the Temple. Otherwise no one would *believe*.

Om stumped along a sandy corridor.

He'd hung around a while after Brutha's disappearance. Hanging around is another thing tortoises are very good at. They're practically world champions.

Bloody useless boy, he thought. Served himself right for trying to talk to a barely coherent novice.

Of course, the skinny old one hadn't been able to hear him. Nor had the chef. Well, the old one was probably deaf. As for the cook ... Om made a note that, when he was restored to his full godly powers, a special fate was going to lie in wait for the cook. He wasn't sure exactly what it was going to be, but it was going to involve boiling water and probably carrots would come into it somewhere.

He enjoyed the thought of that for a moment. But where did it leave him? It left him in this wretched garden, as a tortoise. He knew how he'd got *in* – he glared in dull terror at the tiny dot in the sky that the eye of memory knew was an eagle – and he'd better find a more terrestrial way out unless he wanted to spend the next month hiding under a melon leaf.

Another thought struck him. Good eating!

When he had his power again, he was going to spend *quite some time* devising a few new hells. And a couple of fresh Precepts, too. Thou shalt not eat of the Meat of the Turtle. That was a good one. He was surprised he hadn't thought of it before. Perspective, that's what it was.

And if he'd thought of one like Thou Shalt Bloody Well Pick up Any Distressed Tortoises and Carry Them Anywhere They Want Unless, And This is Important, You're an Eagle a few years ago, he wouldn't be in this trouble now.

Nothing else for it. He'd have to find the Cenobiarch himself. Someone like a High Priest would be bound to be able to hear him.

And he'd be in this place somewhere. High Priests tended to stay put. He should be easy enough to find. And while he might currently be a tortoise, Om was still a god. How hard could it be?

He'd have to go upwards. That's what a hierarchy meant. You found the top man by going upwards.

Wobbling slightly, his shell jerking from side to side, the former Great God Om set off to explore the citadel erected to his greater glory.

He couldn't help noticing things had changed a lot in three thousand years.

'*Me?*' said Brutha. 'But, but –'

'I don't believe he means to punish you,' said Nhumrod. 'Although punishment is what you richly deserve, of course. We *all* richly deserve,' he added piously.

'But *why?*'

'– why? He said he just wants to talk to you.'

'But there is *nothing* I could possibly say that a quisitor wants to hear!' wailed Brutha.

'– Hear. I am sure you are not questioning the deacon's wishes,' said Nhumrod.

'No. No. Of course not,' said Brutha. He hung his head.

'Good boy,' said Nhumrod. He patted as far up Brutha's back as he could reach. 'Just you trot along,' he said. 'I'm sure everything will be all right.' And then, because he too had been brought up in habits of honesty, he added, 'Probably all right.'

There were few steps in the Citadel. The progress of the many processions that marked the complex rituals of Great Om demanded long, gentle slopes. Such steps as there were, were low enough to encompass the faltering steps of very old men. And there were so many very old men in the Citadel.

Sand blew in all the time from the desert. Drifts built up on the steps and in the courtyards, despite everything that an army of brush-wielding novices could do.

But a tortoise has very inefficient legs.

'Thou Shall Build Shallower Steps,' he hissed, hauling himself up.

Feet thundered past him, a few inches away. This was one of the main thoroughfares of the Citadel, leading to the Place of Lamentation, and was trodden by thousands of pilgrims every day.

Once or twice an errant sandal caught his shell and spun him around.

'Your feet to fly from your body and be buried in a termite mound!' he screamed.

It made him feel a little better.

Another foot clipped him and slid him across the stones. He fetched up, with a clang, against a curved metal grille set low in one wall. Only a lightning grab with his jaws stopped him slipping through it. He ended up hanging by his mouth over a cellar.

A tortoise has incredibly powerful jaw muscles. He swayed a bit, legs wobbling. All right. A tortoise in a crevassed, rocky landscape was used to this sort of thing. He just had to get a leg hooked . . .

Faint sounds drew themselves to his attention. There was the clink of metal, and then a very soft whimper.

Om swivelled his eye around.

The grille was high in one wall of a very long, low room. It was brightly illuminated by the light-wells that ran everywhere through the Citadel.

Vorbis had made a point of that. The inquisitors shouldn't work in the shadows, he said, but in the light.

Where they could see, very clearly, what they were doing.

So could Om.

He hung from the grille for some time, unable to take his eye off the row of benches.

On the whole, Vorbis discouraged red-hot irons, spiked chains and things with drills and big screws on, unless it was for a public display on an important Fast day. It was amazing what you could do, he always said, with a simple knife . . .

But many of the inquisitors liked the old ways best.

After a while, Om very slowly hauled himself up to the grille, neck muscles twitching. Like a creature with its mind on something else, the tortoise hooked first one front leg over a bar, then another. His back legs waggled for a while, and then he hooked a claw on to the rough stonework.

He strained for a moment and then pulled himself back into the light.

He walked off slowly, keeping close to the wall to avoid the feet. He had no alternative to walking slowly in any case, but now he was walking slowly because he was thinking. Most gods find it hard to walk and think at the same time.

*

Anyone could go to the Place of Lamentation. It was one of the great freedoms of Omnianism.

There were all sorts of ways to petition the Great God, but they depended largely on how much you could afford, which was right and proper and exactly how things should be. After all, those who had achieved success in the world clearly had done it with the approval of the Great God, because it was impossible to believe that they had managed it with His *disapproval*. In the same way, the Quisition could act without possibility of flaw. Suspicion was proof. How could it be anything else? The Great God would not have seen fit to put the suspicion in the minds of His exquisitors unless it was *right* that it should be there. Life could be very simple, if you believed in the Great God Om. And sometimes quite short, too.

But there were always the improvident, the stupid and those who, because of some flaw or oversight in this life or a past one, were not even able to afford a pinch of incense. And the Great God, in His wisdom and mercy as filtered through His priests, had made provision for them.

Prayers and entreaties could be offered up in the Place of Lamentation. They would assuredly be heard. They might even be heeded.

Behind the Place, which was a square two hundred metres across, rose the Great Temple itself.

There, without a shadow of a doubt, the God listened.

Or somewhere close, anyway . . .

Thousands of pilgrims visited the Place every day.

A heel knocked Om's shell, bouncing him off the wall. On the rebound a crutch caught the edge of his carapace and whirled him away into the crowd, spinning like a coin. He bounced up against the bedroll of an old woman who, like many others, reckoned that the efficacy of her petition was increased by the amount of time she spent in the square.

The God blinked muzzily. This was nearly as bad as eagles. It was nearly as bad as the cellar . . . no, perhaps nothing was as bad as the cellar . . .

He caught a few words before another passing foot kicked him away.

'The drought has been on our village for three years . . . a little rain, oh Lord?'

Rotating on the top of his shell, vaguely wondering if the right answer might stop people kicking him, the Great God muttered, 'No problem.'

Another foot bounced him, unseen by any of the pious, between the forest of legs. The world was a blur.

He caught an ancient voice, steeped in hopelessness, saying, 'Lord, Lord, why must my son be taken to join your Divine Legion? Who now will tend the farm? Could you not take some other boy?'

'Don't worry about it,' squeaked Om.

A sandal caught him under his tail and flicked him several yards across the square. No one was looking down. It was generally believed that staring fixedly at the golden horns on the temple roof while uttering the prayer gave it added potency. Where the presence of the tortoise was dimly registered as a bang on the ankle, it was disposed of by an automatic prod with the other foot.

'... my wife, who is sick with the ...'

'Right!'

Kick –

'... make clean the well in our village, which is foul with ...'

'You got it!'

Kick –

'... every year the locusts come, and ...'

'I promise, only ...!'

Kick –

'... lost upon the seas these five months ...'

'... *stop kicking me!*'

The tortoise landed, right side up, in a brief clear space.

Visible ...

So much of animal life is the recognition of pattern, the shapes of hunter and hunted. To the casual eye the forest is, well, just forest; to the eye of the dove it is so much unimportant fuzzy green background to the hawk which *you* did not notice on the branch of a tree. To the tiny dot of the hunting buzzard in the heights, the whole panorama of the world is just a fog compared to the scurrying prey in the grass.

From his perch on the Horns themselves, the eagle leapt into the sky.

Fortunately, the same awareness of shapes that made the tortoise so prominent in a square full of scurrying humans made the tortoise's one eye swivel upwards in dread anticipation.

Eagles are single-minded creatures. Once the idea of lunch is fixed in their mind, it tends to remain there until satisfied.

There were two Divine Legionaries outside Vorbis's quarters. They looked sideways at Brutha as he knocked timorously at the door, as if looking for a reason to assault him.

A small grey priest opened the door and ushered Brutha into a small, barely furnished room. He pointed meaningfully at a stool.

Brutha sat down. The priest vanished behind a curtain. Brutha took one glance around the room and –

Blackness engulfed him. Before he could move, and Brutha's reflexes were not well coordinated at the best of times, a voice by his ear said, 'Now, brother, do not panic. I order you not to panic.'

There was cloth in front of Brutha's face.

'Just nod, boy.'

Brutha nodded. They put a hood over your face. All the novices knew that. Stories were told in the dormitories. They put a cloth over your face so the inquisitors didn't know who they were working on . . .

'Good. Now, we are going into the next room. Be careful where you tread.'

Hands guided him upright and across the floor. Through the mists of incomprehension he felt the brush of the curtain, and then was jolted down some steps and into a sandy-floored room. The hands spun him a few times, firmly but without apparent ill-will, and then led him along a passageway. There was the swish of another curtain, and then the indefinable sense of a larger space.

Afterwards, long afterwards, Brutha realised: there was no terror. A hood had been slipped over his head in the room of the head of the Quisition, and it never occurred to him to be terrified. Because he had faith.

'There is a stool behind you. Be seated.'

Brutha sat.

'You may remove the hood.'

Brutha removed the hood.

He blinked.

Seated on stools at the far end of the room, with a Holy Legionary on either side of them, were three figures. He recognised the aquiline face of Deacon Vorbis; the other two were a short and stocky man, and a very fat one. Not heavily built, like Brutha, but a genuine lard tub. All three wore plain grey robes.

There was no sign of any branding irons, or even of scalpels.

All three were staring intently.

'Novice Brutha?' said Vorbis.

Brutha nodded.

Vorbis gave a light laugh, the kind made by very intelligent people when they think of something that probably isn't very amusing.

'And, of course, one day we shall have to call you Brother Brutha,' he said. 'Or even Father Brutha? Rather confusing, I think. Best to be avoided. I think we shall have to see to it that you become Subdeacon Brutha just as soon as possible; what do you think of that?'

Brutha did not think anything of it. He was vaguely aware that advancement was being discussed, but his mind had gone blank.

'Anyway, enough of this,' said Vorbis, with the slight exasperation of someone who realises that he is going to have to do a lot of work in this conversation. 'Do you recognise these learned fathers on my left and right?'

Brutha shook his head.

'Good. They have some questions to ask you.'

Brutha nodded.

The very fat man leaned forward.

'Do you have a tongue, boy?'

Brutha nodded. And then, feeling that perhaps this wasn't enough, presented it for inspection.

Vorbis laid a restraining hand on the fat man's arm.

'I think our young friend is a little overawed,' he said mildly.

He smiled.

'Now, Brutha – please put it away – I am going to ask you some questions. Do you understand?'

Brutha nodded.

'When you first came into my apartments, you were for a few seconds in the anteroom. Please describe it to me.'

Brutha stared frog-eyed at him. But the turbines of recollection ground into life without his volition, pouring their words into the forefront of his mind.

'It is a room about three metres square. With white walls. There is sand on the floor except in the corner by the door, where the flagstones are visible. There is a window on the opposite wall, about two metres up. There were three bars in the window. There is a three-legged stool. There is a holy icon of the Prophet Ossory, carved from aphacia wood and set with silver leaf. There is a scratch in the bottom left-hand corner of the frame. There is a shelf under the window. There is nothing on the shelf but a tray.'

Vorbis steepled his long thin fingers in front of his nose.

'On the tray?' he said.

'I am sorry, lord?'

'What was on the tray, my son?'

Images whirled in front of Brutha's eyes.

'On the tray was a thimble. A bronze thimble. And two needles. On the tray was a length of cord. There were knots in the cord. Three knots. And nine coins were on the tray. There was a silver cup on the tray, decorated with a pattern of aphacia leaves. There was a long dagger, I think it was steel, with a black handle with seven ridges on it. There was a small piece of black cloth on the tray. There was a stylus and a slate –'

'Tell me about the coins,' murmured Vorbis.

'Three of them were Citadel cents,' said Brutha promptly. 'Two were showing the Horns, and one the sevenfold-crown. Four of the coins were very small and golden. There was lettering on them which . . . which I could not read, but which if you were to give me a stylus I think I could –'

'This is some sort of trick?' said the fat man.

'I assure you,' said Vorbis, 'the boy could have seen the entire room for no more than a second. Brutha . . . tell us about the other coins.'

'The other coins were large. They were bronze. They were *derechmi* from Ephebe.'

'How do you know this? They are hardly common in the Citadel.'

'I have seen them once before, lord.'

'When was this?'

Brutha's face screwed up with effort.

'I am not sure –' he said.

The fat man beamed at Vorbis.

'Hah,' he said.

'I think . . .' said Brutha '. . . it was in the afternoon. But it may have been the morning. Around midday. On Grune 3, in the year of the Astounded Beetle. Some merchants came to our village.'

'How old were you at that time?' said Vorbis.

'I was within one month of three years old, lord.'

'I don't believe this,' said the fat man.

Brutha's mouth opened and shut once or twice. How did the fat man know? He hadn't been there!

'You could be wrong, my son,' said Vorbis. 'You are a well-grown lad of . . . what . . . seventeen, eighteen years? We feel you could not really recall a chance glimpse of a foreign coin fifteen years ago.'

'We think that you are making it up,' said the fat man.

Brutha said nothing. Why make anything up? When it was just sitting there in his head.

'Can you remember everything that's ever happened to you?' said the stocky man, who had been watching Brutha carefully throughout the exchange. Brutha was glad of the interruption.

'No, lord. Most things.'

'You forget things?'

'Uh. There are sometimes things I don't remember.' Brutha had heard about forgetfulness, although he found it hard to imagine. But there were times in his life, in the first few years of his life especially, when there was . . . nothing. Not an attrition of memory, but great locked rooms in the mansion of his recollection. Not forgotten, any more than a locked room ceases to exist, but . . . locked.

'What is the first thing you can remember, my son?' said Vorbis, kindly.

'There was a bright light, and then someone hit me,' said Brutha.

The three men stared at him blankly. Then they turned to one another. Brutha, through the misery of his terror, heard snatches of whispering.

'. . . is there to lose? . . .' 'Foolishness and probably demonic . . .' 'Stakes are high . . .' 'One chance, and they will be expecting us . . .'

And so on.

He looked around the room.

Furnishing was not a priority in the Citadel. Shelves, stools, tables . . . There was a rumour among the novices that priests towards the top of the hierarchy had golden furniture, but there was no sign of it here. The room was as severe as anything in the novices' quarters although it had, perhaps, a more opulent severity; it wasn't the forced bareness of poverty, but the starkness of intent.

'My son?'

Brutha looked back hurriedly.

Vorbis glanced at his colleagues. The stocky man nodded. The fat man shrugged.

'Brutha,' said Vorbis, 'return to your dormitory now. Before you go, one of the servants will give you something to eat, and a drink. You will report to the Gate of Horns at dawn tomorrow, and you will come with me to Ephebe. You know about the delegation to Ephebe?'

Brutha shook his head.

'Perhaps there is no reason why you should,' said Vorbis. 'We are going to discuss political matters with the Tyrant. Do you understand?'

Brutha shook his head.

'Good,' said Vorbis. 'Very good. Oh, and – Brutha?'

'Yes, lord?'

'You will forget this meeting. You have not been in this room. You have not seen us here.'

Brutha gaped at him. This was nonsense. You couldn't forget things just by wishing. Some things forgot themselves – the things in those locked rooms – but that was because of some mechanism he could not access. What did this man mean?

'Yes, lord,' he said.

It seemed the simplest way.

Gods have no one to pray to.

The Great God Om scurried towards the nearest statue, neck stretched, inefficient legs pumping. The statue happened to be himself as a bull, trampling an infidel, although this was no great comfort.

It was only a matter of time before the eagle stopped circling and swooped.

Om had been a tortoise for only three years, but with the shape he had inherited a grab-bag of instincts, and a lot of them centred around a total terror of the one wild creature that had found out how to eat tortoise.

Gods have no one to pray to.

Om really wished that this was not the case.

But everyone needs *someone*.

'Brutha!'

Brutha was a little uncertain about his immediate future. Deacon Vorbis had clearly cut him loose from his chores as a novice, but he had nothing to do for the rest of the afternoon.

He gravitated towards the garden. There were beans to tie up, and he welcomed the fact. You knew where you were with beans. They didn't tell you to do impossible things, like *forget*. Besides, if he was going to be away for a while, he ought to mulch the melons and explain things to Lu-Tze.

Lu-Tze came with the gardens.

Every organisation has someone like him. They might be pushing a broom in obscure corridors, or wandering among the shelves in the back of the stores (where they are the only person who knows where anything is) or have some ambiguous but essential relationship with the boiler-room. Everyone knows who they are and no one remembers a time when they weren't there, or knows where they go when they're not, well, where they usually are. Just occasionally, people who are slightly more observant than most other people, which is not on the face of it very difficult, stop and wonder about them for a while . . . and then get on with something else.

Strangely enough, given his gentle ambling from garden to garden around the Citadel, Lu-Tze never showed much interest in the plants themselves. He dealt in soil, manure, muck, compost, loam and dust, and the means of moving it about. Generally he was pushing a broom, or turning over a heap. Once anyone put seeds in anything he lost interest.

He was raking the paths when Brutha entered. He was good at raking paths. He left scallop patterns and gentle soothing curves. Brutha always felt apologetic about walking on them.

He hardly ever spoke to Lu-Tze, because it didn't matter much what anyone ever said to Lu-Tze. The old man just nodded and smiled his single-toothed smile in any case.

'I'm going away for a little while,' said Brutha, loudly and distinctly. 'I expect someone else will be sent to look after the gardens, but there are some things that need doing . . .'

Nod, smile. The old man followed him patiently along the rows, while Brutha spoke beans and herbs.

'Understand?' said Brutha, after ten minutes of this.

Nod, smile. Nod, smile, beckon.

'What?'

Nod, smile, beckon. Nod, smile, *beckon*, smile.

Lu-Tze walked his little crab-monkey walk to the little area at the far end of the walled garden which contained his heaps, the flowerpot stacks, and all the other cosmetics of the garden beautiful. The old man slept there, Brutha suspected.

Nod, smile, beckon.

There was a small trestle table in the sun by a stack of bean canes. A straw mat had been spread on it, and on the mat were half a dozen pointy-shaped rocks, none of them bigger than a foot high.

A careful arrangement of sticks had been constructed around them. Bits of thin wood shadowed some parts of the rocks. Small metal mirrors directed sunlight towards other areas. Paper cones at odd angles appeared to be funnelling the breeze to very precise points.

Brutha had never heard about the art of bonsai, and how it was applied to mountains.

'They're ... very nice,' he said uncertainly.

Nod, smile, pick up a small rock, smile, urge, urge.

'Oh, I really couldn't take –'

Urge, urge. Grin, nod.

Brutha took the tiny mountain. It had a strange, unreal heaviness – to his hand it felt like a pound or so, but in his head it weighed thousands of *very, very small* tons.

'Uh. Thank you. Thank you very much.'

Nod, smile, push away politely.

'It's very ... mountainous.'

Nod, grin.

'That can't really be snow on the top, can –'

'*Brutha!*'

His head jerked up. But the voice had come from inside.

Oh, no, he thought wretchedly.

He pushed the little mountain back into Lu-Tze's hands.

'But, er, you keep it for me, yes?'

'*Brutha!*'

All that was a dream, wasn't it? Before I was important and talked to by deacons.

'*No, it wasn't! Help me!*'

The petitioners scattered as the eagle made a pass over the Place of Lamentation.

It wheeled, only a few feet above the ground, and perched on the statue of Great Om trampling the Infidel.

It was a magnificent bird, golden-brown and yellow-eyed, and it surveyed the crowds with blank disdain.

'It's a sign?' said an old man with a wooden leg.

'Yes! A sign!' said a young woman next to him.

'A sign!'

They gathered around the statue.

'It's a bugger,' said a small and totally unheard voice from somewhere around their feet.

'But what's it a sign of?' said an elderly man who had been camping out in the square for three days.

'What do you mean, *of*? It's a sign!' said the wooden-legged man. 'It don't have to be a sign *of* anything. That's a suspicious kind of question to ask, what's it a sign of.'

'Got to be a sign of something,' said the elderly man. 'That's a referential wossname. A gerund. Could be a gerund.'

A skinny figure appeared at the edge of the group, moving surreptitiously yet with surprising speed. It was wearing the *djeliba* of the desert tribes, but around its neck was a tray on a strap. There was an ominous suggestion of sticky sweet things covered in dust.

'It could be a messenger from the Great God himself,' said the woman.

'It's a bloody eagle is what it is,' said a resigned voice from somewhere among the ornamental bronze homicide at the base of the statue.

'Dates? Figs? Sherbets? Holy relics? Nice fresh indulgences? Lizards? Onna stick?' said the man with the tray hopefully.

'I thought when He appeared in the world it was as a swan or a bull,' said the wooden-legged man.

'Hah!' said the unregarded voice of the tortoise.

'Always wondered about that,' said a young novice at the back of the crowd. 'You know ... well ... swans? A bit ... lacking in machismo, yes?'

'May you be stoned to death for blasphemy!' said the woman hotly. 'The Great God hears every irreverent word you utter!'

'Hah!' from under the statue. And the man with the tray oiled forward a little further, saying, 'Klatchian Delight? Honeyed wasps? Get them while they're cold!'

'It's a point, though,' said the elderly man, in a kind of boring, unstoppable voice. 'I mean, there's something very *godly* about an eagle. King of birds, am I right?'

'It's only a better-looking turkey,' said the voice from under the statue. 'Brain the size of a walnut.'

'Very noble bird, the eagle. Intelligent, too,' said the elderly man. 'Interesting fact: eagles are the only birds to work out how to eat tortoises. You know? They pick them up, flying up very high, and drop them on to the rocks. Smashes them right open. Amazing.'

'One day,' said a dull voice from down below, 'I'm going to be back on form again and you're going to be very sorry you said that. For a very long time. I might even go so far as to make even more Time just for you to be sorry in. Or ... no, I'll make *you* a tortoise. See how you like it, eh? That rushing wind around y'shell, the ground getting bigger the whole time. *That*'d be an interesting fact!'

'That sounds dreadful,' said the woman, looking up at the eagle's glare. 'I wonder what passes through the poor little creature's head when he's dropped?'

'His shell, madam,' said the Great God Om, trying to squeeze himself even further under the bronze overhang.

The man with the tray was looking dejected. 'Tell you what,' he said. 'Two bags of sugared dates for the price of one, how about it? And that's cutting my own hand off.'

The woman glanced at the tray.

''Ere, there's flies all over everything!' she said.

'Currants, madam.'

'Why'd they just fly away, then?' the woman demanded.

The man looked down. Then he looked back up into her face.

'A miracle!' he said, waving his hands dramatically. 'The time of miracles is at hand!'

The eagle shifted uneasily.

It recognised humans only as pieces of mobile landscape which, in the lambing season in the high hills, might be associated with thrown stones when it stooped upon the newborn lamb, but which otherwise were as unimportant in the scheme of things as bushes and rocks. But it had never been so close to so many of them. Its mad eyes swivelled backwards and forwards uncertainly.

At that moment trumpets rang out across the Place.

The eagle looked around wildly, its tiny predatory mind trying to deal with this sudden overload.

It leapt into the air. The worshippers fought to get out of its way as it dipped across the flagstones and then rose majestically towards the turrets of the Great Temple and the hot sky.

Below it, the doors of the Great Temple, each one made of forty tons of gilded bronze, opened by the breath (it was said) of the Great God Himself, swung open ponderously and – and this was the holy part – silently.

Brutha's enormous sandals flapped and flapped on the flagstones. Brutha always put a lot of effort into running; he ran from the knees, lower legs thrashing like paddlewheels.

This was too much. There was a tortoise who said he was the God, and this couldn't be true except that it *must* be true, because of what it knew. And he'd been tried by the Quisition. Or something like that. Anyway, it hadn't been as painful as he'd been led to expect.

'*Brutha!*'

The square, normally alive with the susurration of a thousand prayers, had gone quiet. The pilgrims had all turned to face the Temple.

His mind boiling with the events of the day, Brutha shouldered his way through the suddenly silent crowd ...

'Brutha!'

People have reality-dampers.

It is a popular fact that nine-tenths of the brain is not used and, like most popular facts, it is wrong. Not even the most stupid Creator would go to the trouble of making the human head carry around several pounds of unnecessary grey goo if its only real purpose was, for example, to serve as a delicacy for certain remote tribesmen in unexplored valleys. It *is* used. And one of its functions is to make the miraculous seem ordinary and turn the unusual into the usual.

Because if this was *not* the case, then human beings, faced with the daily wondrousness of everything, would go around wearing big stupid grins, similar to those worn by certain remote tribesmen who occasionally get raided by the authorities and have the contents of their plastic greenhouses very seriously inspected. They'd say 'Wow!' a lot. And no one would do much work.

Gods don't like people not doing much work. People who aren't busy all the time might start to *think*.

Part of the brain exists to stop this happening. It is very efficient. It can make people experience boredom in the middle of marvels. And Brutha's was working feverishly.

So he didn't immediately notice that he'd pushed through the last row of people and had trotted out into the middle of a wide pathway, until he turned and saw the procession approaching.

The Cenobiarch was returning to his apartments, after conducting – or at least nodding vaguely while his chaplain conducted on his behalf – the evening service.

Brutha spun around, looking for a way to escape. Then there was a cough beside him, and he stared up into the furious faces of a couple of Lesser Iams and, between them, the bemused and geriatrically good-natured expression of the Cenobiarch himself.

The old man raised his hand automatically to bless Brutha with the holy horns, and then two members of the Divine Legion picked up the novice by the elbows, on the second attempt, and marched him swiftly out of the procession's path and hurled him into the crowd.

'Brutha!'

Brutha bounded across the plaza to the statue and leaned against it, panting.

'I'm going to go to hell!' he muttered. 'For all eternity!'

'*Who cares? Now . . . get me away from here.*'

No one was paying him any attention now. They were all watching the procession. Even watching the procession was a holy act. Brutha knelt down and peered into the scrollwork around the base of the statue.

One beady eye glared back at him.

'How did you get under there?'

'It was touch and go,' said the tortoise. 'I tell you, when I'm back on form, there's going to be a considerable redesigning of eagles.'

'What's the eagle trying to do to you?' said Brutha.

'It wants to carry me off to its nest and give me dinner,' snarled the tortoise. 'What do you *think* it wanted to do?' There was a short pause in which it contemplated the futility of sarcasm in the presence of Brutha; it was like throwing meringues at a castle.

'It wants to *eat* me,' it said patiently.

'But you're a tortoise!'

'I am your *God*!'

'But *currently* in the shape of a tortoise. With a shell on, is what I mean.'

'That doesn't worry eagles,' said the tortoise darkly. 'They pick you up, carry you up a few hundred feet, and then . . . drop you.'

'Urrgh.'

'No. More like . . . crack . . . splat. How did you think I got *in* here?'

'You were dropped? But –'

'Landed on a pile of dirt in your *garden*. That's eagles for you. Whole place built of rock and paved with rock on a big rock and they miss.'

'That was lucky. Million-to-one chance,' said Brutha.

'I never had this trouble when I was a bull. The number of eagles who can pick up a bull, you can count them on the fingers of one head. Anyway,' said the tortoise, 'there's worse here than eagles. There's a –'

'There's good eating on one of them, you know,' said a voice behind Brutha.

He stood up guiltily, the tortoise in his hand.

'Oh, hello, Mr Dhblah,' he said.

Everyone in the city knew Cut-Me-Own-Hand-Off Dhblah, purveyor of suspiciously new holy relics, suspiciously old rancid sweetmeats on a stick, gritty figs and long-past-the-sell-by dates. He was a sort of natural force, like the wind. No one knew where he came from or where he went at night. But he was there every dawn, selling sticky things to the pilgrims. And in this the priests reckoned he was on to a good thing, because most of the pilgrims were coming for the first time and therefore lacked the essential thing you needed in dealing with Dhblah, which was the experience of having dealt with him before. The sight of someone in the Place trying to unstick their jaws with dignity was a familiar one. Many a devout pilgrim, after a thousand miles of perilous journey, was forced to make his petition in sign language.

'Fancy some sherbet for afters?' said Dhblah hopefully. 'Only one cent a glass, and that's cutting me own hand off.'

'Who is this fool?' said Om.

'I'm not going to eat it,' said Brutha hurriedly.

'Going to teach it to do tricks, then?' said Dhblah cheerfully. 'Look through hoops, that kind of thing?'

'Get rid of him,' said Om. 'Smite him on the head, why don't you, and push the body behind the statue.'

'Shut up,' said Brutha, beginning to experience once again the problems that occur when you're talking to someone no one else can hear.

'No need to be like that about it,' said Dhblah.

'I wasn't talking to you,' said Brutha.

'Talking to the tortoise, were you?' said Dhblah. Brutha looked guilty.

'My old mum used to talk to a gerbil,' Dhblah went on. 'Pets are always a great help in times of stress. And in times of starvation too, o'course.'

'This man is not honest,' said Om. 'I can read his mind.'

'Can you?'

'Can I what?' said Dhblah. He gave Brutha a lopsided look. 'Anyway, it'll be company on your journey.'

'What journey?'

'To Ephebe. The secret mission to talk to the infidel.'

Brutha knew he shouldn't be surprised. News went around the enclosed world of the Citadel like bushfire after a drought.

'Oh,' he said. 'That journey.'

'They say Fri'it's going,' said Dhblah. 'And – that other one. The *éminence grease*.'

'Deacon Vorbis is a very nice person,' said Brutha. 'He has been very kind to me. He gave me a drink.'

'What of? Never mind,' said Dhblah. 'Of course, I wouldn't say a word against him, myself,' he added quickly.

'Why are you talking to this stupid person?' Om demanded.

'He's a . . . friend of mine,' said Brutha.

'I wish he was a friend of *mine*,' said Dhblah. 'Friends like that, you never have enemies. Can I press you to a candied sultana? Onna stick?'

There were twenty-three other novices in Brutha's dormitory, on the principle that sleeping alone promoted sin. This always puzzled the novices themselves, since a moment's reflection would suggest that there were whole ranges of sins only available in company. But that was because a moment's reflection was the biggest sin of all. People allowed to be by themselves overmuch might indulge in solitary cogitation. It was well known that this stunted your growth. For one thing, it could lead to your feet being chopped off.

So Brutha had to retire to the garden, with his God screaming at him from the pocket of his robe, where it was being jostled by a ball of garden twine, a pair of shears and some loose seeds.

Finally he was fished out.

'Look, I didn't have a chance to *tell* you,' said Brutha. 'I've been chosen to go on a very important mission. *I'm* going to Ephebe, on a mission to the infidels. Deacon Vorbis *picked* me. He's my friend.'

'Who's he?'

'He's the chief exquisitor. He . . . makes sure you're worshipped properly.'

Om picked up the hesitation in Brutha's voice, and remembered the grating. And the sheer *busyness* below . . .

'He tortures people,' he said coldly.

'Oh, no! The *in*quisitors do that. They work very long hours for not much money, too, Brother Nhumrod says. No, the *ex*quisitors just . . . arrange matters. Every inquisitor wants to become an exquisitor one day, Brother Nhumrod says. That's why they put up with being on duty at all hours. They go for days without sleep, sometimes.'

'Torturing people,' mused the God. No, a mind like that one in the garden wouldn't pick up a knife. Other people would do that. Vorbis would enjoy other methods.

'Letting out the *badness* and the *heresy* in people,' said Brutha.

'But people . . . perhaps . . . don't survive the process?'

'But that doesn't matter,' said Brutha earnestly. 'What happens to us in this life is not really real. There may be a little pain, but that doesn't matter. Not if it ensures less time in the hells after death.'

'But what if the exquisitors are wrong?' said the tortoise.

'They can't be wrong,' said Brutha. 'They are guided by the hand of . . . by your hand . . . your front leg . . . I mean, your claw,' he mumbled.

The tortoise blinked its one eye. It remembered the heat of the sun, the helplessness, and a face watching it not with any cruelty but, worse, with interest. Someone watching something die just to see how long it took. He'd remember that face anywhere. And the mind behind it – that steel ball of a mind.

'But suppose something went wrong,' it insisted.

'I'm not any good at theology,' said Brutha. 'But the testament of Ossory is very clear on the matter. They *must* have done something, otherwise you in your wisdom would not direct the Quisition to them.'

'Would I?' said Om, still thinking of that face. 'It's their fault they get tortured. Did I really say that?'

'"We are judged in life as we are in death" . . . Ossory III, chapter VI, verse 56. My grandmother said that when people die they come before you, they have to cross a terrible desert and you weigh their heart in some scales,' said Brutha. 'And if it weighs less than a feather, they are spared the hells.'

'Goodness me,' said the tortoise. And it added: 'Has it occurred to you, lad, that I might not be able to do that *and* be down here walking around with a shell on?'

'You could do anything you wanted to,' said Brutha.

Om looked up at Brutha.

He really believes, he thought. He doesn't know how to lie.

The strength of Brutha's belief burned in him like a flame.

And then the truth hit Om like the ground hits tortoises after an attack of eagles.

'You've got to take me to this Ephebe place,' he said urgently.

'I'll do whatever you want,' said Brutha. 'Are you going to scourge it with hoof and flame?'

'Could be, could be,' said Om. 'But you've got to take me.' He was trying to keep his innermost thoughts calm, in case Brutha heard. *Don't leave me behind!*

'But you could get there much quicker if I left you,' said Brutha. 'They are very wicked in Ephebe. The sooner it is cleansed, the better. You could stop being a tortoise and fly there like a burning wind and scourge the city.'

A burning wind, thought Om. And the tortoise thought of the silent wastes of the deep desert, and the chittering and sighing of the gods who had faded away to mere djinns and voices on the air.

Gods with no more believers.

Not even one. One was just enough.

Gods who had been *left behind*.

And the thing about Brutha's flame of belief was this: in all the Citadel, in all the day, it was the only one the God had found.

Fri'it was trying to pray.

He hadn't done so for a long time.

Oh, of course there had been the eight compulsory prayers every day, but in the pit of the wretched night he knew them for what they were. A habit. A time for thought, perhaps. And method of measuring time.

He wondered if he'd ever prayed, if he'd ever opened heart and mind to something out there, or up there. He must have done, mustn't he? Perhaps when he was young. He couldn't even remember that. Blood had washed away the memories.

It was his fault. It had to be his fault. He'd been to Ephebe before, and had rather liked the white marble city on its rock overlooking the blue Circle Sea. And he'd visited Djelibeybi, those madmen in their little river valley who believed in gods with funny heads and put their dead in pyramids. He'd even been to far Ankh-Morpork, across the water, where they'd worship any god at all so long as he or she had money. Yes, Ankh-Morpork – where there were streets and streets of gods, squeezed together like a deck of cards. And none of them wanted to set fire to anyone else, or at least any more than was normally the case in Ankh-Morpork. They just wanted to be left in peace, so that everyone went to heaven or hell in their own way.

And he'd drunk too much tonight, from a secret cache of wine whose discovery would deliver him into the machinery of the inquisitors within ten minutes.

Yes, you could say this for old Vorbis. Once upon a time the Quisition had been bribable, but not any more. The chief exquisitor had gone back to fundamentals. Now there was a democracy of sharp knives. Better than that, in fact. The search for heresy was pursued even more vigorously among the higher levels in the

Church. Vorbis had made it clear: the higher up the tree, the blunter the saw.

Give me that old-time religion . . .

He squeezed his eyes shut again, and all he could see was the horns of the temple, or fragmented suggestions of the carnage to come, or . . . the face of Vorbis.

He'd liked that white city.

Even the slaves had been content. There were rules about slaves. There were things you couldn't do to slaves. Slaves had value.

He'd learned about the Turtle, there. It had all made sense. He'd thought: it sounds *right*. It makes *sense*. But sense or not, that thought was sending him to hell.

Vorbis knew about him. He must do. There were spies everywhere. Sasho had been useful. How much had Vorbis got out of him? Had he said what he knew?

Of course he'd say what he knew . . .

Something went snap inside Fri'it.

He glanced at his sword, hanging on the wall.

And why not? After all, he was going to spend all eternity in a thousand hells . . .

The knowledge was freedom, of a sort. When the least they could do to you was everything, then the most they could do to you suddenly held no terror. If he was going to be boiled for a lamb, then he might as well be roasted for a sheep.

He staggered to his feet and, after a couple of tries, got the swordbelt off the wall. Vorbis's quarters weren't far away, if he could manage the steps. One stroke, that's all it would take. He could cut Vorbis in half without trying. And maybe . . . maybe nothing would happen afterwards. There were others who felt like him – somewhere. Or, anyway, he could get down to the stables, be well away by dawn, get to Ephebe, maybe, across the desert . . .

He reached the door and fumbled for the handle.

It turned of its own accord.

Fri'it staggered back as the door swung inwards.

Vorbis was standing there. In the flickering light of the oil lamp, his face registered polite concern.

'Excuse the lateness of the hour, my lord,' he said. 'But I thought we should talk. About tomorrow.'

The sword clattered out of Fri'it's hand.

Vorbis leaned forward.

'Is there something wrong, brother?' he said.

He smiled, and stepped into the room. Two hooded inquisitors slipped in behind him.

'Brother,' Vorbis said again. And shut the door.

'How is it in there?' said Brutha.

'I'm going to rattle around like a pea in a pot,' grumbled the tortoise.

'I could put some more straw in. And, look, I've got these.'

A pile of greenstuff dropped on Om's head.

'From the kitchen,' said Brutha. 'Peelings and cabbage. I stole them,' he added, 'but then I thought it can't be stealing if I'm doing it for you.'

The fetid smell of the half-rotten leaves suggested strongly that Brutha had committed his crime when the greens were halfway to the midden, but Om didn't say so. Not now.

'Right,' he mumbled.

There must be others, he told himself. Sure. Out in the country. This place is too sophisticated. But . . . there had been all those pilgrims in front of the Temple. They weren't just country people, they were the devoutest ones. Whole villages clubbed together to send one person carrying the petitions of many. But there hadn't been the flame. There had been fear, and dread, and yearning, and hope. All those emotions had their flavour. But there hadn't been the flame.

The eagle had dropped him near Brutha. He'd . . . woken up. He could dimly remember all that time as a tortoise. And now he remembered being a god. How far away from Brutha would he still remember? A mile? Ten miles? How would it be . . . feeling the knowledge drain away, dwindling back to nothing but a lowly reptile? Maybe there would be a part of him that would always remember, helplessly . . .

He shuddered.

Currently Om was in a wickerwork box slung from Brutha's shoulder. It wouldn't have been comfortable at the best of times, but now it shook occasionally as Brutha stamped his feet in the pre-dawn chill.

After a while some of the Citadel grooms arrived, with horses. Brutha was the subject of a few odd looks. He smiled at everyone. It seemed the best way.

He began to feel hungry, but didn't dare leave his post. He'd been *told* to be here. But after a while sounds from around the corner made him sidle a few yards to see what was going on.

The courtyard here was U-shaped, around a wing of the Citadel buildings, and around the corner it looked as though another party was preparing to set out.

Brutha knew about camels. There had been a couple in his grandmother's village. There seemed to be hundreds of them here, though, complaining like badly oiled pumps and smelling like a thousand damp carpets. Men in *djeliba* moved among them and occasionally hit them with sticks, which is the approved method of dealing with camels.

Brutha wandered over to the nearest creature. A man was strapping water-bottles round its hump.

'Good morning, brother,' said Brutha.

'Bugger off,' said the man without looking round.

'The Prophet Abbys tells us (chap. XXV, verse 6): "Woe unto he who defiles his mouth with curses *for* his words will be *as* dust",' said Brutha.

'Does he? Well, he can bugger off too,' said the man, conversationally.

Brutha hesitated. Technically, of course, the man had bought himself vacant possession of a thousand hells and a month or two of the attentions of the Quisition, but now Brutha could see that he was a member of the Divine Legion; a sword was half-hidden under the desert robes.

And you had to make special allowances for Legionaries, just as you did for inquisitors. Their often intimate contact with the ungodly affected their minds and put their souls in mortal peril. He decided to be magnanimous.

'And where are you going to with all these camels on this fine morning, brother?'

The soldier tightened a strap.

'Probably to hell,' he said, grinning nastily. 'Just behind you.'

'Really? According to the word of the Prophet Ishkible, a man needs no camel to ride to hell, yea, nor horse, nor mule; a man may ride into hell on his tongue,' said Brutha, letting just a tremor of disapproval enter his voice.

'Does some old prophet say anything about nosy bastards being given a thump alongside the ear?' said the soldier.

'"Woe unto him who raises *his* hand unto his brother, dealing with him as unto an Infidel",' said Brutha. 'That's Ossory, Precepts XI, verse 16.'

'"Sod off and forget you ever saw us otherwise you're going to be in real trouble, my friend." Sergeant Aktar, chapter I, verse 1,' said the soldier.

Brutha's brow wrinkled. He couldn't remember that one.

'Walk away,' said the voice of the God in his head. 'You don't need trouble.'

'I hope your journey is a pleasant one,' said Brutha politely. 'Whatever the destination.'

He backed away and headed towards the gate.

'A man who will have to spend some time in the hells of correction, if I am any judge,' he said. The god said nothing.

The Ephebian travelling group was beginning to assemble now. Brutha stood to attention and tried to keep out of everyone's way. He saw a dozen mounted soldiers, but unlike the camel riders they were in the brightly polished fishmail and black and yellow cloaks that the Legionaries usually only wore on special occasions. Brutha thought they looked very impressive.

Eventually one of the stable servants came up to him.

'What are you doing here, novice?' he demanded.

'I am going to Ephebe,' said Brutha.

The man glared at him and then grinned.

'You? You're not even ordained! You're going to Ephebe?'

'Yes.'

'What makes you think that?'

'Because I told him so,' said the voice of Vorbis, behind the man. 'And here he is, most obedient to my wishes.'

Brutha had a good view of the man's face. The change in his expression was like watching a grease slick cross a pond. Then the stableman turned as though his feet were nailed to a turntable.

'My Lord Vorbis,' he oiled.

'And now he will require a steed,' said Vorbis.

The stableman's face was yellow with dread.

'My pleasure. The very best the sta–'

'My friend Brutha is a humble man before Om,' said Vorbis. 'He will ask for no more than a mule, I have no doubt. Brutha?'

'I – I do not know how to ride, my lord,' said Brutha.

'Any man can get on a mule,' said Vorbis. 'Often many times in a short distance. And now, it would appear, we are all here?'

He raised an eyebrow at the sergeant of the guard, who saluted.

'We are awaiting General Fri'it, lord,' he said.

'Ah. Sergeant Simony, isn't it?'

Vorbis had a terrible memory for names. He knew every one. The sergeant paled a little, and then saluted crisply.

'Yes! Sir!'

'We will proceed without General Fri'it,' said Vorbis.

The B of the word 'But' framed itself on the sergeant's lips, and faded there.

'General Fri'it has other business,' said Vorbis. 'Most pressing and urgent business. Which only he can attend to.'

Fri'it opened his eyes in greyness.

He could see the room around him, but only faintly, as a series of edges in the air.

The sword . . .

He'd dropped the sword, but maybe he could find it again. He stepped forward, feeling a tenuous resistance around his ankles, and looked down.

There was the sword. But his fingers passed through it. It was like being drunk, but he knew he wasn't drunk. He wasn't even sober. He was . . . suddenly clear in his mind.

He turned and looked at the thing that had briefly impeded his progress.

'Oh,' he said.

GOOD MORNING.

'Oh.'

'THERE IS A LITTLE CONFUSION AT FIRST. IT IS ONLY TO BE EXPECTED.

To his horror, Fri'it saw the tall black figure stride away through the grey wall.

'Wait!'

A skull draped in a black hood poked out of the wall.

YES?

'You're Death, aren't you?'

INDEED.

Fri'it gathered what remained of his dignity.

'I know you,' he said. 'I have faced you many times.'

Death gave him a long stare.

NO YOU HAVEN'T.

'I assure you —'

YOU HAVE FACED MEN. IF YOU HAD FACED ME, I ASSURE YOU . . . YOU WOULD HAVE KNOWN.

'But what happens to me now?'

Death shrugged.

DON'T YOU KNOW? he said, and disappeared.

'Wait!'

Fri'it ran at the wall and found to his surprise that it offered no barrier. Now he was out in the empty corridor. Death had vanished.

And then he realised that it wasn't the corridor he remembered, with its shadows and the grittiness of sand underfoot.

That corridor didn't have a glow at the end, that pulled at him like a magnet pulls at an iron filing.

You couldn't put off the inevitable. Because sooner or later, you reached the place when the inevitable just went and waited.

And this was it.

Fri'it stepped through the glow into a desert. The sky was dark and pocked with large stars, but the black sand that stretched away to the distance was nevertheless brightly lit.

A desert. After death, a desert. The desert. No hells, yet. Perhaps there was hope.

He remembered a song from his childhood. Unusually, it wasn't about smiting. No one was trampled underfoot. It wasn't about Om, dreadful in His rage. It was a simple little home-made song, terrifying in its simple forlorn repetition.

You have to walk a lonesome desert . . .

'Where is this place?' he said hoarsely.

THIS IS NO PLACE, said Death.

You have to walk it all alone . . .

'What is at the end of the desert?'

JUDGEMENT.

There is no one to walk it for you . . .

Fri'it stared at the endless, featureless expanse.

'I have to walk it by myself?' he whispered. 'But the song says it's the terrible desert –'

YES? AND NOW, IF YOU WILL EXCUSE ME . . .

Death vanished.

Fri'it took a deep breath, purely out of habit. Perhaps he could find a couple of rocks out there. A small rock to hold and a big rock to hide behind, while he waited for Vorbis . . .

And that thought was habit, too. Revenge? *Here?*

He smiled.

Be sensible, man. You were a soldier. This is a desert. You crossed a few in your time.

And you survive by learning about them. There's whole tribes that know how to live in the worst kinds of desert. Licking water off the shady side of dunes, that sort of thing . . . They think it's *home*. Put 'em in a vegetable garden and they'd think you were mad.

The memory stole over him: a desert is what you think it is. And now, you can think clearly . . .

There were no lies here. All fancies fled away. That's what happened in all deserts. It was just you, and what you believed.

What have I always believed?

That on the whole, and by and large, if a man lived properly, not according to what any priests said, but according to what seemed decent and honest *inside*, then it would, at the end, more or less, turn out all right.

You couldn't get that on a banner. But the desert looked better already.

Fri'it set out.

It was a small mule and Brutha had long legs; if he'd made the effort he could have remained standing and let the mule trot out from underneath.

The order of progression was not as some may have expected. Sergeant Simony and his soldiers rode ahead, on either side of the track.

They were trailed by the servants and clerks and lesser priests. Vorbis rode in the rear, where an exquisitor rode by right, like a shepherd watching over his flock.

Brutha rode with him. It was an honour he would have preferred to avoid. Brutha was one of those people who could raise a sweat on a frosty day, and the dust was settling on him like a gritty skin. But Vorbis seemed to derive some amusement from his company. Occasionally he would ask him questions:

'How many miles have we travelled, Brutha?'

'Four miles and seven *estado*, lord.'

'But how do you know?'

That was a question he couldn't answer. How did he know the sky was blue? It was just something in his head. You couldn't think about how you thought. It was like opening a box with the crowbar that was inside.

'And how long has our journey taken?'

'A little over seventy-nine minutes.'

Vorbis laughed. Brutha wondered why. The puzzle wasn't why he remembered, it was why everyone else seemed to forget.

'Did your fathers have this remarkable faculty?'

There was a pause.

'Could they do it as well?' said Vorbis patiently.

'I don't know. There was only my grandmother. She had – a good memory. For some things.' Transgressions, certainly. 'And very good eyesight and hearing.' What she could apparently see or hear through two walls had, he remembered, seemed phenomenal.

Brutha turned gingerly in the saddle. There was a cloud of dust about a mile behind them on the road.

'Here come the rest of the soldiers,' he said conversationally.

This seemed to shock Vorbis. Perhaps it was the first time in years that anyone had innocently addressed a remark to him.

'The rest of the soldiers?' he said.

'Sergeant Aktar and his men, on ninety-eight camels with many water-bottles,' said Brutha. 'I saw them before we left.'

'You did not see them,' said Vorbis. 'They are not coming with us. You will forget about them.'

'Yes, lord.' The request to do magic again.

After a few minutes the distant cloud turned off the road and started up the long slope that led to the high desert. Brutha watched them surreptitiously, and raised his eyes to the dune mountains.

There was a speck circling up there.

He put his hand to his mouth.

Vorbis heard the gasp.

'What ails you, Brutha?' he said.

'I remembered about the God,' said Brutha, without thinking.

'We should always remember the God,' said Vorbis, 'and trust that He is with us on this journey.'

'He is,' said Brutha, and the absolute conviction in his voice made Vorbis smile.

He strained to hear the nagging internal voice, but there was nothing. For one horrible moment Brutha wondered if the tortoise had fallen out of the box, but there was a reassuring weight on the strap.

'And we must bear with us the certainty that He will be with us in Ephebe, among the infidel,' said Vorbis.

'I am sure He will,' said Brutha.

'And prepare ourselves for the coming of the prophet,' said Vorbis. The cloud had reached the top of the dunes now, and vanished in the silent wastes of the desert.

Brutha tried to put it out of his mind, which was like trying to empty a bucket underwater. No one survived in the high desert. It wasn't just the dunes and the heat. There were terrors in the burning heart, where even the mad tribes never went. An ocean without water, voices without mouths . . .

Which wasn't to say that the immediate future didn't hold terrors enough . . .

He'd seen the sea before, but the Omnians didn't encourage it. This may have been because deserts were so much harder to cross. They kept people in, though. But sometimes the desert barriers *were* a problem, and then you had to put up with the sea.

Il-drim was nothing more than a few shacks around a stone jetty, at one of which was a trireme flying the holy oriflamme. When the Church travelled, the travellers were very senior people indeed, so when the Church travelled it generally travelled in style.

The party paused on a hill and looked at it.

'Soft and corrupt,' said Vorbis. 'That's what we've become, Brutha.'

'Yes, Lord Vorbis.'

'And open to pernicious influence. The sea, Brutha. It washes unholy shores, and gives rise to dangerous ideas. Men should not travel, Brutha. At the centre there is truth. As you travel, so error creeps in.'

'Yes, Lord Vorbis.'

Vorbis sighed.

'In Ossory's day we sailed alone in boats made of hides, and went where the winds of the God took us. That's how a holy man should travel.'

A tiny spark of defiance in Brutha declared that it, personally, would risk a little corruption for the sake of travelling with two decks between its feet and the waves.

'I heard that Ossory once sailed to the island of Erebos on a millstone,' he ventured by way of conversation.

'Nothing is impossible for the strong in faith,' said Vorbis.

'Try striking a match on jelly, mister.'

Brutha stiffened. It was impossible that Vorbis could have failed to hear the voice.

The Voice of the Turtle was heard in the land.

'Who's this bugger?'

'Forward,' said Vorbis. 'I can see that our friend Brutha is agog to get on board.'

The horse trotted on.

'Where are we? Who's that? It's as hot as hell in here and, believe me, I know what I'm talking about.'

'I can't talk now!' hissed Brutha.

'This cabbage stinks like a swamp! Let there be lettuce! Let there be slices of melon!'

The horses edged along the jetty and were led one at a time up the gangplank. By this time the box was vibrating. Brutha kept looking around guiltily, but no one else was taking any notice. Despite his size, Brutha was easy not to notice. Practically everyone had better things to do with their time than notice someone like Brutha. Even Vorbis had switched him off, and was talking to the captain.

He found a place up near the pointed end, where one of the sticking-up bits with the sails on gave him a bit of privacy. Then, with some dread, he opened the box.

The tortoise spoke from deep within its shell.

'Any eagles about?'

Brutha scanned the sky.

'No.'

The head shot out.

'You –' it began.

'I couldn't talk!' said Brutha. 'People were with me all the time! Can't you ... read the words in my mind? Can't you read my thoughts?'

'Mortal thoughts aren't like that,' snapped Om. 'You think it's like watching words paint themselves across the sky? Hah! It's like trying to make sense of a bundle of weeds. *Intentions*, yes. *Emotions*, yes. But not thoughts. Half the time *you* don't know what you're thinking, so why should I?'

'Because you're the God,' said Brutha. 'Abbys, chapter LVI, verse 17: "All of mortal mind he knows, and there are no secrets."'

'Was he the one with the bad teeth?'

Brutha hung his head.

'Listen,' said the tortoise, 'I am what I am. I can't help it if people think something else.'

'But you knew about my thoughts ... in the garden ...' muttered Brutha.

The tortoise hesitated. 'That was different,' it said. 'They weren't ... thoughts. That was guilt.'

'I believe that the Great God is Om, and in His Justice,' said Brutha. 'And I shall go on believing, whatever you say, and whatever you are.'

'Good to hear it,' said the tortoise fervently. 'Hold that thought. Where are we?'

'On a boat,' said Brutha. 'On the sea. Wobbling.'

'Going to Ephebe on a boat? What's wrong with the desert?'

'No one can cross the desert. No one can *live* in the heart of the desert.'

'*I* did.'

'It's only a couple of days' sailing.' Brutha's stomach lurched, even though the boat had hardly cleared the jetty. 'And they say that the God –'

'– me –'

'– is sending us a fair wind.'

'I am? Oh. Yes. Trust me for a fair wind. Flat as a mill-race the whole way, don't you worry.'

'I meant mill-pond! I meant mill-*pond*!'

Brutha clung to the mast.

After a while a sailor came and sat down on a coil of rope and looked at him interestedly.

'You can let go, Father,' he said. 'It stands up all by itself.'

'The sea . . . the waves . . .' murmured Brutha carefully, although there was nothing left to throw up.

The sailor spat thoughtfully.

'Aye,' he said. 'They got to be that shape, see, so's to fit into the sky.'

'But the boat's creaking!'

'Aye. It does that.'

'You mean this isn't a storm?'

The sailor sighed, and walked away.

After a while, Brutha risked letting go. He had never felt so ill in his life.

It wasn't just the seasickness. He didn't know where he was. And Brutha had always known where he was. Where he was, and the existence of Om, had been the only two certainties in his life.

It was something he shared with tortoises. Watch any tortoise walking, and periodically it will stop while it files away the memories of the journey so far. Not for nothing, elsewhere in the multiverse, are the little travelling devices controlled by electric thinking-engines called 'turtles'.

Brutha knew where he was by remembering where he had been – by the unconscious counting of footsteps and the noting of landmarks. Somewhere inside his head was a thread of memory which, if you had wired it directly to whatever controlled his feet, would cause Brutha to amble back through the little pathways of his life all the way to the place he was born.

Out of contact with the ground, on the mutable surface of the sea, the thread flapped loose.

In his box, Om tossed and shook to Brutha's motion as Brutha staggered across the moving deck and reached the rail.

To anyone except the novice, the boat was clipping through the waves on a good sailing day. Seabirds wheeled in its wake. Away to one side – port or starboard or one of those directions – a school of flying fish broke the surface in an attempt to escape the attentions of some dolphins. Brutha stared at the grey shapes as they zigzagged under the keel in a world where they never had to count at all –

'Ah, Brutha,' said Vorbis. 'Feeding the fishes, I see.'

'No, lord,' said Brutha. 'I'm being sick, lord.'

He turned.

There was Sergeant Simony, a muscular young man with the deadpan expression of the truly professional soldier. He was standing next to someone Brutha vaguely recognised as the number one salt or whatever his title was. And there was the exquisitor, smiling.

'*Him! Him!*' screamed the voice of the tortoise.

'Our young friend is not a good sailor,' said Vorbis.

'*Him! Him! I'd know him anywhere!*'

'Lord, I wish I wasn't a sailor at all,' said Brutha. He felt the box trembling as Om bounced around inside.

'*Kill him! Find something sharp! Push him overboard!*'

'Come with us to the prow, Brutha,' said Vorbis. 'There are many interesting things to be seen, according to the captain.'

The captain gave the frozen smirk of those caught between a rock and a hard place. Vorbis could always supply both.

Brutha trailed behind the other three, and risked a whisper.

'What's the matter?'

'Him! The bald one! Push him over the side!'

Vorbis half-turned, caught Brutha's embarrassed attention, and smiled.

'We will have our minds broadened, I am sure,' he said. He turned back to the captain, and pointed to a large bird gliding down the face of the waves.

'The Pointless Albatross,' said the captain promptly. 'Flies from the Hub to the Ri–' he faltered. But Vorbis was gazing with apparent affability at the view.

'He turned me over in the sun! *Look at his mind!*'

'From one pole of the world to the other, every year,' said the captain. He was sweating slightly.

'Really?' said Vorbis. 'Why?'

'No one knows.'

'Excepting the God, of course,' said Vorbis.

The captain's face was a sickly yellow.

'Of course. Certainly,' he said.

'Brutha?' shouted the tortoise. 'Are you listening to me?'

'And over there?' said Vorbis.

The sailor followed his extended arm.

'Oh. Flying fish,' he said. 'But they don't really fly,' he added quickly. 'They just build up speed in the water and glide a little way.'

'One of the God's marvels,' said Vorbis. 'Infinite variety, eh?'

'Yes, indeed,' said the captain. Relief was crossing his face now, like a friendly army.

'And the things down there?' said the exquisitor.

'Them? Porpoises,' said the captain. 'Sort of a fish.'

'Do they always swim around ships like this?'

'Often. Certainly. Especially in the waters off Ephebe.'

Vorbis leaned over the rail, and said nothing. Simony was staring at the horizon, his face absolutely immobile. This left a gap in the conversation which the captain, very stupidly, sought to fill.

'They'll follow a ship for days,' he said.

'Remarkable.' Another pause, a tar-pit of silence ready to snare the mastodons of unthinking comment. Earlier exquisitors had shouted and ranted confessions out of people. Vorbis never did that. He just dug deep silences in front of them.

'They seem to like them,' said the captain. He glanced nervously at Brutha, who was trying to shut the tortoise's voice out of his head. There was no help there.

Vorbis came to his aid instead.

'This must be very convenient on long voyages,' he said.

'Uh. Yes?' said the captain.

'From the provisions point of view,' said Vorbis.

'My lord, I don't quite –'

'It must be like having a travelling larder,' said Vorbis.

The captain smiled. 'Oh no, lord. We don't eat them.'

'Surely not? They look quite wholesome to *me*.'

'Oh, but you know the old saying, lord . . .'

'Saying?'

'Oh, they say that after they die, the souls of dead sailors become –'

The captain saw the abyss ahead, but the sentence had plunged on with a horrible momentum of its own.

For a while there was no sound but the zip of the waves, the distant splash of the porpoises, and the heaven-shaking thundering of the captain's heart.

Vorbis leaned back on the rail.

'But of course *we* are not prey to such superstitions,' he said lazily.

'Well, of course,' said the captain, clutching at this straw. 'Idle sailor talk. If ever I hear it again I shall have the man flog–'

Vorbis was looking past his ear.

'I say! Yes, you there!' he said.

One of the sailors nodded.

'Fetch me a harpoon,' said Vorbis.

The man looked from him to the captain and then scuttled off obediently.

'But, ah, uh, but your lordship should not, uh, ha, attempt such sport,' said the captain. 'Ah. Uh. A harpoon is a dangerous weapon in untrained hands, I am afraid you might do yourself an injury –'

'But *I* will not be using it,' said Vorbis.

The captain hung his head and held out his hand for the harpoon. Vorbis patted him on the shoulder.

'And then,' he said, 'you shall entertain us to lunch. Won't he, sergeant?'

Simony saluted. 'Just as you say, sir.'

'Yes.'

Brutha lay on his back among sails and ropes somewhere under the decking. It was hot, and the air smelled of all air anywhere that has ever come into contact with bilges.

Brutha hadn't eaten all day. Initially he'd been too ill to. Then he just hadn't.

'But being cruel to animals doesn't mean he's a . . . bad person,' he ventured, the harmonics of his tone suggesting that even he didn't believe this. It had been quite a small porpoise.

'He turned me on to my *back*,' said Om.

'Yes, but humans are more important than animals,' said Brutha.

'This is a point of view often expressed by humans,' said Om.

'Chapter IX, verse 16 of the book of –' Brutha began.

'Who cares what any book says?' screamed the tortoise.

Brutha was shaken.

'But you never told any of the prophets that people should be kind to animals,' he said. 'I don't remember anything about that. Not when you were . . . bigger. You don't want people to be kind to animals because they're animals, you just want people to be kind to animals because one of them might be *you*.'

'That's not a bad idea!'

'Besides, he's been kind to me. He didn't have to be.'

'You think that? Is that what you think? Have you looked at the man's *mind*?'

'Of course I haven't! I don't know how to!'

'You don't?'

'No! Humans can't do –'

Brutha paused. Vorbis seemed to do it. He only had to look at someone to know what wicked thoughts they harboured. And grandmother had been the same.

'Humans can't do it, I'm sure,' he said. 'We can't read minds.'

'I don't mean *reading* them, I mean *looking* at them,' said Om. 'Just seeing the shape of them. You can't *read* a mind. You might as well try and read a river. But seeing the shape's *easy*. Witches can do it, no trouble.'

'"The way of the witch shall be as a path strewn with thorns",' said Brutha.

'Ossory?' said Om.

'Yes. But of course you'd know,' said Brutha.

'Never heard it before in my life,' said the tortoise bitterly. 'It was what you might call an educated guess.'

'Whatever you say,' said Brutha, 'I still know that you can't truly be Om. The God would not talk like that about His chosen ones.'

'I never chose anyone,' said Om. 'They chose themselves.'

'If you're really Om, stop being a tortoise.'

'I told you, I can't. You think I haven't tried? Three years! Most of that time I thought I *was* a tortoise.'

'Then perhaps you were. Maybe you're just a tortoise who *thinks* he's a god.'

'Nah. Don't try philosophy again. Start thinking like that and you end up thinking maybe you're just a butterfly dreaming it's a whelk or something. No. One day all I had on my mind was the amount of walking necessary to get to the nearest plant with decent low-growing leaves, the next . . . I had all this memory filling up my head. Three years before the shell. No, don't you tell me I'm a tortoise with big ideas.'

Brutha hesitated. He knew it was wicked to ask, but he wanted to know what the memory *was*. Anyway, could it be wicked? If the God was sitting there talking to you, could you say anything truly wicked? Face to face? Somehow, that didn't seem so bad as saying something wicked when he was up on a cloud or something.

'As far as I can recall,' said Om, 'I'd intended to be a big white bull.'

'Trampling the infidel,' said Brutha.

'Not my basic intention, but no doubt some trampling could have been arranged. Or a swan, I thought. Something impressive. Three years later, I wake up and it turns out I've been a tortoise. I mean, you don't get much lower.' Careful, careful . . . you need his help, but don't tell him everything. Don't tell him what you suspect.

'When did you start think– when did you remember all this?' said Brutha, who found the phenomenon of forgetting a strange and fascinating one, as other men might find the idea of flying by flapping your arms.

'About two hundred feet above your vegetable garden,' said Om, 'which is not a point where it's fun to become sapient, I'm here to tell you.'

'But why?' said Brutha. 'Gods don't have to stay tortoises unless they want to!'

'I don't know,' lied Om.

If he works it out himself I'm done for, he thought. This is a chance in a million. If I get it wrong, it's back to a life where happiness is a leaf you can reach.

Part of him screamed: I'm a god! I don't have to think like this! I don't have to put myself in the power of a human!

But another part, the part that could remember exactly what being a tortoise for three years had been like, whispered: no. You have to. If you want to be up there again. He's stupid and gormless and he's not got a drop of ambition in his big flabby body. And this is what you've got to work with . . .

The god part said: Vorbis would have been better. Be rational. A mind like that could do anything!

He turned me on my back!

No, he turned a *tortoise* on its back.

Yes. Me.

No. You're a god.

Yes, but a persistently tortoise-shaped one.

If he had known you were a god ...

But Om remembered Vorbis's absorbed expression, in a pair of grey eyes in front of a mind as impenetrable as a steel ball. He'd never seen a mind shaped like that on anything walking upright. There was someone who probably *would* turn a god on his back, just to see what would happen. Someone who'd overturn the universe, without thought of consequence, for the sake of the knowledge of what happened when the universe was flat on its back ...

But what *he* had to work with was Brutha, with a mind as incisive as a meringue. And if Brutha found out that ...

Or if Brutha died ...

'How are you feeling?' said Om.

'Ill.'

'Snuggle down under the sails a bit more,' said Om. 'You don't want to catch a chill.'

There's got to be someone else, he thought. It can't be just him who ... the rest of the thought was so terrible he tried to block it from his mind, but he couldn't.

... it can't be just him who believes in me.

Really in me. Not in a pair of golden horns. Not in a great big building. Not in the dread of hot iron and knives. Not in paying your temple dues because everyone else does. Just in the fact that the Great God Om really exists.

And now he's got himself involved with the most unpleasant mind I've ever seen, someone who kills people to see if they die. An eagle kind of person if ever there was one ...

Om was aware of a mumbling.

Brutha was lying face down on the deck.

'What are you doing?' said Om.

Brutha turned his head.

'Praying.'

'That's good. What for?'

'You don't *know*?'

'Oh.'

If Brutha dies ...

The tortoise shuddered in its shell. If Brutha died, then it could already hear in its mind's ear the soughing of the wind in the deep, hot places of the desert.

Where the small gods went.

*

Where do gods come from? Where do they go?

Some attempt to answer this was made by the religious philosopher Koomi of Smale in his book *Ego-Video Liber Deorum*, which translates into the vernacular roughly as *Gods: A Spotter's Guide*.

People said there had to be a Supreme Being because otherwise how could the universe exist, eh?

And of course there clearly had to be, said Koomi, a Supreme Being. But since the universe was a bit of a mess, it was obvious that the Supreme Being hadn't in fact made it. If he had made it he would, being Supreme, have made a much better job of it, with far better thought given, taking an example at random, to things like the design of the common nostril. Or, to put it another way, the existence of a badly put-together watch proved the existence of a blind watchmaker. You only had to look around to see that there was room for improvement practically everywhere.

This suggested that the Universe had probably been put together in a bit of a rush by an underling while the Supreme Being wasn't looking, in the same way that Boy Scouts' Association minutes are done on office photocopiers all over the country.

So, reasoned Koomi, it was not a good idea to address any prayers to a Supreme Being. It would only attract his attention and might cause trouble.

And yet there seemed to be a lot of lesser gods around the place. Koomi's theory was that gods come into being and grow and flourish *because they are believed in*. Belief itself is the food of the gods. Initially, when mankind lived in small primitive tribes, there were probably millions of gods. Now there tended to be only a few very important ones – local gods of thunder and love, for example, tended to run together like pools of mercury as the small primitive tribes joined up and became huge, powerful primitive tribes with more sophisticated weapons. But any god could join. Any god could start small. Any god could grow in stature as its believers increased. And dwindle as they decreased. It was like a great big game of ladders and snakes.

Gods liked games, provided they were winning.

Koomi's theory was largely based on the good old Gnostic heresy, which tends to turn up all over the multiverse whenever men get up off their knees and start thinking for two minutes together, although the shock of the sudden altitude tends to mean the thinking is a little whacked. But it upsets priests, who tend to vent their displeasure in traditional ways.

When the Omnian Church found out about Koomi, they displayed him in every town within the Church's empire to demonstrate the essential flaws in his argument.

There were a lot of towns, so they had to cut him up quite small.

Ragged clouds ripped across the skies. The sails creaked in the rising wind, and Om could hear the shouts of the sailors as they tried to outrun the storm.

It was going to be a big storm, even by the mariners' standards. White water crowned the waves.

Brutha snored in his nest.

Om listened to the sailors. They were not men who dealt in sophistries. Someone had killed a porpoise, and everyone knew what that meant. It meant that there was going to be a storm. It meant that the ship was going to be sunk. It was simple cause and effect. It was worse than women aboard. It was worse than albatrosses.

Om wondered if tortoises could swim. Turtles could, he was pretty sure. But those buggers had the shell for it.

It would be too much to ask (even if a god had anyone to ask) that a body designed for trundling around a dry wilderness had any hydrodynamic properties other than those necessary to sink to the bottom.

Oh, well. Nothing else for it. He was still a god. He had *rights*.

He slid down a coil of rope and crawled carefully to the edge of the swaying deck, wedging his shell against a stanchion so that he could see down into the roiling water.

Then he spoke in a voice audible to nothing that was mortal.

Nothing happened for a while. Then one wave rose higher than the rest, and changed shape as it rose. Water poured upward, filling an invisible mould; it was humanoid, but obviously only because it wanted to be. It could as easily have been a waterspout, or an undertow. The sea is always powerful. So many people believe in it. But it seldom answers prayers.

The water shape rose level with the deck and kept pace with Om.

It developed a face, and opened a mouth.

'Well?' it said.

'Greetings, oh Queen of –' Om began.

The watery eyes focused.

'But you are just a small god. And you dare to summon *me*?'

The wind howled in the rigging.

'I have believers,' said Om. 'So I have the right.'

There was the briefest of pauses. Then the Sea Queen said, '*One* believer?'

'One or many does not matter here,' said Om. 'I have rights.'

'And what rights do you demand, little tortoise?' said the Queen of the Sea.

'Save the ship,' said Om.

The Queen was silent.

'You have to grant the request,' said Om. 'It's the rules.'

'But I can name my price,' said the Sea Queen.

'That's the rules, too.'

'And it will be high.'

'It will be paid.'

The column of water began to collapse back into the waves.

'I will consider this.'

Om stared down into the white sea. The ship rolled, sliding him back down the deck, and then rolled back. A flailing foreclaw hooked itself around the stanchion as Om's shell spun around, and for a moment both hind legs paddled helplessly over the waters.

And then Om was shaken free.

Something white swept down towards him as he seesawed over the edge, and he bit it.

Brutha yelled and pulled his hand up, with Om trailing on the end of it.

'You didn't have to bite!'

The ship pitched into a wave and flung him to the deck. Om let go and rolled away.

When Brutha got to his feet, or at least to his hands and knees, he saw the crewmen standing around him. Two of them grabbed him by the elbows as a wave crashed over the ship.

'What are you doing?'

They were trying to avoid looking at his face. They dragged him towards the rail.

Somewhere in the scuppers Om screamed at the Sea Queen.

'It's the rules! The *rules!*'

Four sailors had got hold of Brutha now. Om could hear, above the roaring of the storm, the silence of the desert.

'Wait,' said Brutha.

'It's nothing personal,' said one of the sailors. 'We don't want to do this.'

'I don't want you to do it either,' said Brutha. 'Is that any help?'

'The sea wants a life,' said the oldest sailor. 'Yours is nearest. Okay, get his —'

'Can I make my peace with my God?'

'What?'

'If you're going to kill me, can I pray to my God first?'

'It's not us that's killing you,' said the sailor. 'It's the sea.'

'"The hand that does the deed is guilty of the crime,"' said Brutha. 'Ossory, chapter LVI, verse 93.'

The sailors looked at one another. At a time like this, it was probably not wise to antagonise *any* god. The ship skidded down the side of a wave.

'You've got ten seconds,' said the oldest sailor. 'That's ten seconds more than many men get.'

Brutha lay down on the deck, helped considerably by another wave that slammed into the timbers.

Om was dimly aware of the prayer, to his surprise. He couldn't make out the words, but the prayer itself was an itch at the back of his mind.

'Don't ask me,' he said, trying to get upright, 'I'm out of options —'

The ship smacked down . . .

. . . on to a calm sea.

The storm still raged, but only around a widening circle with the ship in the middle. The lightning, stabbing at the sea, surrounded them like the bars of a cage.

The circle lengthened ahead of them. Now the ship sped down a narrow channel of calm between grey walls of storm a mile high. Electric fire raged overhead.

And then was gone.

Behind them, a mountain of greyness squatted on the sea. They could hear the thunder dying away.

Brutha got uncertainly to his feet, swaying wildly to compensate for a motion that was no longer there.

'Now I —' he began.

He was alone. The sailors had fled.

'Om?' said Brutha.

'Over here.'

Brutha fished his God out of the seaweed.

'You said you couldn't do anything!' he said accusingly.

'That wasn't m—' Om paused. There will be a price, he thought. It won't be cheap. It can't be cheap. The Sea Queen is a god. I've crushed a few towns in my time. Holy fire, that kind of thing. If the price isn't high, how can people respect you?

'I made arrangements,' he said.

Tidal waves. A ship sunk. A couple of towns disappearing under the sea. It'll be something like that. If people don't respect then they won't fear, and if they don't fear, how can you get them to believe?

Seems unfair, really. One man killed a porpoise. Of course, it doesn't matter to the Queen who gets thrown overboard, just as it didn't matter to *him* which porpoise he killed. And *that's* unfair, because it was Vorbis who did it. He makes people do things they shouldn't do . . .

What am I thinking about? Before I was a tortoise, I didn't even know what *unfair* meant . . .

The hatches opened. People came on deck and hung on the rail. Being on deck in stormy weather always has the possibility of being washed overboard, but that takes on a rosy glow after hours below decks with frightened horses and seasick passengers.

There were no more storms. The ship ploughed on in favourable winds, under a clear sky, in a sea as empty of life as the hot desert.

The days passed uneventfully. Vorbis stayed below decks for most of the time.

The crew treated Brutha with cautious respect. News like Brutha spreads quickly.

The coast here was dunes, with the occasional barren salt marsh. A heat haze hung over the land. It was the kind of coast where shipwrecked landfall is more to be dreaded than drowning. There were no seabirds. Even the birds that had been trailing the ship for scraps had vanished.

'No eagles,' said Om. There was that to be said about it.

Towards the evening of the fourth day the unedifying panorama was punctuated by a glitter of light, high on the dune sea. It flashed with a sort of rhythm. The captain, whose face now looked as if sleep had not been a regular night-time companion, called Brutha over.

'His . . . your . . . the deacon told me to watch out for this,' he said. 'You go and fetch him now.'

Vorbis had a cabin somewhere near the bilges, where the air was as thick as thin soup. Brutha knocked.

'Enter.'*

---

* Words are the litmus paper of the mind. If you find yourself in the power of someone who will use the word 'commence' in cold blood, go somewhere else very quickly. But if they say

There were no portholes down here. Vorbis was sitting in the dark.

'Yes, Brutha?'

'The captain sent me to fetch you, lord. Something's shining in the desert.'

'Good. Now, Brutha. Attend. The captain has a mirror. You will ask to borrow it.'

'Er ... what is a mirror, lord?'

'An unholy and forbidden device,' said Vorbis. 'Which regretfully can be pressed into godly service. He will deny it, of course. But a man with such a neat beard and tiny moustache is vain, and a vain man must have his mirror. So take it. And stand in the sun and move the mirror so that it shines the sun towards the desert. Do you understand?'

'No, lord,' said Brutha.

'Your ignorance is your protection, my son. And then come back and tell me what you see.'

Om dozed in the sun. Brutha had found him a little space near the pointy end where he could get sun with little danger of being seen by the crew – and the crew were jittery enough at the moment not to go looking for trouble in any case.

A tortoise dreams ...

... for millions of years.

It was the dreamtime. The unformed time.

The small gods chittered and whirred in the wilderness places, and the cold places, and the deep places. They swarmed in the darkness, without memory but driven by hope and lust for the one thing, the one thing a god craves – *belief*.

There are no medium-sized trees in the deep forest. There are only the towering ones, whose canopy spreads across the sky. Below, in the gloom, there's light for nothing but mosses and ferns. But when a giant falls, leaving a little space ... *then* there's a race – between the trees on either side, who want to spread *out*, and the seedlings below, who race to grow *up*.

Sometimes, you can make your own space.

Forests were a long way from the wilderness. The nameless voice that was going to be Om drifted on the wind on the edge of the desert, trying to be heard among countless others, trying to avoid being pushed into the centre. It may have whirled for millions of

'Enter', don't stop to pack.

years – it had nothing with which to measure time. All it had was hope, and a certain sense of the presence of things. And a voice.

Then there was a day. In a sense, it was the first day.

Om had been aware of the shepherd for some ti– for a while. The flock had been wandering closer and closer. The rains had been sparse. Forage was scarce. Hungry mouths propelled hungry legs further into the rocks, searching out the hitherto scorned clumps of sun-seared grass.

They were sheep, possibly the most stupid animal in the universe with the possible exception of the duck. But even their uncomplicated minds couldn't hear the voice, because sheep don't listen.

There was a lamb, though. It had strayed a little way. Om saw to it that it strayed a little further. Around a rock. Down the slope. Into the crevice.

Its bleating drew the mother.

The crevice was well hidden and the ewe was, after all, content now that she had her lamb. She saw no reason to bleat, even when the shepherd wandered about the rocks calling, cursing and, eventually, pleading. The shepherd had a hundred sheep, and it might have been surprising that he was prepared to spend days searching for one sheep; in fact, it was *because* he was the kind of man prepared to spend days looking for a lost sheep that he had a hundred sheep.

The voice that was going to be Om waited.

It was on the evening of the second day that he scared up a partridge that had been nesting near the crevice, just as the shepherd was wandering by.

It wasn't much of a miracle, but it was good enough for the shepherd. He made a cairn of stones at the spot and, next day, brought his whole flock into the area. And in the heat of the afternoon he lay down to sleep – and Om spoke to him, inside his head.

Three weeks later the shepherd was stoned to death by the priests of Ur-Gilash, who was at that time the chief god in the area. But they were too late. Om already had a hundred believers, and the number was growing . . .

Only a mile away from the shepherd and his flock was a goatherd and his herd. The merest accident of microgeography had meant that the first man to hear the voice of Om, and who gave Om his view of humans, was a shepherd and not a goatherd. They have quite different ways of looking at the world, and the whole of history might have been different.

For sheep are stupid, and have to be driven. But goats are intelligent, and need to be led.

Ur-Gilash, thought Om. Ah, those were the days... when Ossory and his followers had broken into the temple and smashed the altar and had thrown the priestesses out of the window to be torn apart by wild dogs, which was the correct way of doing things, and there had been a mighty wailing and gnashing of feet and the followers of Om had lit their campfires in the crumbled halls of Gilash just as the Prophet had said, and that counted even though he'd said it only five minutes earlier, when they were only looking for the firewood, because everyone agreed a prophecy is a prophecy and no one said you had to wait a long time for it to come true.

Great days. Great days. Every day fresh converts. The rise of Om had been unstoppable...

He jerked awake.

Old Ur-Gilash. Weather god, wasn't he? Yes. No. Maybe one of your basic giant spider gods? Something like that. Whatever happened to him?

What happened to me? How does it happen? You hang around the astral planes, going with the flow, enjoy the rhythms of the universe, you think that all the, you know, humans are getting on with the believing back down there, you decide to go and stir them up a bit and then... a tortoise. It's like going to the bank and finding the money's been leaking out through a hole. The first you know is when you stroll down looking for a handy mind, and suddenly you're a tortoise and there's no power left to get out.

Three years of looking up at practically everything...

Old Ur-Gilash? Perhaps he was hanging on as a lizard somewhere, with some old hermit as his only believer. More likely he had been blown out into the desert. A small god was lucky to get one chance.

There was something wrong. Om couldn't quite put his finger on it, and not only because he didn't have a finger. Gods rose and fell like bits of onion in a boiling soup, but *this* time was different. There was something wrong this time...

He'd forced out Ur-Gilash. Fair enough. Law of the jungle. But no one was challenging *him*...

Where was Brutha?

'Brutha!'

*

Brutha was counting the flashes of light off the desert.

'It's a good thing I had a mirror, yes?' said the captain hopefully. 'I expect his lordship won't mind about the mirror because it turned out to be useful?'

'I don't think he thinks like that,' said Brutha, still counting.

'No. I don't think he does either,' said the captain gloomily.

'Seven, and then four.'

'It'll be the Quisition for me,' said the captain.

Brutha was about to say, 'Then rejoice that your soul shall be purified.' But he didn't. And he didn't know why he didn't.

'I'm sorry about that,' he said.

A veneer of surprise overlaid the captain's grief.

'You people usually say something about how the Quisition is good for the soul,' he said.

'I'm sure it is,' said Brutha.

The captain was watching his face intently.

'It's flat, you know,' he said quietly. 'I've sailed out into the Rim Ocean. It's flat, and I've seen the Edge, and it moves. Not the Edge. I mean . . . what's down there. They can cut my head off but it will still move.'

'But it will stop moving for you,' said Brutha. 'So I should be careful to whom you speak, captain.'

The captain leaned closer.

'The Turtle Moves!' he hissed, and darted away.

'Brutha!'

Guilt jerked Brutha upright like a hooked fish. He turned around, and sagged with relief. It wasn't Vorbis, it was only God.

He padded over to the place in front of the mast. Om glared up at him.

'Yes?' said Brutha.

'You never come and see me,' said the tortoise. 'I know you're busy,' it added sarcastically, 'but a quick prayer would be nice, even.'

'I checked you first thing this morning,' said Brutha.

'And I'm hungry.'

'You had a whole melon rind last night.'

'And who had the melon, eh?'

'No, he didn't,' said Brutha. 'He eats stale bread and water.'

'Why doesn't he eat fresh bread?'

'He waits for it to get stale.'

'Yes. I expect he does,' said the tortoise.

'Om?'

'What?'

'The captain just said something odd. He said the world is flat and has an edge.'

'Yes? So what?'

'But, I mean, we know the world is a ball, because ...'

The tortoise blinked.

'No, it's not,' he said. 'Who said it's a ball?'

'You did,' said Brutha. Then he added: 'According to Book One of the Septateuch, anyway.'

I've never thought like this before, he thought. I'd never have said 'anyway'.

'Why'd the captain tell me something like that?' he said. 'It's not normal conversation.'

'I told you, I never made the world,' said Om. 'Why should I make the world? It was here already. And if I *did* make a world, I wouldn't make it a ball. People'd fall off. All the sea'd run off the bottom.'

'Not if you told it to stay on.'

'Hah! Will you hark at the man!'

'Besides, the sphere is a perfect shape,' said Brutha. 'Because in the Book of –'

'Nothing amazing about a sphere,' said the tortoise. 'Come to that, a turtle is a perfect shape.'

'A perfect shape for what?'

'Well, the perfect shape for a turtle, to start with,' said Om. 'If it was shaped like a ball, it'd be bobbing to the surface the whole time.'

'But it's a heresy to say the world is flat,' said Brutha.

'Maybe, but it's true.'

'And it's really on the back of a giant turtle?'

'That's right.'

'In that case,' said Brutha triumphantly, 'what does the turtle stand on?'

The tortoise gave him a blank stare.

'It doesn't stand on anything,' it said. 'It's a *turtle*, for heaven's sake. It swims. That's what turtles are for.'

'I ... er ... I think I'd better go and report to Vorbis,' said Brutha. 'He goes very calm if he's kept waiting. What did you want me for? I'll try and bring you some more food after supper.'

'How are you feeling?' said the tortoise.

'I'm feeling all right, thank you.'

'Eating properly, that sort of thing?'

'Yes, thank you.'

'Pleased to hear it. Run along now. I mean, I'm only your *God*.' Om raised its voice as Brutha hurried off. 'And you might visit more often!'

'And pray louder, I'm fed up with straining!' he shouted.

Vorbis was still sitting in his cabin when Brutha puffed along the passage and knocked on the door. There was no reply. After a while, Brutha pushed the door open.

Vorbis did not appear to read. Obviously he wrote, because of the famous Letters, but no one ever saw him do it. When he was alone he spent a lot of time staring at the wall, or prostrate in prayer. Vorbis could humble himself in prayer in a way that made the posturings of power-mad emperors look subservient.

'Um,' said Brutha, and tried to pull the door shut again.

Vorbis waved one hand irritably. Then he stood up. He did not dust off his robe.

'Do you know, Brutha,' he said, 'I do not think there is a single person in the Citadel who would dare to interrupt me at prayer? They would fear the Quisition. *Everyone* fears the Quisition. Except you, it appears. Do you fear the Quisition?'

Brutha looked into the black-on-black eyes. Vorbis looked into a round pink face. There was a special face that people wore when they spoke to an exquisitor. It was flat and expressionless and glistened slightly, and even a half-trained exquisitor could read the barely concealed guilt like a book. Brutha just looked out of breath but then, he always did. It was fascinating.

'No, lord,' he said.

'Why not?'

'The Quisition protects us, lord. It is written in Ossory, chapter VII, verse —'

Vorbis put his head on one side.

'Of course it is. But have you ever thought that the Quisition could be wrong?'

'No, lord,' said Brutha.

'But why not?'

'I do not know why, Lord Vorbis. I just never have.'

Vorbis sat down at a little writing table, no more than a board that folded down from the hull.

'And you are right, Brutha,' he said. 'Because the Quisition *cannot* be wrong. Things can only be as the God wishes them. It is impossible to think that the world could run in any other way, is this not so?'

A vision of a one-eyed tortoise flickered momentarily in Brutha's mind.

Brutha had never been any good at lying. The truth itself had always seemed so incomprehensible that complicating things even further had always been beyond him.

'So the Septateuch teaches us,' he said.

'Where there is punishment, there is always a crime,' said Vorbis. 'Sometimes the crime follows the punishment, which only serves to prove the foresight of the Great God.'

'That's what my grandmother used to say,' said Brutha automatically.

'Indeed? I would like to know more about this formidable lady.'

'She used to give me a thrashing every morning because I would certainly do something to deserve it during the day,' said Brutha.

'A most *complete* understanding of the nature of mankind,' said Vorbis, with his chin on one hand. 'Were it not for the deficiency of her sex, it sounds as though she would have made an excellent inquisitor.'

Brutha nodded. Oh, yes. Yes, indeed.

'And now,' said Vorbis, with no change in his tone, 'you will tell me what you saw in the desert.'

'Uh. There were six flashes. And then a pause of about five heartbeats. And then eight flashes. And another pause. And two flashes.'

Vorbis nodded thoughtfully.

'Three-quarters,' he said. 'All praise to the Great God. He is my staff and guide through the hard places. And you may go.'

Brutha hadn't expected to be told what the flashes meant, and wasn't going to enquire. The Quisition asked the questions. They were known for it.

Next day the ship rounded a headland and the bay of Ephebe lay before it, with the city a white smudge on the horizon which time and distance turned into a spilling of blindingly white houses, all the way up a rock.

It seemed of considerable interest to Sergeant Simony. Brutha had not exchanged a word with him. Fraternisation between clergy and soldiers was not encouraged; there was a certain tendency to *unholiness* about soldiers . . .

Brutha, left to his own devices again as the crew made ready for port, watched the soldier carefully. Most soldiers were a bit slovenly and generally rude to minor clergy. Simony was different. Apart from anything else, he gleamed. His breastplate hurt the eyes. His skin looked scrubbed.

The sergeant stood at the prow, staring fixedly as the city drew nearer. It was unusual to see him very far away from Vorbis. Wherever Vorbis stood there was the sergeant, hand on sword, eyes scanning the surroundings for . . . what?

And always silent, except when spoken to. Brutha tried to be friends.

'Looks very . . . white, doesn't it?' he said. 'The city. Very white. Sergeant Simony?'

The sergeant turned slowly, and stared at Brutha.

Vorbis's gaze was dreadful. Vorbis looked through your head to the sins inside, hardly interested in you except as a vehicle for your sins. But Simony's glance was pure, simple hatred.

Brutha stepped back.

'Oh. I'm sorry,' he muttered. He walked back sombrely to the blunt end, and tried to keep out of the soldier's way.

Anyway, there were more soldiers, soon enough . . .

The Ephebians were expecting them. Soldiers lined the quay, weapons held in a way that stopped just short of being a direct insult. And there were a lot of them.

Brutha trailed along, the voice of the tortoise insinuating itself in his head.

'So the Ephebians want peace, do they?' said Om. 'Doesn't look like that. Doesn't look like we're going to lay down the law to a defeated enemy. Looks like we took a pasting and don't want to take any more. Looks like we're suing for peace. That's what it looks like to me.'

'In the Citadel everyone said it was a glorious victory,' said Brutha. He found he could talk now with his lips hardly moving at all; Om seemed able to pick up his words as they reached his vocal chords.

Ahead of him, Simony shadowed the deacon, staring suspiciously at each Ephebian guard.

'That's a funny thing,' said Om. 'Winners never talk about glorious victories. That's because they're the ones who see what the battlefield looks like afterwards. It's only the losers who have glorious victories.'

Brutha didn't know what to reply. 'That doesn't sound like god talk,' he hazarded.

'It's this tortoise brain.'

'What?'

'Don't you know anything? Bodies aren't just handy things for storing your mind in. Your shape affects how you think. It's all this morphology that's all over the place.'

'What?'

Om sighed. 'If I don't concentrate, I think like a tortoise!'

'What? You mean slowly?'

'No! Tortoises are cynics. They always expect the worst.'

'Why?'

'I don't know. Because it often happens to them, I suppose.'

Brutha stared around at Ephebe. Guards with helmets crested with plumes that looked like horses' tails gone rogue marched on either side of the column. A few Ephebian citizens watched idly from the roadside. They looked surprisingly like the people at home, and not like two-legged demons at all.

'They're people,' he said.

'Full marks for comparative anthropology.'

'Brother Nhumrod said Ephebians eat human flesh,' said Brutha. 'He wouldn't tell lies.'

A small boy regarded Brutha thoughtfully while excavating a nostril. If it was a demon in human form, it was an extremely good actor.

At intervals along the road from the docks were white stone statues. Brutha had never seen statues before. Apart from the statues of the SeptArchs, of course, but that wasn't the same thing.

'What are they?'

'Well, the tubby one with the toga is Tuvelpit, the God of Wine. They call him Smimto in Tsort. And the broad with the hairdo is Astoria, Goddess of Love. A complete bubblehead. The ugly one is Offler the Crocodile God. Not a local boy. He's Klatchian originally, but the Ephebians heard about him and thought he was a good idea. Note the teeth. Good teeth. *Good* teeth. Then the one with the snakepit hairdo is –'

'You talk about them as if they were real,' said Brutha.

'They are.'

'There is no other god but you. You told Ossory that.'

'Well. You know. I exaggerated a bit. But they're not that good. There's one of 'em that sits around playing a flute most of the time and chasing milkmaids. I don't call that very divine. Call that very divine? I don't.'

The road wound up steeply around the rocky hill. Most of the city seemed to be built on outcrops or was cut into the actual rock itself, so that one man's patio was another man's roof. The roads were really a series of shallow steps, accessible to a man or a donkey but sudden death to a cart. Ephebe was a pedestrian place.

More people watched them in silence. So did the statues of the gods. The Ephebians had gods in the same way that other cities had rats.

Brutha got a look at Vorbis's face. The exquisitor was staring straight ahead of himself. Brutha wondered what the man was seeing.

It was all so new!

And devilish, of course. Although the gods in the statues didn't look much like demons – but he could hear the voice of Nhumrod pointing out that this very fact made them even more demonic. Sin crept up on you like a wolf in a sheep's skin.

One of the goddesses had been having some very serious trouble with her dress, Brutha noticed; if Brother Nhumrod had been present, he would have had to hurry off for some very serious lying down.

'Petulia, Goddess of Negotiable Affection,' said Om. 'Worshipped by the ladies of the night and every other time as well, if you catch my meaning.'

Brutha's mouth dropped open.

'They've got a goddess for *painted jezebels?*'

'Why not? Very religious people, I understand. They're used to being on their – they spend so much time looking at the – look, belief is where you find it. Specialisation. That's safe, see. Low risk, guaranteed returns. There's even a God of Lettuce somewhere. I mean, it's not as though anyone else is likely to try to become a God of Lettuce. You just find a lettuce-growing community and hang on. Thunder gods come and go, but it's *you* they turn to every time when there's a bad attack of Lettuce Fly. You've got to . . . uh . . . hand it to Petulia. She spotted a gap in the market and filled it.'

'There's a God of Lettuce?'

'Why not? If enough people believe, you can be god of anything . . .'

Om stopped himself and waited to see if Brutha had noticed. But Brutha seemed to have something else on his mind.

'That's not right. Not treating people like that. Ow.'

He'd walked into the back of a subdeacon. The party had halted, partly because the Ephebian escort had stopped too, but mainly because a man was running down the street.

He was quite old, and in many respects resembled a frog that had been dried out for quite some time. Something about him generally made people think of the word 'spry', but, at the moment, they would be much more likely to think of the words 'mother naked' and possibly also 'dripping wet' and would be one hundred per cent accurate, too. Although there was the beard. It was a beard you could camp out in.

The man thudded down the street without any apparent self-consciousness and stopped outside a potter's shop. The potter didn't seem concerned at being addressed by a little wet naked man; in fact, none of the people in the street had given him a second glance.

'I'd like a Number Nine pot and some string, please,' said the old man.

'Yes sir, Mr Legibus.' The potter reached under his counter and pulled out a towel. The naked man took it in an absent-minded way. Brutha got the feeling that this had happened to both of them before.

'And a lever of infinite length and, um, an immovable place to stand,' said Legibus, drying himself off.

'What you see is what I got, sir. Pots and general household items, but a bit short on axiomatic mechanisms.'

'Well, have you got a piece of chalk?'

'Got some right here from last time,' said the potter.

The little naked man took the chalk and started to draw triangles on the nearest bit of wall. Then he looked down.

'Why haven't I got any clothes on?' he said.

'*We've* been having our *bath* again, haven't we?' said the potter.

'I left my clothes in the bath?'

'I think you probably had an idea while you were in the bath?' prompted the potter.

'That's right! That's right! Got this splendid idea for moving the world around!' said Legibus. 'Simple lever principle. Should work perfectly. It's just a matter of getting the technical details sorted out.'

'That's nice. We can move somewhere warm for the winter,' said the potter.

'Can I borrow the towel?'

'It's yours anyway, Mr Legibus.'

'Is it?'

'I said, you left it here last time. Remember? When you had that idea for the lighthouse?'

'Fine. Fine,' said Legibus, wrapping the towel around himself. He drew a few more lines on the wall. 'Fine. Okay. I'll send someone down later to collect the wall.'

He turned and appeared to see the Omnians for the first time. He peered forward and then shrugged.

'Hmm,' he said, and wandered away.

Brutha tugged at the cloak of one of the Ephebian soldiers.

'Excuse me, but why did we stop?' he said.

'Philosophers have right of way,' said the soldier.

'What's a philosopher?' said Brutha.

'Someone who's bright enough to find a job with no heavy lifting,' said a voice in his head.

'An infidel seeking the just fate he shall surely receive,' said Vorbis. 'An inventor of fallacies. This cursed city attracts them like a dung heap attracts flies.'

'Actually, it's the climate,' said the voice of the tortoise. 'Think about it. If you're inclined to leap out of your bath and run down the street every time you think you've got a bright idea, you don't want to do it somewhere cold. If you *do* do it somewhere cold, you die out. That's natural selection, that is. Ephebe's known for its philosophers. It's better than street theatre.'

'What, a lot of old men running around the streets with no clothes on?' said Brutha, under his breath, as they were marched onward.

'More or less. If you spend your whole time thinking about the universe, you tend to forget the less important bits of it. Like your pants. And ninety-nine out of a hundred ideas they come up with are totally useless.'

'Why doesn't anyone lock them away safely, then? They don't sound much use to *me*,' said Brutha.

'Because the hundredth idea,' said Om, 'is generally a humdinger.'

'What?'

'Look up at the highest tower on the rock.'

Brutha looked up. At the top of the tower, secured by metal bands, was a big disc that glittered in the morning light.

'What is it?' he whispered.

'The reason why Omnia hasn't got much of a fleet any more,' said Om. 'That's why it's always worth having a few philosophers around the place. One minute it's all Is Truth Beauty and Is Beauty

Truth, and Does a Falling Tree in the Forest Make a Sound if There's No one There to Hear It, and then just when you think they're going to start dribbling one of 'em says, Incidentally, putting a thirty-foot parabolic reflector on a high place to shoot the rays of the sun at an enemy's ships would be a very interesting demonstration of optical principles,' he added. 'Always coming up with amazing new ideas, the philosophers. The one before that was some intricate device that demonstrated the principles of leverage by incidentally hurling balls of burning sulphur two miles. Then before that, I think, there was some kind of an underwater thing that shot sharpened logs into the bottom of ships.'

Brutha stared at the disc again. He hadn't understood more than one-third of the words in the last statement.

'Well,' he said, 'does it?'

'Does what?'

'Make a sound. If it falls down when no one's there to hear it.'

'Who cares?'

The party had reached a gateway in the wall that ran around the top of the rock in much the same way that a headband encircles a head. The Ephebian captain stopped, and turned.

'The ... *visitors* ... must be blindfolded,' he said.

'That is outrageous!' said Vorbis. 'We are here on a mission of diplomacy!'

'That is not my business,' said the captain. 'My business is to say: If you go through this gate you go blindfolded. You don't have to be blindfolded. You can stay outside. But if you want to go through, you got to wear a blindfold. This is one of them life choices.'

One of the subdeacons whispered in Vorbis's ear. He held a brief *sotto voce* conversation with the leader of the Omnian guard.

'Very well,' he said, 'under protest.'

The blindfold was quite soft, and totally opaque. But as Brutha was led ...

... ten paces along a passage, and then left five paces, then diagonally forward and left three-and-a-half paces, and right one hundred and three paces, down three steps, and turned around seventeen-and-one-quarter times, and forward nine paces, and left one pace, and forward nineteen paces, and pause three seconds, and right two paces, and back two paces, and left two paces, and turned three-and-a-half times, and wait one second, and up three steps, and right twenty paces, and turned around five-and-a-quarter times, and left fifteen paces, and forward seven paces, and right eighteen paces, and up seven steps, and diagonally forward, and pause two seconds, right four paces, and down a slope that went down a metre every ten paces for thirty paces, and then turned around seven-and-a-half times, and forward six paces . . .

. . . he wondered what good it was supposed to do.

The blindfold was removed in an open courtyard, made of some white stone that turned the sunlight into a glare. Brutha blinked.

Bowmen lined the yard. Their arrows were pointing downwards, but their manner suggested that pointing horizontally could happen any minute.

Another bald man was waiting for them. Ephebe seemed to have an unlimited supply of skinny bald men wearing sheets. This one smiled, with his mouth alone.

No one likes us much, Brutha thought.

'I trust you will excuse this minor inconvenience,' said the skinny man. 'My name is Aristocrates. I am secretary to the Tyrant. Please ask your men to put down their weapons.'

Vorbis drew himself up to his full height. He was a head taller than the Ephebian. Pale though his complexion normally was, it had gone paler.

'We are entitled to retain our arms!' he said. 'We are an emissary to a foreign land!'

'But not a barbarian one,' said Aristocrates mildly. 'Weapons will not be required here.'

'Barbarian?' said Vorbis. 'You burned our ships!'

Aristocrates held up a hand.

'This is a discussion for later,' he said. 'My pleasant task now is to show you to your quarters. I am sure you would like to rest a little after your journey. You are, of course, at liberty to wander anywhere you wish in the palace. And if there is anywhere where *we* do not wish you to wander, the guards will be sure to inform you with speed and tact.'

'And we can leave the palace?' said Vorbis coldly.

Aristocrates shrugged.

'We do not guard the gateway except in times of war,' he said. 'If you can remember the way, you are free to use it. But vague perambulations in the labyrinth are unwise, I must warn you. Our ancestors were sadly very suspicious and put in many traps out of distrust; we keep them well-greased and primed, of course, merely out of a respect for tradition. And now, if you would care to follow me . . .'

The Omnians kept together as they followed Aristocrates through the palace. There were fountains. There were gardens.

Here and there groups of people sat around doing nothing very much except talking. The Ephebians seemed to have only a shaky grasp of the concepts of 'inside' and 'outside' – except for the palace's encircling labyrinth, which was very clear on the subject.

'Danger attends us at every turn,' said Vorbis quietly. 'Any man who breaks rank or fraternises in any way will explain his conduct to the inquisitors. At length.'

Brutha looked at a woman filling a jug from a well. It did not look like a very military act.

He was feeling that strange double feeling again. On the surface there were the thoughts of Brutha, which were exactly the thoughts that the Citadel would have approved of. This was a nest of infidels and unbelievers, its very mundanity a subtle cloak for the traps of wrong thinking and heresy. It might be bright with sunlight, but in reality it was a place of shadows.

But down below were the thoughts of the Brutha that watched Brutha from the inside . . .

Vorbis looked wrong here. Sharp and unpleasant. And any city where potters didn't worry at all when naked, dripping wet old men came and drew triangles on their walls was a place Brutha wanted to find out more about. He felt like a big empty jug. The thing to do with something empty was fill it up.

'Are you doing something to me?' he whispered.

In his box, Om looked at the shape of Brutha's mind. Then he tried to think quickly.

'No,' he said, and that at least was the truth. Had this ever happened before?

Had it been like this back in the first days? It must have been. It was all so hazy now. He couldn't remember the thoughts he'd had then, just the shape of the thoughts. Everything had been highly coloured, everything had been growing every day – *he* had been growing every day; thoughts and the mind that was thinking them were developing at the same speed. Easy to forget things from those times. It was like a fire trying to remember the shape of its flames. But the *feeling* – he could remember that.

He wasn't doing anything to Brutha. Brutha was doing it to himself. Brutha was beginning to think in godly ways. Brutha was starting to become a prophet.

Om wished he had someone to talk to. Someone who understood.

This *was* Ephebe, wasn't it? Where people made a *living* trying to understand?

*

The Omnians were to be housed in little rooms around a central courtyard. There was a fountain in the middle, in a very small grove of sweet-smelling pine trees. The soldiers nudged one another. People think that professional soldiers think a lot about fighting, but *serious* professional soldiers think a lot more about food and a warm place to sleep, because these are two things that are generally hard to get, whereas fighting tends to turn up all the time.

There was a bowl of fruit in Brutha's cell, and a plate of cold meat. But first things first. He fished the God out of the box.

'There's fruit,' he said. 'What're these berries?'

'Grapes,' said Om. 'Raw material for wine.'

'You mentioned that word before. What does it mean?'

There was a cry from outside.

'Brutha!'

'That's Vorbis. I'll have to go.'

Vorbis was standing in the middle of his cell.

'Have you eaten anything?' he demanded.

'No, lord.'

'Fruit and meat, Brutha. And this is a fast day. They seek to insult us!'

'Um. Perhaps they don't know that it is a fast day?' Brutha hazarded.

'Ignorance is itself a sin,' said Vorbis.

'Ossory VII, verse 4,' said Brutha automatically.

Vorbis smiled and patted Brutha's shoulder.

'You are a walking book, Brutha. The *Septateuch perambulatus*.'

Brutha looked down at his sandals.

He's right, he thought. And I had forgotten. Or at least, not wanted to remember.

And then he heard his own thoughts echoed back to him: it's fruit and meat and bread, that's all. That's all it is. Fast days and feast days and Prophets' Days and bread days ... who cares? A God whose only concern about food now is that it's low enough to reach?

I wish he wouldn't keep patting my shoulder.

Vorbis turned away.

'Shall I remind the others?' Brutha said.

'No. Our ordained brothers will not, of course, require reminding. As for soldiers ... a little licence, perhaps, is allowable this far from home ...'

Brutha wandered back to his cell.

Om was still on the table, staring fixedly at the melon.

'I nearly committed a terrible sin,' said Brutha. 'I nearly ate fruit on a fruitless day.'

'That's a terrible thing, a terrible thing,' said Om. 'Now cut the melon.'

'But it is forbidden!' said Brutha.

'No it's not,' said Om. 'Cut the melon.'

'But it was the eating of fruit that caused passion to invade the world,' said Brutha.

'All it caused was flatulence,' said Om. 'Cut the melon!'

'You're tempting me!'

'No I'm not. I'm giving you permission. Special dispensation! Cut the damn melon!'

'Only a bishop or higher is allowed to giv–' Brutha began. And then he stopped.

Om glared at him.

'Yes. Exactly,' he said. 'And now cut the melon.' His tone softened a bit. 'If it makes you feel any better, I shall declare that it is bread. I happen to be the God in this immediate vicinity. I can call it what I damn well like. It's bread. Right? Now cut the damn melon.'

'Loaf,' corrected Brutha.

'Right. And give me a slice without any seeds in it.'

Brutha did so, a bit carefully.

'And eat up quick,' said Om.

'In case Vorbis finds us?'

'Because you've got to go and find a philosopher,' said Om. The fact that his mouth was full didn't make any difference to his voice in Brutha's mind. 'You know, melons grow wild in the wilderness. Not big ones like this. Little green jobs. Skin like leather. Can't bite through 'em. The years I've spent eating dead leaves a goat'd spit out, right next to a crop of melons. Melons should have thinner skins. Remember that.'

'Find a philosopher?'

'Right. Someone who knows how to think. Someone who can help me stop being a tortoise.'

'But . . . Vorbis might want me.'

'You're just going for a stroll. No problem. And hurry up. There's other gods in Ephebe. I don't want to meet them right now. Not looking like this.'

Brutha looked panicky.

'How do I find a philosopher?' he said.

'Around here? Throw a brick, I should think.'

*

The labyrinth of Ephebe is ancient and full of one hundred and one amazing things you can do with hidden springs, razor-sharp knives, and falling rocks. There isn't just one guide through it. There are six, and each one knows his way through one-sixth of the labyrinth. Every year they have a special competition, when they do a little redesigning. They vie with one another to see who can make his section even more deadly than the others to the casual wanderer. There's a panel of judges, and a small prize.

The furthest anyone ever got through the labyrinth without a guide was nineteen paces. Well, more or less. His head rolled a further seven paces, but that probably doesn't count.

At each changeover point there is a small chamber without any traps at all. What it does contain is a small bronze bell. These are the little waiting-rooms where visitors are handed on to the next guide. And here and there, set high in the tunnel roof over the more ingenious traps, are observation windows, because guards like a good laugh as much as anyone else.

All of this was totally lost on Brutha, who padded amiably along the tunnels and corridors without really thinking much about it, and at last pushed open the gate into the late evening air.

It was fragrant with the scent of flowers. Moths whirred through the gloom.

'What do philosophers look like?' said Brutha. 'When they're not having a bath, I mean.'

'They do a lot of thinking,' said Om. 'Look for someone with a strained expression.'

'That might just mean constipation.'

'Well, so long as they're philosophical about it . . .'

The city of Ephebe surrounded them. Dogs barked. Somewhere a cat yowled. There was that general susurration of small comfortable sounds that shows that, out there, a lot of people are living their lives.

And then a door burst open down the street and there was the cracking noise of a quite large wine amphora being broken over someone's head.

A skinny old man in a toga picked himself up from the cobbles where he had landed, and glared at the doorway.

'I'm telling you, listen, a finite intellect, right, cannot by means of comparison reach the absolute truth of things, because being by nature indivisible, truth excludes the concepts of "more" or "less" so that nothing but truth itself can be the exact measure of truth. You bastards,' he said.

Someone from inside the building said, 'Oh yeah? Sez you.'

The old man ignored Brutha but, with great difficulty, pulled a cobblestone loose and hefted it in his hand.

Then he dived back through the doorway. There was a distant scream of rage.

'Ah. Philosophy,' said Om.

Brutha peered cautiously round the door.

Inside the room two groups of very nearly identical men in togas were trying to hold back two of their colleagues. It is a scene repeated a million times a day in bars around the multiverse – both would-be fighters growled and grimaced at one another and fought to escape the restraint of their friends, only of course they did not fight *too* hard, because there is nothing worse than actually *succeeding* in breaking free and suddenly finding yourself all alone in the middle of the ring with a madman who is about to hit you between the eyes with a rock.

'Yep,' said Om, 'that's philosophy, right enough.'

'But they're fighting!'

'A full and free exchange of opinions, yes.'

Now that Brutha could get a clearer view, he could see that there were one or two differences between the men. One had a shorter beard, and was very red in the face, and was waggling a finger accusingly.

'He bloody well accused me of slander!' he was shouting.

'I didn't!' shouted the other man.

'You did! You did! Tell 'em what you said!'

'Look, I merely suggested, to indicate the nature of paradox, right, that if Xeno the Ephebian said, "All Ephebians are liars –"'

'See? See? He did it again!'

'– no, no, listen, listen ... then, since Xeno is himself an Ephebian, this would mean that he himself is a liar and therefore –'

Xeno made a determined effort to break free, dragging four desperate fellow philosophers across the floor.

'I'm going to lay one right *on* you, pal!'

Brutha said, 'Excuse me, please?'

The philosophers froze. Then they turned to look at Brutha. They relaxed by degrees. There was a chorus of embarrassed coughs.

'Are you all philosophers?' said Brutha.

The one called Xeno stepped forward, adjusting the hang of his toga.

'That's right,' he said. 'We're philosophers. We think, therefore we am.'

'Are,' said the luckless paradox manufacturer automatically.

Xeno spun around. 'I've just about had it up to *here* with you, Ibid!' he roared. He turned back to Brutha. 'We *are*, therefore we am,' he said confidently. 'That's it.'

Several of the philosophers looked at one another with interest.

'That's actually quite interesting,' one said. 'The evidence of our existence is the *fact* of our existence, is that what you're saying?'

'Shut up,' said Xeno, without looking around.

'Have you been fighting?' said Brutha.

The assembled philosophers assumed various expressions of shock and horror.

'Fighting? Us? We're *philosophers*,' said Ibid, shocked.

'My word, yes,' said Xeno.

'But you were –' Brutha began.

Xeno waved a hand.

'The cut and thrust of debate,' he said.

'Thesis plus antithesis equals hysteresis,' said Ibid. 'The stringent testing of the universe. The hammer of the intellect upon the anvil of fundamental truth –'

'Shut up,' said Xeno. 'And what can we do for you, young man?'

'Ask them about gods,' Om prompted.

'Uh, I want to find out about gods,' said Brutha.

The philosophers looked at one another.

'Gods?' said Xeno. 'We don't bother with gods. Huh. Relics of an outmoded belief system, gods.'

There was a rumble of thunder from the clear evening sky.

'Except for Blind Io the Thunder God,' Xeno went on, his tone hardly changing.

Lightning flashed across the sky.

'And Cubal the Fire God,' said Xeno.

A gust of wind rattled the windows.

'Flatulus the God of the Winds, he's all right too,' said Xeno.

An arrow materialised out of the air and hit the table by Xeno's hand.

'Fedecks the Messenger of the Gods, one of the all-time greats,' said Xeno.

A bird appeared in the doorway. At least, it looked vaguely like a bird. It was about a foot high, black and white, with a bent beak and an expression that suggested that whatever it was it really dreaded ever happening to it had already happened.

'What's that?' said Brutha.

'A penguin,' said the voice of Om inside his head.

'Patina the Goddess of Wisdom? One of the best,' said Xeno.

The penguin croaked at him and waddled off into the darkness.

The philosophers looked very embarrassed. Then Ibid said, 'Foorgol the God of Avalanches? Where's the snowline?'

'Two hundred miles away,' said someone.

They waited. Nothing happened.

'Relic of an outmoded belief system,' said Xeno.

A wall of freezing white death did not appear anywhere in Ephebe.

'Mere unthinking personification of a natural force,' said one of the philosophers, in a louder voice. They all seemed to feel a lot better about this.

'Primitive nature worship.'

'Wouldn't give you tuppence for him.'

'Simple rationalisation of the unknown.'

'Hah! A clever fiction, a bogey to frighten the weak and stupid!'

The words rose up in Brutha. He couldn't stop himself.

'Is it always this cold?' he said. 'It seemed very chilly on my way here.'

The philosophers all moved away from Xeno.

'Although if there's one thing you can say about Foorgal,' said Xeno, 'it's that he's a very understanding god. Likes a joke as much as the next . . . man.'

He looked both ways, quickly. After a while the philosophers relaxed, and seemed to completely forget about Brutha.

And only now did he really have time to take in the room. He had never seen a tavern before in his life, but that was what it was. The bar ran along one side of the room. Behind it were the typical trappings of an Ephebian bar – the stacks of wine jars, racks of amphora, and the cheery pictures of vestal virgins on cards of salted peanuts and goat jerky, pinned up in the hope that there really *were* people in the world who would slatheringly buy more and more packets of nuts they didn't want in order to look at a cardboard nipple.

'What's all this stuff?' Brutha whispered.

'How should I know?' said Om. 'Let me out so's I can see.'

Brutha unfastened the box and lifted the tortoise out. One rheumy eye looked around.

'Oh. Typical tavern,' said Om. 'Good. Mine's a saucer of whatever they were drinking.'

'A tavern? A place where alcohol is drunk?'

'I very much intend this to be the case, yes.'

'But ... but ... the Septateuch, no less than seventeen times, adjures us most emphatically to refrain from –'

'Beats the hell out of me why,' said Om. 'See that man cleaning the mugs? You say unto him, Give me a –'

'But it mocks the mind of Man, says the Prophet Ossory. And –'

'I'll say this one more time! I never said it! Now talk to the man!'

In fact the man talked to Brutha. He appeared magically on the other side of the bar, still wiping a mug.

'Evening, sir,' he said. 'What'll it be?'

'I'd like a drink of water, please,' said Brutha, very deliberately.

'And something for the tortoise?'

'Wine!' said the voice of Om.

'I don't know,' said Brutha. 'What do tortoises usually drink?'

'The ones we have in here normally have a drop of milk with some bread in it,' said the barman.

'You get a lot of tortoises?' said Brutha loudly, trying to drown out Om's outraged screams.

'Oh, a very useful philosophical animal, your average tortoise. Outrunning metaphorical arrows, beating hares in races ... very handy.'

'Uh ... I haven't got any money,' said Brutha.

The barman leaned towards him. 'Tell you what,' he said. 'Declivities has just bought a round. He won't mind.'

'*Bread and milk?*'

'Oh. Thank you. Thank you very much.'

'Oh, we get all sorts in here,' said the barman, leaning back. 'Stoics. Cynics. Big drinkers, the Cynics. Epicureans. Stochastics. Anamaxandrites. Epistemologists. Peripatetics. Synoptics. All sorts. That's what I always say. What I always say is' – he picked up another mug and started to dry it – 'it takes all sorts to make a world.'

'Bread and milk!' shouted Om. 'You'll feel my wrath for this, right? Now ask him about gods!'

'Tell me,' said Brutha, sipping his mug of water, 'do any of them know much about gods?'

'You'd want a priest for that sort of thing,' said the barman.

'No, I mean about ... what gods are ... how gods came to exist ... *that* sort of thing,' said Brutha, trying to get to grips with the barman's peculiar mode of conversation.

'Gods don't like that sort of thing,' said the barman. 'We get that in here some nights, when someone's had a few. Cosmic speculation about whether gods really exist. Next thing, there's a bolt of lightning through the roof with a note wrapped round it saying "Yes, we do" and a pair of sandals with smoke coming out. That sort of thing, it takes all the interest out of metaphysical speculation.'

'Not even fresh bread,' muttered Om, nose deep in his saucer.

'No, I know gods exist all right,' said Brutha, hurriedly. 'I just want to find out more about . . . them.'

The barman shrugged.

'Then I'd be obliged if you don't stand next to anything valuable,' he said. 'Still, it'll all be the same in a hundred years.' He picked up another mug and started to polish it.

'Are you a philosopher?' said Brutha.

'It kind of rubs off on you after a while,' said the barman.

'This milk's off,' said Om. 'They say Ephebe is a democracy. This milk ought to be allowed to vote.'

'I don't think,' said Brutha carefully, 'that I'm going to find what I want here. Um. Mr Drink Seller?'

'Yes?'

'What was that bird that walked in when the Goddess' – he tasted the unfamiliar word – 'of Wisdom was mentioned?'

'Bit of a problem there,' said the barman. 'Bit of an embarrassment.'

'Sorry?'

'It was,' said the barman, 'a penguin.'

'Is it a wise sort of bird, then?'

'No. Not a lot,' said the barman. 'Not known for its wisdom. Second most confused bird in the world. Can only fly underwater, they say.'

'Then why –'

'We don't like to talk about it,' said the barman. 'It upsets people. Bloody sculptor,' he added, under his breath.

Down the other end of the bar the philosophers had started fighting again.

The barman leaned forward. 'If you haven't got any money,' he said, 'I don't think you're going to get much help. Talk isn't cheap around here.'

'But they just –' Brutha began.

'There's the expenditure on soap and water, for a start. Towels. Flannels. Loofahs. Pumice stones. Bath salts. It all adds up.'

There was a gurgling noise from the saucer. Om's milky head turned to Brutha.

'You've got no money at *all*?' he said.

'No,' said Brutha.

'Well, we've got to have a philosopher,' said the tortoise flatly. 'I can't think and you don't know how to. We've got to find someone who does it all the time.'

'Of course, you could try old Didactylos,' said the barman. 'He's about as cheap as they come.'

'Doesn't use expensive soap?' said Brutha.

'I think it could be said without fear of contradiction,' said the barman solemnly, 'that he doesn't use any soap at all whatsoever in any way.'

'Oh. Well. Thank you,' said Brutha.

'Ask him where this man lives,' Om commanded.

'Where can I find Mr Didactylos?' said Brutha.

'In the palace courtyard. Next door to the Library. You can't miss him. Just follow your nose.'

'We just came –' Brutha said, but his inner voice prompted him not to complete the sentence. 'We'll just be going then.'

'Don't forget your tortoise,' said the barman. 'There's good eating on one of them.'

'May all your wine turn to water!' Om shrieked.

'Will it?' said Brutha, as they stepped out into the night.

'No.'

'Tell me again. Why exactly are we looking for a philosopher?' said Brutha.

'I want to get my power back,' said Om.

'But everyone believes in you!'

'If they believed in me they could talk to me. I could talk to them. I don't know what's gone wrong. No one is worshipping any other gods in Omnia, are they?'

'They wouldn't be allowed to,' said Brutha. 'The Quisition would see to that.'

'Yeah. It's hard to kneel if you have no knees.'

Brutha stopped in the empty street.

'I don't understand you!'

'You're not supposed to. The ways of gods aren't supposed to be understandable to men.'

'The Quisition keeps us on the path of truth! The Quisition works for the greater glory of the Church!'

'And you believe that, do you?' said the tortoise.

Brutha looked, and found that certainty had gone missing. He opened and shut his mouth, but there were no words to be said.

'Come on,' said Om, as kindly as he could manage. 'Let's get back.'

*

In the middle of the night Om awoke. There were noises from Brutha's bed.

Brutha was praying again.

Om listened curiously. He could remember prayers. There had been a lot of them, once. So many that he couldn't make out an individual prayer even if he had felt inclined to, but that didn't matter, because what mattered was the huge cosmic susurration of thousands of praying, *believing* minds. The words weren't worth listening to, anyway.

Humans! They lived in a world where the grass continued to be green and the sun rose every day and flowers regularly turned into fruit, and what impressed them? Weeping statues. And wine made out of water! A mere quantum-mechanistic tunnel effect, that'd happen anyway if you were prepared to wait zillions of years. As if the turning of sunlight into wine, by means of vines and grapes and time and enzymes, wasn't a thousand times more impressive and happened all the time ...

Well, he couldn't even do the most basic of god tricks now. Thunderbolts with about the same effect as the spark off a cat's fur, and you could hardly smite anyone with one of those. He had smitten good and hard in his time. Now he could just about walk through water and feed the One.

Brutha's prayer was a piccolo tune in a world of silence.

Om waited until the novice was quiet again and then unfolded his legs and walked out, rocking from side to side, into the dawn.

The Ephebians walked through the palace courtyards, surrounding the Omnians almost, but not quite, in the manner of a prisoners' escort.

Brutha could see that Vorbis was boiling with fury. A small vein on the side of the exquisitor's bald temple was throbbing.

As if feeling Brutha's eyes on him, Vorbis turned his head.

'You seem ill at ease this morning, Brutha,' he said.

'Sorry, lord.'

'You seem to be looking into every corner. What are you expecting to find?'

'Uh. Just interested, lord. Everything's new.'

'All the so-called wisdom of Ephebe is not worth one line from the least paragraph in the Septateuch,' said Vorbis.

'May we not study the works of the infidel in order to be more alert to the ways of heresy?' said Brutha, surprised at himself.

'Ah. A persuasive argument, Brutha, and one that the inquisitors have heard many times, if a little indistinctly in many cases.'

Vorbis glowered at the back of the head of Aristocrates, who was leading the party. 'It is but a small step from listening to heresy to questioning established truth, Brutha. Heresy is often fascinating. Therein lies its danger.'

'Yes, lord.'

'Hah! And not only do they carve forbidden statues, but they can't even do it properly.'

Brutha was no expert, but even he had to agree that this was true. Now the novelty of them had worn off, the statues that decorated every niche in the palace did have a certain badly made look. Brutha was pretty sure he'd just passed one with two left arms. Another one had one ear larger than the other. It wasn't that someone had set out to carve ugly gods. They had clearly been meant to be quite attractive statues. But the sculptor hadn't been much good at it.

'That woman there appears to be holding a penguin,' said Vorbis.

'Patina, Goddess of Wisdom,' said Brutha automatically, and then realised he'd said it.

'I, er, heard someone mention it,' he added.

'Indeed. And what remarkably good hearing you must have,' said Vorbis.

Aristocrates paused outside an impressive doorway and nodded at the party.

'Gentlemen,' he said, 'the Tyrant will see you now.'

'You will recall everything that is said,' whispered Vorbis.

Brutha nodded.

The doors swung open.

All over the world there were rulers with titles like the Exalted, the Supreme, and Lord High Something or Other. Only in one small country was the ruler elected by the people, who could remove him whenever they wanted – and they called him the Tyrant.

The Ephebians believed that every man should have the vote.[*] Every five years someone was elected to be Tyrant, provided he could prove that he was honest, intelligent, sensible and trustworthy. Immediately after he was elected, of course, it was obvious to everyone that he was a criminal madman and totally out of touch

---

[*] Provided that he wasn't poor, foreign nor disqualified by reason of being mad, frivolous or a woman.

with the view of the ordinary philosopher in the street looking for a towel. And then five years later they elected another one just like him, and really it was amazing how intelligent people kept on making the same mistakes.

Candidates for the Tyrantship were elected by the placing of black or white balls in various urns, thus giving rise to a well-known comment about politics.

The Tyrant was a fat little man with skinny legs, giving people the impression of an egg that was hatching upside down. He was sitting alone in the middle of the marble floor, in a chair surrounded by scrolls and scraps of paper. His feet didn't touch the marble, and his face was pink.

Aristocrates whispered something in his ear. The Tyrant looked up from his paperwork.

'Ah, the Omnian delegation,' he said, and a smile flashed across his face like something small darting across a stone. 'Do be seated, all of you.'

He looked down again.

'I am Deacon Vorbis of the Citadel Quisition,' said Vorbis coldly.

The Tyrant looked up and gave him another lizard smile.

'Yes, I know,' he said. 'You torture people for a living. Please be seated, Deacon Vorbis. And your plump young friend who seems to be looking for something. And the rest of you. Some young women will be along in a moment with grapes and things. This generally happens. It's very hard to stop it, in fact.'

There were benches in front of the Tyrant's chair. The Omnians sat down. Vorbis remained standing.

The Tyrant nodded. 'As you wish,' he said.

'This is intolerable!' snapped Vorbis. 'We have been treated –'

'Much better than you would have treated us,' said the Tyrant mildly. 'You sit or you stand, my lord, because this is Ephebe and indeed you may stand on your head for all I care, but don't expect me to believe that if it was *I*, seeking peace in your Citadel, I would be encouraged to do anything but grovel on what was left of my stomach. Be seated or be upstanding, my lord, but be quiet. I have nearly finished.'

'Finished what?' said Vorbis.

'The peace treaty,' said the Tyrant.

'But that is what we are here to discuss,' said Vorbis.

'No,' said the Tyrant. The lizard scuttled again. 'That is what you are here to sign.'

*

Om took a deep breath and then pushed himself forward.

It was quite a steep flight of steps. He felt every one as he bumped down, but at least he was upright at the bottom.

He was lost, but being lost in Ephebe was preferable to being lost in the Citadel. At least there were no obvious cellars.

Library, library, library . . .

There was a library in the Citadel, Brutha had said. He'd described it, so Om had some idea of what he was looking for.

There would be a book in it.

Peace negotiations were not going well.

'You attacked us!' said Vorbis.

'I would call it pre-emptive defence,' said the Tyrant. 'We saw what happened to Istanzia and Betrek and Ushistan.'

'They saw the truth of Om!'

'Yes,' said the Tyrant. 'We believe they did, eventually.'

'And they are now proud members of the Empire.'

'Yes,' said the Tyrant. 'We believe they are. But we like to remember them as they were. Before you sent them your letters, that put the minds of men in chains.'

'That set the feet of men on the right road,' said Vorbis.

'Chain letters,' said the Tyrant. 'The Chain Letter to the Ephebians. Forget Your Gods. Be Subjugated. Learn to Fear. Do not break the chain – the last people who did woke up one morning to find fifty thousand armed men on their lawn.'

Vorbis sat back.

'What is it you fear?' he said. 'Here in your desert, with your . . . gods? Is it not that, deep in your souls, you know that your gods are as shifting as your sand?'

'Oh, yes,' said the Tyrant. 'We know that. That's always been a point in their favour. We know about sand. And your God is a rock – and we know about rock.'

Om stumped along a cobbled alley, keeping to the shade as much as possible.

There seemed to be a lot of courtyards. He paused at the point where the alley opened into yet another of them.

There were voices. Mainly there was one voice, petulant and reedy.

This was the philosopher Didactylos.

Although one of the most quoted and popular philosophers of all time, Didactylos the Ephebian never achieved the respect of his fellow philosophers. They felt he wasn't philosopher material. He didn't bath often enough or, to put it another way, at all. And he philosophised about the wrong sorts of things. And he was *interested* in the wrong sorts of things. Dangerous things. Other philosophers asked questions like: Is Truth Beauty, and is Beauty Truth? and: Is Reality Created by the Observer? But Didactylos posed the famous philosophical conundrum: 'Yes, But What's It *Really* All About, Then, When You Get Right Down To It, I *Mean* Really'!

His philosophy was a mixture of three famous schools – the Cynics, the Stoics and the Epicureans – and summed up all three of them in his famous phrase, 'You can't trust any bugger further than you can throw him, and there's nothing you can do about it, so let's have a drink. Mine's a double, if you're buying. Thank *you*. And a packet of nuts. Her left bosom is nearly uncovered, eh? Two more packets, then!'

Many people have quoted from his famous *Meditations*:

'It's a rum old world all right. But you've got to laugh, haven't you? *Nil Illegitimo Carborundum* is what I say. The experts don't know everything. Still, where would we be if we were all the same?'

Om crawled closer to the voice, bringing himself around the corner of the wall so that he could see into a small courtyard.

There was a very large barrel against the far wall. Various debris around it – broken wine amphora, gnawed bones, and a couple of lean-to shacks made out of rough boards – suggested that it was someone's home. And this impression was given some weight by the sign chalked on a board and stuck to the wall over the barrel.

It read:

DIDACTYLOS and Nephew
Practical Philosophers

No Proposition Too Large
'We Can Do Your Thinking For You'

Special Rates after 6 pm
Fresh Axioms Every Day

In front of the barrel, a short man in a toga that must have once been white, in the same way that once all continents must have been joined together, was kicking another one who was on the ground.

'You lazy bugger!'

The younger one sat up.

'Honest, Uncle –'

'I turn my back for half an hour and you go to sleep on the job!'

'What job? We haven't had anything since Mr Piloxi the farmer last week –'

'How d'you know? How d'you know? While you were snoring dozens of people could've been goin' past, every one of 'em in need of a pers'nal philosophy!'

'– and he only paid in olives.'

'I shall prob'ly get a good price for them olives!'

'They're *rotten*, Uncle.'

'Nonsense! You said they were green!'

'Yes, but they're supposed to be black.'

In the shadows, the tortoise's head turned back and forth like a spectator's at a tennis match.

The young man stood up.

'Mrs Bylaxis came in this morning,' he said. 'She said the proverb you did for her last week has stopped working.'

Didactylos scratched his head.

'Which one was that?' he said.

'You gave her "It's always darkest before dawn".'

'Nothing wrong with that. Damn good philosophy.'

'She said she didn't feel any better. Anyway, she said she'd stayed up all night because of her bad leg and it was actually quite light just before dawn, so it wasn't true. And her leg still dropped off. So I gave her part exchange on "Still, it does you good to laugh".'

Didactylos brightened up a bit.

'Shifted that one, eh?'

'She said she'd give it a try. She gave me a whole dried squid for it. She said I looked like I needed feeding up.'

'Right? You're learning. That's lunch sorted out at any rate. See, Urn? *Told* you it would work if we stuck at it.'

'I don't call one dried squid and a box of greasy olives much of a return, master. Not for two weeks' thinking.'

'We got three *obols* for doing that proverb for old Grillos the cobbler.'

'No we didn't. He brought it back. His wife didn't like the colour.'

'And you gave him his money back?'

'Yes.'

'What, all of it?'

'Yes.'

'Can't do that. Not after he's put wear and tear on the words. Which one was it?'

'"It's a wise crow that knows which way the camel points".'

'I put a lot of work in on that one.'

'He said he couldn't understand it.'

'I don't understand cobbling, but I know a good pair of sandals when I wears 'em.'

Om blinked his one eye. Then he looked at the shapes of the minds in front of him.

The one called Urn was presumably the nephew, and had a fairly normal sort of mind, even if it did seem to have too many circles and angles in it. But Didactylos's mind bubbled and flashed like a potful of electric eels on full boil. Om had never seen anything like it. Brutha's thoughts took eons to slide into place, it was like watching mountains colliding; Didactylos's thoughts chased after one another with a whooshing noise. No wonder he was bald. Hair would have burned off from the inside.

Om had found a thinker.

A cheap one, too, by the sound of it.

He looked up at the wall behind the barrel. Further along was an impressive set of marble steps leading up to some bronze doors, and over the doors, made of metal letters set in the stone, was the word LIBRVM.

He'd spent too much time looking. Urn's hand clamped itself on to his shell, and he heard Didactylos's voice say, 'Hey . . . there's good eating on one of these things . . .'

Brutha cowered.

'You stoned our envoy!' shouted Vorbis. 'An unarmed man!'

'He brought it upon himself,' said the Tyrant. 'Aristocrates was there. He will tell you.'

The tall man nodded and stood up.

'By tradition anyone may speak in the marketplace,' he began.

'And be stoned?' Vorbis demanded.

Aristocrates held up a hand.

'Ah,' he said, 'anyone can *say* what they like in the square. We have another tradition, though, called free listening. Unfortunately, when people dislike what they hear, they can become a little ... testy.'

'I was there too,' said another advisor. 'Your priest got up to speak and at first everything was fine, because people were laughing. And then he said that Om was the only real God, and everyone went quiet. And then he pushed over a statue of Tuvelpit, the God of Wine. That's when the trouble started.'

'Are you proposing to tell me he was struck by lightning?' said Vorbis.

Vorbis was no longer shouting. His voice was level, without passion. The thought rose in Brutha's mind: this is how the exquisitors speak. When the inquisitors have finished, the exquisitors speak ...

'No. By an amphora. Tuvelpit was in the crowd, you see.'

'And striking honest men is considered proper godly behaviour, is it?'

'Your missionary had said that people who did not believe in Om would suffer endless punishment. I have to tell you that the crowd considered this rude.'

'And so they threw stones at him ...'

'Not many. They only hurt his pride. And only after they'd run out of vegetables.'

'They threw vegetables?'

'When they couldn't find any more eggs.'

'And when we came to remonstrate –'

'I am sure sixty ships intended more than remonstrating,' said the Tyrant. 'And we have warned you, Lord Vorbis. People find in Ephebe what they seek. There will be more raids on your coast. We will harass your ships. Unless you sign.'

'And passage through Ephebe?' said Vorbis.

The Tyrant smiled.

'Across the desert? My lord, if you can cross the desert, I am sure you can go anywhere.' The Tyrant looked away from Vorbis and towards the sky, visible between the pillars.

'And now I see it is nearing noon,' he said. 'And the day heats up. Doubtless you will wish to discuss our ... uh ... proposals with your colleagues. May I suggest we meet again at sunset?'

Vorbis appeared to give this some consideration.

'I think,' he said eventually, 'that our deliberations may take longer. Shall we say ... tomorrow morning?'

The Tyrant nodded.

'As you wish. In the meantime, the palace is at your disposal. There are many fine temples and works of art should you wish to inspect them. When you require meals, mention the fact to the nearest slave.'

'Slave is an Ephebian word. In Om we have no word for slave,' said Vorbis.

'So I understand,' said the Tyrant. 'I imagine that fish have no word for water.' He smiled the fleeting smile again. 'And there are the baths and the Library, of course. Many fine sights. You are our guests.'

Vorbis inclined his head.

'I pray,' he said, 'that one day you will be a guest of mine.'

'And what sights *I* shall see,' said the Tyrant.

Brutha stood up, knocking over his bench and going redder with embarrassment.

He thought: they lied about Brother Murduck. They beat him within an inch of his life, Vorbis said, and flogged him the rest of the way. And Brother Nhumrod said he saw the body, and it was really true. Just for talking! People who would do that sort of thing deserve ... punishment. And they keep slaves. People forced to work against their will. People treated like animals. And they even *call* their ruler a Tyrant!

And why isn't any of this exactly what it seems?

Why don't I believe any of it?

Why do I know it isn't true?

And what did he mean about fish not having a word for water?

The Omnians were half-escorted, half-led back to their compound. Another bowl of fruit was waiting on the table in Brutha's cell, with some more fish and a loaf of bread.

There was also a man, sweeping the floor.

'Um,' said Brutha. 'Are you a slave?'

'Yes, master.'

'That must be terrible.'

The man leaned on his broom. 'You're right. It's terrible. Really terrible. D'you know, I only get one day off a week?'

Brutha, who had never heard the words 'day off' before, and who was in any case unfamiliar with the concept, nodded uncertainly.

'Why don't you run away?' he said.

'Oh, done that,' said the slave. 'Ran away to Tsort once. Didn't like it much. Came back. Run away for a fortnight in Djelibeybi every winter, though.'

'Do you get brought back?' said Brutha.

'Huh!' said the slave. 'No, I don't. Miserable skinflint, Aristocrates. I have to come back by myself. Hitching lifts on ships, that kind of thing.'

'You *come* back?'

'Yeah. Abroad's all right to visit, but you wouldn't want to live there. Anyway, I've only got another four years as a slave and then I'm free. You get the vote when you're free. *And* you get to keep slaves.' His face glazed with the effort of recollection as he ticked off points on his fingers. 'Slaves get three meals a day, at least one with meat. And one free day a week. And two weeks being-allowed-to-run-away every year. And I don't do ovens or heavy lifting, and worldly-wise repartee only by arrangement.'

'Yes, but you're not *free*,' said Brutha, intrigued despite himself.

'What's the difference?'

'Er ... you don't get any days off.' Brutha scratched his head. 'And one less meal.'

'Really? I think I'll give freedom a miss then, thanks.'

'Er ... have you seen a tortoise anywhere around here?' said Brutha.

'No. *And* I cleaned under the bed.'

'Have you seen one anywhere else today?'

'You want one? There's good eating on a –'

'No. No. It's all right –'

'Brutha!'

'It was Vorbis's voice. Brutha hurried out into the courtyard and into Vorbis's cell.

'Ah, Brutha.'

'Yes, lord?'

Vorbis was sitting cross-legged on the floor, staring at the wall.

'You are a young man visiting a new place,' said Vorbis. 'No doubt there is much you wish to see.'

'There is?' said Brutha. Vorbis was using the exquisitor voice again – a level monotone, a voice like a strip of dull steel.

'You may go where you wish. See new things, Brutha. Learn everything you can. You are my eyes and ears. And my memory. Learn about this place.'

'Er. Really, lord?'

'Have I impressed you with my use of careless language, Brutha?'

'No, lord.'

'Go away. Fill yourself. And be back by sunset.'

'Er. Even the Library?' said Brutha.

'Ah? Yes, the Library. The Library that they have here. Of course. Crammed with useless and dangerous and evil knowledge. I can see it in my mind, Brutha. Can you imagine that?'

'No, Lord Vorbis.'

'Your innocence is your shield, Brutha. No. By all means go to the Library. I have no fear of any effect on *you*.'

'Lord Vorbis?'

'Yes?'

'The Tyrant said that they hardly did anything to Brother Murduck . . .'

Silence unrolled its restless length.

Vorbis said, 'He lied.'

'Yes.' Brutha waited. Vorbis continued to stare at the wall. Brutha wondered what he saw there. When nothing else appeared to be forthcoming, he said, 'Thank you.'

He stepped back a bit before he went out, so that he could squint under the deacon's bed.

He's probably in trouble, Brutha thought as he hurried through the palace. Everyone wants to eat tortoises.

He tried to look everywhere while avoiding the friezes of unclad nymphs.

Brutha was technically aware that women were a different shape from men; he hadn't left the village until he was twelve, by which time some of his contemporaries were already married. And Omnianism encouraged early marriage as a preventive against Sin, although any activity involving any part of the human anatomy between neck and knees was more or less Sinful in any case.

Brutha wished he was a better scholar so he could ask his God why this was.

Then he found himself wishing his God was a more intelligent God so it could answer.

He hasn't screamed for me, he thought. I'm sure I would have heard. So maybe no one's cooking him.

A slave polishing one of the statues directed him to the Library. Brutha pounded down an aisle of pillars.

When he reached the courtyard in front of the Library it was crowded with philosophers, all craning to look at something.

Brutha could hear the usual petulant squabbling that showed that philosophical discourse was under way.

In this case:

'I've got ten *obols* here says it can't do it again!'

'Talking money? That's something you don't hear every day, Xeno.'

'Yeah. And it's about to say goodbye.'

'Look, don't be stupid. It's a tortoise. It's just doing a mating dance . . .'

There was a breathless pause. Then a sort of collective sigh.

'There!'

'That's never a right angle!'

'Come *on*! I'd like to see *you* do better in the circumstances!'

'What's it doing now?'

'The hypotenuse, I think.'

'Call that a hypotenuse? It's wiggly.'

'It's *not* wiggly. It's drawing it straight and you're *looking* at it in a wiggly way!'

'I'll bet thirty *obols* it can't do a square!'

'Here's forty *obols* says it can.'

There was another pause, and then a cheer.

'Yeah!'

'That's more of a parallelogram, if you ask me,' said a petulant voice.

'Listen, I knows a square when I sees one! And *that's* a square.'

'All right. Double or nothing then. Bet it can't do a dodecagon.'

'Hah! You bet it couldn't do a septagon just now.'

'Double or nothing. Dodecagon. Worried, eh! Feeling a bit *avis domestica*? Cluck-cluck?'

'It's a shame to take your money . . .'

There was another pause.

'Ten sides? *Ten* sides? Hah!'

'Told you it wasn't any good! Whoever heard of a tortoise doing geometry?'

'Another daft idea, Didactylos?'

'I said so all along. It's just a tortoise.'

'There's good eating on one of those things . . .'

The mass of philosophers broke up, pushing past Brutha without paying him much attention. He caught a glimpse of a circle of damp sand, covered with geometrical figures. Om was sitting in the middle of them. Behind him was a very grubby pair of philosophers, counting out a pile of coins.

'How did we do, Urn?' said Didactylos.

'We're fifty-two *obols* up, master.'

'See? Every day things improve. Pity it didn't know the difference between ten and twelve, though. Cut one of its legs off and we'll have a stew.'

'Cut off a leg?'

'Well, a tortoise like that, you don't eat it all at once.'

Didactylos turned his face towards a plump young man with splayed feet and a red face, who was staring at the tortoise.

'Yes?' he said.

'The tortoise *does* know the difference between ten and twelve,' said the fat boy.

'Damn thing just lost me eighty *obols*,' said Didactylos.

'Yes. But tomorrow . . .' the boy began, his eyes glazing as if he was carefully repeating something he'd just heard '. . . tomorrow . . . you should be able to get odds of at least three to one.'

Didactylos's mouth dropped open.

'Give me the tortoise, Urn,' he said.

The apprentice philosopher reached down and picked up Om, very carefully.

'You know, I thought right at the start there was something funny about this creature,' said Didactylos. 'I said to Urn, there's tomorrow's dinner, and then he says no, it's dragging its tail in the sand and doing geometry. That doesn't come natural to a tortoise, geometry.'

Om's eye turned to Brutha.

'I had to,' he said. 'It was the only way to get his attention. Now I've got him by the curiosity. When you've got 'em by the curiosity, their hearts and minds will follow.'

'He's a God,' said Brutha.

'Really? What's his name?' said the philosopher.

'Don't tell him! Don't tell him! The local gods'll hear!'

'I don't know,' said Brutha.

Didactylos turned Om over.

'The Turtle Moves,' said Urn thoughtfully.

'What?' said Brutha.

'Master did a book,' said Urn.

'Not really a book,' said Didactylos modestly. 'More a scroll. Just a little thing I knocked off.'

'Saying that the world is flat and goes through space on the back of a giant turtle?' said Brutha.

'Have you read it?' Didactylos's gaze was unmoving. 'Are you a slave?'

'No,' said Brutha. 'I am a –'

'Don't mention my name! Call yourself a scribe or something!'

'– scribe,' said Brutha weakly.

'Yeah,' said Urn. 'I can see that. The telltale callus on the thumb where you hold the pen. The inkstains all over your sleeves.'

Brutha glanced at his left thumb. 'I haven't –'

'Yeah,' said Urn, grinning. 'Use your left hand, do you?'

'Er, I use both,' said Brutha. 'But not very well, everyone says.'

'Ah,' said Didactylos. 'Ambi-sinister?'

'What?'

'He means incompetent with both hands,' said Om.

'Oh. Yes. That's me.' Brutha coughed politely. 'Look . . . I'm looking for a philosopher. Um. One that knows about gods.'

He waited.

Then he said, 'You aren't going to say they're a relic of an outmoded belief system?'

Didactylos, still running his fingers over Om's shell, shook his head.

'Nope. I like my thunderstorms a long way off.'

'Oh. Could you stop turning him over and over? He's just told me he doesn't like it.'

'You can tell how old they are by cutting them in half and counting the rings,' said Didactylos.

'Um. He hasn't got much of a sense of humour, either.'

'You're Omnian, by the sound of it.'

'Yes.'

'Here to talk about the treaty?'

'I do the listening.'

'And what do you want to know about gods?'

Brutha appeared to be listening.

Eventually he said: 'How they start. How they grow. And what happens to them afterwards.'

Didactylos put the tortoise into Brutha's hands.

'Costs money, that kind of thinking,' he said.

'Let me know when we've used more than fifty-two *obols* worth,' said Brutha. Didactylos grinned.

'Looks like you can think for yourself,' he said. 'Got a good memory?'

'No. Not exactly a good one.'

'Right? Right. Come on into the Library. It's got an earthed copper roof, you know. Gods really hate that sort of thing.'

Didactylos reached down beside him and picked up a rusty iron lantern.

Brutha looked up at the big white building.

'That's the Library?' he said.

'Yes,' said Didactylos. 'That's why it's got LIBRVM carved over the door in such big letters. But a scribe like you'd know that, of course.'

The Library of Ephebe was – before it burned down – the second biggest on the Disc.

Not as big as the library in Unseen University, of course, but *that* library had one or two advantages on account of its magical nature. No other library anywhere, for example, has a whole gallery of unwritten books – books that *would* have been written if the author hadn't been eaten by an alligator around chapter 1, and so on. Atlases of imaginary places. Dictionaries of illusory words. Spotters' guides to invisible things. Wild thesauri in the Lost Reading Room. A library so big that it distorts reality and has opened gateways to all other libraries, everywhere and everywhen ...

And so unlike the Library at Ephebe, with its four or five hundred volumes. Many of them were scrolls, to save their readers the fatigue of having to call a slave every time they wanted a page turned. Each one lay in its own pigeonhole, though. Books shouldn't be kept too close together, otherwise they interact in strange and unforeseeable ways.

Sunbeams lanced through the shadows, as palpable as pillars in the dusty air.

Although it was the least of the wonders in the Library, Brutha couldn't help noticing a strange construction in the aisles. Wooden laths had been fixed between the rows of stone shelves about two metres from the floor, so that they supported a wider plank of no apparent use whatsoever. Its underside had been decorated with rough wooden shapes.

'The Library,' announced Didactylos.

He reached up. His fingers gently brushed the plank over his head.

It dawned on Brutha.

'You're blind aren't you?' he said.

'That's right.'

'But you carry a lantern?'

'It's all right,' said Didactylos. 'I don't put any oil in it.'

'A lantern that doesn't shine for a man that doesn't see?'

'Yeah. Works perfectly. And of course it's very philosophical.'

'And you live in a barrel.'

'Very fashionable, living in a barrel,' said Didactylos, walking forward briskly, his fingers only occasionally touching the raised patterns on the plank. 'Most of the philosophers do it. It shows contempt and disdain for worldly things. Mind you, Legibus has got a sauna in his. It's amazing the kind of things you can think of in it, he says.'

Brutha looked around. Scrolls protruded from their racks like cuckoos piping the hour.

'It's all so . . . I never met a philosopher before I came here,' he said. 'Last night, they were all . . .'

'You got to remember there's three basic approaches to philosophy in these parts,' said Didactylos. 'Tell him, Urn.'

'There's the Xenoists,' said Urn promptly. 'They say the world is basically complex and random. And there's the Ibidians. They say the world is basically simple and follows certain fundamental rules.'

'And there's me,' said Didactylos, pulling a scroll out of its rack.

'Master says basically it's a funny old world,' said Urn.

'And doesn't contain enough to drink,' said Didactylos.

'And doesn't contain enough to drink.'

'Gods,' said Didactylos, half to himself. He pulled out another scroll. 'You want to know about gods? Here's Xeno's *Reflections*, and old Aristocrates' *Platitudes*, and Ibid's bloody stupid *Discourses*, and Legibus's *Geometries* and Hierarch's *Theologies* . . .'

Didactylos's fingers danced across the racks. More dust filled the air.

'These are all books?' said Brutha.

'Oh, yes. Everyone writes 'em here. You just can't stop the buggers.'

'And people can *read* them?' said Brutha.

Omnia was based on one book. And here were . . . hundreds . . .

'Well, they can if they want,' said Urn. 'But no one comes in here much. These aren't books for reading. They're more for writing.'

'Wisdom of the ages, this,' said Didactylos. 'Got to write a book, see, to prove you're a philosopher. Then you get your scroll and free official philosopher's loofah.'

The sunlight pooled on a big stone table in the centre of the room.

Urn unrolled the length of a scroll. Brilliant flowers glowed in the golden light.

'Orinjcrates' *On the Nature of Plants*,' said Didactylos. 'Six hundred plants and their uses ...'

'They're beautiful,' whispered Brutha.

'Yes, that is one of the uses of plants,' said Didactylos. 'And one which old Orinjcrates neglected to notice, too. Well done. Show him Philo's *Bestiary*, Urn.'

Another scroll unrolled. There were dozens of pictures of animals, thousands of unreadable words.

'But ... pictures of animals ... it's wrong ... isn't it wrong to ...'

'Pictures of just about everything in there,' said Didactylos.

Art was not permitted in Omnia.

'And this is the book Didactylos wrote,' said Urn.

Brutha looked down at a picture of a turtle. There were ... *elephants, they're elephants*, his memory supplied, from the fresh memories of the bestiary sinking indelibly into his mind ... elephants on its back, and on them something with mountains and a waterfall of an ocean around its edge ...

'How can this be?' said Brutha. 'A world on the back of a tortoise? Why does everyone tell me this? This can't be true!'

'Tell that to the mariners,' said Didactylos. 'Everyone who's ever sailed the Rim Ocean knows it. Why deny the obvious?'

'But surely the world is a perfect sphere, spinning about the sphere of the sun, just as the Septateuch tells us,' said Brutha. 'That seems so ... logical. That's how things ought to be.'

'*Ought?*' said Didactylos. 'Well, I don't know about *ought*. That's not a philosophical word.'

'And ... what is this ...' Brutha murmured, pointing to a circle under the drawing of the turtle.

'That's a plan view,' said Urn.

'Map of the world,' said Didactylos.

'Map? What's a map?'

'It's a sort of picture that shows you where you are,' said Didactylos.

Brutha stared in wonderment. 'And how does it know?'

'Hah!'

'Gods,' prompted Om again. 'We're here to ask about gods!'

'But is all this *true*?' said Brutha.

Didactylos shrugged. 'Could be. Could be. We are here and it is now. The way I see it is, after that, everything tends towards guesswork.'

'You mean you don't *know* it's true?' said Brutha.

'I *think* it might be,' said Didactylos. 'I could be wrong. Not being certain is what being a philosopher is all about.'

'Talk about gods,' said Om.

'Gods,' said Brutha weakly.

His mind was on fire. These people made all these books about things, and they weren't *sure*. But he'd been sure, and Brother Nhumrod had been sure, and Deacon Vorbis had a sureness you could bend horseshoes around. Sureness was a rock.

Now he knew why, when Vorbis spoke about Ephebe, his face was grey with hatred and his voice was tense as a wire. If there was no truth, what was there left? And these bumbling old men spent their time kicking away the pillars of the world, and they'd nothing to replace them with but uncertainty. And they were *proud* of this?

Urn was standing on a small ladder, fishing among the shelves of scrolls. Didactylos sat opposite Brutha, his blind gaze still apparently fixed on him.

'You don't like it, do you?' said the philosopher.

Brutha had said nothing.

'You know,' said Didactylos conversationally, 'people'll tell you that us blind people are the real business where the other senses are concerned. It's not true, of course. The buggers just say it because it makes them feel better. It gets rid of the obligation to feel sorry for us. But when you can't see you *do* learn to listen more. The way people breathe, the sounds their clothes make . . .'

Urn reappeared with another scroll.

'You shouldn't do this,' said Brutha wretchedly. 'All this . . .' His voice trailed off.

'I know about sureness,' said Didactylos. Now the light, irascible tone had drained out of his voice. 'I remember, before I was blind, I went to Omnia once. This was before the borders were closed, when you still let people travel. And in your Citadel I saw a crowd stoning a man to death in a pit. Ever seen that?'

'It has to be done,' Brutha mumbled. 'So the soul can be shriven and –'

'Don't know about the soul. Never been that kind of a philosopher,' said Didactylos. 'All I know is, it was a horrible sight.'

'The state of the body is not –'

'Oh, I'm not talking about the poor bugger in the pit,' said the philosopher. 'I'm talking about the people throwing the stones. They were sure all right. They were sure it wasn't them in the pit.

You could see it in their faces. So glad it wasn't them that they were throwing just as hard as they could.'

Urn hovered, looking uncertain.

'I've got Abraxas's *On Religion*,' he said.

'Old "Charcoal" Abraxas,' said Didactylos, suddenly cheerful again. 'Struck by lightning fifteen times so far, and still not giving up. You can borrow this one overnight if you want. No scribbling comments in the margins, mind you, unless they're interesting.'

'This is it!' said Om. 'Come on, let's leave this idiot.'

Brutha unrolled the scroll. There weren't even any pictures. Crabbed writing filled it, line after line.

'He spent years researching it,' said Didactylos. 'Went out into the desert, talked to the small gods. Talked to some of our gods, too. Brave man. He says gods like to see an atheist around. Gives them something to aim at.'

Brutha unrolled a bit more of the scroll. Five minutes ago he would have admitted that he couldn't read. Now the best efforts of the inquisitors couldn't have forced it out of him. He held it up in what he hoped was a familiar fashion.

'Where is he now?' he said.

'Well, someone said they saw a pair of sandals with smoke coming out just outside his house a year or two back,' said Didactylos. 'He might have, you know, pushed his luck.'

'I think,' said Brutha, 'that I'd better be going. I'm sorry to have intruded on your time.'

'Bring it back when you've finished with it,' said Didactylos.

'Is that how people read in Omnia?' said Urn.

'What?'

'Upside down.'

Brutha picked up the tortoise, glared at Urn, and strode as haughtily as possible out of the Library.

'Hmm,' said Didactylos. He drummed his fingers on the tables.

'It was him I saw in the tavern last night,' said Urn. 'I'm sure, master.'

'But the Omnians are staying here in the palace.'

'That's right, master.'

'But the tavern is *outside*.'

'Yes.'

'Then he must have flown over the wall, do you think?'

'I'm sure it was him, master.'

'Then . . . maybe he came later. Maybe he hadn't gone in when you saw him.'

'It can only be that, master. The keepers of the labyrinth are unbribable.'

Didactylos clipped Urn across the back of the head with his lantern.

'Stupid boy! I've told you about that sort of statement.'

'I mean, they are not *easily* bribable, master. Not for all the gold in Omnia, for example.'

'That's more like it.'

'Do you think that tortoise was a god, master?'

'He's going to be in big trouble in Omnia if he is. They've got a bastard of a god there. Did you ever read old Abraxas?'

'No, master.'

'Very big on gods. Big gods man. Always smelled of burnt hair. Naturally resistant.'

Om crawled slowly along the length of a line.

'Stop walking up and down like that,' he said, 'I can't concentrate.'

'How can people talk like that?' Brutha asked the empty air. 'Acting as if they're *glad* they don't know things! Finding out more and more things they don't know! It's like children proudly coming to show you a full potty!'

Om marked his place with a claw.

'But they find things out,' he said. 'This Abraxas was a thinker and no mistake. *I* didn't know some of this stuff. Sit down!'

Brutha obeyed.

'Right,' said Om. 'Now ... listen. Do you know how gods get power?'

'By people believing in them,' said Brutha. 'Millions of people believe in you.'

Om hesitated.

All right, all right. We are here and it is now. Sooner or later he'll find out for himself ...

'They don't believe,' said Om.

'But –'

'It's happened before,' said the tortoise. 'Dozens of times. D'you know Abraxas found the lost city of Ee? Very strange carvings, he says. Belief, he says. Belief *shifts*. People start out believing in the god and end up believing in the structure.'

'I don't understand,' said Brutha.

'Let me put it another way,' said the tortoise. 'I am your God, right?'

'Yes.'

'And you'll obey me.'

'Yes.'

'Good. Now take a rock and go and kill Vorbis.'

Brutha didn't move.

'I'm sure you heard me,' said Om.

'But he'll ... he's ... the Quisition would –'

'*Now* you know what I mean,' said the tortoise. 'You're more afraid of him than you are of me, now. Abraxas says here: "Around the Godde there forms a Shelle of prayers and Ceremonies and Buildings and Priestes and Authority, until at Last the Godde Dies. Ande this maye notte be noticed."'

'That can't be true!'

'I think it is. Abraxas says there's a kind of shellfish that lives in the same way. It makes a bigger and bigger shell until it can't move around any more, and so it dies.'

'But ... but ... that means ... the whole Church ...'

'Yes.'

Brutha tried to keep hold of the idea, but the sheer enormity of it kept wrenching it from his mental grasp.

'But you're not dead,' he managed.

'Next best thing,' said Om. 'And you know what? No other small god is trying to usurp me. Did I ever tell you about old Ur-Gilash? No? He was the god back in what's now Omnia before me. Not much of one. Basically a weather god. Or a snake god. Something, anyway. It took years to get rid of him, though. Wars and everything. So I've been thinking ...'

Brutha said nothing.

'Om still exists,' said the tortoise. 'I mean the shell. All you'd have to do is get people to understand.'

Brutha still said nothing.

'You can be the next prophet,' said Om.

'I can't! Everyone knows Vorbis will be the next prophet!'

'Ah, but you'll be *official*.'

'No!'

'No? I am your God!'

'And I am my me. I'm not a prophet. I can't even write. I can't read. No one will listen to me.'

Om looked him up and down.

'I must admit you're not the chosen one I would have chosen,' he said.

'The great prophets had vision,' said Brutha. 'Even if they ... even if you didn't talk to them, they had something to say. What could I say? I haven't got anything to say to anyone. What could I say?'

'Believe in the Great God Om,' said the tortoise.

'And then what?'

'What do you mean, and then what?'

Brutha looked out glumly at the darkening courtyard.

'Believe in the Great God Om or be stricken with thunderbolts,' he said.

'Sounds good to me.'

'Is that how it always has to be?'

The last rays of the sun glinted off the statue in the centre of the courtyard. It was vaguely feminine. There was a penguin perched on one shoulder.

'Patina, Goddess of Wisdom,' said Brutha. 'The one with a penguin. Why a penguin?'

'Can't imagine,' said Om hurriedly.

'Nothing wise about penguins, is there?'

'Shouldn't think so. Unless you count the fact that you don't get them in Omnia. Pretty wise of them.'

'Brutha!'

'That's Vorbis,' said Brutha, standing up. 'Shall I leave you here?'

'Yes. There's still some melon. I mean loaf.'

Brutha wandered out into the dusk.

Vorbis was sitting on a bench under a tree, as still as a statue in the shadows.

Certainty, Brutha thought. I used to be certain. Now I'm not so sure.

'Ah, Brutha. You will accompany me on a little stroll. We will take the evening air.'

'Yes, lord.'

'You have enjoyed your visit to Ephebe.'

Vorbis seldom asked a question if a statement would do.

'It has been ... interesting.'

Vorbis put one hand on Brutha's shoulder and used the other to haul himself up on his staff.

'And what do you think of it?' he asked.

'They have many gods, and they don't pay them much attention,' said Brutha. 'And they search for ignorance.'

'And they find it in abundance, be sure of that,' said Vorbis.

He pointed his staff into the night. 'Let us walk,' he said.

There was the sound of laughter, somewhere in the darkness, and the clatter of pans. The scent of evening-opening flowers hung thickly in the air. The stored heat of daytime, radiating from the stones, made the night seem like a fragrant soup.

'Ephebe looks to the sea,' said Vorbis after a while. 'You see the way it is built? All on the slope of a hill facing the sea. But the sea is mutable. Nothing lasting comes from the sea. Whereas our dear Citadel looks towards the high desert. And what do we see there?'

Instinctively Brutha turned, and looked over the roof-tops to the black bulk of the desert against the sky.

'I saw a flash of light,' he said. 'And again. On the slope.'

'Ah. The light of truth,' said Vorbis. 'So let us go forth to meet it. Take me to the entrance to the labyrinth, Brutha. You know the way.'

'My lord?' said Brutha.

'Yes, Brutha?'

'I would like to ask you a question.'

'Do so.'

'What happened to Brother Murduck?'

There was the merest suggestion of hesitation in the rhythm of Vorbis's stick on the cobbles. Then the exquisitor said, 'Truth, good Brutha, is like the light. Do you know about light?'

'It . . . comes from the sun. And the moon and stars. And candles. And lamps.'

'And so on,' said Vorbis, nodding. 'Of course. But there is another kind of light. A light that fills even the darkest of places. This has to be. For if this meta-light did not exist, how could darkness be seen?'

Brutha said nothing. This sounded too much like philosophy.

'And so it is with truth,' said Vorbis. 'There are some things which appear to be the truth, which have all the hallmarks of truth, but which are not the *real* truth. The real truth must sometimes be protected by a labyrinth of lies.'

He turned to Brutha. 'Do you understand me?'

'No, Lord Vorbis.'

'I mean, that which appears to our senses is not the *fundamental* truth. Things that are seen and heard and done by the flesh are mere shadows of a deeper reality. This is what you must understand as you progress in the Church.'

'But at the moment, lord, I know only the trivial truth, the truth available on the outside,' said Brutha. He felt as though he was at the edge of a pit.

'That is how we all begin,' said Vorbis kindly.

'So did the Ephebians kill Brother Murduck?' Brutha persisted. Now he was inching out over the darkness.

'I am telling you that in the deepest sense of the truth they did. By their failure to embrace his words, by their intransigence, they surely killed him.'

'But in the *trivial* sense of the truth,' said Brutha, picking every word with the care an inquisitor might give to his patient in the depths of the Citadel, 'in the trivial sense, Brother Murduck died, did he not, in Omnia, because he had *not* died in Ephebe, had been merely mocked, but it was feared that others in the Church might not understand the, the *deeper* truth, and thus it was put about that the Ephebians had killed him in, in the *trivial* sense, thus giving you, and those who saw the truth of the evil of Ephebe, due cause to launch a – a just retaliation.'

They walked past a fountain. The deacon's steel-shod staff clicked in the night.

'I see a great future for you in the Church,' said Vorbis, eventually. 'The time of the eighth Prophet is coming. A time of expansion, and great opportunity for those true in the service of Om.'

Brutha looked into the pit.

If Vorbis was right, and there was a kind of light that made darkness visible, then down there was its opposite, the darkness where no light could ever reach: darkness that blackened light. He thought of blind Didactylos and his empty lantern.

He heard himself say, 'And with people like the Ephebians, there is no truce. No treaty can be held binding, if it is between people like the Ephebians and those who follow a deeper truth?'

Vorbis nodded. 'When the Great God is with us,' he said, 'who can stand against us? You impress me, Brutha.'

There was more laughter in the darkness, and the twang of stringed instruments.

'A feast,' sneered Vorbis. 'The Tyrant invited us to a feast! I sent some of the party, of course. Even their generals are in there! They think themselves safe behind their labyrinth, as a tortoise thinks himself safe in his shell, not realising it is a prison. Onward.'

The inner wall of the labyrinth loomed out of the darkness. Brutha leaned against it. From far above came the chink of metal on metal as a sentry went on his rounds.

The gateway to the labyrinth was wide open. The Ephebians had never seen the point of stopping people entering. Up a short side-tunnel the guide for the first sixth of the way slumbered on a bench, a candle guttering beside him. Above his alcove hung the bronze bell that would-be traversers of the maze used to summon him. Brutha slipped past.

'Brutha?'

'Yes, lord?'

'Lead the way through the labyrinth. I know you can.'

'Lord –'

'This *is* an order, Brutha,' said Vorbis, pleasantly.

There is no hope for it, Brutha thought. It *is* an order.

'Then tread where I tread, lord,' he whispered. 'Not more than one step behind me.'

'Yes, Brutha.'

'If I step around a place on the floor for no reason, you step around it too.'

'Yes, Brutha.'

Brutha thought: perhaps I could do it wrong. No. I took vows and things. You can't just disobey. The whole world ends if you start thinking like that . . .

He let his sleeping mind take control. The way through the labyrinth unrolled in his head like a glowing wire.

. . . diagonally forward and right three-and-a-half paces, and left sixty-three paces, pause two seconds – where a steely swish in the darkness suggested that one of the guardians had devised something that won him a prize – and up three steps . . .

I could run forward, he thought. I could hide, and he'd walk into one of the pits or a deadfall or something, and then I could sneak back to my room and who would ever know?

I would.

. . . forward nine paces, and right one pace, and forward nineteen paces, and left two paces . . .

There was a light ahead. Not the occasional white glow of moonlight from the slits in the roof, but yellow lamplight, dimming and brightening as its owner came nearer.

'Someone's coming,' he whispered. 'It must be one of the guides!'

Vorbis had vanished.

Brutha hovered uncertainly in the passageway as the light bobbed nearer.

An elderly voice said, 'That you, Number Four?'

The light came round a corner. It half-illuminated an old man, who walked up to Brutha and raised the candle to his face.

'Where's Number Four?' he said, peering around Brutha.

A figure appeared behind the man, from out of a side-passage. Brutha had the briefest glimpse of Vorbis, his face strangely peaceful, as he gripped the head of his staff, twisted and pulled. Sharp metal glittered for a moment in the candlelight.

Then the light went out.

Vorbis's voice said, 'Take the lead again.'

Trembling, Brutha obeyed. He felt the soft flesh of an outflung arm under his sandal for a moment.

The pit, he thought. Look into Vorbis's eyes, and there's the pit. And I'm in it with him.

I've got to remember about fundamental truth.

No more guides were patrolling the labyrinth. After a mere million years, the night air blew cool on his face, and Brutha stepped out under the stars.

'Well done. Can you remember the way to the gate?'

'Yes, Lord Vorbis.'

The deacon pulled his hood over his face.

'Carry on.'

There were a few torches lighting the streets, but Ephebe was not a city that stayed awake in darkness. A couple of passers-by paid them no attention.

'They guard their harbour,' said Vorbis, conversationally. 'But the way to the desert . . . everyone knows that no one can cross the desert. I am sure *you* know that, Brutha.'

'But now I suspect that what I know is not the truth,' said Brutha.

'Quite so. Ah. The gate. I believe it had two guards yesterday?'

'I saw two.'

'And now it is night and the gate is shut. But there will be a watchman. Wait here.'

Vorbis disappeared into the gloom. After a while there was a muffled conversation. Brutha stared straight ahead of him.

The conversation was followed by muffled silence. After a while Brutha started to count to himself.

After ten, I'll go back.

Another ten, then.

All right. Make it thirty. And *then* I'll . . .

'Ah, Brutha. Let us go.'

Brutha swallowed his heart again, and turned slowly.

'I did not hear you, lord,' he managed.

'I walk softly.'

'Is there a watchman?'

'Not now. Come help me with the bolts.'

A small wicket gate was set into the main gate. Brutha, his mind numb with hatred, shoved the bolts aside with the heel of his hand. The door opened with barely a creak.

Outside there was the occasional light of a distant farm, and crowding darkness.

Then the darkness poured in.

Hierarchy, Vorbis said later. The Ephebians didn't think in terms of hierarchies.

No army could cross the desert. But maybe a small army could get a quarter of the way, and leave a cache of water. And do that several times. And another small army could use part of that cache to go further, maybe reach halfway, and leave a cache. And another small army . . .

It had taken months. A third of the men had died, of heat and dehydration and wild animals and worse things, the worse things that the desert held . . .

You had to have a mind like Vorbis's to plan it.

And plan it early. Men were already dying in the desert before Brother Murduck went to preach; there was already a beaten track when the Omnian fleet burned in the bay before Ephebe.

You had to have a mind like Vorbis's to plan your retaliation before your attack.

It was over in less than an hour. The fundamental truth was that the handful of Ephebian guards in the palace had no chance at all.

Vorbis sat upright in the Tyrant's chair. It was approaching midnight.

A collection of Ephebian citizens, the Tyrant among them, had been herded in front of him.

He busied himself with some paperwork and then looked up with an air of mild surprise, as if he'd been completely unaware that fifty people were waiting in front of him at crossbow point.

'Ah,' he said, and flashed a little smile.

'Well,' he said, 'I am pleased to say that we can now dispense with the peace treaty. Quite unnecessary. Why prattle of peace when there is no more war? Ephebe is now a diocese of Omnia. There will be no argument.'

He threw a paper on to the floor.

'There will be a fleet here in a few days. There will be no opposition, while we hold the palace. Your infernal mirror is even now being smashed.'

He steepled his fingers and looked at the assembled Ephebians.

'Who built it?'

The Tyrant looked up.

'It was an Ephebian construction,' he said.

'Ah,' said Vorbis, 'democracy. I forgot. Then who' – he signalled one of the guards, who handed him a sack – 'wrote this?'

A copy of *De Chelonian Mobile* was flung on to the marble floor.

Brutha stood beside the throne. It was where he had been told to stand.

He'd looked into the pit and now it was him. Everything around him was happening in some distant circle of light, surrounded by darkness. Thoughts chased one another round his head.

Did the Cenobiarch know about this? Did anyone else know about the two kinds of truth? Who else knew that Vorbis was fighting both sides of a war, like a child playing with soldiers? Was it really wrong if it was for the greater glory of . . .

. . . a god who was a tortoise. A god that only Brutha believed in?

Who did Vorbis talk to when he prayed?

Through the mental storm Brutha heard Vorbis's level tones: 'If the philosopher who wrote this does not own up, the entirety of you will be put to the flame. Do not doubt that I mean it.'

There was a movement in the crowd, and the sound of Didactylos's voice.

'Let go! You heard him! Anyway . . . I always wanted a chance to do this . . .'

A couple of servants were pushed aside and the philosopher stumped out of the crowd, his barren lantern held defiantly over his head.

Brutha watched the philosopher pause for a moment in the empty space, and then turn very slowly until he was directly facing Vorbis. He took a few steps forward then, and held the lantern out as he appeared to regard the deacon critically.

'Hmm,' he said.

'You are the . . . perpetrator?' said Vorbis.

'Indeed. Didactylos is my name.'

'You are blind?'

'Only as far as vision is concerned, my lord.'

'Yet you carry a lantern,' said Vorbis. 'Doubtless for some catchword reason. Probably you'll tell me you're looking for an honest man?'

'I don't know, my lord. Perhaps you could tell me what he looks like?'

'I should strike you down now,' said Vorbis.

'Oh, certainly.'

Vorbis indicated the book.

'These *lies*. This *scandal*. This . . . this *lure* to drag the minds of men from the path of true knowledge. You dare to stand before me and declare' – he pushed the book with a toe – 'that the world is flat and travels through the void on the back of a giant turtle?'

Brutha held his breath.

So did history.

Affirm your belief, Brutha thought. Just once, someone please stand up to Vorbis. I can't. But someone . . .

He found his eyes swivelling towards Simony, who stood on the other side of Vorbis's chair. The sergeant looked transfixed, fascinated.

Didactylos drew himself up to his full height. He half-turned and for a moment his blank gaze passed across Brutha. The lantern was extended at arm's length.

'No,' he said.

'When every honest man knows that the world is a sphere, a perfect shape, bound to spin around the sphere of the Sun as Man orbits the central truth of Om,' said Vorbis, 'and the stars –'

Brutha leaned forward, heart pounding.

'My lord?' he whispered.

'What?' snapped Vorbis.

'He said "no",' said Brutha.

'That's right,' said Didactylos.

Vorbis sat absolutely motionless for a moment. Then his jaw moved a fraction, as if he was rehearsing some words under his breath.

'You *deny* it?' he said.

'Let it be a sphere,' said Didactylos. 'No problem with a sphere. No doubt special arrangements are made for everything to stay on. And the Sun can be another larger sphere, a long way off. Would you like the Moon to orbit the world or the Sun? I advise the world. More hierarchical, and a splendid example to us all.'

Brutha was seeing something he'd never seen before. Vorbis was looking bewildered.

'But you wrote ... you said the world is on the back of a giant turtle! You gave the turtle a *name!*'

Didactylos shrugged. 'Now I know better,' he said. 'Who ever heard of a turtle ten thousand miles long? Swimming through the emptiness of space? Hah. For stupidity! I am embarrassed to think of it now.'

Vorbis shut his mouth. Then he opened it again.

'This is how an Ephebian philosopher behaves?' he said.

Didactylos shrugged again. 'It is how any true philosopher behaves,' he said. 'One must always be ready to embrace new ideas, take account of new proofs. Don't you agree? And you have brought us many new points' – a gesture seemed to take in, quite by accident, the Omnian bowmen around the room – 'for me to ponder. I can always be swayed by powerful argument.'

'Your lies have already poisoned the world!'

'Then I shall write another book,' said Didactylos calmly. 'Think how it will look – proud Didactylos swayed by the arguments of the Omnians. A full retraction. Hmm? In fact, with your permission, lord – I know you have much to do, looting and burning and so on – I will retire to my barrel right away and start work on it. A universe of spheres. Balls spinning through space. Hmm. Yes. With your permission, lord, I will write you more balls than you can imagine ...'

The old philosopher turned and, very slowly, walked towards the exit.

Vorbis watched him go.

Brutha saw him half-raise his hand to signal the guards, and then lower it again.

Vorbis turned to the Tyrant.

'So much for your –' he began.

'*Coo-ee!*'

The lantern sailed through the doorway and shattered against Vorbis's skull.

'*Nevertheless ... the Turtle Moves!*'

Vorbis leapt to his feet.

'I –' he screamed, and then got a grip on himself. He waved irritably at a couple of the guards. 'I want him caught. Now. And ... Brutha?'

Brutha could hardly hear him for the rush of blood in his ears. Didactylos had been a better thinker than he'd thought.

'Yes, lord?'

'You will take a party of men, and you will take them to the Library . . . and then, Brutha, you will burn the Library.'

Didactylos was blind, but it was dark. The pursuing guards could see, except that there was nothing to see by. And they hadn't spent their lives wandering the twisty, uneven and above all many-stepped lanes of Ephebe.

'– eight, nine, ten, eleven,' muttered the philosopher, bounding up a pitch-dark flight of steps and haring around a corner.

'Argh, ow, that was my *knee*,' muttered most of the guards, in a heap about halfway up.

One made it to the top, though. By starlight he could just make out the skinny figure, bounding madly along the street. He raised his crossbow. The old fool wasn't even dodging . . .

A perfect target.

There was a twang.

The guard looked puzzled for a moment. The bow toppled from his hands, firing itself as it hit the cobbles and sending its bolt ricocheting off a statue. He looked down at the feathered shaft sticking out of his chest, and then at the figure detaching itself from the shadows.

'Sergeant Simony?' he whispered.

'I'm sorry,' said Simony. 'I really am. But the Truth is important.'

The soldier opened his mouth to give his opinion of the truth and then slumped forward.

He opened his eyes.

Simony was walking away. Everything looked lighter. It was still dark. But now he could see in the darkness. Everything was shades of grey. And the cobbles under his hand had somehow become a coarse black sand.

He looked up.

ON YOUR FEET, PRIVATE ICHLOS.

He stood up sheepishly. Now he was more than just a soldier, an anonymous figure to chase and be killed and be no more than a shadowy bit-player in other people's lives. Now he was Dervi Ichlos, aged thirty-eight, comparatively blameless in the general scheme of things, and dead.

He raised a hand to his lips uncertainly.

'You're the judge?' he said.

Not me.

Ichlos looked at the sands stretching away. He knew instinctively what he had to do. He was far less sophisticated than General Fri'it, and took more notice of songs he'd learned in his childhood. Besides, he had an advantage. He'd had even less religion than the general.

Judgement is at the end of the desert.

Ichlos tried to smile.

'My mum told me about this,' he said. 'When you're dead, you have to walk a desert. And you see everything properly, she said. And remember everything right.'

Death studiously did nothing to indicate his feelings either way.

'Might meet a few friends on the way, eh?' said the soldier.

Possibly.

Ichlos set out. On the whole, he thought, it could have been worse.

Urn clambered across the shelves like a monkey, pulling books out of their racks and throwing them down to the floor.

'I can carry about twenty,' he said. 'But which twenty?'

'*Always* wanted to do that,' murmured Didactylos happily. 'Upholding truth in the face of tyranny and so on. Hah! One man, unafraid of the –'

'What to take? What to take?' shouted Urn.

'We don't need Grido's *Mechanics*,' said Didactylos. 'Hey, I wish I could have seen the look on his face! Damn good shot, considering. I just hope someone wrote down what I –'

'Principles of gearing! Theory of water expansion!' shouted Urn. 'But we don't need Ibid's *Civics* or Gnomon's *Ectopia*, that's for sure –'

'What? They belong to all mankind!' snapped Didactylos.

'Then if all mankind will come and help us carry them, that's fine,' said Urn. 'But if it's just the two of us, I prefer to carry something useful.'

'Useful? Books on mechanisms?'

'Yes! They can show people how to live better!'

'And *these* show people how to be people,' said Didactylos. 'Which reminds me. Find me another lantern. I feel quite blind without one –'

The Library door shook to a thunderous knocking. It wasn't the knocking of people who expected the door to be opened.

'We could throw some of the others into the –'

The hinges leapt out of the walls. The door thudded down.

Soldiers scrambled over it, swords drawn.

'Ah, gentlemen,' said Didactylos. 'Pray don't disturb my circles.'

The corporal in charge looked at him blankly, and then down at the floor.

'What circles?' he said.

'Hey, how about giving me a pair of compasses and coming back in, say, half an hour?'

'Leave him, corporal,' said Brutha.

He stepped over the door.

'I said leave him.'

'But I got orders to –'

'Are you deaf? If you are, the Quisition can cure that,' said Brutha, astonished at the steadiness of his own voice.

'You don't belong to the Quisition,' said the corporal.

'No. But I know a man who does,' said Brutha. 'You are to search the palace for books. Leave him with me. He's an old man. What harm can he do?'

The corporal looked hesitantly from Brutha to his prisoners.

'Very good, corporal. I will take over.'

They all turned.

'Did you hear me?' said Sergeant Simony, pushing his way forward.

'But the deacon told us –'

'Corporal?'

'Yes, sergeant?'

'The deacon is far away. I am right here.'

'Yes, sergeant.'

'Go!'

'Yes, sergeant.'

Simony cocked an ear as the soldiers marched away.

Then he stuck his sword in the door and turned to Didactylos. He made a fist with his left hand and brought his right hand down on it, palm extended.

'*The Turtle Moves*,' he said.

'That all depends,' said the philosopher, cautiously.

'I mean I am . . . a friend,' he said.

'Why should we trust you?' said Urn.

'Because you haven't got any choice,' said Sergeant Simony briskly.

'Can you get us out of here?' said Brutha.

Simony glared at him. 'You?' he said. 'Why should I get *you* out of here? You're an inquisitor!' He grasped his sword.

Brutha backed away.

'I'm not!'

'On the ship, when the captain sounded you, you just said nothing,' said Simony. 'You're not one of us.'

'I don't think I'm one of them, either,' said Brutha. 'I'm one of mine.'

He gave Didactylos an imploring look, which was a wasted effort, and turned it towards Urn instead.

'I don't know about this soldier,' he said. 'All I know is that Vorbis means to have you killed and he *will* burn your Library. But I can help. I worked it out on the way here.'

'And don't listen to him,' said Simony. He dropped on one knee in front of Didactylos, like a supplicant. 'Sir, there are ... some of us ... who know your book for what it is ... see, I have a copy ...'

He fumbled inside his breastplate.

'We copied it out,' said Simony. 'One copy! That's all we had! But it's been passed around. Some of us who could read, read it to the others! It makes so much sense!'

'Er ...' said Didactylos. 'What?'

Simony waved his hands in excitement. 'Because we know it – I've been to places that – it's true! There *is* a Great Turtle. The turtle *does* move! We don't *need* gods!'

'Urn? No one's stripped the copper off the roof, have they?' said Didactylos.

'Don't think so.'

'Remind me not to talk to this chap outside, then.'

'You don't understand!' said Simony. 'I can save you. You have friends in unexpected places. Come on. I'll just kill this priest ...'

He gripped his sword. Brutha backed away.

'No! I can help, too! That's why I came. When I saw you in front of Vorbis I knew what I could do!'

'What can you do?' sneered Urn.

'I can save the Library.'

'What? Put it on your back and run away?' sneered Simony.

'No. I don't mean that. How many scrolls are there?'

'About seven hundred,' said Didactylos.

'How many of them are important?'

'All of them!' said Urn.

'Maybe a couple of hundred,' said Didactylos, mildly.

'Uncle!'

'All the rest is just wind and vanity publishing,' said Didactylos.

'But they're *books*!'

'I may be able to take more than that,' said Brutha slowly. 'Is there a way out?'

'There . . . could be,' said Didactylos.

'Don't tell him!' said Simony.

'Then all your books will burn,' said Brutha. He pointed to Simony. 'He said you haven't got a choice. So you haven't got anything to lose, have you?'

'He's a –' Simony began.

'Everyone shut up,' said Didactylos. He stared past Brutha's ear.

'There may be a way out,' he said. 'What do you intend?'

'I don't believe this!' said Urn. 'There's Omnians here and you're telling them there's another way out!'

'There's tunnels all through this rock,' said Didactylos.

'Maybe, but we don't *tell* people!'

'I'm inclined to trust this person,' said Didactylos. 'He's got an honest face. Speaking philosophically.'

'*Why* should we trust him?'

'Anyone stupid enough to expect us to trust him in these circumstances *must* be trustworthy,' said Didactylos. 'He'd be too stupid to be deceitful.'

'I can walk out of here right now,' said Brutha. 'And where will your Library be then?'

'You see?' said Simony.

'Just when things apparently look dark, suddenly we have unexpected friends everywhere,' said Didactylos. 'What is your plan, young man?'

'I haven't got one,' said Brutha. 'I just do things, one after the other.'

'And how long will doing things one after another take you?'

'About ten minutes, I think.'

Simony glared at Brutha.

'Now get the books,' said Brutha. 'And I shall need some light.'

'But you can't even read!' said Urn.

'I'm not going to read them.' Brutha looked blankly at the first scroll, which happened to be *De Chelonian Mobile*.

'Oh. My god,' he said.

'Something wrong?' said Didactylos.

'Could someone fetch my tortoise?'

Simony trotted through the palace. No one was paying him much attention. Most of the Ephebian guard was outside the labyrinth, and Vorbis had made it clear to anyone who was thinking of venturing inside just what would happen to the palace's inhabitants. Groups of Omnian soldiers were looting in a disciplined sort of way.

Besides, he was returning to his quarters.

There *was* a tortoise in Brutha's room. It was sitting on the table, between a rolled-up scroll and a gnawed melon rind and, insofar as it was possible to tell with tortoises, was asleep. Simony grabbed it without ceremony, rammed it into his pack, and hurried back towards the Library.

He hated himself for doing it. The stupid priest had ruined everything! But Didactylos had made him promise, and Didactylos was the man who knew the Truth.

All the way there he had the impression that someone was trying to attract his attention.

'You can remember them just by looking?' said Urn.

'Yes.'

'The whole scroll?'

'Yes.'

'I don't believe you.'

'The word LIBRVM outside this building has a chip in the top of the first letter,' said Brutha. 'Xeno wrote *Reflections*, and old Aristocrates wrote *Platitudes*, and Didactylos thinks Ibid's *Discourses* are bloody stupid. There are six hundred paces from the Tyrant's throne room to the Library. There is a –'

'He's got a good memory, you've got to grant him that,' said Didactylos. 'Show him some more scrolls.'

'How will we know he's remembered them?' Urn demanded, unrolling a scroll of geometrical theorems. 'He can't read! And even if he could read, he can't write!'

'We shall have to teach him.'

Brutha looked at a scroll full of maps. He shut his eyes. For a moment the jagged outline glowed against the inside of his eyelids, and then he felt them settle into his mind. They were still there somewhere – he could bring them back at any time. Urn unrolled another scroll. Pictures of animals. This one, drawings of plants and lots of writing. This one, just writing. This one, triangles and things. They settled down in his memory. After a while, he wasn't even aware of the scroll unrolling. He just had to keep looking.

He wondered how much he could remember. But that was stupid. You just remembered everything you saw. A tabletop, or a scroll full of writing. There was as much information in the grain and colouring of the wood as there was in Xeno's *Reflections*.

Even so, he was conscious of a certain heaviness of mind, a feeling that if he turned his head sharply then memory would slosh out of his ears.

Urn picked up a scroll at random and unrolled it partway.

'Describe what an Ambiguous Puzuma looks like,' he demanded.

'Don't know,' said Brutha. He blinked.

'So much for Mr Memory,' said Urn.

'He can't *read*, boy. That's not fair,' said the philosopher.

'All right. I mean – the fourth picture in the third scroll you saw,' said Urn.

'A four-legged creature facing left,' said Brutha. 'A large head similar to a cat's and broad shoulders with the body tapering towards the hindquarters. The body is a pattern of dark and light squares. The ears are very small and laid flat against the head. There are six whiskers. The tail is stubby. Only the hind feet are clawed, three claws on each foot. The fore feet are about the same length as the head and held up against the body. A band of thick hair –'

'That was fifty scrolls ago,' said Urn. 'He saw the whole scroll for a second or two.'

They looked at Brutha. Brutha blinked again.

'You know *everything*?' said Urn.

'I don't know.'

'You've got half the Library in your head!'

'I feel . . . a . . . bit . . .'

The Library of Ephebe was a furnace. The flames burned blue where the melted copper roof dripped on to the shelves.

All libraries, everywhere, are connected by the bookworm holes in space created by the strong space-time distortions found around any large collections of books.

Only a very few librarians learn the secret, and there are

inflexible rules about making *use* of the fact. Because it amounts to time travel, and time travel causes big problems.

But if a library is on fire, and down in the history books as having been on fire . . .

There was a small pop, utterly unheard among the crackling of the bookshelves, and a figure dropped out of nowhere on to a small patch of unburned floor in the middle of the Library.

It looked ape-like, but it moved in a very purposeful way. Long simian arms beat out the flames, pulled scrolls off the shelves, and stuffed them into a sack. When the sack was full, it knuckled back into the middle of the room . . . and vanished, with another pop.

This has nothing to do with the story.

Nor does the fact that, some time later, scrolls thought to have been destroyed in the Great Ephebian Library Fire turned up in remarkably good condition in the Library of Unseen University in Ankh-Morpork.

But it's nice to know, even so.

Brutha awoke with the smell of the sea in his nostrils.

At least it was what people think of as the smell of the sea, which is the stink of antique fish and rotten seaweed.

He was in some sort of shed. Such light as managed to come through its one unglazed window was red, and flickered. One end of the shed was open to the water. The ruddy light showed a few figures clustered around something there.

Brutha gently probed the contents of his memory. Everything seemed to be there, the Library scrolls neatly arranged. The words were as meaningless to him as any other written word, but the pictures were interesting. More interesting than most things in his memory, anyway.

He sat up, carefully.

'You're awake, then,' said the voice of Om, in his head. 'Feel a bit full, do we? Feel a bit like a stack of shelves? Feel like we've got big notices saying "SILENCIOS!" all over the place inside our head? What did you go and do that for?'

'I . . . don't know. It seemed like . . . the next thing to do. Where are you?'

'Your soldier friend has got me in his pack. Thanks for looking after me so carefully, by the way.'

Brutha managed to get to his feet. The world revolved round him for a moment, adding a third astronomical theory to the two currently occupying the minds of local thinkers.

He peered out of the window. The red light was coming from fires all over Ephebe, but there was one huge glow over the Library.

'Guerrilla activity,' said Om. 'Even the slaves are fighting. Can't understand why. You think they'd jump at the chance to be revenged on their masters, eh?'

'I suppose a slave in Ephebe has the chance to be free,' said Brutha.

There was a hiss from the other end of the shed, and a metallic, whirring noise. Brutha heard Urn say, 'There! I told you. Just a block in the tubes. Let's get some more fuel in.'

Brutha tottered towards the group.

They were clustered round a boat. As boats went, it was of normal shape – a pointed end in front, a flat end at the back. But there was no mast. What there was, was a large, copper-coloured ball, hanging in a wooden framework towards the back of the boat. There was an iron basket underneath it, in which someone had already got a good fire going.

And the ball was spinning in its frame, in a cloud of steam.

'I've seen that,' he said. 'In *De Chelonian Mobile*. There was a drawing.'

'Oh, it's the walking Library,' said Didactylos. 'Yes. You're right. Illustrating the principle of reaction. I never asked Urn to build a big one. This is what comes of thinking with your hands.'

'I took it round the lighthouse one night last week,' said Urn. 'No problems at all.'

'Ankh-Morpork is a lot further than that,' said Simony.

'Yes, it is five times further than the distance between Ephebe and Omnia,' said Brutha solemnly. 'There was a scroll of maps,' he added.

Steam rose in scalding clouds from the whirring ball. Now he was closer, Brutha could see that half a dozen very short oars had been joined together in a star-shaped pattern behind the copper globe, and hung over the rear of the boat. Wooden cogwheels and a couple of endless belts filled the intervening space. As the globe spun, the paddles thrashed at the air.

'How does it work?' he said.

'Very simple,' said Urn. 'The fire makes –'

'We haven't got time for this,' said Simony.

'– *makes* the water hot and so it gets angry,' said the apprentice philosopher. 'So it rushes out of the globe through these four little nozzles to get away from the fire. The plumes of steam push the globe around, and the cogwheels and Legibus's screw mechanism transfer the motion to the paddles which turn, pushing the boat through the water.'

'Very philosophical,' said Didactylos.

Brutha felt that he ought to stand up for Omnian progress.

'The great doors of the Citadel weigh tons but are opened solely by the power of faith,' he said. 'One push and they swing open.'

'I should very much like to see that,' said Urn.

Brutha felt a faint sinful twinge of pride that Omnia still had anything he could be proud of.

'Very good balance and some hydraulics, probably.'

'Oh.'

Simony thoughtfully prodded the mechanism with his sword.

'Have you thought of all the possibilities?' he said.

Urn's hands began to weave through the air. 'You mean mighty ships ploughing the wine-dark sea with no –' he began.

'On land, I was thinking,' said Simony. 'Perhaps . . . on some sort of cart . . .'

'Oh, no point in putting a boat on a cart.'

Simony's eyes gleamed with the gleam of a man who had seen the future and found it covered with armour plating.

'Hmm,' he said.

'It's all very well, but it's not philosophy,' said Didactylos. 'Where's the priest?'

'I'm here, but I'm not a –'

'How're you feeling? You went out like a candle back there.'

'I'm . . . better now.'

'One minute upright, next minute a draught-excluder.'

'I'm much better.'

'Happen a lot, does it?'

'Sometimes.'

'Remembering the scrolls okay?'

'I . . . think so. Who set fire to the Library?'

Urn looked up from the mechanism.

'He did,' he said.

Brutha stared at Didactylos.

'*You* set fire to your own Library?'

'I'm the only one qualified,' said the philosopher. 'Besides, it keeps it out of the way of Vorbis.'

'What?'

'Suppose he'd read the scrolls? He's bad enough as it is. He'd be a lot worse with all that knowledge inside him.'

'He wouldn't have read them,' said Brutha.

'Oh, he would. I know that type,' said Didactylos. 'All holy piety in public, and all peeled grapes and self-indulgence in private.'

'Not Vorbis,' said Brutha, with absolute certainty. 'He wouldn't have read them.'

'Well, *anyway*,' said Didactylos, 'if it had to be done, I did it.'

Urn turned away from the bow of the boat, where he was feeding more wood into the brazier under the globe.

'Can we all get on board?' he said.

Brutha eased his way on a rough bench seat amidships, or whatever it was called. The air smelled of hot water.

'Right,' said Urn. He pulled a lever. The spinning paddles hit the water; there was a jerk and then, steam hanging in the air behind it, the boat moved forward.

'What's the name of this vessel?' said Didactylos.

Urn looked surprised.

'Name?' he said. 'It's a boat. A thing, of the nature of things. It doesn't *need* a name.'

'Names are more philosophical,' said Didactylos, with a trace of sulkiness. 'And you should have broken an amphora of wine over it.'

'That would have been a waste.'

The boat chugged out of the boathouse and into the dark harbour. Away to one side, an Ephebian galley was on fire. The whole of the city was a patchwork of flame.

'But you've got an amphora on board?' said Didactylos.

'Yes.'

'Pass it over, then.'

White water trailed behind the boat. The paddles churned.

'No wind. No rowers!' said Simony. 'Do you even begin to understand what you have here, Urn?'

'Absolutely. The operating principles are amazingly simple,' said Urn.

'That wasn't what I meant. I meant the things you could do with this power!'

Urn pushed another log on the fire.

'It's just the transforming of heat into work,' he said. 'I suppose . . . oh, the pumping of water. Mills that can grind even when the wind isn't blowing. That sort of thing? Is that what you had in mind?'

Simony the soldier hesitated.

'Yeah,' he said. 'Something like that.'

Brutha whispered, 'Om?'

'Yes?'

'Are you all right?'

'It smells like a soldier's knapsack in here. Get me out.'

The copper ball spun madly over the fire. It gleamed almost as brightly as Simony's eyes.

Brutha tapped him on the shoulder.

'Can I have my tortoise?'

Simony laughed bitterly.

'There's good eating on one of these things,' he said, fishing out Om.

'Everyone says so,' said Brutha. He lowered his voice to a whisper.

'What sort of place is Ankh?'

'A city of a million souls,' said the voice of Om, 'many of them occupying bodies. And a thousand religions. There's even a temple to the small gods! Sounds like a place where people don't have trouble believing things. Not a bad place for a fresh start, I think. With my brains and your . . . with my brains, we should soon be in business again.'

'You don't want to go back to Omnia?'

'No point,' said the voice of Om. 'It's always possible to overthrow an established god. People get fed up, they want a change. But you can't overthrow yourself, can you?'

'Who're you talking to, priest?' said Simony.

'I . . . er . . . was praying.'

'Hah! To Om? You might as well pray to that tortoise.'

'Yes.'

'I am ashamed for Omnia,' said Simony. 'Look at us. Stuck in the past. Held back by repressive monotheism. Shunned by our neighbours. What good has our God been to us? Gods? Hah!'

'Steady on, steady on,' said Didactylos. 'We're on seawater and that's highly conductive armour you're wearing.'

'Oh, I say nothing about other gods,' said Simony quickly. 'I have not the right. But Om? A bogeyman for the Quisition! If he exists, let him strike me down here and now!'

Simony drew his sword and held it up at arm's length.

Om sat peacefully on Brutha's lap. 'I like this boy,' he said. 'He's almost as good as a believer. It's like love and hate, know what I mean?'

Simony sheathed his sword again.

'Thus I refute Om,' he said.

'Yes, but what's the alternative?'

'Philosophy! Practical philosophy! Like Urn's engine there. It could drag Omnia kicking and screaming into the Century of the Fruitbat!'

'Kicking and screaming,' said Brutha.

'By any means necessary,' said Simony.

He beamed at them.

'Don't worry about him,' said Om. 'We'll be far away. Just as well, too. I don't think Omnia's going to be a popular country when news of last night's work gets about.'

'But it was Vorbis's fault!' said Brutha out loud. 'He started the whole thing! He sent poor Brother Murduck, and then he had him killed so he could blame it on the Ephebians! He never intended any peace treaty! He just wanted to get into the palace!'

'Beats me how he managed that, too,' said Urn. 'No one ever got through the labyrinth without a guide. How did he do it?'

Didactylos's blind eyes sought out Brutha.

'Can't imagine,' he said. Brutha hung his head.

'He really did all that?' said Simony.

'Yes.'

'You idiot! You total sandhead!' screamed Om.

'And you'd tell this to other people?' said Simony, insistently.

'I suppose so.'

'You'd speak out against the Quisition?'

Brutha stared miserably into the night. Behind them, the flames of Ephebe had merged into one orange spark.

'All I can say is what I remember,' he said.

'We're dead,' said Om. 'Throw me over the side, why don't you? This bonehead will want to take us back to Omnia!'

Simony rubbed his chin thoughtfully.

'Vorbis has many enemies,' he said, 'in certain circumstances. Better he should be killed, but some would call that murder. Or even martyrdom. But a trial . . . if there was evidence . . . if they even *thought* there could be evidence . . .'

'I can see his mind working!' Om screamed. 'We'd all be safe if you'd shut up!'

'Vorbis on trial,' Simony mused.

Brutha blanched at the thought. It was the kind of thought that was almost impossible to hold in the mind. It was the kind of thought that made no sense. Vorbis on trial? Trials were things that happened to other people.

He remembered Brother Murduck. And the soldiers who had been lost in the desert. And all the things that had been done to people, even to Brutha.

'Tell him you can't remember!' Om yelled. 'Tell him you can't recall!'

'And if he *was* on trial,' said Simony, 'he'd be found guilty. No one would dare do anything else.'

Thoughts always moved slowly through Brutha's mind, like icebergs. They arrived slowly and left slowly and when they were there they occupied a lot of space, much of it below the surface.

He thought: the worst thing about Vorbis isn't that he's evil, but that he makes good people do evil. He turns people into things like himself. You can't help it. You catch it off him.

There was no sound but the slosh of water against the *Unnamed Boat*'s hull and the spinning of the philosophical engine.

'We'd be caught if we returned to Omnia,' said Brutha slowly.

'We can land away from the ports,' said Simony eagerly.

'Ankh-Morpork!' shouted Om.

'First we should take Mr Didactylos to Ankh-Morpork,' said Brutha. 'Then – I'll come back to Omnia.'

'You can damn well leave *me* there too!' said Om. 'I'll soon find some believers in Ankh-Morpork, don't you worry, they believe anything there!'

'Never seen Ankh-Morpork,' said Didactylos. 'Still, we live and learn. That's what I always say.' He turned to face the soldier. 'Kicking and screaming.'

'There's some exiles in Ankh,' said Simony. 'Don't worry. You'll be safe there.'

'Amazing!' said Didactylos. 'And to think, this morning, I didn't even know I was in danger.'

He sat back in the boat.

'Life in this world,' he said, 'is, as it were, a sojourn in a cave. What can we know of reality? For all we see of the true nature of existence is, shall we say, no more than bewildering and amusing shadows cast upon the inner wall of the cave by the unseen blinding light of absolute truth, from which we may or may not deduce some glimmer of veracity, and we as troglodyte seekers of wisdom can only lift our voices to the unseen and say, humbly, "Go on, do Deformed Rabbit . . . it's my favourite."'

*

Vorbis stirred the ashes with his foot.

'No bones,' he said.

The soldiers stood silently. The fluffy grey flakes collapsed and blew a little way in the dawn breeze.

'And the wrong sort of ash,' said Vorbis.

The sergeant opened his mouth to say something.

'Be assured I know that of which I speak,' said Vorbis.

He wandered over to the charred trap-door, and prodded it with his toe.

'We followed the tunnel,' said the sergeant, in the tones of one who hopes against experience that sounding helpful will avert the wrath to come. 'It comes out near the docks.'

'But if you enter it from the docks it does not come out here,' Vorbis mused. The smoking ashes seemed to hold an endless fascination for him.

The sergeant's brow wrinkled.

'Understand?' said Vorbis. 'The Ephebians wouldn't build a way out that was a way in. The minds that devised the labyrinth would not work like that. There would be ... valves. Sequences of triggerstones, perhaps. Trips that trip only one way. Whirring blades that come out of unexpected walls.'

'Ah.'

'Most intricate and devious, I have no doubt.'

The sergeant ran a dry tongue over his lips. He could not read Vorbis like a book, because there had never been a book like Vorbis. But Vorbis had certain habits of thought that you learned, after a while.

'You wish me to take the squad and follow it up from the docks,' he said hollowly.

'I was just about to suggest it,' said Vorbis.

'Yes, lord.'

Vorbis patted the sergeant on the shoulder.

'But do not worry!' he said cheerfully. 'Om will protect the strong in faith.'

'Yes, lord.'

'And the last man can bring me a full report. But first ... they are not in the city?'

'We have searched it fully, lord.'

'And no one left by the gate? Then they left by sea.'

'All the Ephebian war vessels are accounted for, Lord Vorbis.'

'This bay is lousy with small boats.'

'With nowhere to go but the open sea, sir.'

Vorbis looked out at the Circle Sea. It filled the world from horizon to horizon. Beyond lay the smudge of the Sto plains and the ragged line of the Ramtops, all the way to the towering peaks that the heretics called the Hub but which was, he knew, the Pole, visible around the curve of the world only because of the way light bent in atmosphere, just as it did in water . . . and he saw a smudge of white, curling over the distant ocean.

Vorbis had very good eyesight, from a height.

He picked up a handful of grey ash, which had once been Dykeri's *Principles of Navigation*, and let it drift through his fingers.

'Om has sent us a fair wind,' he said. 'Let us get down to the docks.'

Hope waved optimistically in the waters of the sergeant's despair.

'You won't be wanting us to explore the tunnel, lord?' he said.

'Oh, no. You can do that when we return.'

Urn prodded at the copper globe with a piece of wire while the *Unnamed Boat* wallowed in the waves.

'Can't you beat it?' said Simony, who was not up to speed on the difference between machines and people.

'It's a philosophical engine,' said Urn. 'Beating won't help.'

'But you said machines could be our slaves,' said Simony.

'Not the beating sort,' said Urn. 'The nozzles are bunged up with salt. When the water rushes out of the globe it leaves the salt behind.'

'Why?'

'I don't know. Water likes to travel light.'

'We're becalmed! Can you do anything about it?'

'Yes, wait for it to cool down and then clean it out and put some more water in it.'

Simony looked around distractedly.

'But we're still in sight of the coast!'

'*You* might be,' said Didactylos. He was sitting in the middle of the boat with his hands crossed on the top of his walking-stick, looking like an old man who doesn't often get taken out for an airing and is quite enjoying it.

'Don't worry. No one could see us out here,' said Urn. He prodded at the mechanism. 'Anyway, I'm a bit worried about the screw. It was invented to move water along, not move along on water.'

'You mean it's confused?' said Simony.

'Screwed up,' said Didactylos happily.

Brutha lay in the pointed end, looking down at the water. A small squid siphoned past, just under the surface. He wondered what it was –

– and *knew* it was the common bottle squid, of the class Cephalopoda, phylum Mollusca, and that it had an internal cartilaginous support instead of a skeleton and a well-developed nervous system and large, image-forming eyes that were quite similar to vertebrate eyes.

The knowledge hung in the forefront of his mind for a moment, and then faded away.

'Om?' Brutha whispered.

'What?'

'What're you doing?'

'Trying to get some sleep. Tortoises need a lot of sleep, you know.'

Simony and Urn were bent over the philosophical engine. Brutha stared at the globe –

– a sphere of radius r, which therefore had a volume V = (4/3) (pi) rrr, and surface area A = 4(pi) rr –

'Oh, my god . . .'

'What now?' said the voice of the tortoise.

Didactylos's face turned towards Brutha, who was clutching at his head.

'What's a pi?'

Didactylos reached out a hand and steadied Brutha.

'What's the matter?' said Om.

'I don't know! It's just words! I don't know what's in the books! I can't read!'

'Getting plenty of sleep is vital,' said Om. 'It builds a healthy shell.'

Brutha sagged to his knees in the rocking boat. He felt like a householder coming back unexpectedly and finding the old place full of strangers. They were in every room, not menacing, but just filling the space with their thereness.

'The books are leaking!'

'I don't see how that can happen,' said Didactylos. 'You said you just looked at them. You didn't read them. You don't know what they mean.'

'*They* know what they mean!'

'Listen. They're just books, of the nature of books,' said Didactylos. 'They're not magical. If you could know what books contained just by looking at them, Urn there would be a genius.'

'What's the matter with him?' said Simony.

'He thinks he knows too much.'

'No! I don't know anything! Not really *know*,' said Brutha. 'I just remembered that squids have an internal cartilaginous support!'

'I can see that would be a worry,' said Simony. 'Huh. Priests? Mad, the lot of them.'

'No! I don't know what cartilaginous *means*!'

'Skeletal connective tissue,' said Didactylos. 'Think of bony and leathery at the same time.'

Simony snorted. 'Well, well,' he said, 'we live and learn, just like you said.'

'Some of us even do it the other way round,' said Didactylos.

'Is that supposed to mean something?'

'It's philosophy,' said Didactylos. 'And sit down, boy. You're making the boat rock. We're overloaded as it is.'

'It's being buoyed upward by a force equal to the weight of the displaced fluid,' muttered Brutha, sagging.

'Hmm?'

'Except that I don't know what buoyed means.'

Urn looked up from the sphere. 'We're ready to start again,' he said. 'Just bale some water in here with your helmet, mister.'

'And then we shall go again?'

'Well, we can start getting up steam,' said Urn. He wiped his hands on his toga.

'Y'know,' said Didactylos, 'there *are* different ways of learning things. I'm reminded of the time when old Prince Lasgere of Tsort asked me how he could become learned, especially since he hadn't got any time for this reading business. I said to him, "There is no royal road to learning, sire," and he said to me, "Bloody well build one or I shall have your legs chopped off. Use as many slaves as you like." A refreshingly direct approach, I always thought. Not a man to mince words. People, yes. But not words.'

'Why didn't he chop your legs off?' said Urn.

'I built him his road. More or less.'

'How? I thought that was just a metaphor.'

'You're learning, Urn. So I found a dozen slaves who could read and they sat in his bedroom at night whispering choice passages to him while he slept.'

'Did that work?'

'Don't know. The third slave stuck a six-inch dagger in his ear. Then after the revolution the new ruler let me out of prison and said I could leave the country if I promised not to think of anything on the way to the border. But I don't believe there was anything wrong with the idea in principle.'

Urn blew on the fire.

'Takes a little while to heat up the water,' he explained.

Brutha lay back in the bow again. If he concentrated, he could stop the knowledge flowing. The thing to do was avoid looking at things. Even a cloud –

– devised by natural philosophy as a means of occasioning shade on the surface of the world, thus preventing overheating –

– caused an intrusion. Om was fast asleep.

Knowing without learning, thought Brutha. No. The other way round. Learning without knowing . . .

Nine-tenths of Om dozed in his shell. The rest of him drifted like a fog in the real world of the gods, which is a lot less interesting than the three-dimensional world inhabited by most of humanity.

He thought: we're a little boat. She'll probably not even notice us. There's the whole of the ocean. She can't be everywhere.

Of course, she's got many believers. But we're only a little boat . . .

He felt the minds of inquisitive fishes nosing around the end of the screw. Which was odd, because in the normal course of things fishes were not known for their –

'Greetings,' said the Queen of the Sea.

'Ah.'

'I see you're still managing to exist, little tortoise.'

'Hanging in there,' said Om. 'No problems.'

There was a pause which, if it were taking place between two people in the human world, would have been spent in coughing and looking embarrassed. But gods are never embarrassed.

'I expect,' said Om guardedly, 'you are looking for your price.'

'This vessel and everyone in it,' said the Queen. 'But your believer can be saved, as is the custom.'

'What good are they to you? One of them's an atheist.'

'Hah! They all believe, right at the end.'

'That doesn't seem . . .' Om hesitated. 'Fair?'

Now the Sea Queen paused.

'What's fair?'

'Like . . . underlying justice?' said Om. He wondered why he said it.

'Sounds a human idea to me.'

'They're inventive, I'll grant you. But what I meant was ... I mean ... they've done nothing to deserve it.'

'*Deserve?* They're *human*. What's *deserve* got to do with it?'

Om had to concede this. He wasn't thinking like a god. This bothered him.

'It's just ...'

'You've been relying on one human for too long, little god.'

'I know. I know.' Om sighed. Minds leaked into one another. He was seeing too much from a human point of view. 'Take the boat, then. If you must. I just wish it was –'

'Fair?' said the Sea Queen. She moved forward. Om felt her all around him.

'There's no such thing,' she said. 'Life's like a beach. And then you die.'

Then she was gone.

Om let himself retreat into the shell of his shell.

'Brutha?'

'Yes?'

'Can you swim?'

The globe started to spin.

Brutha heard Urn say, 'There. Soon be on our way.'

'We'd better be.' This was Simony. 'There's a ship out there.'

'This thing goes faster than anything with sails or oars.'

Brutha looked across the bay. A sleek Omnian ship was passing the lighthouse. It was still a long way off, but Brutha stared at it with a dread and expectation that magnified better than telescopes.

'It's moving fast,' said Simony. 'I don't understand it – there's no wind.'

Urn looked round at the flat calm.

'There can't be wind there and not here,' he said.

'I said, can you swim?' The voice of the tortoise was insistent in Brutha's head.

'I don't know,' said Brutha.

'Do you think you could find out quickly?'

Urn looked upwards.

'Oh,' he said.

Clouds had massed over the *Unnamed Boat*. They were visibly spinning.

'You've *got* to know!' shouted Om. 'I thought you had a perfect memory!'

'We used to splash around in the big cistern in the village,' whispered Brutha. 'I don't know if that counts!'

Mist whipped off the surface of the sea. Brutha's ears popped. And still the Omnian ship came on, flying across the waves.

'What do you call it when you've got a dead calm surrounded by winds –' Urn began.

'Hurricane?' said Didactylos.

Lightning crackled between sky and sea. Urn yanked at the lever that lowered the screw into the water. His eyes glowed almost as brightly as the lightning.

'Now *there's* a power,' he said. 'Harnessing the lightning! The dream of mankind!'

The *Unnamed Boat* surged forward.

'Is it? It's not *my* dream,' said Didactylos. 'I always dream of a giant carrot chasing me through a field of lobsters.'

'I mean *metaphorical* dream, master,' said Urn.

'What's a metaphor?' said Simony.

Brutha said, 'What's a dream?'

A pillar of lightning laced the mist. Secondary lightnings sparked off the spinning globe.

'You can get it from cats,' said Urn, lost in a philosophical world, as the *Boat* left a white wake behind it. 'You stroke them with a rod of amber, and you get tiny lightnings . . . if I could magnify that a million times, no man would ever be a slave again and we could catch it in jars and do away with the night . . .'

Lightning struck a few yards away.

'We're in a boat with a large copper ball in the middle of a body of salt water,' said Didactylos. 'Thanks, Urn.'

'And the temples of the gods would be magnificently lit, of course,' said Urn quickly.

Didactylos tapped his stick on the hull. 'It's a nice idea, but you'd never get enough cats,' he said. The sea surged up.

'Jump into the water!' Om shouted.

'Why?' said Brutha.

A wave almost overturned the boat. Rain hissed on the surface of the sphere, sent up a scalding spray.

'I haven't got time to explain! Jump overboard! It's for the best! *Trust* me!'

Brutha stood up, holding the sphere's framework to steady himself.

'Sit down!' said Urn.

'I'm just going out,' said Brutha. 'I may be some time.'

The boat rocked under him as he half-jumped, half-fell into the boiling sea.

398

Lightning struck the sphere.

As Brutha bobbed to the surface he saw, for a moment, the globe glowing white hot and the *Unnamed Boat*, its screw almost out of the water, skimming away through the mists like a comet. It vanished in the clouds and rain. A moment later, above the noise of the storm, there was a muffled 'boom'.

Brutha raised his hand. Om broke the surface, blowing seawater out of his nostrils.

'You said it would be for the best!' screamed Brutha.

'Well? *We're* still alive! And hold me out of the water! Tortoises can't swim!'

'But they might be dead!'

'Do you want to join them?'

A wave submerged Brutha. For a moment the world was a dark green curtain, ringing in his ears.

'I can't swim with one hand!' he shouted, as he broke surface again.

'We'll be saved! She wouldn't dare!'

'What do you mean?'

Another wave slapped at Brutha, and suction dragged at his robes.

'Om?'

'Yes?'

'I don't think I *can* swim . . .'

Gods are not very introspective. It has never been a survival trait. The ability to cajole, threaten and terrify has always worked well enough. When you can flatten entire cities at a whim, a tendency towards quiet reflection and seeing-things-from-the-other-fellow's-point-of-view is seldom necessary.

Which had led, across the multiverse, to men and women of tremendous brilliance and empathy devoting their entire lives to the service of deities who couldn't beat them at a quiet game of dominoes. For example, Sister Sestina of Quirm defied the wrath of a local king and walked unharmed across a bed of coals and propounded a philosophy of sensible ethics on behalf of a goddess whose only real interest was in hairstyles, and Brother Zephilite of Klatch left his vast estates and his family and spent his life ministering to the sick and poor on behalf of the invisible god F'rum, generally considered unable, should he have a backside, to find it with both hands, should he have hands. Gods never need to be very bright when there are humans around to be it for them.

The Sea Queen was considered fairly dumb even by other gods. But there was a certain logic to her thoughts, as she moved deep below the storm-tossed waves. The little boat had been a tempting target... but here was a bigger one, full of people, sailing right into the storm.

This one was fair game.

The Sea Queen had the attention span of an onion *bahji*.

And, by and large, she created her own sacrifices. And she believed in quantity.

The *Fin of God* plunged from wave crest to wave trough, the gale tearing at its sails. The captain fought his way through waist-high water to the prow, where Vorbis stood clutching the rail, apparently oblivious to the fact that the ship was wallowing half-submerged.

'Sir! We *must* reef sail! We can't outrun this!'

Green fire crackled on the tops of the masts. Vorbis turned. The light was reflected in the pit of his eyes.

'It is all for the glory of Om,' he said. 'Trust is our sail, and glory is our destination.'

The captain had had enough. He was unsteady on the subject of religion, but felt fairly confident that after thirty years he knew something about the sea.

'The ocean *floor* is our destination!' he shouted.

Vorbis shrugged. 'I did not say there would not be stops along the way,' he said.

The captain stared at him and then fought his way back across the heaving deck. What he knew about the sea was that storms like this didn't just happen. You didn't just sail from calm water into the midst of a raging hurricane. This wasn't the sea. This was personal.

Lightning struck the mainmast. There was a scream from the darkness as a mass of torn sail and rigging crashed on to the deck.

The captain half-swam, half-climbed up the ladder to the wheel, where the helmsman was a shadow in the spray and the eerie storm glow.

'We'll never make it alive!'

CORRECT.

'We'll have to abandon ship!'

NO. WE WILL TAKE IT WITH US. IT'S A NICE SHIP.

The captain peered closer in the murk.

'Is that you, Bosun Coplei?'

WOULD YOU LIKE ANOTHER GUESS?

The hull hit a submerged rock and ripped open. Lightning struck the remaining mast and, like a paper boat that had been too long in the water, the *Fin of God* folded up. Baulks of timber splintered and fountained up into the whirling sky . . .

And there was a sudden, velvety silence.

The captain found that he had acquired a recent memory. It involved water, and a ringing in his ears, and the sensation of cold fire in his lungs. But it was fading. He walked over to the rail, his footsteps loud in the quietness, and looked over the side. Despite the fact that the recent memory included something about the ship being totally smashed, it now seemed to be whole again. In a way.

'Uh,' he said, 'we appear to have run out of sea.'

YES.

'And land, too.'

The captain tapped the rail. It was greyish, and slightly transparent.

'Uh. Is this wood?'

MORPHIC MEMORY.

'Sorry?'

YOU WERE A SAILOR. YOU HAVE HEARD A SHIP REFERRED TO AS A LIVING THING?

'Oh, yes. You can't spend a night on a ship without feeling that it has a sou–'

YES.

The memory of *Fin of God* sailed on through the silence. There was the distant sighing of wind, or of the memory of wind. The blown-out corpses of dead gales.

'Uh,' said the ghost of the captain, 'did you just say "were"?'

YES.

'I thought you did.'

The captain stared down. The crew was assembling on deck, looking up at him with anxious eyes.

He looked down further. In front of the crew the ship's rats had assembled. There was a tiny robed shape in front of them.

It said, SQUEAK.

He thought: even rats have a Death . . .

Death stood aside and beckoned to the captain.

YOU HAVE THE WHEEL.

'But – but where are we going?'

Who knows?

The captain gripped the spokes helplessly. 'But ... there's no stars that I recognise! No charts! What are the winds here? Where are the currents?'

Death shrugged.

The captain turned the wheel aimlessly. The ship glided on through the ghost of a sea.

Then he brightened up. The worst had already happened. It was amazing how good it felt to know that. And if the worst had already happened ...

'Where's Vorbis?' he growled.

He survived.

'Did he? There's no justice!'

There's just me.

Death vanished.

The captain turned the wheel a bit, for the look of the thing. After all, he was still captain and this was still, in a way, a ship.

'Mr Mate?'

The mate saluted.

'Sir!'

'Um. Where shall we go now?'

The mate scratched his head.

'Well, cap'n, I did hear as the heathen Klatch have got this paradise place where there's drinking and singing and young women with bells on and ... you know ... regardless.'

The mate looked hopefully at his captain.

'Regardless, eh?' said the captain thoughtfully.

'So I did hear.'

The captain felt that he might be due some regardless.

'Any idea how you get there?'

'I think you get given instructions when you're alive,' said the mate.

'Oh.'

'And there're some barbarians up towards the Hub,' said the mate, relishing the word, 'who reckon they go to a big hall where there's all sorts to eat and drink.'

'And women?'

'Bound to be.'

The captain frowned. 'It's a funny thing,' he said, 'but why is it that the heathens and the barbarians seem to have the best places to go when they die?'

'A bit of a poser, that,' agreed the mate. 'I s'pose it makes up for 'em . . . enjoying themselves all the time when they're alive, too?' He looked puzzled. Now that he was dead, the whole thing sounded suspicious.

'I suppose you've no idea of the way to that paradise either?' said the captain.

'Sorry, cap'n.'

'No harm in searching, though.'

The captain looked over the side. If you sailed for long enough, you were bound to strike a shore. And no harm in searching.

A movement caught his eye. He smiled. Good. A sign. Maybe it was all for the best, after all . . .

Accompanied by the ghosts of dolphins, the ghost of a ship sailed on . . .

Seagulls never ventured this far along the desert coast. Their niche was filled by the scalbie, a member of the crow family that the crow family would be the first to disown and never talked about in company. It seldom flew, but walked everywhere in a sort of lurching hop. Its distinctive call put listeners in mind of a malfunctioning digestive system. It looked like other birds looked *after* an oil slick. Nothing ate scalbies, except other scalbies. Scalbies ate things that made a vulture sick. Scalbies would *eat* vulture sick. Scalbies ate *everything*.

One of them, on this bright new morning, sidled across the flea-hopping sand, pecking aimlessly at things in case pebbles and bits of wood had become edible overnight. In the scalbie's experience, practically anything became edible if it was left for long enough. It came across a mound lying on the tideline, and gave it a tentative jab with its beak.

The mound groaned.

The scalbie backed away hurriedly and turned its attention to a small domed rock beside the mound. It was pretty certain this hadn't been there yesterday, either. It essayed an exploratory peck.

The rock extruded a head and said, 'Bugger off, you evil sod.'

The scalbie leapt backwards and then made a kind of running jump, which was the nearest any scalbie ever bothered to come to actual flight, on to a pile of sun-bleached driftwood. Things were looking up. If this rock was alive, then eventually it would be dead.

The Great God Om staggered over to Brutha and butted him in the head with its shell until he groaned.

'Wake up, lad. Rise and shine. Huphuphup. All ashore who's going ashore.'

Brutha opened an eye.

'Wha' happened?' he said.

'You're alive is what happened,' said Om. Life's a beach, he remembered. And then you die.

Brutha pulled himself into a kneeling position.

There are beaches that cry out for brightly coloured umbrellas. There are beaches that speak of the majesty of the sea.

But this beach wasn't like that. It was merely a barren hem where the land met the ocean. Driftwood piled up on the high-tide line, scoured by the wind. The air buzzed with unpleasant small insects. There was a smell that suggested that something had rotted away, a long time ago, somewhere where the scalbies couldn't find it. It was not a good beach.

'Oh. God.'

'Better than drowning,' said Om encouragingly.

'I wouldn't know.' Brutha looked along the beach. 'Is there any water to drink?'

'Shouldn't think so,' said Om.

'Ossory V, verse 3, says that you made living water flow from the dry desert,' said Brutha.

'That was by way of being artistic licence,' said Om.

'You can't even do that?'

'No.'

Brutha looked at the desert again. Behind the driftwood lines, and a few patches of grass that appeared to be dying even while it grew, the dunes marched away.

'Which way to Omnia?' he said.

'We don't want to go to Omnia,' said Om.

Brutha stared at the tortoise. Then he picked him up.

'I think it's this way,' he said.

Om's legs waggled frantically.

'What do you want to go to Omnia for?' he said.

'I don't want to,' said Brutha. 'But I'm going anyway.'

The sun hung high above the beach.

Or possibly it didn't.

Brutha knew things about the sun now. They were leaking into his head. The Ephebians had been very interested in astronomy. Expletius had proved that the Disc was ten thousand miles across.

Febrius, who'd stationed slaves with quick reactions and carrying voices all across the country at dawn, had proved that light travelled at about the same speed as sound. And Didactylos had reasoned that, in that case, in order to pass between the elephants, the sun had to travel at least thirty-five thousand miles in its orbit every day or, to put it another way, twice as fast as its own light. Which meant that mostly you could only ever see where the sun had been, except twice every day when it caught up with itself, and this meant that the whole sun was a faster-than-light particle, a tachyon or, as Didactylos put it, a bugger.

It was still hot. The lifeless sea seemed to steam.

Brutha trudged along, directly above the only piece of shadow for hundreds of miles. Even Om had stopped complaining. It was too hot.

Here and there fragments of wood rolled in the scum at the edge of the sea.

Ahead of Brutha the air shimmered over the sand. In the middle of it was a dark blob.

He regarded it dispassionately as he approached, incapable of any real thought. It was nothing more than a reference point in a world of orange heat, expanding and contracting in the vibrating haze.

Closer to, it turned out to be Vorbis.

The thought took a long time to seep through Brutha's mind.

Vorbis.

Not with a robe. All torn off. Just his singlet with. The nails sewn in. Blood all. Over one leg. Torn by. Rocks. Vorbis.

Vorbis.

Brutha slumped to his knees. On the high-tide line, a scalbie gave a croak.

'He's still . . . alive,' Brutha managed.

'Pity,' said Om.

'We should do something . . . for him.'

'Yes? Maybe you can find a rock and stove his head in,' said Om.

'We can't just leave him here.'

'Watch us.'

'No.'

Brutha got his hand under the deacon and tried to lift him. To his dull surprise, Vorbis weighed almost nothing. The deacon's robe had concealed a body that was just skin stretched over bone. Brutha could have broken him with bare hands.

'What about me?' whined Om.

Brutha slung Vorbis over his shoulder.

'You've got four legs,' he said.

'I am your God!'

'Yes. I know.' Brutha trudged on along the beach.

'What are you going to *do* with him?'

'Take him to Omnia,' said Brutha thickly. 'People must know. What he did.'

'You're mad! You're mad! You think you're going to *carry* him to Omnia?'

'Don't know. Going to try.'

'You! You!' Om pounded a claw on the sand. 'Millions of people in the world and it had to be *you*! Stupid! *Stupid!*'

Brutha was becoming a wavering shape in the haze.

'That's *it*!' shouted Om. 'I don't need you! You think I need you? I don't need you! I can soon find another believer! No problem about that!'

Brutha disappeared.

'And I'm not chasing after you!' Om screamed.

Brutha watched his feet dragging one in front of the other.

He was past the point of thinking now. What drifted through his frying brain were disjointed images and fragments of memory.

Dreams. They were pictures in your head. Coaxes had written a whole scroll about them. The superstitious thought they were messages sent by God, but really they were created by the brain itself, thrown up as it nightly sorted and filed the experiences of the day. Brutha never dreamed. So sometimes . . . blackout, while the mind did the filing. It filed all the books. Now he knew without learning . . .

That was dreams.

God. God needed people. Belief was the food of the gods. But they also needed a shape. Gods became what people believed they ought to be. So the Goddess of Wisdom carried a penguin. It could have happened to any god. It should have been an owl. Everyone knew that. But one bad sculptor who had only ever had an owl described to him makes a mess of a statue, *belief* steps in, next thing you know the Goddess of Wisdom is lumbered with a bird that wears evening dress the whole time and smells of fish.

You gave a god its shape, like a jelly fills a mould.

Gods often became your father, said Abraxas the Agnostic. Gods became a big beard in the sky, because when you were three years old that *was* your father.

Of course Abraxas survived... This thought arrived sharp and cold, out of the part of his own mind that Brutha could still call his own. Gods didn't mind atheists, if they were deep, hot, fiery atheists like Simony, who spend their whole life not believing, spend their whole life hating gods for not existing. That sort of atheism was a rock. It was nearly belief...

Sand. It was what you found in deserts. Crystals of rock, sculpted into dunes. Gordo of Tsort said that sand was worn-down mountains *but* Irexes had found that sandstone was stone pressed out of sand, which suggested that grains were the *fathers* of mountains...

Every one a little crystal. And all of them getting bigger...

Much bigger...

Quietly, without realising it, Brutha stopped falling forward and lay still.

'Bugger *off*!'

The scalbie took no notice. This was *interesting*. It was getting to see whole new stretches of sand it had never seen before and, of course, there was the prospect, even the certainty, of a good meal at the end of it all.

It had perched on Om's shell.

Om stumped along the sand, pausing occasionally to shout at his passenger.

Brutha had come this way.

But here one of the outcrops of rocks, littering the desert like islands in a sea, stretched right down to the water's edge. He'd never have been able to climb it. The footprints in the sand turned inland, towards the deep desert.

'Idiot!'

Om struggled up the side of a dune, digging his feet in to stop himself slaloming backwards.

On the far side of the dune the tracks became a long groove, where Brutha must have fallen. Om retracted his legs and tobogganed down it.

The tracks veered here. He must have thought that he could walk around the next dune and find the rock again on the other side. Om knew about deserts, and one of the things he knew was that this kind of logical thinking had been previously applied by a thousand bleached, lost skeletons.

Nevertheless, he plodded after the tracks, grateful for the brief shade of the dune now that the sun was sinking.

Around the dune and, yes, here they zigzagged awkwardly up a slope about ninety degrees away from where they should be heading. Guaranteed. That was the thing about deserts. They had their own gravity. They sucked you into the centre.

Brutha crawled forward, Vorbis held unsteadily by one limp arm. He didn't dare stop. His grandmother would hit him again. And there was Master Nhumrod, too, drifting in and out of vision.

'I am really disappointed in you, Brutha. Mmm?'

'Want . . . water . . .'

'– water,' said Nhumrod. 'Trust in the Great God.'

Brutha concentrated. Nhumrod vanished.

'Great God?' he said.

Somewhere there was some shade. The desert couldn't go on for ever.

The sun set fast. For a while, Om knew, heat would radiate off the sand and his own shell would store it, but that would soon go and then there would be the bitterness of a desert night.

Stars were already coming on when he found Brutha. Vorbis had been dropped a little way away.

Om pulled himself level with Brutha's ear.

'Hey!'

There was no sound, and no movement. Om butted Brutha gently in the head and then looked at the cracked lips.

There was a pecking noise behind him.

The scalbie was investigating Brutha's toes, but its explorations were interrupted when a tortoise jaw closed around its foot.

'I *old* oo, ugger *ogg*!'

The scalbie gave a burp of panic and tried to fly away, but it was hindered by a determined tortoise hanging on to one leg. Om was bounced along the sand for a few feet before he let go.

He tried to spit, but tortoise mouths aren't designed for the job.

'I hate all birds,' he said, to the evening air.

The scalbie watched him reproachfully from the top of a dune. It ruffled its handful of greasy feathers with the air of one who was prepared to wait all night, if necessary. As long as it took.

Om crawled back to Brutha. Well, there was still breathing going on.

Water . . .

The god gave it some thought. Smiting the living rock. That was one way. Getting water to flow . . . no problem. It was just a matter of molecules and vectors. Water had a natural tendency to flow. You just have to see to it that it flowed *here* instead of *there*. No problem at all to a god in the peak of condition.

How did you tackle it from a tortoise perspective?

The tortoise dragged himself to the bottom of the dune and then walked up and down for a few minutes. Finally he selected a spot and began digging.

This wasn't right. It had been fiery hot. Now he was freezing.

Brutha opened his eyes. Desert stars, brilliant white, looked back at him. His tongue seemed to fill his mouth. Now, what was it . . .

Water.

He rolled over. There had been voices in his head, and now there were voices outside his head. They were faint, but they were definitely there, echoing quietly over the moonlit sands.

Brutha crawled painfully towards the foot of the dune. There was a mound there. In fact, there were several mounds. The muffled voice was coming from one of them. He pulled himself closer.

There was a hole in the mound. Somewhere far underground, someone was swearing. The words were unclear as they echoed backwards and forwards up the tunnel, but the general effect was unmistakable.

Brutha flopped down, and watched.

After a few minutes there was movement at the mouth of the hole and Om emerged, covered with what, if this wasn't a desert, Brutha would have called mud.

'Oh, it's you,' said the tortoise. 'Tear off a bit of your robe and pass it over.'

Dreamlike, Brutha obeyed.

'Turnin' round down there,' said Om, 'is no picnic, let me tell you.'

He took the rag in his jaws, backed around carefully, and disappeared down the hole. After a couple of minutes he was back, still dragging the rag.

It was soaked. Brutha let the liquid dribble into his mouth. It tasted of mud, and sand, and cheap brown dye, and slightly of tortoise, but he would have drunk a gallon of it. He could have swum in a pool of it.

He tore off another strip for Om to take down.

When Om re-emerged, Brutha was kneeling beside Vorbis.

'Sixteen feet down! Sixteen bloody feet!' shouted Om. 'Don't waste it on him! Isn't he dead yet?'

'He's got a fever.'

'Put him out of our misery.'

'We're still taking him back to Omnia.'

'You think *we'll* get there? No food? No water?'

'But you found water. Water in the desert.'

'Nothing miraculous about that,' said Om. 'There's a rainy season near the coast. Flash floods. Wadis. Dried-up river beds. You get aquifers,' he added.

'Sounds like a miracle to me,' croaked Brutha. 'Just because you can explain it doesn't mean it's not still a miracle.'

'Well, there's no food down there, take it from me,' said Om. 'Nothing to eat. Nothing in the sea, *if* we can find the sea again. I *know* the desert. Rocky ridges you have to go round. Everything turning you out of your path. Dunes that move in the night . . . lions . . . other things . . .'

. . . gods.

'What do you want to do, then?' said Brutha. 'You said better alive than dead. You want to go back to Ephebe? We'll be popular there, you think?'

Om was silent.

Brutha nodded.

'Fetch more water, then.'

It was better travelling at night, with Vorbis over one shoulder and Om under one arm.

At this time of year –

– the glow in the sky over *there* is the Aurora Corealis, the hublights, where the magical field of the Discworld constantly discharges itself among the peaks of Cori Celesti, the central mountain. And at this time of year the sun rises over the desert in Ephebe and over the sea in Omnia, so keep the hublights on the left and the sunset glow behind you –

'Did you ever go to Cori Celesti?' said Brutha.

Om, who had been nodding off in the cold, woke up with a start. 'Huh?'

'It's where the gods live.'

'Hah! I could tell you stories,' said Om darkly.

'What?'

'Think they're so bloody élite!'

'You didn't live up there, then?'

'No. Got to be a thunder god or something. Got to have a whole parcel of worshippers to live on Nob Hill. Got to be an anthropomorphic personification, one of them things.'

'Not just a Great God, then?'

Well, this was the desert. And Brutha was going to die.

'May as well tell you,' muttered Om. 'It's not as though we're going to survive ... See, *every* god's a Great God to someone. I never wanted to be *that* great. A handful of tribes, a city or two. It's not much to ask, is it?'

'There's two million people in the empire,' said Brutha.

'Yeah. Pretty good, eh? Started off with nothing but a shepherd hearing voices in his head, ended up with two million people.'

'But you never *did* anything with them,' said Brutha.

'Like what?'

'Well ... tell them not to kill one another, that sort of thing ...'

'Never really given it much thought. Why should I tell them that?'

Brutha sought for something that would appeal to god psychology.

'Well, if people didn't kill one another, there'd be more people to believe in you?' he suggested.

'It's a point,' Om conceded. 'Interesting point. Sneaky.'

Brutha walked along in silence. There was a glimmer of frost on the dunes.

'Have you ever heard,' he said, 'of Ethics?'

'Somewhere in Howondaland, isn't it?'

'The Ephebians were very interested in it.'

'Probably thinking about invading.'

'They seemed to think about it a lot.'

'Long-term strategy, maybe.'

'I don't think it's a place, though. It's more to do with how people live.'

'What, lolling around all day while slaves do the real work? Take it from me, whenever you see a bunch of buggers puttering around talking about truth and beauty and the best way of attacking Ethics, you can bet your sandals it's because dozens of other poor buggers are doing all the real work around the place while those fellows are living like –'

'– gods?' said Brutha.

There was a terrible silence.

'I was going to say kings,' said Om, reproachfully.

'They sound a bit like gods.'

'Kings,' said Om emphatically.

'Why do people need gods?' Brutha persisted.

'Oh, you've *got* to have gods,' said Om, in a hearty, no-nonsense voice.

'But it's *gods* that need *people*,' said Brutha. 'To do the believing. You said.'

Om hesitated. 'Well, okay,' he said. 'But people have got to believe in something. Yes? I mean, why else does it thunder?'

'Thunder,' said Brutha, his eyes glazing slightly. 'I don't –

'– is caused by clouds banging together; after the lightning stroke, there is a hole in the air, and thus the sound is engendered by the clouds rushing to fill the hole and colliding, in accordance with strict cumulodynamic principles.'

'Your voice goes funny when you're quoting,' said Om. 'What does engendered mean?'

'I don't know. No one showed me a dictionary.'

'Anyway, that's just an explanation,' said Om. 'It's not a *reason*.'

'My grandmother said thunder was caused by the Great God Om taking his sandals off,' said Brutha. 'She was in a funny mood that day. Nearly smiled.'

'*Metaphorically* accurate,' said Om. 'But I never did thundering. Demarcation, see. Bloody I've-got-a-big-hammer Blind Io up on Nob Hill does all the thundering.'

'I thought you said there were hundreds of thunder gods,' said Brutha.

'Yeah. And he's all of 'em. Rationalisation. A couple of tribes join up, they've both got thunder gods, right? And the gods kind of run together – you know how amoebas split?'

'No.'

'Well, it's like that, only the other way.'

'I still don't see how one god can be a hundred thunder gods. They all look different . . .'

'False noses.'

'What?'

'And different voices. I happen to know Io's got seventy different hammers. Not common knowledge, that. And it's just the same with mother goddesses. There's only one of 'em. She just got a lot of wigs and of course it's amazing what you can do with a padded bra.'

There was absolute silence in the desert. The stars, smeared slightly by high-altitude moisture, were tiny, motionless rosettes.

Away towards what the Church called the Top Pole, and which Brutha was coming to think of as the Hub, the sky flickered.

Brutha put Om down, and laid Vorbis on the sand.

Absolute silence.

Nothing for miles, except what he had brought with him. This must have been how the prophets felt, when they went into the desert to find ... whatever it was they found, and talk to ... whoever they talked to.

He heard Om, slightly peevish, say: 'People've got to believe in something. Might as well be gods. What else is there?'

Brutha laughed.

'You know,' he said, 'I don't think I believe in anything any more.'

'Except me!'

'Oh, I *know* you exist,' said Brutha. He felt Om relax a little. 'There's something about tortoises. Tortoises I can believe in. They seem to have a lot of existence in one place. It's gods in general I'm having difficulty with.'

'Look, if people stop believing in gods, they'll believe in anything,' said Om. 'They'll believe in young Urn's steam ball. Anything at all.'

'Hmm.'

A green glow in the sky indicated that the light of dawn was chasing frantically after its sun.

Vorbis groaned.

'I don't know why he won't wake up,' said Brutha. 'I can't find any broken bones.'

'How do you know?'

'One of the Ephebian scrolls was all about bones. Can't you do anything for him?'

'Why?'

'You're a god.'

'Well, yes. If I was strong enough, I could probably strike him with lightning.'

'I thought Io did the lightning.'

'No, just the thunder. You're allowed to do as much lightning as you like but you have to contract for the thundering.'

Now the horizon was a broad golden band.

'How about rain?' said Brutha. 'How about something *useful*?'

A line of silver appeared at the bottom of the gold. Sunlight was racing towards Brutha.

'That was a very hurtful remark,' said the tortoise. 'A remark calculated to wound.'

In the rapidly growing light Brutha saw one of the rock islands a little way off. Its sand-blasted pillars offered nothing but shade, but shade, always available in large quantities in the depths of the Citadel, was now in short supply here.

'Caves?' said Brutha.

'Snakes.'

'But still caves?'

'In conjunction with snakes.'

'Poisonous snakes?'

'Guess.'

The *Unnamed Boat* clipped along gently, the wind filling Urn's robe attached to a mast made out of bits of the sphere's framework bound together with Simony's sandal thongs.

'I think I know what went wrong,' said Urn. 'A mere overspeed problem.'

'Overspeed? We left the water!' said Simony.

'It needs some sort of governor device,' said Urn, scratching a design on the side of the boat. 'Something that'd open the valve if there was too much steam. I think I could do something with a pair of revolving balls.'

'It's funny you should say that,' said Didactylos. 'When I felt us leave the water and the sphere exploded I distinctly felt my –'

'That bloody thing nearly killed us!' said Simony.

'So the next one will be better,' said Urn, cheerfully. He scanned the distant coastline.

'Why don't we land somewhere along here?' he said.

'The desert coast?' said Simony. 'What for? Nothing to eat, nothing to drink, easy to lose your way. Omnia's the only destination in this wind. We can land this side of the city. I know people. And those people know people. All across Omnia, there's people who know people. People who believe in the Turtle.'

'You know, I never meant for people to *believe* in the Turtle,' said Didactylos unhappily. 'It's just a big turtle. It just exists. Things just happen that way. I don't think the Turtle gives a damn. I just thought it might be a good idea to write things down and explain things a bit.'

'People sat up all night, on guard, while other people made copies,' said Simony, ignoring him. 'Passing them from hand to hand! Everyone making a copy and passing it on! Like a fire spreading underground!'

'Would this be *lots* of copies?' said Didactylos cautiously.

'Hundreds! Thousands!'

'I suppose it's too late to ask for, say, a five per cent royalty?' said Didactylos, looking hopeful for a moment. 'No. Probably out of the question, I expect. No. Forget I even asked.'

A few flying fish zipped out of the waves, pursued by a dolphin.

'Can't help feeling a bit sorry for that young Brutha,' said Didactylos.

'Priests are expendable,' said Simony. 'There's too many of them.'

'He had all our books,' said Urn.

'He'll probably float with all that knowledge in him,' said Didactylos.

'He was mad, anyway,' said Simony. 'I saw him whispering to that tortoise.'

'I wish we still had it. There's good eating on one of those things,' said Didactylos.

It wasn't much of a cave, just a deep hollow carved by the endless desert winds and, a long time ago, even by water. But it was enough.

Brutha knelt on the stony floor and raised the rock over his head.

There was a buzzing in his ears and his eyeballs felt as though they were set in sand. No water since sunset and no food for a hundred years. He had to do it.

'I'm sorry,' he said, and brought the rock down.

The snake had been watching him intently but in its early-morning torpor it was too slow to dodge. The cracking noise was a sound that Brutha knew his conscience would replay to him, over and over again.

'Good,' said Om, beside him. 'Now skin it, and don't waste the juice. Save the skin, too.'

'I didn't want to do it,' said Brutha.

'Look at it this way,' said Om, 'if you'd walked in the cave without me to warn you, you'd be lying on the floor now with a foot the size of a wardrobe. Do unto others before they do unto you.'

'It's not even a very big snake,' said Brutha.

'And then while you're writhing there in indescribable agony, you imagine all the things you would have done to that damn snake if you'd got to it first,' said Om. 'Well, your wish has been granted. Don't give any to Vorbis,' he added.

'He's running a bad fever. He keeps muttering.'

'Do you really think you'll get him back to the Citadel and they'll believe you?' said Om.

'Brother Nhumrod always said I was very truthful,' said Brutha. He smashed the rock on the cave wall to create a crude cutting edge, and gingerly started dismembering the snake. 'Anyway, there isn't anything else I can do. I couldn't just leave him.'

'Yes you could,' said Om.

'To die in the desert?'

'Yes. It's easy. Much easier than *not* leaving him to die in the desert.'

'No.'

'This is how they do things in Ethics, is it?' said Om sarcastically.

'I don't know. It's how I'm doing it.'

The *Unnamed Boat* bobbed in a gully between the rocks. There was a low cliff beyond the beach. Simony climbed back down it, to where the philosophers were huddling out of the wind.

'I know this area,' he said. 'We're a few miles from the village where a friend lives. All we have to do is wait till nightfall.'

'Why're you doing all this?' said Urn. 'I mean, what's the point?'

'Have you ever heard of a country called Istanzia?' said Simony. 'It wasn't very big. It had nothing anyone wanted. It was just a place for people to live.'

'Omnia conquered it fifteen years ago,' said Didactylos.

'That's right. My country,' said Simony. 'I was just a kid then. But I won't forget. Nor will others. There's lots of people with a reason to hate the Church.'

'I saw you standing close to Vorbis,' said Urn. '*I* thought you were protecting him.'

'Oh, I was, I was,' said Simony. 'I don't want anyone to kill him before I do.'

Didactylos wrapped his toga around himself and shivered.

The sun was riveted to the copper dome of the sky. Brutha dozed in the cave. In his own corner, Vorbis tossed and turned.

Om sat waiting in the cave mouth.

Waited expectantly.
Waited in dread.
And *they* came.

They came out from under scraps of stone, and from cracks in the rock. They fountained up from the sand, they distilled out of the wavering sky. The air was filled with their voices, as faint as the whispering of gnats.

Om tensed.

The language he spoke was not like the language of the high gods. It was hardly language at all. It was a mere modulation of desires and hungers, without nouns and with only a few verbs.

... Want ...

Om replied, *mine*.

There were thousands of them. He was stronger, yes, he had a believer, but they filled the sky like locusts. The longing poured down on him with the weight of hot lead. The only advantage, the *only* advantage, was that the small gods had no concept of working together. That was a luxury that came with evolution.

... Want ...

Mine!

The chittering became a whine.

But you can have the other one, said Om.

... Dull, hard, enclosed, shut-in ...

I know, said Om. But this one, *mine*!

The psychic shout echoed around the desert. The small gods fled.

Except for one.

Om was aware that it had not been swarming with the others, but had been hovering gently over a piece of sun-bleached bone. It had said nothing.

He turned his attention on it.

You. *Mine!*

I know, said the small god. It knew speech, real god speech, although it talked as though every word had been winched from the pit of memory.

Who are you? said Om.

The small god stirred.

There was a city once, said the small god. Not just a city. An empire of cities. I, I, I remember there were canals, and gardens. There was a lake. They had floating gardens on the lake, I recall. I, I. And there were temples. Such temples as you may dream of. Great pyramid temples that reached to the sky. Thousands were sacrificed. To the greater glory.

Om felt sick. This wasn't just a small god. This was a small god who hadn't always been small ...

Who were you?

And there were temples. I, I, me. Such temples as you may dream of. Great pyramid temples that reached to the sky. The glory of. Thousands were sacrificed. Me. To the greater glory.

And there were temples. Me, me, me. Greater glory. Such glory temples as you may dream of. Great pyramid dream temples that reached to the sky. Me, me. Sacrificed. Dream. Thousands were sacrificed. To me the greater sky glory.

You were their God? Om managed.

Thousands were sacrificed. To the greater glory.

Can you hear me?

Thousands sacrificed greater glory. Me, me, me.

What was your name? shouted Om.

Name?

A hot wind blew over the desert, shifting a few grains of sand. The echo of a lost god blew away, tumbling over and over, until it vanished among the rocks.

Who were you?

There was no answer.

That's what happens, Om thought. Being a small god was bad, except at the time you hardly knew that it was bad because you only barely knew anything at all, but all the time there was something which was just possibly the germ of hope, the knowledge and belief that one day you might be more than you were now.

But how much worse to have *been* a god, and to now be no more than a smoky bundle of memories, blown back and forth across the sand made from the crumbled stones of your temples ...

Om turned around and, on stumpy legs, walked purposefully back into the cave until he came to Brutha's head, which he butted.

'Wst?'

'Just checking you're still alive.'

'Fgfl.'

'Right.'

Om staggered back to his guard position at the mouth of the cave.

There were said to be oases in the desert, but they were never in the same place twice. The desert wasn't mappable. It ate mapmakers.

So did the lions. Om could remember them. Scrawny things, not like the lions of the Howondaland veldt. More wolf than lion, more hyena than either. Not brave, but with a kind of vicious, rangy cowardice that was much more dangerous ...

Lions.

Oh, dear ...

He had to find lions.

Lions drank.

Brutha awoke as the afternoon light dragged across the desert. His mouth tasted of snake.

Om was butting him on the foot.

'Come on, come on, you're missing the best of the day.'

'Is there any water?' Brutha murmured thickly.

'There will be. Only five miles off. Amazing luck.'

Brutha pulled himself up. Every muscle ached.

'How do you know?'

'I can sense it. I *am* a god, you know.'

'You said you could only sense minds.'

Om cursed. Brutha didn't forget things.

'It's more complicated than that,' lied Om. 'Trust me. Come on, while there's some twilight. And don't forget Mister Vorbis.'

Vorbis was curled up. He looked at Brutha with unfocused eyes, stood up like a man still asleep when Brutha helped him.

'I think he might have been poisoned,' said Brutha. 'There's sea creatures with stings. And poisonous corals. He keeps moving his lips, but I can't make out what he's trying to say.'

'Bring him along,' said Om. 'Bring him along. Oh, yes.'

'You wanted me to abandon him last night,' said Brutha.

'Did I?' said Om, his very shell radiating innocence. 'Well, maybe I've been to Ethics. Had a change of heart. I can see he's with us for a purpose now. Good old Vorbis. Bring him along.'

Simony and the two philosophers stood on the cliff-top, looking across the parched farmlands of Omnia to the distant rock of the Citadel. Two of them looking, anyway.

'Give *me* a lever and a place to stand, and I'd smash that place like an egg,' said Simony, leading Didactylos down the narrow path.

'Looks big,' said Urn.

'See the gleam? Those are the doors.'

'Look massive.'

'I was wondering,' said Simony, 'about the boat. The way it moved. Something like that could smash the doors, right?'

'You'd have to flood the valley,' said Urn.

'I mean if it was on wheels.'

'Hah, yes,' said Urn, sarcastically. It had been a long day. 'Yes, if I had a forge and half a dozen blacksmiths and a lot of help. Wheels? No problem. But –'

'We shall have to see,' said Simony, 'what we can do.'

The sun was on the horizon when Brutha, his arm around Vorbis's shoulders, reached the next rock island. It was bigger than the one with the snake. The wind had carved the stones into gaunt, unlikely shapes, like fingers. There were even plants lodging in crevices in the rock.

'There's water somewhere,' said Brutha.

'There's always water, even in the worst deserts,' said Om. 'One, oh, maybe two inches of rain a year.'

'I can smell something,' said Brutha, as his feet stopped treading on sand and crunched up the limestone scree around the boulders. 'Something rank.'

'Hold me over your head.'

Om scanned the rocks.

'Right. Now bring me down again. And head for that rock that looks like . . . that looks very unexpected, really.'

Brutha stared. 'It does, too,' he croaked, eventually. 'Amazing to think it was carved by the wind.'

'The wind god has a sense of humour,' said Om. 'Although it's pretty basic.'

Near the foot of the rock huge slabs had fallen over the years, forming a jagged pile with, here and there, shadowy openings.

'That smell –' Brutha began.

'Probably animals come to drink the water,' said Om.

Brutha's foot kicked against something yellow-white, which bounced away among the rocks making a noise like a sackful of coconuts. In the stifling empty silence of the desert, it echoed loudly.

'What was that?'

'Definitely not a skull,' lied Om. 'Don't worry . . .'

'There's bones everywhere!'

'Well? What did you expect? This is a desert! People die here! It's a very popular occupation in this vicinity!'

Brutha picked up a bone. He was, as he well knew, stupid. But people didn't gnaw their own bones after they died.

'Om –'

'There's water here!' shouted Om. 'We need it! But – there's probably one or two drawbacks!'

'What kind of drawbacks?'

'As in natural hazards!'

'Like –?'

'Well, you know lions?' said Om desperately.

'There's lions here?'

'Well . . . slightly.'

'*Slightly* lions?'

'Only one lion.'

'Only one –'

'– generally a solitary creature. Most to be feared are the old males, who are forced into the most inhospitable regions by their younger rivals. They are evil-tempered and cunning and in their extremity have lost all fear of man –'

The memory faded, letting go of Brutha's vocal chords.

'That kind?' Brutha finished.

'It won't take any notice of us once it's fed,' said Om.

'Yes?'

'They go to sleep.'

'After feeding –?'

Brutha looked round at Vorbis, who was slumped against a rock.

'Feeding?' he repeated.

'It'll be a kindness,' said Om.

'To the lion, yes! You want to use him as *bait*?'

'He's not going to survive the desert. Anyway, he's done much worse to thousands of people. He'll be dying for a good cause.'

'A good cause?'

'*I* like it.'

There was a growl, from somewhere in the stones. It wasn't loud, but it was a sound with sinews in it. Brutha backed away.

'We don't just throw people to the lions!'

'He does.'

'Yes. I don't.'

'All right, we'll get on top of a slab and when the lion starts on him you can brain it with a rock. He'll probably get away with an arm or a leg. He'll never miss it.'

'No! You can't do that to people just because they're helpless!'

'You know, I can't think of a better time?'

There was another growl from the rock pile. It sounded closer.

Brutha looked down desperately at the scattered bones. Among them, half-hidden by debris, was a sword. It was old, and not well made, and scoured by sand. He picked it up gingerly by the blade.

'Other end,' said Om.

'I know!'

'Can you use one?'

'I don't know!'

'I really hope you're a fast learner.'

The lion emerged, slowly.

Desert lions, it has been said, are not like the lions of the veldt. They had been, when the great desert had been verdant woodland.* Then there had been time to lie around for most of the day, looking majestic, in between regular meals of goat.† But the woodland had become scrubland, the scrubland had become, well, poorer scrubland, and the goats and the people and, eventually, even the cities, went away.

The lions stayed. There's always something to eat, if you're hungry enough. People still had to cross the desert. There were lizards. There were snakes. It wasn't much of an ecological niche, but the lions were hanging on to it like grim death, which was what happened to most people who met a desert lion.

Someone had already met this one.

Its mane was matted. Ancient scars criss-crossed its pelt. It dragged itself towards Brutha, back legs trailing uselessly.

'It's hurt,' said Brutha.

'Oh, good. And there's plenty of eating on one of those,' said Om. 'A bit stringy, but –'

The lion collapsed, its toast-rack chest heaving. A spear was protruding from its flank. Flies, which can always find something to eat in any desert, flew up in a swarm.

Brutha put down the sword. Om stuck his head in his shell.

'Oh no,' he murmured. 'Twenty *million* people in this world, and the only one who believes in me is a suicide –'

'We can't just leave it,' said Brutha.

'We *can*. We *can*. It's a *lion*. You leave lions *alone*.'

Brutha knelt down. The lion opened one crusted yellow eye, too weak even to bite him.

'You're going to die, you're going to *die*. I'm not going to find *anyone* to believe in me out here –'

---

* ie, before the inhabitants had let goats graze everywhere. Nothing makes a desert like a goat.

† But not enough.

Brutha's knowledge of animal anatomy was rudimentary. Although some of the inquisitors had an enviable knowledge of the insides of the human body that is denied to all those who are not allowed to open it while it's still working, medicine as such was frowned upon in Omnia. But somewhere, in every village, was someone who officially *didn't* set bones and who *didn't* know a few things about certain plants, and who stayed out of reach of the Quisition because of the fragile gratitude of their patients. And every peasant picked up a smattering of knowledge. Acute toothache can burn through all but the strongest in faith.

Brutha grasped the spear-haft. The lion growled as he moved it.

'Can't you speak to it?' said Brutha.

'It's an *animal*.'

'So are you. You could try to calm it down. Because if it gets excited –'

Om snapped into concentration.

In fact the lion's mind contained nothing but pain, a spreading nebula of the stuff, overcoming even the normal background hunger. Om tried to encircle the pain, make it flow away . . . and not to think about what would happen if it went. By the feel of things, the lion had not eaten for days.

The lion grunted as Brutha withdrew the spear-head.

'Omnian,' he said. 'It hasn't been there long. It must have met the soldiers when they were on the way to Ephebe. They must have passed close by.' He tore another strip from his robe, and tried to clean the wound.

'We want to *eat* it, not cure it!' shouted Om. 'What're you thinking of? You think it's going to be grateful?'

'It wanted to be helped.'

'And soon it will want to be fed, have you thought about that?'

'It's looking pathetically at me.'

'Probably never seen a week's meals all walking around on one pair of legs before.'

That wasn't true, Om reflected. Brutha was shedding weight like an ice-cube, out here in the desert. That kept him alive! The boy was a two-legged camel.

Brutha crunched towards the rock pile, shards and bones shifting under his feet. The boulders formed a maze of half-open tunnels and caves. By the smell, the lion had lived there for a long time, and had quite often been ill.

He stared at the nearest cave for some time.

'What's so fascinating about a lion's den?' said Om.
'The way it's got steps down into it, I think,' said Brutha.

Didactylos could *feel* the crowd. It filled the barn.
'How many are there?' he said.
'Hundreds!' said Urn. 'They're even sitting on the rafters! And... master?'
'Yes?'
'There's even one or two priests! And dozens of soldiers!'
'Don't worry,' said Simony, joining them on the makeshift platform made of fig barrels. 'They are Turtle believers, just like you. We have friends in unexpected places!'
'But I *don't* –' Didactylos began, helplessly.
'There isn't anyone here who doesn't hate the Church with all their soul,' said Simony.
'But that's not –'
'They're just waiting for someone to lead them!'
'But I never –'
'I know you won't let us down. You're a man of reason. Urn, come over here. There's a blacksmith I want you to meet –'
Didactylos turned his face to the crowd. He could feel the hot, hushed silence of their stares.

Each drop took minutes.
It was hypnotic. Brutha found himself staring at each developing drip. It was almost impossible to see it grow, but they had been growing and dripping for thousands of years.
'How?' said Om.
'Water seeps down after the rains,' said Brutha. 'It lodges in the rocks. Don't gods know these things?'
'We don't need to.' Om looked around. 'Let's go. I hate this place.'
'It's just an old temple. There's nothing here.'
'That's what I mean.'
Sand and rubble half-filled it. Light lanced in through the broken roof high above, on to the slope that they had climbed down. Brutha wondered how many of the wind-carved rocks in the desert had once been buildings. This one must have been huge, perhaps a mighty tower. And then the desert had come.
There were no whispering voices here. Even the small gods kept away from abandoned temples, for the same reason that people

kept away from graveyards. The only sound was the occasional plink of the water.

It dripped into a shallow pool in front of what looked like an altar. From the pool it had worn a groove in the slabs of the floor all the way to a round pit, which appeared to be bottomless. There were a few statues, all of them toppled; they were heavy-proportioned, lacking any kind of detail, each one a child's clay model chiselled in granite. The distant walls had once been covered with some kind of bas-relief, but it had crumbled away except in a few places, which showed strange designs that mainly consisted of tentacles.

'Who were the people who lived here?' said Brutha.

'I don't know.'

'What god did they worship?'

'I don't know.'

'The statues are made of granite, but there's no granite near here.'

'They were very devout, then. They dragged it all the way.'

'And the altar block is covered in grooves.'

'Ah. *Extremely* devout. That would be to let the blood run off.'

'You really think they did human sacrifice?'

'I don't know! I want to get out of here!'

'Why? There's water and it's cool –'

'Because ... a god lived here. A powerful god. Thousands worshipped it. I can feel it. You know? It comes out of the walls. A Great God. Mighty were his dominions and magnificent was his word. Armies went forth in his name and conquered and slew. That kind of thing. And now no one, not you, not me, no one, even knows who the god was or his name or what he looked like. Lions drink in the holy places and those little squidgy things with eight legs, there's one by your foot, what d'you call 'em, the ones with the antennae, crawl beneath the altar. Now do you understand?'

'No,' said Brutha.

'Don't you fear death? You're a human!'

Brutha considered this. A few feet away, Vorbis stared mutely at the patch of sky.

'He's awake. He's just not speaking.'

'Who cares? I didn't ask you about him.'

'Well ... sometimes ... when I'm on catacomb duty ... it's the kind of place where you can't help ... I mean, all the skulls and things ... and the Book says ...'

'There you are,' said Om, a note of bitter triumph in his voice.

'You don't *know*. That's what stops everyone going mad, the uncertainty of it, the feeling that it might work out all right after all. But it's different for gods. We *do* know. You know that story about the sparrow flying through a room?'

'No.'

'Everyone knows it.'

'Not me.'

'About life being like a sparrow flying through a room? Nothing but darkness outside? And it flies through the room and there's just a moment of warmth and light?'

'There are windows open?' said Brutha.

'Can't you imagine what it's like to *be* that sparrow, and know about the darkness? To know that afterwards there'll be nothing to remember, ever, except that one moment of the light?'

'No.'

'No. Of course you can't. But that's what it's like, being a god. And this place . . . it's a morgue.'

Brutha looked around at the ancient, shadowy temple.

'Well . . . do you know what it's like, being human?'

Om's head darted into his shell for a moment, the nearest he was capable of to a shrug.

'Compared to a god? Easy. Get born. Obey a few rules. Do what you're told. Die. Forget.'

Brutha stared at him.

'Is something wrong?'

Brutha shook his head. Then he stood up and walked over to Vorbis.

The deacon had drunk water from Brutha's cupped hands. But there was a switched-off quality about him. He walked, he drank, he breathed. Or something did. His body did. The dark eyes opened, but appeared to be looking at nothing that Brutha could see. There was no sense that anyone was looking out through them. Brutha was certain that if he walked away, Vorbis would sit on the cracked flagstones until he very gently fell over. Vorbis's body was present, but the whereabouts of his mind was probably not locatable on any normal atlas.

It was just that, here and now and suddenly, Brutha felt so alone that even Vorbis was good company.

'Why do you bother with him? He's had thousands of people killed!'

'Yes, but perhaps he thought you wanted it.'

'I never said I wanted that.'

'You didn't care,' said Brutha.

'But I –'

'Shut up!'

Om's mouth opened in astonishment.

'You could have helped people,' said Brutha. 'But all you did was stamp around and roar and try to make people afraid. Like . . . like a man hitting a donkey with a stick. But people like Vorbis made the stick so good, that's all the donkey ends up believing in.'

'That could use some work, as a parable,' said Om sourly.

'This is real life I'm talking about!'

'It's not my fault if people misuse the –'

'It is! It has to be! If you muck up people's minds just because you want them to believe in you, what they do is all your fault!'

Brutha glared at the tortoise, and then stamped off towards the pile of rubble that dominated one end of the ruined temple. He rummaged around in it.

'What are you looking for?'

'We'll need to carry water,' said Brutha.

'There won't be anything,' said Om. 'People just left. The land ran out and so did the people. They took everything with them. Why bother to look?'

Brutha ignored him. There was something under the rocks and sand.

'Why worry about Vorbis?' Om whined. 'In a hundred years' time, he'll be dead anyway. We'll all be dead.'

Brutha tugged at the piece of curved pottery. It came away, and turned out to be about two-thirds of a wide bowl, broken right across. It had been almost as wide as Brutha's outstretched arms, but had been too broken for anyone to loot.

It was useful for nothing. But it had once been useful for something. There were embossed figures round its rim. Brutha peered at them, for want of something to distract himself, while Om's voice droned on in his head.

The figures looked more or less human. And they were engaged in religion. You could tell by the knives (it's not murder if you do it for a god). In the centre of the bowl was a larger figure, obviously important, some kind of god they were doing it for . . .

'What?' he said.

'I *said*, in a hundred years' time we'll all be dead.'

Brutha stared at the figures round the bowl. No one knew who their god was, and they were gone. Lions slept in the holy places and –

– *Chilopoda aridius*, the common desert centipede, his memory resident library supplied –

– scuttled beneath the altar.

'Yes,' said Brutha. 'We will.' He raised the bowl over his head, and turned.

Om ducked into his shell.

'But here –' Brutha gritted his teeth as he staggered under the weight. 'And now –'

He threw the bowl. It landed against the altar. Fragments of ancient pottery fountained up, and clattered down again. The echoes boomed around the temple.

'– we are alive!'

He picked up Om, who had withdrawn completely into his shell.

'And we'll make it home. All of us,' he said. 'I know it.'

'It's written, is it?' said Om, his voice muffled.

'It is *said*. And if you argue – a tortoise shell is a pretty good water container, I expect.'

'You wouldn't.'

'Who knows? I might. In a hundred years' time we'll all be dead, you said.'

'Yes! Yes!' said Om desperately. 'But here and now –'

'Right.'

Didactylos smiled. It wasn't something that came easily to him. It wasn't that he was a sombre man, but he could not see the smiles of others. It took several dozen muscle movements to smile, and there was no return on his investment.

He'd spoken many times to crowds in Ephebe, but they were invariably made up of other philosophers, whose shouts of 'Bloody daft!', 'You're making it up as you go along!' and other contributions to the debate always put him at his ease. That was because no one really paid any attention. They were just working out what *they* were going to say next.

But this crowd put him in mind of Brutha. Their listening was like a huge pit waiting for his words to fill it. The trouble was that he was talking in philosophy, but they were listening in gibberish.

'You *can't* believe in Great A 'Tuin,' he said. 'Great A 'Tuin *exists*. There's no point in believing in things that exist.'

'Someone's put up their hand,' said Urn.

'Yes?'

'Sir, surely only things that exist are worth believing in?' said the enquirer, who was wearing a uniform of a sergeant of the Holy Guard.

'If they exist, you don't have to believe in them,' said Didactylos. 'They just are.' He sighed. 'What can I tell you? What do you want to hear? I just wrote down what people know. Mountains rise and fall, and under them the Turtle swims onwards. Men live and die, and the Turtle Moves. Empires grow and crumble, and the Turtle Moves. Gods come and go, and still the Turtle Moves. The Turtle *Moves*.'

From the darkness came a voice, 'And that is really true?'

Didactylos shrugged. 'The Turtle *exists*. The world is a flat disc. The sun turns round it once every day, dragging its light behind it. And this will go on happening, whether you believe it is true or not. It is real. I don't know about truth. Truth is a lot more complicated than that. I don't think the Turtle gives a bugger whether it's true or not, to tell you the truth.'

Simony pulled Urn to one side as the philosopher went on talking.

'This isn't what they came to hear! Can't you do anything?'

'Sorry?' said Urn.

'They don't want philosophy. They want a reason to move against the Church! Now! Vorbis is dead, the Cenobiarch is gaga, the hierarchy are busy stabbing one another in the back. The Citadel is like a big rotten plum.'

'Still a few wasps in it, though,' said Urn. 'You said you've only got a tenth of the army.'

'But they're free men,' said Simony. 'Free in their heads. They'll be fighting for more than fifty cents a day.'

Urn looked down at his hands. He often did that when he was uncertain about anything, as if they were the only things he was sure of in all the world.

'They'll get the odds down to three to one before the rest know what's happening,' said Simony grimly. 'Did you talk to the blacksmith?'

'Yes.'

'Can you do it?'

'I . . . think so. It wasn't what I . . .'

'They tortured his father. Just for having a horseshoe hanging up in his forge, when everyone knows that smiths have to have their little rituals. And they took his son off into the army. But he's got a lot of helpers. They'll work through the night. All you have to do is tell them what you want.'

'I've made some sketches . . .'

'Good,' said Simony. '*Listen*, Urn. The Church is run by people like Vorbis. That's how it all works. Millions of people have died for – for nothing but lies. We can stop all that –'

Didactylos had stopped talking.

'He's muffed it,' said Simony. 'He could have done *anything* with them. And he just told them a lot of facts. You can't inspire people with facts. They need a cause. They need a symbol.'

They left the temple just before sundown. The lion had crawled into the shade of some rocks, but stood up unsteadily to watch them go.

'It'll track us,' moaned Om. 'They do that. For miles and miles.'

'We'll survive.'

'I wish I had your confidence.'

'Ah, but I have a God to have faith in.'

'There'll be no more ruined temples.'

'There'll be something else.'

'And not even snake to eat.'

'But I walk with my God.'

'Not as a snack, though. *And* you're walking the wrong way, too.'

'No. I'm still heading away from the coast.'

'That's what I mean.'

'How far can a lion go with a spear wound like that in him?'

'What's that got to do with anything?'

'Everything.'

And, half an hour later, a black shadowy line on the silver moonlit desert, there were the tracks.

'The soldiers came this way. We just have to follow the tracks back. If we head where they've come from, we'll get where we're going.'

'We'll never do it!'

'We're travelling light.'

'Oh, yeah. They were burdened by all the food and water they had to carry,' said Om bitterly. 'How lucky for us we haven't got any.'

Brutha glanced at Vorbis. He was walking unaided now, provided that you gently turned him around whenever you needed to change direction.

But even Om had to admit that the tracks were some comfort. In a way they were alive, in the same way that an echo is alive. People had been this way, not long ago. There were other people in the world. Someone, somewhere, was surviving.

Or not. After an hour or so they came across a mound beside the track. There was a helmet atop it, and a sword stuck in the sand.

'A lot of soldiers died to get here quickly,' said Brutha.

Whoever had taken enough time to bury their dead had also drawn a symbol in the sand of the mound. Brutha half-expected it to be a turtle, but the desert wind had not quite eroded the crude shape of a pair of horns.

'I don't understand that,' said Om. 'They don't *really* believe I exist, but they go and put something like that on a grave.'

'It's hard to explain. I think it's because they believe *they* exist,' said Brutha. 'It's because they're people, and so was he.'

He pulled the sword out of the sand.

'What do you want that for?'

'Might be useful.'

'Against who?'

'Might be useful.'

An hour later the lion, who was limping after Brutha, also arrived at the grave. It had lived in the desert for sixteen years, and the reason it had lived so long was that it had not died, and it had not died because it never wasted handy protein. It dug.

Humans have always wasted handy protein ever since they started wondering who had lived in it.

But, on the whole, there are worse places to be buried than inside a lion.

There were snakes and lizards on the rock islands. They were probably very nourishing and every one was, in its own way, a taste explosion.

There was no more water.

But there were plants . . . more or less. They looked like groups of stones, except where a few had put up a central flower spike that was a brilliant pink and purple in the dawn light.

'Where do they get the water from?'

'Fossil seas.'

'Water that's turned to stone?'

'No. Water that sank down thousands of years ago. Right down in the bedrock.'

'Can you dig down to it?'

'Don't be stupid.'

Brutha glanced from the flower to the nearest rock island.

'Honey,' he said.

'What?'

The bees had a nest high on the side of a spire of rock. The buzzing could be heard from ground level. There was no possible way up.

'Nice try,' said Om.

The sun was up. Already the rocks were warm to the touch. 'Get some rest,' said Om, kindly. 'I'll keep watch.'

'Watch for what?'

'I'll watch and find out.'

Brutha led Vorbis into the shade of a large boulder, and gently pushed him down. Then he lay down too.

The thirst wasn't too bad yet. He'd drunk from the temple pool until he squelched as he walked. Later on, they might find a snake ... When you considered what some people in the world had, life wasn't too bad.

Vorbis lay on his side, his black-on-black eyes staring at nothing. Brutha tried to sleep.

He had never dreamed. Didactylos had been quite excited about that. Someone who remembered everything and didn't dream would have to think slowly, he said. Imagine a heart,[*] he said, that was nearly all memory, and had hardly any beats to spare for the everyday purposes of thinking. That would explain why Brutha moved his lips while he thought.

So this couldn't have been a dream. It must have been the sun.

He heard Om's voice in his head. The tortoise sounded as though he was holding a conversation with people Brutha could not hear.

Mine!

Go away!

No.

Mine!

Both of them!

Mine!

Brutha turned his head.

The tortoise was in a gap between two rocks, neck extended and

---

[*] Like many early thinkers, the Ephebians believed that thoughts originated in the heart and that the brain was merely a device to cool the blood.

weaving from side to side. There was another sound, a sort of gnat-like whining, that came and went . . . and promises in his head.

They flashed past . . . faces talking to him, shapes, visions of greatness, moments of opportunity, picking him up, taking him high above the world, all this was his, he could do anything, all he had to do was believe, in *me*, in *me*, in *me* –

An image formed in front of him. There, on a stone beside him, was a roast pig surrounded by fruit, and a mug of beer so cold the air was frosting on the sides.

Mine!

Brutha blinked. The voices faded. So did the food.

He blinked again.

There were strange after-images, not seen but felt. Perfect though his memory was, he could not remember what the voices had said or what the other pictures had been. All that lingered was a memory of roast pork and cold beer.

'That's because they don't know what to offer you,' said Om's voice, quietly. 'So they try to offer you anything. Generally they start with visions of food and carnal gratification.'

'They got as far as the food,' said Brutha.

'Good job I overcame them, then,' said Om. 'No telling what they might have achieved with a young man like yourself.'

Brutha raised himself on his elbows.

Vorbis had not moved.

'Were they trying to get through to him, too?'

'I suppose so. Wouldn't work. Nothing gets in, nothing gets out. Never seen a mind so turned in on itself.'

'Will they be back?'

'Oh, yes. It's not as if they've got anything else to do.'

'When they do,' said Brutha, feeling lightheaded, 'could you wait until they've shown me visions of carnal gratification?'

'Very bad for you.'

'Brother Nhumrod was very down on them. But I think perhaps we should know our enemies, yes?'

Brutha's voice faded to a croak.

'I could have done with the vision of the drink,' he said, wearily. The shadows were long. He looked around in amazement.

'How long were they trying?'

'All day. Persistent devils, too. Thick as flies.'

Brutha learned why at sunset.

He met St Ungulant the anchorite, friend of all small gods. Everywhere.

*

'Well, well, well,' said St Ungulant. 'We don't get very many visitors up here. Isn't that so, Angus?'

He addressed the air beside him.

Brutha was trying to keep his balance, because the cartwheel rocked dangerously every time he moved. They'd left Vorbis seated on the desert twenty feet below, hugging his knees and staring at nothing.

The wheel had been nailed flat on top of a slim pole. It was just wide enough for one person to lie uncomfortably. But St Ungulant looked designed to lie uncomfortably. He was so thin that even skeletons would say, 'Isn't he thin?' He was wearing some sort of minimalist loin-cloth, insofar as it was possible to tell under the beard and hair.

It had been quite hard to ignore St Ungulant, who had been capering up and down at the top of his pole shouting 'Coo-ee!' and 'Over here!' There was a slightly smaller pole a few feet away, with an old-fashioned half-moon-cut-out-on-the-door privy on it. Just because you were an anchorite, St Ungulant said, didn't mean you had to give up *everything*.

Brutha had heard of anchorites, who were a kind of one-way prophet. They went out into the desert but did not come back, preferring a hermit's life of dirt and hardship and dirt and holy contemplation and dirt. Many of them liked to make life even more uncomfortable for themselves by being walled up in cells or living, quite appropriately, at the top of a pole. The Omnian Church encouraged them, on the basis that it was best to get madmen as far away as possible where they couldn't cause any trouble and could be cared for by the community, insofar as the community consisted of lions and buzzards and dirt.

'I was thinking of adding another wheel,' said St Ungulant, 'just over there. To catch the morning sun, you know.'

Brutha looked around him. Nothing but flat rock and sand stretched away on every side.

'Don't you get the sun everywhere all the time?' he said.

'But it's much more important in the morning,' said St Ungulant. 'Besides, Angus says we ought to have a patio.'

'He could barbecue on it,' said Om, inside Brutha's head.

'Um,' said Brutha. 'What ... religion ... are you a saint of, exactly?'

An expression of embarrassment crossed the very small amount of face between St Ungulant's eyebrows and his moustache.

'Uh. None, really. That was all rather a mistake,' he said. 'My parents named me Sevrian Thaddeus Ungulant, and then one day, of course, most amusing, someone drew attention to the initials. After that, it all seemed rather inevitable.'

The wheel rocked slightly. St Ungulant's skin was almost blackened by the desert sun.

'I've had to pick up herming as I went along, of course,' he said. 'I taught myself. I'm entirely self-taught. You can't find a hermit to teach you herming, because of course that rather spoils the whole thing.'

'Er ... but there's ... Angus?' said Brutha, staring at the spot where he believed Angus to be, or at least where he believed St Ungulant believed Angus to be.

'He's over here now,' said the saint sharply, pointing to a different part of the wheel. 'But he doesn't do any of the herming. He's not, you know, trained. He's just company. My word, I'd have gone quite *mad* if it wasn't for Angus cheering me up all the time!'

'Yes ... I expect you would,' said Brutha. He smiled at the empty air, in order to show willing.

'Actually, it's a pretty good life. The hours are rather long but the food and drink are extremely worthwhile.'

Brutha had a distinct feeling that he knew what was going to come next.

'Beer cold enough?' he said.

'Extremely frosty,' said St Ungulant, beaming.

'And the roast pig?'

St Ungulant's smile was manic.

'All brown and crunchy round the edges, yes,' he said.

'But I expect, er ... you eat the occasional lizard or snake, too?'

'Funny you should say that. Yes. Every once in a while. Just for a bit of variety.'

'And mushrooms, too?' said Om.

'Any mushrooms in these parts?' said Brutha innocently.

St Ungulant nodded happily.

'After the annual rains, yes. Red ones with yellow spots. The desert becomes really *interesting* after the mushroom season.'

'Full of giant purple singing slugs? Talking pillars of flame? Exploding giraffes? That sort of thing?' said Brutha carefully.

'Good heavens, yes,' said the saint. 'I don't know why. I think they're attracted by the mushrooms.'

Brutha nodded.

'You're catching on, kid,' said Om.

'And I expect sometimes you drink ... water?' said Brutha.

'You know, it's odd, isn't it,' said St Ungulant. 'There's all this wonderful stuff to drink but every so often I get this, well, I can only call it a *craving*, for a few sips of water. Can you explain that?'

'It must be . . . a little hard to come by,' said Brutha, still talking very carefully, like someone playing a fifty-pound fish on a fifty-one-pound breaking-strain fishing-line.

'Strange, really,' said St Ungulant. 'When ice-cold beer is so readily available, too.'

'Where, uh, do you get it? The water?' said Brutha.

'You know the stone plants?'

'The ones with the big flowers?'

'If you cut open the fleshy part of the leaves, there's up to half a pint of water,' said the saint. 'It tastes like weewee, mind you.'

'I think we could manage to put up with that,' said Brutha, through dry lips. He backed towards the rope-ladder that was the saint's contact with the ground.

'Are you sure you won't stay?' said St Ungulant. 'It's Wednesday. We get sucking pig plus chef's selection of sun-drenched dew-fresh vegetables on Wednesdays.'

'We, uh, have lots to do,' said Brutha, halfway down the swaying ladder.

'Sweets from the trolley?'

'I think perhaps . . .'

St Ungulant looked down sadly at Brutha helping Vorbis away across the wilderness.

'And afterwards there's probably mints!' he shouted, through cupped hands. 'No?'

Soon the figures were mere dots on the sand.

'There may be visions of sexual grati – no, I tell a lie, that's Fridays . . .' St Ungulant murmured.

Now that the visitors had gone, the air was once again filled with the zip and whine of the small gods. There were billions of them.

St Ungulant smiled.

He was, of course, mad. He'd occasionally suspected this. But he took the view that madness should not be wasted. He dined daily on the food of the gods, drank the rarest vintages, ate fruits that were not only out of season but out of reality. Having to drink the occasional mouthful of brackish water and chew the odd lizard leg for medicinal purposes was a small price to pay.

He turned back to the laden table that shimmered in the air. All this . . . and all the little gods wanted was someone to know about them, someone to even believe that they existed.

There was jelly and ice-cream today, too.
'All the more for us, eh, Angus?'
Yes, said Angus.

The fighting was over in Ephebe. It hadn't lasted long, especially when the slaves joined in. There were too many narrow streets, too many ambushes and, above all, too much terrible determination. It's generally held that free men will always triumph over slaves, but perhaps it all depends on your point of view.

Besides, the Ephebian garrison commander had declared somewhat nervously that slavery would henceforth be abolished, which infuriated the slaves. What would be the point of saving up to become free if you couldn't own slaves afterwards? Besides, how'd they eat?

The Omnians couldn't understand, and uncertain people fight badly. And Vorbis had gone. Certainties seemed less certain when those eyes were elsewhere.

The Tyrant was released from his prison. He spent his first day of freedom carefully composing messages to the other small countries along the coast.

It was time to do something about Omnia.

Brutha sang.

His voice echoed off the rocks. Flocks of scalbies shook off their lazy pedestrian habits and took off frantically, leaving feathers behind in their rush to get airborne. Snakes wriggled into cracks in the stone.

You could live in the desert. Or at least survive . . .

Getting back to Omnia could only be a matter of time. One more day . . .

Vorbis trooped along a little behind him. He said nothing and, when spoken to, gave no sign that he had understood what had been said to him.

Om, bumping along in Brutha's pack, began to feel the acute depression that steals over every realist in the presence of an optimist.

The strained strains of *Claws of Iron shall Rend the Ungodly* faded away. There was a small rockslide, some way off.

'We're alive,' said Brutha.

'For now.'

'And we're close to home.'

'Yes?'

'I saw a wild goat on the rocks back there.'

'There's still a lot of 'em about.'

'Goats?'

'Gods. And the ones we had back there were the puny ones, mind you.'

'What do you mean?'

Om sighed. 'It's *reasonable*, isn't it? Think about it. The stronger ones hang around the edge, where there's prey . . . I mean, people. The weak ones get pushed out to the sandy places, where people hardly ever go –'

'The strong gods,' said Brutha, thoughtfully. 'Gods that know about being strong.'

'That's right.'

'Not gods that know what it feels like to be weak . . .'

'What? They wouldn't last five minutes. It's a god-eat-god world.'

'Perhaps that explains something about the nature of gods. Strength is hereditary. Like sin.'

His face clouded.

'Except that . . . it isn't. Sin, I mean. I think, perhaps, when we get back, I shall talk to some people.'

'Oh, and they'll listen, will they?'

'Wisdom comes out of the wilderness, they say.'

'Only the wisdom that people want. And mushrooms.'

When the sun was starting to climb Brutha milked a goat. It stood patiently while Om soothed its mind. And Om didn't suggest killing it, Brutha noticed.

Then they found shade again. There were bushes here, low-growing, spiky, every tiny leaf barricaded behind its crown of thorns.

Om watched for a while, but the small gods on the edge of the wilderness were more cunning and less urgent. They'd be here, probably at noon, when the sun turned the landscape into a hellish glare. He'd hear them. In the meantime, he could eat.

He crawled through the bushes, their thorns scraping harmlessly along his shell. He passed another tortoise, which wasn't inhabited by a god and gave him that vague stare that tortoises employ when they're deciding whether something is there to be eaten or made love to, which are the only things on a normal tortoise mind. He avoided it, and found a couple of leaves it had missed.

Periodically he'd stomp back through the gritty soil and watch the sleepers.

And then he saw Vorbis sit up, look around him in a slow methodical way, pick up a stone, study it carefully, and then bring it down sharply on Brutha's head.

Brutha didn't even groan.

Vorbis got up and strode directly towards the bushes that hid Om. He tore the branches aside, regardless of the thorns, and pulled out the tortoise Om had just met.

For a moment it was held up, legs moving slowly, before the deacon threw it overarm into the rocks.

Then he picked up Brutha with some effort, slung him across his shoulders, and set off towards Omnia.

It happened in seconds.

Om fought to stop his head and legs retracting automatically into his shell, a tortoise's instinctive panic reaction.

Vorbis was already disappearing round some rocks.

He disappeared.

Om started to move forward and then ducked into his shell as a shadow skimmed over the ground. It was a familiar shadow, and one filled with tortoise dread.

The eagle swept down and towards the spot where the stricken tortoise was struggling and, with barely a pause in the stoop, snatched the reptile and soared back up into the sky with long, lazy sweeps of its wings.

Om watched it until it became a dot, and then looked away as a smaller dot detached itself and tumbled over and over towards the rocks below.

The eagle descended slowly, preparing to feed.

A breeze rattled the thorn-bushes and stirred the sand. Om thought he could hear the taunting, mocking voices of all the small gods.

St Ungulant, on his bony knees, smashed open the hard swollen leaf of a stone plant.

Nice lad, he thought. Talked to himself a lot, but that was only to be expected. The desert took some people like that, didn't it, Angus?

Yes, said Angus.

Angus didn't want any of the brackish water. He said it gave him wind.

'Please yourself,' said St Ungulant. 'Well, well! Here's a little treat.'

You didn't often get *Chilopoda aridius* out here in the open desert, and here were three, all under one rock!

Funny how you felt like a little nibble, even after a good meal of *Petit porc rôti avec pommes de terre nouvelles et légumes du jour et bière glacée avec figment de l'imagination.*

He was picking the legs of the second one out of his tooth when the lion padded to the top of the nearest dune behind him.

The lion was feeling odd sensations of gratitude. It felt it should catch up with the nice food that had tended to it and, well, refrain from eating it in some symbolic way. And now here was some more food, hardly paying it any attention. Well, it didn't owe *this* one anything . . .

It padded forward, then lumbered up into a run.

Oblivious to his fate, St Ungulant started on the third centipede. The lion leapt . . .

And things would have looked very bad for St Ungulant if Angus hadn't caught it right behind the ear with a rock.

Brutha was standing in the desert, except that the sand was as black as the sky and there was no sun, although everything was brilliantly lit.

Ah, he thought. So *this* is dreaming.

There were thousands of people walking across the desert. They paid him no attention. They walked as if completely unaware that they were in the middle of a crowd.

He tried to wave at them, but he was nailed to the spot. He tried to speak, and the words evaporated in his mouth.

And then he woke up.

The first thing he saw was the light, slanting through a window. Against the light was a pair of hands, raised in the sign of the holy horns.

With some difficulty, his head screaming pain at him, Brutha followed the hands along a pair of arms to where they joined not far under the bowed head of –

'Brother Nhumrod?'

The master of novices looked up.

'Brutha?'

'Yes?'

'Om be praised!'

Brutha craned his neck to look around.

'Is he here?'

'– here? How do you feel?'

'I –'

His head ached, his back felt as though it was on fire, and there was a dull pain in his knees.

'You were very badly sunburned,' said Nhumrod. 'And that was a nasty knock on the head you had in the fall.'

'What fall?'

'– fall. From the rocks. In the desert. You were with the *Prophet*,' said Nhumrod. 'You walked with the Prophet. One of *my* novices.'

'I remember . . . the desert . . .' said Brutha, touching his head gingerly. 'But . . . the . . . Prophet . . .?'

'– Prophet. People are saying you could be made a bishop, or even an Iam,' said Nhumrod. 'There's a precedent, you know. The Most Holy St Bobby was made a bishop because he was in the desert with the Prophet Ossory, and *he* was a donkey.'

'But I don't . . . remember . . . any Prophet. There was just me and –'

Brutha stopped. Nhumrod was beaming.

'*Vorbis?*'

'He most graciously told me all about it,' said Nhumrod. 'I was privileged to be in the Place of Lamentation when he arrived. It was just after the Sestine prayers. The Cenobiarch was just departing . . . well, you know the ceremony. And there was Vorbis. Covered in dust and leading a donkey. I'm afraid you were across the back of the donkey.'

'I don't remember a donkey,' said Brutha.

'– donkey. He'd picked it up at one of the farms. There was quite a crowd with him!'

Nhumrod was flushed with excitement.

'And he's declared a month of Jhaddra, and double penances, and the Council has given him the Staff and the Halter, and the Cenobiarch has gone off to the hermitage in Skant!'

'Vorbis is the eighth Prophet,' said Brutha.

'– Prophet. Of course.'

'And . . . was there a tortoise? Has he mentioned anything about a tortoise?'

'– tortoise? What have tortoises got to do with anything?' Nhumrod's expression softened. 'But, of course, the Prophet said the sun had affected you. He said you were raving – excuse me – about all sorts of strange things.'

'He did?'

'He sat by your bed for three days. It was ... inspiring.'

'How long ... since we came back?'

'– back? Almost a week.'

'A week!'

'He said the journey exhausted you very much.'

Brutha stared at the wall.

'And he left orders that you were to be brought to him as soon as you were fully conscious,' said Nhumrod. 'He was very definite about that.' His tone of voice suggested that he wasn't quite sure of Brutha's state of consciousness, even now. 'Do you think you can walk? I can get some novices to carry you, if you'd prefer.'

'I have to go and see him now?'

'– now. Right away. I expect you'll want to thank him.'

Brutha had known about these parts of the Citadel only by hearsay. Brother Nhumrod had never seen them, either. Although he had not been specifically included in the summons, he had come nevertheless, fussing importantly around Brutha as two sturdy novices carried him in a kind of sedan chair normally used by the more crumbling of the senior clerics.

In the centre of the Citadel, behind the Temple, was a walled garden. Brutha looked at it with an expert eye. There wasn't an inch of natural soil on the bare rock – every spadeful that these shady trees grew in must have been carried up by hand.

Vorbis was there, surrounded by bishops and Iams. He looked round as Brutha approached.

'Ah, my desert companion,' he said, amiably. 'And Brother Nhumrod, I believe. My brothers, I should like you to know that I have it in mind to raise our Brutha to archbishophood.'

There was a very faint murmur of astonishment from the clerics, and then a clearing of a throat. Vorbis looked at Bishop Treem, who was the Citadel's archivist.

'Well, technically he is not yet even ordained,' said Bishop Treem, doubtfully. 'But of course we all know there has been a precedent.'

'Ossory's ass,' said Brother Nhumrod promptly. He put his hand over his mouth and went red with shame and embarrassment.

Vorbis smiled.

'Good Brother Nhumrod is correct,' he said. 'Who had also not been ordained, unless the qualifications were somewhat relaxed in those days.'

There was a chorus of nervous laughs, such as there always is from people who owe their jobs and possibly their lives to a whim of the person who has just cracked the not very amusing line.

'Although the donkey was only made a bishop,' said Bishop 'Deathwish' Treem.

'A role for which it was *highly* qualified,' said Vorbis sharply. 'And now, you will all leave. Including Sub-deacon Nhumrod,' he added. Nhumrod went from red to white at this sudden preferment. 'But Archbishop Brutha will remain. We wish to talk.'

The clergy withdrew.

Vorbis sat down on a stone chair under an elder tree. It was huge and ancient, quite unlike its short-lived relatives outside the garden, and its berries were ripening.

The Prophet sat with his elbows on the stone arms of the chair, his hands interlocked in front of him, and gave Brutha a long, slow stare.

'You are . . . recovered?' he said, eventually.

'Yes, lord,' said Brutha. 'But, lord, I cannot be a bishop, I cannot even —'

'I assure you the job does not require much intelligence,' said Vorbis. 'If it did, bishops would not be able to do it.'

There was another long silence.

When Vorbis next spoke, it was as if every word was being winched up from a great depth.

'We spoke once, did we not, of the nature of reality?'

'Yes.'

'And about how often what is perceived is not that which is *fundamentally* true?'

'Yes.'

Another pause. High overhead, an eagle circled, looking for tortoises.

'I am sure you have confused memories of our wanderings in the wilderness.'

'No.'

'It is only to be expected. The sun, the thirst, the hunger . . .'

'No, lord. My memory does not confuse readily.'

'Oh, yes. I recall.'

'So do I, lord.'

Vorbis turned his head slightly, looking sidelong at Brutha as if he was trying to hide behind his own face.

'In the desert, the Great God Om spoke to me.'

'Yes, lord. He did. Every day.'

'You have a mighty if simple faith, Brutha. When it comes to people, I am a great judge.'

'Yes, lord. Lord?'

'Yes, my Brutha?'

'Nhumrod said *you* led *me* through the desert, lord.'

'Remember what I said about fundamental truth, Brutha? Of course you do. There was a physical desert, indeed, but also a desert of the soul. My God led me, and I led you.'

'Ah. Yes. I see.'

Overhead, the spiralling dot that was the eagle appeared to hang motionless in the air for a moment. Then it folded its wings and fell –

'Much was given to me in the desert, Brutha. Much was learned. Now I must tell the world. That is the duty of a prophet. To go where others have not been, and bring back the truth of it.'

– faster than the wind, its whole brain and body existing only as a mist around the sheer intensity of its purpose –

'I did not expect it to be this soon. But Om guided my steps. And now that we have the Cenobiarchy, we shall . . . make use of it.'

Somewhere out on the hillsides the eagle swooped, picked something up, and strove for height . . .

'I'm just a novice, Lord Vorbis. I am not a bishop, even if everyone calls me one.'

'You will get used to it.'

It sometimes took a long time for an idea to form in Brutha's mind, but one was forming now. It was something about the way Vorbis was sitting, something about the edge in his voice.

Vorbis was afraid of him.

Why me? Because of the desert? Who would care? For all I know, it was always like this – probably it was Ossory's ass that carried him in the wilderness, who found the water, who kicked a lion to death.

Because of Ephebe? Who would listen? Who would care? He is the Prophet and the Cenobiarch. He could have me killed just like that. Anything he does is right. Anything he says is true.

Fundamentally true.

'I have something to show you that may amuse you,' said Vorbis, standing up. 'Can you walk?'

'Oh, yes. Nhumrod was just being kind. It's mainly sunburn.'

As they moved away, Brutha saw something he hadn't noticed

before. There were members of the Holy Guard, armed with bows, in the garden. They were in the shade of trees, or amongst bushes – not too obvious, but not exactly hidden.

Steps led from the garden to the maze of underground tunnels and rooms that underlay the Temple and, indeed, the whole of the Citadel. Noiselessly, a couple of guards fell in behind them at a respectful distance.

Brutha followed Vorbis through the tunnels to the artificers' quarter, where forges and workshops clustered around one wide, deep light-well. Smoke and fumes billowed up around the hewn rock walls.

Vorbis walked directly to a large alcove that glowed red with the light of forge fires. Several workers were clustered around something wide and curved.

'There,' said Vorbis. 'What do you think?'

It was a turtle.

The iron-founders had done a pretty good job, even down to the patterning on the shell and the scales on the legs. It was about eight feet long.

Brutha heard a rushing noise in his ears as Vorbis spoke.

'They speak poisonous gibberish about turtles, do they not? They think they live on the back of a Great Turtle. Well, let them die on one.'

Now Brutha could see the shackles attached to each iron leg. A man, or a woman, could with great discomfort lie spreadeagled on the back of the turtle and be chained firmly at the wrists and ankles.

He bent down. Yes, there was the firebox underneath. Some aspects of Quisition thinking never changed.

That much iron would take ages to heat up to the point of pain. Much time, therefore, to reflect on things . . .

'What do you think?' said Vorbis.

A vision of the future flashed across Brutha's mind.

'Ingenious,' he said.

'And it will be a salutary lesson for all others tempted to stray from the path of true knowledge,' said Vorbis.

'When do you intend to, uh, demonstrate it?'

'I am sure an occasion will present itself,' said Vorbis.

When Brutha straightened up, Vorbis was staring at him so intently that it was as if he was reading Brutha's thoughts off the back of his head.

'And now, please leave,' said Vorbis. 'Rest as much as you can . . . my son.'

Brutha walked slowly across the Place, deep in unaccustomed thought.

'Afternoon, Your Reverence.'

'You know already?'

Cut-Me-Own-Hand-Off Dhblah beamed over the top of his lukewarm ice-cold sherbet stand.

'Heard it on the grapevine,' he said. 'Here, have a slab of Klatchian Delight. Free. Onna stick.'

The Place was more crowded than usual. Even Dhblah's hot cakes were selling like hot cakes.

'Busy today,' said Brutha, hardly thinking about it.

'Time of the Prophet, see,' said Dhblah, 'when the Great God is manifest in the world. And if you think it's busy now, you won't be able to swing a goat here in a few days' time.'

'What happens then?'

'You all right? You look a bit peaky.'

'What happens then?'

'The Laws. *You* know. The Book of Vorbis? I suppose –' Dhblah leaned towards Brutha – you wouldn't have a hint, would you? I suppose the Great God didn't happen to say anything of benefit to the convenience food industry?'

'I don't know. I think he'd like people to grow more lettuce.'

'Really?'

'It's only a guess.'

Dhblah grinned evilly. 'Ah, yes, but it's *your* guess. A nod's as good as a poke with a sharp stick to a deaf camel, as they say. I know where I can get my hands on a few acres of well-irrigated land, funnily enough. Perhaps I ought to buy now, ahead of the crowd?'

'Can't see any harm in it, Mr Dhblah.'

Dhblah sidled closer. This was not hard. Dhblah sidled everywhere. *Crabs* thought he walked sideways.

'Funny thing,' he said. 'I mean . . . Vorbis?'

'Funny?' said Brutha.

'Makes you think. Even Ossory must have been a man who walked around, just like you and me. Got wax in his ears, just like ordinary people. Funny thing.'

'What is?'

'The whole thing.'

Dhblah gave Brutha another conspiratorial grin and then sold a footsore pilgrim a bowl of hummus that he would come to regret.

Brutha wandered down to his dormitory. It was empty at this time of day, hanging around dormitories being discouraged in case the presence of the rock-hard mattresses engendered thoughts of sin. His few possessions were gone from the shelf by his bunk. Probably he had a room of his own somewhere, although no one had told him.

Brutha felt totally lost.

He lay down on the bunk, just in case, and offered up a prayer to Om. There was no reply. There had been no reply for almost all of his life, and that hadn't been too bad, because he'd never expected one. And before, there'd always been the comfort that perhaps Om was listening and simply not deigning to say anything.

Now, there was nothing to hear.

He might as well be talking to himself, and listening to himself. Like Vorbis.

That thought wouldn't go away. Mind like a steel ball, Om had said. Nothing got in or out. So all Vorbis could hear were the distant echoes of his own soul. And out of the distant echoes he would forge a Book of Vorbis, and Brutha suspected he knew what the commandments would be. There would be talk of holy wars and blood and crusades and blood and piety and blood.

Brutha got up, feeling like a fool. But the thoughts wouldn't go away.

He was a bishop, but he didn't know what bishops did. He'd only seen them in the distance, drifting along like earthbound clouds. There was only one thing he felt he knew how to do.

Some spotty boy was hoeing the vegetable garden. He looked at Brutha in amazement when he took the hoe, and was stupid enough to try to hang on to it for a moment.

'I am a *bishop*, you know,' said Brutha. 'Anyway, you aren't doing it right. Go and do something else.'

Brutha jabbed viciously at the weeds around the seedlings. Only away a few weeks and already there was a haze of green on the soil.

You're a bishop. For being good. And here's the iron turtle. In case you're bad. Because . . .

. . . there were two people in the desert, and Om spoke to one of them.

It had never occurred to Brutha like that before.

Om had spoken to him. Admittedly, he hadn't said the things

that the Great Prophets said he said. Perhaps he'd never said things like that . . .

He worked his way along to the end of the row. Then he tidied up the bean vines.

Lu-Tze watched Brutha carefully from his little shed by the soil heaps.

It was another barn. Urn was seeing a lot of barns.

They'd started with a cart, and invested a lot of time in reducing its weight as much as possible. Gearing had been a problem. He'd been doing a lot of thinking about gears. The ball wanted to spin much faster than the wheels wanted to turn. That was probably a metaphor for something or other.

'And I can't get it to go backwards,' he said.

'Don't worry,' said Simony. 'It won't have to go backwards. What about armour?'

Urn waved a distracted hand around his workshop.

'This is a village forge!' he said. 'This thing is twenty feet long! Zacharos can't make plates bigger than a few feet across. I've tried nailing them on a framework, but it just collapses under the weight.'

Simony looked at the skeleton of the steam car and the pile of plates stacked beside it.

'Ever been in a battle, Urn?' he said.

'No. I've got flat feet. And I'm not very strong.'

'Do you know what a tortoise is?'

Urn scratched his head. 'Okay. The answer isn't a little reptile in a shell, is it? Because you *know* I know that.'

'I mean a shield tortoise. When you're attacking a fortress or a wall, and the enemy is dropping everything he's got on you, every man holds his shield overhead so that it . . . kind of . . . slots into all the shields around it. Can take a lot of weight.'

'Overlapping,' murmured Urn.

'Like scales,' said Simony.

Urn looked reflectively at the cart.

'A tortoise,' he said.

'And the battering-ram?' said Simony.

'Oh, that's no problem,' said Urn, not paying much attention. 'Tree-trunk bolted to the frame. Big iron rammer. They're only bronze doors, you say?'

'Yes. But very big.'

'Then they're probably hollow. Or cast bronze plates on wood. That's what I'd do.'

'Not solid bronze? Everyone says they're solid bronze.'

'That's what I'd say, too.'

'Excuse me, sirs.'

A burly man stepped forward. He wore the uniform of the palace guards.

'This is Sergeant Fergmen,' said Simony. 'Yes, sergeant?'

'The doors is reinforced with Klatchian steel. Because of all the fighting in the time of the False Prophet Zog. And they opens outwards only. Like lock gates on a canal, you understand? If you push on 'em, they only locks more firmly together.'

'How are they opened, then?' said Urn.

'The Cenobiarch raises his hand and the breath of God blows them open,' said the sergeant.

'In a *logical* sense, I meant.'

'Oh. Well, one of the deacons goes behind a curtain and pulls a lever. But . . . when I was on guard down in the crypts, sometimes, there was a room . . . there was gratings and things . . . well, you could hear water gushing . . .'

'Hydraulics,' said Urn. 'Thought it would be hydraulics.'

'Can you get in?' said Simony.

'To the room? Why not? No one bothers with it.'

'Could he make the doors open?' said Simony.

'Hmm?' said Urn.

Urn was rubbing his chin reflectively with a hammer. He seemed to be lost in a world of his own.

'I said, could Fergmen make these hydra haulics work?'

'Hmm? Oh. Shouldn't think so,' said Urn, vaguely.

'Could you?'

'What?'

'Could you make them work?'

'Oh. Probably. It's just pipes and pressures, after all. Um.'

Urn was still staring thoughtfully at the steam cart. Simony nodded meaningfully at the sergeant, indicating that he should go away, and then tried the mental interplanetary journey necessary to get to whatever world Urn was in.

He tried looking at the cart, too.

'How soon can you have it all finished?'

'Hmm?'

'I said –'

'Late tomorrow night. If we work through tonight.'

'But we'll need it for the next dawn! We won't have time to see if it works!'

'It'll work first time,' said Urn.

'Really?'

'I built it. I know about it. You know about swords and spears and things. I know about things that go round and round. It will work first time.'

'Good. Well, there are other things I've got to do –'

'Right.'

Urn was left alone in the barn. He looked reflectively at his hammer, and then at the iron cart.

They didn't know how to cast bronze properly here. Their iron was pathetic, just pathetic. Their copper? It was terrible. They seemed to be able to make steel that shattered at a blow. Over the years the Quisition had weeded out all the good smiths.

He'd done the best he could, but . . .

'Just don't ask me about the second or third time,' he said quietly to himself.

Vorbis sat in the stone chair in his garden, papers strewn around him.

'Well?'

The kneeling figure did not look up. Two guards stood over it, with drawn swords.

'The Turtle people . . . the people are plotting something,' it said, the voice shrill with terror.

'Of course they are. Of course they are,' said Vorbis. 'And what is this plot?'

'There is some kind of . . . when you are confirmed as Cenobiarch . . . some kind of device, some machine that goes by itself . . . it will smash down the doors of the Temple . . .'

The voice faded away.

'And where is this device now?' said Vorbis.

'I don't know. They've bought iron from me. That's all I know.'

'An iron device.'

'Yes.' The man took a deep breath – half-breath, half-gulp. 'People say . . . the guards said . . . you have my father in prison and you might . . . I plead . . .'

Vorbis looked down at the man.

'But you *fear*,' he said, 'that I might have you thrown into the cells as well. You think I am that sort of person. You fear that I may think, this man has associated with heretics and blasphemers in familiar circumstances ...'

The man continued to stare fixedly at the ground. Vorbis's fingers curled gently around his chin and raised his head until they were eye to eye.

'What you have done is a *good* thing,' he said. He looked at one of the guards. 'Is this man's father still alive?'

'Yes, lord.'

'Still capable of walking?'

The inquisitor shrugged. 'Ye-es, lord.'

'Then release him this instant, put him in the charge of his dutiful son here, and send them both back home.'

The armies of hope and fear fought in the informant's eyes.

'Thank you, lord,' he said.

'Go in peace.'

Vorbis watched one of the guards escort the man from the garden. Then he waved a hand vaguely at one of the head inquisitors.

'Do we know where he lives?'

'Yes, lord.'

'Good.'

The inquisitor hesitated.

'And this ... device, lord?'

'Om has spoken to me. A machine that goes by itself? Such a thing is against all reason. Where are its muscles? Where is its mind?'

'Yes, lord.'

The inquisitor, whose name was Deacon Cusp, had got where he was today, which was a place he wasn't sure right now that he wanted to be, because he liked hurting people. It was a simple desire, and one that was satisfied in abundance within the Quisition. And he was one of those who were terrified in a very particular way by Vorbis. Hurting people because you enjoyed it ... that was understandable. Vorbis just hurt people because he'd decided that they should be hurt, without passion, even with a kind of hard love.

In Cusp's experience, people didn't make things up, ultimately, not in front of an exquisitor. Or course there were no such things as devices that moved by themselves, but he made a mental note to increase the guard –

'However,' said Vorbis, 'there will be a disturbance during the ceremony tomorrow.'

'Lord?'

'I have . . . special knowledge,' said Vorbis.

'Of course, lord.'

'You know the breaking strain of sinews and muscles, Deacon Cusp.'

Cusp had formed an opinion that Vorbis was somewhere on the other side of madness. Ordinary madness he could deal with. In his experience there were quite a lot of mad people in the world, and many of them became even more insane in the tunnels of the Quisition. But Vorbis had passed right through that red barrier and had built some kind of logical structure on the other side. Rational thoughts made out of insane components . . .

'Yes, lord,' he said.

'I know the breaking strain of people.'

It was night, and cold for the time of year.

Lu-Tze crept through the gloom of the barn, sweeping industriously. Sometimes he took a rag from the recesses of his robe and polished things.

He polished the outside of the Moving Turtle, which loomed low and menacing in the shadows.

And he swept his way towards the forge, where he watched for a while.

It takes extreme concentration to pour good steel. No wonder gods have always clustered around isolated smithies. There are so many things that can go wrong. A slight mis-mix of ingredients, a moment's lapse –

Urn, who was almost asleep on his feet, grunted as he was nudged awake and something was put in his hands.

It was a cup of tea. He looked into the little round face of Lu-Tze.

'Oh,' he said. 'Thank you. Thank you very much.'

Nod, smile.

'Nearly done,' said Urn, more or less to himself. 'Just got to let it cool now. Got to let it cool really *slowly*. Otherwise it crystallises, you see.'

Nod, smile, nod.

It was *good* tea.

''S'not 'n important cast anyway,' said Urn, swaying. 'Jus' the control levers –'

Lu-Tze caught him carefully and steered him to a seat on a heap of charcoal. Then he went and watched the forge for a while. The bar of steel was glowing in the mould.

He poured a bucket of cold water over it, watched the great cloud of steam spread and disperse, and then put his broom over his shoulder and ran away hurriedly.

People to whom Lu-Tze was a vaguely glimpsed figure behind a very slow broom would have been surprised at his turn of speed, especially in a man six thousand years old who ate nothing but brown rice and drank only green tea with a knob of rancid butter in it.

A little way away from the Citadel's main gates he stopped running and started sweeping. He swept up to the gates, swept around the gates themselves, nodded and smiled at a soldier who glared at him and then realised that it was only the daft old sweeper, polished one of the handles of the gates, and swept his way by passages and cloisters to Brutha's vegetable garden.

He could see a figure crouched among the melons.

Lu-Tze found a rug and padded back out into the garden, where Brutha was sitting hunched up with his hoe over his knees.

Lu-Tze had seen many agonised faces in his time, which was a longer time than most whole civilisations managed to see. Brutha's was the worst. He tugged the rug over the bishop's shoulders.

'I can't hear him,' said Brutha hoarsely. 'It may mean that he's too far away. I keep on thinking that. He might be out there somewhere. Miles away!'

Lu-Tze smiled and nodded.

'It'll happen all over again. *He* never told anyone to do anything. Or not to do anything. He didn't care!'

Lu-Tze nodded and smiled again. His teeth were yellow. They were in fact his two-hundredth set.

'He should have cared.'

Lu-Tze disappeared into his corner again and returned with a shallow bowl full of some kind of tea. He nodded and smiled and proffered it until Brutha took it and had a sip. It tasted like hot water with a lavender bag in it.

'You don't understand anything I'm talking about, do you?' said Brutha.

'Not much,' said Lu-Tze.

'You *can* talk?'

Lu-Tze put a wizened finger to his lips.

'Big secret,' he said.

Brutha looked at the little man. How much did he know about him? How much did anyone know about him?

'You talk to God,' said Lu-Tze.

'How do you know that?'

'Signs. Man who talk to God have difficult life.'

'You're right!' Brutha stared at Lu-Tze over the cup. 'Why are you here?' he said. 'You're not Omnian. Or Ephebian.'

'Grew up near Hub. Long time ago. Now Lu-Tze a stranger everywhere he goes. Best way. Learned religion in temple at home. Now go where job is.'

'Carting soil and pruning plants?'

'Sure. Never been bishop or high panjandrum. Dangerous life. Always be man who cleans pews or sweeps up behind altar. No one bother useful man. No one bother small man. No one remember name.'

'That's what I was going to do! But it doesn't work for me.'

'Then find other way. I learn in temple. Taught by ancient master. When trouble, always remember wise words of ancient and venerable master.'

'What were they?'

'Ancient master say: "That boy there! What you eating? Hope you brought enough for everybody!" Ancient master say: "You bad boy! Why you no do homework?" Ancient master say: "What boy laughing? No tell what boy laughing, whole dojo stay in after school!" When remember these wise words, nothing seems so bad.'

'What shall I do? I can't hear *him*!'

'You do what you must. I learn anything, it you have to walk it all alone.'

Brutha hugged his knees.

'But he told me nothing! Where's all this wisdom? All the other prophets came back with commandments!'

'Where they get them?'

'I ... suppose they made them up.'

'You get them from same place.'

'You call this philosophy?' roared Didactylos, waving his stick.

Urn cleaned pieces of the sand mould from the lever.

'Well ... *natural* philosophy,' he said.

The stick whanged down on the Moving Turtle's flanks.

'I never taught you this sort of thing!' shouted the philosopher. 'Philosophy is supposed to make life *better*!'

'This *will* make it better for a lot of people,' said Urn, calmly. 'It will help overthrow a tyrant.'

'And then?' said Didactylos.

'And then what?'

'And then you'll take it to bits, will you?' said the old man. 'Smash it up? Take the wheels off? Get rid of all those spikes? Burn the plans? Yes? When it's served its purpose, yes?'

'Well –' Urn began.

'Aha!'

'Aha what? What if we do keep it? It'll be a . . . a deterrent to other tyrants!'

'You think tyrants won't build 'em too?'

'Well . . . I can build bigger ones!' Urn shouted.

Didactylos sagged. 'Yes,' he said. 'No doubt you can. So that's all right, then. My word. And to think I was worrying. And now . . . I think I'll go and have a rest somewhere . . .'

He looked hunched up, and suddenly old.

'Master?' said Urn.

'Don't "master" me,' said Didactylos, feeling his way along the barn walls to the door. 'I can see you know every bloody thing there is to know about human nature now. Hah!'

The Great God Om slid down the side of an irrigation ditch and landed on his back in the weeds at the bottom. He righted himself by gripping a root with his mouth and hauling himself over.

The shape of Brutha's thoughts flickered back and forth in his mind. He couldn't make out any actual words, but he didn't need to, any more than you needed to see the ripples to know which way the river flowed.

Occasionally, when he could see the Citadel as a gleaming dot in the twilight, he'd try shouting his own mind back as loudly as he could:

'Wait! Wait! You don't want to do that! We can go to Ankh-Morpork! Land of opportunity! With my brains and your . . . with you, the world is our mollusc! Why throw it all away . . .'

And then he'd slide into another furrow. Once or twice he saw the eagle, forever circling.

'Why put your hand into a grinder? This place *deserves* Vorbis! Sheep *deserve* to be led!'

It had been like this when his very first believer had been stoned to death. Of course, by then he had dozens of other believers. But it had been a wrench. It had been upsetting. You never forgot your first believer. They gave you shape.

Tortoises are not well equipped for cross-country navigation. They need longer legs or shallower ditches.

Om estimated that he was doing less than a fifth of a mile an hour in a direct line, and the Citadel was at least twenty miles away. Occasionally he made good time between the trees in an olive grove, but that was more than pulled back by rocky ground and field walls.

All the time, as his legs whirred, Brutha's thoughts buzzed in his head like a distant bee.

He tried shouting in his mind again.

'What've you got? He's got an army! You've got an army? How many divisions have you got?'

But thoughts like that needed energy, and there was a limit to the amount of energy available in one tortoise. He found a bunch of fallen grapes and gobbled them until the juice covered his head, but it didn't make a lot of difference.

And then there was nightfall. Nights here weren't as cold as the desert, but they weren't as warm as the day. He'd slow down at night as his blood cooled. He wouldn't be able to think as fast. Or walk as fast.

He was losing heat already. Heat meant speed.

He pulled himself up on to an ant-hill –

'You're going to die! You're going to die!'

– and slid down the other side.

Preparations for the inauguration of the Cenobiarch Prophet began many hours before the dawn. Firstly, and not according to ancient tradition, there was a very careful search of the temple by Deacon Cusp and some of his colleagues. There was a prowling for tripwires and a poking of odd corners for hidden archers. Although it was against the thread, Deacon Cusp had his head screwed on. He also sent a few squads into the town to round up the usual suspects. The Quisition always found it advisable to leave a few suspects at large. Then you knew where to find them when you needed them.

After that a dozen lesser priests arrived to shrive the premises and drive out all afreets, djinns and devils. Deacon Cusp watched them without comment. He'd never had any personal dealings with supernatural entities, but he knew what a well-placed arrow would do to an unexpecting stomach.

Someone tapped him on the rib-cage. He gasped at the sudden linkage of real life into the chain of thought, and reached instinctively for his dagger.

'Oh,' he said.

Lu-Tze nodded and smiled and indicated with his broom that Deacon Cusp was standing on a patch of floor that he, Lu-Tze, wished to sweep.

'Hello, you ghastly little yellow fool,' said Deacon Cusp.

Nod, smile.

'Never say a bloody word, do you?' said Deacon Cusp.

Smile, smile.

'Idiot.'

Smile. Smile. Watch.

Urn stood back.

'Now,' he said, 'you sure you've got it all?'

'Easy,' said Simony, who was sitting in the Turtle's saddle.

'Tell me again,' said Urn.

'We-stoke-up-the-firebox,' said Simony. 'Then-when-the-red-needle-points-to-xxvi, turn-the-brass-tap; when-the-bronze-whistle-blows, pull-the-big-lever. And steer by pulling the ropes.'

'Right,' said Urn. But he still looked doubtful. 'It's a precision device,' he said.

'And I am a professional soldier,' said Simony. 'I'm not a superstitious peasant.'

'Fine, fine. Well ... if you're *sure* ...'

They'd had time to put a few finishing touches to the Moving Turtle. There were serrated edges to the shell and spikes on the wheels. And of course the waste steam pipe ... he was a little uncertain about the waste steam pipe ...

'It's merely a device,' said Simony. 'It does not present a problem.'

'Give us an hour, then. You should just get to the Temple by the time we get the doors open.'

'Right. Understood. Off you go. Sergeant Fergmen knows the way.'

Urn looked at the steam pipe and bit his lip. I don't know what effect it's going to have on the enemy, he thought, but it scares the hells out of me.

*

Brutha woke up, or at least ceased trying to sleep. Lu-Tze had gone. Probably sweeping somewhere.

He wandered through the deserted corridors of the novice section. It would be hours before the new Cenobiarch was crowned. There were dozens of ceremonies to be undertaken first. Everyone who was anyone would be in the Place and the surrounding piazzas, and so would the even greater number of people who were no one very much. The sestinas were empty, the endless prayers left unsung. The Citadel might have been dead, were it not for the huge indefinable background roar of tens of thousands of people being silent. Sunlight filtered down through the light-wells.

Brutha had never felt more alone. The wilderness had been a feast of fun compared to this. Last night . . . last night, with Lu-Tze, it had all seemed so clear. Last night he had been in a mood to confront Vorbis there and then. Last night there seemed to be a chance. Anything was possible last night. That was the trouble with last nights. They were always followed by this mornings.

He wandered out into the kitchen level, and then into the outside world. There were one or two cooks around, preparing the ceremonial meal of meat, bread and salt, but they paid him no attention at all.

He sat down outside one of the slaughterhouses. There was, he knew, a back gate somewhere around. Probably no one would stop him, today, if he walked out. Today they would be looking for unwanted people walking in.

He could just walk away. The wilderness had seemed quite pleasant, apart from the thirst and hunger. St Ungulant with his madness and his mushrooms seemed to have life exactly right. It didn't matter if you fooled yourself provided you didn't let yourself know it, and did it well. Life was so much simpler, in the desert.

But there were a dozen guards by the gate. They had an unsympathetic look. He went back to his seat, which was tucked away in a corner, and stared gloomily at the ground.

If Om was alive, surely he could send a sign?

A grating by Brutha's sandals lifted itself up a few inches and slid aside. He stared at the hole.

A hooded head appeared, stared back, and disappeared again. There was a subterranean whispering. The head reappeared, and was followed by a body. It pulled itself on to the cobbles. The hood was pushed back. The man grinned conspiratorially at Brutha, put his finger to his lips and then, without warning, launched himself at him with violent intent.

Brutha rolled across the cobbles and raised his hands frantically as he saw the gleam of metal. One filthy hand clamped against his mouth. A knifeblade made a dramatic and very final silhouette against the light –

'No!'

'Why not? We said the first thing we'll do, we'll kill all the priests!'

'Not that one!'

Brutha dared to swivel his eyes sideways. Although the second figure rising from the hole was also wearing a filthy robe, there was no mistaking the paintbrush hairstyle.

He tried to say 'Urn?'

'Shut up, you,' said the other man, pressing the knife to his throat.

'Brutha?' said Urn. 'You're alive?'

Brutha moved his eyes from his captor to Urn in a way which he hoped would indicate that it was too soon to make any commitment on this point.

'He's all right,' said Urn.

'All right? He's a priest!'

'But he's on our side. Aren't you, Brutha?'

Brutha tried to nod, and thought: I'm on everyone's side. It'd be nice if, just for once, someone was on mine.

The hand was unclamped from his mouth, but the knife remained resting on his throat. Brutha's normally careful thought processes ran like quicksilver.

'The Turtle Moves?' he ventured.

The knife was withdrawn, with obvious reluctance.

'I don't trust him,' said the man. 'We should shove him down the hole at least.'

'Brutha's one of us,' said Urn.

'That's right. That's *right*,' said Brutha. 'Which ones are you?'

Urn leaned closer.

'How's your memory?'

'Unfortunately, it is fine.'

'Good. Good. Uh. It would be a good idea to stay out of trouble, d'you hear . . . if anything happens. Remember the Turtle. Well, of course you would.'

'What things?'

Urn patted him on the shoulder, making Brutha think for a moment of Vorbis. Vorbis, who never touched another person inside his head, was a great toucher with his hands.

'Best if you don't know what's happening,' said Urn.

'But I don't know what's happening,' said Brutha.

'Good. That's the way.'

The burly man gestured with his knife towards the tunnels that led into the rock.

'Are we going, or what?' he demanded.

Urn ran after him and then stopped briefly and turned.

'Be careful,' he said. 'We need what's in your head!'

Brutha watched them go.

'So do I,' he murmured.

And then he was alone again.

But he thought: Hold on. I don't have to be. I'm a bishop. At least I can watch. Om's gone and soon the world will end, so at least I might as well watch it happen.

Sandals flapping, Brutha set off towards the Place.

Bishops move diagonally. That's why they often turn up where the kings don't expect them to be.

'You godawful idiot! Don't go *that* way!'

The sun was well up now. In fact it was probably setting, if Didactylos's theories about the speed of light were correct, but in matters of relativity the point of view of the observer is very important, and from Om's point of view the sun was a golden ball in a flaming orange sky.

He pulled himself up another slope, and stared blearily at the distant Citadel. In his mind's eye, he could hear the mocking voices of all small gods.

They didn't like a god who had failed. They didn't like that at all. It let them all down. It reminded them of mortality. He'd be thrust out into the deep desert, where no one would ever come. Ever. Until the end of the world.

He shivered in his shell.

Urn and Fergmen walked nonchalantly through the tunnels of the Citadel, using the kind of nonchalant walk which, had there been anyone to take an interest in it, would have drawn detailed and arrow-sharp attention to them within seconds. But the only people around were those with vital jobs to do. Besides, it was not a good idea to stare too hard at the guards, in case they stared back.

Simony had told Urn he'd agreed to this. He couldn't quite

remember doing so. The sergeant knew a way into the Citadel, that was sensible. And Urn knew about hydraulics. Fine. Now he was walking through these dry tunnels with his toolbelt clinking. There was a logical connection, but it had been made by someone else.

Fergmen turned a corner and stopped by a large grille, which stretched from floor to ceiling. It was very rusty. It might once have been a door – there was a suggestion of hinges, rusted into the stone. Urn peered through the bars. Beyond, in the gloom, there were pipes.

'Eureka,' he said.

'Going to have a bath, then?' said Fergmen.

'Just keep watch.'

Urn selected a short crowbar from his belt and inserted it between the grille and the stonework. Give me a foot of good steel and a wall to brace . . . my . . . foot . . . against – the grille ground forward and then popped out with a leaden sound – and I can change the world . . .

He stepped inside the long, dark, damp room, and gave a whistle of admiration.

No one had done any maintenance for – well, for as long as it took iron hinges to become a mass of crumbling rust – but all this still worked?

He looked up at lead and iron buckets bigger than he was, and a tangle of man-sized pipes.

This was the breath of God.

Probably the last man who knew how it worked had been tortured to death years before. Or as soon as it was installed. Killing the creator was a traditional method of patent-protection.

There were the levers and *there*, hanging over pits in the rock floor, were the two sets of counterweights. Probably it'd only take a few hundred gallons of water to swing the balance either way. Of course, the water'd have to be pumped up –

'Sergeant?'

Fergmen peered round the door. He looked nervous, like an atheist in a thunderstorm.

'What?'

Urn pointed.

'There's a big shaft through the wall there, see? At the bottom of the gear-chain?'

'The what?'

'The big knobbly wheels?'

'Oh. Yeah.'

'Where does the shaft go to?'

'Don't know. There's the big Treadmill of Correction through there.'

Ah.

The breath of God was ultimately the sweat of men. Didactylos would have appreciated the joke, Urn thought.

He was aware of a sound that had been there all the time but was only now penetrating through his concentration. It was tinny and faint and full of echoes, but it was voices. From the pipes.

The sergeant, to judge by his expression, had heard them too.

Urn put his ear to the metal. There was no possibility of making out words, but the general religious rhythm was familiar enough.

'It's just the service going on in the Temple,' he said. 'It's probably resonating off the doors and the sound's being carried down the pipes.'

Fergmen did not look reassured.

'No gods are involved in any way,' Urn translated. He turned his attention to the pipes again.

'Simple principle,' said Urn, more to himself than to Fergmen. 'Water pours into the reservoirs on the weights, disturbing the equilibrium. One lot of weights descends and the other rises up the shaft in the wall. The weight of the door is immaterial. As the bottom weights descend, these buckets *here* tip over, pouring the water out. Probably quite a smooth action. Perfect equilibrium at either end of the movement, too. Nicely thought out.'

He caught Fergmen's expression.

'Water goes in and out and the doors swing open,' he translated. 'So all we've got to do is wait for . . . what did he say the sign would be?'

'They'll blow a trumpet when they're through the main gate,' said Fergmen, pleased to be of service.

'Right.' Urn eyed the weights and the reservoirs overhead. The bronze pipes dripped with corrosion.

'But perhaps we'd better just check that we know what we're doing,' he said. 'It probably takes a minute or two before the doors start moving.' He fumbled under his robe and produced something that looked, to Fergmen's eye, very much like a torture instrument. This must have communicated itself to Urn, who said very slowly and kindly: 'This is an ad-just-ab-ble span-ner.'

'Yes?'

'It's for twisting nuts off.'

Fergmen nodded miserably.

'Yes?' he said.

'And this is a bottle of penetrating oil.'

'Oh, good.'

'Just give me a leg up, will you? It'll take time to unhook the linkage to the valve, so we might as well make a start.' Urn heaved himself into the ancient machinery while, above, the ceremony droned on.

Cut-Me-Own-Hand-Off Dhblah was all for new prophets. He was even in favour of the end of the world, if he could get the concession to sell religious statues, cut-price icons, rancid sweetmeats, fermenting dates and putrescent olives on a stick to any watching crowds.

Subsequently, this was his testament. There never was a Book of the Prophet Brutha, but an enterprising scribe, during what came to be called the Renovation, did assemble some notes, and Dhblah had this to say:

'I. I was standing right by the statue of Ossory, right, when I noticed Brutha just beside me. Everyone was keeping away from him because of him being a bishop and they do things to you if you jostle bishops.

'II. I said to him, hello, Your Graciousness, and offered him a yoghurt practically free.

'III. He responded, no.

'IV. I said, it's very healthy, it's a *live* yoghurt.

'V. He said, yes, he could see.

'VI. He was staring at the doors. This was about the time of the third gong, right, so we all knew we'd got hours to wait. He was looking a bit down and it's not as if he even et the yoghurt, which I admit was on the hum a bit, what with the heat. I mean, it was more alive than usual. I mean, I had to keep hitting it with a spoon to stop it getting out of the . . . all right. I was just explaining about the yoghurt. All *right*. I mean, you want to put a bit of colour in, don't you? People like a bit of colour. It was green.

'VII. He just stood there, staring. So I said, got a problem, Your Reverence? Upon which he vouchsafed, I cannot hear him. I said, what is this he to whom what you refer? He said, if he was here, he would send me a sign.

'VIII. There is no truth whatsoever in the rumour that I ran away at this juncture. It was just the pressure of the crowd. I have never been a friend of the Quisition. I might have sold them food, but I always charged them extra.

'IX. Anyway, right, then he pushed through the line of guards what was holding the crowd back and stood right in front of the doors, and they weren't sure what to do about bishops, and I heard him say something like, I carried you in the desert, I believed all my life, just give me this one thing.

'X. Something like that, anyway. How about some yoghurt? Bargain offer. Onna stick.'

Om lifted himself over a creeper-clad wall by grasping tendrils in his beak and hauling himself up by the neck muscles. Then he fell down the other side. The Citadel was as far away as ever.

Brutha's mind was flaming like a beacon in Om's senses. There's a streak of madness in everyone who spends quality time with gods, and it was driving the boy now.

'It's too soon!' Om yelled. 'You need followers! It can't be just *you*! You can't do it by *yourself*! You have to get disciples first!'

Simony turned to look down the length of the Turtle. Thirty men were crouched under the shell, looking very apprehensive.

A corporal saluted.

'The needle's there, sergeant.'

The brass whistle whistled.

Simony picked up the steering ropes. This was what war should be, he thought. No uncertainty. A few more Turtles like this, and no one would ever fight again.

'Stand by,' he said.

He pulled the big lever hard.

The brittle metal snapped in his hand.

Give anyone a lever long enough and they can change the world. It's unreliable levers that are the problem.

In the depths of the Temple's hidden plumbing, Urn grasped a bronze pipe firmly with his spanner and gave the nut a cautious turn. It resisted. He changed position, and grunted as he used more pressure.

With a sad little metal sound, the pipe twisted – and broke . . .

Water gushed out, hitting him in the face. He dropped the tool and tried to block the flow with his fingers, but it spurted around his hands and gurgled down the channel towards one of the weights.

'Stop it! Stop it!' he shouted.

'What?' said Fergmen, several feet below him.

'Stop the water!'

'How?'

'The pipe's broken!'

'I thought that's what we wanted to do?'

'Not yet!'

'Stop shouting, mister! There's guards around!'

Urn let the water gush for a moment as he struggled out of his robe, and then he rammed the sodden material into the pipe. It shot out again with some force and slapped wetly against the lead funnel, sliding down until it blocked the tube that led to the weights. The water piled up behind it and then spilled over on to the floor.

Urn glanced at the weight. It hadn't begun to move. He relaxed slightly. Now, provided there was still enough water to make the weight drop . . .

'Both of you – stand still.'

He looked around, his mind going numb.

There was a heavy-set man in a black robe standing in the stricken doorway. Behind him, a guard held a sword in a meaningful manner.

'Who are you? Why are you here?'

Urn hesitated for only a moment.

He gestured with his spanner.

'Well, it's the seating, innit,' he said. 'You've got shocking seepage around the seating. Amazing it holds together.'

The man stepped into the room. He glared uncertainly at Urn for a moment and then turned his attention to the gushing pipe. And then back to Urn.

'But you're not –' he began.

He spun around as Fergmen hit the guard hard with a length of broken pipe. When he turned back, Urn's spanner caught him full in the stomach. Urn wasn't strong, but it was a long spanner, and the well-known principles of leverage did the rest. He doubled up and then sagged backwards against one of the weights.

What happened next happened in frozen time. Deacon Cusp grabbed at the weight for support. It sank down, ponderously, his extra poundage adding to the weight of the water. He clawed higher. It sank further, dropping below the lip of the pit. He sought for balance again, but this time it was against fresh air, and he tumbled on top of the falling weight.

Urn saw his face staring up at him as the weight fell into the gloom.

With a lever, he could change the world. It had certainly changed it for Deacon Cusp. It had made it stop existing.

Fergmen was standing over the guard, his pipe raised.

'I know this one,' he said. 'I'm going to give him a –'

'Never mind about that!'

'But –'

Above them linkage clanked into action. There was a distant creaking of bronze against bronze.

'Let's get out of here,' said Urn. 'Only the gods know what's happening up there.'

And blows rained on the unmoving Moving Turtle's carapace.

'Damn! Damn! Damn!' shouted Simony, thumping it again. 'Move! I command you to move! Can you understand plain Ephebian! Move!'

The unmoving machine leaked steam and sat there.

And Om pulled himself up the slope of a small hill. So it came to this, then. There was only one way to get to the Citadel now.

It was a million-to-one chance, with any luck.

And Brutha stood in front of the huge doors, oblivious to the crowd and the muttering guards. The Quisition could arrest anyone, but the guards weren't certain what happened to you if you apprehended an archbishop, especially one so recently favoured by the Prophet.

Just a sign, Brutha thought, in the loneliness of his head.

The doors trembled, and swung slowly outwards.

Brutha stepped forward. He wasn't fully conscious now, not in any coherent way as understood by normal people. Just one part of him was still capable of looking at the state of his own mind and thinking: perhaps the Great Prophets felt like this *all the time*.

The thousands inside the temple were looking around in confusion. The choirs of lesser Iams paused in their chant. Brutha walked on up the aisle, the only one with a purpose in the suddenly bewildered throng.

Vorbis was standing in the centre of the temple, under the vault of the dome. Guards hurried towards Brutha, but Vorbis raised a hand in a gentle but very positive movement.

Now Brutha could take in the scene. There was the staff of Ossory, and Abbys's cloak, and the sandals of Cena. And, supporting the dome, the massive statues of the first four prophets. He'd never seen them. He'd heard about them every day of his childhood.

And what did they mean now? They didn't mean anything. Nothing meant anything, if Vorbis was Prophet. Nothing meant anything, if the Cenobiarch was a man who'd heard nothing in the inner spaces of his own head but his own thoughts.

He was aware that Vorbis's gesture had not only halted the guards, although they surrounded him like a hedge. It had also filled the temple with silence. Into which Vorbis spoke.

'Ah. My Brutha. We had looked for you in vain. And now even you are here . . .'

Brutha stopped a few feet away. The moment of . . . whatever it had been . . . that had propelled him through the doors had drained away.

Now all there was, was Vorbis.

Smiling.

The part of him still capable of thought was thinking: there is nothing you can say. No one will listen. No one will care. It doesn't matter what you tell people about Ephebe, and Brother Murduck, and the desert. It won't be *fundamentally* true.

Fundamentally true. That's what the world is, with Vorbis in it.

Vorbis said, 'There is something wrong? Something you wish to say?'

The black-on-black eyes filled the world, like two pits.

Brutha's mind gave up, and Brutha's body took over. It brought his hand back and raised it, oblivious to the sudden rush forward of the guards.

He saw Vorbis turn his cheek, and smile.

Brutha stopped, and lowered his hand.

He said, 'No. I won't.'

Then, for the first and only time, he saw Vorbis really enraged. There had been times before when the deacon had been angry, but it had been something driven by the brain, switched on and off as the need arose. This was something else, something out of control. And it flashed across his face only for a moment.

As the hands of the guards closed on him, Vorbis stepped forward and patted him on the shoulder. He looked Brutha in the eye for a moment and then said softly:

'Thrash him within an inch of his life and burn him the rest of the way.'

An Iam began to speak, but stopped when he saw Vorbis's expression.

'Do it *now*.'

A world of silence. No sound up here, except the rush of wind through the feathers.

Up here the world is round, bordered by a band of sea. The viewpoint is from horizon to horizon, the sun is closer.

And yet, looking down, looking for shapes . . .

. . . down in the farmland on the edge of the wilderness . . .

. . . on a small hill . . .

. . . a tiny moving dome, ridiculously exposed . . .

No sound but the rush of wind through feathers as the eagle pulls in its wings and drops like an arrow, the world spinning around the little moving shape that is the focus of all the eagle's attention.

Closer and . . .

. . . talons down . . .

. . . *grip* . . .

. . . and rise . . .

Brutha opened his eyes.

His back was merely agonising. He'd long ago got used to switching off pain.

But he was spreadeagled on a surface, his arms and legs chained to something he couldn't see. Sky above. The towering frontage of the temple to one side.

By turning his head a little he could see the silent crowd. And the brown metal of the iron turtle. He could smell smoke.

Someone was just tightening the shackles on his hand. Brutha looked over at the inquisitor. Now, what was it he had to say? Oh, yes.

'The Turtle Moves?' he mumbled.

The man sighed.

'Not this one, friend,' he said.

*

The world spun under Om as the eagle sought for shell-cracking height, and his mind was besieged by the tortoise's existential dread of being off the ground. And Brutha's thoughts, bright and clear this close to death . . .

I'm on my back and getting hotter and I'm going to die . . .

Careful, careful. Concentrate, *concentrate*. It'll let go any second . . .

Om stuck out his long scrawny neck, stared at the body just above him, picked what he hoped was about the right spot, plunged his beak through the brown feathers between the talons, and *gripped*.

The eagle blinked. No tortoise had ever done that to an eagle, anywhere else in history.

Om's thoughts arrived in the little silvery world of its mind:

'We don't want to hurt one another, now do we?'

The eagle blinked again.

Eagles have never evolved much imagination or forethought, beyond that necessary to know that a turtle smashes when you drop it on the rocks. But it was forming a mental picture of what happened when you let go of a heavy tortoise that was still intimately gripping an essential bit of you.

Its eyes watered.

Another thought crept into its mind.

'Now. You play, uh, ball with me, I'll play . . . ball with you. Understand? This is important. This is what I want you to do . . .'

The eagle soared on a thermal off the hot rocks, and sped towards the distant gleam of the Citadel.

No tortoise had ever done this before. No tortoise in the whole universe. But no tortoise had ever been a god, and knew the unwritten motto of the Quisition: *Cuius testiculos habes, habeas cardia et cerebellum*.

When you have their full attention in your grip, their hearts and minds will follow.

Urn pushed his way through the crowds, with Fergmen trailing behind. That was the best and the worst of civil war, at least at the start – everyone wore the same uniform. It was much easier when you picked enemies who were a different colour or at least spoke with a funny accent. You could call them 'gooks' or something. It made things easier.

Hey, Urn thought. This is nearly philosophy. Pity I probably won't live to tell anyone.

The big doors were ajar. The crowd was silent, and very attentive. He craned forward to see, and then looked up at the soldier beside him.

It was Simony.

'I thought –'

'It didn't work,' said Simony, bitterly.

'Did you –?'

'We did everything! Something broke!'

'It must be the steel they make here,' said Urn. 'The link pins on –'

'That doesn't matter now,' said Simony.

The flat tones of his voice made Urn follow the eyes of the crowd.

There was another iron turtle there – a proper model of a turtle, mounted on a sort of open gridwork of metal bars in which a couple of inquisitors were even now lighting a fire. And chained to the back of the turtle –

'Who's that?'

'Brutha.'

'*What?*'

'I don't know what happened. He hit Vorbis, or didn't hit him. Or something. Enraged him anyway. Vorbis stopped the ceremony, right there and then.'

Urn glanced at the deacon. Not Cenobiarch yet, so uncrowned. Among the Iams and bishops standing uncertainly in the open doorway, his bald head gleamed in the morning light.

'Come on, then,' said Urn.

'Come on what?'

'We can rush the steps and save him!'

'There's more of them than there are of us,' said Simony.

'Well, haven't there always been? There's not magically more of them than there are of us just because they've got Brutha, are there?'

Simony grabbed his arm.

'Think logically, will you?' he said. 'You're a philosopher, aren't you? Look at the crowd!'

Urn looked at the crowd.

'Well?'

'They don't like it.' Simony turned. 'Look, Brutha's going to die anyway. But this way it'll mean something. People don't understand, really understand, about the shape of the universe and all that stuff, but they'll remember what Vorbis did to a man. Right? We can make Brutha's death a symbol for people, don't you see?'

Urn stared at the distant figure of Brutha. It was naked, except for a loin-cloth.

'A symbol?' he said. His throat was dry.

'It has to be.'

He remembered Didactylos saying the world was a funny place. And, he thought distantly, it really was. Here people were about to roast someone to death, but they'd left his loin-cloth on, out of respectability. You had to laugh. Otherwise you'd go mad.

'You know,' he said, turning to Simony. 'Now I *know* Vorbis is evil. He burned my city. Well, the Tsorteans do it sometimes, and we burn theirs. It's just war. It's all part of history. And he lies and cheats and claws power for himself, and lots of people do that, too. But do you know what's special? Do you know what it is?'

'Of course,' said Simony. 'It's what he's doing to –'

'It's what he's done to *you*.'

'What?'

'He turns other people into copies of himself.'

Simony's grip was like a vice. 'You're saying *I'm* like *him*?'

'Once you said you'd cut him down,' said Urn. 'Now you're thinking like him ...'

'So we rush them, then?' said Simony. 'I'm sure of – maybe four hundred on our side. So I give the signal and a few hundred of us attack thousands of them? And he dies anyway and we die too? What difference does that make?'

Urn's face was grey with horror now.

'You mean you don't know?' he said.

Some of the crowd looked round curiously at him.

'You don't *know*?' he said.

The sky was blue. The sun wasn't high enough yet to turn it into Omnia's normal copper bowl.

Brutha turned his head again, towards the sun. It was about a width above the horizon, although if Didactylos's theories about the speed of light were correct, it was really setting, thousands of years in the future.

It was eclipsed by the head of Vorbis.

'Hot yet, Brutha?' said the deacon.

'Warm.'

'It will get warmer.'

There was a disturbance in the crowd. Someone was shouting. Vorbis ignored it.

'Nothing you want to say?' he said. 'Can't you manage even a curse? Not even a curse?'

'You never heard Om,' said Brutha. 'You never believed. You never, ever heard his voice. All you heard were the echoes inside your own mind.'

'Really? But I am the Cenobiarch and you are going to burn for treachery and heresy,' said Vorbis. 'So much for Om, perhaps?'

'There will be justice,' said Brutha. 'If there is no justice, there is nothing.'

He was aware of a small voice in his head, too faint yet to distinguish words.

'Justice?' said Vorbis. The idea seemed to enrage him. He spun around to the crowd of bishops. 'Did you hear him? There will be justice? Om *has* judged! Through *me*! This *is* justice!'

There was a speck in the sun now, speeding towards the Citadel. And the little voice was saying *left left left up up left right a bit up left* – The mass of metal under him was getting uncomfortably hot.

'He comes now,' said Brutha.

Vorbis waved his hand to the great facade of the temple. 'Men built this. We built this,' he said. 'And what did Om do? Om comes? Let him come! Let him judge between us!'

'He comes now,' Brutha repeated. 'The God.'

People looked apprehensively upwards. There was that moment, just one moment, when the world holds its breath and against all experience waits for a miracle.

– *up left now, when I say three, one, two, THREE* –

'Vorbis?' croaked Brutha.

'What?' snapped the deacon.

'You're going to die.'

It was hardly a whisper, but it bounced off the bronze doors and carried across the Place . . .

It made people uneasy, although they couldn't quite say why.

The eagle sped across the square, so low that people ducked. Then it cleared the roof of the temple and curved away towards the mountains. The watchers relaxed. It was only an eagle. For a moment there, just for a moment . . .

No one saw the tiny speck, tumbling down from the sky.

Don't put your faith in gods. But you can believe in turtles.

A feeling of rushing wind in Brutha's mind, and a voice . . .

-obuggerbuggerbuggerhelpaarghnoNoNoAarghBuggerNONOAARGH –

Even Vorbis got a grip of himself. There had been just a moment, when he'd seen the eagle – but, no . . .

He extended his arms and smiled beatifically at the sky.

'I'm sorry,' said Brutha.

One or two people, who had been watching Vorbis closely, said later that there was just time for his expression to change before two pounds of tortoise, travelling at three metres a second, hit him between the eyes.

It was a revelation.

And that does something to people watching. For a start, they believe with all their heart.

Brutha was aware of feet running up the steps, and hands pulling at the chains.

And then a voice:

I. He is Mine.

The Great God rose over the Temple, billowing and changing as the belief of thousands of people flowed into him. There were shapes there, of eagle-headed men, and bulls, and golden horns, but they tangled and flamed and fused into one another.

Four bolts of fire whirred out of the cloud and burst the chains holding Brutha.

II. He Is Cenobiarch And *Prophet Of Prophets.*

The voice of theophany rumbled off the distant mountains.

III. Do I Hear Any Objections? No? Good.

The cloud had by now condensed into a shimmering golden figure, as tall as the Temple. It leaned down until its face was a few feet away from Brutha, and in a whisper that boomed across the Place said:

IV. Don't Worry. This Is Just The Start. You and Me, Kid! People Are Going To Find Out What Wailing and Gnashing Of Teeth Really Is.

Another shaft of flame shot out and struck the Temple doors. They slammed shut, and then the white-hot bronze melted, erasing the commandments of the centuries.

V. What Shall It Be, Prophet?

Brutha stood up, unsteadily. Urn supported him by one arm, and Simony by the other.

'Mm?' he said, muzzily.

VI. Your Commandments?

'I thought they were supposed to come from you,' said Brutha. 'I don't know if I can think of any . . .'

The world waited.

'How about "Think for Yourself"?' said Urn, staring in horrified fascination at the manifestation.

'No,' said Simony. 'Try something like "Social Cohesiveness is the Key to Progress".'

'Can't say it rolls off the tongue,' said Urn.

'If I can be of any help,' said Cut-Me-Own-Hand-Off Dhblah, from the crowd, 'something of benefit to the convenience food industry would be very welcome.'

'Not killing people. We could do with one like that,' said someone else.

'It'd be a good start,' said Urn.

They looked at the Chosen One. He shook himself free of their grip and stood alone, swaying a little.

'No-oo,' said Brutha. 'No. I thought like that once, but it wouldn't. Not really.'

Now, he said. Only now. Just one point in history. Not tomorrow, not next month, it'll always be too late unless it's *now*.

They stared at him.

'Come *on*,' said Simony. 'What's wrong with it? You can't argue with it.'

'It's hard to explain,' said Brutha. 'But I think it's got something to do with how people should behave. I think . . . you should do things because they're right. Not because gods say so. They might say something different another time.'

VII. I Like *One About Not Killing*, said Om, from far above.

VIII. It's Got A Good Ring To It. Hurry Up, I've Got Some Smiting To Do.

'You see?' said Brutha. 'No. No smiting. No commandments unless you obey them too.'

Om thumped on the roof of the Temple.

IX. You Order Me? Here? NOW? ME?

'No. I ask.'

X. That's Worse Than Ordering!

'Everything works both ways.'

Om thumped his Temple again. A wall caved in. That part of the crowd that hadn't managed to stampede from the Place redoubled its efforts.

XI. There Must Be Punishment! Otherwise There Will Be No Order!

'No.'

XII. I Do Not Need You! I Have Believers Enough Now!

'But only through me. And, perhaps, not for long. It will all happen again. It's happened before. It happens all the time. That's why gods die. They never believe in people. But you have a chance. All you need to do is . . . believe.'

XIII. What? Listen To Stupid Prayers? Watch Over Small Children? Make It Rain?

'Sometimes. Not always. It could be a bargain.'

XIV. BARGAIN! I don't Bargain! Not With Humans!

'Bargain now,' said Brutha. 'While you have the chance. Or one day you'll have to bargain with Simony, or someone like him. Or Urn, or someone like *him*.'

XV. I Could Destroy You Utterly.

'Yes. I am entirely in your power.'

XVI. I Could Crush You Like An Egg!

'Yes.'

Om paused.

Then he said: *XVII. You Can't Use Weakness As A Weapon.*

'It's the only one I've got.'

XVIII. Why Should I Yield, Then?

'Not yield. Bargain. Deal with me in weakness. Or one day you'll have to bargain with someone in a position of strength. The world changes.'

XIX. Hah! You Want A Constitutional Religion?

'Why not? The other sort didn't work.'

Om leaned on the Temple, his temper subsiding.

Chap. II v.I. Very Well, Then. But Only For A Time. A grin spread across the enormous, smoking face. *For One Hundred Years, Yes?*

'And after a hundred years?'

II. We Shall See.

'Agreed.'

A finger the length of a tree unfolded, descended, touched Brutha.

III. You Have A Persuasive Way. You Will Need It. A Fleet Approaches.

'Ephebians?' said Simony.

IV. And Tsorteans. And Djelibeybians. And Klatchians. Every Free Country Along The Coast. To Stamp Out Omnia For Good. Or Bad.

'You don't have many friends, do you?' said Urn.

'Even I don't like us much, and I *am* us,' said Simony. He looked up at the god.

'Will you help?'

V. *You Don't Even Believe In Me!*

'Yes, but I'm a practical man.'

VI. *And Brave, Too, To Declare Atheism Before Your God.*

'This doesn't change anything, you know!' said Simony. 'Don't think you can get round me by existing!'

'No help,' said Brutha, firmly.

'What?' said Simony. 'We'll need a mighty army against that lot!'

'Yes. And we haven't got one. So we'll do it another way.'

'You're crazy!'

Brutha's calmness was like a desert.

'This may be the case.'

'We have to fight!'

'Not yet.'

Simony clenched his fists in anger.

'Look . . . *listen* . . . We died for lies, for *centuries* we died for lies.' He waved a hand towards the god. 'Now we've got a truth to die for!'

'No. Men should die for lies. But the truth is too precious to die for.'

Simony's mouth opened and shut soundlessly as he sought for words. Finally, he found some from the dawn of his education.

'I was told it was the finest thing to die for a god,' he mumbled.

'Vorbis said that. And he was . . . stupid. You can die for your country or your people or your family, but for a god you should live fully and busily, every day of a long life.'

'And how long is that going to be?'

'We shall see.'

Brutha looked up at Om.

'You will not show yourself like this again?'

Chap. III v.I. No. Once Is Enough.

'Remember the desert.'

II. I Will Remember.

'Walk with me.'

Brutha went over to the body of Vorbis and picked it up.

'I think,' he said, 'that they will land on the beach on the Ephebian side of the forts. They won't use the rock shore and they can't use the cliffs. I'll meet them there.' He glanced down at Vorbis. 'Someone should.'

'You can't mean you want to go by yourself?'

'Ten thousand won't be sufficient. One might be enough.'

He walked down the steps.

Urn and Simony watched him go.

'He's going to die,' said Simony. 'He won't even be a patch of grease on the sand.' He turned to Om. 'Can you stop him?'

III. It May Be That I Cannot.

Brutha was already halfway across the Place.

'Well, we're not deserting him,' said Simony.

IV. Good.

Om watched them go, too. And then he was alone, except for the thousands watching him, crammed around the edges of the great square. He wished he knew what to say to them. That's why he needed people like Brutha. That's why all gods needed people like Brutha.

'Excuse me?'

The god looked down.

V. Yes?

'Um. I can't sell you anything, can I?'

VI. What Is Your Name?

'Dhblah, god.'

VII. Ah, Yes. And What Is It You Wish?

The merchant hopped anxiously from one foot to the other.

'You couldn't manage just a small commandment? Something about eating yoghurt on Wednesdays, say? It's always very difficult to shift, midweek.'

VIII. You Stand Before Your God And Look For Business Opportunities?

'We-ell,' said Dhblah, 'we could come to an arrangement. Strike while the iron is hot, as the inquisitors say. Haha. Twenty percent? How about it? After expenses, of course –'

The Great God Om smiled.

IX. I Think You Will Make A Little Prophet, Dhblah, he said.

'Right. Right. That's all I'm looking for. Just trying to make both ends hummus.'

X. Tortoises Are To Be Left Alone.

Dhblah put his head on one side.

'Doesn't *sing*, does it?' he said. 'But ... tortoise necklaces ... hmm ... brooches, of course. Tortoiseshel–'

XI. NO!

'Sorry, sorry. See what you mean. All right. Tortoise statues. Ye-ess. I thought about them. Nice shape. Incidentally, you couldn't make a statue wobble every now and again, could you? Very good for business, wobbling statues. The statue of Ossory wobbles every Fast of Ossory, reg'lar. By means of a small piston device operated in the basement, it is said. But very good for the prophets, all the same.'

XII. You Make Me Laugh, Little Prophet. Sell Your Tortoises, By All Means.

'Tell you the truth,' said Dhblah, 'I've already drawn a few designs just now . . .'

Om vanished. There was a brief thunderclap. Dhblah looked reflectively at his sketches.

'. . . but I suppose I'll have to take the little figure off them,' he said, more or less to himself.

The shade of Vorbis looked around.

'Ah. The desert,' he said. The black sand was absolutely still under the starlit sky. It looked cold.

He hadn't planned on dying yet. In fact . . . he couldn't quite remember how he'd died . . .

'The desert,' he repeated, and this time there was a hint of uncertainty. He'd never been uncertain about anything in his . . . life. The feeling was unfamiliar and terrifying. Did ordinary people feel like this?

He got a grip on himself.

Death was impressed. Very few people managed this, managed to hold on to the shape of their old thinking after death.

Death took no pleasure in his job. It was an emotion he found hard to grasp. But there was such a thing as satisfaction.

'So,' said Vorbis. 'The desert. And at the end of the desert –?'

JUDGEMENT.

'Yes, yes, of course.'

Vorbis tried to concentrate. He couldn't. He could feel certainty draining away. And he'd always *been* certain.

He hesitated, like a man opening a door to a familiar room and finding nothing there but a bottomless pit. The memories were still there. He could feel them. They had the right shape. It was just that he couldn't remember what they *were*. There had been a voice . . . Surely, there had been a voice? But all he could remember was the sound of his own thoughts, bouncing off the inside of his own head.

Now he had to cross the desert. What could there be to fear –

The desert was what you believed.

Vorbis looked inside himself.

And went on looking.

He sagged to his knees.

I CAN SEE THAT YOU ARE BUSY, said Death.

'Don't leave me! It's so *empty*!'

Death looked around at the endless desert. He snapped his fingers and a large white horse trotted up.

I SEE A HUNDRED THOUSAND PEOPLE, he said, swinging himself into the saddle.

'Where? Where?'

HERE. WITH YOU.

'I can't see them!'

Death gathered up the reins.

NEVERTHELESS, he said. His horse trotted forward a few steps.

'I don't understand!' screamed Vorbis.

Death paused. YOU HAVE PERHAPS HEARD THE PHRASE, he said, THAT HELL IS OTHER PEOPLE?

'Yes. Yes, of course.'

Death nodded. IN TIME, he said, YOU WILL LEARN THAT IT IS WRONG.

The first boats grounded in the shallows, and the troops leapt into shoulder-high surf.

No one was quite sure who was leading the fleet. Most of the countries along the coast hated one another, not in any personal sense, but simply on a kind of historical basis. On the other hand, how much leadership was necessary? Everyone knew where Omnia was. None of the countries in the fleet hated the others worse than they did Omnia. Now it was necessary for it . . . not to exist.

General Argavisti of Ephebe considered that he was in charge, because although he didn't have the most ships he was avenging the attack on Ephebe. But Imperiator Borvorius of Tsort knew that *he* was in charge, because there were more Tsortean ships than any others. And Admiral Rham-ap-Efan of Djelibeybi knew that *he* was in charge, because he was the kind of person who always thought he was in charge of anything. The only captain who did not, in fact, think that he was commanding the fleet was Fasta Benj, a fisherman from a very small nation of marsh-dwelling nomads of whose existence all the other countries were in complete ignorance, and whose small reed boat had been in the path of the fleet and had got swept along. Since his tribe believed that there were only fifty-one people in the world, worshipped a giant newt, spoke a very personal language which no one else understood, and had never seen metal or fire before, he was spending a lot of time wearing a puzzled grin.

Clearly they had reached a shore, not of proper mud and reeds, but of very small gritty bits. He lugged his little reed boat up the sand, and sat down with interest to see what the men in the feathery hats and shiny fish-scale vests were going to do next.

General Argavisti scanned the beach.

'They must have seen us coming,' he said. 'So why would they let us establish a beach-head?'

Heat haze wavered over the dunes. A dot appeared, growing and contracting in the shimmering air.

More troops poured ashore.

General Argavisti shaded his eyes against the sun.

'Fella's just standing there,' he said.

'Could be a spy,' said Borvorius.

'Don't see how he could be a spy in his own country,' said Argavisti. 'Anyway, if he was a spy he'd be creepin' around. That's how you can tell.'

The figure had stopped at the foot of the dunes. There was something about it that drew the eye. Argavisti had faced many an opposing army, and this was normal. One patiently waiting figure was not. He found he kept turning to look at it.

''S'carrying something,' he said eventually. 'Sergeant? Go and bring that man here.'

A few minutes later the sergeant returned.

'Says he'll meet you in the middle of the beach, sir,' he reported.

'Didn't I tell you to bring him here?'

'He didn't want to come, sir.'

'You've got a sword, haven't you?'

'Yessir. Prodded him a bit, but he dint want to move, sir. And he's carrying a dead body, sir.'

'On a battlefield? It's not bring-your-own, you know.'

'And . . . sir?'

'What?'

'Says he's probably the Cenobiarch, sir. Wants to talk about a peace treaty.'

'Oh, he does? Peace treaty? We know about peace treaties with Omnia. Go and tell . . . no. Take a couple of men and bring him here.'

Brutha walked back between the soldiers, through the organised pandemonium of the camp. I ought to feel afraid, he thought. I was always afraid in the Citadel. But not now. This is through fear and out the other side.

Occasionally one of the soldiers would give him a push. It's not allowed for an enemy to walk freely into a camp, even if he wants to.

He was brought before a trestle table, behind which sat half a dozen large men in various military styles, and one small olive-skinned man who was gutting a fish and grinning hopefully at everyone.

'Well, now,' said Argavisti, 'Cenobiarch of Omnia, eh?'

Brutha dropped Vorbis's body on to the sand. Their gaze followed it.

'I know him –' said Borvorius. 'Vorbis! Someone killed him at last, eh? And will you stop trying to sell me fish? Does anyone know who this man is?' he added, indicating Fasta Benj.

'It was a tortoise,' said Brutha.

'Was it? Not surprised. Never did trust them, always creeping around. *Look*, I said no fish! He's not one of mine, I know that. Is he one of yours?'

Argavisti waved a hand irritably. 'Who sent you, boy?'

'No one. I came by myself. But you could say I come from the future.'

'Are you a philosopher? Where's your sponge?'

'You've come to wage war on Omnia. This would not be a good idea.'

'From Omnia's point of view, yes.'

'From everyone's. You will probably defeat us. But not all of us. And then what will you do? Leave a garrison? For ever? And eventually a new generation will retaliate. Why you did this won't mean anything to them. You'll be the oppressors. They'll fight. They might even win. And there'll be another war. And one day people will say: why didn't they sort it all out, back then? On the beach. Before it all started. Before all those people died. Now we have that chance. Aren't we lucky?'

Argavisti stared at him. Then he nudged Borvorius.

'What did he say?'

Borvorius, who was better at thinking than the others, said, 'Are you talking about surrender?'

'Yes. If that's the word.'

Argavisti exploded.

'You can't do that!'

'Someone will have to. Please listen to me. Vorbis is dead. He's paid.'

'Not enough. What about your soldiers? They tried to sack our city!'

'Do your soldiers obey your orders?'

'Certainly!'

'And they'd cut me down here and now if you commanded it?'

'I should say so!'

'And I'm unarmed,' said Brutha.

The sun beat down on an awkward pause.

'When I say they'd obey –' Argavisti began.

'We were not sent here to parley,' said Borvorius abruptly. 'Vorbis's death changes nothing fundamental. We are here to see that Omnia is no longer a threat.'

'It is not. We will send materials and people to help rebuild Ephebe. And gold, if you like. We will reduce the size of our army. And so on. Consider us beaten. We will even open Omnia to whatever other religions wish to build holy places here.'

A voice echoed in his head, like the person behind you who says, 'Put the red Queen on the black King,' when you think you have been playing all by yourself . . .

I. What?

'This will encourage . . . local effort,' said Brutha.

II. Other Gods? Here?

'There will be free trade along the coast. I wish to see Omnia take its place among its fellow nations.'

III. I heard You Mention Other Gods.

'Its place is at the bottom,' said Borvorius.

'No. That won't work.'

IV. Could We Please Get Back To The Matter Of Other Gods?

'Will you please excuse me a moment?' said Brutha, brightly. 'I need to pray.'

Even Argavisti raised no objection as Brutha walked off a little way up the beach. As St Ungulant preached to any who would listen, there were plus points in being a madman. People hesitated to stop you, in case it made things worse.

'Yes?' said Brutha, under his breath.

V. I Don't Seem To Recall Any Discussion About Other Gods Being Worshipped In Omnia?

'Ah, but it'll work *for* you,' said Brutha. 'People will soon see that those other ones are no good at all, won't they?' He crossed his fingers behind his back.

VI. This Is Religion, Boy. Not Comparison Bloody Shopping! You Shall Not Subject Your God To Market Forces!

'I'm sorry. I can see that you would be worried about –'

VII. Worried? Me? By A Bunch Of Primping Women And Musclebound Posers In Curly Beards?

'Fine. Is that settled, then?'

VIII. They Won't Last Five Minutes! . . . what?

'And now I'd better go and talk to these men one more time.'

His eye was caught by a movement among the dunes.

'Oh, no,' he said. 'The idiots . . .'

He turned and ran desperately towards the beached fleet.

'No! It's not like that! Listen! *Listen!*'

But they had seen the army, too.

It looked impressive, perhaps more impressive than it really was. When news gets through that a huge enemy fleet has beached with the intent of seriously looting, pillaging and – because they are from civilised countries – whistling and making catcalls at the women and impressing them with their flash bloody uniforms and wooing them away with their flash bloody consumer goods, I don't know, show them a polished bronze mirror and it goes right to their heads, you'd think there was something wrong with the local lads . . . *then* people either head for the hills or pick up some handy, swingable object, get Granny to hide the family treasures in her drawers, and prepare to make a fight of it.

And, in the lead, the iron cart. Steam poured out of its funnel. Urn must have got it working again.

'Stupid! Stupid!' Brutha shouted, to the world in general, and carried on running.

The fleet was already forming battle-lines, and its commander, whichever he was, was amazed to see an apparent attack by one man.

Borvorius caught him as he plunged towards a line of spears.

'I *see*,' he said. 'Keep us talking while your soldiers got into position, eh?'

'No! I didn't want that!'

Borvorius's eyes narrowed. He had not survived the many wars of his life by being a stupid man.

'No,' he said, 'maybe you didn't. But it doesn't matter. Listen to me, my innocent little priest. Sometimes there has to be a war. Things go too far for words. There's . . . other forces. Now . . . go back to your people. Maybe we'll both be alive when all this is over and *then* we can talk. Fight first, talk after. That's how it works, boy. That's *history*. Now, go back.'

Brutha turned away.

I. Shall I Smite Them?

'No!'

II. I Could Make Them As Dust. Just Say The Word.

'No. That's worse than war.'

III. But You Said A God Must Protect His People –

'What would we be if I told you to crush honest men?'

IV. Not Stuck Full Of Arrows?

'No.'

The Omnians were assembling among the dunes. A lot of them had clustered around the iron-shielded cart. Brutha looked at it through a mist of despair.

'Didn't I say I'd go down there alone?' he said.

Simony, who was leaning against the Turtle, gave him a grim smile.

'Did it work?' he said.

'I think . . . it didn't.'

'I knew it. Sorry you had to find out. Things have a way of wanting to happen, see? Sometimes you get people facing off and . . . that's it.'

'But if only people would –'

'Yeah. You could use *that* as a commandment.'

There was a clanging noise, and a hatch opened on the side of the Turtle. Urn emerged, backwards, holding a spanner.

'What is this thing?' said Brutha.

'It's a machine for fighting,' said Simony. 'The Turtle Moves, eh?'

'For fighting Ephebians?' said Brutha.

Urn turned around.

'What?' he said.

'You've built this . . . thing . . . to fight Ephebians?'

'Well . . . no . . . no,' said Urn, looking bewildered. 'We're fighting Ephebians?'

'Everyone,' said Simony.

'But I never . . . *I'm* an . . . I never –'

Brutha looked at the spiked wheels and the saw-edged plates around the edge of the Turtle.

'It's a device that goes by itself,' said Urn. 'We were going to use it for . . . I mean . . . look, I never wanted it to . . .'

'We need it now,' said Simony.

'Which we?'

'What comes out of the big long spout thing at the front?' said Brutha.

'Steam,' said Urn dully. 'It's connected to the safety valve.'

'Oh.'

'It comes out very hot,' said Urn, sagging even more.

'Oh?'

'Scalding, in fact.'

Brutha's gaze drifted from the steam funnel to the rotating knives.

'Very philosophical,' he said.

'We were going to use it against Vorbis,' said Urn.

'And now you're not. It's going to be used against Ephebians. You know, I used to think *I* was stupid, and then I met philosophers.'

Simony broke the silence by patting Brutha on the shoulder.

'It will all work out,' he said. 'We won't lose. After all,' he smiled encouragingly, '*we* have God on our side.'

Brutha turned. His fist shot out. It wasn't a scientific blow, but it was hard enough to spin Simony around. He clutched his chin.

'What was *that* for? Isn't this what you wanted?'

'We get the gods we deserve,' said Brutha, 'and I think we don't deserve any. Stupid. Stupid. The sanest man I've met this year lives up a pole in the desert. Stupid. I think I ought to join him.'

I. Why?

'Gods and men, men and gods,' said Brutha. 'Everything happens because things have happened before. Stupid.'

II. But You Are The Chosen One.

'Choose someone else.'

Brutha strode off through the ragged army. No one tried to stop him. He reached the path that led up to the cliffs, and did not even turn to look at the battle-lines.

'Aren't you going to watch the battle? I need someone to watch the battle.'

Didactylos was sitting on a rock, his hands folded on his stick.

'Oh, hello,' said Brutha, bitterly. 'Welcome to Omnia.'

'It helps if you're philosophical about it,' said Didactylos.

'But there's no reason to fight!'

'Yes there is. Honour and revenge and duty and things like that.'

'Do you really think so? I thought philosophers were supposed to be logical?'

Didactylos shrugged.

'Well, the way I see it, logic is only a way of being ignorant by numbers.'

'I thought it would all be over when Vorbis was dead.'

Didactylos stared into his inner world.

'It takes a long time for people like Vorbis to die. They leave echoes in history.'

'I know what you mean.'

'How's Urn's steam machine?' said Didactylos.

'I think he's a bit upset about it,' said Brutha.

Didactylos cackled and banged his stick on the ground.

'Hah! He's learning! Everything works both ways!'

'It should do,' said Brutha.

Something like a golden comet sped across the sky of the Discworld. Om soared like an eagle, buoyed up by the freshness, by the *strength* of the belief. For as long as it lasted, anyway. Belief this hot, this desperate, never lasted long. Human minds could not sustain it. But while it did last, he was *strong*.

The central spire of Cori Celesti rises up from the mountains at the Hub, ten vertical miles of green ice and snow, topped by the turrets and domes of Dunmanifestin.

There the gods of the Discworld live.

At the least, any god who is anybody. And it is strange that, although it takes years of effort and work and scheming for a god to get there, once there they never seem to do a lot apart from drink too much and indulge in a little mild corruption. Many systems of government follow the same broad lines.

They play games. They tend to be very simple games, because gods are easily bored by complicated things. It is strange that, while small gods can have one aim in mind for millions of years, *are* in fact one aim, large gods seem to have the attention span of the common mosquito.

And style? If the gods of the Discworld were people they would think that three plaster ducks is a bit avant-garde.

There was a double door at the end of the main hall.

It rocked to a thunderous knocking.

The gods looked up vaguely from their various preoccupations, shrugged and turned away.

The doors burst inward.

Om strode through the debris, looking around with the air of one who has a search to complete and not a lot of time to do it in.

'Right,' he said.

Io, God of Thunder, looked up from his throne and waved his hammer threateningly.

'Who are you?'

Om strode towards the throne, picked up Io by his toga, and gave a quick jab with his forehead.

Hardly anyone really believes in thunder gods any more . . .

'Ow!'

'Listen, friend, I've got no time for talking to some pantywaister in a sheet. Where's the gods of Ephebe and Tsort?'

Io, clutching at his nose, waved vaguely towards the centre of the hall.

'You nidn't naf to ndo dat!' he said reproachfully.

Om strode across the hall.

In the centre of the room was what at first looked like a round table, and then looked like a model of the Discworld, Turtle, elephants and all, and then in some undefinable way looked like the *real* Discworld, seen from far off yet brought up close to. There was something subtly wrong about the distances, a feeling of vast space curled up small. But possibly the real Discworld wasn't covered with a network of glowing lines, hovering just above the surface. Or perhaps miles above the surface?

Om hadn't seen this before, but he knew what it was. Both a wave and a particle; both a map and the place mapped. If he focused on the tiny glittering dome on top of the tiny Cori Celesti, he would undoubtedly see himself, looking down on an even smaller model . . . and so on, down to the point where the universe coiled up like the tail of an ammonite, a kind of creature that lived millions of years ago and never believed in any gods at all . . .

The gods clustered around it, watching intently.

Om elbowed aside a minor Goddess of Plenty.

There were dice floating just above the world, and a mess of little clay figures and gaming counters. You didn't need to be even slightly omnipotent to know what was going on.

'He hid by nose!'

Om turned around.

'I never forget a face, friend. Just take yours away, right? While you still have some left?'

He turned back to the game.

'S'cuse me,' said a voice by his waist. He looked down at a very large newt.

'Yes?'

'You not supposed do that here. No Smiting. Not up *here*. It the rules. You want fight, you get your humans fight his humans.'

'Who're you?'

'P'tang-P'tang, me.'

'*You're* a god?'

'Definite.'

'Yeah? How many worshippers have you got?'

'Fifty-one!'

The newt looked at him hopefully, and added, 'Is that lots? Can't count.'

It pointed at a rather crudely moulded figure on the beach in Omnia and said, 'But got a stake!'

Om looked at the figure of the little fisherman.

'When he dies, you'll have fifty worshippers,' he said.

'That more or less than fifty-one?'

'A lot less.'

'Definite?'

'Yes.'

'No one tell me that.'

There were several dozen gods watching the beach. Om vaguely remembered the Ephebian statues. There was the goddess with the badly carved owl. Yes.

Om rubbed his head. This wasn't god-like thinking. It seemed simpler when you were up here. It was all a game. You forgot that it wasn't a game down there. People died. Bits got chopped off. We're like eagles up here, he thought. Sometimes we show a tortoise how to fly.

Then we let go.

He said, to the occult world in general, 'There's people going to die down there.'

A Tsortean God of the Sun did not even bother to look round.

'That's what they're for,' he said. In his hand he was holding a dice box that looked very much like a human skull with rubies in the eye-sockets.

'Ah, yes,' said Om. 'I forgot that, for a moment.' He looked at the skull, and then turned to the little Goddess of Plenty.

'What's this, love? A cornucopia? Can I have a look? Thanks.'

Om emptied some of the fruit out. Then he nudged the Newt God.

'If I was you, friend, I'd find something long and hefty,' he said.

'Is one less than fifty-one?' said P'Tang-P'Tang.

'It's the same,' said Om, firmly. He eyed the back of the Tsortean God's head.

'But you have thousands,' said the Newt God. 'You fight for thousands.'

Om rubbed his forehead. I spent too long down there, he thought. I can't stop thinking at ground level.

'I think,' he said, 'I think, if you want thousands, you have to fight for one.' He tapped the Solar God on the shoulder. 'Hey, sunshine?'

When the God looked around, Om broke the cornucopia over his head.

It wasn't a normal thunderclap. It stuttered like the shyness of supernovas, great ripping billows of sound that tore up the sky. Sand fountained up and whirled across the recumbent bodies lying face down on the beach. Lightning stabbed down, and sympathetic fire leapt from spear-tip and sword-point.

Simony looked up at the booming darkness.

'What the hell's happening?' He nudged the body next to him.

It was Argavisti. They stared at one another.

More thunder smashed across the sky. Waves climbed up one another to rip into the fleet. Hull drifted with awful grace into hull, giving the bass line of the thunder a counterpoint of groaning wood.

A broken spar thudded into the sand by Simony's head.

'We're dead if we stay here,' he said. 'Come on.'

They staggered through the spray and sand, amidst groups of cowering and praying soldiers, fetching up against something hard, half-covered.

They crawled into the calm under the Turtle.

Other people had already had the same idea. Shadowy figures sat or sprawled in the darkness. Urn sat dejectedly on his toolbox. There was a hint of gutted fish.

'The gods are angry,' said Borvorius.

'Bloody furious,' said Argavisti.

'I'm not that happy myself,' said Simony. 'Gods? Huh!'

'This is no time for impiety,' said Rham-ap-Efan.

There was a shower of grapes outside.

'Can't think of a better one,' said Simony.

A piece of cornucopia shrapnel bounced off the roof of the Turtle, which rocked on its spiked wheels.

'But why be angry with us?' said Argavisti. 'We're doing what they want.'

Borvorius tried to smile. 'Gods, eh?' he said. 'Can't live with 'em, can't live without 'em.'

Someone nudged Simony, and passed him a soggy cigarette. It was a Tsortean soldier. Despite himself, he took a puff.

'It's good tobacco,' he said. 'The stuff we grow tastes like camel's droppings.'

He passed it along to the next hunched figure.

THANK YOU.

Borvorius produced a flask from somewhere.

'Will you go to hell if you have a drop of spirit?' he said.

'So it seems,' said Simony, absently. Then he noticed the flask. 'Oh, you mean alcohol? Probably. But who cares? I won't be able to get near the fire for priests. Thanks.'

'Pass it round.'

THANK YOU.

The Turtle rocked to a thunderbolt.

'G'n y'himbe bo?'

They all looked at the pieces of raw fish, and Fasta Benj's hopeful expression.

'I could rake some of the coals out of the firebox from here,' said Urn, after a while.

Someone tapped Simony on the shoulder, creating a strange tingling sensation.

THANK YOU. I HAVE TO GO.

As he took it he was aware of the rush of air, a sudden breath in the universe. He looked around in time to see a wave lift a ship out of the water and smash it against the dunes.

A distant scream coloured the wind.

The soldiers stared.

'There were people under there,' said Argavisti.

Simony dropped the flask.

'Come on,' he said.

And no one, as they hauled on timbers in the teeth of the gale, as Urn applied everything he knew about levers, as they used their helmets as shovels to dig under the wreckage, asked who it was they were digging for, or what kind of uniform they'd been wearing.

Fog rolled in on the wind, hot and flashing with electricity, and still the sea pounded down.

Simony hauled on a spar, and then found the weight lessen as someone grasped the other end. He looked up into Brutha's eyes.

'Don't say anything,' said Brutha.

'Gods are doing this to us?'

'Don't say anything!'

'I've got to know!'

'It's better than *us* doing this to us, isn't it?'

'There's still people who never got off the ships!'

'No one ever said it was going to be nice!'

Simony pulled aside some planking. There was a man there, armour and leathers so stained as to be unrecognisable, but alive.

'Listen,' said Simony, as the wind whipped at him, 'I'm not giving in! You've haven't won! I'm not doing this for any sort of god, whether they exist or not! I'm doing it for other people! *And stop smiling like that!*'

A couple of dice dropped on to the sand. They sparkled and crackled for a while and then evaporated.

The sea calmed. The fog went ragged and curled into nothingness. There was still a haze in the air, but the sun was at least visible again, if only as a brighter area in the dome of the sky.

Once again, there was the sensation of the universe drawing breath.

The gods appeared, transparent and shimmering in and out of focus. The sun glinted off a hint of golden curls, and wings, and lyres.

When they spoke, they spoke in unison, their voices drifting ahead or trailing behind the others, as always happens when a group of people are trying to faithfully repeat something they've been told to say.

Om was in the throng, standing right behind the Tsortean God of Thunder with a faraway expression on his face. It was noticeable, if only to Brutha, that the Thunder God's right arm disappeared up behind his own back in a way that, if such a thing could be imagined, would suggest that someone was twisting it to the edge of pain.

What the gods said was heard by each combatant in his own language, and according to his own understanding. It boiled down to:

I. This is Not a Game.

II. Here and Now, You are Alive.

And then it was over.

'You'd make a good bishop,' said Brutha.

'Me?' said Didactylos. 'I'm a philosopher!'

'Good. It's about time we had one.'

'And an Ephebian!'

'Good. You can think up a better way of ruling the country. Priests shouldn't do it. They can't think about it properly. Nor can soldiers.'

'Thank you,' said Simony.

They were sitting in the Cenobiarch's garden. Far overhead an eagle circled, looking for anything that wasn't a tortoise.

'I like the idea of democracy. You have to have someone everyone distrusts,' said Brutha. 'That way, everyone's happy. Think about it. Simony?'

'Yes?'

'I'm making you head of the Quisition.'

'What?'

'I want it stopped. And I want it stopped the hard way.'

'You want me to kill all the inquisitors? Right!'

'No. That's the easy way. I want as few deaths as possible. Those who enjoyed it, perhaps. But only those. Now . . . where's Urn?'

The Moving Turtle was still on the beach, wheels buried in the sand blown about by the storm. Urn had been too embarrassed to try to unearth it.

'The last I saw, he was tinkering with the door mechanism,' said Didactylos. 'Never happier than when he's tinkering with things.'

'Yes. We shall have to find things to keep him occupied. Irrigation. Architecture. That sort of thing.'

'And what are *you* going to do?' said Simony.

'I've got to copy out the Library,' said Brutha.

'But you can't read and write,' said Didactylos.

'No. But I can see and draw. Two copies. One to keep here.'

'Plenty of room when we burn the Septateuch,' said Simony.

'No burning of anything. You have to take a step at a time,' said Brutha. He looked out at the shimmering line of the desert. Funny. He'd been as happy as he'd ever been in the desert.

'And then . . .' he began.

'Yes?'

Brutha lowered his eyes, to the farmlands and villages around the Citadel. He sighed.

'And then we'd better get on with things,' he said. 'Every day.'

Fasta Benj rowed home, in a thoughtful frame of mind.

It had been a very good few days. He'd met a lot of new people and sold quite a lot of fish. P'Tang-P'Tang, with his lesser servants, had talked personally to him, making him promise not to wage war on some place he'd never heard of. He'd agreed.*

Some of the new people had shown him this amazing way of making lightning. You hit this rock with this piece of hard stuff and you got little bits of lightning which dropped on to dry stuff which got red and hot like the sun. If you put more wood on it got bigger and if you put a fish on it got black but if you were quick it didn't get black but got brown and tasted better than anything he'd ever tasted, although this was not difficult. And he'd been given some knives not made out of rock and cloth not made out of reeds and, all in all, life was looking up for Fasta Benj and his people.

He wasn't sure why *lots* of people would want to hit Pacha Moj's uncle with a big rock, but it definitely escalated the pace of technological progress.

No one, not even Brutha, noticed that old Lu-Tze wasn't around any more. Not being noticed, either as being present or absent, is part of a history monk's stock in trade.

In fact he'd packed his broom and his bonsai mountains and had gone by secret tunnels and devious means to the hidden valley in the central peaks, where the abbot was waiting for him. The abbot was playing chess in the long gallery that overlooked the valley. Fountains bubbled in the gardens, and swallows flew in and out of the windows.

'All went well?' said the abbot, without looking up.

'Very well, lord,' said Lu-Tze. 'I had to *nudge* things a little, though.'

'I wish you wouldn't do that sort of thing,' said the abbot, fingering a pawn. 'You'll overstep the mark one day.'

'It's the history we've got these days,' said Lu-Tze. 'Very shoddy stuff, lord. I have to patch it up all the time –'

'Yes, yes –'

'We used to get much better history in the old days.'

'Things were always better than they are now. It's in the nature of things.'

---

* Fasta Benj's people had no word for war, since they had no one to fight and life was quite tough enough as it was. P'Tang-P'Tang's words had arrived as: 'remember when Pacha Moj hit his uncle with big rock? Like that, only more worse.'

'Yes, lord. Lord?'

The abbot looked up in mild exasperation.

'Er . . . you know the books say that Brutha died and there was a century of terrible warfare?'

'You know my eyesight isn't what it was, Lu-Tze.'

'Well . . . it's not entirely like that now.'

'Just so long as it all turns out all right in the end,' said the abbot.

'Yes, lord,' said the history monk.

'There are a few weeks before your next assignment. Why don't you have a little rest?'

'Thank you, lord. I thought I might go down to the forest and watch a few falling trees.'

'Good practice. Good practice. Mind always on the job, eh?'

As Lu-Tze left, the abbot glanced up at his opponent.

'Good man, that,' he said. 'Your move.'

The opponent looked long and hard at the board.

The abbot waited to see what long-term, devious strategies were being evolved. Then his opponent tapped a piece with a bony finger.

REMIND ME AGAIN, he said, HOW THE LITTLE HORSE-SHAPED ONES MOVE.

Eventually Brutha died, in unusual circumstances.

He had reached a great age, but this at least was not unusual in the Church. As he said, you had to keep busy, every day.

He rose at dawn, and wandered over to the window. He liked to watch the sunrise.

They hadn't got around to replacing the Temple doors. Apart from anything else, even Urn hadn't been able to think of a way of removing the weirdly contorted heap of molten metal. So they'd just built steps over them. And after a year or two people had quite accepted it, and said it was probably a symbol. Not *of* anything, exactly, but still a symbol. Definitely symbolic.

But the sun did shine off the copper dome of the Library. Brutha made a mental note to enquire about the progress of the new wing. There were too many complaints about overcrowding these days.

People came from everywhere to visit the Library. It was the biggest non-magical library in the world. Half the philosophers of Ephebe seemed to live there now, and Omnia was even producing one or two of its own. And even priests were coming to spend some time in it, because of the collection of religious books. There were one thousand, two hundred and eighty-three religious books in there now, each one – according to itself – the only book any man need ever read. It was sort of nice to see them all together. As Didactylos used to say, you had to laugh.

It was while Brutha was eating his breakfast that the subdeacon whose job it was to read him his appointments for the day, and tactfully make sure he wasn't wearing his underpants on the outside, shyly offered him congratulations.

'Mmm?' said Brutha, his gruel dripping off the spoon.

'One hundred years,' said the subdeacon. 'Since you walked in the desert, sir.'

'Really? I thought it was, mm, fifty years? Can't be more than sixty years, boy.'

'Uh, one hundred years, lord. We had a look in the records.'

'Really. One hundred years? One hundred years' time?' Brutha laid down his spoon very carefully, and stared at the plain white wall opposite him. The subdeacon found himself turning to see what it was the Cenobiarch was looking at, but there was nothing, only the whiteness of the wall.

'One hundred years,' mused Brutha. 'Mmm. Good lord. I forgot.' He laughed. 'I *forgot*. One hundred years, eh? But here and now, we –'

The subdeacon turned round.

'Cenobiarch?'

He stepped closer, the blood draining from his face.

'Lord?'

He turned and ran for help.

Brutha's body toppled forward almost gracefully, smacking into the table. The bowl overturned, and gruel dripped down on to the floor.

And then Brutha stood up, without a second glance at his corpse.

'Hah. I wasn't expecting you,' he said.

Death stopped leaning against the wall.

How fortunate you were.

'But there's still such a lot to be done . . .'

Yes. There always is.

Brutha followed the gaunt figure through the wall where, instead of the privy that occupied the far side in normal space, there was . . .

. . . black sand.

The light was brilliant, crystalline, in a black sky filled with stars.

'Ah. There really *is* a desert. Does everyone get this?' said Brutha.

WHO KNOWS?

'And what is at the end of the desert?'

JUDGEMENT.

Brutha considered this.

'*Which* end?'

Death grinned and stepped aside.

What Brutha had thought was a rock in the sand was a hunched figure, sitting clutching its knees. It looked paralysed with fear.

He stared.

'Vorbis?' he said.

He looked at Death.

'But Vorbis died a hundred years ago!'

YES. HE HAD TO WALK IT ALL ALONE. ALL ALONE WITH HIMSELF. IF HE DARED.

'He's been here for a hundred years?'

POSSIBLY NOT. TIME IS DIFFERENT HERE. IT IS . . . MORE PERSONAL.

'Ah. You mean a hundred years can pass like a few seconds?'

A HUNDRED YEARS CAN PASS LIKE INFINITY.

The black-on-black eyes stared imploringly at Brutha, who reached out automatically, without thinking . . . and then hesitated.

HE WAS A MURDERER, said Death. AND A CREATOR OF MURDERERS. A TORTURER. WITHOUT PASSION. CRUEL. CALLOUS. COMPASSIONLESS.

'Yes. I know. He's Vorbis,' said Brutha. Vorbis changed people. Sometimes he changed them into dead people. But he always changed them. That was his triumph.

He sighed.

'But I'm me,' he said.

Vorbis stood up, uncertainly, and followed Brutha across the desert.

Death watched them walk away.

HOGFATHER

To the guerilla bookshop
manager known to friends as
'ppint' for asking me, many years
ago, the question Susan asks in
this book. I'm surprised more
people haven't asked it . . .

And to too many absent friends.

Everything starts somewhere, although many physicists disagree.

But people have always been dimly aware of the problem with the start of things. They wonder aloud how the snowplough driver gets to work, or how the makers of dictionaries look up the spelling of the words. Yet there is the constant desire to find some point in the twisting, knotting, ravelling nets of space-time on which a metaphorical finger can be put to indicate that *here*, here, is the point where it all began . . .

Something began when the Guild of Assassins enrolled Mister Teatime, who saw things differently from other people, and one of the ways that he saw things differently from other people was in seeing other people as things (later, Lord Downey of the Guild said, 'We took pity on him because he'd lost both parents at an early age. I think that, on reflection, we should have wondered a bit more about that.').

But it was much earlier even than that when most people forgot that the very oldest stories are, sooner or later, about blood. Later on they took the blood out to make the stories more acceptable to children, or at least to the people who had to read them to children rather than the children themselves (who, on the whole, are quite keen on blood provided it's being shed by the deserving[*]), and then wondered where the stories went.

And earlier still when something in the darkness of the deepest caves and gloomiest forests thought: what *are* they, these creatures? I will observe them . . .

And much, much earlier than that, when the Discworld was formed, drifting onwards through space atop four elephants on the shell of the giant turtle, Great A'Tuin.

Possibly, as it moves, it gets tangled like a blind man in a cobwebbed house in those highly specialized little space-time strands that try to breed in every history they encounter, stretching them and breaking them and tugging them into new shapes.

---

[*] That is to say, those who deserve to shed blood. Or possibly not. You never quite know with some kids.

Or possibly not, of course. The philosopher Didactylos has summed up an alternative hypothesis as 'Things just happen. What the hell.'

The senior wizards of Unseen University stood and looked at the door.

There was no doubt that whoever had shut it wanted it to stay shut. Dozens of nails secured it to the door frame. Planks had been nailed right across. And finally it had, up until this morning, been hidden by a bookcase that had been put in front of it.

'And there's the sign, Ridcully,' said the Dean. 'You *have* read it, I assume. You know? The sign which says "Do not, under any circumstances, open this door"?'

'Of course I've read it,' said Ridcully. 'Why d'yer think I want it opened?'

'Er . . . why?' said the Lecturer in Recent Runes.

'To see why they wanted it shut, of course.'*

He gestured to Modo, the University's gardener and odd-job dwarf, who was standing by with a crowbar.

'Go to it, lad.'

The gardener saluted. 'Right you are, sir.'

Against a background of splintering timber, Ridcully went on: 'It says on the plans that this was a bathroom. There's nothing frightening about a bathroom, for gods' sake. I *want* a bathroom. I'm fed up with sluicing down with you fellows. It's unhygienic. You can catch stuff. My father told me that. Where you get lots of people bathing together, the Verruca Gnome is running around with his little sack.'

'Is that like the Tooth Fairy?' said the Dean sarcastically.

'I'm in charge here and I want a bathroom of my own,' said Ridcully firmly. 'And that's all there is to it, all right? I want a bathroom in time for Hogswatchnight, understand?'

And that's a problem with beginnings, of course. Sometimes, when you're dealing with occult realms that have quite a different attitude to time, you get the effect a little way before the cause.

From somewhere on the edge of hearing came a *glingleglingleglingle* noise, like little silver bells.

*

* This exchange contains almost all you need to know about human civilization. At least, those bits of it that are now under the sea, fenced off or still smoking.

At about the same time as the Archchancellor was laying down the law, Susan Sto-Helit was sitting up in bed, reading by candlelight.

Frost patterns curled across the windows.

She enjoyed these early evenings. Once she had put the children to bed she was more or less left to herself. Mrs Gaiter was pathetically scared of giving her any instructions even though she paid Susan's wages.

Not that the wages were important, of course. What was important was that she was being her Own Person and holding down a Real Job. And being a governess *was* a real job. The only tricky bit had been the embarrassment when her employer found out that she was a duchess, because in Mrs Gaiter's book, which was a rather short book with big handwriting, the upper crust wasn't supposed to work. It was supposed to loaf around. It was all Susan could do to stop her curtseying when they met.

A flicker made her turn her head.

The candle flame was streaming out horizontally, as though in a howling wind.

She looked up. The curtains billowed away from the window, which –

– flung itself open with a clatter.

But there was no wind.

At least, no wind in this world.

Images formed in her mind. A red ball . . . The sharp smell of snow . . . And then they were gone, and instead there were . . .

'Teeth?' said Susan, aloud. 'Teeth, *again?*'

She blinked. When she opened her eyes the window was, as she knew it would be, firmly shut. The curtain hung demurely. The candle flame was innocently upright. Oh, no, not again. Not after all this time. Everything had been going so well –

'Thusan?'

She looked around. Her door had been pushed open and a small figure stood there, barefoot in a nightdress.

She sighed. 'Yes, Twyla?'

'I'm afraid of the monster in the cellar, Thusan. It's going to eat me up.'

Susan shut her book firmly and raised a warning finger.

'What have I told you about trying to sound ingratiatingly cute, Twyla?' she said.

The little girl said, 'You said I mustn't. You said that exaggerated lisping is a hanging offence and I only do it to get attention.'

'Good. Do you know what monster it is this time?'

'It's the big hairy one wif —'

Susan raised the finger. 'Uh?' she warned.

'— *with* eight arms,' Twyla corrected herself.

'What, again? Oh, all right.'

She got out of bed and put on her dressing gown, trying to stay quite calm while the child watched her. *So they were coming back.* Oh, not the monster in the cellar. That was all in a day's work. But it looked as if she was going to start remembering the future again.

She shook her head. However far you ran away, you always caught yourself up.

But *monsters* were easy, at least. She'd learned how to deal with monsters. She picked up the poker from the nursery fender and went down the back stairs, with Twyla following her.

The Gaiters were having a dinner party. Muffled voices came from the direction of the dining room.

Then, as she crept past, a door opened and yellow light spilled out and a voice said, 'Ye gawds, there's a gel in a nightshirt out here with a *poker!*'

She saw figures silhouetted in the light and made out the worried face of Mrs Gaiter.

'Susan? Er . . . what are you doing?'

Susan looked at the poker and then back at the woman. 'Twyla said she's afraid of a monster in the cellar, Mrs Gaiter.'

'And yer going to attack it with a poker, eh?' said one of the guests. There was a strong atmosphere of brandy and cigars.

'Yes,' said Susan simply.

'Susan's our governess,' said Mrs Gaiter. 'Er . . . I told you about her.'

There was a change in the expression on the faces peering out from the dining room. It became a sort of amused respect.

'She beats up monsters with a poker?' said someone.

'Actually, that's a very clever idea,' said someone else. 'Little gel gets it into her head there's a monster in the cellar, you go in with the poker and make a few bashing noises while the child listens, and then everything's all right. Good thinkin', that girl. Ver' sensible. Ver' modern.'

'Is that what you're doing, Susan?' said Mrs Gaiter anxiously.

'Yes, Mrs Gaiter,' said Susan obediently.

'This I've got to watch, by Io! It's not every day you see monsters beaten up by a gel,' said the man behind her. There was a swish of silk and a cloud of cigar smoke as the diners poured out into the hall.

Susan sighed again and went down the cellar stairs, while Twyla sat demurely at the top, hugging her knees.

A door opened and shut.

There was a short period of silence and then a terrifying scream. One woman fainted and a man dropped his cigar.

'You don't have to worry, everything will be all right.' said Twyla calmly. 'She always wins. Everything will be all right.'

There were thuds and clangs, and then a whirring noise, and finally a sort of bubbling.

Susan pushed open the door. The poker was bent at right angles. There was nervous applause.

'Ver' well done,' said a guest. 'Ver' persykological. Clever idea, that, bendin' the poker. And I expect you're not afraid any more, eh, little girl?'

'No,' said Twyla.

'Ver' persykological.'

'Susan says don't get afraid, get angry,' said Twyla.

'Er, thank you, Susan,' said Mrs Gaiter, now a trembling bouquet of nerves. 'And, er, now, Sir Geoffrey, if you'd all like to come back into the parlour – I mean, the drawing room –'

The party went back up the hall. The last thing Susan heard before the door shut was 'Dashed convincin', the way she bent the poker like that –'

She waited.

'Have they all gone, Twyla?'

'Yes, Susan.'

'Good.' Susan went back into the cellar and emerged towing something large and hairy with eight legs. She managed to haul it up the steps and down the other passage to the back yard, where she kicked it out. It would evaporate before dawn.

'That's what *we* do to monsters,' she said.

Twyla watched carefully.

'And now it's bed for you, my girl,' said Susan, picking her up.

'C'n I have the poker in my room for the night?'

'All right.'

'It only kills monsters, doesn't it . . .?' the child said sleepily, as Susan carried her upstairs.

'That's right,' Susan said. 'All kinds.'

She put the girl to bed next to her brother and leaned the poker against the toy cupboard.

The poker was made of some cheap metal with a brass knob on

the end. She would, Susan reflected, give quite a lot to be able to use it on the children's previous governess.

'G'night.'

'Goodnight.'

She went back to her own small bedroom and got back into bed, watching the curtains suspiciously.

It would be nice to think she'd imagined it. It would also be *stupid* to think that, too. But she'd been nearly normal for two years now, making her own way in the real world, never remembering the future at all . . .

Perhaps she *had* just dreamed things (but even dreams could be real . . .).

She tried to ignore the long thread of wax that suggested the candle had, just for a few seconds, streamed in the wind.

As Susan sought sleep, Lord Downey sat in his study catching up on the paperwork.

Lord Downey was an assassin. Or, rather, an Assassin. The capital letter was important. It separated those curs who went around murdering people for money from the gentlemen who were occasionally consulted by other gentlemen who wished to have removed, for a consideration, any inconvenient razorblades from the candyfloss of life.

The members of the Guild of Assassins considered themselves cultured men who enjoyed good music and food and literature. And they knew the value of human life. To a penny, in many cases.

Lord Downey's study was oak-panelled and well carpeted. The furniture was very old and quite worn, but the wear was the wear that comes only when very good furniture is carefully used over several centuries. It was *matured* furniture.

A log fire burned in the grate. In front of it a couple of dogs were sleeping in the tangled way of large hairy dogs everywhere.

Apart from the occasional doggy snore or the crackle of a shifting log, there were no other sounds but the scratching of Lord Downey's pen and the ticking of the longcase clock by the door . . . small, private noises which only served to define the silence.

At least, this was the case until someone cleared their throat.

The sound suggested very clearly that the purpose of the exercise was not to erase the presence of a troublesome bit of biscuit, but merely to indicate in the politest possible way the presence of the throat.

Downey stopped writing but did not raise his head.

Then, after what appeared to be some consideration, he said in a businesslike voice, 'The doors are locked. The windows are barred. The dogs do not appear to have woken up. The squeaky floorboards haven't. Other little arrangements which I will not specify seem to have been bypassed. That severely limits the possibilities. I really doubt that you are a ghost and gods generally do not announce themselves so politely. You could, of course, be Death, but I don't believe he bothers with such niceties and, besides, I am feeling quite well. Hmm.'

Something hovered in the air in front of his desk.

'My teeth are in fine condition so you are unlikely to be the Tooth Fairy. I've always found that a stiff brandy before bedtime quite does away with the need for the Sandman. And, since I can carry a tune quite well, I suspect I'm not likely to attract the attention of Old Man Trouble. Hmm.'

The figure drifted a little nearer.

'I suppose a gnome could get through a mousehole, but I have traps down,' Downey went on. 'Bogeymen can walk through walls but would be very loath to reveal themselves. Really, you have me at a loss. Hmm?'

And then he looked up.

A grey robe hung in the air. It appeared to be occupied, in that it had a shape, although the occupant was not visible.

The prickly feeling crept over Downey that the occupant wasn't invisible, merely not, in any physical sense, there at all.

'Good evening,' he said.

The robe said, Good evening, Lord Downey.

His brain registered the words. His ears swore they hadn't heard them.

But you did not become head of the Assassins' Guild by taking fright easily. Besides, the thing wasn't frightening. It was, thought Downey, astonishingly dull. If monotonous drabness could take on a shape, this would be the shape it would choose.

'You appear to be a spectre,' he said.

Our nature is not a matter for discussion, arrived in his head. We offer you a commission.

'You wish someone inhumed?' said Downey.

Brought to an end.

Downey considered this. It was not as unusual as it appeared. There were precedents. Anyone could buy the services of the Guild. Several zombies had, in the past, employed the Guild to settle scores with their murderers. In fact the Guild, he liked to think, practised the ultimate democracy. You didn't need intelligence, social position, beauty or charm to hire it. You just needed money which, unlike the other stuff, was available to everyone. Except for the poor, of course, but there was no helping some people.

'Brought to an end ...' That was an odd way of putting it.

'We can –' he began.

The payment will reflect the difficulty of the task.

'Our scale of fees –'

The payment will be three million dollars.

Downey sat back. That was four times higher than any fee yet earned by any member of the Guild, and *that* had been a special family rate, including overnight guests.

'No questions asked, I assume?' he said, buying time.

No questions answered.

'But does the suggested fee represent the difficulty involved? The client is heavily guarded?'

Not guarded at all. But almost certainly impossible to delete with conventional weapons.

Downey nodded. This was not necessarily a big problem, he said to himself. The Guild had amassed quite a few unconventional weapons over the years. Delete? An unusual way of putting it ...

'We like to know for whom we are working,' he said.

We are sure you do.

'I mean that we need to know your name. Or names. In strict client confidentiality, of course. We have to write something down in our files.'

You may think of us as ... the Auditors.

'Really? What is it you audit?'

Everything.

'I think we need to know something about you.'

We are the people with three million dollars.

Downey took the point, although he didn't like it. Three million dollars could buy a lot of no questions.

'Really?' he said. 'In the circumstances, since you are a new client, I think we would like payment in advance.'

As you wish. The gold is now in your vaults.

'You mean that it will shortly be in our vaults,' said Downey.

No. It has always been in your vaults. We know this because we have just put it there.

Downey watched the empty hood for a moment, and then without shifting his gaze he reached out and picked up the speaking tube.

'Mr Winvoe?' he said, after whistling into it. 'Ah. Good. Tell me, how much do we have in our vaults at the moment? Oh, approximately. To the nearest million, say.' He held the tube away from his ear for a moment, and then spoke into it again. 'Well, be a good chap and check anyway, will you?'

He hung up the tube and placed his hands flat on the desk in front of him.

'Can I offer you a drink while we wait?' he said.

Yes. We believe so.

Downey stood up with some relief and walked over to his large drinks cabinet. His hand hovered over the Guild's ancient and valuable tantalus, with its labelled decanters of Mur, Nig, Trop and Yksihw.*

'And what would you like to drink?' he said, wondering where the Auditor kept its mouth. His hand hovered for just a moment over the smallest decanter, marked Nosiop.

We do not drink.

'But you did just say I could offer you a drink . . .'

Indeed. We judge you fully capable of performing that action.

'Ah.' Downey's hand hesitated over the whisky decanter, and then he thought better of it. At that point, the speaking tube whistled.

'Yes, Mr Winvoe? Really? Indeed? I myself have frequently found loose change under sofa cushions, it's amazing how it mou . . . No, no, I wasn't being . . . Yes, I *did* have some reason to . . . No, no blame attaches to you in any . . . No, I could hardly see how it . . . Yes, go and have a rest, what a good idea. Thank you.'

He hung up the tube again. The cowl hadn't moved.

'We will need to know where, when and, of course, *who*,' he said, after a moment.

The cowl nodded. The location is not on any map. We would like the task to be completed within the week. This is essential. As for the who . . .

A drawing appeared on Downey's desk and in his head arrived the words: Let us call him the Fat Man.

'Is this a joke?' said Downey.

We do not joke.

No, you don't, do you, Downey thought. He drummed his fingers.

---

* It's a sad and terrible thing that high-born folk really have thought that the servants would be totally fooled if spirits were put into decanters that were cunningly labelled *backwards*. And also throughout history the more politically conscious butler has taken it on trust, and with rather more justification, that his employers will not notice if the whisky is topped up with eniru.

'There are many who would say this . . . person does not exist,' he said.

He must exist. How else could you so readily recognize his picture? And many are in correspondence with him.

'Well, yes, of course, in a *sense* he exists . . .'

In a sense everything exists. It is cessation of existence that concerns us here.

'Finding him would be a little difficult.'

You will find persons on any street who can tell you his approximate address.

'Yes, of course,' said Downey, wondering why anyone would call them 'persons'. It was an odd usage. 'But, as you say, I doubt that they could give a map reference. And even then, *how* could the . . . the Fat Man *be* inhumed? A glass of poisoned sherry, perhaps?'

The cowl had no face to crack a smile.

You misunderstand the nature of employment, it said in Downey's head.

He bridled at this. Assassins were never *employed*. They were engaged or retained or commissioned, but never *employed*. Only servants were employed.

'What is it that I misunderstand, exactly?' he said.

We pay. You find the ways and means.

The cowl began to fade.

'How can I contact you?' said Downey.

We will contact *you*. We know where you are. We know where everyone is.

The figure vanished. At the same moment the door was flung open to reveal the distraught figure of Mr Winvoe, the Guild Treasurer.

'Excuse me, my lord, but I really had to come up!' He flung some discs on the desk. 'Look at them!'

Downey carefully picked up a golden circle. It looked like a small coin, but –

'No denomination!' said Winvoe. 'No heads, no tails, no milling! It's just a blank disc! They're all just blank discs!'

Downey opened his mouth to say, 'Valueless?' He realized that he was half hoping that this was the case. If they, whoever *they* were, had paid in worthless metal then there wasn't even the glimmering of a contract. But he could see this wasn't the case. Assassins learned to recognize money early in their careers.

'Blank discs,' he said, 'of pure gold.'

Winvoe nodded mutely.

'That,' said Downey, 'will do nicely.'

'It *must* be magical!' said Winvoe. 'And we *never* accept magical money!'

Downey bounced the coin on the desk a couple of times. It made a satisfyingly rich thunking noise. It *wasn't* magical. Magical money would look real, because its whole purpose was to deceive. But this didn't need to ape something as human and adulterated as mere currency. This is gold, it told his fingers. Take it or leave it.

Downey sat and thought, while Winvoe stood and worried.

'We'll take it,' he said.

'But –'

'Thank you, Mr Winvoe. That is my decision,' said Downey. He stared into space for a while, and then smiled. 'Is Mister Teatime still in the building?'

Winvoe stood back. 'I thought the council had agreed to dismiss him,' he said stiffly. 'After that business with –'

'Mister Teatime does not see the world in quite the same way as other people,' said Downey, picking up the picture from his desk and looking at it thoughtfully.

'Well, indeed, I think *that* is certainly true.'

'Please send him up.'

The Guild attracted all sorts of people, Downey reflected. He found himself wondering how it had come to attract Winvoe, for one thing. It was hard to imagine him stabbing anyone in the heart in case he got blood on the victim's wallet. Whereas Mister Teatime . . .

The problem was that the Guild took young boys and gave them a splendid education and incidentally taught them how to kill, cleanly and dispassionately, for money and for the good of society, or at least that part of society that had money, and what other kind of society was there?

But very occasionally you found you'd got someone like Mister Teatime, to whom the money was merely a distraction. Mister Teatime had a truly brilliant mind, but it was brilliant like a fractured mirror, all marvellous facets and rainbows but, ultimately, also something that was broken.

Mister Teatime enjoyed himself too much. And other people, also.

Downey had privately decided that some time soon Mister Teatime was going to meet with an accident. Like many people with no actual morals, Lord Downey *did* have standards, and Teatime repelled him. Assassination was a careful game, usually played against people who knew the rules themselves or at least could afford the services of those who did. There was considerable satisfaction in a clean kill. What there wasn't supposed to be was pleasure in a messy one. That sort of thing led to talk.

On the other hand, Teatime's corkscrew of a mind was exactly the tool to deal with something like this. And if he didn't . . . well, that was hardly Downey's fault, was it?

He turned his attention to the paperwork for a while. It was amazing how the stuff mounted up. But you had to deal with it. It wasn't as though they were murderers, after all . . .

There was a knock at the door. He pushed the paperwork aside and sat back.

'Come in, Mister Teatime,' he said. It never hurt to put the other fellow slightly in awe of you.

In fact the door was opened by one of the Guild's servants, carefully balancing a tea tray.

'Ah, Carter,' said Lord Downey, recovering magnificently. 'Just put it on the table over there, will you?'

'Yes, sir,' said Carter. He turned and nodded. 'Sorry, sir, I will go and fetch another cup directly, sir.'

'What?'

'For your visitor, sir.'

'What visitor? Oh, when Mister Teati—'

He stopped. He turned.

There was a young man sitting on the hearthrug, playing with the dogs.

'Mister Teatime!'

'It's pronounced Teh-ah-tim-eh, sir,' said Teatime, with just a hint of reproach. 'Everyone gets it wrong, sir.'

'How did you do *that*?'

'Pretty well, sir. I got mildly scorched on the last few feet, of course.'

There were some lumps of soot on the hearthrug. Downey realized he'd heard them fall, but that hadn't been particularly extraordinary. No one could get down the chimney. There was a heavy grid firmly in place near the top of the flue.

'But there's a blocked-in fireplace behind the old library,' said Teatime, apparently reading his thoughts. 'The flues connect, under the bars. It was really a stroll, sir.'

'Really . . .'

'Oh, yes, sir.'

Downey nodded. The tendency of old buildings to be honeycombed with sealed chimney flues was a fact you learned early in your career. And then, he told himself, you forgot. It always paid to put the other fellow in awe of you, too. He had forgotten they taught *that*, too.

'The dogs seem to like you,' he said.

'I get on well with animals, sir.'

Teatime's face was young and open and friendly. Or, at least, it smiled all the time. But the effect was spoiled for most people by the fact that it had only one eye. Some unexplained accident had taken the other one, and the missing orb had been replaced by a ball of glass. The result was disconcerting. But what bothered Lord Downey far more was the man's other eye, the one that might loosely be called normal. He'd never seen such a small and sharp pupil. Teatime looked at the world through a pinhole.

He found he'd retreated behind his desk again. There was that about Teatime. You always felt happier if you had something between you and him.

'You like animals, do you?' he said. 'I have a report here that says you nailed Sir George's dog to the ceiling.'

'Couldn't have it barking while I was working, sir.'

'Some people would have drugged it.'

'Oh.' Teatime looked despondent for a moment, but then he brightened. 'But I definitely fulfilled the contract, sir. There can be no doubt about that, sir. I checked Sir George's breathing with a mirror as instructed. It's in my report.'

'Yes, indeed.' Apparently the man's head had been several feet from his body at that point. It was a terrible thought that Teatime might see nothing incongruous about this.

'And ... the servants ...?' he said.

'Couldn't have them bursting in, sir.'

Downey nodded, half hypnotized by the glassy stare and the pinhole eyeball. No, you couldn't have them bursting in. And an Assassin might well face serious professional opposition, possibly even by people trained by the same teachers. But an old man and a maidservant who'd merely had the misfortune to be in the house at the time ...

There was no actual *rule*, Downey had to admit. It was just that, over the years, the Guild had developed a certain ethos and members tended to be very neat about their work, even shutting doors behind them and generally tidying up as they went. Hurting the harmless was worse than a transgression against the moral fabric of society, it was a breach of *good manners*. It was worse even than that. It was *bad taste*. But there was no actual *rule* ...

'That was all right, wasn't it, sir?' said Teatime, with apparent anxiety.

'It, uh . . . lacked elegance,' said Downey.

'Ah. Thank you, sir. I am always happy to be corrected. I shall remember that next time.'

Downey took a deep breath.

'It's about that I wish to talk,' he said. He held up the picture . . . what had the thing called him? . . . the Fat Man?

'As a matter of interest,' he said, 'how would you go about inhuming this . . . gentleman?'

Anyone else, he was sure, would have burst out laughing. They would have said things like 'Is this a joke, sir?' Teatime merely leaned forward, with a curious intent expression.

'Difficult, sir.'

'Certainly,' Downey agreed.

'I would need some time to prepare a plan, sir,' Teatime went on.

'Of course, and –'

There was a knock at the door and Carter came in with another cup and saucer. He nodded respectfully to Lord Downey and crept out again.

'Right, sir,' said Teatime.

'I'm sorry?' said Downey, momentarily distracted.

'I have now thought of a plan, sir,' said Teatime, patiently.

'You have?'

'Yes, sir.'

'As quickly as that?'

'Yes, sir.'

'Ye gods!'

'Well, sir, you know we are encouraged to consider hypothetical problems . . .?'

'Oh, yes. A very valuable exercise –' Downey stopped, and then looked shocked.

'You mean you have actually devoted time to considering how to inhume the Hogfather?' he said weakly. 'You've actually sat down and thought out how to do it? You've actually devoted your spare time to the problem?'

'Oh, yes, sir. And the Soul Cake Duck. And the Sandman. And Death.'

Downey blinked again. 'You've actually sat down and considered how to –'

'Yes, sir. I've amassed quite an interesting file. In my own time, of course.'

'I want to be quite certain about this, Mister Teatime. You . . . have . . . applied . . . yourself to a study of ways of killing *Death*?'

'Only as a hobby, sir.'

'Well, *yes*, hobbies, yes, I mean, I used to collect butterflies myself,' said Downey, recalling those first moments of awakening pleasure at the use of poison and the pin, 'but –'

'Actually, sir, the basic methodology is exactly the same as it would be for a human. Opportunity, geography, technique . . . You just have to work with the known facts about the individual concerned. Of course, with *this* one such a lot is known.'

'And you've worked it all out, have you?' said Downey, almost fascinated.

'Oh, a long time ago, sir.'

'When, may I ask?'

'I think it was when I was lying in bed one Hogswatchnight, sir.'

My gods, thought Downey, and to think that *I* just used to listen for sleigh bells.

'My word,' he said aloud.

'I may have to check some details, sir. I'd appreciate access to some of the books in the Dark Library. But, yes, I think I can see the basic shape.'

'And yet . . . this person . . . some people might say that he is technically immortal.'

'Everyone has their weak point, sir.'

'Even Death?'

'Oh, yes. Absolutely. Very much so.'

'Really?'

Downey drummed his fingers on the desk again. The boy couldn't possibly have a *real* plan, he told himself. He certainly had a skewed mind – skewed? It was a positive helix – but the Fat Man wasn't just another target in some mansion somewhere. It was reasonable to assume that people had tried to trap him before.

He felt happy about this. Teatime would fail, and possibly even fail fatally if his plan was stupid enough. And maybe the Guild would lose the gold, but maybe not.

'Very well,' he said. 'I don't need to know what your plan is.'

'That's just as well, sir.'

'What do you mean?'

'Because I don't propose to tell you, sir. You'd be obliged to disapprove of it.'

'I am amazed that you are so confident that it can work, Teatime.'

'I just think logically about the problem, sir,' said the boy. He sounded reproachful.

'Logically?' said Downey.

'I suppose I just see things differently from other people,' said Teatime.

It was a quiet day for Susan, although on the way to the park Gawain trod on a crack in the pavement. On purpose.

One of the many terrors conjured up by the previous governess's happy way with children had been the bears that waited around in the street to eat you if you stood on the cracks.

Susan had taken to carrying the poker under her respectable coat. One wallop generally did the trick. They were amazed that anyone else saw them.

'Gawain?' she said, eyeing a nervous bear who had suddenly spotted her and was now trying to edge away nonchalantly.

'Yes?'

'You meant to tread on that crack so that I'd have to thump some poor creature whose only fault is wanting to tear you limb from limb.'

'I was just skipping –'

'Quite. Real children don't go hoppity-skip unless they are on drugs.'

He grinned at her.

'If I catch you being twee again I will knot your arms behind your head,' said Susan levelly.

He nodded, and went to push Twyla off the swings.

Susan relaxed, satisfied. It was her personal discovery. Ridiculous threats didn't worry them at all, but they were obeyed. Especially the ones in graphic detail.

The previous governess had used various monsters and bogeymen as a form of discipline. There was always something waiting to eat or carry off bad boys and girls for crimes like stuttering or defiantly and aggravatingly persisting in writing with their left hand. There was always a Scissor Man waiting for a little girl who sucked her thumb, always a bogeyman in the cellar. Of such bricks is the innocence of childhood constructed.

Susan's attempts at getting them to disbelieve in the things only caused the problems to get worse.

Twyla had started to wet the bed. This may have been a crude form of defence against the terrible clawed creature that she was certain lived under it.

Susan had found out about this one the first night, when the child had woken up crying because of a bogeyman in the closet.

She'd sighed and gone to have a look. She'd been so angry that she'd pulled it out, hit it over the head with the nursery poker, dislocated its shoulder as a means of emphasis and kicked it out of the back door.

The children refused to disbelieve in the monsters because, frankly, they knew damn well the things were there.

But she'd found that they could, very firmly, also believe in the poker.

Now she sat down on a bench and read a book. She made a point of taking the children, every day, somewhere where they could meet others of the same age. If they got the hang of the playground, she thought, adult life would hold no fears. Besides, it was nice to hear the voices of little children at play, provided you took care to be far enough away not to hear what they were actually saying.

There were lessons later on. These were going a lot better now she'd got rid of the reading books about bouncy balls and dogs called Spot. She'd got Gawain on to the military campaigns of General Tacticus, which were suitably bloodthirsty but, more importantly, considered too difficult for a child. As a result his vocabulary was doubling every week and he could already use words like 'disembowelled' in everyday conversation. After all, what was the point of teaching children to be children? They were naturally good at it.

And she was, to her mild horror, naturally good with them. She wondered suspiciously if this was a family trait. And if, to judge by the way her hair so readily knotted itself into a prim bun, she was destined for jobs like this for the rest of her life.

It was her parents' fault. They hadn't meant it to turn out like this. At least, she hoped charitably that they hadn't.

They'd wanted to protect her, to keep her away from the worlds outside this one, from what people thought of as the occult, from . . . well, from her grandfather, to put it bluntly. This had, she felt, left her a little twisted up.

Of course, to be fair, that was a parent's job. The world was so full of sharp bends that if they didn't put a few twists in you, you wouldn't stand a chance of fitting in. And they'd been conscientious and kind and given her a good home and even an education.

It had been a good education, too. But it had only been later on that she'd realized that it had been an education in, well, education. It meant that if ever anyone needed to calculate the volume of a cone, then they could confidently call on Susan Sto-Helit. Anyone at a loss to recall the campaigns of General Tacticus or the square root of 27.4 would not find her wanting. If you needed someone who could talk about household items and things to buy in the shops in five languages, then Susan was at the head of the queue. Education had been easy.

Learning things had been harder.

Getting an education was a bit like a communicable sexual disease. It made you unsuitable for a lot of jobs and then you had the urge to pass it on.

She'd become a governess. It was one of the few jobs a known lady could do. And she'd taken to it well. She'd sworn that if she did indeed ever find herself dancing on rooftops with chimney sweeps she'd beat herself to death with her own umbrella.

After tea she read them a story. They liked her stories. The one in the book was pretty awful, but the Susan version was well received. She translated as she read.

'... and then Jack chopped down the beanstalk, adding murder and ecological vandalism to the theft, enticement and trespass charges already mentioned, but he got away with it and lived happily ever after without so much as a guilty twinge about what he had done. Which proves that you can be excused just about anything if you're a hero, because no one asks inconvenient questions. And now,' she closed the book with a snap, 'it's time for bed.'

The previous governess had taught them a prayer which included the hope that some god or other would take their soul if they died while they were asleep and, if Susan was any judge, had the underlying message that this would be a good thing.

One day, Susan averred, she'd hunt that woman down.

'Susan,' said Twyla, from somewhere under the blankets.

'Yes?'

'You know last week we wrote letters to the Hogfather?'

'Yes?'

'Only ... in the park Rachel says he doesn't exist and it's your father really. And everyone else said she was right.'

There was a rustle from the other bed. Twyla's brother had turned over and was listening surreptitiously.

Oh dear, thought Susan. She had hoped she could avoid this. It was going to be like that business with the Soul Cake Duck all over again.

'Does it matter if you get the presents anyway?' she said, making a direct appeal to greed.

''es.'

Oh dear, oh dear. Susan sat down on the bed, wondering how the hell to get through this. She patted the one visible hand.

'Look at it this way, then,' she said, and took a deep mental breath. 'Wherever people are obtuse and absurd . . . and wherever they have, by even the most generous standards, the attention span of a small chicken in a hurricane and the investigative ability of a one-legged cockroach . . . and wherever people are inanely credulous, pathetically attached to the certainties of the nursery and, in general, have as much grasp of the realities of the physical universe as an oyster has of mountaineering . . . *yes*, Twyla: there *is* a Hogfather.'

There was silence from under the bedclothes, but she sensed that the tone of voice had worked. The words had meant nothing. That, as her grandfather might have said, was humanity all over.

'G'night.'

'Goodnight,' said Susan.

It wasn't even a bar. It was just a room where people drank while they waited for other people with whom they had business. The business usually involved the transfer of ownership of something from one person to another, but then, what business doesn't?

Five businessmen sat round a table, lit by a candle stuck in a saucer. There was an open bottle between them. They were taking some care to keep it away from the candle flame.

''s gone six,' said one, a huge man with dreadlocks and a beard you could keep goats in. 'The clocks struck ages ago. He ain't coming. Let's go.'

'Sit *down*, will you? Assassins are always late. 'cos of style, right?'

'This one's mental.'

'Eccentric.'

'What's the difference?'

'A bag of cash.'

The three that hadn't spoken yet looked at one another.

'What's this? You never said he was an Assassin,' said Chickenwire.

'He never said the guy was an Assassin, did he, Banjo?'

There was a sound like distant thunder. It was Banjo Lilywhite clearing his throat.

'Dat's right,' said a voice from the upper slopes. 'Youse never said.'

The others waited until the rumble died away. Even Banjo's *voice* hulked.

'He's' – the first speaker waved his hands vaguely, trying to get across the point that someone was a hamper of food, several folding chairs, a tablecloth, an assortment of cooking gear and an entire colony of ants short of a picnic – '*mental*. And he's got a funny eye.'

'It's just glass, all right?' said the one known as Catseye, signalling a waiter for four beers and a glass of milk. 'And he's paying ten thousand dollars each. I don't care what kind of eye he's got.'

'I heard it was made of the same stuff they make them fortune-telling crystals out of. You can't tell *me* that's right. And he looks at you with it,' said the first speaker. He was known as Peachy, although no one had ever found out why.*

Catseye sighed. Certainly there was something odd about Mister Teatime, there was no doubt about that. But there was something weird about all Assassins. And the man paid well. Lots of Assassins used informers and locksmiths. It was against the rules, technically, but standards were going down everywhere, weren't they? Usually they paid you late and sparsely, as if *they* were doing the favour. But Teatime was OK. True, after a few minutes talking to him your eyes began to water and you felt you needed to scrub your skin even on the inside, but no one was perfect, were they?

Peachy leaned forward. 'You know what?' he said. 'I reckon he could be here already. In disguise! Laughing at us! Well, if he's in here laughing at us –' He cracked his knuckles.

Medium Dave Lilywhite, the last of the five, looked around. There were indeed a number of solitary figures in the low, dark room. Most of them wore cloaks with big hoods. They sat alone, in corners, hidden by the hoods. None of them looked very friendly.

'Don't be daft, Peachy,' Catseye murmured.

'That's the sort of thing they do,' Peachy insisted. 'They're masters of disguise!'

'With that eye of his?'

'That guy sitting by the fire has got an eye patch,' said Medium Dave. Medium Dave didn't speak much. He watched a lot.

---

* Peachy was not someone you generally asked questions of, except the sort that go like: 'If-if-if-if I give you all my money could you possibly not break the other leg, thank you so much?'

520

The others turned to stare.

'He'll wait till we're off our guard then go ahahaha,' said Peachy.

'They can't kill you unless it's for money,' said Catseye. But now there was a soupçon of doubt in his voice.

They kept their eyes on the hooded man. He kept his eye on them.

If asked to describe what they did for a living, the five men around the table would have said something like 'This and that' or 'The best I can', although in Banjo's case he'd have probably said 'Dur?' They were, by the standards of an uncaring society, criminals, although they wouldn't have thought of themselves as such and couldn't even *spell* words like 'nefarious'. What they generally did was move things around. Sometimes the things were on the wrong side of a steel door, say, or in the wrong house. Sometimes the things were in fact people who were far too unimportant to trouble the Assassins' Guild with, but who were nevertheless inconveniently positioned where they were and could much better be located on, for example, a sea bed somewhere.[*] None of the five belonged to any formal guild and they generally found their clients among those people who, for their own dark reasons, didn't want to put the guilds to any trouble, sometimes because they were guild members themselves. They had plenty of work. There was always something that needed transferring from A to B or, of course, to the bottom of the C.

'Any minute now,' said Peachy, as the waiter brought their beers.

Banjo cleared his throat. This was a sign that another thought had arrived.

'What I don' unnerstan,' he said, 'is . . .'

'Yes?' said his brother.[†]

'What I don' unnerstan is, how longaz diz place had waiters?'

'Good evening,' said Teatime, putting down the tray.

They stared at him in silence.

He gave them a friendly smile.

Peachy's huge hand slapped the table.

---

[*] Chickenwire had got his name from his own individual contribution to the science of this very specialized 'concrete overshoe' form of waste disposal. An unfortunate drawback of the process was the tendency for bits of the client to eventually detach and float to the surface, causing much comment in the general population. Enough chickenwire, he'd pointed out, would solve that, while also allowing the ingress of crabs and fish going about their vital recycling activities.

[†] Ankh-Morpork's underworld, which was so big that the overworld floated around on top of it like a very small hen trying to mother a nest of ostrich chicks, already had Big Dave, Fat Dave, Mad Dave, Wee Davey, and Lanky Dai. Everyone had to find their niche.

'You crept up on us, you little –' he began.

Men in their line of business develop a certain prescience. Medium Dave and Catseye, who were sitting on either side of Peachy, leaned away nonchalantly.

'Hi!' said Teatime. There was a blur, and a knife shuddered in the table between Peachy's thumb and index finger.

He looked down at it in horror.

'My name's Teatime,' said Teatime. 'Which one are you?'

''m . . . Peachy,' said Peachy, still staring at the vibrating knife.

'That's an interesting name,' said Teatime. 'Why are you called Peachy, Peachy?'

Medium Dave coughed.

Peachy looked up into Teatime's face. The glass eye was a mere ball of faintly glowing grey. The other eye was a little dot in a sea of white. Peachy's only contact with intelligence had been to beat it up and rob it whenever possible, but a sudden sense of self-preservation glued him to his chair.

''cos I don't shave,' he said.

'Peachy don't like blades, mister,' said Catseye.

'And do you have a lot of friends, Peachy?' said Teatime.

'Got a few, yeah . . .'

With a sudden whirl of movement that made the men start, Teatime spun away, grabbed a chair, swung it up to the table and sat down on it. Three of them had already got their hands on their swords.

'I don't have many,' he said, apologetically. 'Don't seem to have the knack. On the other hand . . . I don't seem to have *any* enemies at all. Not one. Isn't that nice?'

Teatime had been thinking, in the cracking, buzzing firework display that was his head. What he had been thinking about was immortality.

He might have been quite, quite insane, but he was no fool. There were, in the Assassins' Guild, a number of paintings and busts of famous members who had, in the past, put . . . no, of course, that wasn't right. There were paintings and busts of the famous *clients* of members, with a noticeably modest brass plaque screwed somewhere nearby, bearing some unassuming little comment like 'Departed this vale of tears on Grune 3, Year of the Sideways Leech, with the assistance of the Hon. K.W. Dobson (Viper House)'.

Many fine old educational establishments had dignified memorials in some hall listing the Old Boys who had laid down their lives for monarch and country. The Guild's was very similar, except for the question of whose life had been laid.

Every Guild member wanted to be up there somewhere. Because getting up there represented immortality. And the bigger your client, the more incredibly discreet and restrained would be the little brass plaque, so that everyone couldn't help but notice your name.

In fact, if you were very, very renowned, they wouldn't even have to write down your name at all . . .

The men around the table watched him. It was always hard to know what Banjo was thinking, or even if he was thinking at all, but the other four were thinking along the lines of: bumptious little tit, like all Assassins. Thinks he knows it all. I could take him down one-handed, no trouble. But . . . you hear stories. Those eyes give me the creeps . . .

'So what's the job?' said Chickenwire.

'We don't do jobs,' said Teatime. 'We perform services. And the service will earn each of you ten thousand dollars.'

'That's a lot more'n Thieves' Guild rate,' said Medium Dave.

'I've never liked the Thieves' Guild,' said Teatime, without turning his head.

'Why not?'

'They ask too many questions.'

'We don't ask questions,' said Chickenwire quickly.

'We shall suit one another perfectly,' said Teatime. 'Do have another drink while we wait for the other members of our little troupe.'

Chickenwire saw Medium Dave's lips start to frame the opening letters 'Who –'. These letters he deemed inauspicious at this time. He kicked Medium Dave's leg under the table.

The door opened slightly. A figure came in, but only just. It inserted itself in the gap and sidled along the wall in a manner calculated not to attract attention. Calculated, that is, by someone not good at this sort of calculation.

It looked at them over its turned-up collar.

'That's a *wizard*,' said Peachy.

The figure hurried over and dragged up a chair.

'No I'm not!' it hissed. 'I'm incognito!'

'Right, Mr Gnito,' said Medium Dave. 'You're just someone in a pointy hat. This is my brother Banjo, that's Peachy, this is Chick –'

The wizard looked desperately at Teatime.

'I didn't want to come!'

'Mr Sideney here is indeed a wizard,' said Teatime. 'A student, anyway. But down on his luck at the moment, hence his willingness to join us this venture.'

'Exactly how far down on his luck?' said Medium Dave.

The wizard tried not to meet anyone's gaze.

'I made a misjudgement to do with a wager,' he said.

'Lost a bet, you mean?' said Chickenwire.

'I paid up on time,' said Sideney.

'Yes, but Chrysoprase the troll has this odd little thing about money that turns into lead the next day,' said Teatime cheerfully. 'So our friend needs to earn a little cash in a hurry and in a climate where arms and legs stay on.'

'No one said anything about there being magic in all this,' said Peachy.

'Our destination is ... probably you should think of it as something like a wizard's tower, gentlemen,' said Teatime.

'It isn't an actual wizard's tower, is it?' said Medium Dave. 'They got a very odd sense of humour when it comes to booby traps.'

'No.'

'Guards?'

'I believe so. According to legend. But nothing very much.'

Medium Dave narrowed his eyes. 'There's valuable stuff in this ... tower?'

'Oh, yes.'

'Why ain't there many guards, then?'

'The ... person who owns the property probably does not realize the value of what ... of what they have.'

'Locks?' said Medium Dave.

'On our way we shall be picking up a locksmith.'

'Who?'

'Mr Brown.'

They nodded. Everyone – at least, everyone in 'the business', and everyone in 'the business' knew what 'the business' was, and if you didn't know what 'the business' was you weren't a businessman – knew Mr Brown. His presence anywhere around a job gave it a certain kind of respectability. He was a neat, elderly man who'd invented most of the tools in his big leather bag. No matter what cunning you'd used to get into a place, or overcome a small army, or find the secret treasure room, sooner or later you sent for Mr Brown, who'd turn up with his leather bag and his little springy things and his little bottles of strange alchemy and his neat little boots. And he'd do nothing for ten minutes but look at the lock, and then he'd select a piece of bent metal from a ring of several hundred almost identical pieces, and under an hour later he'd be walking away with a neat ten per cent of the takings. Of course, you didn't *have* to use Mr Brown's services. You could always opt to spend the rest of your life looking at a locked door.

'All right. Where is this place?' said Peachy.

Teatime turned and smiled at him. 'If I'm paying you, why isn't it me who's asking the questions?'

Peachy didn't even try to outstare the glass eye a second time.

'Just want to be prepared, that's all,' he mumbled.

'Good reconnaissance is the essence of a successful operation,' said Teatime. He turned and looked up at the bulk that was Banjo and added, 'What is this?'

'This is Banjo,' said Medium Dave, rolling himself a cigarette.

'Does it do tricks?'

Time stood still for a moment. The other men looked at Medium Dave. He was known to Ankh-Morpork's professional underclass as a thoughtful, patient man, and considered something of an intellectual because some of his tattoos were spelled right. He was reliable in a tight spot and, above all, he was honest, because good criminals have to be honest. If he had a fault, it was a tendency to deal out terminal and definitive retribution to anyone who said anything about his brother.

If he had a virtue, it was a tendency to pick his time. Medium Dave's fingers tucked the tobacco into the paper and raised it to his lips.

'No,' he said.

Chickenwire tried to defrost the conversation. 'He's not what you'd call bright, but he's always useful. He can lift two men in each hand. By their necks.'

'Yur,' said Banjo.

'He looks like a volcano,' said Teatime.

'*Really?*' said Medium Dave Lilywhite. Chickenwire reached out hastily and pushed him back down in his seat.

Teatime turned and smiled at him.

'I do so hope we're going to be friends, Mr Medium Dave,' he said. 'It really hurts to think I might not be among friends.' He gave him another bright smile. Then he turned back to the rest of the table.

'Are we resolved, gentlemen?'

They nodded. There was some reluctance, given the consensus

view that Teatime belonged in a room with soft walls, but ten thousand dollars was ten thousand dollars, possibly even more.

'Good,' said Teatime. He looked Banjo up and down. 'Then I suppose we might as well make a start.'

And he hit Banjo very hard in the mouth.

Death in person did not turn up upon the cessation of every life. It was not necessary. Governments govern, but prime ministers and presidents do not personally turn up in people's homes to tell them how to run their lives, because of the mortal danger this would present. There are laws instead.

But from time to time Death checked up to see that things were functioning properly or, to put it another and more accurate way, properly *ceasing* to function in the less significant areas of his jurisdiction.

And now he walked through dark seas.

Silt rose in clouds around his feet as he strode along the trench bottom. His robes floated out around him.

There was silence, pressure and utter, utter darkness. But there was life down here, even this far below the waves. There were giant squid, and lobsters with teeth on their eyelids. There were spidery things with their stomachs on their feet, and fish that made their own light. It was a quiet, black nightmare world, but life lives everywhere that life can. Where life can't, this takes a little longer.

Death's destination was a slight rise in the trench floor. Already the water around him was getting warmer and more populated, by creatures that looked as though they had been put together from the bits left over from everything else.

Unseen but felt, a vast column of scalding hot water was welling up from a fissure. Somewhere below were rocks heated to near incandescence by the Disc's magical field.

Spires of minerals had been deposited around this vent. And, in this tiny oasis, a type of life had grown up. It did not need air or light. It did not even need food in the way that most other species would understand the term.

It just grew at the edge of the streaming column of water, looking like a cross between a worm and a flower.

Death kneeled down and peered at it, because it was so small. But for some reason, in this world without eyes or light, it was also a brilliant red. The profligacy of life in these matters never ceased to amaze him.

He reached inside his robe and pulled out a small roll of black material, like a jeweller's toolkit. With great care he took from one of its pouches a scythe about an inch long, and held it expectantly between thumb and forefinger.

Somewhere overhead a shard of rock was dislodged by a stray current and tumbled down, raising little puffs of silt as it bounced off the tubes.

It landed just beside the living flower and then rolled, wrenching it from the rock.

Death flicked the tiny scythe just as the bloom faded ...

The omnipotent eyesight of various supernatural entities is often remarked upon. It is said they can see the fall of every sparrow.

And this may be true. But there is only one who is always there when it hits the ground.

The soul of the tube worm was very small and uncomplicated. It wasn't bothered about sin. It had never coveted its neighbour's polyps. It had never gambled or drunk strong liquor. It had never bothered itself with questions like 'Why am I here?' because it had no concept at all of 'here' or, for that matter, of 'I'.

Nevertheless, something was cut free under the surgical edge of the scythe and vanished in the roiling waters.

Death carefully put the instrument away and stood up. All was well, things were functioning satisfactorily, and –

– but they weren't.

In the same way that the best of engineers can hear the tiny change that signals a bearing going bad long before the finest of instruments would detect anything wrong, Death picked up a discord in the symphony of the world. It was one wrong note among billions but all the more noticeable for that, like a tiny pebble in a very large shoe.

He waved a finger in the waters. For a moment a blue, door-shaped outline appeared. He stepped through it and was gone.

The tube creatures didn't notice him go. They hadn't noticed him arrive. They never ever noticed anything.

A cart trundled through the freezing foggy streets, the driver hunched in his seat. He seemed to be all big thick brown overcoat.

A figure darted out of the swirls and was suddenly on the box next to him.

'Hi!' it said. 'My name's Teatime. What's yours?'

''ere, you get down, I ain't allowed to give li–'

The driver stopped. It was amazing how Teatime had been able to thrust a knife through four layers of thick clothing and stop it just at the point where it pricked the flesh.

'Sorry?' said Teatime, smiling brightly.

'Er – there ain't nothing valuable, y'know, nothing valuable, only a few bags of –'

'Oh, dear,' said Teatime, his face a sudden acre of concern. 'Well, we'll just have to see, won't we . . . What *is* your name, sir?'

'Ernie. Er. Ernie,' said Ernie. 'Yes. Ernie. Er . . .'

Teatime turned his head slightly.

'Come along, gentlemen. This is my friend Ernie. He's going to be our driver for tonight.'

Ernie saw half a dozen figures emerge from the fog and climb into the cart behind him. He didn't turn to look at them. By the pricking of his kidneys he knew this would not be an exemplary career move. But it seemed that one of the figures, a huge shambling mound of a creature, was carrying a long bundle over its shoulder. The bundle moved and made muffled noises.

'Do stop shaking, Ernie. We just need a lift,' said Teatime, as the cart rumbled over the cobbles.

'Where to, mister?'

'Oh, we don't mind. But first, I'd like you to stop in Sator Square, near the second fountain.'

The knife was withdrawn. Ernie stopped trying to breathe through his ears.

'Er . . .'

'What is it? You do seem tense, Ernie. I always find a neck massage helps.'

'I ain't rightly allowed to carry passengers, see. Charlie'll give me a right telling-off . . .'

'Oh, don't you worry about *that*,' said Teatime, slapping him on the back. 'We're all friends here!'

'What're we bringing the girl for?' said a voice behind them.

''s not right, hittin' girls,' said a deep voice. 'Our mam said no hittin' girls. Only bad boys do that, our mam said –'

'You be quiet, Banjo.'

'Our mam said –'

'Shssh! Ernie here doesn't want to listen to our troubles,' said Teatime, not taking his gaze off the driver.

'Me? Deaf as a post, me,' burbled Ernie, who in some ways was a very quick learner. 'Can't hardly see more'n a few feet, neither. Got no recollection for them faces that I do see, come to that. Bad memory? Hah! Talk about bad memory. Cor, sometimes I can be like as it were on the cart, talking to people, hah, just like I'm talking to you now, and then when they're gone, hah, try as I might, do you think I can remember anything about them or how many they were or what they were carrying or anything about any girl or anything?' By this time his voice was a high-pitched wheeze. 'Hah! Sometimes I forget me own name!'

'It's *Ernie*, isn't it?' said Teatime, giving him a happy smile. 'Ah, and here we are. Oh dear. There seems to be some excitement.'

There was the sound of fighting somewhere ahead, and then a couple of masked trolls ran past with three Watchmen after them. They all ignored the cart.

'I heard the De Bris gang were going to have a go at Packley's strongroom tonight,' said a voice behind Ernie.

'Looks like Mr Brown won't be joining us, then,' said another voice. There was a snigger.

'Oh, I don't know about that, Mr Lilywhite, I don't know about that at all,' said a third voice, and this one was from the direction of the fountain. 'Could you take my bag while I climb up, please? Do be careful, it's a little heavy.'

It was a neat little voice. The owner of a voice like that kept his money in a shovel purse and always counted his change carefully. Ernie thought all this, and then tried very hard to forget that he had.

'On you go, Ernie,' said Teatime. 'Round behind the University, I think.'

As the cart rolled on, the neat little voice said, 'You grab all the money and then you get out very smartly. Am I right?'

There was a murmur of agreement.

'Learned that on my mother's knee, yeah.'

'You learned a lot of stuff across your ma's knee, Mr Lilywhite.'

'Don't you say nuffin' about our mam!' The voice was like an earthquake.

'This is *Mr Brown*, Banjo. You smarten up.'

'He dint ort to tork about our mam!'

'All right! All right! Hello, Banjo ... I think I may have a sweet somewhere ... Yes, there you are. Yes, your ma knew the way all right. You go in quietly, you take your time, you get what you came for and you leave smartly and in good order. You *don't* hang around at the scene to count it out and tell one another what brave lads you are, am I right?'

'You seem to have done all right, Mr Brown.' The cart rattled towards the other side of the square.

'Just a little for expenses, Mr Catseye. A little Hogswatch present, you might say. Never take the lot and run. Take a little and walk. Dress neat. That's my motto. Dress neat and walk away slowly. Never run. *Never* run. The Watch'll always chase a running man. They're like terriers for giving chase. No, you walk out slow, you walk round the corner, you wait till there's a lot of excitement, then you turn around and walk back. They can't cope with that, see. Half the time they'll stand aside to let you walk past. "Good evening, officers," you say, and then you go home for your tea.'

'Wheee! Gets you out of trouble, I can see that. If you've got the nerve.'

'Oh, no, Mr Peachy. Doesn't get you out of. *Keeps* you out of.'

It was like a very good schoolroom, Ernie thought (and immediately tried to forget). Or a back-street gym when a champion prizefighter had just strolled in.

'What's up with your mouth, Banjo?'

'He lost a tooth, Mr Brown,' said another voice, and sniggered.

'Lost a toot', Mr Brown,' said the thunder that was Banjo.

'Keep your eyes on the road, Ernie,' said Teatime beside him. 'We don't want an accident, do we . . .'

The road here was deserted, despite the bustle of the city behind them and the bulk of the University nearby. There were a few streets, but the buildings were abandoned. And something was happening to the sound. The rest of Ankh-Morpork seemed very far away, the sounds arriving as if through quite a thick wall. They were entering that scorned little corner of Ankh-Morpork that had long been the site of the University's rubbish pits and was now known as the Unreal Estate.

'Bloody wizards,' muttered Ernie, automatically.

'I beg your pardon?' said Teatime.

'My great-grandpa said we used t'own prop'ty round here. Low levels of magic, my arse! Hah, it's all right for them wizards, they got all kindsa spells to protect 'em. Bit of magic here, bit of magic there . . . Stands to reason it's got to go somewhere, right?'

'There used to be warning signs up,' said the neat voice from behind.

'Yeah, well, warning signs in Ankh-Morpork might as well have "Good firewood" written on them,' said someone else.

'I mean, stands to reason, they chuck out an old spell for exploding this, and another one for twiddlin' that, and another one for making carrots grow, they finish up interfering with one another, who knows what they'll end up doing?' said Ernie. 'Great-grandpa said sometimes they'd wake up in the morning and the cellar'd be higher than the attic. And that weren't the worst,' he added darkly.

'Yeah, I heard where it got so bad you could walk down the street and meet yourself coming the other way,' someone supplied. 'It got so's you didn't know it was bum or breakfast time, I heard.'

'The dog used to bring home all kinds of stuff,' said Ernie. 'Great-grandpa said half the time they used to dive behind the sofa if it came in with anything in its mouth. Corroded fire spells startin' to fizz, broken wands with green smoke coming out of 'em and I don't know what else . . . and if you saw the cat playing with anything, it was best not to try to find out what it was, I can tell you.'

He twitched the reins, his current predicament almost forgotten in the tide of hereditary resentment.

'I mean, they *say* all the old spell books and stuff was buried deep and they recycle the used spells now, but that don't seem much comfort when your potatoes started walkin' about,' he grumbled. 'My great-grandpa went to see the head wizard about it, and *he* said' – he put on a strangled nasal voice which was his idea of how you talked when you'd got an education – '"Oh, there might be some temp'ry inconvenience now, my good man, but just you come back in fifty thousand years." Bloody wizards.'

The horse turned a corner.

This was a dead-end street. Half-collapsed houses, windows smashed, doors stolen, leaned against one another on either side.

'I heard they said they were going to clean up this place,' said someone.

'Oh, *yeah*,' said Ernie, and spat. When it hit the ground it ran away. 'And you know what? You get loonies coming in all the time now, poking around, pulling things about –'

'Just at the wall up ahead,' said Teatime conversationally. 'I think you generally go through just where there's a pile of rubble by the old dead tree, although you wouldn't see it unless you looked closely. But I've never seen how you *do* it . . .'

''ere, I can't take you lot through,' said Ernie. 'Lifts is one thing, but not taking people through –'

Teatime sighed. 'And we were getting on *so* well. Listen, Ernie . . . Ern . . . you will take us through or, and I say this with very considerable regret, I will have to kill you. You seem a nice man. Conscientious. A very serious overcoat and sensible boots.'

'But if'n I take you through –'

'What's the worst that can happen?' said Teatime. 'You'll lose your job. Whereas if you don't, you'll die. So if you look at it like that, we're actually doing you a favour. Oh, *do* say yes.'

'Er . . .' Ernie's brain felt twisted up. The lad was definitely what Ernie thought of as a toff, and he seemed nice and friendly, but it didn't all add up. The tone and the content didn't match.

'Besides,' said Teatime, 'if you've been coerced, it's not your fault, is it? No one can blame you. No one could blame *anyone* who'd been coerced at knife point.'

'Oh, well, I s'pose, if we're talking *coerced* . . .' Ernie muttered. Going along with things seemed to be the only way.

The horse stopped and stood waiting with the patient look of an animal that probably knows the route better than the driver.

Ernie fumbled in his overcoat pocket and took out a small tin, rather like a snuff box. He opened it. There was glowing dust inside.

'What do you do with that?' said Teatime, all interest.

'Oh, you just takes a pinch and throws it in the air and it goes *twing* and it opens the soft place,' said Ernie.

'So . . . you don't need any special training or anything?'

'Er . . . you just chucks it at the wall there and it goes *twing*,' said Ernie.

'Really? May I try?'

Teatime took the tin from his unresisting hand and threw a pinch of dust into the air in front of the horse. It hovered for a moment and then produced a narrow, glittering arch in the air. It sparkled and went . . .

. . . *twing*.

'Aw,' said a voice behind them. 'Innat nice, eh, our Davey?'

'Yeah.'

'All pretty sparkles . . .'

'And then you just drive forward?' said Teatime.

'That's right,' said Ernie. 'Quick, mind. It only stays open for a little while.'

Teatime pocketed the little tin. 'Thank you very much, Ernie. Very much indeed.'

His other hand lashed out. There was a glint of metal. The carter blinked, and then fell sideways off his seat.

There was silence from behind, tinted with horror and possibly just a little terrible admiration.

'Wasn't he *dull*?' said Teatime, picking up the reins.

*

Snow began to fall. It fell on the recumbent shape of Ernie, and it also fell through several hooded grey robes that hung in the air.

There appeared to be nothing inside them. You could believe they were there merely to make a certain point in space.

Well, said one, we are frankly impressed.

Indeed, said another. We would never have thought of doing it *this* way.

He is certainly a resourceful human, said a third.

The beauty of it all, said the first – or it may have been the second, because absolutely nothing distinguished the robes – is that there is so much else we will control.

Quite, said another. It is really amazing how they think. A sort of ... illogical logic.

Children, said another. Who would have thought it? But today the children, tomorrow the world.

Give me a child until he is seven and he's mine for life, said another.

There was a dreadful pause.

The consensus beings that called themselves the Auditors did not believe in anything, except possibly immortality. And the way to be immortal, they knew, was to avoid living. Most of all they did not believe in personality. To be a personality was to be a creature with a beginning and an end. And since they reasoned that in an infinite universe any life was by comparison unimaginably short, they died instantly. There was a flaw in their logic, of course, but by the time they found this out it was always too late. In the meantime, they scrupulously avoided any comment, action or experience that set them apart ...

You said 'me', said one.

Ah. Yes. But, you see, we were quoting, said the other one hurriedly. Some religious person said that. About educating children. And so would logically say 'me'. But I wouldn't use that term of myself, of – *damn*!

The robe vanished in a little puff of smoke.

Let that be a lesson to us, said one of the survivors, as another and totally indistinguishable robe popped into existence where the stricken colleague had been.

Yes, said the newcomer. Well, it certainly appears –

It stopped. A dark shape was approaching through the snow.

It's *him*, it said.

They faded hurriedly – not simply vanishing, but spreading out and thinning until they were just lost in the background.

*

The dark figure stopped by the dead carter and reached down.

COULD I GIVE YOU A HAND?

Ernie looked up gratefully.

'Cor, yeah,' he said. He got to his feet, swaying a little. 'Here, your fingers're cold, mister!'

SORRY.

'What'd he go and do that for? I *did* what he said. He could've *killed* me.'

Ernie felt inside his overcoat and pulled out a small and, at this point, strangely transparent silver flask.

'I always keep a nip on me these cold nights,' he said. 'Keeps me spirits up.'

YES INDEED. Death looked around briefly and sniffed the air.

'How'm I going to explain all this, then, eh?' said Ernie, taking a pull.

SORRY? THAT WAS VERY RUDE OF ME. I WASN'T PAYING ATTENTION.

'I said what'm I going to tell people? Letting some blokes ride off with my cart neat as you like . . . That's gonna be the sack for sure, I'm gonna be in *big* trouble . . .'

AH. WELL. THERE AT LEAST I HAVE SOME GOOD NEWS, ERNEST. AND, THEN AGAIN, I HAVE SOME BAD NEWS.

Ernie listened. Once or twice he looked at the corpse at his feet. He looked smaller from the outside. He was bright enough not to argue. Some things are fairly obvious when it's a seven-foot skeleton with a scythe telling you them.

'So I'm dead, then,' he concluded.

CORRECT.

'Er . . . The priest said that . . . you know . . . after you're dead . . . it's like going through a door and on one side of it there's . . . He . . . well, a terrible place . . .?'

Death looked at his worried, fading face.

THROUGH A DOOR . . .

'That's what he said . . .'

I EXPECT IT DEPENDS ON THE DIRECTION YOU'RE WALKING IN.

When the street was empty again, except for the fleshy abode of the late Ernie, the grey shapes came back into focus.

Honestly, he gets worse and worse, said one.

He was looking for us, said another. Did you notice? He suspects something. He gets so . . . *concerned* about things.

Yes . . . but the beauty of this plan, said a third, is that he *can't* interfere.

He can go everywhere, said one.

No, said another. Not quite *everywhere*.

And, with ineffable smugness, they faded into the foreground.

It started to snow quite heavily.

It was the night before Hogswatch. All through the house . . .

. . . one creature stirred. It was a mouse.

And someone, in the face of all appropriateness, had baited a trap. Although, because it was the festive season, they'd used a piece of pork crackling. The smell of it had been driving the mouse mad all day but now, with no one about, it was prepared to risk it.

The mouse didn't know it was a trap. Mice aren't good at passing on information. Young mice aren't taken up to famous trap sites and told, 'This is where your Uncle Arthur passed away.' All it knew was that, what the hey, here was something to eat. On a wooden board with some wire round it.

A brief scurry later and its jaw had closed on the rind.

Or, rather, passed through it.

The mouse looked around at what was now lying under the big spring, and thought, 'Oops . . .'

Then its gaze went up to the black-clad figure that had faded into view by the wainscoting.

'Squeak?' it asked.

SQUEAK, said the Death of Rats.

And that was *it*, more or less.

Afterwards, the Death of Rats looked around with interest. In the nature of things his very important job tended to take him to rickyards and dark cellars and the inside of cats and all the little dank holes where rats and mice finally found out if there was a Promised Cheese. This place was different.

It was brightly decorated, for one thing. Ivy and mistletoe hung in bunches from the bookshelves. Brightly coloured streamers festooned the walls, a feature seldom found in most holes or even quite civilized cats.

The Death of Rats took a leap on to a chair and from there on to the table and in fact right into a glass of amber liquid, which tipped over and broke. A puddle spread around four turnips and began to soak into a note which had been written rather awkwardly on pink writing paper.

It read:

> Dere HogFather,
>   For Hogswatch I would like a drum an a dolly an a teddybear an a Gharstley Omnian Inquisision Torchure Chamber with Wind-up Rack and Nearly Real Blud You Can Use Agian, you can get it from the toyshoppe in Short Strete, it is $5.99p. I have been good an here is a gluss of Sherre an a pork pie for you and turnips for Gouger an Tusker an Rooter an ~~Snot~~ Snouter. I hop the chimney is big enough but my friend Willaim says you are your father really.   Yrs. Virginua Prood.

The Death of Rats nibbled a bit of the pork pie because when you are the personification of the death of small rodents you have to behave in certain ways. He also piddled on one of the turnips for the same reason, although only metaphorically, because when you are a small skeleton in a black robe there are also some things you technically cannot do.

Then he leapt down from the table and left sherry-flavoured footprints all the way to the tree that stood in a pot in the corner. It was really only a bare branch of oak, but so much shiny holly and mistletoe had been wired on to it that it gleamed in the light of the candles.

There was tinsel on it, and glittering ornaments, and small bags of chocolate money.

The Death of Rats peered at his hugely distorted reflection in a glass ball, and then looked up at the mantelpiece.

He reached it in one jump, and ambled curiously through the cards that had been ranged along it. His grey whiskers twitched at messages like 'Wishing you Joye and all Goode Cheer at Hogswatchtime & All Through The Yeare'. A couple of them had pictures of a big jolly fat man carrying a sack. In one of them he was riding in a sledge drawn by four enormous pigs.

The Death of Rats sniffed at a couple of long stockings that had been hung from the mantelpiece, over the fireplace in which a fire had died down to a few sullen ashes.

He was aware of a subtle tension in the air, a feeling that here was a scene that was also a stage, a round hole, as it were, waiting for a round peg –

There was a scraping noise. A few lumps of soot thumped into the ashes.

The Grim Squeaker nodded to himself.

The scraping became louder, and was followed by a moment of silence and then a clang as something landed in the ashes and knocked over a set of ornamental fire irons.

The rat watched carefully as a red-robed figure pulled itself upright and staggered across the hearthrug, rubbing its shin where it had been caught by the toasting fork.

It reached the table and read the note. The Death of Rats thought he heard a groan.

The turnips were pocketed and so, to the Death of Rats' annoyance, was the pork pie. He was pretty sure it was meant to be eaten here, not taken away.

The figure scanned the dripping note for a moment, and then turned around and approached the mantelpiece. The Death of Rats pulled back slightly behind *'Season's Greetings!'*

A red-gloved hand took down a stocking. There was some creaking and rustling and it was replaced, looking a lot fatter – the larger box sticking out of the top had, just visible, the words 'Victim Figures Not Included. 3–10 yrs'.

The Death of Rats couldn't see much of the donor of this munificence. The big red hood hid all the face, apart from a long white beard.

Finally, when the figure finished, it stood back and pulled a list out of its pocket. It held it up to the hood and appeared to be consulting it. It waved its other hand vaguely at the fireplace, the sooty footprints, the empty sherry glass and the stocking. Then it bent forward, as if reading some tiny print.

AH, YES, it said. ER . . . HO. HO. HO.

With that, it ducked down and entered the chimney. There was some scrabbling before its boots gained a purchase, and then it was gone.

The Death of Rats realized he'd begun to gnaw his little scythe's handle in sheer shock.

SQUEAK?

He landed in the ashes and swarmed up the sooty cave of the

chimney. He emerged so fast that he shot out with his legs still scrabbling and landed in the snow on the roof.

There was a sledge hovering in the air by the gutter.

The red-hooded figure had just climbed in and appeared to be talking to someone invisible behind a pile of sacks.

HERE'S ANOTHER PORK PIE.

'Any mustard?' said the sacks. 'They're a treat with mustard.'

IT DOES NOT APPEAR SO.

'Oh, well. Pass it over anyway.'

IT LOOKS VERY BAD.

'Nah, 's just where something's nibbled it –'

I MEAN THE SITUATION. MOST OF THE LETTERS . . . THEY DON'T REALLY *BELIEVE*. THEY PRETEND TO BELIEVE, JUST IN CASE.* I FEAR IT MAY BE TOO LATE. IT HAS SPREAD SO FAST AND BACK IN TIME, TOO.

'Never say die, master. That's our motto, eh?' said the sacks, apparently with their mouth full.

I CAN'T SAY IT'S EVER REALLY BEEN MINE.

'I meant we're not going to be intimidated by the certain prospect of complete and utter failure, master.'

AREN'T WE? OH, GOOD. WELL, I SUPPOSE WE'D BETTER BE GOING. The figure picked up the reins. UP, GOUGER! UP, ROOTER! UP, TUSKER! UP, SNOUTER! GIDDYUP!

The four large boars harnessed to the sledge did not move.

WHY DOESN'T THAT WORK? said the figure in a puzzled, heavy voice.

'Beats me, master,' said the sacks.

IT WORKS ON HORSES.

'You could try "Pig-hooey!"'

PIG-HOOEY. They waited. NO . . . DOESN'T SEEM TO REACH THEM.

There was some whispering.

REALLY? YOU THINK THAT WOULD WORK?

'It'd bloody well work on me if I was a pig, master.'

VERY WELL, THEN.

The figure gathered up the reins again.

APPLE! SAUCE!

The pigs' legs blurred. Silver light flicked across them, and exploded outwards. They dwindled to a dot, and vanished.

SQUEAK?

The Death of Rats skipped across the snow, slid down a drainpipe and landed on the roof of a shed.

---

* This is very similar to the suggestion put forward by the Quirmian philosopher Ventre, who said, 'Possibly the gods exist, and possibly they do not. So why not believe in them in any case? If it's all true you'll go to a lovely place when you die, and if it isn't then you've lost nothing, right?' When he died he woke up in a circle of gods holding nasty-looking sticks and one of them said, 'We're going to show you what we think of Mr Clever Dick in these parts . . .'

There was a raven perched there. It was staring disconsolately at something.

Squeak!

'Look at that, willya?' said the raven rhetorically. It waved a claw at a bird table in the garden below. 'They hangs up half a bloody coconut, a lump of bacon rind, a handful of peanuts in a bit of wire and they think they're the gods' gift to the nat'ral world. Huh. Do I see eyeballs? Do I see entrails? I think *not*. Most intelligent bird in the temperate latitudes an' I gets the cold shoulder just because I can't hang upside down and go twit, twit. Look at robins, now. Stroppy little evil buggers, fight like demons, but all they got to do is go bob-bob-bobbing along and they can't move for breadcrumbs. Whereas me myself can recite poems and repeat many hum'rous phrases –'

Squeak!

'Yes? What?'

The Death of Rats pointed at the roof and then the sky and jumped up and down excitedly. The raven swivelled one eye upwards.

'Oh, yes. *Him*,' he said. 'Turns up at this time of year. Tends to be associated distantly with robins, which –'

Squeak! Squee ik ik ik! The Death of Rats pantomimed a figure landing in a grate and walking around a room. Squeak eek ik ik, squeak 'heek heek heek'! Ik ik *squeak*!

'Been overdoing the Hogswatch cheer, have you? Been rootling around in the brandy butter?'

Squeak?

The raven's eyes revolved.

'Look, Death's *Death*. It's a full-time job, right? It's not as though you can run, like, a window cleaning round on the side or nip round after work cutting people's lawns.'

Squeak!

'Oh, please yourself.'

The raven crouched a little to allow the tiny figure to hop on to its back, and then lumbered into the air.

'Of course, they can go mental, your occult types,' it said, as it swooped over the moonlit garden. 'Look at Old Man Trouble, for one –'

Squeak.

'Oh, I'm not suggesting –'

Susan didn't like Biers but she went there anyway, when the

pressure of being normal got too much. Biers, despite the smell and the drink and the company, had one important virtue. In Biers no one took any notice. Of anything. Hogswatch was traditionally supposed to be a time for families but the people who drank in Biers probably didn't have families; some of them looked as though they might have had litters, or clutches. Some of them looked as though they'd probably eaten their relatives, or at least *someone*'s relatives.

Biers was where the undead drank. And when Igor the barman was asked for a Bloody Mary, he didn't mix a metaphor.

The regular customers didn't ask questions, and not only because some of them found anything above a growl hard to articulate. None of them was in the answers business. Everyone in Biers drank alone, even when they were in groups. Or packs.

Despite the decorations put up inexpertly by Igor the barman to show willing,* Biers was not a family place.

Family was a subject Susan liked to avoid.

Currently she was being aided in this by a gin and tonic. In Biers, unless you weren't choosy, it paid to order a drink that was transparent because Igor also had undirected ideas about what you could stick on the end of a cocktail stick. If you saw something spherical and green, you just had to hope that it was an olive.

She felt hot breath on her ear. A bogeyman had sat down on the stool beside her.

'Woss a normo doin' in a place like this, then?' it rumbled, causing a cloud of vaporized alcohol and halitosis to engulf her. 'Hah, you fink it's *cool* comin' down here an' swannin' around in a black dress wid all the lost boys, eh? Dabblin' in a bit of designer darkness, eh?'

Susan moved her stool away a little. The bogeyman grinned.

'Want a bogeyman under yer bed, eh?'

'Now then, Shlimazel,' said Igor, without looking up from polishing a glass.

'Well, woss she down here for, eh?' said the bogeyman. A huge hairy hand grabbed Susan's arm. 'O' course, maybe what she wants is —'

'I ain't telling you again, Shlimazel,' said Igor.

He saw the girl turn to face Shlimazel.

Igor wasn't in a position to see her face fully, but the bogeyman was. He shot back so quickly that he fell off his stool.

And when the girl spoke, what she said was only partly words

---

* He'd done his best. But black and purple and vomit yellow weren't a good colour combination for paperchains, and no Hogswatch fairy doll should be nailed up by its head.

but also a statement, written in stone, of how the future was going to be.

'Go away and stop bothering me.'

She turned back and gave Igor a polite and slightly apologetic smile. The bogeyman struggled frantically out of the wreckage of his stool and loped towards the door.

Susan felt the drinkers turn back to their private preoccupations. It was amazing what you could get away with in Biers.

Igor put down the glass and looked up at the window. For a drinking den that relied on darkness it had rather a large one but, of course, some customers did arrive by air.

Something was tapping on it now.

Igor lurched over and opened it.

Susan looked up.

'Oh, no ...'

The Death of Rats leapt down on to the counter, with the raven fluttering after it.

Squeak squeak eek! Eek! Squeak ik ik 'heek heek heek'! Sq–

'Go away,' said Susan coldly. 'I'm not interested. You're just a figment of my imagination.'

The raven perched on a bowl behind the bar and said, 'Ah, great.'

Squeak!

'What're these?' said the raven, flicking something off the end of its beak. '*Onions?* Pfah!'

'Go on, go away, the pair of you,' said Susan.

'The rat says your granddad's gone mad,' said the raven. 'Says he's pretending to be the Hogfather.'

'Listen, I just don't – What?'

'Red cloak, long beard –'

Heek! Heek! Heek!

'– going "Ho, ho, ho", driving around in the big sledge drawn by the four piggies, the whole thing ...'

'Pigs? What happened to Binky?'

'Search me. O' course, it can happen, as I was telling the rat only just now –'

Susan put her hands over her ears, more for desperate theatrical effect than for the muffling they gave.

'I don't want to know! I don't *have* a grandfather!'

She had to hold on to that.

The Death of Rats squeaked at length.

'The rat says you must remember, he's tall, not what you'd call fleshy, he carries a scythe –'

'Go *away*! And take the ... the *rat* with you!'

She waved her hand wildly and, to her horror and shame, knocked the little hooded skeleton over an ashtray.

Eek?

The raven took the rat's cowl in its beak and tried to drag him away, but a tiny skeletal fist shook its scythe.

Eek *ik* eek squeak!

'He says, you don't mess with the rat,' said the raven.

In a flurry of wings they were gone.

Igor closed the window. He didn't pass any comment.

'They weren't real,' said Susan, hurriedly. 'Well, that is ... the raven's probably real, but he hangs around with the rat –'

'Which isn't real,' said Igor.

'That's right!' said Susan, gratefully. 'You probably didn't see a thing.'

'That's right,' said Igor. 'Not a thing.'

'Now ... how much do I owe you?' said Susan.

Igor counted on his fingers.

'That'll be a dollar for the drinks,' he said, 'and fivepence because the raven that wasn't here messed in the pickles.'

It was the night before Hogswatch.

In the Archchancellor's new bathroom Modo wiped his hands on a piece of rag and looked proudly at his handiwork. Shining porcelain gleamed back at him. Copper and brass shone in the lamplight.

He was a little worried that he hadn't been able to test everything, but Mr Ridcully had said, 'I'll test it when I use it,' and Modo never argued with the Gentlemen, as he thought of them. He knew that they all knew a lot more than he knew, and was quite happy knowing this. *He* didn't meddle with the fabric of time and space, and *they* kept out of his greenhouses. The way he saw it, it was a partnership.

He'd been particularly careful to scrub the floors. Mr Ridcully had been very specific about that.

'Verruca Gnome,' he said to himself, giving a tap a last polish. 'What an imagination the Gentlemen do have ...'

Far off, unheard by anyone, was a faint little noise, like the ringing of tiny silver bells.

Glingleglinglegingle ...

And someone landed abruptly in a snowdrift and said, 'Bugger!', which is a terrible thing to say as your first word ever.

*

Overhead, heedless of the new and somewhat angry life that was even now dusting itself off, the sledge soared onwards through time and space.

I'M FINDING THE BEARD A BIT OF A TRIAL, said Death.

'Why've you got to have the beard?' said the voice from among the sacks. 'I thought you said people see what they expect to see.'

CHILDREN DON'T. TOO OFTEN THEY SEE WHAT'S THERE.

'Well, at least it's keeping you in the right frame of mind, master. In character, sort of thing.'

BUT GOING DOWN THE CHIMNEY? WHERE'S THE SENSE IN THAT? I CAN JUST WALK THROUGH THE WALLS.

'Walking through the walls is not right, neither,' said the voice from the sacks.

IT WORKS FOR ME.

'It's got to be chimneys. Same as the beard, really.'

A head thrust itself out from the pile. It appeared to belong to the oldest, most unpleasant pixie in the universe. The fact that it was underneath a jolly little green hat with a bell on it did not do anything to improve matters.

It waved a crabbed hand containing a thick wad of letters, many of them on pastel-coloured paper, often with bunnies and teddy bears on them, and written mostly in crayon.

'You reckon these little buggers'd be writing to someone who walked through walls?' it said. 'And the "Ho, ho, ho" could use some more work, if you don't mind my saying so.'

HO. HO. HO.

'No, no, *no*!' said Albert. 'You got to put a bit of life in it, sir, no offence intended. It's got to be a big fat laugh. You got to ... you got to sound like you're pissing brandy and crapping plum pudding, sir, excuse my Klatchian.'

REALLY? HOW DO YOU KNOW ALL THIS?

'I *was* young once, sir. Hung up my stocking like a good boy every year. For to get it filled with toys, just like you're doing. Mind you, in those days basically it was sausages and black puddings if you were lucky. But you always got a pink sugar piglet in the toe. It wasn't a good Hogswatch unless you'd eaten so much you were sick as a pig, master.'

Death looked at the sacks.

It was a strange but demonstrable fact that the sacks of toys carried by the Hogfather, no matter what they really contained, always appeared to have sticking out of the top a teddy bear, a toy soldier in the kind of colourful uniform that would stand out in a disco, a drum and a red-and-white candy cane. The actual contents always turned out to be something a bit garish and costing $5.99.

Death had investigated one or two. There had been a Real Agatean Ninja, for example, with Fearsome Death Grip, and a Captain Carrot One-Man Night Watch with a complete wardrobe of toy weapons, each of which cost as much as the original wooden doll in the first place.

Mind you, the stuff for the girls was just as depressing. It seemed to be nearly all horses. Most of them were grinning. Horses, Death felt, shouldn't grin. Any horse that was grinning was planning something.

He sighed again.

Then there was this business of deciding who'd been naughty or nice. He'd never had to think about that sort of thing before. Naughty or nice, it was ultimately all the same.

Still, it had to be done *right*. Otherwise it wouldn't *work*.

The pigs pulled up alongside another chimney.

'Here we are, here we are,' said Albert. 'James Riddle, aged eight.'

HAH, YES. HE ACTUALLY SAYS IN *HIS* LETTER, 'I BET YOU DON'T EXIST 'COS EVERYONE KNOWS ITS YORE PARENTS.' OH *YES*, said Death, with what almost sounded like sarcasm, I'M SURE HIS PARENTS ARE JUST *IMPATIENT* TO BANG THEIR ELBOWS IN TWELVE FEET OF NARROW UNSWEPT CHIMNEY, I DON'T THINK. I SHALL TREAD EXTRA SOOT INTO HIS CARPET.

'Right, sir. Good thinking. Speaking of which – down you go, sir.'

HOW ABOUT IF I DON'T GIVE HIM ANYTHING AS A PUNISHMENT FOR NOT BELIEVING?

'Yeah, but what's that going to prove?'

Death sighed. I SUPPOSE YOU'RE RIGHT.

'Did you check the list?'

YES. TWICE. ARE YOU SURE THAT'S ENOUGH?

'Definitely.'

COULDN'T REALLY MAKE HEAD OR TAIL OF IT, TO TELL YOU THE TRUTH. HOW CAN I *TELL* IF HE'S BEEN NAUGHTY OR NICE, FOR EXAMPLE?

'Oh, well . . . I don't know . . . Has he hung his clothes up, that sort of thing . . .'

AND IF HE HAS BEEN GOOD I MAY GIVE HIM THIS KLATCHIAN WAR CHARIOT WITH REAL SPINNING SWORD BLADES?

'That's right.'

AND IF HE'S BEEN BAD?

Albert scratched his head. 'When I was a lad, you got a bag of bones. 's'mazing how kids got better behaved towards the end of the year.'

OH DEAR. AND NOW?

Albert held a package up to his ear and rustled it. 'Sounds like socks.'

'Could be a woolly vest.'

SERVE HIM RIGHT, IF I MAY VENTURE TO EXPRESS AN OPINION . . .

Albert looked across the snowy rooftops and sighed. This wasn't right. He was helping because, well, Death was his master and that's all there was to it, and if the master *had* a heart it would be in the right place. But . . .

'Are you *sure* we ought to be doing this, master?'

Death stopped, halfway out of the chimney.

CAN YOU THINK OF A BETTER ALTERNATIVE, ALBERT?

And that was it. Albert couldn't.

Someone had to do it.

There were bears on the street again.

Susan ignored them and didn't even make a point of not treading on the cracks.

They just stood around, looking a bit puzzled and slightly transparent, visible only to children and Susan. News like Susan gets around. The bears had heard about the poker. Nuts and berries, their expressions seemed to say. That's what we're here for. Big sharp teeth? What big shar– Oh, *these* big sharp teeth? They're just for, er, cracking nuts. And some of these berries can be really vicious.

The city's clocks were striking six when she got back to the house. She was allowed her own key. It wasn't as if she was a servant, exactly.

You couldn't be a duchess *and* a servant. But it was all right to be a governess. It was understood that it wasn't exactly what you *were*, it was merely a way of passing the time until you did what every girl, or gel, was supposed to do in life, i.e., marry some man. It was understood that you were playing.

The parents were in awe of her. She was the daughter of a duke whereas Mr Gaiter was a man to be reckoned with in the wholesale boots and shoes business. Mrs Gaiter was bucking for a transfer into the Upper Classes, which she currently hoped to achieve by reading books on etiquette. She treated Susan with the kind of worried deference she thought was due to anyone who'd known the difference between a serviette and a napkin from *birth*.

Susan had never before come across the idea that you could rise in Society by, as it were, gaining marks, especially since such noblemen as she'd met in her father's house had used neither serviette nor napkin but a state of mind, which was 'Drop it on the floor, the dogs'll eat it.'

When Mrs Gaiter had tremulously asked her how one addressed the second cousin of a queen, Susan had replied without thinking, 'We called him Jamie, usually,' and Mrs Gaiter had had to go and have a headache in her room.

Mr Gaiter just nodded when he met her in a passage and never said very much to her. He was pretty sure he knew where he stood in boots and shoes and that was that.

Gawain and Twyla, who'd been named by people who apparently loved them, had been put to bed by the time Susan got in, at their own insistence. It's a widely held belief at a certain age that going to bed early makes tomorrow come faster.

She went to tidy up the schoolroom and get things ready for the morning, and began to pick up the things the children had left lying around. Then something tapped at a window pane.

She peered out at the darkness, and then opened the window. A drift of snow fell down outside.

In the summer the window opened into the branches of a cherry tree. In the winter dark, they were little grey lines where the snow had settled on them.

'Who's that?' said Susan.

Something hopped through the frozen branches.

'Tweet tweet tweet, would you believe?' said the raven.

'Not *you* again?'

'You wanted maybe some dear little robin? Listen, your grand–'

'Go *away*!'

Susan slammed the window and pulled the curtains across. She put her back to them, to make sure, and tried to concentrate on the room. It helped to think about ... *normal* things.

There was the Hogswatch tree, a rather smaller version of the grand one in the hall. She'd helped the children to make paper decorations for it. Yes. Think about that.

There were the paperchains. There were the bits of holly, thrown out from the main rooms for not having enough berries on them, and now given fake modelling clay berries and stuck in anyhow on shelves and behind pictures.

There were two stockings hanging from the mantelpiece of the small schoolroom grate. There were Twyla's paintings, all blobby blue skies and violently green grass and red houses with four square windows. There were ...

Normal things ...

She straightened up and stared at them, her fingernails beating a thoughtful tattoo on a wooden pencil case.

The door was pushed open. It revealed the tousled shape of Twyla, hanging on to the doorknob with one hand.

'Susan, there's a monster under my bed *again* ...'

The click of Susan's fingernails stopped.

'... I can hear it moving about ...'

Susan sighed and turned towards the child.

'All right, Twyla. I'll be along directly.'

The girl nodded and went back to her room, leaping into bed from a distance as a precaution against claws.

There was a metallic *tzing* as Susan withdrew the poker from the little brass stand it shared with the tongs and the coal shovel.

She sighed. Normality was what you made it.

She went into the children's bedroom and leaned over as if to tuck Twyla up. Then her hand darted down and under the bed. She grabbed a handful of hair. She pulled.

The bogeyman came out like a cork but before it could get its balance it found itself spreadeagled against the wall with one arm behind its back. But it did manage to turn its head, to see Susan's face glaring at it from a few inches away.

Gawain bounced up and down on his bed.

'Do the Voice on it! Do the Voice on it!' he shouted.

'Don't do the Voice, don't do the Voice!' pleaded the bogeyman urgently.

'Hit it on the head with the poker!'

'Not the poker! Not the poker!'

'It's you, isn't it,' said Susan. 'From this afternoon ...'

'Aren't you going to poke it with the poker?' said Gawain.

'Not the poker!' whined the bogeyman.

'New in town?' whispered Susan.

'Yes!' The bogeyman's forehead wrinkled with puzzlement. 'Here, how come you can see me?'

'Then this is a friendly warning, understand? Because it's Hogswatch.'

The bogeyman tried to move. 'You call this friendly?'

'Ah, you want to try for *un*friendly?' said Susan, adjusting her grip.

'No, no, no, I *like* friendly!'

'This house is out of bounds, right?'

'You a witch or something?' moaned the bogeyman.

'I'm just . . . something. Now . . . you won't be around here again, will you? Otherwise it'll be the *blanket* next time.'

'No!'

'I mean it. We'll put your head under the blanket.'

'No!'

'It's got *fluffy bunnies* on it . . .'

'*No!*'

'Off you go, then.'

The bogeyman half fell, half ran towards the door.

''s not right,' it mumbled. 'You're not *s'posed* to see us if you ain't dead or magic . . .'s not fair . . .'

'Try number nineteen,' said Susan, relenting a little. 'The governess there doesn't believe in bogeymen.'

'Right?' said the monster hopefully.

'She believes in algebra, though.'

'Ah. Nice.' The bogeyman grinned hugely. It was amazing the sort of mischief that could be caused in a house where no one in authority thought you existed.

'I'll be off, then,' it said. 'Er. Happy Hogswatch.'

'Possibly,' said Susan, as it slunk away.

'That wasn't as much fun as the one last month,' said Gawain, getting between the sheets again. 'You know, when you kicked him in the trousers –'

'Just you two get to sleep now,' said Susan.

'Verity said the sooner we got to sleep the sooner the Hogfather would come,' said Twyla conversationally.

'Yes,' said Susan. 'Unfortunately, that might be the case.'

The remark passed right over their heads. She wasn't sure why it had gone through hers, but she knew enough to trust her senses.

She *hated* that kind of sense. It ruined your life. But it was the sense she had been born with.

The children were tucked in, and she closed the door quietly and went back to the schoolroom.

Something had changed.

She glared at the stockings, but they were unfulfilled. A paperchain rustled.

She stared at the tree. Tinsel had been twined around it, badly pasted-together decorations had been hung on it. And on top was the fairy made of –

She crossed her arms, looked up at the ceiling, and sighed theatrically.

'It's you, isn't it?' she said.

SQUEAK?

'Yes, it *is*. You're sticking out your arms like a scarecrow and you've stuck a little star on your scythe, haven't you . . .?'

The Death of Rats hung his head guiltily.

SQUEAK.

'You're not fooling *anyone*.'

SQUEAK.

'Get down from there this minute!'

SQUEAK.

'And *what* did you do with the fairy?'

'It's shoved under a cushion on the chair,' said a voice from the shelves on the other side of the room. There was a clicking noise and the raven's voice added, 'These damn eyeballs are hard, aren't they?'

Susan raced across the room and snatched the bowl away so fast that the raven somersaulted and landed on its back.

'They're *walnuts*!' she shouted, as they bounced around her. '*Not* eyeballs! This is a *schoolroom*! And the difference between a school and a-a-a raven delicatessen is that they hardly *ever* have eyeballs lying around in bowls in case a raven drops in for a quick snack! Understand? *No* eyeballs! The world is full of small round things that *aren't* eyeballs! OK?'

The raven's own eyes revolved.

''n' I suppose a bit of warm liver's out of the question –'

'Shut up! I want both of you out of here right now! I don't know how you got in here –'

'There's a law against coming down the chimney on Hogswatchnight?'

'– but I *don't* want you back in my life, understand?'

'The rat said you ought to be warned even if you *were* crazy,' said the raven sulkily. 'I didn't want to come, there's a donkey dropped dead just outside the city gates, I'll be lucky now if I get a hoof –'

'Warned?' said Susan.

There it was again. The change in the weather of the mind, a sensation of tangible time . . .

The Death of Rats nodded.

There was a scrabbling sound far overhead. A few flakes of soot dropped down the chimney.

SQUEAK, said the rat, but very quietly.

Susan was aware of a new sensation, as a fish might be aware of a new tide, a spring of fresh water flowing into the sea. Time was pouring into the world.

She glanced up at the clock. It was just on half past six.

The raven scratched its beak.

'The rat says . . . The rat says: you'd better watch out . . .'

There were others at work on this shining Hogswatch Eve. The Sandman was out and about, dragging his sack from bed to bed. Jack Frost wandered from window pane to window pane, making icy patterns.

And one tiny hunched shape slid and slithered along the gutter, squelching its feet in slush and swearing under its breath.

It wore a stained black suit and, on its head, the type of hat known in various parts of the multiverse as 'bowler', 'derby' or 'the one that makes you look a bit of a tit'. The hat had been pressed down very firmly and, since the creature had long pointy ears, these had been forced out sideways and gave it the look of a small malignant wing-nut.

The thing was a gnome by shape but a fairy by profession. Fairies aren't necessarily little twinkly creatures. It's purely a job description, and the commonest ones aren't even visible.* A fairy is simply any creature currently employed under supernatural laws to take things away or, as in the case of the small creature presently climbing up the inside of a drainpipe and swearing, to bring things.

Oh, yes. He does. Someone has to do it, and he looks the right gnome for the job.

Oh, yes.

Sideney was worried. He didn't like violence, and there had been a lot of it in the last few days, if days passed in this place. The men . . . well, they only seemed to find life interesting when they were doing something sharp to someone else and, while they didn't bother him much in the same way that lions don't trouble themselves with ants, they certainly worried him.

---

* Such as the Electric Drill Chuck Key Fairy.

But not as much as Teatime did. Even the brute called Chickenwire treated Teatime with caution, if not respect, and the monster called Banjo just followed him around like a puppy.

The enormous man was watching him now.

He reminded Sidney too much of Ronnie Jenks, the bully who'd made his life miserable at Gammer Wimblestone's dame school. Ronnie hadn't been a pupil. He was the old woman's grandson or nephew or something, which gave him a licence to hang around the place and beat up any kid smaller or weaker or brighter than he was, which more or less meant he had the whole world to choose from. In those circumstances, it was particularly unfair that he always chose Sidney.

Sidney hadn't hated Ronnie. He'd been too frightened. He'd wanted to be his friend. Oh, so much. Because that way, just possibly, he wouldn't have his head trodden on such a lot and would actually get to eat his lunch instead of having it thrown in the privy. And it had been a *good* day when it had been his lunch.

And then, despite all Ronnie's best efforts, Sidney had grown up and gone to university. Occasionally his mother told him how Ronnie was getting on (she assumed, in the way of mothers, that because they had been small boys at school together they had been friends). Apparently he ran a fruit stall and was married to a girl called Angie.[*] This was not enough punishment, Sidney considered.

Banjo even *breathed* like Ronnie, who had to concentrate on such an intellectual exercise and always had one blocked nostril. And his mouth open all the time. He looked as though he was living on invisible plankton.

He tried to keep his mind on what he was doing and ignore the laboured gurgling behind him. A change in its tone made him look up.

'Fascinating,' said Teatime. 'You make it look so *easy*.'

Sidney sat back, nervously.

'Um . . . it should be fine now, sir,' he said. 'It just got a bit scuffed when we were piling up the . . .' He couldn't bring himself to say it, he even had to avert his eyes from the heap, it was the *sound* they'd made. '. . . the things,' he finished.

---

[*] Who was (according to Sidney's mother) a bit of a catch since her father owned a half-share in an eel pie shop in Gleam Street, you must know her, got all her own teeth and a wooden leg you'd hardly notice, got a sister called Continence, lovely girl, why didn't she invite her along for tea next time he was over, not that she hardly saw her son the big wizard at all these days, but you never knew and if the magic thing didn't work out then a quarter-share in a thriving eel pie business was not to be sneezed at . . .

'We don't need to repeat the spell?' said Teatime.

'Oh, it'll keep going for ever,' said Sidney. 'The simple ones do. It's just a state change, powered by the ... the ... it just keeps going ...'

He swallowed.

'So,' he said, 'I was thinking ... since you don't actually *need* me, sir, perhaps ...'

'Mr Brown seems to be having some trouble with the locks on the top floor,' said Teatime. 'That door we couldn't open, remember? I'm sure you'll want to help.'

Sideney's face fell.

'Um, I'm not a locksmith ...'

'They appear to be magical.'

Sideney opened his mouth to say, 'But I'm very bad at magical locks,' and then thought much better of it. He had already fathomed that if Teatime wanted you to do something, and you weren't very good at it, then your best plan, in fact quite possibly your *only* plan, was to learn to be good at it very quickly. Sideney was not a fool. He'd seen the way the others reacted around Teatime, and *they* were men who did things he'd only dreamed of.*

At which point he was relieved to see Medium Dave walk down the stairs, and it said a lot for the effect of Teatime's stare that anyone could be relieved to have it punctuated by someone like Medium Dave.

'We've found another guard, sir. Up on the sixth floor. He's been hiding.'

Teatime stood up. 'Oh dear,' he said. 'Not trying to be heroic, was he?'

'He's just scared. Shall we let him go?'

'Let him go?' said Teatime. 'Far too messy. I'll go up there. Come along, Mr Wizard.'

Sideney followed him reluctantly up the stairs.

The tower – if that's what it was, he thought; he was used to the odd architecture at Unseen University and this made UU look normal – was a hollow tube. No fewer than four spiral staircases climbed the inside, criss-crossing on landings and occasionally passing through one another in defiance of generally accepted physics. But that was practically normal for an alumnus of Unseen University, although technically Sideney had not alumed. What threw the eye was the absence of shadows. You didn't notice

---

* Not, that is, things that he wanted to do, or wanted done to him. Just things that he dreamed of, in the armpit of a bad night.

shadows, how they delineated things, how they gave texture to the world, until they weren't there. The white marble, if that's what it was, seemed to glow from the inside. Even when the impossible sun shone through a window it barely caused faint grey smudges where honest shadows should be. The tower seemed to avoid darkness.

That was even more frightening than the times when, after a complicated landing, you found yourself walking *up* by stepping *down* the underside of a stair and the distant floor now hung overhead like a ceiling. He'd noticed that even the other men shut their eyes when that happened. Teatime, though, took those stairs three at a time, laughing like a kid with a new toy.

They reached an upper landing and followed a corridor. The others were gathered by a closed door.

'He's barricaded himself in,' said Chickenwire.

Teatime tapped on it. 'You in there,' he said. 'Come on out. You have my word you won't be harmed.'

'No!'

Teatime stood back. 'Banjo, knock it down,' he said.

Banjo lumbered forward. The door withstood a couple of massive kicks and then burst open.

The guard was cowering behind an overturned cabinet. He cringed back as Teatime stepped over it. 'What're you doing here?' he shouted. 'Who *are* you?'

'Ah, I'm glad you asked. I'm your worst nightmare!' said Teatime cheerfully.

The man shuddered.

'You mean ... the one with the giant cabbage and the sort of whirring knife thing?'

'Sorry?' Teatime looked momentarily nonplussed.

'Then you're the one about where I'm falling, only instead of ground underneath it's all –'

'No, in fact I'm –'

The guard sagged. 'Awww, *not* the one where there's all this kind of, you know, mud and then everything goes blue –'

'No, I'm –'

'Oh, *shit*, then you're the one where there's this door only there's no floor beyond it and then there's these claws –'

'No,' said Teatime. 'Not that one.' He withdrew a dagger from his sleeve. 'I'm the one where this man comes out of nowhere and kills you stone dead.'

The guard grinned with relief. 'Oh, *that* one,' he said. 'But that one's not very –'

He crumpled around Teatime's suddenly out-thrust fist. And then, just like the others had done, he faded.

'Rather a charitable act there, I feel,' Teatime said as the man vanished. 'But it *is* nearly Hogswatch, after all.'

Death, pillow slipping gently under his red robe, stood in the middle of the nursery carpet . . .

It was an old one. Things ended up in the nursery when they had seen a complete tour of duty in the rest of the house. Long ago, someone had made it by carefully knotting long bits of brightly coloured rag into a sacking base, giving it the look of a deflated Rastafarian hedgehog. Things lived among the rags. There were old rusks, bits of toy, buckets of dust. It had seen life. It may even have evolved some.

Now the occasional lump of grubby melting snow dropped on to it.

Susan was crimson with anger.

'I mean, *why?*' she demanded, walking around the figure. 'This is *Hogswatch!* It's supposed to be jolly, with mistletoe and holly, and – and other things ending in olly! It's a time when people want to feel good about things and eat until they explode! It's a time when they want to see all their relatives –'

She stopped *that* sentence.

'I mean it's a time when humans are really human,' she said. 'And they *don't* want a . . . a skeleton at the feast! Especially one, I might add, who's wearing a false beard and has got a damn cushion shoved up his robe! I mean, *why?*'

Death looked nervous.

Albert said it would help me get into the spirit of the thing. Er . . . It's good to see you again –

There was a small squelchy noise.

Susan spun around, grateful right now for any distraction.

'Don't think I can't hear you! They're *grapes*, understand? And the other things are satsumas! Get *out* of the fruit bowl!'

'Can't blame a bird for trying,' said the raven sulkily, from the table.

'And you, you leave those nuts alone! They're for tomorrow!'

Skqueaf, said the Death of Rats, swallowing hurriedly.

Susan turned back to Death. The Hogfather's artificial stomach was now at groin level.

'This is a *nice* house,' she said. 'And this is a good job. And it's real, with normal people. And I was looking forward to a real life, where normal things happen! And suddenly the old circus comes to town. Look at yourselves. Three Stooges, No Waiting! Well, I don't know what's going on, but you can all leave again, right? This is *my* life. It doesn't belong to any of you. It's not going to –'

There was a muffled curse, a rush of soot, and a skinny old man landed in the grate.

'Bum!' he said.

'Good *grief*!' raged Susan. 'And here is Pixie Albert! Well, well, well! Come along in, do! If the real Hogfather doesn't come soon there's not going to be *room*.'

HE WON'T BE JOINING US, said Death. The pillow slid softly on to the rug.

'Oh, and why not? Both of the children did letters to him,' said Susan. 'There's *rules*, you know.'

YES. THERE ARE RULES. AND THEY'RE ON THE LIST. I CHECKED IT.

Albert pulled the pointy hat off his head and spat out some soot. 'Right. He did. Twice,' he said. 'Anything to drink around here?'

'So what have *you* turned up for?' Susan demanded. 'And if it's for business reasons, I will add, then that outfit is in extremely poor taste –'

THE HOGFATHER IS ... UNAVAILABLE.

'Unavailable? At Hogswatch?'

YES.

'Why?'

HE IS ... LET ME SEE ... THERE ISN'T AN ENTIRELY APPROPRIATE HUMAN WORD, SO ... LET'S SETTLE FOR ... DEAD. YES. HE IS DEAD.

Susan had never hung up a stocking. She'd never looked for eggs laid by the Soul Cake Duck. She'd never put a tooth under her pillow in the serious expectation that a dentally inclined fairy would turn up.

It wasn't that her parents didn't believe in such things. They didn't *need* to believe in them. They knew they existed. They just wished they didn't.

Oh, there had been presents, at the right time, with a careful label saying who they were from. And a superb egg on Soul Cake Morning, filled with sweets. Juvenile teeth earned no less than a dollar each from her father, without argument.[*] But it was all *straightforward*.

---

[*] In fact, when she was eight she'd found a collection of animal skulls in an attic, relict of some former duke of an enquiring turn of mind. Her father had been a bit preoccupied with affairs of state and she'd made twenty-seven dollars before being found out. The hippopotamus

She knew now that they'd been trying to protect her. She hadn't known then that her father had been Death's apprentice for a while, and that her mother was Death's adopted daughter. She'd had very dim recollections of being taken a few times to see someone who'd been quite, well, jolly, in a strange, thin way. And the visits had suddenly stopped. And she'd met him later and, yes, he had his good side, and for a while she'd wondered why her parents had been so unfeeling and –

She knew now why they'd tried to keep her away. There was far more to genetics than little squirmy spirals.

She could walk through walls when she really had to. She could use a tone of voice that was more like actions than words, that somehow reached inside people and operated all the right switches. And her hair . . .

That had only happened recently, though. It used to be unmanageable, but at around the age of seventeen she had found it more or less managed itself.

That had lost her several young men. Someone's hair rearranging itself into a new style, the tresses curling around themselves like a nest of kittens, could definitely put the crimp on any relationship.

She'd been making good progress, though. She could go for *days* now without feeling anything other than entirely human.

But it was always the case, wasn't it? You could go out into the world, succeed on your own terms, and sooner or later some embarrassing old relative was bound to turn up.

Grunting and swearing, the gnome clambered out of another drainpipe, jammed its hat firmly on its head, threw its sack on to a snowdrift and jumped down after it.

''s a good one,' he said. 'Ha, take 'im *weeks* to get rid of *that* one!'

He took a crumpled piece of paper out of a pocket and examined it closely. Then he looked at an elderly figure working away quietly at the next house.

It was standing by a window, drawing with great concentration on the glass.

The gnome wandered up, interested, and watched critically.

molar had, with hindsight, been a mistake.
Skulls never frightened her, even then.

'Why just fern patterns?' he said, after a while. 'Pretty, yeah, but you wouldn't catch me puttin' a penny in your hat for fern patterns.'

The figure turned, brush in hand.

'I happen to like fern patterns,' said Jack Frost coldly.

'It's just that people expect, you know, sad big-eyed kids, kittens lookin' out of boots, little doggies, that sort of thing.'

'I do ferns.'

'Or big pots of sunflowers, happy seaside scenes ...'

'And ferns.'

'I mean, s'posing some big high priest wanted you to paint the temple ceiling with gods 'n' angels and suchlike, what'd you do then?'

'He could have as many gods and angels as he liked, provided they –'

'– looked like ferns?'

'I resent the implication that I am solely fern-fixated,' said Jack Frost. 'I can also do a very nice paisley pattern.'

'What's that look like, then?'

'Well ... it does, admittedly, have a certain ferny quality to the uninitiated eye.' Frost leaned forward. 'Who're you?'

The gnome took a step backwards.

'You're not a tooth fairy, are you? I see more and more of them about these days. Nice girls.'

'Nah. Nah. Not teeth,' said the gnome, clutching his sack.

'What, then?'

The gnome told him.

'Really?' said Jack Frost. 'I thought they just turned up.'

'Well, come to *that*, I thought frost on the windows just happened all by itself,' said the gnome. "ere, you don't half look spiky. I bet you go through a lot of bedsheets.'

'I don't sleep,' said Frost icily, turning away. 'And now, if you'll excuse me, I have a large number of windows to do. Ferns aren't easy. You need a steady hand.'

'What do you mean dead?' Susan demanded. 'How can the Hogfather be *dead*? He's ... isn't he what you are? An –'

Anthropomorphic personification. Yes. He has become so. The spirit of Hogswatch.

'But ... how? How can anyone kill the Hogfather? Poisoned sherry? Spikes in the chimney?'

There are ... more subtle ways.

'Coff. Coff. Coff. Oh dear, this soot,' said Albert loudly. 'Chokes me up something cruel.'

'And you've taken over?' said Susan, ignoring him. 'That's *sick!*'

Death contrived to look hurt.

'I'll just go and have a look somewhere,' said Albert, brushing past her and opening the door.

She pushed it shut quickly.

'And what are you doing here, Albert?' she said, clutching at the straw. 'I thought you'd die if you ever came back to the world!'

AH, BUT WE ARE NOT IN THE WORLD, said Death. WE ARE IN THE SPECIAL CONGRUENT REALITY CREATED FOR THE HOGFATHER. NORMAL RULES HAVE TO BE SUSPENDED. HOW ELSE COULD ANYONE GET AROUND THE ENTIRE WORLD IN ONE NIGHT?

''s right,' said Albert, leering. 'One of the Hogfather's Little Helpers, me. Official. Got the pointy green hat and everything.' He spotted the glass of sherry and couple of turnips that the children had left on the table, and bore down on them.

Susan looked shocked. A couple of days earlier she'd taken the children to the Hogfather's Grotto in one of the big shops in The Maul. Of course, it wasn't the real one, but it had turned out to be a fairly good actor in a red suit. There had been people dressed up as pixies, and a picket outside the shop by the Campaign for Equal Heights.*

None of the pixies had looked anything like Albert. If they had, people would have only gone into the grotto armed.

'Been good, 'ave yer?' said Albert, and spat into the fireplace.

Susan stared at him.

Death leaned down. She stared up into the blue glow of his eyes.

YOU ARE KEEPING WELL? he said.

'Yes.'

SELF-RELIANT? MAKING YOUR OWN WAY IN THE WORLD?

'Yes!'

GOOD. WELL, COME, ALBERT. WE WILL LOAD THE STOCKINGS AND GET ON WITH THINGS.

A couple of letters appeared in Death's hand.

SOMEONE CHRISTENED THE CHILD TWYLA?

---

* The CEH was always ready to fight for the rights of the differently tall, and was not put off by the fact that most pixies and gnomes weren't the least interested in dressing up in little pointy hats with bells on when there were other far more interesting things to do. All that tinkly-wee stuff was for the old folks back home in the forest – when a tiny man hit Ankh-Morpork he preferred to get drunk, kick some serious ankle, and search for tiny women. In fact the CEH now had to spend so much time explaining to people that they hadn't got enough rights that they barely had any time left to fight for them.

'I'm afraid so, but why –'
AND THE OTHER ONE GAWAIN?
'Yes. But look, how –'
WHY GAWAIN?
'I . . . suppose it's a good strong name for a fighter . . .'
A SELF-FULFILLING PROPHECY, I SUSPECT. I SEE THE GIRL WRITES IN GREEN CRAYON ON PINK PAPER WITH A MOUSE IN THE CORNER. THE MOUSE IS WEARING A DRESS.

'I ought to point out that she decided to do that so the Hogfather would think she was sweet,' said Susan. 'Including the deliberate bad spelling. But look, why are *you* –'
SHE SAYS SHE IS FIVE YEARS OLD.
'In years, yes. In cynicism, she's about thirty-five. Why are *you* doing the –'
BUT SHE BELIEVES IN THE HOGFATHER?
'She'd believe in anything if there was a dolly in it for her. But you're *not* going to leave without telling me –'
Death hung the stockings back on the mantelpiece.
NOW WE MUST BE GOING. HAPPY HOGSWATCH. ER . . . OH, YES: HO. HO. HO.
'Nice sherry,' said Albert, wiping his mouth.
Rage overtook Susan's curiosity. It had to travel quite fast.
'You've actually been drinking the actual drinks little children leave out for the actual Hogfather?' she said.
'Yeah, why not? *He* ain't drinking 'em. Not where *he's* gone.'
'And how many have you had, may I ask?'
'Dunno, ain't counted,' said Albert happily.
ONE MILLION, EIGHT HUNDRED THOUSAND, SEVEN HUNDRED AND SIX, said Death. AND SIXTY-EIGHT THOUSAND, THREE HUNDRED AND NINETEEN PORK PIES. AND ONE TURNIP.
'It looked pork-pie shaped,' said Albert. 'Everything does, after a while.'
'Then why haven't you exploded?'
'Dunno. Always had a good digestion.'
TO THE HOGFATHER, ALL PORK PIES ARE AS ONE PORK PIE. EXCEPT THE ONE LIKE A TURNIP. COME, ALBERT. WE HAVE TRESPASSED ON SUSAN'S TIME.
'*Why are you doing this*?' Susan screamed.
I AM SORRY. I CANNOT TELL YOU. FORGET YOU SAW ME. IT'S NOT YOUR BUSINESS.
'Not my business? How can –'
AND NOW . . . WE MUST BE GOING . . .

'Nighty-night,' said Albert.

The clock struck, twice, for the half-hour. It was still half past six. And they were gone.

The sledge hurtled across the sky.

'She'll try to find out what this is all about, you know,' said Albert.

OH DEAR.

'Especially after you told her not to.'

YOU THINK SO?

'Yeah,' said Albert.

DEAR ME. I STILL HAVE A LOT TO LEARN ABOUT HUMANS, DON'T I?

'Oh ... I dunno ...' said Albert.

OBVIOUSLY IT WOULD BE QUITE WRONG TO INVOLVE A HUMAN IN ALL THIS. THAT IS WHY, YOU WILL RECALL, I CLEARLY FORBADE HER TO TAKE AN INTEREST.

'Yeah ... you did ...'

BESIDES, IT'S AGAINST THE RULES.

'You said them little grey buggers had already broken the rules.'

YES, BUT I CAN'T JUST WAVE A MAGIC WAND AND MAKE IT ALL BETTER. THERE MUST BE PROCEDURES. Death stared ahead for a moment and then shrugged. AND WE HAVE SO MUCH TO DO. WE HAVE PROMISES TO KEEP.

'Well, the night is young,' said Albert, sitting back in the sacks.

THE NIGHT IS OLD. THE NIGHT IS ALWAYS OLD.

The pigs galloped on. Then, 'No, it ain't.'

I'M SORRY?

'The night isn't any older than the day, master. It stands to reason. There must have been a day before anyone knew what the night was.'

YES, BUT IT'S MORE DRAMATIC.

'Oh. Right, then.'

Susan stood by the fireplace.

It wasn't as though she *disliked* Death. Death considered as an individual rather than life's final curtain was someone she couldn't help liking, in a strange kind of way.

Even so ...

The idea of the Grim Reaper filling the Hogswatch stockings of the world didn't fit well in her head, no matter which way she twisted it. It was like trying to imagine Old Man Trouble as the Tooth Fairy. Oh, yes. Old Man Trouble ... now *there* was a nasty one for you ...

But *honestly*, what kind of *sick* person went round creeping into little children's bedrooms all night?

Well, the Hogfather, of course, but ...

There was a little tinkling sound from somewhere near the base of the Hogswatch tree.

The raven backed away from the shards of one of the glittering balls.

'Sorry,' it mumbled. 'Bit of a species reaction there. You know ... round, glittering ... sometimes you just gotta peck –'

'That chocolate money belongs to the children!'

SQUEAK? said the Death of Rats, backing away from the shiny coins.

'Why's he doing this?'

SQUEAK.

'You don't know either?'

SQUEAK.

'Is there some kind of trouble? Did he *do* something to the real Hogfather?'

SQUEAK.

'Why won't he tell me?'

SQUEAK.

'Thank you. You've been very helpful.'

Something ripped, behind her. She turned and saw the raven carefully removing a strip of red wrapping paper from a package.

'Stop that this minute!'

It looked up guiltily.

'It's only a little bit,' it said. 'No one's going to miss it.'

'What do you want it for, anyway?'

'We're attracted to bright colours, right? Automatic reaction.'

'That's jackdaws!'

'Damn. Is it?'

The Death of Rats nodded. SQUEAK.

'Oh, so suddenly you're Mr Ornithologist, are you?' snapped the raven.

Susan sat down and held out her hand.

The Death of Rats leapt on to it. She could feel its claws, like tiny pins.

It was just like those scenes where the sweet and pretty heroine sings a little duet with Mr Bluebird.

Similar, anyway.

In general outline, at least. But with more of a PG rating.

'*Has* he gone funny in the head?'

SQUEAK. The rat shrugged.

'But it could happen, couldn't it? He's very old, and I suppose he sees a lot of terrible things.'

SQUEAK.

'All the trouble in the world,' the raven translated.

'I understood,' said Susan. That was a talent, too. She didn't understand what the rat said. She just understood what it meant.

'There's something wrong and he won't tell me?' said Susan.

That made her even more angry.

'But Albert is in on it too,' she added.

She thought: thousands, *millions* of years in the same job. Not a nice one. It isn't always cheerful old men passing away at a great age. Sooner or later, it was bound to get anyone down.

Someone had to do something. It was like that time when Twyla's grandmother had started telling everyone that she was the Empress of Krull and had stopped wearing clothes.

And Susan was bright enough to know that the phrase 'Someone ought to do something' was not, by itself, a helpful one. People who used it *never* added the rider 'and that someone is me'. But someone ought to do something, and right now the whole pool of someones consisted of her, and no one else.

Twyla's grandmother had ended up in a nursing home overlooking the sea at Quirm. That sort of option probably didn't apply here. Besides, he'd be unpopular with the other residents.

She concentrated. *This* was the simplest talent of them all. She was amazed that other people couldn't do it. She shut her eyes, placed her hands palm down in front of her at shoulder height, spread her fingers and lowered her hands.

When they were halfway down she heard the clock stop ticking. The last tick was long-drawn-out, like a death rattle.

Time stopped.

But *duration* continued.

She'd always wondered, when she was small, why visits to her grand-father could go on for days and yet, when they got back, the calendar was still plodding along as if they'd never been away.

Now she knew the why, although probably no human being would ever really understand the how. Sometimes, somewhere, somehow, the numbers on the clock did not count.

Between every rational moment were a billion irrational ones. Somewhere behind the hours there was a place where the Hogfather rode, the tooth fairies climbed their ladders, Jack Frost drew his pictures, the Soul Cake Duck laid her chocolate eggs. In the endless spaces between the clumsy seconds Death moved like a witch dancing through raindrops, never getting wet.

Humans could liv– No, humans couldn't *live* here, no, because even when you diluted a glass of wine with a bathful of water you might have more liquid but you still have the same amount of wine. A rubber band was still the same rubber band no matter how far it was stretched.

Humans could *exist* here, though.

It was never too cold, although the air did prickle like winter air on a sunny day. But out of human habit Susan got her cloak out of the closet.

Squeak.

'Haven't you got some mice and rats to see to, then?'

'Nah, 's pretty quiet just before Hogswatch,' said the raven, who was trying to fold the red paper between his claws. 'You get a lot of gerbils and hamsters and that in a few days, mind. When the kids forget to feed them or try to find out what makes them go.'

Of course, she'd be leaving the children. But it wasn't as if anything could happen to them. There wasn't any time for it to happen to them in.

She hurried down the stairs and let herself out of the front door.

Snow hung in the air. It was not a poetic description. It hovered like the stars. When flakes touched Susan they melted with little electric flashes.

There was a lot of traffic in the street, but it was fossilized in Time. She walked carefully between it until she reached the entrance to the park.

The snow had done what even wizards and the Watch couldn't do, which was clean up Ankh-Morpork. It hadn't had time to get dirty. In the morning it'd probably look as though the city had been covered in coffee meringue, but for now it mounded the bushes and trees in pure white.

There was no noise. The curtains of snow shut out the city lights. A few yards into the park and she might as well be in the country.

She stuck her fingers into her mouth and whistled.

'Y'know, that could've been done with a bit more ceremony,' said the raven, who'd perched on a snow-encrusted twig.

'Shut up.'

''s good, though. Better than most women could do.'

'Shut up.'

They waited.

'Why have you stolen that piece of red paper from a little girl's present?' said Susan.

'I've got plans,' said the raven darkly.

They waited again.

She wondered what would happen if it didn't work. She wondered if the rat would snigger. It had the most annoying snigger in the world.

Then there were hoofbeats and the floating snow burst open and the horse was there.

Binky trotted round in a circle, and then stood and steamed.

He wasn't saddled. Death's horse didn't let you fall.

If I get on, Susan thought, it'll all start again. I'll be out of the light and into the world beyond this one. I'll fall off the tightrope.

But a voice inside her said, *You want to, though . . . don't you . . . ?*

Ten seconds later, there was only the snow.

The raven turned to the Death of Rats.

'Any idea where I can get some string?'

SQUEAK.

She was watched.

One said, Who is she?

One said, Do we remember that Death adopted a daughter? The young woman is *her* daughter.

One said, She is human?

One said, Mostly.

One said, Can she be killed?

One said, Oh, yes.

One said, Well, that's all right, then.

One said, Er . . . we don't think we're going to get into trouble over this, do we? All this is not exactly . . . authorized. We don't want questions asked.

One said, We have a duty to rid the universe of sloppy thinking.

One said, Everyone will be grateful when they find out.

*

Binky touched down lightly on Death's lawn.

Susan didn't bother with the front door but went round the back, which was never locked.

There had been changes. One significant change, at least.

There was a cat-flap in the door.

She stared at it.

After a second or two a ginger cat came through the flap, gave her an I'm-not-hungry-and-you're-not-interesting look, and padded off into the gardens.

Susan pushed open the door into the kitchen.

Cats of every size and colour covered every surface. Hundreds of eyes swivelled to watch her.

It was Mrs Gammage all over again, she thought. The old woman was a regular in Biers for the company and was quite gaga, and one of the symptoms of those going completely yoyo was that they broke out in chronic cats. Usually cats who'd mastered every detail of feline existence except the whereabouts of the dirt box.

Several of them had their noses in a bowl of cream.

Susan had never been able to see the attraction in cats. They were owned by the kind of people who liked puddings. There were actual people in the world whose idea of heaven would be a chocolate cat.

'Push off, the lot of you,' she said. 'I've never known him have *pets*.'

The cats gave her a look to indicate that they were intending to go somewhere else in any case and strolled off, licking their chops.

The bowl slowly filled up again.

They were obviously living cats. Only life had colour here. Everything else was created by Death. Colour, along with plumbing and music, were arts that escaped the grasp of his genius.

She left them in the kitchen and wandered along to the study.

There were changes here, too. By the look of it, he'd been trying to learn to play the violin again. He'd never been able to understand why he couldn't play music.

The desk was a mess. Books lay open, piled on one another. They were the ones Susan had never learned to read. Some of the characters hovered above the pages or moved in complicated little patterns as they read you while you read them.

Intricate devices had been scattered across the top. They looked vaguely navigational, but on what oceans and under which stars?

Several pages of parchment had been filled up with Death's own handwriting. It was immediately recognizable. No one else Susan had ever met had handwriting with serifs.

It looked as though he'd been trying to work something out.

> NOT KLATCH. NOT HOWONDALAND. NOT THE EMPIRE.
> LET US SAY 20 MILLION CHILDREN AT 2LB OF TOYS PER CHILD.
> EQUALS 17,857 TONS. 1,785 TONS PER HOUR.
> MEMO: DON'T FORGET THE SOOTY FOOTPRINTS. MORE PRACTICE ON THE HO HO HO.
> CUSHION.

She put the paper back carefully.

Sooner or later it'd get to you. Death was fascinated by humans, and study was never a one-way thing. A man might spend his life peering at the private life of elementary particles and then find he either knew who he was or where he was, but not both. Death had picked up ... humanity. Not the real thing, but something that might pass for it until you examined it closely.

The house even imitated human houses. Death had created a bedroom for himself, despite the fact that he never slept. If he really picked things up from humans, had he tried insanity? It was very popular, after all.

Perhaps, after all these millennia, he wanted to be nice.

She let herself into the Room of Lifetimers. She'd liked the sound of it, when she was a little girl. But now the hiss of sand from millions of hourglasses, and the little *pings* and *pops* as full ones vanished and new empty ones appeared, was not so enjoyable. *Now* she knew what was going on. Of course, everyone died sooner or later. It just wasn't right to be listening to it happening.

She was about to leave when she noticed the open door in a place where she had never seen a door before.

It was disguised. A whole section of shelving, complete with its whispering glasses, had swung out.

Susan pushed it back and forth with a finger. When it was shut, you'd have to look hard to see the crack.

There was a much smaller room on the other side. It was merely the size of, say, a cathedral. And it was lined floor to ceiling with more hourglasses that Susan could just see dimly in the light from the big room. She stepped inside and snapped her fingers.

'Light,' she commanded. A couple of candles sprang into life.

The hourglasses were ... wrong.

The ones in the main room, however metaphorical they might be, were solid-looking things of wood and brass and glass. But *these* looked as though they were made of highlights and shadows with no real substance at all.

She peered at a large one.

The name in it was: OFFLER.

'The crocodile god?' she thought.

Well, gods had a life, presumably. But they never actually died, as far as she knew. They just dwindled away to a voice on the wind and a footnote in some textbook on religion.

There were other gods lined up. She recognized a few of them.

But there were smaller lifetimers on the shelf. When she saw the labels she nearly burst out laughing.

'The Tooth Fairy? The Sandman? John Barleycorn? The Soul Cake Duck? The God of – *what?*'

She stepped back, and something crunched under her feet.

There were shards of glass on the floor. She reached down and picked up the biggest. Only a few letters remained of the name etched into the glass –

HOGFA . . .

'Oh, no . . . it's *true*. Granddad, what have you *done?*'

When she left, the candles winked out. Darkness sprang back.

And, in the darkness, among the spilled sand, a faint sizzle and a tiny spark of light . . .

Mustrum Ridcully adjusted the towel around his waist.

'How're we doing, Mr Modo?'

The University gardener saluted.

'The tanks are full, Mr Archchancellor sir!' he said brightly. 'And I've been stoking the hot-water boilers all day!'

The other senior wizards clustered in the doorway.

'Really, Mustrum, I really think this is *most* unwise,' said the Lecturer in Recent Runes. 'It was surely sealed up for a purpose.'

'Remember what it said on the door,' said the Dean.

'Oh, they just wrote that on it to keep people out,' said Ridcully, opening a fresh bar of soap.

'Well, yes,' said the Chair of Indefinite Studies. 'That's right. That's what people do.'

'It's a *bathroom*,' said Ridcully. 'You are all acting as if it's some kind of a torture chamber.'

'A bathroom,' said the Dean, 'designed by Bloody Stupid Johnson.

Archchancellor Weatherwax only used it once and then had it sealed up! Mustrum, I beg you to reconsider! It's a *Johnson*!'

There was something of a pause, because even Ridcully had to adjust his mind around this.

The late (or at least severely delayed) Bergholt Stuttley Johnson was generally recognized as the worst inventor in the world, yet in a very specialized sense. Merely *bad* inventors made things that failed to operate. He wasn't among these small fry. Any fool could make something that did absolutely nothing when you pressed the button. He scorned such fumble-fingered amateurs. Everything he built worked. It just didn't do what it said on the box. If you wanted a small ground-to-air missile, you asked Johnson to design an ornamental fountain. It amounted to pretty much the same thing. But this never discouraged him, or the morbid curiosity of his clients. Music, landscape gardening, architecture – there was no start to his talents.

Nevertheless, it was a little bit surprising to find that Bloody Stupid had turned to bathroom design. But, as Ridcully said, it was known that he had designed and built several large musical organs and, when you got right down to it, it was all just plumbing, wasn't it?

The other wizards, who'd been there longer than the Archchancellor, took the view that if Bloody Stupid Johnson had built a fully functional bathroom he'd actually meant it to be something else.

'Y'know, I've always felt that Mr Johnson was a much maligned man,' said Ridcully, eventually.

'Well, yes, of *course* he was,' said the Lecturer in Recent Runes, clearly exasperated. 'That's like saying that jam attracts wasps, you see.'

'Not everything he made worked badly,' said Ridcully stoutly, flourishing his scrubbing brush. 'Look at that thing they use down in the kitchens for peelin' the potatoes, for example.'

'Ah, you mean the thing with the brass plate on it saying "Improved Manicure Device", Archchancellor?'

'Listen, it's just water,' snapped Ridcully. 'Even Johnson couldn't do much harm with water. Modo, open the sluices!'

The rest of the wizards backed away as the gardener turned a couple of ornate brass wheels.

'I'm fed up with groping around for the soap like you fellows!' shouted the Archchancellor, as water gushed through hidden channels. 'Hygiene. That's the ticket!'

'Don't say we didn't warn you,' said the Dean, shutting the door.

'Er, I still haven't worked out where all the pipes lead, sir,' Modo ventured.

'We'll find out, never you fear,' said Ridcully happily. He removed his hat and put on a shower cap of his own design. In deference to his profession, it was pointy. He picked up a yellow rubber duck.

'Man the pumps, Mr Modo. Or dwarf them, of course, in your case.'

'Yes, Archchancellor.'

Modo hauled on a lever. The pipes started a hammering noise and steam leaked out of a few joints.

Ridcully took a last look around the bathroom.

It was a hidden treasure, no doubt about it. Say what you like, old Johnson must sometimes have got it right, even if it was only by accident. The entire room, including the floor and ceiling, had been tiled in white, blue and green. In the centre, under its crown of pipes, was Johnson's Patent 'Typhoon' Superior Indoor Ablutorium with Automatic Soap Dish, a sanitary poem in mahogany, rosewood and copper.

He'd got Modo to polish every pipe and brass tap until they gleamed. It had taken ages.

Ridcully shut the frosted door behind him.

The inventor of the ablutionary marvel had decided to make a mere shower a fully controllable experience, and one wall of the large cubicle held a marvellous panel covered with brass taps cast in the shape of mermaids and shells and, for some reason, pomegranates. There were separate feeds for salt water, hard water and soft water and huge wheels for accurate control of temperature. Ridcully inspected them with care.

Then he stood back, looked around at the tiles and sang, 'Mi, mi, mi!'

His voice reverberated back at him.

'A perfect echo!' said Ridcully, one of nature's bathroom baritones.

He picked up a speaking tube that had been installed to allow the bather to communicate with the engineer.

'All cisterns go, Mr Modo!'

'Aye aye, sir!'

Ridcully opened the tap marked 'Spray' and leapt aside, because part of him was still well aware that Johnson's inventiveness didn't just push the edge of the envelope but often went across the room and out through the wall of the sorting office.

A gentle shower of warm water, almost a caressing mist, enveloped him.

'My word!' he exclaimed, and tried another tap.

'Shower' turned out to be a little more invigorating. 'Torrent' made him gasp for breath and 'Deluge' sent him groping to the panel because the top of his head felt that it was being removed. 'Wave' sloshed a wall of warm salt water from one side of the cubicle to the other before it disappeared into the grating that was set into the middle of the floor.

'Are you all right, sir?' Modo called out.

'Marvellous! And there's a dozen knobs I haven't tried yet!'

Modo nodded, and tapped a valve. Ridcully's voice, raised in what he considered to be song, boomed out through the thick clouds of steam.

'Oh, IIIIIIII knew a . . . er . . . an agricultural worker of some description, possibly a thatcher,

And I knew him well, and he – he was a farmer, now I come to think of it – and he had a daughter and her name I can't recall at the moment,

And . . . Where was I? Ah yes. Chorus:

Something something, a humorously shaped vegetable, a turnip, I believe, something something and the sweet nightingaleeeeaarg-goooooohARRGHH oh oh oh –'

The song shut off suddenly. All Modo could hear was a ferocious gushing noise.

'Archchancellor?'

After a moment a voice answered from near the ceiling. It sounded somewhat high and hesitant.

'Er . . . I wonder if you would be so very good as to shut the water off from out there, my dear chap? Er . . . quite gently, if you wouldn't mind . . .'

Modo carefully spun a wheel. The gushing sound gradually subsided.

'Ah. Well done,' said the voice, but now from somewhere nearer floor level. 'Well. Jolly good job. I think we can definitely call it a success. Yes, indeed. Er. I wonder if you could help me walk for a moment. I inexplicably feel a little unsteady on my feet . . .'

Modo pushed open the door and helped Ridcully out and on to a bench. He looked rather pale.

'Yes, indeed,' said the Archancellor, his eyes a little glazed. 'Astoundingly successful. Er. Just a minor point, Modo –'

'Yes, sir?'

'There's a tap in there we perhaps should leave alone for now,' said Ridcully. 'I'd esteem it a service if you could go and make a little sign to hang on it.'

'Yes, sir?'

'Saying "Do not touch at all", or something like that.'

'Right, sir.'

'Hang it on the one marked "Old Faithful".'

'Yes, sir.'

'No need to mention it to the other fellows.'

'Yes, sir.'

'Ye gods, I've never felt so *clean*.'

From a vantage point among some ornamental tilework near the ceiling a small gnome in a bowler hat watched Ridcully carefully.

When Modo had gone the Archchancellor slowly began to dry himself on a big fluffy towel. As he got his composure back, so another song wormed its way under his breath.

'*On the second day of Hogswatch I . . . sent my true love back A nasty little letter,* hah, yes indeed, *and a partridge in a pear tree –*'

The gnome slid down on to the tiles and crept up behind the briskly shaking shape.

Ridcully, after a few more trial runs, settled on a song which evolves somewhere on every planet where there are winters. It's often dragooned into the service of some local religion and a few words are changed, but it's really about things that have to do with gods only in the same way that roots have to do with leaves.

'*– the rising of the sun, and the running of the deer –*'

Ridcully spun. A corner of wet towel caught the gnome on the ear and flicked it on to its back.

'I saw you creeping up!' roared the Archchancellor. 'What's the game, then? Small-time thief, are you?'

The gnome slid backwards on the soapy surface.

"ere, what's *your* game, mister, you ain't supposed to be able to see me!'

'I'm a wizard! We can see things that are really there, you know,' said Ridcully. 'And in the case of the Bursar, things that aren't there, too. What's in this bag?'

'You don't wanna open the bag, mister! You really don't wanna open the bag!'

'Why? What have you got in it?'

The gnome sagged.' It ain't what's in it, mister. It's what'll come out. I has to let 'em out one at a time, no knowin' what'd happen if they all gets out at once!'

Ridcully looked interested, and started to undo the string.

'You'll really wish you hadn't, mister!' the gnome pleaded.

'Will I? What're you doing here, young man?'

The gnome gave up.

'Well . . . you know the Tooth Fairy?'

'Yes. Of course,' said Ridcully.

'Well . . . I ain't her. But . . . it's sort of like the same business . . .'

'What? You take things away?'

'Er . . . not take away, as such. More sort of . . . bring . . .'

'Ah . . . like new teeth?'

'Er . . . like new verrucas,' said the gnome.

Death threw the sack into the back of the sledge and climbed in after it.

'You're doing well, master,' said Albert.

THIS CUSHION IS STILL UNCOMFORTABLE, said Death, hitching his belt. I AM NOT USED TO A BIG FAT STOMACH.

'Just *a* stomach's the best I could do, master. You're starting off with a handicap, sort of thing.'

Albert unscrewed the top off a bottle of cold tea. All the sherry had made him thirsty.

'Doing well, master,' he repeated, taking a pull. 'All the soot in the fireplace, the footprints, them swigged sherries, the sleigh tracks all over the roofs . . . it's got to work.'

YOU THINK SO?

'Sure'.

AND I MADE SURE SOME OF THEM SAW ME. I KNOW IF THEY ARE PEEPING, Death added proudly.

'Well done, sir.'

YES.

'Though here's a tip, though. *Just* "Ho. Ho. Ho," will do. Don't say, "Cower, brief mortals" unless you want them to grow up to be moneylenders or some such.'

HO. HO. HO.

'Yes, you're really getting the hang of it.' Albert looked down hurriedly at his notebook so that Death wouldn't see his face. 'Now, I got to tell you, master, what'll *really* do some good is a public appearance. Really.'

OH. I DON'T NORMALLY DO THEM.

'The Hogfather's more've a public figure, master. And one good public appearance'll do more good than any amount of letting kids see you by accident. Good for the old belief muscles.'

REALLY? HO. HO. HO.

'Right, right, that's really *good*, master. Where was I . . . yes . . . the shops'll be open late. Lots of kiddies get taken to see the Hogfather, you see. Not the *real* one, of course. Just some ole geezer with a pillow up his jumper, saving yer presence, master.'

NOT REAL? HO. HO. HO.

'Oh, no. And you don't need –'

THE CHILDREN KNOW THIS? HO. HO. HO.

Albert scratched his nose. 'S'pose so, master.'

THIS SHOULD NOT BE. NO WONDER THERE HAS BEEN . . . THIS DIFFICULTY. BELIEF WAS COMPROMISED? HO. HO. HO.

'Could be, master. Er, the "ho, ho –"'

WHERE DOES THIS TRAVESTY TAKE PLACE? HO. HO. HO.

Albert gave up. 'Well, Crumley's in The Maul, for one. Very popular, the Hogfather Grotto. They always have a good Hogfather, apparently.'

LET'S GET THERE AND SLEIGH THEM. HO. HO. HO.

'Right you are, master.'

THAT WAS A PUNE OR PLAY ON WORDS, ALBERT. I DON'T KNOW IF YOU NOTICED.

'I'm laughing like hell deep down, sir.'

HO. HO. HO.

Archchancellor Ridcully grinned.

He often grinned. He was one of those men who grinned even when they were annoyed, but right now he grinned because he was proud. A little sore still, perhaps, but still proud.

'Amazing bathroom, ain't it?' he said. 'They had it walled up, you know. Damn silly thing to do. I mean, perhaps there were a few teething troubles,' he shifted gingerly, 'but that's only to be expected. It's got everything, d'you see? Foot baths in the shape of clam shells, look. A whole wardrobe for dressing gowns. And that tub over there's got a big blower thingy so's you get bubbly water without even havin' to eat starchy food. And this thingy here with the mermaids holdin' it up's a special pot for your toenail clippings. It's got everything, this place.'

'A special pot for nail clippings?' said the Verruca Gnome.

'Oh, can't be too careful,' said Ridcully, lifting the lid of an ornate jar marked BATH SALTS and pulling out a bottle of wine. 'Get hold of something like someone's nail clipping and you've got 'em under your control. That's real old magic. Dawn of time stuff.'

He held the wine bottle up to the light.

'Should be cooled nicely by now,' he said, extracting the cork. 'Verrucas, eh?'

'Wish I knew why,' said the gnome.

'You mean you don't know?'

'Nope. Suddenly I wake up and I'm the Verruca Gnome.'

'Puzzling, that,' said Ridcully. 'My dad used to say the Verruca Gnome turned up if you walked around in bare feet but I never knew you *existed*. I thought he just made it up. I mean, tooth fairies, yes, and them little buggers that live in flowers, used to collect 'em myself as a lad, but can't recall anything about verrucas.' He drank thoughtfully. 'Got a distant cousin called Verruca, as a matter of fact. It's quite a nice sound, when you come to think of it.'

He looked at the gnome over the top of his glass.

You didn't become Archchancellor without a feeling for subtle wrongness in a situation. Well, that wasn't quite true. It was more accurate to say that you didn't *remain* Archchancellor for very long.

'Good job, is it?' he said thoughtfully.

'Dandruff'd be better,' said the gnome. 'At least I'd be out in the fresh air.'

'I think we'd better check up on this,' said Ridcully. 'Of course, it might be nothing.'

'Oh, thank you,' said the Verruca Gnome, gloomily.

It was a magnificent Grotto this year, Vernon Crumley told himself. The staff had worked really hard. The Hogfather's sleigh was a work of art in itself, and the pigs looked really real and a *wonderful* shade of pink.

The Grotto took up nearly all of the first floor. One of the pixies had been Disciplined for smoking behind the Magic Tinkling Waterfall and the clockwork Dolls of All Nations showing how We Could All Get Along were a bit jerky and giving trouble but all in all, he told himself, it was a display to Delight the Hearts of Kiddies everywhere.

The kiddies were queueing up with their parents and watching the display owlishly.

And the money was coming in. Oh, how the money was coming in.

So that the staff would not be Tempted, Mr Crumley had set up an arrangement of overhead wires across the ceilings of the store. In the middle of each floor was a cashier in a little cage. Staff took money from customers, put it in a little clockwork cable car, sent it whizzing overhead to the cashier, who'd make change and start it rattling back again. Thus there was no possibility of Temptation, and the little trolleys were shooting back and forth like fireworks.

Mr Crumley loved Hogswatch. It was for the Kiddies, after all. He tucked his fingers in the pockets of his waistcoat and beamed.

'Everything going well, Miss Harding?'

'Yes, Mr Crumley,' said the cashier, meekly.

'*Jolly* good.' He looked at the pile of coins.

A bright little zig-zag crackled off them and earthed itself on the metal grille.

Mr Crumley blinked. In front of him sparks flashed off the steel rims of Miss Harding's spectacles.

The Grotto display changed. For just a fraction of a second Mr Crumley had the sensation of speed, as though what appeared had screeched to a halt. Which was *ridiculous*.

The four pink papier-maché pigs exploded. A cardboard snout bounced off Mr Crumley's head.

There, sweating and grunting in the place where the little piggies had been, were ... well, he assumed they were pigs, because hippopotamuses didn't have pointy ears and rings through their noses. But the creatures were huge and grey and bristly and a cloud of acrid mist hung over each one.

And they didn't look sweet. There was nothing charming about them. One turned to look at him with small, red eyes, and didn't go 'oink', which was the sound that Mr Crumley, born and raised in the city, had always associated with pigs.

It went '*Ghnaaarrrwnnkh?*'

The sleigh had changed, too. He'd been very pleased with that sleigh. It had delicate silver curly bits on it. He'd personally supervised the gluing on of every twinkling star. But the splendour of it was lying in glittering shards around a sledge that looked as though it had been built of crudely sawn tree trunks laid on two massive wooden runners. It looked ancient and there were faces carved on the wood, nasty crude grinning faces that looked quite out of place.

Parents were yelling and trying to pull their children away, but they weren't having much luck. The children were gravitating towards it like flies to jam.

Mr Crumley ran towards the terrible thing, waving his hands. 'Stop that! Stop that!' he screamed. 'You'll frighten the Kiddies!'

He heard a small boy behind him say, 'They've got tusks! *Cool*!'

His sister said, 'Hey, look, that one's doing a wee!' A tremendous cloud of yellow steam arose. 'Look, it's going all the way to the stairs! All those who can't swim hold on to the banisters!'

'They eat you if you're bad, you know,' said a small girl with obvious approval. 'All up. Even the bones. They *crunch* them.'

Another, older, child opined: 'Don't be childish. They're not real. They've just got a wizard in to do the magic. Or it's all done by clockwork. Everyone knows they're not really r–'

One of the boars turned to look at him. The boy moved behind his mother.

Mr Crumley, tears of anger streaming down his face, fought through the milling crowd until he reached the Hogfather's Grotto. He grabbed a frightened pixie.

'It's the Campaign for Equal Heights that've done this, isn't it!' he shouted. 'They're out to ruin me! And they're ruining it for all the Kiddies! Look at the lovely dolls!'

The pixie hesitated. Children were clustering around the pigs, despite the continued efforts of their mothers. The small girl was giving one of them an orange.

But the animated display of Dolls of All Nations was definitely in trouble. The musical box underneath was still playing 'Wouldn't It Be Nice If Everyone Was Nice' but the rods that animated the figures had got twisted out of shape, so that the Klatchian boy was rhythmically hitting the Omnian girl over the head with his ceremonial spear, while the girl in Agatean national costume was kicking a small Llamedosian druid repeatedly in the ear. A chorus of small children was cheering them on indiscriminately.

'There's, er, there's more trouble in the Grotto, Mr Crum–' the pixie began.

A red and white figure pushed its way through the crush and rammed a false beard into Mr Crumley's hands.

'That's *it*,' said the old man in the Hogfather costume. 'I don't mind the smell of oranges and the damp trousers but I ain't putting up with *this*.'

He stamped off through the queue. Mr Crumley heard him add, 'And he's not even doin' it right!'

Mr Crumley forced his way onward.

Someone was sitting in the big chair. There was a child on his knee. The figure was . . . strange. It was definitely in something like a Hogfather costume but Mr Crumley's eye kept slipping, it wouldn't focus, it skittered away and tried to put the figure on the very edge of vision. It was like trying to look at your own ear.

'What's going on here? What's going on here?' Crumley demanded.

A hand took his shoulder firmly. He turned round and looked into the face of a Grotto Pixie. At least, it was wearing the costume of a Grotto Pixie, although somewhat askew, as if it had been put on in a hurry.

'Who are *you*?'

The pixie took the soggy cigarette end out of its mouth and leered at him.

'Call me Uncle Heavy,' he said.

'You're not a pixie!'

'Nah, I'm a fairy cobbler, mister.'

Behind Crumley, a voice said:

AND WHAT DO *YOU* WANT FOR HOGSWATCH, SMALL HUMAN?

Mr Crumley turned in horror.

In front of – well, he had to think of it as the usurping Hogfather – was a small child of indeterminate sex who seemed to be mostly woollen bobble hat.

Mr Crumley knew how it was supposed to go. It was supposed to go like this: the child was always struck dumb and the attendant mother would lean forward and catch the Hogfather's eye and say very pointedly, in that voice adults use when they're conspiring against children: 'You want a Baby Tinkler Doll, don't you, Doreen? And the Just Like Mummy Cookery Set you've got in the window. And the Cut-Out Kitchen Range Book. And what do you say?'

And the stunned child would murmur ''nk you' and get given a balloon or an orange.

This time, though, it didn't work like that.

Mother got as far as 'You want a –'

WHY ARE YOUR HANDS ON BITS OF STRING, CHILD?

The child looked down the length of its arms to the dangling mittens affixed to its sleeves. It held them up for inspection.

'Glubs,' it said.

I SEE. VERY PRACTICAL.

'Are you weal?' said the bobble hat.

WHAT DO *YOU* THINK?

The bobble hat sniggered. 'I saw your piggie do a wee!' it said, and implicit in the tone was the suggestion that this was unlikely to be dethroned as the most enthralling thing the bobble hat had ever seen.

Oh. Er ... Good.

'It had a gwate big –'

What do you want for Hogswatch? said the Hogfather hurriedly.

Mother took her economic cue again, and said briskly: 'She wants a –'

The Hogfather snapped his fingers impatiently. The mother's mouth slammed shut.

The child seemed to sense that here was a once-in-a-lifetime opportunity and spoke quickly.

'I wanta narmy. Anna big castle wif pointy bits,' said the child. 'Anna swored.'

What do you say? prompted the Hogfather.

'A *big* swored?' said the child, after a pause for deep cogitation.

That's right.

Uncle Heavy nudged the Hogfather.

They're supposed to *thank* you,' he said.

Are you sure? People don't, normally.

'I meant they thank the *Hogfather*,' Albert hissed. 'Which is you, right?'

Yes, of course. Ahem. You're supposed to say thank you.

''nk you.'

And be good. This is part of the arrangement.

''es.'

Then we have a contract. The Hogfather reached into his sack and produced

– a very large model castle with, as correctly interpreted, pointy blue cone roofs on turrets suitable for princesses to be locked in –

– a box of several hundred assorted knights and warriors –

– and a sword. It was four feet long and glinted along the blade. The mother took a deep breath.

'You can't give her that!' she screamed. 'It's not safe!'

It's a sword, said the Hogfather. They're not *meant* to be safe.

'She's a child!' shouted Crumley.

It's educational.

'What if she cuts herself?'

That will be an important lesson.

Uncle Heavy whispered urgently.

Really? Oh, well. It's not for me to argue, I suppose.

The blade went wooden.

'And she doesn't want all that other stuff!' said Doreen's mother, in the face of previous testimony. 'She's a girl! Anyway, I can't afford big posh stuff like that!'

I THOUGHT I GAVE IT AWAY, said the Hogfather, sounding bewildered.

'You do?' said the mother.

'You *do?*' said Crumley, who'd been listening in horror. 'You *don't*! That's our Merchandise! You can't give it away! Hogswatch isn't about giving it all away! I mean . . . yes, of course, of *course* things are given away,' he corrected himself, aware that people were watching, 'but first they have to be bought, d'you see, I mean . . . haha.' He laughed nervously, increasingly aware of the strangeness around him and the rangy look of Uncle Heavy. 'It's not as though the toys are made by little elves at the Hub, ahaha . . .'

'Damn right,' said Uncle Heavy sagely. 'You'd have to be a maniac even to think of giving an elf a chisel, less'n you want their initials carved on your forehead.'

'You mean this is all free?' said Doreen's mother sharply, not to be budged from what she saw as the central point.

Mr Crumley looked helplessly at the toys. They certainly didn't look like any of his stock.

Then he tried to look hard at the new Hogfather. Every cell in his brain was telling him that here was a fat jolly man in a red and white suit.

Well . . . nearly every cell. A few of the sparkier ones were saying that his eyes were reporting something else, but they couldn't agree on what. A couple had shut down completely.

The words escaped through his teeth.

'It . . . seems to be,' he said.

Although it was Hogswatch the University buildings were bustling. Wizards didn't go to bed early in any case,* and of course there was

---

* Often they lived to a timescale to suit themselves. Many of the senior ones, of course, lived entirely in the past, but several were like the Professor of Anthropics, who had invented an entire temporal system based on the belief that all the other ones were a mere illusion.

† Many people are aware of the Weak and Strong Anthropic Principles. The Weak One says, basically, that it was jolly amazing of the universe to be constructed in such a way that humans could evolve to a point where they make a living in, for example, universities, while the Strong One says that, on the contrary, the whole point of the universe was that humans should not only work in universities but also write for huge sums books with words like 'Cosmic' and 'Chaos' in the titles.†

The UU Professor of Anthropics had developed the Special and Inevitable Anthropic Principle, which was that the entire reason for the existence of the universe was the eventual evolution of the UU Professor of Anthropics. But this was only a formal statement of the theory which absolutely everyone, with only some minor details of a 'Fill in name here' nature, secretly the Hogswatchnight Feast to look forward to at midnight.

It would give some idea of the scale of the Hogswatchnight Feast that a light snack at UU consisted of a mere three or four courses, not counting the cheese and nuts.

Some of the wizards had been practising for weeks. The Dean in particular could now lift a twenty-pound turkey on one fork. Having to wait until midnight merely put a healthy edge on appetites already professionally honed.

There was a general air of pleasant expectancy about the place, a general sizzling of salivary glands, a general careful assembling of the pills and powders against the time, many hours ahead, when eighteen courses would gang up somewhere below the ribcage and mount a counter-attack.

Ridcully stepped out into the snow and turned up his collar. The lights were all on in the High Energy Magic Building.

'I don't know, I don't know,' he muttered. 'Hogswatchnight and they're *still* working. It's just not natural. When I was a student I'd have been sick twice by now –'

In fact Ponder Stibbons and his group of research students *had* made a concession to Hogswatchnight. They'd draped holly over Hex and put a paper hat on the big glass dome containing the main ant heap.

Every time he came in here, it seemed to Ridcully, something more had been done to the ... engine, or thinking machine, or whatever it was. Sometimes stuff turned up overnight. Occasionally, according to Stibbons, Hex hims– *itself* would draw plans for extra bits that he – *it* needed. It all gave Ridcully the willies, and an additional willy was engendered right now when he saw the Bursar sitting in front of the thing. For a moment, he forgot all about verrucas.

'What're you doing here, old chap?' he said. 'You should be inside, jumping up and down to make more room for tonight.'

'Hooray for the pink, grey and green,' said the Bursar.

'Er ... we thought Hex might be of ... you know ... help, sir,' said Ponder Stibbons, who liked to think of himself as the University's token sane person. 'With the Bursar's problem. We thought it might be a nice Hogswatch present for him.'

---

believes to be true.

† And they are correct. The universe clearly operates for the benefit of humanity. This can be readily seen from the convenient way the sun comes up in the morning, when people are ready to start the day.

'Ye gods, Bursar's got no problems,' said Ridcully, and patted the aimlessly smiling man on the head while mouthing the words 'mad as a spoon'. 'Mind just wanders a bit, that's all. I said MIND WANDERS A BIT, EH? Only to be expected, spends far too much time addin' up numbers. Doesn't get out in the fresh air. I said, YOU DON'T GET OUT IN THE FRESH AIR, OLD CHAP!'

'We thought, er, he might like someone to talk to,' said Ponder.

'What? What? But I talk to him all the time! I'm always trying to take him out of himself,' said Ridcully. 'It's important to stop him mopin' around the place.'

'Er . . . yes . . . certainly,' said Ponder diplomatically. He recalled the Bursar as a man whose idea of an exciting time had once been a soft-boiled egg. 'So . . . er . . . well, let's give it another try, shall we? Are you ready, Mr Dinwiddie?'

'Yes, thank you, a green one with cinnamon if it's not too much trouble.'

'Can't see how he can talk to a machine,' said Ridcully, in a sullen voice. 'The thing's got no damn ears.'

'Ah, well, in fact we made it *one* ear,' said Ponder. 'Er . . .'

He pointed to a large drum in a maze of tubes.

'Isn't that old Windle Poons' ear trumpet sticking out of the end?' said Ridcully suspiciously.

'Yes, Archchancellor.' Ponder cleared his throat. 'Sound, you see, comes in waves –'

He stopped. Wizardly premonitions rose in his mind. He just *knew* Ridcully was going to assume he was talking about the sea. There was going to be one of those huge bottomless misunderstandings that always occurred whenever anyone tried to explain anything to the Archchancellor. Words like 'surf', and probably 'ice cream' and 'sand' were just . . .

'It's all done by magic, Archchancellor,' he said, giving up.

'Ah. Right,' said Ridcully. He sounded a little disappointed. 'None of that complicated business with springs and cogwheels and tubes and stuff, then.'

'That's right, sir,' said Ponder. 'Just magic. Sufficiently *advanced* magic.'

'Fair enough. What's it do?'

'Hex can hear what you say.'

'Interesting. Saves all that punching holes in bits of cards and hitting keys you lads are forever doing, then –'

'Watch this, sir,' said Ponder. 'All right, Adrian, initialize the GBL.'

'How do you do that, then?' said Ridcully, behind him.

'It ... it means pull the great big lever,' Ponder said, reluctantly.

'Ah. Takes less time to say.'

Ponder sighed. 'Yes, that's right, Archchancellor.'

He nodded to one of the students, who pulled a large red lever marked 'Do Not Pull'. Gears spun, somewhere inside Hex. Little trapdoors opened in the ant farms and millions of ants began to scurry along the networks of glass tubing. Ponder tapped at the huge wooden keyboard.

'Beats me how you fellows remember how to do all this stuff,' said Ridcully, still watching him with what Ponder considered to be amused interest.

'Oh, it's largely intuitive, Archchancellor,' said Ponder. 'Obviously you have to spend a lot of time learning it first, though. Now, then, Bursar,' he added. 'If you'd just like to say something ...'

'He says, SAY SOMETHING, BURSAAAR!' yelled Ridcully helpfully, into the Bursar's ear.

'Corkscrew? It's a tickler, that's what Nanny says,' said the Bursar.

Things started to spin inside Hex. At the back of the room a huge converted waterwheel covered with sheep skulls began to turn, ponderously.

And the quill pen in its network of springs and guiding arms started to write:

+++ Why Do You Think You Are A Tickler? +++

For a moment the Bursar hesitated. Then he said, 'I've got a spoon of my own, you know.'

+++ Tell Me About Your Spoon +++

'Er ... it's a little spoon ...'

+++ Does Your Spoon Worry You? +++

The Bursar frowned. Then he seemed to rally. 'Whoops, here comes Mr Jelly,' he said, but he didn't sound as though his heart was in it.

+++ How Long Have You Been Mr Jelly? +++

The Bursar glared. 'Are you making *fun* of me?' he said.

'Amazin'!' said Ridcully. 'It's got him stumped! 's better than dried frog pills! How did you work it out?'

'Er ...' said Ponder. 'It sort of just happened ...'

'Amazin',' said Ridcully. He knocked the ashes out of his pipe on Hex's 'Anthill Inside' sticker, causing Ponder to wince. 'This thing's a kind of big artificial brain, then?'

'You *could* think of it like that,' said Ponder, carefully. 'Of course,

Hex doesn't actually think. Not as such. It just *appears* to be thinking.'

'Ah. Like the Dean,' said Ridcully. 'Any chance of fitting a brain like this into the Dean's head?'

'It does weigh ten tons, Archchancellor.'

'Ah. Really? Oh. Quite a large crowbar would be in order, then.' He paused, and then reached into his pocket. 'I knew I'd come here for something,' he added. 'This here chappie is the Verruca Gnome –'

'Hello,' said the Verruca Gnome shyly.

' – who seems to have popped into existence to be with us here tonight. And, you know, I thought: this is a bit odd. Of course, there's always something a *bit* unreal about Hogswatchnight,' said Ridcully. 'Last night of the year and so on. The Hogfather whizzin' around and so forth. Time of the darkest shadows and so on. All the old year's occult rubbish pilin' up. Anythin' could happen. I just thought you fellows might check up on this. Probably nothing to worry about.'

'A *Verruca* Gnome?' said Ponder.

The gnome clutched his sack protectively.

'Makes about as much sense as a lot of things, I suppose,' said Ridcully. 'After all, there's a Tooth Fairy, ain' there? You might as well wonder why we have a God of Wine and not a God of Hangovers –'

He stopped.

'Anyone else hear that noise just then?' he said.

'Sorry, Archchancellor?'

'Sort of *glingleglingleglingle*? Like little tinkly bells?'

'Didn't hear anything like that, sir.'

'Oh.' Ridcully shrugged. 'Anyway ... what was I saying ... yes ... no one's ever *heard* of a Verruca Gnome until tonight.'

'That's right,' said the gnome. 'Even *I've* never heard of me until tonight, and I'm *me*.'

'We'll see what we can find out, Archchancellor,' said Ponder diplomatically.

'Good man.' Ridcully put the gnome back in his pocket and looked up at Hex.

'Amazin',' he said again. 'He just *looks* as though he's thinking, right?'

'Er ... yes.'

'But he's not actually thinking?'

'Er ... no.'

'So . . . he just gives the *impression* of thinking but really it's just a show?'

'Er . . . yes.'

'Just like everyone else, then, really,' said Ridcully.

The boy gave the Hogfather an appraising stare as he sat down on the official knee.

'Let's be absolutely clear. I know you're just someone dressed up,' he said. 'The Hogfather is a biological and temporal impossibility. I hope we understand one another.'

AH. SO I DON'T EXIST?

'Correct. This is just a bit of seasonal frippery and, I may say, rampantly commercial. My mother's already bought my presents. I instructed her as to the right ones, of course. She often gets things wrong.'

The Hogfather glanced briefly at the smiling, worried image of maternal ineffectiveness hovering nearby.

HOW OLD ARE YOU, BOY?

The child rolled his eyes. 'You're not supposed to say that,' he said. 'I *have* done this before, you know. You have to start by asking me my name.'

AARON FIDGET, 'THE PINES', EDGEWAY ROAD, ANKH-MORPORK.

'I expect someone told you,' said Aaron. 'I expect these people dressed up as pixies get the information from the mothers.'

AND YOU ARE EIGHT, GOING ON . . . OH, ABOUT FORTY-FIVE, said the Hogfather.

'There's forms to fill in when they pay, I expect,' said Aaron.

AND YOU WANT WALNUT'S *INOFFENSIVE* REPTILES OF THE STO PLAINS, A DISPLAY CABINET, A COLLECTOR'S ALBUM, A KILLING JAR AND A LIZARD PRESS. WHAT IS A LIZARD PRESS?

'You can't glue them in when they're still fat, or didn't you know that? I expect she told you about them when I was momentarily distracted by the display of pencils. Look, shall we end this charade? Just give me my orange and we'll say no more about it.'

I CAN GIVE FAR MORE THAN ORANGES.

'Yes, yes, I saw all that. Probably done in collusion with accomplices to attract gullible customers. Oh dear, you've even got a false beard. By the way, old chap, did you know that your pig –'

YES.

'All done by mirrors and string and pipes, I expect. It all looked very artificial to *me*.'

The Hogfather snapped his fingers.

'That's probably a signal, I expect,' said the boy, getting down. 'Thank you very much.'

Happy Hogswatch, said the Hogfather as the boy walked away.

Uncle Heavy patted him on the shoulder.

'Well done, master,' he said. 'Very patient. I'd have given him a clonk athwart the earhole, myself.'

Oh, I'm sure he'll see the error of his ways. The red hood turned so that only Albert could see into its depths. Right around the time he opens those boxes his mother was carrying . . .

Ho. Ho. Ho.

'Don't tie it so tight! Don't tie it so *tight!*'

Squeak.

There was a bickering behind Susan as she sought along the shelves in the canyons of Death's huge library, which was so big that clouds would form in it if they dared.

'Right, right,' said the voice she was trying to ignore. 'That's about right. I've got to be able to move my wings, right?'

Squeak.

'Ah,' said Susan, under her breath. 'The Hogfather . . .'

He had several shelves, not just one book. The first volume seemed to be written on a roll of animal skin. The Hogfather was *old*.

'OK, OK. How does it look?'

Squeak.

'Miss?' said the raven, seeking a second opinion.

Susan looked up. The raven bounced past, its breast bright red.

'Twit, twit,' it said. 'Bobbly bobbly bob. Hop hop hopping along . . .'

'You're fooling no one but yourself,' said Susan. 'I can see the string.'

She unrolled the scroll.

'Maybe I should sit on a snowy log,' mumbled the raven behind her. 'That's probably the trick, right enough.'

'I can't read this!' said Susan. 'The letters are all . . . odd . . .'

'Ethereal runes,' said the raven. 'The Hogfather ain't human, after all.'

Susan ran her hands over the thin leather. The . . . shapes flowed around her fingers.

She couldn't read them but she could *feel* them. There was the sharp smell of snow, so vivid that her breath condensed in the air. There were sounds, hooves, the snap of branches in a freezing forest —

A bright shining ball . . .

Susan jerked awake and thrust the scroll aside. She unrolled the next one, which looked as though it was made of strips of bark. Characters hovered over the surface. Whatever they were, they had never been designed to be read by the eye; you could believe they were a Braille for the touching mind. Images ribboned across her senses — wet fur, sweat, pine, soot, iced air, the tang of damp ash, pig . . . manure, her governess mind hastily corrected. There was blood . . . and the taste of . . . beans? It was all images without words. Almost . . . animal.

'But none of this is right! Everyone knows he's a jolly old fat man who hands out presents to kids!' she said aloud.

'*Is. Is*. Not *was*. You know how it is,' said the raven.

'Do I?'

'It's like, you know, industrial re-training,' said the bird. 'Even gods have to move with the times, am I right? He was probably quite different thousands of years ago. Stands to reason. No one wore stockings, for one thing.' He scratched at his beak.

'Yersss,' he continued expansively, 'he was probably just your basic winter demi-urge. You know . . . blood on the snow, making the sun come up. Starts off with animal sacrifice, y'know hunt, some big hairy animal to death, that kind of stuff. You know there's some people up on the Ramtops who kill a wren at Hogswatch and walk around from house to house singing about it? With a whack-fol-oh-diddle-dildo. Very folkloric, very myffic.'

'A *wren*? Why?'

'I dunno. Maybe someone said, hey, how'd you like to hunt this evil bustard of an eagle with his big sharp beak and great ripping talons, sort of thing, or how about instead you hunt this wren, which is basically about the size of a pea and goes "twit"? Go on, *you* choose. Anyway, then later on it sinks to the level of religion and then they start this business where some poor bugger finds a special bean in his tucker, oho, everyone says, you're *king*, mate, and he thinks "This is a bit of all right" only they don't say it wouldn't be a good idea to start any long books, 'cos next thing he's legging it over the snow with a dozen other buggers chasing him with holy sickles so's the earth'll come to life again and all this snow'll go away. Very, you know . . . *ethnic*. Then some bright spark thought, hey, looks like that damn sun comes up *anyway*, so how come we're giving those druids all this free grub? Next thing you know, there's a job vacancy. That's the thing about gods. They'll always find a way to, you know . . . hang on.'

'The damn sun comes up anyway,' Susan repeated. 'How do you know that?'

'Oh, observation. It happens every morning. I *seen* it.'

'I meant all that stuff about holy sickles and things.'

The raven contrived to look smug.

'Very occult bird, your basic raven,' he said. 'Blind Io the Thunder God used to have these myffic ravens that flew everywhere and told him everything that was going on.'

'Used to?'

'Weeelll . . . you know how he's not got eyes in his face, just these, like, you know, free-floating eyeballs that go and zoom around . . .' The raven coughed in species embarrassment. 'Bit of an accident waiting to happen, really.'

'Do you ever think of *anything* except eyeballs?'

'Well . . . there's entrails.'

SQUEAK.

'He's right, though,' said Susan. 'Gods don't die. Never completely die . . .'

There's always somewhere, she told herself. Inside some stone, perhaps, or the words of a song, or riding the mind of some animal, or maybe in a whisper on the wind. They never entirely go, they hang on to the world by the tip of a fingernail, always fighting to find a way back. Once a god, always a god. Dead, perhaps, but only like the world in winter –

'All right,' she said. 'Let's see what happened to him . . .'

She reached out for the last book and tried to open it at random . . .

The feeling lashed at her out of the book, like a whip . . .

. . . *hooves, fear, blood, snow, cold, night* . . .

She dropped the scroll. It slammed shut.

SQUEAK?

'I'm . . . all right.'

She looked down at the book and knew that she'd been given a friendly warning, such as a pet animal might give when it was crazed with pain but just still tame enough not to claw and bite the hand that fed it – this time. Wherever the Hogfather was – dead, alive, *somewhere* – he wanted to be left alone . . .

She eyed the Death of Rats. His little eye sockets flared blue in a disconcertingly familiar way.

SQUEAK. EEK?

'The rat says, if *he* wanted to find out about the Hogfather, he'd go to the Castle of Bones.'

'Oh, that's just a nursery tale,' said Susan. 'That's where the letters are supposed to go that are posted up the chimney. That's just an old story.'

She turned. The rat and the raven were staring at her. And she realized that she'd been too normal.

SQUEAK?

'The rat says, "What d'you mean, *just*?"' said the raven.

Chickenwire sidled towards Medium Dave in the garden. If you could call it a garden. It was the land round the ... house. If you could call it a house. No one said much about it, but every so often you just had to get out. It didn't feel right, inside.

He shivered. 'Where's *himself*?' he said.

'Oh, up at the top,' said Medium Dave. 'Still trying to open that room.

'The one with all the locks?'

'Yeah.'

Medium Dave was rolling a cigarette. Inside the house ... or tower, or both, or whatever ... you couldn't smoke, not properly. When you smoked inside it tasted horrible and you felt sick.

'What for? We done what we came to do, didn't we? Stood there like a bunch of kids and watched that wet wizard do all his chanting, it was all I could do to keep a straight face. What's he after now?'

'He just said if it was locked that bad he wanted to see inside.'

'I thought we were supposed to do what we came for and go!'

'Yeah? You tell him. Want a roll-up?'

Chickenwire took the bag of tobacco and relaxed. 'I've seen some bad places in my time, but this takes the serious biscuit.'

'Yeah.'

'It's the cute that wears you down. And there's got to be something else to eat than apples.'

'Yeah.'

'And that damn sky. That damn sky is really getting on my nerves.'

'Yeah.'

They kept their eyes averted from that damn sky. For some reason, it made you feel that it was about to fall on you. And it was worse if you let your eyes stray to the gap where a gap shouldn't be. The effect was like getting toothache in your eyeballs.

In the distance Banjo was swinging on a swing. Odd, that, Dave thought. Banjo seemed perfectly happy here.

'He found a tree that grows lollipops yesterday,' he said moodily. 'Well, I say *yesterday*, but how can you tell? And he follows the man around like a dog. *No one* ever laid a punch on Banjo since our mam died. He's just like a little boy, you know. Inside. Always has been. Looks to me for everything. Used to be, if I told him "punch someone", he'd do it.'

'And they stayed punched.'

'Yeah. Now he follows him around everywhere. It makes me sick.'

'What are you doing here, then?'

'Ten thousand dollars. And *he* says there's more, you know. More than we can imagine.'

He was always Teatime.

'He ain't just after money.'

'Yeah, well, I didn't sign up for world domination,' said Medium Dave. 'That sort of thing gets you into trouble.'

'I remember your mam saying that sort of thing,' said Chickenwire. Medium Dave rolled his eyes. Everyone remembered Ma Lilywhite. 'Very straight lady, was your ma. Tough but fair.'

'Yeah ... tough.'

'I recall that time she strangled Glossy Ron with his own leg,' Chickenwire went on. 'She had a *wicked* right arm on her, your mam.'

'Yeah. Wicked.'

'She wouldn't have stood for someone like Teatime.'

'Yeah,' said Medium Dave.

'That was a lovely funeral you boys gave her. Most of the Shades turned up. Very respectful. All them flowers. An' everyone looking so . . .' Chickenwire floundered '. . . happy. In a sad way, o' course.'

'Yeah.'

'Have you got any idea how to get back home?'

Medium Dave shook his head.

'Me neither. Find the place again, I suppose.' Chickenwire shivered. 'I mean, what he did to that carter ... I mean, well, I wouldn't even act like that to me own dad –'

'Yeah.'

'Ordinary mental, yes, I can deal with that. But he can be talking quite normal, and then –'

'Yeah.'

'Maybe the both of us could creep up on him and –'

'Yeah, yeah. And how long'll we live? In seconds.'

'We could get lucky –' Chickenwire began.

'Yeah? You've seen him. This isn't one of those blokes who threatens you. This is one of those blokes who'd kill you soon as look at you. Easier, too. We got to hang on, right? It's like that saying about riding a tiger.'

'What saying about riding a tiger?' said Chickenwire suspiciously.

'Well . . .' Medium Dave hesitated. 'You . . . well, you get branches slapping you in the face, fleas, that sort of thing. So you got to hang on. Think of the money. There's bags of it in there. You saw it.'

'I keep thinking of that glass eye watching me. I keep thinking it can see right in my head.'

'Don't worry, he doesn't suspect you of anything.'

'How d'you know?'

'You're still alive, yeah?'

In the Grotto of the Hogfather, a round-eyed child.

HAPPY HOGSWATCH. HO. HO. HO. AND YOUR NAME IS . . . EUPHRASIA GOAT, CORRECT?

'Go on, dear, answer the nice man.'

"'s.'

AND YOU ARE SIX YEARS OLD.

'Go on, dear. They're all the same at this age, aren't they . . .'

"'s.'

AND YOU WANT A PONY –

"'s.' A small hand pulled the Hogfather's hood down to mouth level. Uncle Heavy heard a ferocious whispering. Then the Hogfather leaned back.

YES, I KNOW. WHAT A NAUGHTY PIG IT WAS, INDEED.

His shape flickered for a moment, and then a hand went into the sack.

HERE IS A BRIDLE FOR YOUR PONY, AND A SADDLE, AND A RATHER STRANGE HARD HAT AND A PAIR OF THOSE TROUSERS THAT MAKE YOU LOOK AS THOUGH YOU HAVE A LARGE RABBIT IN EACH POCKET.

'But we can't have a pony, can we, Euffie, because we live on the third floor . . .'

OH, YES. IT'S IN THE KITCHEN.

'I'm sure you're making a little joke, Hogfather,' said Mother, sharply.

Ho. Ho. Yes. What a jolly fat man I am. In the kitchen? What a joke. Dollies and so on will be delivered later as per your letter.

'What do you say, Euffie?'

"nk you.'

"ere, you didn't really put a pony in their kitchen, did you?' said Heavy Uncle Albert as the line moved on.

Don't be foolish, Albert. I said that to be jolly.

'Oh, right. Hah, for a minute –'

It's in the bedroom.

'Ah . . .'

More hygienic.

'Well, it'll make sure of one thing,' said Albert. 'Third floor? They're going to believe all right.'

Yes. You know, I think I'm getting the hang of this. Ho. Ho. Ho.

At the Hub of the Discworld, the snow burned blue and green. The Aurora Corealis hung in the sky, curtains of pale cold fire that circled the central mountains and cast their spectral light over the ice.

They billowed, swirled and then trailed a ragged arm on the end of which was a tiny dot that became, when the eye of imagination drew nearer, Binky.

He trotted to a halt and stood on the air. Susan looked down.

And then found what she was looking for. At the end of a valley of snow-mounded trees something gleamed brightly, reflecting the sky.

The Castle of Bones.

Her parents had sat her down one day when she was about six or seven and explained how such things as the Hogfather did not *really* exist, how they were pleasant little stories that it was fun to know, how they were not *real*. And she had believed it. All the fairies and bogeymen, all those stories from the blood and bone of humanity, were not really *real*.

They'd lied. A seven-foot skeleton had turned out to be her grandfather. Not a flesh and blood grandfather, obviously. But a grandfather, you could say, in the bone.

Binky touched down and trotted over the snow.

Was the Hogfather a god? Why not? thought Susan. There were sacrifices, after all. All that sherry and pork pie. And he made commandments and rewarded the good and he knew what you were doing. If you believed, nice things happened to you. Sometimes you found him in a grotto, and sometimes he was up there in the sky . . .

The Castle of Bones loomed over her now. It certainly deserved the capital letters, up this close.

She'd seen a picture of it in one of the children's books. Despite its name, the woodcut artist had endeavoured to make it look . . . sort of jolly.

It wasn't jolly. The pillars at the entrance were hundreds of feet high. Each of the steps leading up was taller than a man. They were the grey-green of old ice.

Ice. Not bone. There were faintly familiar shapes to the pillars, possibly a suggestion of femur or skull, but it was made of ice.

Binky was not challenged by the high stairs. It wasn't that he flew. It was simply that he walked on a ground level of his own devising.

Snow had blown over the ice. Susan looked down at the drifts. Death left no tracks, but there were the faint outlines of booted footprints. She'd be prepared to bet they belonged to Albert. And . . . yes, half obscured by the snow . . . it looked as though a sledge had stood here. Animals had milled around. But the snow was covering everything.

She dismounted. This was certainly the place described, but it still wasn't right. It was supposed to be a blaze of light and abuzz with activity, but it looked like a giant mausoleum.

A little way beyond the pillars was a very large slab of ice, cracked into pieces. Far above, stars were visible through the hole it had left in the roof. Even as she stared up, a few small lumps of ice thumped into a snowdrift.

The raven popped into existence and fluttered wearily on to a stump of ice beside her.

'This place is a morgue,' said Susan.

''s goin' to be mine, if I do . . . any more flyin' tonight,' panted the raven, as the Death of Rats got off its back. 'I never signed up for all this long-distance, faster'n time stuff. I should be back in a forest somewhere, making excitingly decorated constructions to attract females.'

'That's bower birds,' said Susan. 'Ravens don't do that.'

'Oh, so it's type-casting now, is it?' said the raven. 'I'm missing meals here, you do know that?'

It swivelled its independently sprung eyes.

'So where's all the lights?' it said. 'Where's all the noise? Where's all the jolly little buggers in pointy hats and red and green suits, hitting wooden toys unconvincingly yet rhythmically with hammers?'

'This is more like the temple of some old thunder god,' said Susan.

Squeak.

'No, I read the map right. Anyway, Albert's been here too. There's fag ash all over the place.'

The rat jumped down and walked around for a moment, bony snout near the ground. After a few moments of snuffling it gave a squeak and hurried off into the gloom.

Susan followed. As her eyes grew more accustomed to the faint blue-green light she made out something rising out of the floor. It was a pyramid of steps, with a big chair on top.

Behind her, a pillar groaned and twisted slightly.

Squeak.

'That rat says this place reminds him of some old mine,' said the raven. 'You know, after it's been deserted and no one's been paying attention to the roof supports and so on? We see a lot of them.'

At least these steps were human sized, Susan thought, ignoring the chatter. Snow had come in through another gap in the roof. Albert's footprints had stamped around quite a lot here.

'Maybe the old Hogfather crashed his sleigh,' the raven suggested.

Squeak?

'Well, it *could've* happened. Pigs are not notably aerodynamic, are they? And with all this snow, you know, poor visibility, big cloud ahead turns out too late to be a mountain, there's buggers in saffron robes looking down at you, poor devil tries to remember whether you're supposed to shove someone's head between your legs, then WHAM, and it's all over bar some lucky mountaineers making an awful lot of sausages and finding the flight recorder.'

Squeak!

'Yes, but he's an old man. Probably shouldn't be in the sky at his time of life.'

Susan pulled at something half buried in the snow.

It was a red-and-white-striped candy cane.

She kicked the snow aside elsewhere and found a wooden toy soldier in the kind of uniform that would only be inconspicuous if you wore it in a nightclub for chameleons on hard drugs. Some further probing found a broken trumpet.

There was some more groaning in the darkness.

The raven cleared its throat.

'What the rat meant about this place being like a mine,' he said, 'was that abandoned mines tend to creak and groan in the same way, see? No one looking after the pit props. Things fall in. Next thing you know you're a squiggle in the sandstone. We shouldn't hang around is what I'm saying.'

Susan walked further in, lost in thought.

This was all wrong. The place looked as though it had been deserted for years, which couldn't be true.

The column nearest her creaked and twisted slightly. A fine haze of ice crystals dropped from the roof.

Of course, this wasn't exactly a normal place. You couldn't build an ice palace this big. It was a bit like Death's house. If he abandoned it for too long all those things that had been suspended, like time and physics, would roll over it. It would be like a dam bursting.

She turned to leave and heard the groan again. It wasn't dissimilar to the tortured sounds being made by the ice, except that ice, afterwards, didn't moan 'Oh, *me* . . .'

There was a figure lying in a snowdrift. She'd almost missed it because it was wearing a long white robe. It was spreadeagled, as though it had planned to make snow angels and had then decided against it.

And it wore a little crown, apparently of vine leaves.

And it kept groaning.

She looked up. The roof was open here, too. But no one could have fallen that far and survived.

No one human, anyway.

He *looked* human and, in theory, quite young. But it was only in theory because, even by the second-hand light of the glowing snow, his face looked like someone had been sick with it.

'Are you all right?' she ventured.

The recumbent figure opened its eyes and stared straight up.

'I wish I was dead . . .' it moaned. A piece of ice the size of a house fell down in the far depths of the building and exploded in a shower of sharp little shards.

'You may have come to the right place,' said Susan. She grabbed the boy under his arms and hauled him out of the snow. 'I think leaving would be a very good idea around now, don't you? This place is going to fall apart.'

'Oh, *me* . . .'

She managed to get one of his arms around her neck.

'Can you walk?'

'Oh, *me* . . .'

'It might help if you stopped saying that and tried walking.'

'I'm sorry, but I seem to have . . . too many legs. Ow.'

Susan did her best to prop him up as, swaying and slipping, they made their way back to the exit.

'My head,' said the boy. 'My head. My head. My head. Feels awful. My head. Feels like someone's hitting it. My head. With a hammer.'

Someone was. There was a small green and purple imp sitting amid the damp curls and holding a very large mallet. It gave Susan a friendly nod and brought the hammer down again.

'Oh, *me* . . .'

'That wasn't necessary!' said Susan.

'You telling me my job?' said the imp. 'I suppose you could do it better, could you?'

'I wouldn't do it at all!'

'Well, *someone's* got to do it,' said the imp.

'He's part. Of the. Arrangement,' said the boy.

'Yeah, see?' said the imp. 'Can you hold the hammer while I go and coat his tongue with yellow gunk?'

'Get down right now!'

Susan made a grab for the creature. It leapt away, still clutching the hammer, and grabbed a pillar.

'I'm part of the arrangement, I am!' it yelled.

The boy clutched his head.

'I feel awful,' he said. 'Have you got any ice?'

Whereupon, because there are conventions stronger than mere physics, the building fell in.

The collapse of the Castle of Bones was stately and impressive and seemed to go on for a long time. Pillars fell in, the slabs of the roof slid down, the ice crackled and splintered. The air above the tumbling wreckage filled with a haze of snow and ice crystals.

Susan watched from the trees. The boy, who she'd leaned against a handy trunk, opened his eyes.

'That was amazing,' he managed.

'Why, you mean the way it's all turning back into snow?'

'The way you just picked me up and ran. Ouch!'

'Oh, *that*.'

The grinding of the ice continued. The fallen pillars didn't stop moving when they collapsed, but went on tearing themselves apart.

When the fog of ice settled there was nothing but drifted snow.

'As though it was never there,' said Susan, aloud. She turned to the groaning figure.

'All right, what were you doing there?'

'I don't know. I just opened my. Eyes and there I was.'

'Who *are* you?'

'I ... *think* my name is Bilious. I'm the ... I'm the oh God of Hangovers.'

'There's a God of Hangovers?'

'An *oh god*,' he corrected. 'When people witness me, you see, they clutch their head and say, "Oh God ..." How many of you are standing here?'

'What? There's just me!'

'Ah. Fine. Fine.'

'I've never heard of a God of Hangovers ...'

'You've heard of Bibulous, the God of Wine? Ouch.'

'Oh, yes.'

'Big fat man, wears vine leaves round his head, always pictured with a glass in his hand ... Ow. Well, you know *why* he's so cheerful? Him and his big face? It's because he knows he's going to feel good in the morning! It's because it's *me* that –'

'– gets the hangovers?' said Susan.

'I don't even drink! Ow! But who is it who ends up head down in the privy every morning? Arrgh.' He stopped and clutched at his head. 'Should your skull feel like it's lined with dog hair?'

'I don't think so.'

'Ah.' Bilious swayed. 'You know when people say "I had fifteen lagers last night and when I woke up my head was clear as a bell" ?'

'Oh, yes.'

'Bastards! That's because *I* was the one who woke up groaning in a pile of recycled chilli. Just once, I mean just *once*, I'd like to open my eyes in the morning without my head sticking to something.' He paused. 'Are there any giraffes in this wood?'

'Up here? I shouldn't think so.'

He looked nervously past Susan's head.

'Not even indigo-coloured ones which are sort of stretched and keep flashing on and off?'

'Very unlikely.'

'Thank goodness for that.' He swayed back and forth. 'Excuse me, I think I'm about to throw up my breakfast.'

'It's the middle of the evening!'

'Is it? In that case, I think I'm about to throw up my dinner.'

He folded up gently in the snow behind the tree.

'He's a long streak of widdle, isn't he?' said a voice from a branch. It was the raven. 'Got a neck with a knee in it.'

The oh god reappeared after a noisy interlude.

'I *know* I must eat,' he mumbled. 'It's just that the only time I remember seeing my food it's always going the other way . . .'

'What were you doing in there?' said Susan.

'Ouch! Search me,' said the oh god. 'It's only a mercy I wasn't holding a traffic sign and wearing a –' he winced and paused '– having some kind of women's underwear about my person.' He sighed. 'Someone somewhere has a lot of fun,' he said wistfully. 'I wish it was me.'

'Get a drink inside you, that's my advice,' said the raven. 'Have a hair of the dog that bit someone else.'

'But why *there*?' Susan insisted.

The oh god stopped trying to glare at the raven. 'I don't know, where was *there* exactly?'

Susan looked back at where the castle had been. It was entirely gone.

'There was a very important building there a moment ago,' she said.

The oh god nodded carefully.

'I often see things that weren't there a moment ago,' he said. 'And they often aren't there a moment later. Which is a blessing in most cases, let me tell you. So I don't usually take a lot of notice.'

He folded up and landed in the snow again.

There's just snow now, Susan thought. Nothing but snow and the wind. There's not even a ruin.

The certainty stole over her again that the Hogfather's castle wasn't *simply* not there any more. No . . . it had never been there. There was no ruin, no trace.

It had been an odd enough place. It was where the Hogfather lived, according to the legends. Which was odd, when you thought about it. It *didn't* look like the kind of place a cheery old toymaker would live in.

The wind soughed in the trees behind them. Snow slid off branches. Somewhere in the dark there was a flurry of hooves.

A spidery little figure leapt off a snowdrift and landed on the oh god's head. It turned a beady eye up towards Susan.

'All right by you, is it?' said the imp, producing its huge hammer. 'Some of us have a job to do, you know, even if we are of a metaphorical, nay, folkloric persuasion.'

'Oh, go *away*.'

'If you think *I'm* bad, wait until you see the little pink elephants,' said the imp.

'I don't believe you.'

'They come out of his ears and fly around his head making tweeting noises.'

'Ah,' said the raven, sagely. 'That sounds more like robins. I wouldn't put anything past *them*.

The oh god grunted.

Susan suddenly felt that she didn't want to leave him. He was human. Well, human shaped. Well, at least he had two arms and legs. He'd freeze to death here. Of course, gods, or even oh gods, probably couldn't, but humans didn't think like that. You couldn't just *leave* someone. She prided herself on this bit of normal thinking.

Besides, he might have some answers, if she could make him stay awake enough to understand the questions.

From the edge of the frozen forest, animal eyes watched them go.

Mr Crumley sat on the damp stairs and sobbed. He couldn't get any nearer to the toy department. Every time he tried he got lifted off his feet by the mob and dumped at the edge of the crowd by the current of people.

Someone said, 'Top of the evenin', squire,' and he looked up blearily at the small yet irregularly formed figure that had addressed him thusly.

'Are you one of the pixies?' he said, after mentally exhausting all the other possibilities.

'No, sir. I am not in fact a pixie, sir, I am in fact Corporal Nobbs of the Watch. And this is Constable Visit, sir.' The creature looked at a piece of paper in its paw. 'You Mr Crummy?'

'Crumley!'

'Yeah, right. You sent a runner to the Watch House and we have hereby responded with commendable speed, sir,' said Corporal Nobbs. 'Despite it being Hogswatchnight and there being a lot of strange things happening and most importantly it being the occasion of our Hogswatchly piss-up, sir. But this is all right because Washpot, that's Constable Visit here, he doesn't drink, sir, it being against his religion, and although I *do* drink, sir, I volunteered to come because it is my civic duty, sir.' Nobby tore off a salute, or what he liked to believe was a salute. He did *not* add,

'And turning out for a rich bugger such as your good self is bound to put the officer concerned in the way of a seasonal bottle or two or some other tangible evidence of gratitude,' because his entire stance said it for him. Even Nobby's ears could look suggestive.

Unfortunately, Mr Crumley wasn't in the right receptive frame of mind. He stood up and waved a shaking finger towards the top of the stairs.

'I want you to go up there,' he said, 'and arrest him!'

'Arrest who, sir?' said Corporal Nobbs.

'The Hogfather!'

'What for, sir?'

'Because he's sitting up there as bold as brass in his Grotto, giving away presents!'

Corporal Nobbs thought about this.

'You haven't been having a festive drink, have you, sir?' he said hopefully.

'I do not drink!'

'Very wise, sir,' said Constable Visit. 'Alcohol is the tarnish of the soul. Ossory, Book Two, Verse Twenty-four.'

'Not quite up to speed here, sir,' said Corporal Nobbs, looking perplexed. 'I thought the Hogfather is *s'posed* to give away stuff, isn't he?'

This time Mr Crumley had to stop and think. Up until now he hadn't quite sorted things out in his head, other than recognizing their essential wrongness.

'This one is an Imposter!' he declared. 'Yes, that's right! He smashed his way into here!'

'Y'know, I always thought that,' said Nobby. 'I thought, every year, the Hogfather spends a fortnight sitting in a wooden grotto in a shop in Ankh-Morpork? At his busy time, too? Hah! Not likely! Probably just some old man in a beard, I thought.'

'I meant ... he's not the Hogfather we usually have,' said Crumley, struggling for firmer ground. 'He just barged in here!'

'Oh, a *different* imposter? Not the real imposter at all?'

'Well ... yes ... no ...'

'And started giving stuff away?' said Corporal Nobbs.

'That's what I said! That's got to be a Crime, hasn't it?'

Corporal Nobbs rubbed his nose.

'Well, *nearly*,' he conceded, not wishing to totally relinquish the chance of any festive remuneration. Realization dawned. 'He's giving away *your* stuff, sir?'

'No! No, he brought it in with him!'

'Ah? Giving away *your* stuff, now, if he was doing that, yes, I could see the problem. That's a sure sign of crime, stuff going missing. Stuff turning up, weerlll, that's a tricky one. Unless it's stuff like arms and legs, o' course. We'd be on safer ground if he was nicking stuff, sir, to tell you the truth.'

'This is a *shop*,' said Mr Crumley, finally getting to the root of the problem. 'We do *not* give Merchandise *away*. How can we expect people to buy things if some Person is *giving* them away? Now please go and get him out of here.'

'Arrest the Hogfather, style of thing?'

'Yes!'

'On Hogswatchnight?'

'Yes!'

'In your shop?'

'*Yes!*'

'In front of all those kiddies?'

'Y–' Mr Crumley hesitated. To his horror, he realized that Corporal Nobbs, against all expectation, had a point. 'You think that will look bad?' he said.

'Hard to see how it could look good, sir.'

'Could you not do it surreptitiously?' he said.

'Ah, well, surreption, yes, we could give that a try,' said Corporal Nobbs. The sentence hung in the air with its hand out.

'You won't find me ungrateful,' said Mr Crumley, at last.

'Just you leave it to us,' said Corporal Nobbs, magnanimous in victory. 'You just nip down to your office and treat yourself to a nice cup of tea and we'll sort this out in no time. You'll be ever so grateful.'

Crumley gave him a look of a man in the grip of serious doubt, but staggered away nonetheless. Corporal Nobbs rubbed his hands together.

'You don't have Hogswatch back where you come from, do you, Washpot?' he said, as they climbed the stairs to the first floor. 'Look at this carpet, you'd think a pig'd pissed on it . . .'

'We call it the Fast of St Ossory,' said Visit, who was from Omnia. 'But it is not an occasion for superstition and crass commercialism. We simply get together in family groups for a prayer meeting and a fast.'

'What, turkey and chicken and that?'

'A *fast*, Corporal Nobbs. We don't eat *anything*.'

'Oh, right. Well, each to his own, I s'pose. And at least you don't have to get up early in the morning and find that the nothing you've got is too big to fit in the oven. No presents neither?'

They stood aside hurriedly as two children scuttled down the stairs carrying a large toy boat between them.

'It is sometimes appropriate to exchange new religious pamphlets, and of course there are usually copies of the *Book of Ossory* for the children,' said Constable Visit. 'Sometimes with *illustrations*,' he added, in the guarded way of a man hinting at licentious pleasures.

A small girl went past carrying a teddy bear larger than herself. It was pink.

'They always gives *me* bath salts,' complained Nobby. 'And bath soap and bubble bath and herbal bath lumps and tons of bath stuff and I can't think why, 'cos it's not as if I hardly ever *has* a bath. You'd think they'd take the hint, wouldn't you?'

'Abominable, I call it,' said Constable Visit.

The first floor was a mob.

'Huh, look at them. Mr Hogfather never brought *me* anything when I was a kid,' said Corporal Nobbs, eyeing the children gloomily. 'I used to hang up my stocking every Hogswatch, regular. All that ever happened was my dad was sick in it once.' He removed his helmet.

Nobby was not by any measure a hero, but there was the sudden gleam in his eye of someone who'd seen altogether too many empty stockings plus one rather full and dripping one. A scab had been knocked off some wound in the corrugated little organ of his soul.

'I'm going in,' he said.

In between the university's Great Hall and its main door is a rather smaller circular hall or vestibule known as Archchancellor Bowell's Remembrance, although no one now knows why, or why an extant bequest pays for one small currant bun and one copper penny to be placed on a high stone shelf on one wall every second Wednesday.[*] Ridcully stood in the middle of the floor, looking upwards.

'Tell me, Senior Wrangler, we never invited any *women* to the Hogswatchnight Feast, did we?'

'Of course not, Archchancellor,' said the Senior Wrangler. He looked up in the dust-covered rafters, wondering what had caught

---

[*] The ceremony still carries on, of course. If you left off traditions because you didn't know why they started you'd be no better than a foreigner.

Ridcully's eye. 'Good heavens, no. They'd spoil everything. I've always said so.'

'And all the maids have got the evening off until midnight?'

'A very generous custom, I've always said,' said the Senior Wrangler, feeling his neck crick.

'So why, every year, do we hang a damn great bunch of mistletoe up there?'

The Senior Wrangler turned in a circle, still staring upwards.

'Well, er ... it's ... well, it's ... it's symbolic, Archchancellor.'

'Ah?'

The Senior Wrangler felt that something more was expected. He groped around in the dusty attics of his education.

'Of ... the leaves, d'y'see ... they're symbolic of ... of green, d'y'see, whereas the berries, in fact, yes, the berries symbolize ... symbolize white. Yes. White and green. Very ... symbolic.'

He waited. He was not, unfortunately, disappointed.

'What of?'

The Senior Wrangler coughed.

'I'm not sure there *has* to *be* an *of*,' he said.

'Ah? So,' said the Archchancellor, thoughtfully, 'it could be said that the white and green symbolize a small parasitic plant?'

'Yes, indeed,' said the Senior Wrangler.

'So mistletoe, in fact, symbolizes mistletoe?'

'Exactly, Archchancellor,' said the Senior Wrangler, who was now just hanging on.

'Funny thing, that,' said Ridcully, in the same thoughtful tone of voice. 'That statement is either so deep it would take a lifetime to fully comprehend every particle of its meaning, or it is a load of absolute tosh. Which is it, I wonder?'

'It could be both,' said the Senior Wrangler desperately.

'And *that* comment,' said Ridcully, 'is either very perceptive, or very trite.'

'It might be bo–'

'Don't push it, Senior Wrangler.'

There was a hammering on the outer door.

'Ah, that'll be the wassailers,' said the Senior Wrangler, happy for the distraction. 'They call on us first every year. I personally have always liked "The Lily-white Boys", you know.'

The Archchancellor glanced up at the mistletoe, gave the beaming man a sharp look, and opened the little hatch in the door.

'Well, now, wassailing you fellows –' he began. 'Oh. Well, I must say you might've picked a better time ...'

A hooded figure stepped through the wood of the door, carrying a limp bundle over its shoulder.

The Senior Wrangler stepped backwards quickly.

'Oh ... no, not *tonight* ...'

And then he noticed that what he had taken for a robe had lace around the bottom, and the hood, while quite definitely a hood, was nevertheless rather more stylish than the one he had first mistaken it for.

'Putting down or taking away?' said Ridcully.

Susan pushed back her hood.

'I need your help, Mr Ridcully,' she said.

'You're ... aren't you Death's granddaughter?' said Ridcully. 'Didn't I meet you a few –'

'Yes,' sighed Susan.

'And ... are you helping out?' said Ridcully. His waggling eyebrows indicated the slumbering figure over her shoulder.

'I need you to wake him up,' said Susan.

'Some sort of miracle, you mean?' said the Senior Wrangler, who was a little behind.

'He's not dead,' said Susan. 'He's just resting.'

'That's what they all say,' the Senior Wrangler quavered.

Ridcully, who was somewhat more practical, lifted the oh god's head. There was a groan.

'Looks a bit under the weather,' he said.

'He's the God of Hangovers,' said Susan. 'The *Oh* God of Hangovers.'

'Really?' said Ridcully. 'Never had one of those myself. Funny thing, I can drink all night and feel as fresh as a daisy in the morning.'

The oh god's eyes opened. Then he soared towards Ridcully and started beating him on the chest with both fists.

'You utter, utter bastard! I hate you hate you hate you hate you –'

His eyes shut, and he slid down to the floor.

'What was all that about?' said Ridcully.

'I think it was some kind of nervous reaction,' said Susan diplomatically. 'Something nasty's happening tonight. I'm hoping he can tell me what it is. But he's got to be able to think straight first.'

'And you brought him *here*?' said Ridcully.

Ho. Ho. Ho. Yes indeed, hello, small child called Verruca Lumpy,

WHAT A LOVELY NAME, AGED SEVEN, I BELIEVE? GOOD. YES, I KNOW IT DID. ALL OVER THE NICE CLEAN FLOOR, YES. THEY DO, YOU KNOW. THAT'S ONE OF THE THINGS ABOUT REAL PIGS. HERE WE ARE, DON'T MENTION IT. HAPPY HOGSWATCH AND BE GOOD. I WILL KNOW IF YOU'RE GOOD OR BAD, YOU KNOW. HO. HO. HO.

'Well, you brought some magic into *that* little life,' said Albert, as the next child was hurried away.

IT'S THE EXPRESSION ON THEIR LITTLE FACES I LIKE, said the Hogfather.

'You mean sort of fear and awe and not knowing whether to laugh or cry or wet their pants?'

YES. NOW *THAT* IS WHAT I CALL BELIEF.

The oh god was carried into the Great Hall and laid out on a bench. The senior wizards gathered round, ready to help those less fortunate than themselves remain that way.

'I know what's good for a hangover,' said the Dean, who was feeling in a party mood.

They looked at him expectantly.

'Drinking heavily the previous night!' he said.

He beamed at them.

'That was a good word joke,' he said, to break the silence.

The silence came back.

'Most amusing,' said Ridcully. He turned back and stared thoughtfully at the oh god.

'Raw eggs are said to be good –' he glared at the Dean '– I mean *bad* for a hangover,' he said. 'And fresh orange juice.'

'Klatchian coffee,' said the Lecturer in Recent Runes, firmly.

'But this fellow hasn't just got *his* hangover, he's got *everyone's* hangover,' said Ridcully.

'I've tried it,' mumbled the oh god. 'It just makes me feel suicidal *and* sick.'

'A mixture of mustard and horseradish?' said the Chair of Indefinite Studies. 'In cream, for preference. With anchovies.'

'Yoghurt,' said the Bursar.

Ridcully looked at him, surprised.

'That sounded almost relevant,' he said. 'Well done. I should leave it at that if I were you, Bursar. Hmm. Of course, my uncle always used to swear at Wow-Wow Sauce,' he added.

'You mean swear *by*, surely?' said the Lecturer in Recent Runes.

'Possibly both,' said Ridcully. 'I know he once drank a whole bottle of it as a hangover cure and it certainly seemed to cure him. He looked very peaceful when they came to lay him out.'

'Willow bark,' said the Bursar.

'That's a good idea,' said the Lecturer in Recent Runes. 'It's an analgesic.'

'Really? Well, possibly, though it's probably better to give it to him by mouth,' said Ridcully. 'I say, are you feeling yourself, Bursar? You seem somewhat coherent.'

The oh god opened his crusted eyes.

'Will all that stuff help?' he mumbled.

'It'll probably kill you,' said Susan.

'Oh. Good.'

'We could add Englebert's Enhancer,' said the Dean. 'Remember when Modo put some on his peas? We could only manage one each!'

'Can't you do something more, well, magical?' said Susan. 'Magic the alcohol out of him or something?'

'Yes, but it's not alcohol by this time, is it?' said Ridcully. 'It'll have turned into a lot of nasty little poisons all dancin' round on his liver.'

'Spold's Unstirring Divisor would do it,' said the Lecturer in Recent Runes. 'Very simply, too. You'd end up with a large beaker full of all the nastiness. Not difficult at all, if you don't mind the side effects.'

'Tell me about the side effects,' said Susan, who had met wizards before.

'The main one is that the rest of him would end up in a somewhat larger beaker,' said the Lecturer in Recent Runes.

'Alive?'

The Lecturer in Recent Runes screwed up his face and waggled his hands. '*Broadly*, yes,' he said. 'Living tissue, certainly. And definitely sober.'

'I think we had in mind something that would leave him the same shape and still breathing,' said Susan.

'Well, you might've *said* . . .'

Then the Dean repeated the mantra that has had such a marked effect on the progress of knowledge throughout the ages.

'Why don't we just mix up absolutely everything and see what happens?' he said.

And Ridcully responded with the traditional response.

'It's got to be worth a try,' he said.

*

The big glass beaker for the cure had been placed on a pedestal in the middle of the floor. The wizards liked to make a ceremony of everything in any case, but felt instinctively that if they were going to cure the biggest hangover in the world it needed to be done with style.

Susan and Bilious watched as the ingredients were added. Round about halfway the mixture, which was an orange-brown colour, went *gloop*.

'Not a lot of improvement, I feel,' said the Lecturer in Recent Runes.

Englebert's Enhancer was the penultimate ingredient. The Dean dropped in a greenish ball of light that sank under the surface. The only apparent effect was that it caused purple bubbles to creep over the sides of the beaker and drip on to the floor.

'That's *it*?' said the oh god.

'I think the yoghurt probably wasn't a good idea,' said the Dean.

'I'm not drinking *that*,' said Bilious firmly, and then clutched at his head.

'But gods are practically unkillable, aren't they?' said the Dean.

'Oh, *good*,' muttered Bilious. 'Why not stick my legs in a meat grinder, then?'

'Well, if you think it might help –'

'I anticipated a certain amount of resistance from the patient,' said the Archchancellor. He removed his hat and fished out a small crystal ball from a pocket in the lining. 'Let's see what the God of Wine is up to at the moment, shall we? Shouldn't be too difficult to locate a fun-loving god like him on an evening like this . . .'

He blew on the glass and polished it. Then he brightened up.

'Why, here he is, the little rascal! On Dunmanifestin, I do believe. Yes . . . yes . . . reclining on his couch, surrounded by naked maenads.'

'What? Maniacs?' said the Dean.

'He means . . . excitable young women,' said Susan. And it seemed to her that there was a general ripple of movement among the wizards, a sort of nonchalant drawing towards the glittering ball.

'Can't quite see what he's doing . . .' said Ridcully.

'Let me see if I can make it out,' said the Chair of Indefinite Studies hopefully. Ridcully half turned to keep the ball out of his reach.

'Ah, yes,' he said. 'It looks like he's drinking . . . yes, could very well be lager and blackcurrant, if I'm any judge . . .'

'Oh, *me* . . .' moaned the oh god.

'These young women, now –' the Lecturer in Recent Runes began.

'I can see there's some bottles on the table,' Ridcully continued. 'That one, hmm, yes, could be scumble which, as you know, is made from apples –'

'*Mainly* apples,' the Dean volunteered. 'Now, about these poor mad girls –'

The oh god slumped to his knees.

'. . . and there's . . . that drink, you know, there's a worm in the bottle . . .'

'Oh, *me* . . .'

'. . . and . . . there's an empty glass, a big one, can't quite see what it contained, but there's a paper umbrella in it. And some cherries on a stick. Oh, and an amusing little monkey.'

'. . . ooohhh . . .'

'. . . of course, there's a lot of other bottles too,' said Ridcully, cheerfully. 'Different coloured drinks, mainly. The sort made from melons and coconuts and chocolate and suchlike, don'tcherknow. Funny thing is, all the glasses on the table are pint mugs . . .'

Bilious fell forward.

'All right,' he murmured. 'I'll drink the wretched stuff.'

'It's not quite ready yet,' said Ridcully. 'Ah, thank you, Modo.'

Modo tiptoed in, pushing a trolley. There was a large metal bowl on it, in which a small bottle stood in the middle of a heap of crushed ice.

'Only just made this for Hogswatch dinner,' said Ridcully. 'Hasn't had much time to mature yet.'

He put down the crystal and fished a pair of heavy gloves out of his hat.

The wizards spread like an opening flower. One moment they were gathered around Ridcully, the next they were standing close to various items of heavy furniture.

Susan felt she was present at a ceremony and hadn't been told the rules.

'What's that?' she said, as Ridcully carefully lifted up the bottle.

'Wow-Wow Sauce,' said Ridcully. 'Finest condiment known to man. A happy accompaniment to meat, fish, fowl, eggs and many types of vegetable dishes. It's not safe to drink it when sweat's still condensing on the bottle, though.' He peered at the bottle, and then rubbed at it, causing a glassy, squeaky noise. 'On the other hand,' he said brightly, 'if it's a kill-or-cure remedy then we are, given that the patient is practically immortal, probably on to a winner.'

He placed a thumb over the cork and shook the bottle vigorously. There was a crash as the Chair of Indefinite Studies and the Senior Wrangler tried to get under the same table.

'And these fellows seem to have taken against it for some reason,' he said, approaching the beaker.

'I prefer a sauce that doesn't mean you mustn't make any jolting movements for half an hour after using it,' muttered the Dean.

'And that can't be used for breaking up small rocks,' said the Senior Wrangler.

'Or getting rid of tree roots,' said the Chair of Indefinite Studies.

'And which isn't actually outlawed in three cities,' said the Lecturer in Recent Runes.

Ridcully cautiously uncorked the bottle. There was a brief hiss of indrawn air.

He allowed a few drops to splash into the beaker. Nothing happened.

A more generous helping was allowed to fall. The mixture remained irredeemably inert.

Ridcully sniffed suspiciously at the bottle.

'I wonder if I added enough grated wahooni?' he said, and then upturned the sauce and let most of it slide into the mixture.

It merely went *gloop*.

The wizards began to stand up and brush themselves off, giving one another the rather embarrassed grins of people who know that they've just been part of a synchronized making-a-fool-of-yourself team.

'I know we've had that asafoetida rather a long time,' said Ridcully. He turned the bottle round, peering at it sadly.

Finally he tipped it up for the last time and thumped it hard on the base.

A trickle of sauce arrived on the lip of the bottle and glistened there for a moment. Then it began to form a bead.

As if drawn by invisible strings, the heads of the wizards turned to look at it.

Wizards wouldn't be wizards if they couldn't see a *little* way into the future.

As the bead swelled and started to go pear-shaped they turned and, with a surprising turn of speed for men so wealthy in years and waistline, began to dive for the floor.

The drop fell.

It went *gloop*.

And that was all.

Ridcully, who'd been standing like a statue, sagged in relief.

'I don't know,' he said, turning away, 'I wish you fellows would show some backbone –'

The fireball lifted him off his feet. Then it rose to the ceiling, where it spread out widely and vanished with a pop, leaving a perfect chrysanthemum of scorched plaster.

Pure white light filled the room. And there was a sound.
TINKLE. TINKLE.
FIZZ.

The wizards risked looking around.

The beaker gleamed. It was filled with a liquid glow, which bubbled gently and sent out sparkles like a spinning diamond.

'My word . . .' breathed the Lecturer in Recent Runes.

Ridcully picked himself up off the floor. Wizards tended to roll well, or in any case are well padded enough to bounce.

Slowly, the flickering brilliance casting their long shadows on the walls, the wizards gravitated towards the beaker.

'Well, what *is* it?' said the Dean.

'I remember my father tellin' me some very valuable advice about drinks,' said Ridcully. 'He said, "Son, never drink any drink with a paper umbrella in it, never drink any drink with a humorous name, and never drink any drink that changes colour when the last ingredient goes in. And never, ever, do this –"'

He dipped his finger into the beaker.

It came out with one glistening drop on the end.

'Careful, Archchancellor,' warned the Dean. 'What you have there might represent pure sobriety.'

Ridcully paused with the finger halfway to his lips.

'Good point,' he said. 'I don't want to start being sober at my time of life.' He looked around. 'How do we usually test stuff?'

'Generally we ask for student volunteers,' said the Dean.

'What happens if we don't get any?'

'We give it to them anyway.'

'Isn't that a bit unethical?'

'Not if we don't tell them, Archchancellor.'

'Ah, good point.'

'I'll try it,' the oh god mumbled.

'Something these clo– gentlemen have cooked up?' said Susan. 'It might kill you!'

'You've never *had* a hangover, I expect,' said the oh god. 'Otherwise you wouldn't talk such rot.'

He staggered up to the beaker, managed to grip it on the second go, and drank the lot.

'There'll be fireworks now,' said the raven, from Susan's shoulder. 'Flames coming out of the mouth, screams, clutching at the throat, lying down under the cold tap, that sort of thing –'

Death found, to his amazement, that dealing with the queue was very enjoyable. Hardly anyone had ever been pleased to see him before.

NEXT! AND WHAT'S YOUR NAME, LITTLE . . . He hesitated, but rallied, and continued . . . PERSON?

'Nobby Nobbs, Hogfather,' said Nobby. Was it him, or was this knee he was sitting on a lot bonier than it should be? His buttocks argued with his brain, and were sat on.

AND HAVE YOU BEEN A GOOD BO . . . A GOOD DWA . . . A GOOD GNO . . . A GOOD INDIVIDUAL?

And suddenly Nobby found he had no control at all of his tongue. Of its own accord, gripped by a terrible compulsion, it said:

"S."

He struggled for self-possession as the great voice went on: So I EXPECT YOU'LL WANT A PRESENT FOR A GOOD MON . . . A GOOD HUM . . . A GOOD MALE?

Aha, got you bang to rights, you'll be coming along with *me*, my old chummy, I bet you don't remember the cellar at the back of the shoelace maker's in Old Cobblers, eh, all those Hogswatch mornings with a little hole in my world, eh?

The words rose in Nobby's throat but were overridden by something ancient before they reached his voice box, and to his amazement were translated into:

"S."

SOMETHING NICE?

"S."

There was hardly anything left of Nobby's conscious will now. The world consisted of nothing but his naked soul and the Hogfather, who filled the universe.

AND YOU WILL OF COURSE BE GOOD FOR ANOTHER YEAR?

The tiny remnant of basic Nobbyness wanted to say, 'Er, how exactly do you define "good", mister? Like, suppose there was just some stuff that no one'd miss, say? Or, f'r instance, say a friend of mine was on patrol, sort of thing, and found a shopkeeper had left his door unlocked at night. I mean, anyone could walk in, right, but suppose this friend took one or two things, sort of like, you know, a *gratuity*, and then called the shopkeeper out and got him to lock up, that counts as "good", does it?'

Good and bad were, to Nobby's way of thinking, entirely relative terms. Most of his relatives, for example, were criminals. But, again, this invitation to philosophical debate was ambushed somewhere in his head by sheer dread of the big beard in the sky.

''s,' he squeaked.

Now, I wonder what you would like?

Nobby gave up, and sat mute. Whatever was going to happen next was going to happen, and there was not a thing he could do about it ... Right now, the light at the end of his mental tunnel showed only more tunnel.

Ah, yes ...

The Hogfather reached into his sack and pulled out an awkwardly shaped present wrapped in festive Hogswatch paper which, owing to some slight confusion on the current Hogfather's part, had merry ravens on it. Corporal Nobbs took it in nervous hands.

What do you say?

''nk you.'

Off you go.

Corporal Nobbs slid down gratefully and barged his way through the crowds, stopping only when he was fielded by Constable Visit.

'What happened? What happened? I couldn't see!'

'I dunno,' mumbled Nobby. 'He gave me *this*.'

'What is it?'

'I dunno ...'

He clawed at the raven-bedecked paper.

'This is disgusting, this whole business,' said Constable Visit. 'It's the worship of idols –'

'It's a genuine Burleigh and Stronginthearm double-action triple-cantilever crossbow with a polished walnut stock and engraved silver facings!'

'– a crass commercialization of a date which is purely of astronomical significance,' said Visit, who seldom paid attention when he was in mid-denounce. 'If it is to be celebrated at all, then –'

'*I saw this in* Bows and Ammo*! It got Editor's Choice in the "What to Buy When Rich Uncle Sidney Dies" category! They had to break both the reviewer's arms to get him to let go of it!*'

'– ought to be commemorated in a small service of –'

'It must cost more'n a year's salary! They only make 'em to order! You have to wait ages!'

'– religious significance.' It dawned on Constable Visit that something behind him was amiss.

'Aren't we going to arrest this imposter, corporal?' he said.

Corporal Nobbs looked blearily at him through the mists of possessive pride.

'You're foreign, Washpot,' he said. 'I can't expect you to know the real meaning of Hogswatch.'

The oh god blinked.

'Ah,' he said. 'That's better. Oh, *yes*. That's a lot better. Thank you.'

The wizards, who shared the raven's belief in the essential narrative conventions of life, watched him cautiously.

'Any minute now,' said the Lecturer in Recent Runes confidently, 'it'll probably start with some kind of amusing yell –'

'You know,' said the oh god, 'I think I could just possibly eat a soft-boiled egg.'

'– or maybe the ears spinning round –'

'And perhaps drink a glass of milk,' said the oh god.

Ridcully looked nonplussed.

'You really feel better?' he said.

'Oh, yes,' said the oh god. 'I really think I could risk a smile without the top of my head falling off.'

'No, no, no,' said the Dean. 'This can't be right. Everyone knows that a good hangover cure has got to involve a lot of humorous shouting, ekcetra.'

'I could possibly tell you a joke,' said the oh god carefully.

'You don't have this pressing urge to run outside and stick your head in a water butt?' said Ridcully.

'Er . . . not really,' said the oh god. 'But I'd like some toast, if that helps.'

The Dean took off his hat and pulled a thaumometer out of the point. '*Something* happened,' he said. 'There was a massive thaumic surge.'

'Didn't it even taste a bit . . . well, spicy?' said Ridcully.

'It didn't taste of anything, really,' said the oh god.

'Oh, look, it's obvious,' said Susan. 'When the God of Wine drinks, Bilious here gets the after-effects, so when the God of Hangovers drinks a hangover cure then the effects must jump back across the same link.'

'That could be right,' said the Dean. 'He is, after all, basically a conduit.'

'I've always thought of myself as more of a tube,' said the oh god.

'No, no, she's right,' said Ridcully. 'When he drinks, this lad here gets the nasty result. So, logically, when our friend here takes a hangover cure the side effects should head back the same way –'

'Someone mentioned a crystal ball just now,' said the oh god in a voice suddenly clanging with vengeance. 'I want to *see* this –'

It was a big drink. A very big and a very long drink. It was one of those special cocktails where each very sticky, very strong ingredient is poured in very slowly, so that they layer on top of one another. Drinks like this tend to get called Traffic Lights or Rainbow's Revenge or, in places where truth is more highly valued, Hello and Goodbye, Mr Brain Cell.

In addition, this drink had some lettuce floating in it. And a slice of lemon *and* a piece of pineapple hooked coquettishly on the side of the glass, which had sugar frosted round the rim. There were *two* paper umbrellas, one pink and one blue, and they each had a cherry on the end.

And someone had taken the trouble to freeze ice cubes in the shape of little elephants. After that, there's no hope. You might as well be drinking in a place called the Cococobana.

The God of Wine picked it up lovingly. It was his kind of drink.

There was a rumba going on in the background. There were also a couple of young ladies snuggling up to him. It was going to be a good night. It was always a good night.

'Happy Hogswatch, everyone!' he said, and raised the glass.

And then: 'Can anyone hear something?'

Someone blew a paper squeaker at him.

'No, seriously . . . like a sort of descending note . . .?'

Since no one paid this any attention he shrugged, and nudged one of his fellow drinkers.

'How about we have a couple more and go to this club I know?' he said.

And then –

The wizards leaned back, and one or two of them grimaced.

Only the oh god stayed glued to the glass, face contorted in a vicious smile.

'We have eructation!' he shouted, and punched the air. 'Yes! Yes! *Yes*! The worm is on the other boot now, eh? Hah! How do you like *them* apples, huh?'

'Well, *mainly* apples –' said the Dean.

'Looked like a lot of other things to me,' said Ridcully. 'It seems we have reversed the cause-effect flow ...'

'Will it be permanent?' said the oh god hopefully.

'I shouldn't think so. After all, you *are* the God of Hangovers. It'll probably just reverse itself again when the potion wears off.'

'Then I may not have much time. Bring me ... let's see ... twenty pints of lager, some pepper vodka and a bottle of coffee liqueur! With an umbrella in it! Let's see how he enjoys that, Mr You've Got Room For Another One In There!'

Susan grabbed his hand and pulled him over to a bench.

'I didn't have you sobered up just so you could go on a binge!' she said.

He blinked at her. 'You didn't?'

'I want you to help me!'

'Help you what?'

'You said you'd never been human before, didn't you?'

'Er ...' The oh god looked down at himself. 'That's right,' he said. 'Never.'

'You've never incarnated?' said Ridcully.

'Surely that's a rather personal question, isn't it?' said the Chair of Indefinite Studies.

'That's ... right,' said the oh god. 'Odd, that. I remember always having headaches ... but never having a head. That can't be right, can it?'

'You existed in potentia?' said Ridcully.

'Did I?'

'Did he?' said Susan.

Ridcully paused. 'Oh dear,' he said. 'I think *I* did it, didn't I? I said something to young Stibbons about drinking and hangovers, didn't I ...?'

'And you created him just like that?' said the Dean. 'I find that *very* hard to believe, Mustrum. Hah! Out of thin air? I suppose we can *all* do that, can we? Anyone care to think up some new pixie?'

'Like the Hair Loss Fairy?' said the Lecturer in Recent Runes. The other wizards laughed.

'I am *not* losing my hair!' snapped the Dean. 'It is just very finely spaced.'

'Half on your head and half on your hairbrush,' said the Lecturer in Recent Runes.

'No sense in bein' bashful about goin' bald,' said Ridcully evenly. 'Anyway, you know what they say about bald men, Dean.'

'Yes, they say, "Look at him, he's got no hair,"' said the Lecturer in Recent Runes. The Dean had been annoying him lately.

'For the last time,' shouted the Dean, 'I am *not* – '

He stopped.

There was a *glingleglingleglingle* noise.

'I wish I knew where that was coming from,' said Ridcully.

'Er . . .' the Dean began. 'Is there . . . something on my head?'

The other wizards stared.

Something was moving under his hat.

Very carefully, he reached up and removed it.

The very small gnome sitting on his head had a clump of the Dean's hair in each hand. It blinked guiltily in the light.

'Is there a problem?' it said.

'Get it off me!' the Dean yelled.

The wizards hesitated. They were all vaguely aware of the theory that very small creatures could pass on diseases, and while the gnome was larger than such creatures were generally thought to be, no one wanted to catch Expanding Scalp Sickness.

Susan grabbed it.

'Are you the Hair Loss Fairy?' she said.

'Apparently,' said the gnome, wriggling in her grip.

The Dean ran his hands desperately through his hair.

'What have you been doing with my hair?' he demanded.

'Well, some of it I think I have to put on hairbrushes,' said the gnome, 'but sometimes I think I weave it into little mats to block up the bath with.'

'What do you mean, you *think*?' said Ridcully.

'Just a minute,' said Susan. She turned to the oh god. 'Where exactly *were* you before I found you in the snow?'

'Er . . . sort of . . . everywhere, I think,' said the oh god. 'Anywhere where drink had been consumed in beastly quantities some time previously, you could say.'

'Ah-*ha*,' said Ridcully. 'You were an immanent vital force, yes?'

'I suppose I could have been,' the oh god conceded.

'And when we joked about the Hair Loss Fairy it suddenly focused on the Dean's head,' said Ridcully, 'where its operations have been noticeable to all of us in recent months although of course we have been far too polite to pass comment on the subject.'

'You're calling things into being,' said Susan.

'Things like the Give the Dean a Huge Bag of Money Goblin?' said the Dean, who could think very quickly at times. He looked around hopefully. 'Anyone hear any fairy tinkling?'

'Do you often get given huge bags of money, sir?' said Susan.

'Not on what you'd call a daily basis, no,' said the Dean. 'But if – '

'Then there probably isn't any occult room for a Huge Bags of Money Goblin,' said Susan.

'I personally have always wondered what happens to my socks,' said the Bursar cheerfully. 'You know how there's always one missing? When I was a lad I always thought that something was taking them . . .'

The wizards gave this some thought. Then they all heard it – the little crinkly tinkling noise of magic taking place.

The Archchancellor pointed dramatically skywards.

'To the laundry!' he said.

'It's downstairs, Ridcully,' said the Dean.

'*Down* to the laundry!'

'And you know Mrs Whitlow doesn't like us going in there,' said the Chair of Indefinite Studies.

'And who is Archchancellor of this university, may I ask?' said Ridcully. 'Is it Mrs Whitlow? I don't think so! Is it me? Why, how amazing, I do believe it is!'

'Yes, but you know what she can be like,' said the Chair.

'Er, yes, that's true – ' Ridcully began.

'I believe she's gone to her sister's for the holiday,' said the Bursar.

'We certainly don't have to take orders from any kind of housekeeper!' said the Archchancellor. 'To the laundry!'

The wizards surged out excitedly, leaving Susan, the oh god, the Verruca Gnome and the Hair Loss Fairy.

'Tell me again who those people were,' said the oh god.

'Some of the cleverest men in the world,' said Susan.

'And I'm sober, am I?'

'Clever isn't the same as sensible,' said Susan, 'and they do say that if you wish to walk the path to wisdom then for your first step you must become as a small child.'

'Do you think they've heard about the second step?'

Susan sighed. 'Probably not, but sometimes they fall over it while they're running around shouting.'

'Ah.' The oh god looked around. 'Do you think they have any soft drinks here?' he said.

*

The path to wisdom does, in fact, begin with a single step.

Where people go wrong is in ignoring all the thousands of other steps that come after it. They make the single step of deciding to become one with the universe, and for some reason forget to take the logical next step of living for seventy years on a mountain and a daily bowl of rice and yak-butter tea that would give it any kind of meaning. While evidence says that the road to Hell is paved with good intentions, they're probably all on first steps.

The Dean was always at his best at times like this. He led the way between the huge, ancient copper vats, prodding with his staff into dark corners and going 'Hut! Hut!' under his breath.

'Why would it turn up here?' whispered the Lecturer in Recent Runes.

'Point of reality instability,' said Ridcully, standing on tip-toe to look into a bleaching cauldron. 'Every damn thing turns up here. You should know that by now.'

'But why *now*?' said the Chair of Indefinite Studies.

'No talking!' hissed the Dean, and leapt out into the next alleyway, staff held protectively in front of him.

'Hah!' he screamed, and then looked disappointed.

'Er, how big would this sock-stealing thing be?' said the Senior Wrangler.

'Don't know,' said Ridcully. He peered behind a stack of washboards. 'Come to think of it, I must've lost a ton of socks over the years.'

'Me too,' said the Lecturer in Recent Runes.

'So . . . should we be looking in small places or very *large* places?' the Senior Wrangler went on, in the voice of one whose train of thought has just entered a long dark tunnel.

'Good point,' said Ridcully. 'Dean, why do you keep referring to sheds all the time?'

'It's "hut", Mustrum,' said the Dean. 'It means . . . it means . . .'

'Small wooden building?' Ridcully suggested.

'Well, sometimes, agreed, but other times . . . well, you just have to say "hut".'

'This sock creature . . . Does it just steal them, or does it *eat* them?' said the Senior Wrangler.

'Valuable contribution, that man,' said Ridcully, giving up on the Dean. 'Right, pass the word along: no one is to look like a sock, understand?'

'How can you –' the Dean began, and stopped.

They all heard it.

... grnf, grnf, grnf ...

It was a busy sound, the sound of something with a serious appetite to satisfy.

'The Eater of Socks,' moaned the Senior Wrangler, with his eyes shut.

'How many tentacles would you expect it to have?' said the Lecturer in Recent Runes. 'I mean, roughly speaking?'

'It's a very *large* sort of noise, isn't it?' said the Bursar.

'To the nearest dozen, say,' said the Lecturer in Recent Runes, edging backwards.

... grnf, grnf, grnf ...

'It'd probably tear our socks off as soon as look at us ...' wailed the Senior Wrangler.

'Ah. So at least five or six tentacles, then, would you say?' said the Lecturer in Recent Runes.

'Seems to me it's coming from one of the washing engines,' said the Dean.

The engines were each two storeys high, and usually only used when the University's population soared during term time. A huge treadmill connected to a couple of big bleached wooden paddles in each vat, which were heated via the fireboxes underneath. In full production the washing engines needed at least half a dozen people to manhandle the loads, maintain the fires and oil the scrubbing arms. Ridcully had seen them at work once, when it had looked like a picture of a very clean and hygienic Hell, the kind of place soap might go to when it died.

The Dean stopped by the door to the boiler area.

'Something's in here,' he whispered. 'Listen!'

... grnf ...

'It's stopped! It knows we're here!' he hissed. 'All right? Ready? Hut!'

'No!' squeaked the Lecturer in Recent Runes. 'I'll open the door and you be ready to stop it! One ... two ... *three*! Oh ...'

The sleigh soared into the snowy sky.

ON THE WHOLE, I THINK THAT WENT VERY WELL, DON'T YOU?

'Yes, master,' said Albert.

I WAS RATHER PUZZLED BY THE LITTLE BOY IN THE CHAIN MAIL, THOUGH.

'I think that was a Watchman, master.'

REALLY? WELL, HE WENT AWAY HAPPY, AND THAT'S THE MAIN THING.

'Is it, master?' There was worry in Albert's voice. Death's osmotic nature tended to pick up new ideas altogether too quickly. Of course, Albert understood why they had to do all this, but the master ... well, sometimes the master lacked the necessary mental equipment to work out what should be true and what shouldn't ...

AND I THINK I'VE GOT THE LAUGH WORKING REALLY WELL NOW. HO. HO. HO.

'Yeah, sir, very jolly,' said Albert. He looked down at the list. 'Still, work goes on, eh? The next one's pretty close, master, so I should keep them down low if I was you.'

JOLLY GOOD. HO. HO. HO.

'Sarah the little match girl, doorway of Thimble's Pipe and Tobacco Shop, Money Trap Lane, it says here.'

AND WHAT DOES *SHE* WANT FOR HOGSWATCH? HO. HO. HO.

'Dunno. Never sent a letter. By the way, just a tip, you don't have to say "Ho, ho, ho," *all* the time, master. Let's see ... It says here ...' Albert's lips moved as he read.

I EXPECT A DOLL IS ALWAYS ACCEPTABLE. OR A SOFT TOY OF SOME DESCRIPTION. THE SACK SEEMS TO KNOW. WHAT'VE WE GOT FOR HER, ALBERT? HO. HO. HO.

Something small was dropped into his hand.

'This,' said Albert.

OH.

There was a moment of horrible silence as they both stared at the lifetimer.

'You're for life, not just for Hogswatch,' prompted Albert. 'Life goes on, master. In a manner of speaking.'

BUT THIS IS *HOGSWATCHNIGHT*.

'Very traditional time for this sort of thing, I understand,' said Albert.

I THOUGHT IT WAS THE SEASON TO BE JOLLY, said Death.

'Ah, well, yes, you see, one of the things that makes folks even more jolly is knowing there're people who ain't,' said Albert, in a matter-of-fact voice. 'That's how it goes, master. Master?'

NO. Death stood up. THIS IS HOW IT SHOULDN'T GO.

The University's Great Hall had been set for the Hogswatchnight Feast. The tables were already groaning under the weight of the cutlery, and it would be hours before any real food was put on them.

It was hard to see where there would be space for any among the drifts of ornamental fruit bowls and forests of wine glasses.

The oh god picked up a menu and turned to the fourth page.

'Course four: molluscs and crustaceans. A medley of lobster, crab, king crab, prawn, shrimp, oyster, clam, giant mussel, green-lipped mussel, thin-lipped mussel and Fighting Tiger Limpet. With a herb and butter dipping sauce. Wine: "Three Wizards" Chardonnay, Year of the Talking Frog. Beer: Winkles' Old Peculiar.' He put it down. 'That's *one* course?' he said.

'They're big men in the food department,' said Susan.

He turned the menu over. On the cover was the University's coat of arms and, over it, three large letters in ancient script:

η β π

'Is this some sort of magic word?'

'No.' Susan sighed. 'They put it on all their menus. You might call it the unofficial motto of the University.'

'What's it mean?'

'Eta Beta Pi.'

Bilious gave her an expectant look.

'Yes . . .?'

'Er . . . like, Eat a Better Pie?' said Susan.

'That's what you just said, yes,' said the oh god.

'Um. No. You see, the letters are Ephebian characters which just *sound* a bit like "eat a better pie".'

'Ah.' Bilious nodded wisely. 'I can see that might cause confusion.'

Susan felt a bit helpless in the face of the look of helpful puzzlement. 'No,' she said, 'in fact they are *supposed* to cause a little bit of confusion, and then you laugh. It's called a pune or play on words. Eta Beta Pi.' She eyed him carefully. 'You laugh,' she said. 'With your mouth. Only, in *fact*, you don't laugh, because you're not supposed to laugh at things like this.'

'Perhaps I could find that glass of milk,' said the oh god helplessly, peering at the huge array of jugs and bottles. He'd clearly given up on sense of humour.

'I gather the Archchancellor won't have milk in the University,' said Susan. 'He says he knows where it comes from and it's unhygienic. And that's a man who eats three eggs for breakfast every day, mark you. How do you know about milk, by the way?'

'I've got . . . memories,' said the oh god. 'Not exactly of anything, er, specific. Just, you know, memories. Like, I know trees usually grow green-end up . . . that sort of thing. I suppose gods just know things.'

'Any special god-like powers?'

'I might be able to turn water into an enervescent drink.' He pinched the bridge of his nose. 'Is that any help? And it's just possible I can give people a blinding headache.'

'I need to find out why my grandfather is ... acting strange.'

'Can't you ask him?'

'He won't tell me!'

'Does he throw up a lot?'

'I shouldn't think so. He doesn't often eat. The occasional curry, once or twice a month.'

'He must be pretty thin.'

'You've no idea.'

'Well, then ... Does he often stare at himself in the mirror and say "Arrgh"? Or stick out his tongue and wonder why it's gone yellow? You see, it's possible I might have some measure of influence over people who are hung over. If he's been drinking a lot, I might be able to find him.'

'I can't see him doing any of those things. I think I'd better tell you ... My grandfather is Death.'

'Oh, I'm sorry to hear that.'

'I said *Death*.'

'Sorry?'

'Death. You know ... Death?'

'You mean the robes, the –'

'– scythe, white horse, bones ... yes. Death.'

'I just want to make sure I've got this clear,' said the oh god in a reasonable tone of voice. 'You think your grandfather is Death and you think *he's* acting strange?'

The Eater of Socks looked up at the wizards, cautiously. Then its jaws started to work again.

... *grnf, grnf* ...

'Here, that's one of mine!' said the Chair of Indefinite Studies, making a grab. The Eater of Socks backed away hurriedly.

It looked like a very small elephant with a very wide, flared trunk, up which one of the Chair's socks was disappearing.

'Funny lookin' little thing, ain't it?' said Ridcully, leaning his staff against the wall.

'Let go, you wretched creature!' said the Chair, making a grab for the sock. 'Shoo!'

The sock eater tried to get away while remaining where it was.

This should be impossible, but it is in fact a move attempted by many small animals when they are caught eating something forbidden. The legs scrabble hurriedly but the neck and feverishly working jaws merely stretch and pivot around the food. Finally the last of the sock disappeared up the snout with a faint sucking noise and the creature lumbered off behind one of the boilers. After a while it poked one suspicious eye around the corner to watch them.

'They're expensive, you know, with the flax-reinforced heel,' muttered the Chair of Indefinite Studies.

Ridcully pulled open a drawer in his hat and extracted his pipe and a pouch of herbal tobacco. He struck a match on the side of the washing engine. This was turning out to be a far more interesting evening than he had anticipated.

'We've got to get this sorted out,' he said, as the first few puffs filled the washing hall with the scent of autumn bonfires. 'Can't have creatures just popping into existence because someone's thought about them. It's unhygienic.'

The sleigh slewed around at the end of Money Trap Lane.

COME ON, ALBERT.

'You know you're not supposed to do this sort of thing, master. You know what happened last time.'

THE HOGFATHER CAN DO IT, THOUGH.

'But ... little match girls dying in the snow is part of what the Hogswatch spirit is all *about*, master,' said Albert desperately. 'I mean, people hear about it and say, "We may be poorer than a disabled banana and only have mud and old boots to eat, but at least we're better off than the poor little match girl," master. It makes them feel happy and grateful for what they've got, see.'

I KNOW WHAT THE SPIRIT OF HOGSWATCH IS, ALBERT.

'Sorry, master. But, look, it's all right, anyway, because she wakes up and it's all bright and shining and tinkling music and there's angels, master.'

Death stopped.

AH. THEY TURN UP AT THE LAST MINUTE WITH WARM CLOTHES AND A HOT DRINK?

Oh dear, thought Albert. The master's really in one of his funny moods now.

'Er. No. Not exactly at the *last* minute, master. Not as such.'

WELL?

'More sort of just *after* the last minute.' Albert coughed nervously.

You mean after she's —

'Yes. That's how the story goes, master. 's not my fault.'

Why not turn up before? An angel has quite a large carrying capacity.

'Couldn't say, master. I suppose people think it's more ... satisfying the other way ...' Albert hesitated, and then frowned. 'You know, now that I come to tell someone ...'

Death looked down at the shape under the falling snow. Then he set the lifetimer on the air and touched it with a finger. A spark flashed across.

'You ain't really allowed to do that,' said Albert, feeling wretched.

The Hogfather can. The Hogfather gives presents. There's no better present than a future.

'Yeah, but —'

Albert.

'All right, master.'

Death scooped up the girl and strode to the end of the alley.

The snowflakes fell like angel's feathers. Death stepped out into the street and accosted two figures who were tramping through the drifts.

Take her somewhere warm and give her a good dinner, he commanded, pushing the bundle into the arms of one of them. And I may well be checking up later.

Then he turned and disappeared into the swirling snow.

Constable Visit looked down at the little girl in his arms, and then at Corporal Nobbs.

'What's all this about, corporal?'

Nobby pulled aside the blanket.

'Search me,' he said. 'Looks like we've been chosen to do a bit of charity.'

'*I* don't call it very charitable, just dumping someone on people like this.'

'Come on, there'll still be some grub left in the Watch-house,' said Nobby. He'd got a very deep and certain feeling that this was expected of him. He remembered a big man in a grotto, although he couldn't quite remember the face. And he couldn't quite remember the face of the person who had handed over the girl, so that meant it must be the same one.

Shortly afterwards there was some tinkling music and a very bright light and two rather affronted angels appeared at the other end of the alley, but Albert threw snowballs at them until they went away.

*

Hex worried Ponder Stibbons. He didn't know how it worked, but everyone else assumed that he did. Oh, he had a good idea about *some* parts, and he was pretty certain that Hex thought about things by turning them all into numbers and crunching them (a clothes wringer from the laundry, or CWL, had been plumbed in for this very purpose), but why did it need a lot of small religious pictures? And there was the mouse. It didn't seem to do much, but whenever they forgot to give it its cheese Hex stopped working. There were all those ram skulls. The ants wandered over to them occasionally but they didn't seem to *do* anything.

What Ponder was worried about was the fear that he was simply engaged in a cargo cult. He'd read about them. Ignorant[*] and credulous[†] people, whose island might once have been visited by some itinerant merchant vessel that traded pearls and coconuts for such fruits of civilization as glass beads, mirrors, axes and sexual diseases, would later make big model ships out of bamboo in the hope of once again attracting this magical cargo. Of course, they were far too ignorant and credulous to know that just because you built the shape you didn't get the substance ...

He'd built the shape of Hex and, it occurred to him, he'd built it in a magical university where the border between the real and 'not real' was stretched so thin you could almost see through it. He got the horrible suspicion that, somehow, they were merely making solid a sketch that was hidden somewhere in the air.

Hex knew what it ought to be.

All that business about the electricity, for example. Hex had raised the subject one night, not long after it'd asked for the mouse.

Ponder prided himself that he knew pretty much all there was to know about electricity. But they'd tried rubbing balloons and glass rods until they'd been able to stick Adrian on to the ceiling, and it hadn't had any effect on Hex. Then they'd tried tying a lot of cats to a wheel which, when revolved against some beads of amber, caused

---

[*] Ignorant: a state of not knowing what a pronoun is, or how to find the square root of 27.4, and merely knowing childish and useless things like which of the seventy almost identical-looking species of the purple sea snake are the deadly ones, how to treat the poisonous pith of the Sago-sago tree to make a nourishing gruel, how to foretell the weather by the movements of the tree-climbing Burglar Crab, how to navigate across a thousand miles of featureless ocean by means of a piece of string and a small clay model of your grandfather, how to get essential vitamins from the liver of the ferocious Ice Bear, and other such trivial matters. It's a strange thing that when everyone becomes educated, everyone knows about the pronoun but no one knows about the Sago-sago.

[†] Credulous: having views about the world, the universe and humanity's place in it that are shared only by very unsophisticated people and the most intelligent and advanced mathematicians and physicists.

any amount of electricity all over the place. The wretched stuff hung around for *days*, but there didn't seem any way of ladling it into Hex and anyway no one could stand the noise.

So far the Archchancellor had vetoed the lightning rod idea.

All this depressed Ponder. He was certain that the world ought to work in a more efficient way.

And now even the things that he thought were going right were going wrong.

He stared glumly at Hex's quill pen in its tangle of springs and wire.

The door was thrown open. Only one person could make a door bang on its hinges like that. Ponder didn't even turn round.

'Hello again, Archchancellor.'

'That thinking engine of yours working?' said Ridcully. 'Only there's an interesting little —'

'It's not working,' said Ponder.

'It ain't? What's this, a half-holiday for Hogswatch?'

'Look,' said Ponder.

Hex wrote: +++ Whoops! Here Comes The Cheese! +++ MELON MELON MELON +++ Error At Address: 14, Treacle Mine Road, Ankh-Morpork +++ !!!!! +++ Oneoneoneoneoneone +++ Redo From Start +++

'What's going on?' said Ridcully, as the others pushed in behind them.

'I know it sounds stupid, Archchancellor, but we think it might have caught something off the Bursar.'

'Daftness, you mean?'

'That's ridiculous, boy!' said the Dean. 'Idiocy is *not* a communicable disease.'

Ridcully puffed his pipe.

'I used to think that, too,' he said. 'Now I'm not so sure. Anyway, you can catch wisdom, can't you?'

'No, you can't,' snapped the Dean. 'It's not like 'flu, Ridcully. Wisdom is . . . well, instilled.'

'We bring students here and hope they catch wisdom off us, don't we?' said Ridcully.

'Well, *metaphorically*,' said the Dean.

'And if you hang around with a bunch of idiots you're bound to become pretty daft yourself,' Ridcully went on.

'I suppose in a manner of speaking . . .'

'And you've only got to talk to the poor old Bursar for five minutes and you think you're going a bit potty yourself, am I right?'

The wizards nodded glumly. The Bursar's company, although quite harmless, had a habit of making one's brain squeak.

'So Hex here has caught daftness off the Bursar,' said Ridcully. 'Simple. Real stupidity beats artificial intelligence every time.' He banged his pipe on the side of Hex's listening tube and shouted: 'FEELING ALL RIGHT, OLD CHAP?'

Hex wrote: +++ Hi Mum Is Testing +++ MELON MELON MELON +++ Out Of Cheese Error +++ !!!!! +++ Mr Jelly! Mr Jelly! +++

'Hex seems perfectly able to work out anything purely to do with numbers but when it tries anything else it does this,' said Ponder.

'See? Bursar Disease,' said Ridcully. 'The bee's knees when it comes to adding up, the pig's ear at everything else. Try giving him dried frog pills?'

'Sorry, sir, but that is a very uninformed suggestion,' said Ponder. 'You can't give medicine to machines.'

'Don't see why not,' said Ridcully. He banged on the tube again and bellowed, 'SOON HAVE YOU BACK ON YOUR ... your ... yes, indeed, old chap! Where's that board with all the letter and number buttons, Mr Stibbons? Ah, good.' He sat down and typed, with one finger, as slowly as a company chairman:

D-R-Y-D-F-R-O-R-G-$\frac{1}{2}$P-I-L-L-S

Hex's pipes jangled.

'That can't possibly work, sir,' said Ponder.

'It ought to,' said Ridcully. 'If he can get the idea of being ill, he can get the idea of being cured.'

He typed: L-O-T-S-O-F-D-R-Y-D-F-R-O-R-G-P-$\frac{1}{4}$-L-L-S

'Seems to me,' he said, 'that this thing believes what it's told, right?'

'Well, it's true that Hex has, if you want to put it that way, no idea of an untruth.'

'Right. Well, I've just told the thing it's had a lot of dried frog pills. It's not going to call me a liar, is it?'

There were some clickings and whirrings within the structure of Hex.

Then it wrote: +++ Good Evening, Archchancellor. I Am Fully Recovered And Enthusiastic About My Tasks +++

'Not mad, then?'

+++ I Assure You I Am As Sane As The Next Man +++

'Bursar, just move away from the machine, will you?' said Ridcully. 'Oh well, I expect it's the best we're going to get. Right, let's get all this sorted out. We want to find out what's going on.'

'Anywhere specific or just everywhere?' said Ponder, a shade sarcastically.

There was a scratching noise from Hex's pen. Ridcully glanced down at the paper.

'Says here "Implied Creation Of Anthropomorphic Personification",' he said. 'What's that mean?'

'Er ... I think Hex has tried to work out the answer,' said Ponder.

'Has it, bigods? *I* hadn't even worked out what the question was yet ...'

'It heard you talking, sir.'

Ridcully raised his eyebrows. Then he leaned down towards the speaking tube.

'CAN YOU HEAR ME IN THERE?'

The pen scratched.

+++ Yes +++

'LOOKIN' AFTER YOU ALL RIGHT, ARE THEY?'

'You don't have to shout, Archchancellor,' said Ponder.

'What's this Implied Creation, then?' said Ridcully.

'Er, I think I've heard of it, Archchancellor,' said Ponder. 'It means the existence of some things automatically brings into existence other things. If some things exist, certain other things have to exist as well.'

'Like ... crime and punishment, say?' said Ridcully. 'Drinking and hangovers ... of course ...'

'*Something* like that, sir, yes.'

'So ... if there's a Tooth Fairy there has to be a Verruca Gnome?' Ridcully stroked his beard. 'Makes a sort of sense, I suppose. But why not a Wisdom Tooth Goblin? You know, bringing them extra ones? Some little devil with a bag of big teeth?'

There was silence. But in the depths of the silence there was a little tinkly fairy bell sound.

'Er ... do you think I might have –' Ridcully began.

'Sounds logical to me,' said the Senior Wrangler. 'I remember the agony I had when *my* wisdom teeth came through.'

'Last week?' said the Dean, and smirked.

'Ah,' said Ridcully. He didn't look embarrassed because people like Ridcully are never, ever embarrassed about anything, although often people are embarrassed on their behalf. He bent down to the ear trumpet again.

'YOU STILL IN THERE?'

Ponder Stibbons rolled his eyes.

'MIND TELLING US WHAT THE REALITY IS LIKE ROUND HERE?'

The pen wrote: +++ On A Scale Of One To Ten – Query +++

'FINE,' Ridcully shouted.

+++ Divide By Cucumber Error. Please Reinstall Universe And Reboot +++

'Interestin',' said Ridcully. 'Anyone know what that means?'

'Damn,' said Ponder. 'It's crashed again.'

Ridcully looked mystified. 'Has it? I never even saw it take off.'

'I mean it's . . . it's sort of gone a little bit mad,' said Ponder.

'Ah,' said Ridcully. 'Well, we're experts at that around here.'

He thumped on the drum again.

'WANT SOME MORE DRIED FROG PILLS, OLD CHAP?' he shouted.

'Er, I should let us sort it out, Archchancellor,' said Ponder, trying to steer him away.

'What does "divide by cucumber" mean?' said Ridcully.

'Oh, Hex just says that if it comes up with an answer that it knows can't possibly be real,' said Ponder.

'And this "rebooting" business? Give it a good kicking, do you?'

'Oh, no, of course, we . . . that is . . . well, yes, in fact,' said Ponder. 'Adrian goes round the back and . . . er . . . prods it with his foot. But in a *technical* way,' he added.

'Ah. I think I'm getting the hang of this thinkin' engine business,' said Ridcully cheerfully. 'So it reckons the universe needs a kicking, does it?'

Hex's pen was scratching across the paper. Ponder glanced at the figures.

'It must do. These figures can't be right!'

Ridcully grinned again. 'You mean either the whole world has gone wrong or your machine is wrong?'

'Yes!'

'Then I'd imagine the answer's pretty easy, wouldn't you?' said Ridcully.

'Yes. It certainly is. Hex gets thoroughly tested every day,' said Ponder Stibbons.

'Good point, that man,' said Ridcully. He banged on Hex's listening tube once more.

'YOU DOWN THERE –'

'You really *don't* need to shout, Archchancellor,' said Ponder.

'– what's this *Anthropomorphic* Personification, then?'

+++ Humans Have Always Ascribed Random, Seasonal, Natural

Or Inexplicable Actions To Human-Shaped Entities. Such Examples Are Jack Frost, The Hogfather, The Tooth Fairy And Death +++

'Oh, *them*. Yes, but they exist,' said Ridcully. 'Met a couple of 'em myself.'

+++ Humans Are Not Always Wrong +++

'All right, but I'm damn sure there's never been an Eater of Socks or God of Hangovers.'

+++ But There Is No Reason Why There Should Not Be +++

'The thing's right, you know,' said the Lecturer in Recent Runes. 'A little man who carries verrucas around is no more ridiculous than someone who takes away children's teeth for money, when you come to think about it.'

'Yes, but what about the Eater of Socks?' said the Chair of Indefinite Studies. 'Bursar just said he always thought something was eating his socks and, bingo, there it was.'

'But we all believed him, didn't we? I know *I* did. Seems like the best possible explanation for all the socks *I've* lost over the years. I mean, if they'd just fallen down the back of the drawer or something there'd be a mountain of the things by now.'

'I know what you mean,' said Ponder. 'It's like pencils. I must have bought hundreds of pencils over the years, but how many have I ever actually worn down to the stub? Even I've caught myself thinking that something's creeping up and eating them –'

There was a faint *glingleglingle* noise. He froze.

'What was that?' he said. 'Should I look round? Will I see something horrible?'

'Looks like a very puzzled bird,' said Ridcully.

'With a very odd-shaped beak,' said the Lecturer in Recent Runes.

'I wish I knew who's making that bloody tinkling noise,' said the Archchancellor.

The oh god listened attentively. Susan was amazed. He didn't seem to disbelieve anything. She'd never been able to talk like this before, and said so.

'I think that's because I haven't got any pre-conceived ideas,' said the oh god. 'It comes of not having been conceived, probably.'

'Well, that's how it is, anyway,' said Susan. 'Obviously I haven't inherited . . . physical characteristics. I suppose I just look at the world in a certain way.'

'What way?'

'It . . . doesn't always present barriers. Like this, for example.'

She closed her eyes. She felt better if she didn't see what she was doing. Part of her would keep on insisting it was impossible.

All she felt was a faintly cold, prickling sensation.

'What did I just do?' she said, her eyes still shut.

'Er . . . you waved your hand through the table,' said the oh god.

'You see?'

'Um . . . I assume that most humans can't do that?'

'No!'

'You don't have to shout. I'm not very experienced about humans, am I? Apart from around the point the sun shines through the gap in the curtains. And then they're mainly wishing that the ground would open up and swallow them. I mean the humans, not the curtains.'

Susan leaned back in her chair – and knew that a tiny part of her brain was saying, yes, there is a chair here, it's a real thing, you can sit on it.

'There's other things,' she said. 'I can remember things. Things that haven't happened yet.'

'Isn't that useful?'

'No! Because I never know what they – look, it's like looking at the future through a keyhole. You see bits of things but you never really know what they mean until you arrive where they are and see where the bit fits in.'

'That could be a problem,' said the oh god politely.

'Believe me. It's the waiting that's the worst part. You keep watching out for one of the bits to go past. I mean I don't usually remember anything *useful* about the future, just twisted little clues that don't make sense until it's too late. Are you *sure* you don't know why you turned up at the Hogfather's castle?'

'No. I just remember being a . . . well, can you understand what I mean by a disembodied mind?'

'Oh, yes.'

'Good. Now can you understand what I mean by a disembodied headache? And then, next moment, I was lying on a back I didn't used to have in a lot of cold white stuff I'd never seen before. But I suppose if you're going to pop into existence, you've got to do it *somewhere*.'

'Somewhere where someone else, who should have existed, didn't,' said Susan, half to herself.

'Pardon?'

'The Hogfather wasn't there,' said Susan. 'He shouldn't have been there *anyway*, not tonight, but this time he wasn't there not because he was somewhere else but because he wasn't anywhere any more. Even his castle was vanishing.'

'I expect I shall get the hang of this incarnation business as I go along,' said the oh god.

'Most people –' Susan began. A shudder ran through her body. 'Oh, no. What's he doing? WHAT'S HE DOING?'

A JOB WELL DONE, I FANCY.

The sleigh thundered across the night. Frozen fields passed underneath.

'Hmph,' said Albert. He sniffed.

WHAT DO YOU CALL THAT WARM FEELING YOU GET INSIDE?

'Heartburn!' Albert snapped.

DO I DETECT A NOTE OF UNSEASONAL GRUMPINESS? said Death. NO SUGAR PIGGYWIGGY FOR *YOU*, ALBERT.

'I don't want any present, master.' Albert sighed. 'Except maybe to wake up and find it's all back to normal. Look, you know it always goes wrong when you start changing things . . .'

BUT THE HOGFATHER *CAN* CHANGE THINGS. LITTLE MIRACLES ALL OVER THE PLACE, WITH MANY A MERRY HO, HO, HO. TEACHING PEOPLE THE REAL MEANING OF HOGSWATCH, ALBERT.

'What, you mean that the pigs and cattle have all been slaughtered and with any luck everyone's got enough food for the winter?'

WELL, WHEN I SAY THE *REAL* MEANING –

'Some wretched devil's had his head chopped off in a wood somewhere 'cos he found a bean in his dinner and now the summer's going to come back?'

NOT EXACTLY THAT, BUT –

'Oh, you mean that they've chased down some poor beast and shot arrows up into their apple trees and now the shadows are going to go away?'

THAT IS DEFINITELY *A* MEANING, BUT I –

'Ah, then you're talking about the one where they light a bloody big bonfire to give the sun a hint and tell it to stop lurking under the horizon and do a proper day's work?'

Death paused, while the hogs hurtled over a range of hills.

YOU'RE NOT HELPING, ALBERT.

'Well, they're all the real meanings that *I* know.'

I THINK YOU COULD WORK WITH ME ON THIS.

'It's all about the sun, master. White snow and red blood and the sun. Always has been.'

VERY WELL, THEN. THE HOGFATHER CAN TEACH PEOPLE THE *UNREAL* MEANING OF HOGSWATCH.

Albert spat over the side of the sleigh. 'Hah! "Wouldn't It Be Nice If Everyone Was Nice", eh?'

THERE ARE WORSE BATTLE CRIES.

'Oh dear, oh dear, oh dear . . .'

EXCUSE ME . . .

Death reached into his robe and pulled out an hourglass.

TURN THE SLEIGH AROUND, ALBERT. DUTY CALLS.

'Which one?'

A MORE POSITIVE ATTITUDE WOULD ASSIST AT THIS POINT, THANK YOU SO VERY MUCH.

'Fascinatin'. Anyone got another pencil?' said Ridcully.

'It's had four already,' said the Lecturer in Recent Runes. 'Right down to the stub, Archchancellor. And you *know* we buy our own these days.'

It was a sore point. Like most people with no grasp whatsoever of real economics, Mustrum Ridcully equated 'proper financial control' with the counting of paperclips. Even senior wizards had to produce a pencil stub to him before they were allowed a new one out of the locked cupboard below his desk. Since of course hardly anyone retained a half-used pencil, the wizards had been reduced to sneaking out and buying new ones with their own money.

The reason for the dearth of short pencils was perched in front of them, whirring away as it chewed an HB down to the eraser on the end, which it spat at the Bursar.

Ponder Stibbons had been making notes.

'I think it works like this,' he said. 'What we're getting is the personification of forces, just like Hex said. But it only works if the thing is . . . well, logical.' He swallowed. Ponder was a great believer in logic, in the face of all the local evidence, and he hated having to use the word in this way. 'I don't mean it's *logical* that there's a creature that eats socks, but it . . . a . . . it makes a sort of sense . . . I mean it's a working hypothesis.'

'Bit like the Hogfather,' said Ridcully. 'When you're a kiddie, he's as good an explanation as any, right?'

'What's not logical about there being a goblin that brings me huge bags of money?' said the Dean sulkily. Ridcully fed the Stealer of Pencils another pencil.

'Well, sir . . . firstly, you've never mysteriously received huge bags of money and needed to find a hypothesis to explain them, and secondly, no one else would think it at all likely.'

'Huh!'

'Why's it happening now?' said Ridcully. 'Look, it's hopped on to my finger! Anyone got another pencil?'

'Well, these . . . forces have always been here,' said Ponder. 'I mean, socks and pencils have always inexplicably gone missing, haven't they? But why they're suddenly getting personified like this . . . I'm afraid I don't know.'

'Well, we'd better find out, hadn't we?' said Ridcully. 'Can't have this sort of thing going on. Daft anti-gods and miscellaneous whatnots being created just because people've thought about 'em? We could have anything turn up, anyway. Supposing some idiot says there must be a god of indigestion, eh?'

Glingleglingleglingle.

'Er . . . I think someone just did, sir,' said Ponder.

'What's the matter? What's the matter?' said the oh god. He took Susan by the shoulders.

They felt bony under his hands.

'DAMN,' said Susan. She pushed him away and steadied herself on the table, taking care that he didn't see her face.

Finally, with a measure of the self-control she'd taught herself over the last few years, she managed to get her own voice back.

'He's slipping out of character,' she muttered, to the hall in general. 'I can *feel* him doing it. And *that* drags me in. What's he doing it all *for*?'

'Search me,' said the oh god, who'd backed away hurriedly. 'Er . . . just then . . . before you turned your face away . . . it looked as though you were wearing *very* dark eye shadow . . . only you weren't . . .'

'Look, it's very simple,' said Susan, spinning round. She could feel her hair restyling itself, which it always did when it was anxious. 'You know how stuff runs in families? Blue eyes, buck teeth, that sort of thing? Well, Death runs in *my* family.'

'Er . . . in everybody's family, doesn't it?' said the oh god.

'Just shut up, please, don't gabble,' said Susan. 'I didn't mean death, I meant Death with a capital D. I remember things that haven't happened yet and I can TALK THAT TALK and stalk that stalk and . . . if he gets sidetracked, then I'll have to do it. And he *does* get sidetracked. I don't know what's really happened to the real Hogfather or why Grandfather's doing his job, but I know a bit about how he thinks and he's got no . . . no mental shields like we have. He doesn't know how to forget things or ignore things. He takes everything literally and logically and doesn't understand why that doesn't always work –'

She saw his bemused expression.

'Look . . . how would you make sure everyone in the world was well fed?' she demanded.

'Me? Oh, well, I . . .' The oh god spluttered for a moment. 'I suppose you'd have to think about the prevalent political systems, and the proper division and cultivation of arable land, and –'

'Yes, yes. But *he'd* just give everyone a good meal,' said Susan.

'Oh, I see. Very impractical. Hah, it's as silly as saying you could clothe the naked by, well, giving them some clothes.'

'Yes! I mean, no. Of course not! I mean, *obviously* you'd give – oh, you *know* what I mean!'

'Yes, I suppose so.'

'But *he* wouldn't.'

There was a crash beside them.

A burning wheel always rolls out of flaming wreckage. Two men carrying a large sheet of glass always cross the road in front of any comedy actor involved in a crazy car chase. Some narrative conventions are so strong that equivalents happen even on planets where the rocks boil at noon. And when a fully laden table collapses, one miraculously unbroken plate always rolls across the floor and spins to a halt.

Susan and the oh god watched it, and then turned their attention to the huge figure now lying in what remained of an enormous centre-piece made of fruit.

'He just . . . came right out of the air,' whispered the oh god.

'Really? Don't just stand there. Give me a hand to help him up, will you?' said Susan, pulling at a large melon.

'Er, that's a bunch of grapes behind his ear –'

'Well?'

'I don't like even to *think* about grapes –'

'Oh, come *on.*'

Together they managed to get the newcomer on to his feet.

'Toga, sandals . . . he looks a bit like you,' said Susan, as the fruit victim swayed heavily.

'Was I that green colour?'

'Close.'

'Is ... is there a privy nearby?' mumbled their burden, through clammy lips.

'I believe it's through that arch over there,' said Susan. 'I've heard it's not very pleasant, though.'

'That's not a rumour, that's a forecast,' said the fat figure, and lurched off. 'And then can I please have a glass of water and one charcoal biscuit ...'

They watched him go.

'Friend of yours?' said Susan.

'God of Indigestion, I think. Look ... I ... er ... I think I *do* remember *something*,' said the oh god. 'Just before I, um, incarnated. But it sounds stupid ...'

'Well?'

'Teeth,' said the oh god.

Susan hesitated.

'You don't mean something attacking you, do you?' she said flatly.

'No. Just ... a sensation of toothiness. Probably doesn't mean much. As God of Hangovers I see a lot worse, I can tell you.'

'Just teeth. Lots of teeth. But not horrible teeth. Just lots and lots of little teeth. Almost ... sad?'

'Yes! How did you know?'

'Oh, I ... maybe I remember you telling me before you told me. I don't know. How about a big shiny red globe?'

The oh god looked thoughtful for a moment and then said, 'No, can't help you there, I'm afraid. It's just teeth. Rows and rows of teeth.'

'I don't remember rows,' said Susan. 'I just felt ... teeth were important.'

'Nah, it's amazing what you can do with a beak,' said the raven, who'd been investigating the laden table and had succeeded in levering a lid off a jar.

'What have you got there?' said Susan wearily.

'Eyeballs,' said the raven. 'Hah, wizards know how to live all right, eh? They don't want for nothing around here, I can tell you.'

'They're olives,' said Susan.

'Tough luck,' said the raven. 'They're mine now.'

'They're a kind of fruit! Or a vegetable or something!'

'You sure?' The raven swivelled one doubtful eye on the jar and the other on her.

'Yes!'

The eyes swivelled again.

'So you're an eyeball expert all of a sudden?'

'Look, they're *green*, you stupid bird!'

'They could be very *old* eyeballs,' said the raven defiantly. 'Sometimes they go like that –'

SQUEAK, said the Death of Rats, who was halfway through a cheese.

'And not so much of the stupid,' said the raven. 'Corvids are exceptionally bright with reasoning and, in the case of some forest species, tool-using abilities!'

'Oh, so *you* are an expert on ravens, are you?' said Susan.

'Madam, I happen to *be* a –'

SQUEAK, said the Death of Rats again.

They both turned. It was pointing at its grey teeth.

'The Tooth Fairy?' said Susan. 'What about her?'

SQUEAK.

'Rows of teeth,' said the oh god again. 'Like . . . rows, you know? What's the Tooth Fairy?'

'Oh, you see her around a lot these days,' said Susan. 'Or them, rather. It's a sort of franchise operation. You get the ladder, the moneybelt and the pliers and you're set up.'

'Pliers?'

'If she can't make change she has to take an extra tooth on account. But, look, the tooth fairies are harmless enough. I've met one or two of them. They're just working girls. They don't *menace* anyone.'

SQUEAK.

'I just hope Grandfather doesn't take it into his head to do *their* job as well. Good grief, the thought of it –'

'They collect teeth?'

'Yes. Obviously.'

'Why?'

'Why? It's their *job*.'

'I meant why, where do they take the teeth after they collect them?'

'*I* don't know! They just . . . well, they just take the teeth and leave the money,' said Susan. 'What sort of question is that – "Where do they take the teeth?"?'

'I just wondered, that's all. Probably all humans know, I'm probably very silly for asking, it's probably a well-known fact.'

Susan looked thoughtfully at the Death of Rats.

'Actually . . . where *do* they take the teeth?'

SQUEAK?

'He says search him,' said the raven. 'Maybe they sell 'em?' It pecked at another jar. 'How about these, these look nice and wrinkl–'

'Pickled walnuts,' said Susan absently. 'What do they do with the teeth? What use is there for a lot of teeth? But . . . what harm can a tooth fairy do?'

'Have we got time to find one and ask her?' said the oh god.

'Time isn't the problem,' said Susan.

There are those who believe knowledge is something that is acquired – a precious ore hacked, as it were, from the grey strata of ignorance.

There are those who believe that knowledge can only be recalled, that there was some Golden Age in the distant past when everything was known and the stones fit together so you could hardly put a knife between them, you know, and it's obvious they had flying machines, right, because of the way the earthworks can only be seen from above, yeah? and there's this museum I read about where they found a pocket calculator under the altar of this ancient temple, you know what I'm saying? but the government hushed it up . . .*

Mustrum Ridcully believed that knowledge could be acquired by shouting at people, and was endeavouring to do so. The wizards were sitting around the Uncommon Room table, which was piled high with books.

'It *is* Hogswatch, Archchancellor,' said the Dean reproachfully, thumbing through an ancient volume.

'Not until midnight,' said Ridcully. 'Sortin' this out will give you fellows an appetite for your dinner.'

---

* It's amazing how good governments are, given their track record in almost every other field, at hushing up things like alien encounters.

One reason may be that the aliens themselves are too embarrassed to talk about it.

It's not known why most of the space-going races of the universe want to undertake rummaging in Earthling underwear as a prelude to formal contact. But representatives of several hundred races have taken to hanging out, unsuspected by one another, in rural corners of the planet and, as a result of this, keep on abducting other would-be abductees. Some have been in fact abducted while waiting to carry out an abduction on a couple of other aliens trying to abduct the aliens who were, as a result of misunderstood instructions, trying to form cattle into circles and mutilate crops.

The planet Earth is now banned to all alien races until they can compare notes and find out how many, if any, real humans they have actually got. It is gloomily suspected that there is only one – who is big, hairy and has very large feet.

The truth may be out there, but lies are inside your head.

'I think I might have something, Archchancellor,' said the Chair of Indefinite Studies. 'This is *Woddeley's Basic Gods*. There's some stuff here about lares and penates that seems to fit the bill.'

'Lares and penates? What were they when they were at home?' said Ridcully.

'Hahaha,' said the Chair.

'What?' said Ridcully.

'I thought you were making a rather good joke, Archchancellor,' said the Chair.

'Was I? I didn't *mean* to,' said Ridcully.

'Nothing new there,' said the Dean, under his breath.

'What was that, Dean?'

'Nothing, Archchancellor.'

'I thought you made the reference "at home" because they are, in fact, household gods. Or were, rather. They seemed to have faded away long ago. They were ... little spirits of the house, like, for example –'

Three of the other wizards, thinking quite fast for wizards, clapped their hands over his mouth.

'Careful!' said Ridcully. 'Careless talk creates lives! That's why we've got a big fat God of Indigestion being ill in the privy. By the way, where's the Bursar?'

'He was in the privy, Archchancellor,' said the Lecturer in Recent Runes.

'What, when the –?'

'*Yes*, Archchancellor.'

'Oh, well, I'm sure he'll be all right,' said Ridcully, in the matter-of-fact voice of someone contemplating something nasty that was happening to someone else out of earshot. 'But we don't want any more of these ... what're they, Chair?'

'Lares and penates, Archchancellor, but I wasn't suggesting –'

'Seems clear to me. Something's gone wrong and these little devils are coming back. All we have to do is find out what's gone wrong and put it right.'

'Oh, well, I'm glad that's all sorted out,' said the Dean.

'Household gods,' said Ridcully. 'That's what they are, Chair?' He opened the drawer in his hat and took out his pipe.

'Yes, Archchancellor. It says here they used to be the ... local spirits, I suppose. They saw to it that the bread rose and the butter churned properly.'

'Did they eat pencils? What was their attitude in the socks department?'

'This was back in the time of the First Empire,' said the Chair of Indefinite Studies. 'Sandals and togas and so on.'

'Ah. Not noticeably socked?'

'Not excessively so, no. And it was nine hundred years before Osric Pencillium first discovered, in the graphite-rich sands of the remote island of Sumtri, the small bush which, by dint of careful cultivation, he induced to produce the long –'

'Yes, we can all see you've got the encyclopaedia open under the table, Chair,' said Ridcully. 'But I daresay things have changed a bit. Moved with the times. Bound to have been a few developments. Once they looked after the bread rising, now we have things that eat pencils and socks and see to it that you can never find a clean towel when you want one –'

There was a distant tinkling.

He stopped.

'I just said that, didn't I?' he said.

The wizards nodded glumly.

'And this is the first time anyone's mentioned it?'

The wizards nodded again.

'Well, dammit, it's amazing, you *can* never find a clean towel when –'

There was a rising *wheeee* noise. A towel went by at shoulder height. There was a suggestion of many small wings.

'That was mine,' said the Lecturer in Recent Runes reproachfully. The towel disappeared in the direction of the Great Hall.

'Towel Wasps,' said the Dean. 'Well done, Archchancellor.'

'Well, I mean, *dammit*, it's human nature, isn't it?' said Ridcully hotly. 'Things go wrong, things get lost, it's *natural* to invent little creatures that – All right, all right, I'll be careful. I'm just saying man is naturally a mythopoeic creature.'

'What's that mean?' said the Senior Wrangler.

'Means we make things up as we go along,' said the Dean, not looking up.

'Um . . . excuse me, gentlemen,' said Ponder Stibbons, who had been scribbling thoughtfully at the end of the table. 'Are we suggesting that things are coming back? Do we think that's a viable hypothesis?'

The wizards looked at one another around the table.

'Definitely viable.'

'Viable, right enough.'

'Yes, that's the stuff to give the troops.'

'What is? What's the stuff to give the troops?'

'Well . . . tinned rations? Decent weapons, good boots . . . that sort of thing.'

'What's that got to do with anything?'

'Don't ask *me*. *He* was the one who started talking about giving stuff to the troops.'

'Will you lot shut up? No one's giving anything to the troops!'

'Oh, shouldn't they have something? It's Hogswatch, after all.'

'Look, it was just a figure of speech, all right? I just meant I was fully in agreement. It's just colourful language. Good grief, you surely can't think I'm actually suggesting giving stuff to the troops, at Hogswatch or any other time!'

'You weren't?'

'No!'

'That's a bit mean, isn't it?'

Ponder just let it happen. It's because their minds are so often involved with deep and problematic matters, he told himself, that their mouths are allowed to wander around making a nuisance of themselves.

'I don't hold with using that thinking machine,' said the Dean. 'I've said this before. It's meddling with the Cult. The *occult* has always been good enough for me, thank you very much.'

'On the other hand it's the only person round here who can think straight and it does what it's told,' said Ridcully.

The sleigh roared through the snow, leaving rolling trails in the sky.

'Oh, what fun,' muttered Albert, hanging on tightly.

The runners hit a roof near the University and the pigs trotted to a halt.

Death looked at the hourglass again.

Odd, he said.

'It's a scythe job, then?' said Albert. 'You won't be wanting the false beard and the jolly laugh?' He looked around, and puzzlement replaced sarcasm. 'Hey . . . how could anyone be dead up here?'

Someone was. A corpse lay in the snow.

It was clear that the man had only just died. Albert squinted up at the sky.

'There's nowhere to fall from and there's no footprints in the snow,' he said, as Death swung his scythe. 'So where did he come from? Looks like someone's personal guard. Been stabbed to death. Nasty knife wound there, see?'

'It's not good,' agreed the spirit of the man, looking down at himself.

Then he stared from himself to Albert to Death and his phantom expression went from shock to concern.

'They got the teeth! All of them! They just walked in . . . and . . . they . . . no, wait . . .'

He faded and was gone.

'Well, what was *that* all about?' said Albert.

I HAVE MY SUSPICIONS.

'See that badge on his shirt? Looks like a drawing of a tooth.'

YES. IT DOES.

'Where's that come from?'

A PLACE I CANNOT GO.

Albert looked down at the mysterious corpse and then back up at Death's impassive skull.

'I keep thinking it was a funny thing, us bumping into your granddaughter like that,' he said.

YES.

Albert put his head on one side. 'Given the large number of chimneys and kids in the world, ekcetra.'

INDEED.

'Amazing coincidence, really.'

IT JUST GOES TO SHOW.

'Hard to believe, you might say.'

LIFE CERTAINLY SPRINGS A FEW SURPRISES.

'Not just life, I reckon,' said Albert. 'And she got *real* worked up, didn't she? Flew right off the ole handle. Wouldn't be surprised if she started asking questions.'

THAT'S PEOPLE FOR YOU.

'But Rat is hanging around, ain't he? He'll probably keep an eye socket on her. Guide her path, prob'ly.'

HE IS A LITTLE SCAMP, ISN'T HE?

Albert knew he couldn't win. Death had the ultimate poker face.

I'M SURE SHE'LL ACT SENSIBLY.

'Oh, yeah,' said Albert, as they walked back to the sleigh. 'It runs in the family, acting sensibly.'

Like many barmen, Igor kept a club under the bar to deal with those little upsets that occurred around closing time, although in fact Biers never closed and no one could ever remember not seeing

Igor behind the bar. Nevertheless, things sometimes got out of hand. Or paw. Or talon.

Igor's weapon of choice was a little different. It was tipped with silver (for werewolves), hung with garlic (for vampires) and wrapped around with a strip of blanket (for bogeymen). For everyone else the fact that it was two feet of solid bog-oak usually sufficed.

He'd been watching the window. The frost was creeping across it. For some reason the creeping fingers were forming into a pattern of three little dogs looking out of a boot.

Then someone had tapped him on the shoulder. He spun around, club already in his hand, and relaxed.

'Oh . . . it's you, miss. I didn't hear the door.'

There hadn't been the door. Susan was in a hurry.

'Have you seen Violet lately, Igor?'

'The tooth girl?' Igor's one eyebrow writhed in concentration. 'Nah, haven't seen her for a week or two.'

The eyebrow furrowed into a V of annoyance as he spotted the raven, which tried to shuffle behind a half-empty display card of beer nuts.

'You can get that out of here, miss,' he said. 'You *know* the rule 'bout pets and familiars. If it can't turn back into human on demand, it's out.'

'Yeah, well, some of us have more brain cells than fingers,' muttered a voice from behind the beer nuts.

'Where does she live?'

'Now, miss, you know I never answers questions like that –'

'Where does she live, Igor?'

'Shamlegger Street, next to the picture framers,' said Igor automatically. The eyebrow knotted in anger as he realized what he'd said.

'Now, *miss*, you *know* the rules! I don't get bitten, I don't get me froat torn out and no one hides behind me door! And *you* don't try your granddad's voice on me! I could *ban* you for messin' me about like that!'

'Sorry, it's important,' said Susan. Out of the corner of her eye she could see that the raven had crept on to the shelves and was pecking the top off a jar.

'Yeah, well, suppose one of the vampires decides it's important he's missed his tea?' grumbled Igor, putting the club away.

There was a *plink* from the direction of the pickled egg jar. Susan tried hard not to look.

'Can we go?' said the oh god. 'All this alcohol makes me nervous.'

Susan nodded and hurried out.

Igor grunted. Then he went back to watching the frost, because Igor never demanded much out of life. After a while he heard a muffled voice say:

'I 'ot 'un! I *ot* 'un!'

It was indistinct because the raven had speared a pickled egg with its beak.

Igor sighed, and picked up his club. And it would have gone very hard for the raven if the Death of Rats hadn't chosen that moment to bite Igor on the ear.

DOWN THERE, said Death.

The reins were hauled so sharply so quickly that the hogs ended up facing the other way.

Albert fought his way out of a drift of teddy bears, where he'd been dozing.

'What's up? What's up? Did we hit something?' he said.

Death pointed downwards. An endless white snowfield lay below, only the occasional glow of a window candle or a half-covered hut indicating the presence on this world of brief mortality.

Albert squinted, and then saw what Death had spotted.

''s some old bugger trudging through the snow,' he said. 'Been gathering wood, by the look of it. A bad night to be out,' he said. 'And I'm out in it too, come to that. Look, master, I'm sure you've done enough now to make sure –'

SOMETHING'S HAPPENING DOWN THERE. HO. HO. HO.

'Look, he's all *right*,' said Albert, hanging on as the sleigh tumbled downwards. There was a brief wedge of light below as the wood-gatherer opened the door of a snow-drifted hovel. 'See, over there, there's a couple of blokes catching him up, look, they're weighed down with parcels and stuff, see? He's going to have a decent Hogswatch after all, no problem there. *Now* can we go –'

Death's glowing eye sockets took in the scene in minute detail.

IT'S WRONG.

'Oh, no ... here we go *again*.'

The oh god hesitated.

'What do you mean, you can't walk through the door?' said Susan. 'You walked through the door in the bar.'

'That was different. I have certain god-like powers in the presence of alcohol. Anyway, we've knocked and she hasn't answered and whatever happened to Mr Manners?'

Susan shrugged, and walked through the cheap woodwork. She knew she probably shouldn't. Every time she did something like this she used up a certain amount of, well, *normal*. And sooner or later she'd forget what doorknobs were for, just like Grandfather.

Come to think of it, he'd never found *out* what doorknobs were for.

She opened the door from the inside. The oh god stepped in and looked around. This did not take long. It was not a large room. It had been subdivided from a room that itself hadn't been all that big to start with.

'*This* is where the Tooth Fairy lives?' Bilious said. 'It's a bit ... poky, isn't it? Stuff all over the floor ... What're these things hanging from this line?'

'They're ... women's clothes,' said Susan, rummaging through the paperwork on a small rickety table.

'They're not very big,' said the oh god. 'And a bit thin ...'

'Tell me,' said Susan, without looking up. 'These memories you arrived here with ... They weren't very complicated, were they ...? Ah ...'

He looked over her shoulder as she opened a small red notebook.

'I've only talked to Violet a few times,' she said. 'I think she delivers the teeth somewhere and gets a percentage of the money. It's not a highly paid line of work. You know, they say you can Earn $$$ in Your Spare Time but she says really she could earn more money waiting on tables – Ah, this looks right ...'

'What's that?'

'She said she gets given the names every week.'

'What, of the children who're going to lose teeth?'

'Yes. Names and addresses,' said Susan, flicking through the pages.

'That doesn't sound very likely.'

'Pardon me, but are you the God of Hangovers? Oh, look, here's Twyla's tooth last month.' She smiled at the neat grey writing. 'She practically hammered it out because she needed the half-dollar.'

'Do you *like* children?' said the oh god.

She gave him a look. 'Not raw,' she said. 'Other people's are OK. Hold on ...'

She flicked some pages back and forth.

'There's just blank days,' she said. 'Look, the last few days, all unticked. No names. But if you go back a week or two, look, they're all properly marked off and the money added up at the bottom of the page, see? And ... *this* can't be right, can it?'

There were only five names entered on the first unticked night, for the previous week. Most children instinctively knew when to push their luck and only the greedy or dentally improvident called out the Tooth Fairy around Hogswatch.

'Read the names,' said Susan.

'William Wittles, a.k.a. Willy (home), Tosser (school), 2nd flr bck bdrm, 68 Kicklebury Street;

Sophie Langtree, a.k.a. Daddy's Princess, attic bdrm, 5 The Hippo;

The Hon. Jeffrey Bibbleton, a.k.a. Trouble In Trousers (home), Foureyes (school), 1st flr bck, Scrote Manor, Park Lane –'

He stopped. 'I say, this is a bit intrusive, isn't it?'

'It's a whole new world,' said Susan. 'You haven't got there yet. Keep going.'

'Nuhakme Icta, a.k.a. Little Jewel, basement, The Laughing Falafel, Klatchistan Take-Away and All-Nite Grocery, cnr. Soake and Dimwell;

Reginald Lilywhite, a.k.a. Banjo, The Park Lane Bully, Have You Seen This Man?, The Goose Gate Grabber, The Nap Hill Lurker, Rm 17, YMPA.

'YMPA?'

'It's what we generally call the Young-Men's-Reformed-Cultists-of-the-Ichor-God-Bel-Shamharoth-Association,' said Susan. 'Does that sound to you like someone who'd expect a visit from a tooth fairy?'

'No.'

'Me neither. He sounds like someone who'd expect a visit from the Watch.'

Susan looked around. It really was a crummy room, the sort rented by someone who probably took it never intending to stay long, the sort where walking across the floor in the middle of the night would be accompanied by the crack of cockroaches in a death flamenco. It was amazing how many people spent their whole lives in places where they never intended to stay.

Cheap, narrow bed, crumbling plaster, tiny window –

She opened the window and fished around below the ledge, and felt satisfied when her questing fingers closed on a piece of string which was attached to an oilcloth bag. She hauled it in.

'What's that?' said the oh god, as she opened it on the table.

'Oh, you see them a lot,' said Susan, taking out some packages wrapped in second-hand waxed paper. 'You live alone, mice and roaches eat everything, there's nowhere to store food — but outside the window it's cold and safe. More or less safe. It's an old trick. Now ... look at this. Leathery bacon, a green loaf and a bit of cheese you could shave. She hasn't been back home for some time, believe me.'

'Oh dear. What now?'

'Where would she take the teeth?' said Susan, to the world in general but mainly to herself. 'What the hell does the Tooth Fairy *do* with —'

There was a knock at the door. Susan opened it.

Outside was a small bald man in a long brown coat. He was holding a clipboard and blinked nervously at the sight of her.

'Er ...' he began.

'Can I help you?' said Susan.

'Er, I saw the light, see, I thought Violet was in,' said the little man. He twiddled the pencil that was attached to his clipboard by a piece of string. 'Only she's a bit behind with the teeth and there's a bit of money owing and Ernie's cart ain't come back and it's got to go in my report and I come round in case ... in case she was ill or something, it not being nice being alone and ill at Hogswatch —'

'She's not here,' said Susan.

The man gave her a worried look and shook his head sadly.

'There's nearly thirteen dollars in pillow money, see. I'll have to report it.'

'Who to?'

'It has to go higher up, see. I just hope it's not going to be like that business in Quirm where the girl started robbing houses. We never heard the end of that one —'

'Report to who?'

'And there's the ladder and the pliers,' the man went on, in a litany against a world that had no understanding of what it meant to have to fill in an AF17 report in triplicate. 'How can I keep track of stocktaking if people go around taking stock?' He shook his head. 'I dunno, they get the job, they think it's all nice sunny nights, they get a bit of sharp weather and suddenly it's goodbye Charlie I'm off to be a waitress in the warm. And then there's Ernie. I know him. It's a nip to keep out the cold, and then another one to keep it company, and then a third in case the other two get lost ... It's all going to have to go down in my report, you know, and who's going to get the blame? I'll tell you —'

'It's going to be you, isn't it?' said Susan. She was almost hypnotized. The man even had a fringe of worried hair and a small, worried moustache. And the voice suggested exactly that here was a man who, at the end of the world, would worry that it would be blamed on him.

'That's *right*,' he said, but in a slightly grudging voice. He was not about to allow a bit of understanding to lighten his day. 'And the girls all go on about the job but I tell them they've got it easy, it's just basic'ly ladder work, they don't have to spend their evenings knee-deep in paper *and* making shortfalls good out of their own money, I might add –'

'You employ the tooth fairies?' said Susan quickly. The oh god was still vertical but his eyes had glazed over.

The little man preened slightly. '*Sort* of,' he said. 'Basic'ly I run Bulk Collection and Despatch –'

'Where to?'

He stared at her. Sharp, direct questions weren't his forte.

'I just sees to it they gets on the cart,' he mumbled. 'When they're on the cart and Ernie's signed the GV19 for 'em, that's it done and finished, only like I said he ain't turned up this week and –'

'A whole cart for a handful of teeth?'

'Well, there's the food for the guards, and –'ere, who are you, anyway? What're you doing here?'

Susan straightened up. 'I don't have to put up with this,' she said sweetly, to no one in particular. She leaned forward again.

'WHAT CART ARE WE TALKING ABOUT HERE, CHARLIE?' The oh god jolted away. The man in the brown coat shot backwards and splayed against the corridor wall as Susan advanced.

'Comes Tuesdays,' he panted. ''ere, what –'

'AND WHERE DOES IT GO?'

'Dunno! Like I said, when he's –'

'Signed the GV19 for them it's you done and finished,' said Susan, in her normal voice. 'Yes. You said. What's Violet's full name? She never mentioned it.'

The man hesitated.

'I SAID –'

'Violet Bottler!'

'Thank you.'

'An' Ernie's gorn too,' said Charlie, continuing more or less on auto-pilot. 'I call that suspicious. I mean, he's got a wife and everything. Won't be the first man to get his head turned by thirteen dollars and a pretty ankle and, o' course, no one thinks about muggins who has to carry the can, I mean, supposing we was all to get it in our heads to run off with young wimmin?'

He gave Susan the stern look of one who, if it was not for the fact that the world needed him, would even now be tiring of painting naked young ladies on some tropical island somewhere.

'What happens to the teeth?' said Susan.

He blinked at her. A bully, thought Susan. A very small, weak, very *dull* bully, who doesn't manage any real bullying because there's hardly anyone smaller and weaker than him, so he just makes everyone's lives just that little bit more difficult . . .

'What sort of question is that?' he managed, in the face of her stare.

'You never wondered?' said Susan, and added to herself, *I didn't. Did anyone?*

'Well, 's not my job, I just –'

'Oh, yes. You said,' said Susan. 'Thank you. You've been very helpful. Thank you very much.'

The man stared at her, and then turned and ran down the stairs.

'Drat,' said Susan.

'That's a very unusual swearword,' said the oh god nervously.

'It's *so* easy,' said Susan. 'If I want to, I can find *anybody*. It's a family trait.'

'Oh. Good.'

'No. Have you any *idea* how hard it is to be normal? The things you have to remember? How to go to sleep? How to forget things? What doorknobs are for?'

Why ask him, she thought, as she looked at his shocked face. All that's normal for *him* is remembering to throw up what someone else drank.

'Oh, come on,' she said, and hurried towards the stairs.

It was so easy to slip into immortality, to ride the horse, to know everything. And every time you did, it brought closer the day when you could never get off and never forget.

Death *was* hereditary.

You got it from your ancestors.

'Where are we going now?' said the oh god.

'Down to the YMPA,' said Susan.

The old man in the hovel looked uncertainly at the feast spread in front of him. He sat on his stool as curled up on himself as a spider in a flame.

'I'd got a bit of a mess of beans cooking,' he mumbled, looking at his visitors through filmy eyes.

'Good heavens, you can't eat *beans* at Hogswatch,' said the king, smiling hugely. 'That's terribly unlucky, eating beans at Hogswatch. My word, yes!'

'Di'nt know that,' the old man said, looking down desperately at his lap.

'*We've* brought you this *magnificent* spread. Don't you think so?'

'I bet you're incredibly grateful for it, too,' said the page, sharply.

'Yes, well, o' course, it's very kind of you gennelmen,' said the old man, in a voice the size of a mouse. He blinked, uncertain of what to do next.

'The turkey's hardly been touched, still *plenty* of meat on it,' said the king. 'And do have some of this *cracking* good widgeon stuffed with swan's liver.'

'– only I'm partial to a bowl of beans and I've never been beholden to no one nor nobody,' the old man said, still staring at his lap.

'Good heavens, man, you don't need to worry about *that*,' said the king heartily. 'It's Hogswatch! I was only just now looking out of the window and I saw you plodding through the snow and I said to young Jermain here, I said, "Who's that chappie?" and he said "Oh, he's some peasant fellow who lives up by the forest," and I said, "Well, I couldn't eat another thing and it's Hogswatch, after all," and so we just bundled everything up and here we are!'

'And I expect you're pathetically thankful,' said the page. 'I expect we've brought a ray of light into your dark tunnel of a life, hmm?'

'– yes, well, o' course, only I'd been savin' 'em for weeks, see, and there's some bakin' potatoes under the fire, I found 'em in the cellar 'n' the mice'd hardly touched 'em.' The old man never raised his eyes from knee level. ''n' our dad brought me up never to ask for –'

'Listen,' said the king, raising his voice a little, 'I've walked *miles* tonight and I bet you've never seen food like this in your whole life, eh?'

Tears of humiliated embarrassment were rolling down the old man's face.

'– well, I'm sure it's very kind of you fine gennelmen but I ain't sure I knows how to eat swans and suchlike, but if you want a bit o' my beans you've only got to say –'

'Let me make myself *absolutely* clear,' said the king sharply. 'This is some genuine Hogswatch charity, d'you understand? And we're going to sit here and watch the smile on your grubby but honest face, is that understood?'

'And what do you say to the good king?' the page prompted.

The peasant hung his head.

'nk you.'

'Right,' said the king, sitting back. 'Now, pick up your fork –'

The door burst open. An indistinct figure strode into the room, snow swirling around it in a cloud.

WHAT'S GOING ON HERE?

The page started to stand up, drawing his sword. He never worked out how the *other* figure could have got behind him, but there it was, pressing him gently down again.

'Hello, son, my name is Albert,' said a voice by his ear. 'Why don't you put that sword back very slowly? People might get hurt.'

A finger prodded the king, who had been too shocked to move.

WHAT DO YOU THINK YOU ARE DOING, SIRE?

The king tried to focus on the figure. There was an impression of red and white, but black, too.

To Albert's secret amazement, the man managed to get to his feet and draw himself up as regally as he could.

'What is going on here, whoever you are, is some fine old Hogswatch charity! And who –'

NO, IT'S NOT.

'What? How dare you –'

WERE YOU HERE LAST MONTH? WILL YOU BE HERE NEXT WEEK? NO. BUT TONIGHT YOU WANTED TO FEEL ALL WARM INSIDE. TONIGHT YOU WILL WANT THEM TO SAY: WHAT A GOOD KING HE IS.

'Oh, no, he's going too far again –' muttered Albert under his breath. He pushed the page down again. 'No, you stay still, sonny. Else you'll just be a paragraph.'

'Whatever it is, it's more than he's got!' snapped the king. 'And all we've had from him is ingratitude –'

YES, THAT DOES SPOIL IT, DOESN'T IT? Death leaned forward. *Go* AWAY.

To the king's own surprise his body took over and marched him out of the door.

Albert patted the page on the shoulder. 'And you can run along too,' he said.

'– I didn't mean to go upsetting anyone, it's just that I never asked no one for nothing –' mumbled the old man, in a small humble world of his own, his hands tangling themselves together out of nervousness.

'Best if you leave this one to me, master, if you don't mind,' said

Albert. 'I'll be back in just a tick.' Loose ends, he thought, that's my job. Tying up loose ends. The master never thinks things through.

He caught up with the king outside.

'Ah, there you are, your sire,' he said. 'Just before you go, won't keep you a minute, just a minor point –' Albert leaned close to the stunned monarch. 'If anyone was thinking about making a mistake, you know, like maybe sending the guards down here tomorrow, tipping the old man out of his hovel, chuckin' him in prison, anything like that ... werrlll ... that's the kind of mistake he ought to treasure on account of it being the last mistake he'll ever make. A word to the wise men, right?' He tapped the side of his nose conspiratorially. 'Happy Hogswatch.'

Then he hurried back into the hovel.

The feast had vanished. The old man was looking blearily at the bare table.

HALF-EATEN LEAVINGS, said Death. WE COULD CERTAINLY DO BETTER THAN THIS. He reached into the sack.

Albert grabbed his arm before he could withdraw his hand.

'Mind taking a bit of advice, master? I was brung up in a place like this.'

DOES IT BRING TEARS TO YOUR EYES?

'A box of matches to me hand, more like. Listen ...'

The old man was only dimly aware of some whispering. He sat hunched up, staring at nothing.

WELL, IF YOU ARE SURE ...

'Been there, done that, chewed the bones,' said Albert. 'Charity ain't giving people what you wants to give, it's giving people what they need to get.'

VERY WELL.

Death reached into the sack again.

HAPPY HOGSWATCH. HO. HO. HO.

There was a string of sausages. There was a side of bacon. And a small tub of salt pork. And a mass of chitterlings wrapped up in greased paper. There was a black pudding. There were several other tubs of disgusting yet savoury pork-adjacent items highly prized in any pig-based economy. And, laid on the table with a soft thump, there was –

'A pig's head,' breathed the old man. 'A *whole* one! Ain't had brawn in years! And a basin of pig knuckles! And a bowl of pork dripping!'

Ho. Ho. Ho.

'Amazing,' said Albert. 'How did you get the head's expression to look like the king?'

I THINK THAT'S ACCIDENTAL.

Albert patted the old man on the back.

'Have yourself a ball,' he said. 'In fact, have two. Now I think we ought to be going, master.'

They left the old man staring at the laden board.

WASN'T THAT NICE? said Death, as the hogs accelerated.

'Oh, yes,' said Albert, shaking his head. 'Poor old devil. Beans at Hogswatch? Unlucky, that. Not a night for a man to find a bean in his bowl.'

I FEEL I WAS CUT OUT FOR THIS SORT OF THING, YOU KNOW.

'Really, master?'

IT'S NICE TO DO A JOB WHERE PEOPLE LOOK FORWARD TO SEEING YOU.

'Ah,' said Albert glumly.

THEY DON'T NORMALLY LOOK FORWARD TO SEEING ME.

'Yes, I expect so.'

EXCEPT IN SPECIAL AND RATHER UNFORTUNATE CIRCUMSTANCES.

'Right, right.'

AND THEY SELDOM LEAVE A GLASS OF SHERRY OUT.

'I expect they don't, no.'

I COULD GET INTO THE HABIT OF DOING THIS, IN FACT.

'But you won't need to, will you, master?' said Albert hurriedly, with the horrible prospect of being a permanent Pixie Albert looming in his mind again. 'Because we'll get the Hogfather back, right? That's what you *said* we were going to do, right? And young Susan's probably bustling around . . .'

YES. OF COURSE.

'Not that you asked her to, of course.'

Albert's jittery ears didn't detect any enthusiasm.

Oh dear, he thought.

I HAVE ALWAYS CHOSEN THE PATH OF DUTY.

'Right, master.'

The sleigh sped on.

I AM THOROUGHLY IN CONTROL AND FIRM OF PURPOSE.

'No problem there, then, master,' said Albert.

NO NEED TO WORRY AT ALL.

'Pleased to hear it, master.'

IF I HAD A FIRST NAME, 'DUTY' WOULD BE MY MIDDLE NAME.

'Good.'

NEVERTHELESS . . .

Albert strained his ears and thought he heard, just on the edge of hearing, a voice whisper sadly.

Ho. Ho. Ho.

There was a party going on. It seemed to occupy the entire building.

'Certainly very energetic young men,' said the oh god carefully, stepping over a wet towel. 'Are women allowed in here?'

'No,' said Susan. She stepped through a wall into the superintendent's office.

A group of young men went past, manhandling a barrel of beer.

'You'll feel bad about it in the morning,' said Bilious. 'Strong drink is a mocker, you know.'

They set it up on a table and knocked out the bung.

'Someone's going to have to be sick after all that,' he said, raising his voice above the hubbub. 'I hope you realize that. You think it's clever, do you, reducing yourself to the level of the beasts of the field ... er ... or the level they'd sink to if they drank, I mean.'

They moved away, leaving one mug of beer by the barrel.

The oh god glanced at it, and picked it up and sniffed at it.

'Ugh.'

Susan stepped out of the wall.

'He hasn't been back for – What're you doing?'

'I thought I'd see what beer tastes like,' said the oh god guiltily.

'*You* don't know what beer tastes like?'

'Not on the way *down*, no. It's ... quite different by the time it gets to me,' he said sourly. He took another sip, and then a longer one. 'I can't see what all the fuss is about,' he added.

He tipped up the empty pot.

'I suppose it comes out of this tap here,' he said. 'You know, for once in my existence I'd like to get drunk.'

'Aren't you always?' said Susan, who wasn't really paying attention.

'No. I've always *been* drunk. I'm sure I explained.'

'He's been gone a couple of days,' said Susan. 'That's odd. And he didn't say where he was going. The last night he was here was the night he was on Violet's list. But he paid for his room for the week, and I've got the number.'

'And the key?' said the oh god.

'What a strange idea.'

Mr Lilywhite's room was small. That wasn't surprising. What was surprising was how neat it was, how carefully the little bed had been made, how well the floor had been swept. It was hard to imagine anyone living in it, but there were a few signs. On the simple table by the bed was a small, rather crude portrait of a bulldog in a wig, although on closer inspection it might have been a woman. This tentative hypothesis was borne out by the inscription 'To a Good Boy, from his Mother' on the back.

A book lay next to it. Susan wondered what kind of reading someone with Mr Banjo's background would buy.

It turned out to be a book of six pages, one of those that were supposed to enthral children with the magic of the printed word by pointing out that they could See Spot Run.

There were no more than ten words on each page and yet, carefully placed between pages four and five, was a bookmark.

She turned back to the cover. The book was called *Happy Tales*. There was a blue sky and trees and a couple of impossibly pink children playing with a jolly-looking dog.

It looked as though it had been read frequently, if slowly.

And that was it.

A dead end.

No. Perhaps not . . .

On the floor by the bed, as if it had been accidentally dropped, was a small, silvery half-dollar piece.

Susan picked it up and tossed it idly. She looked the oh god up and down. He was swilling a mouthful of beer from cheek to cheek and looking thoughtfully at the ceiling.

She wondered about his likelihood of survival incarnate in Ankh-Morpork at Hogswatch, especially if the cure wore off. After all, the only purpose of his existence was to have a headache and throw up. There were not a great many post-graduate jobs for which these were the main qualifications.

'Tell me,' she said. 'Have you ever ridden a horse?'

'I don't know. What's a horse?'

In the depths of the library of Death, a squeaking noise.

It was not loud, but it appeared louder than mere decibels would suggest in the furtive, scribbling hush of the books.

Everyone, it is said, has a book inside them. In this library, everyone was inside a book.

The squeaking got louder. It had a rhythmical, circular quality.

Book on book, shelf on shelf . . . and in every one, at the page of the ever-moving now, a scribble of handwriting following the narrative of every life . . .

The squeaking came round the corner.

It was issuing from what looked like a very rickety edifice, several storeys high. It looked rather like a siege tower, open at the sides. At the base, between the wheels, was a pair of geared treadles which moved the whole thing.

Susan clung to the railing of the topmost platform.

'Can't you hurry up?' she said. 'We're only at the Bi's at the moment.'

'I've been pedalling for ages!' panted the oh god.

'Well, "A" is a very popular letter.'

Susan stared up at the shelves. A was for Anon, among other things. All those people who, for one reason or another, never officially got a name.

They tended to be short books.

'Ah . . . Bo . . . Bod . . . Bog . . . turn left . . .'

The library tower squeaked ponderously around the next corner.

'Ah, Bo . . . blast, the Bots are at least twenty shelves up.'

'Oh, how nice,' said the oh god grimly.

He heaved on the lever that moved the drive chain from one sprocket to another, and started to pedal again.

Very ponderously, the creaking tower began to telescope upwards.

'Right, we're there,' Susan shouted down, after a few minutes of slow rise. 'Here's . . . let's see . . . Aabana Bottler . . .'

'I expect Violet will be a lot further,' said the oh god, trying out irony.

'Onwards!'

Swaying a little, the tower headed down the Bs until:

'Stop!'

It rocked as the oh god kicked the brake block against a wheel.

'I think this is her,' said a voice from above. 'OK, you can lower away.'

A big wheel with ponderous lead weights on it spun slowly as the tower concertina'd back, creaking and grinding. Susan climbed down the last few feet.

'*Everyone*'s in here?' said the oh god, as she thumbed through the pages.

'Yes.'

'Even gods?'

'Anything that's alive and self-aware,' said Susan, not looking up.

'This is . . . odd. It looks as though she's in some sort of . . . prison. Who'd want to lock up a tooth fairy?'

'Someone with very sensitive teeth?'

Susan flicked back a few pages. 'It's all . . . hoods over her head and people carrying her and so on. But . . .' she turned a page '. . . it says the last job she did was on Banjo and . . . yes, she got the tooth . . . and then she felt as though someone was behind her and . . . there's a ride on a cart . . . and the hood's come off . . . and there's a causeway . . . and . . .'

'All that's in a *book*?'

'The autobiography. Everyone has one. It writes down your life as you go along.'

'I've got one?'

'I expect so.'

'Oh, dear. "Got up, was sick, wanted to die." Not a gripping read, really.'

Susan turned the page.

'A tower,' she said. 'She's in a tower. From what she saw, it was tall and white inside . . . but not outside? It didn't look real. There were apple trees around it, but the trees, the trees didn't look right. And a river, but that wasn't right either. There were goldfish in it . . . but they were on *top* of the water.'

'Ah. Pollution,' said the oh god.

'I don't think so. It says here she saw them swimming.'

'Swimming on top of the water?'

'That's how she thinks she saw it.'

'Really? You don't think she'd been eating any of that mouldy cheese, do you?'

'And there was blue sky but . . . she must have got this wrong . . . it says here there was only blue sky *above* . . .'

'Yep. Best place for the sky,' said the oh god. 'Sky underneath you, that probably means trouble.'

Susan flicked a page back and forth. 'She means . . . sky overhead but not around the edges, I think. No sky on the horizon.'

'Excuse me,' said the oh god. 'I'm not long in this world, I appreciate that, but I think you have to have sky on the horizon. That's how you can tell it's the horizon.'

A sense of familiarity was creeping up on Susan, but surreptitiously, dodging behind things whenever she tried to concentrate on it.

'I've *seen* this place,' she said, tapping the page. 'If only she'd looked harder at the trees . . . She says they've got brown trunks and green leaves and it says here she thought they were odd. And ...' She concentrated on the next paragraph. 'Flowers. Growing in the grass. With big round petals.'

She stared unseeing at the oh god again.

'This isn't a proper landscape,' she said.

'It doesn't sound too unreal to me,' said the oh god. 'Sky. Trees. Flowers. Dead fish.'

'*Brown* tree trunks? Really they're mostly a sort of greyish mossy colour. You only ever see brown tree trunks in one place,' said Susan. 'And it's the same place where the sky is only ever overhead. The blue never comes down to the ground.'

She looked up. At the far end of the corridor was one of the very tall, very thin windows. It looked out on to the black gardens. Black bushes, black grass, black trees. Skeletal fish cruising in the black waters of a pool, under black water lilies.

There was colour, in a sense, but it was the kind of colour you'd get if you could shine a beam of black through a prism. There were hints of tints, here and there a black you might persuade yourself was a very deep purple or a midnight blue. But it was basically black, under a black sky, because this was the world belonging to Death and that was all there was to it.

The shape of Death was the shape people had created for him, over the centuries. Why bony? Because bones were associated with death. He'd got a scythe because agricultural people could spot a decent metaphor. And he lived in a sombre land because the human imagination would be rather stretched to let him live somewhere nice with flowers.

People like Death lived in the human imagination, and got their shape there, too. He wasn't the only one ...

... but he didn't like the script, did he? He'd started to take an interest in people. Was that a thought, or just a memory of something that hadn't happened yet?

The oh god followed her gaze.

'Can we go after her?' said the oh god. 'I say *we*, I think I've just got drafted in because I was in the wrong place.'

'She's alive. That means she is mortal,' said Susan. 'That means I can find her, too.' She turned and started to walk out of the library.

'If she says the sky is just blue overhead, what's between it and the horizon?' said the oh god, running to keep up.

'You don't *have* to come,' said Susan. 'It's not your problem.'

'Yes, but given that my problem is that my whole purpose in life is to feel rotten, anything's an improvement.'

'It could be dangerous. I don't think she's there of her own free will. Would you be any good in a fight?'

'Yes. I could be sick on people.'

It was a shack, somewhere out on the outskirts of the Plains town of Scrote. Scrote had a lot of outskirts, spread so widely – a busted cart here, a dead dog there – that often people went through it without even knowing it was there, and really it only appeared on the maps because cartographers get embarrassed about big empty spaces.

Hogswatch came after the excitement of the cabbage harvest when it was pretty quiet in Scrote and there was nothing much to look forward to until the fun of the sprout festival.

This shack had an iron stove, with a pipe that went up through the thick cabbage-leaf thatch.

Voices echoed faintly within the pipe.

THIS IS REALLY, REALLY STUPID.

'I think the tradition got started when everyone had them big chimneys, master.' *This* voice sounded as though it was coming from someone standing on the roof and shouting down the pipe.

INDEED? IT'S ONLY A MERCY IT'S UNLIT.

There was some muffled scratching and banging, and then a thump from within the pot belly of the stove.

DAMN.

'What's up, master?'

THE DOOR HAS NO HANDLE ON THE INSIDE. I CALL THAT INCONSIDERATE.

There were some more bumps, and then a scrape as the stove lid was lifted up and pushed sideways. An arm came out and felt around the front of the stove until it found the handle.

It played with it for a while, but it was obvious that the hand did not belong to a person used to opening things.

In short, Death came out of the stove. Exactly how would be difficult to describe without folding the page. Time and space were, from Death's point of view, merely things that he'd heard described. When it came to Death, they ticked the box marked Not Applicable. It might help to think of the universe as a rubber sheet, or perhaps not.

'Let us in, master,' a pitiful voice echoed down from the roof. 'It's brass monkeys out here.'

Death went over to the door. Snow was blowing underneath it.

He peered nervously at the woodwork. There was a thump outside and Albert's voice sounded a lot closer.

'What's up, master?'

Death stuck his head through the wood of the door.

THERE'S THESE METAL THINGS —

'Bolts, master. You slide them,' said Albert, sticking his hands under his armpits to keep them warm.

AH.

Death's head disappeared. Albert stamped his feet and watched his breath cloud in the air while he listened to the pathetic scrabbling on the other side of the door.

Death's head appeared again.

ER . . .

'It's the latch, master,' said Albert wearily.

RIGHT. RIGHT.

'You put your thumb on it and push it down.'

RIGHT.

The head disappeared. Albert jumped up and down a bit, and waited.

The head appeared.

ER . . . I WAS WITH YOU UP TO THE THUMB . . .

Albert sighed. 'And then you press down and pull, master.'

AH. RIGHT. GOT YOU.

The head disappeared.

Oh dear, thought Albert. He just can't get the hang of them, can he . . .?

The door jerked open. Death stood behind it, beaming proudly, as Albert staggered in, snow blowing in with him.

'Blimey, it's getting really parky,' said Albert. 'Any sherry?' he added hopefully.

IT APPEARS NOT.

Death looked at the sock hooked on to the side of the stove. It had a hole in it.

A letter, in erratic handwriting, was attached to it. Death picked it up.

THE BOY WANTS A PAIR OF TROUSERS THAT HE DOESN'T HAVE TO SHARE, A HUGE MEAT PIE, A SUGAR MOUSE, 'A LOT OF TOYS' AND A PUPPY CALLED SCRUFF.

'Ah, sweet,' said Albert. 'I shall wipe away a tear, 'cos what he's gettin', see, is this little wooden toy and an apple.' He held them out.

BUT THE LETTER CLEARLY —

'Yes, well, it's socio-economic factors again, right?' said Albert. 'The world'd be in a right mess if everyone got what they asked for, eh?'

I GAVE THEM WHAT THEY WANTED IN THE STORE . . .

'Yeah, and that's gonna cause a *lot* of trouble, master. All them "toy pigs that really work". I didn't say nothing 'cos it was getting the job done but you can't go on like that. What good's a god who gives you everything you want?'

YOU HAVE ME THERE.

'It's the *hope* that's important. Big part of belief, hope. Give people jam today and they'll just sit and eat it. Jam tomorrow, now – that'll keep them going for ever.'

AND YOU MEAN THAT BECAUSE OF THIS THE POOR GET POOR THINGS AND THE RICH GET RICH THINGS?

''s right,' said Albert. 'That's the meaning of Hogswatch.'

Death nearly wailed.

BUT I'M THE HOGFATHER! He looked embarrassed. AT THE MOMENT, I MEAN.

'Makes no difference,' said Albert, shrugging. 'I remember when I was a nipper, one Hogswatch I had my heart set on this huge model horse they had in the shop . . .' His face creased for a moment in a grim smile of recollection. 'I remember I spent *hours* one day, cold as charity the weather was, I spent *hours* with my nose pressed up against the window . . . until they heard me callin', and unfroze me. I saw them take it out of the window, someone was in there buying it, and, y'know, just for a second I thought it really was going to be for me . . . Oh. I *dreamed* of that toy horse. It were red and white with a real saddle and everything. And rockers. I'd've *killed* for that horse.' He shrugged again. 'Not a chance, of course, 'cos we didn't have a pot to piss in and we even 'ad to spit on the bread to make it soft enough to eat –'

PLEASE ENLIGHTEN ME. WHAT IS SO IMPORTANT ABOUT HAVING A POT TO PISS IN?

'It's . . . it's more like a figure of speech, master. It means you're as poor as a church mouse.'

ARE THEY POOR?

'Well . . . yeah.'

BUT SURELY NOT MORE POOR THAN ANY OTHER MOUSE? AND, AFTER ALL, THERE TEND TO BE LOTS OF CANDLES AND THINGS THEY COULD EAT.

'Figure of speech again, master. It doesn't have to make sense.'

OH. I SEE. DO CARRY ON.

'O' course, I still hung up my stocking on Hogswatch Eve, and in the morning, you know, you know what? Our dad had put in this little horse he'd carved his very own self . . .'

AH, said Death. AND THAT WAS WORTH MORE THAN ALL THE EXPENSIVE TOY HORSES IN THE WORLD, EH?

Albert gave him a beady look. 'No!' he said. 'It *weren't*. All I could think of was it wasn't the big horse in the window.'

Death looked shocked.

BUT HOW MUCH BETTER TO HAVE A TOY CARVED WITH –

'No. Only grown-ups think like that,' said Albert. 'You're a selfish little bugger when you're seven. Anyway, Dad got ratted after lunch and trod on it.'

LUNCH?

'All right, mebbe we had a bit of pork dripping for the bread . . .'

EVEN SO, THE SPIRIT OF HOGSWATCH –

Albert sighed. 'If you like, master. If you like.'

Death looked perturbed.

BUT SUPPOSING THE HOGFATHER HAD BROUGHT YOU THE WONDERFUL HORSE –

'Oh, Dad would've flogged it for a couple of bottles,' said Albert.

BUT WE HAVE BEEN INTO HOUSES WHERE THE CHILDREN HAD MANY TOYS AND BROUGHT THEM EVEN *MORE* TOYS, AND IN HOUSES LIKE THIS THE CHILDREN GET PRACTICALLY NOTHING.

'Huh, we'd have given *anything* to get *practically* nothing when I were a lad,' said Albert.

BE HAPPY WITH WHAT YOU'VE GOT, IS THAT THE IDEA?

'That's about the size of it, master. A good god line, that. Don't give 'em too much and tell 'em to be happy with it. Jam tomorrow, see.'

THIS IS WRONG. Death hesitated. I MEAN . . . IT'S *RIGHT* TO BE HAPPY WITH WHAT YOU'VE GOT. BUT YOU'VE GOT TO HAVE SOMETHING TO BE HAPPY ABOUT HAVING. THERE'S NO POINT IN BEING HAPPY ABOUT HAVING NOTHING.

Albert felt a bit out of his depth in this new tide of social philosophy.

'Dunno,' he said. 'I suppose people'd say they've got the moon and the stars and suchlike.'

I'M SURE THEY WOULDN'T BE ABLE TO PRODUCE THE PAPERWORK.

'All I know is, if Dad'd caught *us* with a big bag of pricey toys we'd just have got a ding round the earhole for nicking 'em.'

IT IS . . . UNFAIR.

'That's life, master.'

BUT I'M NOT.

'I meant this is how it's supposed to go, master,' said Albert.

No. You mean this is how it goes.

Albert leaned against the stove and rolled himself one of his horrible thin cigarettes. It was best to let the master work his own way through these things. He got over them eventually. It was like that business with the violin. For three days there was nothing but twangs and broken strings, and then he'd never touched the thing again. That was the trouble, really. Everything the master did *was* a bit like that. When things got into his head you just had to wait until they leaked out again.

He'd thought that Hogswatch was all ... plum pudding and brandy and ho ho ho and he didn't have the kind of mind that could ignore all the other stuff. And so it hurt him.

It is Hogswatch, said Death, and people die on the streets. People feast behind lighted windows and other people have no homes. Is this fair?

'Well, of course, that's the big issue –' Albert began.

The peasant had a handful of beans and the king had so much he would not even notice that which he gave away. Is this fair?

'Yeah, but if you gave it all to the peasant then in a year or two he'd be just as snooty as the king –' began Albert, jaundiced observer of human nature.

Naughty and nice? said Death. But it's *easy* to be nice if you're rich. Is this fair?

Albert wanted to argue. He wanted to say, Really? In that case, how come so many of the rich buggers is bastards? And being poor don't mean being naughty, neither. We was poor when I were a kid, but we was honest. Well, more stupid than honest, to tell the truth. But basically honest.

He didn't argue, though. The master wasn't in any mood for it. He always did what needed to be done.

'You *did* say we just had to do this so's people'd believe –' he began, and then stopped and started again. 'When it comes to *fair*, master, you yourself –'

I am even-handed to rich and poor alike, snapped Death. But this should not be a sad time. This is supposed to be the season to be jolly. He wrapped his red robe around him. And other things ending in olly, he added.

'There's no blade,' said the oh god. 'It's just a sword hilt.'

Susan stepped out of the light and her wrist moved. A sparkling blue line flashed in the air, for a moment outlining an edge too thin to be seen.

The oh god backed away.

'What's *that*?'

'Oh, it cuts tiny bits of the air in half. It can cut the soul away from the body, so stand back, please.'

'Oh, I will, I will.'

Susan fished the black scabbard out of the umbrella stand.

Umbrella stand! It never rained here, but Death had an umbrella stand. Practically no one else Susan knew had an umbrella stand. In any list of useful furniture, the one found at the bottom would be the umbrella stand.

Death lived in a black world, where nothing was alive and everything was dark and his great library only had dust and cobwebs because he'd created them for effect and there was never any sun in the sky and the air never moved and he had an umbrella stand. And a pair of silver-backed hairbrushes by his bed. He wanted to be something more than just a bony apparition. He tried to create these flashes of personality but somehow they betrayed themselves, they tried too hard, like an adolescent boy going out wearing an aftershave called 'Rampant'.

Grandfather *always* got things wrong. He saw life from outside and never quite understood.

'That looks dangerous,' said the oh god.

Susan sheathed the sword.

'I hope so,' she said.

'Er . . . where are we going? Exactly?'

'Somewhere under an overhead sky,' said Susan. 'And . . . I've seen it before. Recently. I *know* the place.'

They walked out to the stable yard. Binky was waiting.

'I said you don't have to come,' said Susan, grasping the saddle. 'I mean, you're a . . . an innocent bystander.'

'But I'm a god of hangovers who's been cured of hangovers,' said the oh god. 'I haven't really got any function at all.'

He looked so forlorn when he said this that she relented.

'All right. Come on, then.'

She pulled him up behind her.

'Just hang on,' she said. And then she said, 'Hang on somewhere differently, I mean.'

'I'm sorry, was that a problem?' said the oh god, shifting his grip.

'It might take too long to explain and you probably don't know all the words. Around the *waist*, please.'

Susan took out Violet's hourglass and held it up. There was a lot of sand left to run, but she couldn't be certain that was a good sign.

All she could be certain of was that the horse of Death could go anywhere.

The sound of Hex's quill as it scrabbled across the paper was like a frantic spider trapped in a matchbox.

Despite his dislike of what was going on, there was a part of Ponder Stibbons that was very, very impressed.

In the past, when Hex had been recalcitrant about its calculations, when it had got into a mechanical sulk and had started writing things like '+++ Out Of Cheese Error +++' and '+++ Redo From Start +++' Ponder had tried to sort things out calmly and logically.

It had never, ever occurred to him to contemplate hitting Hex with a mallet. But this was, in fact, what Ridcully was threatening to do.

What was *impressive*, and also more than a little worrying, was that Hex seemed to understand the concept.

'Right,' said Ridcully, putting the mallet aside. 'Let's have no more of this "Insufficient dates" business, shall we? There's boxes of the damn things back in the Great Hall. You can have the lot as far as I'm concerned –'

'It's *data*, not dates,' said Ponder helpfully.

'What? You mean like . . . more than dates? Extra sticky?'

'No, no, data is Hex's word for . . . well, facts,' said Ponder.

'Ridiculous way to behave,' said Ridcully brusquely. 'If he's stumped for an answer, why can't he write "You've got me there" or "Damned if I know" or "That's a bit of a puzzler and no mistake"? All this "Insufficient data" business is just pure contrariness, to my mind. It's just swank.' He turned back to Hex. 'Right, you. Hazard a guess.'

The quill started to write '+++ Insuff' and then stopped. After quivering for a moment it went down a line and started again.

+++ This Is Just Calculating Aloud, You Understand +++

'Fair enough,' said Ridcully.

+++ The Amount Of Belief In The World Must Be Subject To An Upper Limit +++

'What an odd question,' said the Dean.

'Sounds sensible,' said Ridcully. 'I suppose people just . . . believe in stuff. Obviously there's a limit to what you can believe in. I've always said so. So what?'

+++ Creatures Have Appeared That Were Once Believed In +++

'Yes. Yes, you could put it like that.'

+++ They Disappeared Because They Were Not Believed In +++

'Seems reasonable,' said Ridcully.

+++ People Were Believing In Something Else – Query? +++

Ridcully looked at the other wizards. They shrugged.

'Could be,' he said guardedly. 'People can only believe in so many things.'

+++ It Follows That If A Major Focus Of Belief Is Removed, There Will Be Spare Belief +++

Ridcully stared at the words.

'You mean . . . sloshing around?'

The big wheel with the ram skulls on it began to turn ponderously. The scurrying ants in the glass tubes took on a new urgency.

'What's happening?' said Ridcully, in a loud whisper.

'I think Hex is looking up the word "sloshing",' said Ponder. 'It may be in long-term storage.'

A large hourglass came down on the spring.

'What's that for?' said Ridcully.

'Er . . . it shows Hex is working things out.'

'Oh. And that buzzing noise? Seems to be coming from the other side of the wall.'

Ponder coughed.

'That *is* the long-term storage, Archchancellor.'

'And how does that work?'

'Er . . . well, if you think of memory as a series of little shelves or, or, or holes, Archchancellor, in which you can put things, well, we found a way of making a sort of memory which, er, interfaces neatly with the ants, in fact, but more importantly can expand its size depending on how much we give it to remember and, er, is possibly a bit slow but –'

'It's a very *loud* buzzing,' said the Dean. 'Is it going wrong?'

'No, that shows it's working,' said Ponder. 'It's, er, beehives.'

He coughed.

'Different types of pollen, different thicknesses of honey, placement of the eggs . . . It's actually amazing how much information you can store on one honeycomb.'

He looked at their faces. 'And it's very secure because anyone trying to tamper with it will get stung to death and Adrian believes that when we shut it down in the summer holidays we should get a nice lot of honey, too.' He coughed again. 'For our ... sand ... wiches,' he said.

He felt himself getting smaller and hotter under their gazes.

Hex came to his rescue. The hourglass bounced away and the quill pen was jerked in and out of its inkwell.

+++ Yes. Sloshing Around. Accreting +++

'That means forming around new centres, Archchancellor,' said Ponder helpfully.

'I know *that*,' said Ridcully. 'Blast. Remember when we had all that life force all over the place? A man couldn't call his trousers his own! So . . . there's spare belief sloshing around, thank you, and these little devils are taking advantage of it? Coming back? Household gods?'

+++ This Is Possible +++

'All right, then, so what are people *not* believing in all of a sudden?'

+++ Out Of Cheese Error +++ MELON MELON MELON +++ Redo From Start +++

'Thank you. A simple "I don't know" would have been sufficient,' said Ridcully, sitting back.

'One of the major gods?' said the Chair of Indefinite Studies.

'Hah, we'd soon know about it if one of *those* vanished.'

'It's Hogswatch,' said the Dean. 'I *suppose* the Hogfather is around, is he?'

'You believe in him?' said Ridcully.

'Well, he's for kids, isn't he?' said the Dean. 'But I'm sure *they* all believe in him. *I* certainly did. It wouldn't be Hogswatch when I was a kid without a pillowcase hanging by the fire –'

'A pillowcase?' said the Senior Wrangler, sharply.

'Well, you can't get much in a stocking,' said the Dean.

'Yes, but a whole pillowcase?' the Senior Wrangler insisted.

'Yes. What of it?'

'Is it just me, or is that a rather greedy and selfish way to behave? In *my* family we just hung up very small socks,' said the Senior Wrangler. 'A sugar pig, a toy soldier, a couple of oranges and that was it. Hah, turns out people with whole pillowcases were cornering the market, eh?'

'Shut up and stop squabbling, both of you,' said Ridcully. 'There must be a simple way to check up. How can you tell if the Hogfather exists?'

'Someone's drunk the sherry, there's sooty footprints on the carpet, sleigh tracks on the roof and your pillowcase is full of presents,' said the Dean.

'Hah, *pillowcase*,' said the Senior Wrangler darkly. 'Hah. I expect *your* family were the stuck-up sort that didn't even open their presents until after Hogswatch dinner, eh? One of them with a big snooty Hogswatch tree in the hall?'

'What if –' Ridcully began, but he was too late.

'Well?' said the Dean. 'Of course we waited until after lunch –'

'You know, it really used to wind me *right* up, people with big snooty Hogswatch trees. And I just bet you had one of those swanky fancy nutcrackers like a big thumbscrew,' said the Senior Wrangler. '*Some* people had to make do with the coal hammer out of the outhouse, of course. *And* had dinner in the middle of the day instead of lah-di-dah posh dinner in the evening.'

'I can't help it if my family had money,' said the Dean, and that might have defused things a bit had he not added, 'and standards.'

'And big pillowcases!' shouted the Senior Wrangler, bouncing up and down in rage. '*And* I bet you *bought* your holly, eh?'

The Dean raised his eyebrows. 'Of course! We didn't go creeping around the country pinching it out of other people's hedges, like *some* people did,' he snapped.

'That's traditional! That's part of the fun!'

'Celebrating Hogswatch with stolen greenery?'

Ridcully put his hand over his eyes.

The word for this, he had heard, was 'cabin fever'. When people had been cooped up for too long in the dark days of the winter, they always tended to get on one another's nerves, although there was probably a school of thought that would hold that spending your time in a university with more than five thousand known rooms, a huge library, the best kitchens in the city, its own brewery, dairy, extensive wine cellar, laundry, barber shop, cloisters and skittle alley was testing the definition of 'cooped up' a little. Mind you, wizards could get on one another's nerves in opposite corners of a very large field.

'Just shut up, will you?' he said. 'It's Hogswatch! That's *not* the time for silly arguments, all right?'

'Oh, yes it is,' said the Chair of Indefinite Studies glumly. 'It's exactly the time for silly arguments. In our family we were lucky to get through dinner without a reprise of What A Shame Henry Didn't Go Into Business With Our Ron. Or Why Hasn't Anyone Taught Those Kids To Use A Knife? That was another favourite.'

'And the sulks,' said Ponder Stibbons.

'Oh, the sulks,' said the Chair of Indefinite Studies. 'Not a proper Hogswatch without everyone sitting staring at different walls.'

'The games were worse,' said Ponder.

'Worse than the kids hitting one another with their toys, d'you think? Not a proper Hogswatch afternoon without wheels and bits of broken dolly everywhere and everyone whining. Assault and battery included.'

'We had a game called Hunt the Slipper,' said Ponder. 'Someone hid a slipper. And then we had to find it. And then we had a row.'

'It's not *really* bad,' said the Lecturer in Recent Runes. 'I mean, not proper *Hogswatch* bad, unless everyone's wearing a paper hat. There's always that bit, isn't there, when someone's horrible great-aunt puts on a paper hat and smirks at everyone because she's being so bohemian.'

'I'd forgotten about the paper hats,' said the Chair of Indefinite Studies. 'Oh, dear.'

'And then later on someone'll suggest a board game,' said Ponder.

'That's right. Where no one exactly remembers all the rules.'

'Which doesn't stop someone suggesting that you play for pennies.'

'And five minutes later there's two people not speaking to one another for the rest of their lives because of tuppence.'

'And some horrible little kid –'

'I know, I know! Some little kid who's been allowed to stay up wins everyone's money by being a nasty little cut-throat swot!'

'Right!'

'Er . . .' said Ponder, who rather suspected that he had *been* that child.

'And don't forget the presents,' said the Chair of Indefinite Studies, as if reading off some internal list of gloom. 'How . . . how full of potential they seem in all that paper, how pregnant with possibilities . . . and then you open them and basically the wrapping paper was *more* interesting and you have to say "How thoughtful, that *will* come in handy." It's not better to give than to receive, in my opinion, it's just less embarrassing.'

'I've worked out,' said the Senior Wrangler, 'that over the years I have been a net exporter of Hogswatch presents –'

'Oh, everyone is,' said the Chair. 'You spend a fortune on other people and what you get when all the paper is cleared away is one slipper that's the wrong colour and a book about earwax.'

Ridcully sat in horrified amazement. He'd always enjoyed Hogswatch, every bit of it. He'd enjoyed seeing ancient relatives, he'd enjoyed the food, he'd been *good* at games like Chase My Neighbour Up The Passage and Hooray Jolly Tinker. He was always the first to don a paper hat. He felt that paper hats lent a special festive air to the occasion. And he always very carefully read the messages on Hogswatch cards and found time for a few kind thoughts about the sender.

Listening to his wizards was like watching someone kick apart a doll's house.

'At least the Hogswatch cracker mottoes are fun ...?' he ventured.

They all turned to look at him, and then turned away again.

'If you have the sense of humour of a wire coathanger,' said the Senior Wrangler.

'Oh dear,' said Ridcully. 'Then perhaps there *isn't* a Hogfather if all you chaps are sitting around with long faces. He's not the sort to let people go around being miserable!'

'Ridcully, he's just some old winter god,' said the Senior Wrangler wearily. 'He's not the Cheerful Fairy or anything.'

The Lecturer in Recent Runes raised his chin from his hands. 'What Cheerful Fairy?'

'Oh, it's just something my granny used to go on about if it was a wet afternoon and we were getting on her nerves,' said the Senior Wrangler. 'She'd say "I'll call the Cheerful Fairy if you're ..."' He stopped, looking guilty.

The Archchancellor held a hand to his ear in a theatrical gesture denoting 'Hush. What was that I heard?'

'Someone tinkled,' he said. 'Thank you, Senior Wrangler.'

'Oh no,' the Senior Wrangler moaned. 'No, no, no!'

They listened for a moment.

'We might have got away with it,' said Ponder. '*I* didn't hear anything ...'

'Yes, but you can just imagine her, can't you?' said the Dean. 'The moment you said it, I had this picture in my mind. She's going to have a whole bag of word games, for one thing. Or she'll suggest we go outdoors for our health.'

The wizards shuddered. They weren't against the outdoors, it was simply their place in it they objected to.

'Cheerfulness has always got me down,' said the Dean.

'Well, if some wretched little ball of cheerfulness turns up I shan't have it for one,' said the Senior Wrangler, folding his arms. 'I've put up with monsters and trolls and big green things with teeth, so I'm not sitting still for any kind of –'

'Hello!! Hello!!'

The voice was the kind of voice that reads suitable stories to children. Every vowel was beautifully rounded. And they could hear the extra exclamation marks, born of a sort of desperate despairing jollity, slot into place. They turned.

The Cheerful Fairy was quite short and plump in a tweed skirt and shoes so sensible they could do their own tax returns, and was pretty much like the first teacher you get at school, the one who has special training in dealing with nervous incontinence and little boys whose contribution to the wonderful world of sharing consists largely of hitting a small girl repeatedly over the head with a wooden horse. In fact, this picture was helped by the whistle on a string around her neck and a general impression that at any moment she would clap her hands.

The tiny gauzy wings just visible on her back were probably just for show, but the wizards kept on staring at her shoulder.

'Hello –' she said again, but a lot more uncertainly. She gave them a suspicious look. 'You're rather *big* boys,' she said, as if they'd become so in order to spite her. She blinked. 'It's my job to chase those blues away,' she added, apparently following a memorized script. Then she seemed to rally a bit and went on. 'So chins up, everyone, and let's see a lot of bright shining faces!!'

Her gaze met that of the Senior Wrangler, who had probably never had a bright shining face in his entire life. He specialized in dull, sullen ones. The one he was wearing now would have won prizes.

'Excuse me, madam,' said Ridcully. 'But is that a chicken on your shoulder?'

'It's, er, it's, er, it's the Blue Bird of Happiness,' said the Cheerful Fairy. Her voice now had the slightly shaking tone of someone who doesn't quite believe what she has just said but is going to go on saying it anyway, just in case saying it will eventually make it true.

'I beg your pardon, but it is a chicken. A live chicken,' said Ridcully. 'It just went cluck.'

'It *is* blue,' she said hopelessly.

'Well, that at least is true,' Ridcully conceded, as kindly as he could manage. 'Left to myself, I expect I'd have imagined a slightly more *streamlined* Blue Bird of Happiness, but I can't actually fault you there.'

The Cheerful Fairy coughed nervously and fiddled with the buttons on her sensible woolly jumper.

'How about a nice game to get us all in the mood?' she said. 'A guessing game, perhaps? Or a painting competition? There may be a small prize for the winner.'

'Madam, we're wizards,' said the Senior Wrangler. 'We don't do cheerful.'

'Charades?' said the Cheerful Fairy. 'Or perhaps you've been playing them already? How about a sing-song? Who knows "Row Row Row Your Boat"?'

Her bright little smile hit the group scowl of the assembled wizards. 'We don't want to be Mr Grumpy, do we?' she added hopefully.

'Yes,' said the Senior Wrangler.

The Cheerful Fairy sagged, and then patted frantically at her shapeless sleeves until she tugged out a balled-up handkerchief. She dabbed at her eyes.

'It's all going wrong again, isn't it?' she said, her chin trembling. 'No one ever wants to be cheerful these days, and I really *do* try. I've made a Joke Book and I've got three boxes of clothes for charades and ... and ... and whenever I try to cheer people up they all look embarrassed ... and really I *do* make an effort ...'

She blew her nose loudly.

Even the Senior Wrangler had the grace to look embarrassed.

'Er ...' he began.

'Would it hurt anyone just *occasionally* to try to be a *little* bit cheerful?' said the Cheerful Fairy.

'Er ... in what way?' said the Senior Wrangler, feeling wretched.

'Well, there's so many nice things to be cheerful about,' said the Cheerful Fairy, blowing her nose again.

'Er ... raindrops and sunsets and that sort of thing?' said the Senior Wrangler, managing some sarcasm, but they could tell his heart wasn't in it. 'Er, would you like to borrow my handkerchief? It's nearly fresh.'

'Why don't you get the lady a nice sherry?' said Ridcully. 'And some corn for her chicken ...'

'Oh, I *never* drink alcohol,' said the Cheerful Fairy, horrified.

'Really?' said Ridcully. 'We find it's something to be cheerful about. Mr Stibbons ... would you be so kind as to step over here for a moment?'

He beckoned him up close.

'There's got to be a lot of belief sloshing around to let *her* be created,' he said. 'She's a good fourteen stone, if I'm any judge. If we wanted to contact the Hogfather, how would we go about it? Letter up chimney?'

'Yes, but not *tonight*, sir,' said Ponder. 'He'll be out delivering.'

'No telling where he'll be, then,' said Ridcully. 'Blast.'

'Of course, he might not have come *here* yet,' said Ponder.

'Why should he come here?' said Ridcully.

The Librarian pulled the blankets over himself and curled up.

As an orang-utan he hankered for the warmth of the rainforest. The problem was that he'd never even *seen* a rainforest, having been turned into an orang-utan when he was already a fully grown human. Something in his bones knew about it, though, and didn't like the cold of winter at all. But he was also a librarian in those same bones and he flatly refused to allow fires to be lit in the library. As a result, pillows and blankets went missing everywhere else in the University and ended up in a sort of cocoon in the reference section, in which the ape lurked during the worst of the winter.

He turned over and wrapped himself in the Bursar's curtains.

There was a creaking outside his nest, and some whispering.

'No, don't light the lamp.'

'I wondered why I hadn't seen him all evening.'

'Oh, he goes to bed early on Hogswatch Eve, sir. Here we are . . .'

There was some rustling.

'We're in luck. It hasn't been filled,' said Ponder. 'Looks like he's used one of the Bursar's.'

'He puts it up every year?'

'Apparently.'

'But it's not as though he's a child. A certain child-like simplicity, perhaps.'

'It might be different for orang-utans, Archchancellor.'

'Do they do it in the jungle, d'you think?'

'I don't imagine so, sir. No chimneys, for one thing.'

'And quite short legs, of course. Extremely under-funded in the sock area, orang-utans. They'd be quids in if they could hang up gloves, of course. Hogfather'd be on double shifts if they could hang up their gloves. On account of the length of their arms.'

'Very good, Archchancellor.'

'I say, what's this on the . . . my word, a glass of sherry. Well, waste not, want not.' There was a damp glugging noise in the darkness.

'I think that was supposed to be for the Hogfather, sir.'

'And the banana?'

'I *imagine* that's been left out for the pigs, sir.'

'Pigs?'

'Oh, *you* know, sir. Tusker and Snouter and Gouger and Rooter. I mean,' Ponder stopped, conscious that a grown man shouldn't be able to remember this sort of thing, 'that's what children believe.'

'Bananas for pigs? That's not traditional, is it? I'd have thought acorns, perhaps. Or apples or swedes.'

'Yes, sir, but the Librarian likes bananas, sir.'

'Very nourishin' fruit, Mr Stibbons.'

'Yes, sir. Although, funnily enough it's not actually a fruit, sir.'

'Really?'

'Yes, sir. Botanically, it's a type of fish, sir. According to my theory it's cladistically associated with the Krullian pipefish, sir, which of course is also yellow and goes around in bunches or shoals.'

'And lives in trees?'

'Well, not usually, sir. The banana is obviously exploiting a new niche.'

'Good heavens, really? It's a funny thing, but I've never much liked bananas and I've always been a bit suspicious of fish, too. That'd explain it.'

'Yes, sir.'

'Do they attack swimmers?'

'Not that I've heard, sir. Of course, they may be clever enough to only attack swimmers who're far from land.'

'What, you mean sort of . . . high up? In the trees, as it were?'

'Possibly, sir.'

'Cunning, eh?'

'Yes, sir.'

'Well, we might as well make ourselves comfortable, Mr Stibbons.'

'Yes, sir.'

A match flared in the darkness as Ridcully lit his pipe.

The Ankh-Morpork wassailers had practised for weeks.

The custom was referred to by Anaglypta Huggs, organizer of the best and most select group of the city's singers, as an occasion for fellowship and good cheer.

One should always be wary of people who talk unashamedly of 'fellowship and good cheer' as if it were something that can be applied to life like a poultice. Turn your back for a moment and they may well organize a Maypole dance and, frankly, there's no option then but to try and make it to the treeline.

The singers were halfway down Park Lane now, and halfway through 'The Red Rosy Hen' in marvellous harmony.* Their collecting tins were already full of donations for the poor of the city, or at least those sections of the poor who in Mrs Huggs' opinion were suitably picturesque and not too smelly and could be relied upon to say thank you. People had come to their doors to listen. Orange light spilled on to the snow. Candle lanterns glowed among the tumbling flakes. If you could have taken the lid off the scene, there would have been chocolates inside. Or at least an interesting biscuit assortment.

Mrs Huggs had heard that wassailing was an ancient ritual, and you didn't need anyone to tell you what *that* meant, but she felt she'd carefully removed all those elements that would affront the refined ear.

And it was only gradually that the singers became aware of the discord.

Around the corner, slipping and sliding on the ice, came another band of singers.

Some people march to a different drummer. The drummer in question here must have been trained elsewhere, possibly by a different species on another planet.

In front of the group was a legless man on a small wheeled trolley, who was singing at the top of his voice and banging two saucepans together. His name was Arnold Sideways. Pushing him along was Coffin Henry, whose croaking progress through an entirely different song was punctuated by bouts of off-the-beat coughing. He was accompanied by a perfectly ordinary-looking man in torn, dirty and yet expensive clothing, whose pleasant tenor voice was drowned out by the quacking of a duck on his head. He answered to the name of Duck Man, although he never seemed to understand why, or why he was always surrounded by people who seemed to see ducks where no ducks could be. And finally, being towed along by a small grey dog on a string, was Foul Ole Ron, generally regarded in Ankh-Morpork as the deranged beggars'

---

* 'The red rosy hen greets the dawn of the day'. In fact the hen is not the bird traditionally associated with heralding a new sunrise, but Mrs Huggs, while collecting many old folk songs for posterity, had taken care to rewrite them where necessary to avoid, as she put it, 'offending those of a refined disposition with unwarranted coarseness'. Much to her surprise, people often couldn't spot the unwarranted coarseness until it had been pointed out to them.

Sometimes a chicken is nothing but a bird.

deranged beggar. He was probably incapable of singing, but at least he was attempting to swear in time to the beat, or beats.

The wassailers stopped and watched them in horror.

Neither party noticed, as the beggars oozed and ambled up the street, that little smears of black and grey were spiralling out of drains and squeezing out from under tiles and buzzing off into the night. People have always had the urge to sing and clang things at the dark stub of the year, when all sorts of psychic nastiness has taken advantage of the long grey days and the deep shadows to lurk and breed. Lately people had taken to singing harmoniously, which rather lost the effect. Those who really understood just clanged something and shouted.

The beggars were not in fact this well versed in folkloric practice. They were just making a din in the well-founded hope that people would give them money to stop.

It was just possible to make out a consensus song in there somewhere.

> 'Hogswatch is coming,
> The pig is getting fat,
> Please put a dollar in the old man's hat
> If you ain't got a dollar a penny will do –'

'And if you ain't got a penny,' Foul Ole Ron yodelled, solo, 'then – fghfgh yffg mfmfmf . . .'

The Duck Man had, with great presence of mind, clamped a hand over Ron's mouth.

'So sorry about this,' he said, 'but *this* time I'd like people not to slam their doors on us. And it doesn't scan, anyway.'

The nearby doors slammed regardless. The other wassailers fled hastily to a more salubrious location. Goodwill to all men was a phrase coined by someone who hadn't met Foul Ole Ron.

The beggars stopped singing, except for Arnold Sideways, who tended to live in his own small world.

'– nobody knows how good we can live, on boots three times a day . . .'

Then the change in the air penetrated even his consciousness.

Snow thumped off the trees as a contrary wind brushed them. There was a whirl of flakes and it was just possible, since the beggars did not always have their mental compasses pointing due Real, that they heard a brief snatch of conversation.

'It just ain't that simple, master, that's all I'm saying —'

IT IS BETTER TO GIVE THAN TO RECEIVE, ALBERT.

'No, master, it's just a lot more expensive. You can't just go around —'

Things rained down on the snow.

The beggars looked at them. Arnold Sideways carefully picked up a sugar pig and bit its nose off. Foul Ole Ron peered suspiciously into a cracker that had bounced off his hat, and then shook it against his ear.

The Duck Man opened a bag of sweets.

'Ah, humbugs?' he said.

Coffin Henry unlooped a string of sausages from around his neck.

'Buggrit?' said Foul Ole Ron.

'It's a cracker,' said the dog, scratching its ear. 'You pull it.'

Ron waved the cracker aimlessly by one end.

'Oh, give it here,' said the dog, and gripped the other end in its teeth.

'My word,' said the Duck Man, fishing in a snowdrift. 'Here's a whole roast pig! *And* a big dish of roast potatoes, miraculously uncracked! And ... look ... isn't this caviar in the jar? Asparagus! Potted shrimp! My goodness! What were we going to have for Hogswatch dinner, Arnold?'

'Old boots,' said Arnold. He opened a fallen box of cigars and licked them.

'Just old boots?'

'Oh, no. Stuffed with mud, and with roast mud. 's good mud, too. I bin saving it up.'

'Now we can have a merry feast of goose!'

'All right. Can we stuff it with old boots?'

There was a pop from the direction of the cracker. They heard Foul Ole Ron's thinking-brain dog growl.

'No, no, no, you put the *hat* on your *head* and you *read* the hum'rous *mottar*.'

'Millennium hand and shrimp?' said Ron, passing the scrap of paper to the Duck Man. The Duck Man was regarded as the intellectual of the group.

He peered at the motto.

'Ah, yes, let's see now ... It says "Help Help Help Ive Fallen in the Crakker Machine I Cant Keep Runin on this Roller Please Get me Ou–".' He turned the paper over a few times. 'That appears to be it, except for the stains.'

'Always the same ole mottars,' said the dog. 'Someone slap Ron on the back, will you? If he laughs any more he'll – oh, he has. Oh well, nothing new about that.'

The beggars spent a few more minutes picking up hams, jars and bottles that had settled on the snow. They packed them around Arnold on his trolley and set off down the street.

'How come we got all this?'

''s Hogswatch, right?'

'Yeah, but who hung up their stocking?'

'I don't think we've got any, have we?'

'I hung up an old boot.'

'Does that count?'

'Dunno. Ron ate it.'

I'm waiting for the Hogfather, thought Ponder Stibbons. I'm in the dark waiting for the Hogfather. Me. A believer in Natural Philosophy. I can find the square root of 27.4 in my head.[*] I shouldn't be doing this.

It's not as if I've hung a stocking up. There'd be some *point* if . . .

He sat rigid for a moment, and then pulled off his pointy sandal and rolled down a sock. It helped if you thought of it as the scientific testing of an interesting hypothesis.

From out of the darkness Ridcully said, 'How long, do you think?'

'It's generally believed that all deliveries are completed well before midnight,' said Ponder, and tugged hard.

'Are you all right, Mr Stibbons?'

'Fine, sir. Fine. Er . . . do you happen to have a drawing pin about you? Or a small nail, perhaps?'

'I don't believe so.'

'Oh, it's all right. I've found a penknife.'

After a while Ridcully heard a faint scratching noise in the dark.

'How do you spell "electricity", sir?'

Ridcully thought for a while. 'You know, I don't think I ever do.'

There was silence again, and then a clang. The Librarian grunted in his sleep.

'What are you doing?'

---

[*] He'd have to admit that the answer would be 'five and a bit', but at least he could come up with it.

'I just knocked over the coal shovel.'

'Why are you feeling around on the mantelpiece?'

'Oh, just ... you know, just ... just looking. A little ... experiment. After all, you never know.'

'You never know what?'

'Just ... never know, you know.'

'*Sometimes* you know,' said Ridcully. 'I think I know quite a lot that I didn't used to know. It's amazing what you *do* end up knowing, I sometimes think. I often wonder what new stuff I'll know.'

'Well, you never know.'

'That's a fact.'

High over the city Albert turned to Death, who seemed to be trying to avoid his gaze.

'You didn't get *that* stuff out of the sack! Not cigars and peaches in brandy and grub with fancy foreign names!'

YES, IT CAME OUT OF THE SACK.

Albert gave him a suspicious look.

'But you put it in the sack in the first place, didn't you?'

NO.

'You did, didn't you?' Albert stated.

NO.

'You put all those things in the sack.'

NO.

'You got them from somewhere and put them in the sack.'

NO.

'You *did* put them in the sack, didn't you?'

NO.

'You put them in the sack.'

YES.

'I *knew* you put them in the sack. Where did you get them?'

THEY WERE JUST LYING AROUND.

'Whole roast pig does not, in my experience, just lie around.'

NO ONE SEEMED TO BE USING THEM, ALBERT.

'Couple of chimneys ago we were over that big posh restaurant ...'

REALLY? I DON'T REMEMBER.

'And it seemed to me you were down there a bit longer than usual, if you don't mind me saying so.'

REALLY.

'How exactly were they just inverted comma lying around inverted comma?'

JUST ... LYING AROUND. YOU KNOW. RECUMBENT.

'In a kitchen?'

THERE WAS A CERTAIN CULINARINESS ABOUT THE PLACE, I RECALL.

Albert pointed a trembling finger.

'You nicked someone's Hogswatch dinner, master!'

IT'S GOING TO BE EATEN, said Death defensively. ANYWAY, YOU THOUGHT IT WAS A GOOD IDEA WHEN I SHOWED THAT KING THE DOOR.

'Yeah, well, that was a bit different,' said Albert, lowering his voice. 'But, I mean, the Hogfather doesn't drop down the chimney and pinch people's grub!'

THE BEGGARS WILL ENJOY IT, ALBERT.

'Well, yes, but –'

IT WASN'T STEALING. IT WAS JUST ... REDISTRIBUTION. IT WILL BE A GOOD DEED IN A NAUGHTY WORLD.

'No, it won't!'

THEN IT WILL BE A NAUGHTY DEED IN A NAUGHTY WORLD AND WILL PASS COMPLETELY UNNOTICED.

'Yeah, but you might at least have thought about the people whose grub you pinched.'

THEY HAVE BEEN PROVIDED FOR, OF COURSE. I AM NOT *COMPLETELY* HEARTLESS. IN A METAPHORICAL SENSE. AND NOW – ONWARDS AND UPWARDS.

'We're heading down, master.'

ONWARDS AND DOWNWARDS, THEN.

There were ... swirls. Binky galloped easily through them, except that he did not seem to move. He might have been hanging in the air.

'Oh, me,' said the oh god weakly.

'What?' said Susan.

'Try shutting your eyes –'

Susan shut her eyes. Then she reached up to touch her face.

'I'm still seeing ...'

'I thought it was just me. It's usually just me.'

The swirls vanished.

There was greenery below.

And *that* was odd. It *was* greenery. Susan had flown a few times over countryside, even swamps and jungles, and there had never been a green as green as this. If green could be a primary colour, this was it.

And that wiggly thing –

'That's not a river!' she said.

'Isn't it?'

'It's blue!'

The oh god risked a look down.

'Water's blue,' he said.

'Of course it's not!'

'Grass is green, water's blue . . . I can remember that. It's some of the stuff I just know.'

'Well, in a *way* . . .' Susan hesitated. Everyone *knew* grass was green and water was blue. Quite often it wasn't true, but everyone knew it in the same way they knew the sky was blue, too.

She made the mistake of looking up as she thought that.

There was the sky. It was, indeed, blue. And down there was the land. It was green.

And in between was nothing. Not white space. Not black night. Just . . . nothing, all round the edges of the world. Where the brain said there should be, well, sky and land, meeting neatly at the horizon, there was simply a void that sucked at the eyeball like a loose tooth.

And there was the sun.

It *was* under the sky, floating above the land.

And it was yellow.

Buttercup yellow.

Binky landed on the grass beside the river. Or at least on the green. It felt more like sponge, or moss. He nuzzled it.

Susan slid off, trying to keep her gaze low. That meant she was looking at the vivid blue of the water.

There were orange fish in it. They didn't look quite right, as if they'd been created by someone who really *did* think a fish was two curved lines and a dot and a triangular tail. They reminded her of the skeletal fish in Death's quiet pool. Fish that were . . . appropriate to their surroundings. And she could see them, even though the water was just a block of colour which part of her insisted ought to be opaque . . .

She knelt down and dipped her hand in. It felt like water, but what poured through her fingers was liquid blue.

And now she knew where she was. The last piece clicked into place and the knowledge bloomed inside her. She knew if she saw a house just how its windows would be placed, and just how the smoke would come out of the chimney.

There would almost certainly be apples on the trees. And they would be red, because everyone knew that apples were red. And the sun was yellow. And the sky was blue. And the grass was green.

But there was *another* world, called the real world by the people who believed in it, where the sky could be anything from off-white to sunset red to thunderstorm yellow. And the trees would be anything from bare branches, mere scribbles against the sky, to red flames before the frost. And the sun was white or yellow or orange. And water was brown and grey and green . . .

The colours *here* were springtime colours, and not the springtime of the world. They were the colours of the springtime of the eye.

'This is a child's painting,' she said.

The oh god slumped on to the green.

'Every time I look at the gap my eyes water,' he mumbled. 'I feel awful.'

'I said this is a child's painting,' said Susan.

'Oh, *me* . . . I think the wizards' potion is wearing off . . .'

'I've seen dozens of pictures of it,' said Susan, ignoring him. 'You put the sky overhead because the sky's above you and when you are a couple of feet high there's not a lot of sideways to the sky in any case. And everyone tells you grass is green and water is blue. *This is the landscape you paint. Twyla paints like that. I painted like that.* Grandfather saved some of –'

She stopped.

'All children do it, anyway,' she muttered. 'Come on, let's find the house.'

'What house?' the oh god moaned. 'And can you speak quieter, please?'

'There'll be a house,' said Susan, standing up. 'There's *always* a house. With four windows. And the smoke coming out of the chimney all curly like a spring. Look, this is a place like gr– Death's country. It's not really geography.'

The oh god walked over to the nearest tree and banged his head on it as if he hoped it was going to hurt.

'Feels like geo'fy,' he muttered.

'But have you ever seen a tree like that? A big green blob on a brown stick? It looks like a lollipop!' said Susan, pulling him along.

'Dunno. Firs' time I ever saw a tree. Arrgh. Somethin' dropped on m'head.' He blinked owlishly at the ground. ''s red.'

'It's an apple,' she said. She sighed. 'Everyone knows apples are red.'

There were no bushes. But there were flowers, each with a couple of green leaves. They grew individually, dotted around the rolling green.

And then they were out of the trees and there, by a bend in the river, was the house.

It didn't look very big. There were four windows and a door. Corkscrew smoke curled out of the chimney.

'You know, it's a funny thing,' said Susan, staring at it. 'Twyla draws houses like that. And she practically lives in a mansion. I drew houses like that. And I was born in a palace. Why?'

'P'raps it's all this house,' muttered the oh god miserably.

'What? You really think so? Kids' paintings are all of this place? It's in our heads?'

'Don't ask me, I was just making conversation,' said the oh god.

Susan hesitated. The words What Now? loomed. Should she just go and knock?

And she realized that was *normal* thinking . . .

In the glittering, clattering, chattering atmosphere a head waiter was having a difficult time. There were a lot of people in, and the staff should have been fully stretched, putting bicarbonate of soda in the white wine to make very expensive bubbles and cutting the vegetables very small to make them cost more.

Instead they were standing in a dejected group in the kitchen.

'Where did it all go?' screamed the manager. 'Someone's been through the cellar, too!'

'William said he felt a cold wind,' said the waiter. He'd been backed up against a hot plate, and now *knew* why it was called a hot plate in a way he hadn't fully comprehended before.

'I'll give him a cold wind! Haven't we got *anything*?'

'There's odds and ends . . .'

'You don't mean odds and ends, you mean *des curieux et des bouts*,' corrected the manager.

'Yeah, right, yeah. And, er, and, er . . .'

'There's nothing else?'

'Er . . . old boots. Muddy old boots.'

'Old –?'

'Boots. Lots of 'em,' said the waiter. He felt he was beginning to singe.

'How come we've got . . . vintage footwear?'

'Dunno. They just turned up, sir. The oven's full of old boots. So's the pantry.'

'There's a hundred people booked in! All the shops'll be shut! Where's Chef?'

'William's trying to get him to come out of the privy, sir. He's locked himself in and is having one of his Moments.'

'*Something's* cooking. What's that I can smell?'

'Me, sir.'

'Old boots . . .' muttered the manager. 'Old boots . . . old boots . . . Leather, are they? Not clogs or rubber or anything?'

'Looks like . . . just boots. And lots of mud, sir.'

The manager took off his jacket. 'All right. Got any cream, have we? Onions? Garlic? Butter? Some old beef bones? A bit of pastry?'

'Er, yes . . .'

The manager rubbed his hands together. '*Right*,' he said, taking an apron off a hook. 'You there, get some water boiling! Lots of water! And find a really large hammer! And *you*, chop some onions! The rest of you, start sorting out the boots. I want the tongues out and the soles off. We'll do them . . . let's see . . . *Mousse de la Boue dans une Panier de la Pâte de Chaussures* . . .'

'Where're we going to get that from, sir?'

'Mud mousse in a basket of shoe pastry. Get the idea? It's not our fault if even Quirmians don't understand restaurant Quirmian. It's not like lying, after all.'

'Well, it's a *bit* like –' the waiter began. He'd been cursed with honesty at an early stage.

'Then there's *Brodequin rôti Façon Ombres* . . .' The manager sighed at the head waiter's panicky expression. 'Soldier's boot done in the Shades fashion,' he translated.

'Er . . . Shades fashion?'

'In mud. But if we cook the tongues separately we can put on *Languette braisée*, too.'

'There's some ladies' shoes, sir,' said an under-chef.

'Right. Add to the menu . . . Let's see now . . . Sole *d'une Bonne Femme* . . . and . . . yes . . . *Servis dans un Coulis de Terre en l'Eau*. That's mud, to you.'

'What about the laces, sir?' said another under-chef.

'Good thinking. Dig out that recipe for Spaghetti Carbonara.'

'Sir?' said the head waiter.

'I started off as a chef,' said the manager, picking up a knife. 'How do you think I was able to afford this place? I know how it's done. Get the look and the sauce right and you're three-quarters there.'

'But it's all going to be old boots!' said the waiter.

'Prime aged beef,' the manager corrected him. 'It'll tenderize in no time.'

'Anyway . . . anyway . . . we haven't got any soup –'

'Mud. And a lot of onions.'

'There's the puddings –'

'Mud. Let's see if we can get it to caramelize, you never know.'

'I can't even find the coffee . . . Still, they probably won't last till the coffee . . .'

'Mud. *Café de Terre*,' said the manager firmly. 'Genuine ground coffee.'

'Oh, they'll spot that, sir!'

'They haven't up till now,' said the manager darkly.

'We'll never get away with it, sir. Never.'

In the country of the sky on top, Medium Dave Lilywhite hauled another bag of money down the stairs.

'There must be thousands here,' said Chickenwire.

'Hundreds of thousands,' said Medium Dave.

'And what's all this stuff?' said Catseye, opening a box. "s just paper.' He tossed it aside.

Medium Dave sighed. He was all for class solidarity, but sometimes Catseye got on his nerves.

'They're title deeds,' he said. 'And they're better than money.'

'Paper's better'n money?' said Catseye. 'Hah, if you can burn it you can't spend it, that's what I say.'

'Hang on,' said Chickenwire. 'I know about them. The Tooth Fairy owns property?'

'Got to raise money somehow,' said Medium Dave. 'All those half-dollars under the pillow.'

'If we steal them, do they become ours?'

'Is that a trick question?' said Catseye, smirking.

'Yeah, but . . . ten thousand each doesn't sound such a lot, when you see all this.'

'He won't miss a –'

'*Gentlemen* . . .'

They turned. Teatime was in the doorway.

'We were just . . . we were just piling up the stuff,' said Chickenwire.

'Yes. I know. I told you to.'

'Right. That's right. You did,' said Chickenwire gratefully.

'And there's such a lot,' said Teatime. He gave them a smile. Catseye coughed.

''s got to be thousands,' said Medium Dave. 'And what about all these deeds and so on? Look, this one's for that pipe shop in Honey Trap Lane! In Ankh-Morpork! I buy my tobacco there! Old Thimble is always moaning about the rent, too!'

'Ah. So you opened the strongboxes,' said Teatime pleasantly.

'Well . . . yes . . .'

'Fine. Fine,' said Teatime. 'I didn't ask you to, but . . . fine, fine. And how did you think the Tooth Fairy made her money? Little gnomes in some mine somewhere? Fairy gold? But *that* turns to trash in the morning!'

He laughed. Chickenwire laughed. Even Medium Dave laughed. And then Teatime was on him, pushing him irresistibly backwards until he hit the wall.

There was a blur and he tried to blink and his left eyelid was suddenly a rose of pain.

Teatime's good eye was close to him, if you could call it good. The pupil was a dot. Medium Dave could just make out his hand, right by Medium Dave's face.

It was holding a knife. The point of the blade could only be the merest fraction of an inch from Medium Dave's right eye.

'I know people say I'd kill them as soon as look at them,' whispered Teatime. 'And in fact I'd *much* rather kill you than look at you, Mr Lilywhite. You stand in a castle of gold and plot to steal pennies. Oh, dear. What am I to do with you?'

He relaxed a little, but his hand still held the knife to Medium Dave's unblinking eye.

'You're thinking that Banjo is going to help you,' he said. 'That's how it's always been, isn't it? But Banjo likes me. He really does. Banjo is *my* friend.'

Medium Dave managed to focus beyond Teatime's ear. His brother was just standing there, with the blank face he had while he waited for another order or a new thought to turn up.

'If I thought you were feeling bad thoughts about me I would be so downcast,' said Teatime. 'I do not have many friends left, Mr Medium Dave.'

He stood back and smiled happily. 'All friends now?' he said, as Medium Dave slumped down. 'Help him, Banjo.'

On cue, Banjo lumbered forward.

'Banjo has the heart of a little child,' said Teatime, the knife disappearing somewhere about his clothing. 'I believe I have, too.'

The others were frozen in place. They hadn't moved since the attack. Medium Dave was a heavy-set man and Teatime was a matchstick model, but he'd lifted Medium Dave off his feet like a feather.

'As far as the money goes, in fact, I really have no use for it,' said Teatime, sitting down on a sack of silver. 'It is small change. You may share it out amongst yourselves, and no doubt you'll squabble and double-cross one another more tiresomely. Oh, dear. It is so awful when friends fall out.'

He kicked the sack. It split. Silver and copper fell in an expensive trickle.

'And you'll swagger and spend it on drink and women,' he said, as they watched the coins roll into every corner of the room. 'The thought of *investment* will never cross your scarred little minds –'

There was a rumble from Banjo. Even Teatime waited patiently until the huge man had assembled a sentence. The result was:

'I gotta piggy bank.'

'And what would you do with a million dollars, Banjo?' said Teatime.

Another rumble. Banjo's face twisted up.

'Buy ... a ... bigger piggy bank?'

'Well done.' The Assassin stood up. 'Let's go and see how our wizard is getting on, shall we?'

He walked out of the room without looking back. After a moment Banjo followed.

The others tried not to look at one another's faces. Then Chickenwire said, 'Was he saying we could take the money and go?'

'Don't be bloody stupid, we wouldn't get ten yards,' said Medium Dave, still clutching his face. 'Ugh, this *hurts*. I think he cut the eyelid ... he cut the damn *eyelid* ...'

'Then let's just leave the stuff and go! I never joined up to ride on tigers!'

'And what'll you do when he comes after you?'

'Why'd he bother with the likes of us?'

'He's got time for his friends,' said Medium Dave bitterly. 'For gods' sakes, someone get me a clean rag or something ...'

'OK, but ... but he can't look everywhere.'

Medium Dave shook his head. He'd been through Ankh-Morpork's very own university of the streets and had graduated with his life and an intelligence made all the keener by constant friction. You only had to look into Teatime's mismatched eyes to know one thing, which was this: that if Teatime wanted to find you he would *not* look everywhere. He'd look in only one place, which would be the place where you were hiding.

'How come your brother likes him so much?'

Medium Dave grimaced. Banjo had always done what he was told, simply because Medium Dave had told him. Up to now, anyway.

It must have been that punch in the bar. Medium Dave didn't like to think about it. He'd always promised their mother that he'd look after Banjo,* and Banjo had gone back like a falling tree. And when Medium Dave had risen from his seat to punch Teatime's unbalanced lights out he'd suddenly found the Assassin already behind him, holding a knife. In front of everyone. It was humiliating, that's what it was –

And then Banjo had sat up, looking puzzled, and spat out a tooth –

'If it wasn't for Banjo going around with him all the time we could gang up on him,' said Catseye.

Medium Dave looked up, one hand clamping a handkerchief to his eye.

'*Gang up on him?*' he said.

'Yeah, it's all your fault,' Chickenwire went on.

'Oh, yeah? So it wasn't you who said, wow, ten thousand dollars, count me in?'

Chickenwire backed away. 'I didn't know there was going to be all this creepy stuff! I want to go home!'

Medium Dave hesitated, despite his pain and rage. This wasn't normal talk for Chickenwire, for all that he whined and grumbled. This was a strange place, no lie about that, and all that business with the teeth had been very ... odd, but he'd been out with Chickenwire when jobs had gone wrong and both the Watch *and* the Thieves' Guild had been after them and he'd been as cool as anyone. And if the Guild had been the ones to catch them they'd have nailed their ears to their ankles and thrown them in the river. In Medium Dave's book, which was a simple book and largely written in mental crayon, things didn't get creepier than that.

'What's up with you?' he said. 'All of you – you're acting like little kids!'

'Would he deliver to apes *earlier* than humans?'

* It had been Ma Lilywhite's dying wish, although she hadn't known it at the time. Her last words to her son were 'You try and get to the horses, I'll try to hold 'em off on the stairs, and if anything happens to me, take care of the dummy!'

'Interesting point, sir. Possibly you're referring to my theory that humans may have in fact descended from apes, of course,' said Ponder. 'A bold hypothesis which ought to sweep away the ignorance of centuries if the grants committee could just see their way clear to letting me hire a boat and sail around to the islands of –'

'I just thought he might deliver alphabetically,' said Ridcully.

There was a patter of soot in the cold fireplace.

'That's presumably him now, do you think?' Ridcully went on. 'Oh, well, I thought we should check –'

Something landed in the ashes. The two wizards stood quietly in the darkness while the figure picked itself up. There was a rustle of paper.

LET ME SEE NOW –

There was a click as Ridcully's pipe fell out of his mouth.

'Who the hell are you?' he said. 'Mr Stibbons, light a candle!'

Death backed away.

I'M THE HOGFATHER, OF COURSE. ER. HO. HO. HO. WHO WOULD YOU EXPECT TO COME DOWN A CHIMNEY ON A NIGHT LIKE THIS, MAY I ASK?

'No you're not!'

I AM. LOOK, I'VE GOT THE BEARD AND THE PILLOW AND EVERYTHING!

'You look extremely thin in the face!'

I'M . . . I . . . I'M NOT WELL. IT'S ALL . . . YES, IT'S ALL THIS SHERRY. AND RUSHING AROUND. I AM A BIT ILL.

'Terminally, I should say.' Ridcully grabbed the beard. There was a twang as the string gave way.

'It's a false beard!'

NO IT'S NOT, said Death desperately.

'Here's the hooks for the ears, which must have given *you* a bit of trouble, I must say!'

Ridcully flourished the incriminating evidence.

'What were you doing coming down the chimney?' he continued. 'Not in marvellous taste, I think.'

Death waved a small grubby scrap of paper defensively.

OFFICIAL LETTER TO THE HOGFATHER. SAYS HERE . . . he began, and then looked at the paper again. WELL, QUITE A LOT, IN FACT. IT'S A LONG LIST. LIBRARY STAMPS, REFERENCE BOOKS, PENCILS, BANANAS . . .

'The Librarian asked the Hogfather for those things?' said Ridcully. 'Why?'

I DON'T KNOW, said Death. This was a diplomatic answer. He kept his finger over a reference to the Archchancellor. The orang-utan for 'duck's bottom' was quite an interesting squiggle.

'I've got plenty in my desk drawer,' mused Ridcully. 'I'm quite happy to give them out to any chap provided he can prove he's used up the old one.'

THEY MUST SHOW YOU AN ABSENCE OF PENCIL?

'Of course. If he needed essential materials he need only have come to me. No man can tell you I'm an unreasonable chap.'

Death checked the list carefully.

THAT IS PRECISELY CORRECT, he confirmed, with anthropological exactitude.

'Except for the bananas, of course. I wouldn't keep fish in my desk.'

Death looked down at the list and then back up at Ridcully.

GOOD? he said, in the hope that this was the right response.

Wizards know when they are going to die.* Ridcully had no such premonitions, and to Ponder's horror prodded Death in the cushion.

'Why *you*?' he said. 'What's happened to the other fellow?'

I SUPPOSE I MUST TELL YOU.

In the house of Death, a whisper of shifting sand and the faintest chink of moving glass, somewhere in the darkness of the floor . . .

And, in the dry shadows, the sharp smell of snow and a thud of hooves.

Sideney almost swallowed his tongue when Teatime appeared beside him.

'Are we making progress?'

'Gnk–'

'I'm sorry?' said Teatime.

Sideney recovered himself. 'Er . . . some,' he said. 'We think we've worked out . . . er . . . one lock.'

Light gleamed off Teatime's eye.

'I believe there are seven of them?' said the Assassin.

'Yes, but . . . they're half magic and half real and half not there . . . I mean . . . there's parts of them that don't exist all the time –'

Mr Brown, who had been working at one of the locks, laid down his pick.

---

* They generally know in time to have their best robe cleaned, do some serious damage to the wine cellar and have a really good last meal. It's a nicer version of Death Row, with the bonus of no lawyers.

't's no good, mister,' he said. 'Can't even get a purchase with a crowbar. Maybe if I went back to the city and got a couple of dragons we could do something. You can melt through steel with them if you twist their necks right and feed 'em carbon.'

'I was told you were the best locksmith in the city,' said Teatime.

Behind him, Banjo shifted position.

Mr Brown looked annoyed . . .

'Well, *yes*,' he said. 'But locks don't generally alter 'emselves while you're working on 'em, that's what I'm saying.'

'And *I* thought you could open any lock anyone ever made,' said Teatime.

'Made by humans,' said Mr Brown sharply. 'And most dwarfs. I dunno *what* made these. You never said anything about magic.'

'That's a shame,' said Teatime. 'Then really I have no more need of your services. You may as well go back home.'

'I won't be sorry.' Mr Brown started putting things back into his tool bag. 'What about my money?'

'Do I owe you any?'

'I came along with you. I don't see it's my fault that this is all magic business. I should get *something*.'

'Ah, yes, I see your point,' said Teatime. 'Of course, you should get what you deserve. Banjo?'

Banjo lumbered forward, and then stopped.

Mr Brown's hand had come out of the bag holding a crowbar.

'You must think I was born yesterday, you slimy little bugger,' he said. 'I know your type. You think it's all some kind of game. You make little jokes to yourself and you think no one else notices and you think you're so smart. Well, Mr Teacup, I'm leaving, right? Right now. With what's coming to me. And you ain't stopping me. And Banjo certainly ain't. I knew old Ma Lilywhite back in the good old days. You think you're nasty? You think *you're* mean? Ma Lilywhite'd tear your ears off and spit 'em in your eye, you cocky little devil. And I worked with her, so you don't scare me and nor does little Banjo, poor sod that he is.'

Mr Brown glared at each of them in turn, flourishing the crowbar. Sideney cowered in front of the doors.

He saw Teatime nod gracefully, as if the man had made a small speech of thanks.

'I appreciate your point of view,' said Teatime. 'And, I have to repeat, it's Teh-ah-tim-eh. Now, please, Banjo.'

Banjo loomed over Mr Brown, reached down and lifted him up by the crowbar so sharply that his feet came out of his boots.

'Here, you know me, Banjo!' the locksmith croaked, struggling in mid-air. 'I remembers you when you was little, I used to sit you on my knees, I often used to work for your ma –'

'D'you like apples?' Banjo rumbled.

Brown struggled.

'You got to say yes,' Banjo said.

'Yes!'

'D'you like pears? You got to say yes.'

'All right, yes!'

'D'you like falling down the stairs?'

Medium Dave held up his hands for quiet.

He glared at the gang.

'This place is getting to you, right? But we've all been in bad places before, right?'

'Not this bad,' said Chickenwire. 'I've never been anywhere where it hurts to look at the sky. It give me the creeps.'

'Chick's a little baby, nyer nyer nyer,' sang Catseye.

They looked at him. He coughed nervously.

'Sorry ... don't know why I said that ...'

'If we stick together we'll be fine –'

'Eeeny meeny miney mo ...' mumbled Catseye.

'What? What are you talking about?'

'Sorry ... it just sort of slipped out ...'

'What I'm trying to say,' said Medium Dave, 'is that if –'

'Peachy keeps making faces at me!'

'I didn't!'

'Liar, liar, pants on fire!'

Two things happened at this point. Medium Dave lost his temper, and Peachy screamed.

A small wisp of smoke was rising from his trousers.

He hopped around, beating desperately at himself.

'Who did that? Who did that?' demanded Medium Dave.

'I didn't see anyone,' said Chickenwire. 'I mean, no one was *near* him. Catseye said "pants on fire" and next minute –'

'Now he's sucking his thumb!' Catseye jeered. 'Nyer nyer nyer! Crying for Mummy! You know what happens to kids who suck their thumbs, there's this big monster with scissors all –'

'Will you stop talking like that!' shouted Medium Dave. 'Blimey, it *is* like dealing with a bunch of –'

Someone screamed, high above. It went on for a while and

seemed to be getting nearer, but then it stopped and was replaced by a rush of thumping and an occasional sound like a coconut being bounced on a stone floor.

Medium Dave got to the door just in time to see the body of Mr Brown the locksmith tumble past, moving quite fast and not at all neatly. A moment later his bag somersaulted around the curve of the stairs. It split as it bounced and there was a jangle as tools and lockpicks bounced out and followed their late owner.

He'd been moving quite fast. He'd probably roll all the way to the bottom.

Medium Dave looked up. Two turns above him, on the opposite side of the huge shaft, Banjo was watching him.

Banjo didn't know right from wrong. He'd always left that sort of thing to his brother.

'Er . . . poor guy must've slipped,' Medium Dave mumbled.

'Oh, yeah . . . slipped,' said Peachy.

He looked up, too.

It was funny. He hadn't noticed them before. The white tower had seemed to glow from within. But now there were shadows, moving across the stone. *In* the stone.

'What was that?' he said. 'That sound . . .'

'What sound?'

'It sounded . . . like knives scraping,' said Peachy. 'Really close.'

'There's only us here!' said Medium Dave. 'What're you afraid of? Attack by daisies? Come on . . . let's go and help him . . .'

She *couldn't* walk through the door. It simply resisted any such effort. She ended up merely bruised. So Susan turned the doorknob instead.

She heard the oh god gasp. But she was used to the idea of buildings that were bigger on the inside. Her grandfather had never been able to get a handle on dimensions.

The second thing the eye was drawn to were the staircases. They started opposite one another in what was now a big round tower, its ceiling lost in the haze. The spirals circled into infinity.

Susan's eyes went back to the first thing.

It was a large conical heap in the middle of the floor.

It was white. It glistened in the cool light that shone down from the mists.

'It's teeth,' she said.

'I think I'm going to throw up,' said the oh god miserably.

'There's nothing that scary about teeth,' said Susan. She didn't mean it. The heap was very horrible indeed.

'Did I say I was scared? I'm just hung over again . . . Oh, *me* . . .'

Susan advanced on the heap, moving warily.

They were *small* teeth. Children's teeth. Whoever had piled them up hadn't been very careful about it, either. A few had been scattered across the floor. She knew because she trod on one, and the slippery little crunching sound made her desperate not to tread on any more.

Whoever had piled them up had presumably been the one who'd drawn the chalk marks around the obscene heap.

'There're so *many*,' whispered Bilious.

'At least twenty million, given the size of the average milk tooth,' said Susan. She was shocked to find that it came almost automatically.

'How can you possibly know that?'

'Volume of a cone,' said Susan. 'Pi times the square of the radius times the height divided by three. I bet Miss Butts never thought it'd come in handy in a place like this.'

'That's amazing. You did it in your head?'

'This isn't right,' said Susan quietly. 'I don't think this is what the Tooth Fairy is all about. All that effort to get the teeth, and then just to dump them like this? No. Anyway, there's a cigarette end on the floor. I don't see the Tooth Fairy as someone who rolls her own.'

She stared down at the chalk marks.

Voices high above her made her look up. She thought she saw a head look over the stair rail, and then draw back again. She didn't see much of the face, but what she saw didn't look fairylike.

She glanced back at the circle of chalk around the teeth. Someone had wanted all the teeth in one place and had drawn a circle to show people where they had to go.

There were a few symbols scrawled around the circle.

She had a good memory for small details. It was another family trait. And a small detail stirred in her memory like a sleepy bee.

'Oh, *no*,' she breathed. 'Surely no one would try to –'

Someone shouted, someone up in the whiteness.

A body rolled down the stairs nearest her. It had been a skinny, middle-aged man. Technically it still was, but the long spiral staircase had not been kind.

It tumbled across the white marble and slid to a boneless halt.

Then, as she hurried towards the body, it faded away, leaving nothing behind but a smear of blood.

A jingle noise made her look back up the stairs. Spinning over and over, making salmon leaps in the air, a crowbar bounded over the last dozen steps and landed point first on a flagstone, staying upright and vibrating.

Chickenwire reached the top of the stairs, panting.

'There's people down there, Mister Teatime!' he wheezed. 'Dave and the others've gone down to catch them, Mister Teatime!'

'Teh-ah-tim-eh,' said Teatime, without taking his eyes off the wizard.

'That's right, sir!'

'Well?' said Teatime. 'Just ... do away with them.'

'Er ... one of them's a girl, sir.'

Teatime still didn't look round. He waved a hand vaguely.

'Then do away with them *politely*.'

'Yes, Mister ... yes, right ...' Chickenwire coughed. 'Don't you want to find out why they're here, sir?'

'Good heavens, no. Why should I want to do that? Now go away.'

Chickenwire stood there for a moment, and then hurried off.

As he scurried down the stairs he thought he heard a creak, as of an ancient wooden door.

He went pale.

It was just a door, said the sensible bit in front of his brain. There were hundreds of them in this place, although, come to think of it, none of them had creaked.

The other bit, the bit that hung around in dark places nearly at the top of his spinal column, said: But it's not one of them, and you know it, because you know which door it really is ...

He hadn't heard that creak for thirty years.

He gave a little yelp and started to take the stairs four at a time.

In the hollows and corners, the shadows grew darker.

Susan ran up a flight of stairs, dragging the oh god behind her.

'Do you know what they've been doing?' she said. 'You know why they've got all those teeth in a circle? The *power* ... oh my ...'

'I'm not going to,' said the head waiter, firmly.

'Look, I'll buy you a better pair after Hogswatch –'

'There's two more Shoe Pastry, one for *Purée de la Terre* and three more *Tourte à la Boue*,' said a waiter, hurrying in.

'Mud pies!' moaned the waiter. 'I can't believe we're selling mud pies. And now you want *my* boots!'

'With cream and sugar, mind you. A real taste of Ankh-Morpork. And we can get at least four helpings off those boots. Fair's fair. We're all in our socks –'

'Table seven says the steaks were lovely but a bit tough,' said a waiter, rushing past.

'Right. Use a larger hammer next time and boil them for longer.' The manager turned back to the suffering head waiter. 'Look, Bill,' he said, taking him by the shoulder. 'This isn't food. No one expects it to be food. If people wanted food they'd stay at home, isn't that so? They come here for ambience. For the experience. This isn't cookery, Bill. This is *cuisine*. See? And they're coming back for more.'

'Yeah, but *old boots* . . .'

'Dwarfs eats rats,' said the manager. 'And trolls eat rocks. There's folks in Howondaland that eat insects and folks on the Counterweight Continent eat soup made out of bird spit. At least the boots have been on a cow.'

'And mud?' said the head waiter, gloomily.

'Isn't there an old proverb that says a man must eat a bushel of dirt before he dies?'

'Yes, but not all at once.'

'Bill?' said the manager, kindly, picking up a spatula.

'Yes, boss?'

'Get those damn boots off right now, will you?'

When Chickenwire reached the bottom of the tower he was trembling, and not just from the effort. He headed straight for the door until Medium Dave grabbed him.

'Let me out! It's after me!'

'Look at his *face*,' said Catseye. 'Looks like he's seen a ghost!'

'Yeah, well, it *ain't* a ghost,' muttered Chickenwire. 'It's *worse'n* a ghost –'

Medium Dave slapped him across the face.

'Pull yourself together! Look around! Nothing's chasing you! Anyway, it's not as though we couldn't put up a fight, right?'

Terror had had time to drain away a little. Chickenwire looked back up the stairs. There was nothing there.

'Good,' said Medium Dave, watching his face. 'Now ... What happened?'

Chickenwire looked at his feet.

'I thought it was the wardrobe,' he muttered. 'Go on, laugh ...'

They didn't laugh.

'What wardrobe?' said Catseye.

'Oh, when I was a kid ...' Chickenwire waved his arms vaguely. 'We had this big ole wardrobe, if you must know. Oak. It had this ... this ... on the door there was this ... sort of ... *face*.' He looked at their faces, which were equally wooden. 'I mean, not an actual face, there was ... all this ... decoration round the keyhole, sort of flowers and leaves and stuff, but if you looked at it in the ... right way ... it was a face and they put it in my room 'cos it was so big and in the night ... in the night ... in the night –'

They were grown men or at least had lived for several decades, which in some societies is considered the same thing. But you had to stare at a man so creased up with dread.

'Yes?' said Catseye hoarsely.

'... it whispered things,' said Chickenwire, in a quiet little voice, like a vole in a dungeon.

They looked at one another.

'What things?' said Medium Dave.

'I don't *know*! I always had my head under the pillow! Anyway, it's just something from when I was a kid, all right? Our dad got rid of it in the finish. Burned it. And I *watched*.'

They mentally shook themselves, as people do when their minds emerge back into the light.

'It's like me and the dark,' said Catseye.

'Oh, don't you start,' said Medium Dave. 'Anyway, you *ain't* afraid of the dark. You're famed for it. I been working with you in all kinds of cellars and stuff. I mean, that's how you got your *name*. Catseye. Sees like a cat.'

'Yeah, well ... you try an' make up for it, don't you?' said Catseye. ''Cos when you're grown you know it's just shadows and stuff. Besides, it ain't like the dark we used to have in the cellar.'

'Oh, they had a special kind of a dark when you was a lad, did they?' said Medium Dave. 'Not like the kind of dark you get these days, eh?'

Sarcasm didn't work.

'No,' said Catseye, simply. 'It wasn't. In our cellar, it wasn't.'

'Our mam used to wallop us if we went down to the cellar,' said Medium Dave. 'She had her still down there.'

'Yeah?' said Catseye, from somewhere far off. 'Well, *our* dad used to wallop us if we tried to get out. Now shut up talking about it.'

They reached the bottom of the stairs.

There was an absence of anybody. And any body.

'He couldn't have survived that, could he?' said Medium Dave.

'I saw him as he went past,' said Catseye. 'Necks aren't supposed to bend that way –'

He squinted upwards.

'Who's that moving up there?'

'How are their *necks* moving?' quavered Chickenwire.

'Split up!' said Medium Dave. 'And this time all take a stairway. Then they can't come back down!'

'Who're they? Why're they here?'

'Why're *we* here?' said Peachy. He started, and looked behind him.

'Taking our money? After us putting up with *him*?'

'Yeah . . .' said Peachy distantly, trailing after the others. 'Er . . . did you hear that noise just then?'

'What noise?'

'A sort of clipping, snipping . . .?'

'No.'

'No.'

'No. You must have imagined it.'

Peachy nodded miserably.

As he walked up the stairs, little shadows raced through the stone and followed his feet.

Susan darted off the stairs and dragged the oh god along a corridor lined with white doors.

'I think they saw us,' she said. 'And if they're tooth fairies there's been a really *stupid* equal opportunities policy . . .'

She pushed open a door.

There were no windows to the room, but it was lit perfectly well by the walls themselves. Down the middle of the room was something like a display case, its lid gaping open. Bits of card littered the floor.

She reached down and picked one up and read: 'Thomas Ague, aged 4 and nearly three quarters, 9 Castle View, Sto Lat'. The writing was in a meticulous rounded script.

She crossed the passage to another room, where there was the same scene of devastation.

'So now we know where the teeth were,' she said. 'They must've taken them out of everywhere and carried them downstairs.'

'What for?'

She sighed. 'It's such old magic it isn't even magic any more,' she said. 'If you've got a piece of someone's hair, or a nail clipping, or a tooth – you can control them.'

The oh god tried to focus.

'That heap's controlling millions of children?'

'Yes. Adults too, by now.'

'And you . . . you could make them think things and do things?'

She nodded. 'Yes.'

'You could get them to open Dad's wallet and post the contents to some address?'

'Well, I hadn't thought of *that*, but yes, I suppose you could . . .'

'Or go downstairs and smash all the bottles in the drinks cabinet and promise never to take a drink when they grow up?' said the oh god hopefully.

'What are you talking about?'

'It's all right for you. You don't wake up every morning and see your whole life flush before your eyes.'

Medium Dave and Catseye ran down the passage and stopped where it forked.

'You go that way, I'll –'

'Why don't we stick together?' said Catseye.

'What's got into everyone? I saw you bite the throats out of a coupla guard dogs when we did that job in Quirm! Want me to hold your hand? You check the doors down there, I'll check them along here.'

He walked off.

Catseye peered down the other passage.

There weren't many doors down there. It wasn't very long. And, as Teatime had said, there was nothing dangerous here that they hadn't brought with them.

He heard voices coming from a doorway and sagged with relief.

He could *deal* with humans.

As he approached, a sound made him look round.

Shadows were racing down the passage behind him. They cascaded down the walls and flowed over the ceiling.

Where shadows met they became darker. And darker.

And rose. And leapt.

*

'What was that?' said Susan.

'Sounded like the start of a scream,' said Bilious.

Susan threw open the door.

There was no one outside.

There was movement, though. She saw a patch of darkness in the corner of a wall shrink and fade, and another shadow slid around the bend of the corridor.

And there was a pair of boots in the centre of the corridor.

She hadn't remembered any boots there before.

She sniffed. The air tasted of rats, and damp, and mould.

'Let's get out of here,' she said.

'How're we going to find this Violet in all these rooms?'

'I don't know. I should be able to . . . sense her, but I can't.' Susan peered around the end of the corridor. She could hear men shouting, some way off.

They slipped out on to the stairs again and managed another flight. There were more rooms here, and in each one a cabinet that had been broken open.

Shadows moved in the corners. The effect was as though some invisible light source was gently shifting.

'This reminds me a lot of your . . . um . . . of your grandfather's place,' said the oh god.

'I know,' said Susan. 'There aren't any rules except the ones he makes up as he goes along. I can't see *him* being very happy if someone got in and started pulling the library apart –'

She stopped. When she spoke again her voice had a different tone.

'This is a children's place,' she said. 'The rules are what children believe.'

'Well, that's a relief.'

'You think so? Things aren't going to be *right*. In the Soul Cake Duck's country ducks *can* lay chocolate eggs, in the same way that Death's country is black and sombre because that's what people believe. He's very conventional about that sort of thing. Skull and bone decorations all over the place. And *this* place –'

'Pretty flowers and an odd sky.'

'I think it's going to be a lot worse than that. And very odd, too.'

'More odd than it is now?'

'I don't think it's possible to die here.'

'That man who fell down the stairs looked pretty dead to *me*.'

'Oh, you die. But not here. You . . . let's see . . . yes . . . you go somewhere else. Away. You're just not seen any more. That's about all you understand when you're three. Grandfather said it wasn't like that fifty years ago. He said you often couldn't see the bed for everyone having a good cry. Now they just tell the child that Grandma's gone. For three weeks Twyla thought her uncle'd been buried in the sad patch behind the garden shed along with Buster and Meepo and all three Bulgies.'

'Three Bulgies?'

'Gerbils. They tend to die a lot,' said Susan. 'They trick is to replace them when she's not looking. You really don't know *anything*, do you?'

'Er ... hello?'

The voice came from the corridor.

They worked their way round to the next room.

There, sitting on the floor and tied to the leg of a white display case, was Violet. She looked up in apprehension, and then in bewilderment, and finally in growing recognition.

'Aren't you –?'

'Yes, yes, we see each other sometimes in Biers, and when you came for Twyla's last tooth you were so shocked that I could see you I had to give you a drink to get your nerves back,' said Susan, fumbling with the ropes. 'I don't think we've got a lot of time.'

'And who's he?'

The oh god tried to push his lank hair into place.

'Oh, he's just a god,' said Susan. 'His name's Bilious.'

'Do you drink at all?' said the oh god.

'What sort of quest –'

'He needs to know before he decides whether he hates you or not,' said Susan. 'It's a god thing.'

'No, I don't,' said Violet. 'What an idea. I've got the blue ribbon!'

The oh god raised his eyebrows at Susan.

'That means she's a member of Offler's League of Temperance,' said Susan. 'They sign a pledge not to touch alcohol. I can't think why. Of course, Offler's a crocodile. They don't go in bars much. They're into water.'

'Not touch alcohol at all?' said the oh god.

'Never!' said Violet. 'My dad's very strict about that sort of thing!'

After a moment Susan felt forced to wave a hand across their locked gaze.

'Can we get on?' she said. 'Good. Who brought you here, Violet?'

'I don't know! I was doing the collection as usual, and then I thought I heard someone following me, and then it all went dark, and when I came to we were ... Have you seen what it's like outside?'

'Yes.'

'Well, we were there. The big one was carrying me. The one they call Banjo. He's not bad, just a bit ... odd. Sort of ... slow. He just watches me. The others are thugs. Watch out for the one with the glass eye. They're all afraid of him. Except Banjo.'

'Glass eye?'

'He's dressed like an Assassin. He's called Teatime. I think they're trying to steal something ... They spent *ages* carting the teeth out. Little teeth everywhere ... It was horrible! Thank you,' she added to the oh god, who had helped her on to her feet.

'They've piled them up in a magic circle downstairs,' said Susan.

Violet's eyes and mouth formed three Os. It was like looking at a pink bowling ball.

'What for?'

'I think they're using them to control the children. By magic.'

Violet's mouth opened wider.

'That's *horrid*.'

Horrible, thought Susan. The word is 'horrible'. 'Horrid' is a childish word selected to impress nearby males with one's fragility, if I'm any judge. She knew it was unkind and counter-productive of her to think like that. She also knew it was probably an accurate observation, which only made it worse.

'Yes,' she said.

'There was a wizard! He's got a pointy hat!'

'I think we should get her out of here,' said the oh god, in a tone of voice that Susan considered was altogether too dramatic.

'Good idea,' she conceded. 'Let's go.'

Catseye's boots had snapped their laces. It was as if he'd been pulled upwards so fast they simply couldn't keep up.

That worried Medium Dave. So did the smell. There was no smell at all in the rest of the tower, but just here there was a lingering odour of mushrooms.

His forehead wrinkled. Medium Dave was a thief and a murderer and therefore had a highly developed moral sense. He preferred not to steal from poor people, and not only because they never had anything worth stealing. If it was necessary to hurt anyone, he tried to leave wounds that would heal. And when in the course of his activities he had to kill people then he made some effort to see that they did not suffer much or at least made as few noises as possible.

This whole business was getting on his nerves. Usually, he didn't even notice that he had any. There was a wrongness to everything that grated on his bones.

And a pair of boots was all that remained of old Catseye.

He drew his sword.

Above him, the creeping shadows moved and flowed away.

Susan edged up to the entrance to the stairways and peered around into the point of a crossbow.

'Now, all of you step out where I can see you,' said Peachy conversationally. 'And don't touch that sword, lady. You'll probably hurt yourself.'

Susan tried to make herself unseen, and failed. Usually it was so easy to do that that it happened automatically, usually with embarrassing results. She could be idly reading a book while people searched the room for her. But here, despite every effort, she seemed to remain obstinately visible.

'You don't own this place,' she said, stepping back.

'No, but you see this crossbow? I own this crossbow. So you just walk ahead of me, right, and we'll all go and see Mister Teatime.'

'Excuse me, I just want to check something,' said Bilious. To Susan's amazement he leaned over and touched the point of the arrow.

'Here! What did you do that for?' said Peachy, stepping back.

'I felt it, but of course a certain amount of pain sensation would be part of normal sensory response,' said the oh god. 'I warn you, there's a very good chance that I might be immortal.'

'Yes, but we probably aren't,' said Susan.

'Immortal, eh?' said Peachy. 'So if I was to shoot you inna head, you wouldn't die?'

'I suppose when you put it like that . . . I do know I feel pain . . .'

'Right. You just keep moving, then.'

'When something happens,' said Susan, out of the corner of her mouth, 'you two try to get downstairs and out, all right? If the worst comes to the worst, the horse will take you out of here.'

'If something happens,' whispered the oh god.

'When,' said Susan.

Behind them, Peachy looked around. He knew he'd feel a lot

better when any of the others turned up. It was almost a relief to have prisoners.

Out of the corner of her eye Susan saw something move on the stairs on the opposite side of the shaft. For a moment she thought she saw several flashes like metal blades catching the light.

She heard a gasp behind her.

The man with the crossbow was standing very still and staring at the opposite stairs.

'Oh, noooo,' he said, under his breath.

'What is it?' said Susan.

He stared at her. 'You can see it too?'

'The thing like a lot of blades clicking together?' said Susan.

'Oh, *noooo* . . .'

'It was only there for a moment,' said Susan. 'It's gone now,' she said. 'Somewhere else,' she added.

'It's the Scissor Man . . .'

'Who's he?' said the oh god.

'No one!' snapped Peachy, trying to pull himself together. 'There's no such thing as the Scissor Man, all right?'

'Ah . . . *yes*. When you were little, did you suck your thumb?' said Susan. 'Because the only Scissor Man I know is the one people used to frighten children with. They said he'd turn up and –'

'Shutupshutupshutup!' said Peachy, prodding her with the crossbow. 'Kids believe all kinds of crap! But I'm grown up now, right, and I can open beer bottles with other people's teeth an– oh, *gods* . . .'

Susan heard the snip, snip. It sounded very close now.

Peachy had his eyes shut.

'Is there anything behind me?' he quavered.

Susan pushed the others aside and waved frantically towards the bottom of the stairs.

'No,' she said, as they hurried away.

'Is there anything standing on the stairs at all?'

'No.'

'Right! If you see that one-eyed bastard you tell him he can keep the money!'

He turned and ran.

When Susan turned to go up the stairs the Scissor Man was there.

It wasn't man-shaped. It was something like an ostrich, and something like a lizard on its hind legs, but almost entirely like something made out of blades. Every time it moved a thousand blades went snip, snip.

Its long silver neck curved and a head made of shears stared down at her.

'You're not looking for me,' she said. 'You're not *my* nightmare.'

The blades tilted this way and that. The Scissor Man was trying to think.

'I remember you came for Twyla,' said Susan, stepping forward. 'That damn governess had told her what happens to little girls who suck their thumbs, remember? Remember the *poker*? I bet you needed a hell of a lot of sharpening afterwards ...'

The creature lowered its head, stepped carefully around her in as polite a way as it could manage, and clanked on down the stairs after Peachy.

Susan ran on towards the top of the tower.

Sideney put a green filter over his lantern and pressed down with a small silver rod that had an emerald set on its tip. A piece of the lock moved. There was a whirring from inside the door and something went click.

He sagged with relief. It is said that the prospect of hanging concentrates the mind wonderfully, but it was Valium compared to being watched by Mister Teatime.

'I, er, think that's the third lock,' he said. 'Green light is what opens it. I remember the fabulous lock of the Hall of Murgle, which could only be opened by the Hubward wind, although that was –'

'I commend your expertise,' said Teatime. 'And the other four?'

Sideney looked up nervously at the silent bulk of Banjo, and licked his lips.

'Well, of course, if I'm right, and the locks depend on certain conditions, well, we could be here for years ...' he ventured. 'Supposing they can only be opened by, say, a small blond child holding a mouse? On a Tuesday? In the rain?'

'You can find out what the nature of the spell is?' said Teatime.

'Yes, yes, of course, yes.' Sideney waved his hands urgently. 'That's how I worked out this one. Reverse thaumaturgy, yes, certainly. Er. In time.'

'We have lots of time,' said Teatime.

'Perhaps a *little* more time than that,' Sideney quavered. 'The processes are very, very, very ... difficult.'

'Oh, dear. If it's too much for you, you've only got to say,' said Teatime.

'No!' Sideney yipped, and then managed to get some self-control. 'No. No. No, I can ... I'm sure I shall work them out soon –'

'*Jolly* good,' said Teatime.

The student wizard looked down. A wisp of vapour oozed from the crack between the doors.

'Do you know what's in here, Mister Teatime?'

'No.'

'Ah. Right.' Sideney stared mournfully at the fourth lock. It was amazing how much you remembered when someone like Teatime was around.

He gave him a nervous look. 'There's not going to be any more violent deaths, are there?' he said. 'I just can't *stand* the sight of violent deaths!'

Teatime put a comforting arm around his shoulders. 'Don't worry,' he said. 'I'm on *your* side. A violent death is the last thing that'll happen to you.'

'Mister Teatime?'

He turned. Medium Dave stepped on to the landing.

'Someone else is in the tower,' he said.' 'They've got Catseye. I don't know how. I've got Peachy watching the stairs and I ain't sure where Chickenwire is.'

Teatime looked back to Sideney, who started prodding at the fourth lock again in a feverish attempt not to die.

'Why are you telling me? I thought I was paying you big strong men a lot of money to deal with this sort of thing.'

Medium Dave's lips framed some words, but when he spoke he said, 'All right, but what are we up against here? Eh? Old Man Trouble or the bogeyman or what?'

Teatime sighed.

'Some of the Tooth Fairy's employees, I assume,' he said.

'Not if they're like the ones that were here,' said Medium Dave. 'They were just civilians. It looks like the ground opened and swallowed Catseye up.' He thought about this. 'I mean the ceiling,' he corrected himself. A horrible image had just passed across his under-used imagination.

Teatime walked across to the stairwell and looked down. Far below, the pile of teeth looked like a white circle.

'And the girl's gone,' said Medium Dave.

'Really? I thought I said she should be killed.'

Medium Dave hesitated. The boys had been brought up by Ma

Lilywhite to be respectful to women as delicate and fragile creatures, and were soundly thrashed if disrespectful tendencies were perceived by Ma's incredibly sensitive radar. And it was truly incredibly sensitive. Ma could hear what you were doing three rooms away, a terrible thing for a growing lad.

That sort of thing leaves a mark. Ma Lilywhite certainly could. As for the others, they had no objections in practice to the disposal of anyone who got between them and large sums of money, but there was a general unspoken resentment at being told by Teatime to kill someone just because he had no further use for them. It wasn't that it was unprofessional. Only Assassins thought like that. It was just that there were things you did do, and things you didn't do. And this was one of the things you didn't do.

'We thought . . . well, you never know . . .'

'She wasn't necessary,' said Teatime. 'Few people are.'

Sideney thumbed hurriedly through his notebooks.

'Anyway, the place is a maze –' Medium Dave said.

'Sadly, this is so,' said Teatime. 'But I am sure they will be able to find us. It's probably too much to hope that they intend something heroic.'

Violet and the oh god hurried down the stairs.

'Do you know how to get back?' said Violet.

'Don't you?'

'I think there's a . . . a kind of soft place. If you walk at it knowing it's there you go *through*.'

'You know where it is?'

'No! I've never been here before! They had a bag on my head when we came! All I ever did was take the teeth from under the pillows!' Violet started to sob. 'You just get this list and about five minutes' training and they even dock you ten pence a week for the ladder and I know I made that mistake with little William Rubin but they should of *said*, you're *supposed* to take any teeth you –'

'Er . . . mistake?' said Bilious, trying to get her to hurry.

'Just because he slept with his head under the pillow but they give you the pliers *anyway* and no one told *me* that you shouldn't –'

She certainly *did* have a pleasant voice, Bilious told himself. It was just that in a funny way it grated, too. It was like listening to a talking flute.

'I think we'd just better get outside,' he said. 'In case they hear us,' he hinted.

'What sort of godding do you do?' said Violet.

'Er . . . oh, I . . . this and that . . . I . . . er . . .' Bilious tried to think through the pounding headache. And then he had one of those ideas, the kind that only sound good after a lot of alcohol. Someone else may have drunk the drinks, but he managed to snag the idea.

'I'm actually self-employed,' he said, as brightly as he could manage.

'How can you be a self-employed god?'

'Ah, well, you see, if any other god wants, perhaps, you know, a holiday or something, I cover for them. Yes. That's what I do.'

Unwisely, in the circumstances, he let his inventiveness impress him.

'Oh, yes. I'm very busy. Rushed off my feet. They're always employing me. You've no idea. They don't think twice about pushing off for a month as a big white bull or a swan or something and it's always, "Oh, Bilious, old chap, just take care of things while I'm away, will you? Answer the prayers and so on." I hardly get a minute to myself but of course you can't turn down work these days.'

Violet was round-eyed with fascination.

'And are you covering for anyone right now?' she asked.

'Um, yes . . . the God of Hangovers, actually . . .'

'A God of Hangovers? How awful!'

Bilious looked down at his stained and wretched toga.

'I suppose it is . . .' he mumbled.

'You're not very good at it.'

'You don't have to tell me.'

'You're more cut out to be one of the important gods,' said Violet, admiringly. 'I can just see you as Io or Fate or one of those.'

Bilious stared at her with his mouth open.

'I could tell at once you weren't right,' she went on. 'Not for some horrible little god. You could even be Offler with calves like yours.'

'Could I? I mean . . . oh, yes. Sometimes. Of course, I have to wear fangs –'

And then someone was holding a sword to his throat.

'What's this?' said Chickenwire. 'Lover's Lane?'

'You leave him alone, you!' shouted Violet. 'He's a god! You'll be really sorry!'

Bilious swallowed, but very gently. It was a sharp sword.

'A god, eh?' said Chickenwire. 'What of?'

Bilious tried to swallow again.

'Oh, bit o' this, bit o' that,' he mumbled.

'Cor,' said Chickenwire. 'Well, I'm impressed. I can see I'm going to have to be dead careful here, eh? Don't want you smiting me with thunderbolts, do I? Puts a crimp in the day, that sort of thing –'

Bilious didn't dare move his head. But out of the corner of his eye he was sure he could see shadows moving very fast across the walls.

'Dear me, out of thunderbolts, are we?' Chickenwire sneered. 'Well, y'know, I've never –'

There was a creak.

Chickenwire's face was a few inches from Bilious. The oh god saw his expression change.

The man's eyes rolled. His lips said '. . . nur . . .'

Bilious risked stepping back. Chickenwire's sword didn't move. He stood there, trembling slightly, like a man who wants to turn round to see what's behind him but doesn't dare to in case he does.

As far as Bilious was concerned, it had just been a creak.

He looked up at the thing on the landing above.

'Who put that there?' said Violet.

It was just a wardrobe. Dark oak, a bit of fancy woodwork glued on in an effort to diguise the undisguisable fact that it was just an upright box. It was a wardrobe.

'You didn't, you know, try to cast a thunderbolt and go on a few letters too many?' she went on.

'Huh?' said Bilious, looking from the stricken man to the wardrobe. It was so ordinary it was . . . odd.

'I mean, thunderbolts begin with T and wardrobes . . .'

Violet's lips moved silently. Part of Bilious thought: I'm attracted to a girl who actually has to shut down all other brain functions in order to think about the order of the letters of the alphabet. On the other hand, *she's* attracted to someone who's wearing a toga that looks as though a family of weasels have had a party in it, so maybe I'll stop this thought right here.

But the major part of his brain thought: why's this man making little bubbling noises? It's just a *wardrobe*, for my sake!

'No, no,' mumbled Chickenwire. 'I don't *wanna!*'

The sword clanged on the floor.

He took a step backwards up the stairs, but very slowly, as if he was doing it despite every effort his muscles could muster.

'Don't want to what?' said Violet.

Chickenwire spun round. Bilious had never seen that happen before. People turned round quickly, yes, but Chickenwire just revolved as if some giant hand had been placed on his head and twisted a hundred and eighty degrees.

'No. No. No,' Chickenwire whined. 'No.'

He tottered up the steps.

'You got to help me,' he whispered.

'What's the matter?' said Bilious. 'It's just a wardrobe, isn't it? It's for putting all your old clothes in so that there's no room for your *new* clothes.'

The doors of the wardrobe swung open.

Chickenwire managed to thrust out his arms and grab the sides and, for a moment, he stood quite still.

Then he was pulled into the wardrobe in one sudden movement and the doors slammed shut.

The little brass key turned in the lock with a click.

'We ought to get him out,' said the oh god, running up the steps.

'Why?' Violet demanded. 'They are *not* very nice people! I know that one. When he brought me food he made ... suggestive comments.'

'Yes, but ...' Bilious hadn't ever seen a face like that, outside of a mirror. Chickenwire had looked very, very sick.

He turned the key and opened the doors.

'Oh dear ...'

'I don't want to see! I don't want to see!' said Violet, looking over his shoulder.

Bilious reached down and picked up a pair of boots that stood neatly in the middle of the wardrobe's floor.

Then he put them back carefully and walked around the wardrobe. It was plywood. The words 'Dratley and Sons, Phedre Road, Ankh-Morpork' were stamped in one corner in faded ink.

'Is it magic?' said Violet nervously.

'I don't know if something magic has the maker's name on it,' said Bilious.

'There *are* magic wardrobes,' said Violet nervously. 'If you go into them, you come out in a magic land.'

Bilious looked at the boots again.

'Um ... yes,' he said.

I THINK I MUST TELL YOU SOMETHING, said Death.

'Yes, I think you should,' said Ridcully. 'I've got little devils running round the place eating socks and pencils, earlier tonight we sobered up someone who thinks he's a God of Hangovers and half my wizards are trying to cheer up the Cheerful Fairy. *We* thought something must've happened to the Hogfather. We were right, right?'

'*Hex* was right, Archchancellor,' Ponder corrected him.

Hex? What is Hex?

'Er . . . Hex thinks – that is, *calculates* – that there's been a big change in the nature of belief today,' said Ponder. He felt, he did not know why, that Death was probably not in favour of unliving things that thought.

Mr Hex was remarkably astute. The Hogfather has been . . . Death paused. There is no sensible human word. Dead, in a way, but not exactly . . . A god cannot be killed. Never completely killed. He has been, shall we say, severely reduced.

'Ye gods!' said Ridcully. 'Who'd want to kill off the old boy?'

He has enemies.

'What did he do? Miss a chimney?'

Every living thing has enemies.

'What, everything?'

Yes. Everything. Powerful enemies. But they have gone too far this time. Now they are using people.

'Who are?'

Those who think the universe should be a lot of rocks moving in curves. Have you ever heard of the Auditors?

'I suppose the Bursar may have done –'

Not auditors of money. Auditors of reality. They think of life as a stain on the universe. A pestilence. Messy. Getting in the way.

'In the way of what?'

The efficient running of the universe.

'I thought it *was* run for us . . . Well, for the Professor of Applied Anthropics, actually, but we're allowed to tag along,' said Ridcully. He scratched his chin. 'And I could certainly run a marvellous university here if only we didn't have to have these damn students underfoot all the time.'

Quite so.

'They want to get *rid* of us?'

They want you to be . . . less . . . Damn, I've forgotten the word. Untruthful? The Hogfather is a symbol of this . . . Death snapped his fingers, causing echoes to bounce off the walls, and added, wistful lying?

'Untruthful?' said Ridcully. '*Me?* I'm as honest as the day is long! Yes, what is it *this* time?'

Ponder had tugged at his robe and now he whispered something in his ear. Ridcully cleared his throat.

'I am reminded that this is in fact the shortest day of the year,' he said. 'However, this does *not* undermine the point that I just made, although I thank my colleague for his invaluable support and constant readiness to correct minor if not downright trivial errors. I am a remarkably truthful man, sir. Things said at University council meetings don't count.'

I MEAN HUMANITY IN GENERAL. ER ... THE ACT OF TELLING THE UNIVERSE IT IS OTHER THAN IT IS?

'You've got me there,' said Ridcully. 'Anyway, why're *you* doing the job?'

SOMEONE MUST. IT IS VITALLY IMPORTANT. THEY MUST BE SEEN, AND BELIEVED. BEFORE DAWN, THERE MUST BE ENOUGH BELIEF IN THE HOGFATHER.

'Why?' said Ridcully.

SO THAT THE SUN WILL COME UP.

The two wizards gawped at him.

I SELDOM JOKE, said Death.

At which point there was a scream of horror.

'That sounded like the Bursar,' said Ridcully. 'And he's been doing so well up to now.'

The reason for the Bursar's scream lay on the floor of his bedroom.

It was a man. He was dead. No one alive had that kind of expression.

Some of the other wizards had got there first. Ridcully pushed his way through the crowd.

'Ye gods,' he said. 'What a face! He looks as though he died of fright! What happened?'

'Well,' said the Dean, 'as far as I can tell, the Bursar opened his wardrobe and found the man inside.'

'Really? I wouldn't have said the poor old Bursar was all that frightening.'

'No, Archchancellor. The corpse fell out on him.'

The Bursar was standing in the corner, wearing his old familiar expression of good-humoured concussion.

'You all right, old fellow?' said Ridcully. 'What's eleven per cent of 1,276?'

'One hundred and forty point three six,' said the Bursar promptly.

'Ah, right as rain,' said Ridcully cheerfully.

'I don't see why,' said the Chair of Indefinite Studies. 'Just because he can do things with numbers doesn't mean everything else is fine.'

'Doesn't need to be,' said Ridcully. 'Numbers is what he has to do. The poor chap might be slightly yoyo, but I've been reading about it. He's one of these idiot servants.'

'Savants,' said the Dean patiently. 'The word is savants, Ridcully.'

'Whatever. Those chaps who can tell you what day of the week the first of Grune was a hundred years ago –'

'– Tuesday –' said the Bursar.

'– but can't tie their bootlaces,' said Ridcully. 'What was a corpse doing in his wardrobe? And no one is to say "Not a lot," or anythin' tasteless like that. Haven't had a corpse in a wardrobe since that business with Archchancellor Buckleby.'

'We all warned Buckleby that the lock was too stiff,' said the Dean.

'Just out of interest, why was the Bursar fiddling with his wardrobe at this time of night?' said Ridcully.

The wizards looked sheepish.

'We were . . . playing Sardines, Archchancellor,' said the Dean.

'What's that?'

'It's like Hide and Seek, but when you find someone you have to squeeze in with them,' said the Dean.

'I just want to be clear about this,' said Ridcully. 'My senior wizards have spent the evening playing Hide and Seek?'

'Oh, not the whole evening,' said the Chair of Indefinite Studies. 'We played Grandmother's Footsteps and I Spy for quite a while until the Senior Wrangler made a scene just because we wouldn't let him spell chandelier with an S.'

'Party games? *You* fellows?'

The Dean sidled closer.

'It's Miss Smith,' he mumbled. 'When we don't join in she bursts into tears.'

'Who's Miss Smith?'

'The Cheerful Fairy,' said the Lecturer in Recent Runes glumly. 'If you don't say yes to everything her lip wobbles like a plate of jelly. It's unbearable.'

'We just joined in to stop her weeping,' said the Dean. 'It's amazing how one woman can be so soggy.'

'If we're not cheerful she bursts into tears,' said the Chair of

Indefinite Studies. 'The Senior Wrangler's doing some juggling for her at the moment.'

'But he can't juggle!'

'I think that's cheering her up a bit.'

'What you're tellin' me, then, is that my wizards are prancing around playin' children's games just to cheer up some dejected fairy?'

'Er . . . yes.'

'I thought you had to clap your hands and say you believed in 'em,' said Ridcully. 'Correct me if I'm wrong.'

'That's just for the little shiny ones,' said the Lecturer in Recent Runes. 'Not for the ones in saggy cardigans with half a dozen hankies stuffed up their sleeves.'

Ridcully looked at the corpse again.

'Anyone know who he is? Looks a bit of a ruffian to me. And where's his boots, may I ask?'

The Dean took a small glass cube from his pocket and ran it over the corpse.

'Quite a large thaumic reading, gentlemen,' he said. 'I think he got here by magic.'

He rummaged in the man's pockets and pulled out a handful of small white things.

'Ugh,' he said.

'Teeth?' said Ridcully. 'Who goes around with a pocket full of teeth?'

'A very bad fighter?' said the Chair of Indefinite Studies. 'I'll go and get Modo to take the poor fellow away, shall I?'

'If we can get a reading off the thaumometer, perhaps Hex –' Ridcully began.

'Now, Ridcully,' said the Dean, 'I really think there must be some problems that can be resolved without having to deal with that damn thinking mill.'

Death looked up at Hex.

A MACHINE FOR THINKING?

'Er . . . yes, sir,' said Ponder Stibbons. 'You see, when you said . . . well, you see, Hex believes everything . . . but, look, the sun really will come up, won't it? That's its *job*.'

LEAVE US.

Ponder backed away, and then scurried out of the room.

The ants flowed along their tubes. Cogwheels spun. The big

wheel with the sheep skulls on it creaked around slowly. A mouse squeaked, somewhere in the works.

WELL? said Death.

After a while, the pen began to write.

+++ Big Red Lever Time +++ Query +++

NO. THEY SAY YOU ARE A THINKER. EXTEND LOGICALLY THE RESULT OF THE HUMAN RACE CEASING TO BELIEVE IN THE HOGFATHER. WILL THE SUN COME UP? ANSWER.

It took several minutes. The wheels spun. The ants ran. The mouse squeaked. An eggtimer came down on a spring. It bounced aimlessly for a while, and then jerked back up again.

Hex wrote: +++ The Sun Will Not Come Up +++

CORRECT. HOW MAY THIS BE PREVENTED? ANSWER.

+++ Regular And Consistent Belief +++

GOOD. I HAVE A TASK FOR YOU, THINKING ENGINE.

+++ Yes. I Am Preparing An Area Of Write-Only Memory +++

WHAT IS THAT?

+++ You Would Say: To Know In Your Bones +++

GOOD. HERE IS YOUR INSTRUCTION. BELIEVE IN THE HOGFATHER.

+++ Yes +++

DO YOU BELIEVE? ANSWER.

+++ Yes +++

DO ... YOU ... BELIEVE? ANSWER.

+++ **YES** +++

There was a change in the ill-assembled heap of pipes and tubes that was Hex. The big wheel creaked into a new position. From the other side of the wall came the hum of busy bees.

GOOD.

Death turned to leave the room, but stopped when Hex began to write furiously. He went back and looked at the emerging paper.

+++ Dear Hogfather, For Hogswatch I Want –

OH, NO. *YOU* CAN'T WRITE LETT– Death paused, and then said, YOU CAN, CAN'T YOU.

+++ Yes. I Am Entitled +++

Death waited until the pen had stopped, and picked up the paper.

BUT YOU ARE A MACHINE. THINGS HAVE NO DESIRES. A DOORKNOB WANTS NOTHING, EVEN THOUGH IT IS A COMPLEX MACHINE.

+++ All Things Strive +++

YOU HAVE A POINT, said Death. He thought of tiny red petals in the black depths, and read to the end of the list.

I DON'T KNOW WHAT MOST OF THESE THINGS ARE. I DON'T THINK THE SACK WILL, EITHER.

+++ I Regret This +++
But we will do the best we can, said Death. Frankly, I shall be glad when tonight's over. It's much harder to give than to receive. He rummaged in his sack. Let me see ... How old are you?

Susan crept up the stairs, one hand on the hilt of the sword.

Ponder Stibbons had been worried to find himself, as a wizard, awaiting the arrival of the Hogfather. It's amazing how people define roles for themselves and put handcuffs on their experience and are constantly surprised by the things a roulette universe spins at them. Here am I, they say, a mere wholesale fishmonger, at the controls of a giant airliner because as it turns out all the crew had the Coronation Chicken. Who'd have thought it? Here am I, a housewife who merely went out this morning to bank the proceeds of the Playgroup Association's Car Boot Sale, on the run with one million in stolen cash and a rather handsome man from the Battery Chickens' Liberation Organization. Amazing! Here am I, a perfectly ordinary hockey player, suddenly realizing I'm the Son of God with five hundred devoted followers in a nice little commune in Empowerment, Southern California. Who'd have thought it?

Here am I, thought Susan, a very practically minded governess who can add up faster upside down than most people can the right way up, climbing up a tooth-shaped tower belonging to the Tooth Fairy and armed with a sword belonging to Death ...

Again! I wish one month, just one damn *month*, could go by without something like this happening to me.

She could hear voices above her. Someone said something about a lock.

She peered over the edge of the stairwell.

It looked as though people had been camping out up here. There were boxes and sleeping rolls strewn around. A couple of men were sitting on boxes watching a third man who was working on a door in one curved wall. One of the men was the biggest Susan had ever seen, one of those huge fat men who contrive to indicate that a lot of the fat under their shapeless clothes is muscle. The other –

'Hello,' said a cheerful voice by her ear. 'What's *your* name?'

She made herself turn her head slowly.

First she saw the grey, glinting eye. Then the yellow-white one with the tiny dot of a pupil came into view.

Around them was a friendly pink and white face topped by curly hair. It was actually quite pretty, in a boyish sort of way, except that those mismatched eyes staring out of it suggested that it had been stolen from someone else.

She started to move her hand but the boy was there first, dragging the sword scabbard out of her belt.

'Ah, ah!' he chided, turning and fending her off as she tried to grab it. 'Well, well, well. My word. White bone handle, rather tasteless skull and bone decoration ... Death himself's second favourite weapon, am I right? Oh, my! This must be Hogswatch! And this must mean that you are Susan Sto-Helit. Nobility. I'd bow,' he added, dancing back, 'but I'm afraid you'd do something dreadful –'

There was a click, and a little gasp of excitement from the wizard working on the door.

'Yes! Yes! Left-handed using a wooden pick! That's *simple*!'

He saw that even Susan was looking at him, and coughed nervously.

'Er, I've got the fifth lock open, Mister Teatime! *Not* a problem! They're just based on Woddeley's Occult Sequence! Any fool could do it if they knew that!'

'*I* know it,' said Teatime, without taking his eyes off Susan. 'Ah ...'.

It was not technically audible, but nevertheless Susan could almost hear the wizard's mind back-pedalling. Up ahead was the conclusion that Teatime had no time for people he didn't need.

'... with ... inter ... est ... ing subtleties,' he said slowly. 'Yes. Very tricky. I'll, er, just have a look at number six ...'

'How do you know who I am?' said Susan.

'Oh, *easy*,' said Teatime. '*Twurp's Peerage*. Family motto *Non temetis messor*. We have to read it, you know, in class. Hah, old Mericet calls it the Guide to the Turf. No one laughs except him, of course. Oh yes, I know about you. Quite a lot. Your father was well known. Went a long way very fast. As for your grandfather ... honestly, that motto. Is that good taste? Of course, *you* don't need to fear him, do you? Or do you?'

Susan tried to fade. It didn't work. She could feel herself staying embarrassingly solid.

'I don't know what you're talking about,' she said. 'Who are you, anyway?'

'I beg your pardon. My name is Teatime, Jonathan Teatime. At your service.'

Susan lined up the syllables in her head.

'You mean ... like around four o'clock in the afternoon?' she said.

'No. I did say Teh-ah-tim-eh,' said Teatime. 'I spoke very clearly. Please don't try to break my concentration by annoying me. I only get annoyed at important things. How are you getting on, Mr Sideney? If it's just according to Woddeley's sequence, number six should be copper and blue-green light. Unless, of course, there are any *subtleties* . . .'

'Er, doing it right now, Mister Teatime –'

'Do you think your grandfather will try to rescue you? Do you think he will? But now I have his sword, you see. I wonder –'

There was another click.

'Sixth lock, Mister Teatime!'

'Really.'

'Er . . . don't you want me to start on the seventh?'

'Oh, well, if you like. Pure white light will be the key,' said Teatime, still not looking away from Susan. 'But it may not be all important now. Thank you, anyway. You've been most helpful.'

'Er –'

'Yes, you may go.'

Susan noticed that Sideney didn't even bother to pick up his books and tools, but hurried down the stairs as if he expected to be called back and was trying to run faster than the sound.

'Is that all you're here for?' she said. 'A robbery?' He was dressed like an Assassin, after all, and there was always one way to annoy an Assassin. 'Like a thief?'

Teatime danced excitedly. 'A thief? Me? I'm not a thief, madam. But if I were, I would be the kind that steals fire from the gods.'

'We've already got fire.'

'There must be an upgrade by now. No, *these* gentlemen are thieves. Common robbers. Decent types, although you wouldn't necessarily want to watch them eat, for example. That's Medium Dave and exhibit B is Banjo. He can talk.'

Medium Dave nodded at Susan. She saw the look in his eyes. Maybe there was something she could use . . .

She'd need something. Even her hair was a mess. She couldn't step behind time, she couldn't fade into the background, and now even her hair had let her down.

She was normal. Here, she was what she'd always wanted to be. Bloody, bloody damn.

Sideney prayed as he ran down the stairs. He didn't believe in any gods, since most wizards seldom like to encourage them, but he prayed anyway the fervent prayers of an atheist who hopes to be wrong.

But no one called him back. And no one ran after him.

So, being of a serious turn of mind under his normal state of subcritical fear, he slowed down in case he lost his footing.

It was then that he noticed that the steps underfoot weren't the smooth whiteness they had been everywhere else but were very large, pitted flagstones. And the light had changed, and then they weren't stairs any more and he staggered as he encountered flat ground where steps should have been.

His outstretched hand brushed against a crumbling brick.

And the ghosts of the past poured in, and he knew where he was. He was in the yard of Gammer Wimblestone's dame school. His mother wanted him to learn his letters and be a wizard, but she also thought that long curls on a five-year-old boy looked very smart.

This was the hunting ground of Ronnie Jenks.

Adult memory and understanding said that Ronnie was just an unintelligent bullet-headed seven-year-old bully with muscles where his brain should have been. The eye of childhood, rather more accurately, dreaded him as a force like a personalized earthquake with one nostril bunged up with bogies, both knees scabbed, both fists balled and all five brain cells concentrated in a kind of cerebral grunt.

Oh, gods. There was the tree Ronnie used to hide behind. It looked as big and menacing as he remembered it.

But ... if somehow he'd ended up back there, gods knew how, well, he might be a bit on the skinny side but he was a damn sight bigger than Ronnie Jenks now. Gods, *yes*, he'd kick those evil little trousers all the –

And then, as a shadow blotted out the sun, he realized he was wearing curls.

Teatime looked thoughtfully at the door.

'I suppose I should open it,' he said, 'after coming all this way ...'

'You're controlling children by their teeth,' said Susan.

'It does sound odd, doesn't it, when you put it like that,' said Teatime. 'But that's sympathetic magic for you. Is your grandfather going to try to rescue you, do you think? But no ... I don't think he can. Not here, I think. I don't think that he can come here. So he sent you, did he?'

'Certainly not! He –' Susan stopped. Oh, he *had*, she told herself, feeling even more of a fool. He certainly had. He was learning about humans, all right. For a walking skeleton, he could be quite clever . . .

But . . . how clever was Teatime? Just a bit too excited at his cleverness to realize that if Death – She tried to stamp on the thought, just in case Teatime could read it in her eyes.

'I don't think he'll try,' she said. 'He's not as clever as you, Mister Teatime.'

'Teh-ah-tim-eh,' said Teatime, automatically. 'That's a shame.'

'Do you think you're going to get away with this?'

'Oh, dear. Do people really say that?' And suddenly Teatime was much closer. 'I've *got* away with it. No more Hogfather. And that's only the start. We'll keep the teeth coming in, of course. The possibilities –'

There was a rumble like an avalanche, a long way off. The dormant Banjo had awakened, causing tremors on his lower slopes. His enormous hands, which had been resting on his knees, started to bunch.

'What's dis?' he said.

Teatime stopped and, for a moment, looked puzzled.

'What's this what?'

'You said no more Hogfather,' said Banjo. He stood up, like a mountain range rising gently in the squeeze between colliding continents. His hands still stayed in the vicinity of his knees.

Teatime stared at him and then glanced at Medium Dave.

'He does *know* what we've been doing, does he?' he said. 'You did *tell* him?'

Medium Dave shrugged.

'Dere's got to be a Hogfather,' said Banjo. 'Dere's always a Hogfather.'

Susan looked down. Grey blotches were speeding across the white marble. She was standing in a pool of grey. So was Banjo. And around Teatime the dots bounced and recoiled like wasps around a pot of jam.

Looking for something, she thought.

'You don't believe in the Hogfather, do you?' said Teatime. 'A big boy like you?'

'Yeah,' said Banjo. 'So what's dis' "no more Hogfather"?'

Teatime pointed at Susan.

'*She* did it,' he said. 'She killed him.'

The sheer playground effrontery of it shocked Susan.

'No I didn't,' she said. 'He –'

'Did!'

'Didn't!'

'Did!'

Banjo's big bald head turned towards her.

'What's dis about the Hogfather?' he said.

'I don't think he's dead,' said Susan. 'But Teatime *has* made him very ill –'

'Who cares?' said Teatime, dancing away. 'When this is over, Banjo, you'll have as many presents as you want. Trust me!'

'Dere's got to be a Hogfather,' Banjo rumbled. 'Else dere's no Hogswatch.'

'It's just another solar festival,' said Teatime. 'It –'

Medium Dave stood up. He had his hand on his sword.

'We're going, Teatime,' he said. 'Me and Banjo are going. I don't like any of this. I don't mind robbing, I don't mind thieving, but *this* isn't *honest*. Banjo? You come with me right now!'

'What's dis about no more Hogfather?' said Banjo.

Teatime pointed to Susan.

'You grab her, Banjo. It's all her fault!'

Banjo lumbered a few steps in Susan's direction, and then stopped.

'Our mam said no hittin' girls,' he rumbled. 'No pullin' dere hair . . .'

Teatime rolled his one good eye. Around his feet the greyness seemed to be boiling in the stone, following his feet as they moved. And it was around Banjo, too.

Searching, Susan thought. It's looking for a way in.

'I think I know you, Teatime,' she said, as sweetly as she could for Banjo's sake. 'You're the mad kid they're all scared of, right?'

'Banjo?' snapped Teatime. 'I said grab her –'

'Our mam said –'

'The giggling excitable one even the bullies never touched because if they did he went insane and kicked and bit,' said Susan. 'The kid who didn't know the difference between chucking a stone at a cat and setting it on fire.'

To her delight he glared at her.

'Shut up,' he said.

'I *bet* no one wanted to *play* with you,' said Susan. 'Not the kid with no friends. Kids know about a mind like yours even if they don't know the right words for it –'

'I *said* shut up! *Get* her, Banjo!'

That was it. She could hear it in Teatime's voice. There was a touch of vibrato that hadn't been there before.

'The kind of little boy,' she said, watching his face, 'who looks up dolls' dresses ...'

'I *didn't*!'

Banjo looked worried.

'Our mam said –'

'Oh, to blazes with your mam!' snapped Teatime.

There was a whisper of steel as Medium Dave drew his sword.

'What'd you say about our mam?' he whispered.

Now he's having to concentrate on three people, Susan thought.

'I bet *no one* ever played with you,' she said. 'I bet there were things people had to hush up, eh?'

'Banjo! You do what I tell you!' Teatime screamed.

The monstrous man was beside her now. She could see his face twisted in an agony of indecision. His enormous fists clenched and unclenched and his lips moved as some kind of horrible debate raged in his head.

'Our ... our mam ... our mam said ...'

The grey marks flowed across the floor and formed a pool of shadow which grew darker and higher with astonishing speed. It towered over the three men, and grew a shape.

'Have you been a bad boy, you little perisher?'

The huge woman towered over all three men. In one meaty hand it was holding a bundle of birch twigs as thick as a man's arm.

The thing growled.

Medium Dave looked up into the enormous face of Ma Lilywhite. Every pore was a pothole. Every brown tooth was a tombstone.

'You been letting him get into trouble, our Davey? You have, ain't you?'

He backed away. 'No, Mum ... no, Mum ...'

'You need a good hiding, Banjo? You been playing with girls again?'

Banjo sagged on to his knees, tears of misery rolling down his face.

'Sorry Mum sorry sorry Mum noooohhh Mum sorry Mum sorry sorry –'

Then the figure turned to Medium Dave again.

The sword dropped out of his hand. His face seemed to melt.

Medium Dave started to cry.

'No Mum no Mum no Mum nooooh Mum –'

He gave a gurgle and collapsed, clutching his chest. And vanished.

Teatime started to laugh.

Susan tapped him on the shoulder and, as he looked round, hit him as hard as she could across the face.

That was the plan, at least. His hand moved faster and caught her wrist. It was like striking an iron bar.

'Oh, *no*,' he said. 'I don't *think* so.'

Out of the corner of her eye Susan saw Banjo crawling across the floor to where his brother had been. Ma Lilywhite had vanished.

'This place gets into your head, doesn't it?' Teatime said. 'It pokes around to find out how to deal with you. Well, *I'm* in touch with my inner child.'

He reached out with his other hand and grabbed her hair, pulling her head down.

Susan screamed.

'And it's much more fun,' he whispered.

Susan felt his grip lessen. There was a wet thump like a piece of steak hitting a slab and Teatime went past her, on his back.

'No pullin' girls' hair,' rumbled Banjo. 'That's *bad*.'

Teatime bounced up like an acrobat and steadied himself on the railing of the stairwell.

Then he drew the sword.

The blade was invisible in the bright light of the tower.

'It's true what the stories say, then,' he said. 'So thin you can't see it. I'm going to have such *fun* with it.' He waved it at them. 'So light.'

'You wouldn't *dare* use it. My grandfather will come after you,' said Susan, walking towards him.

She saw one eye twitch.

'He comes after everyone. But I'll be ready for him,' said Teatime.

'He's very single-minded,' said Susan, closer now.

'Ah, a man after my own heart.'

'Could be, Mister *Tea*time.'

He brought the sword around. She didn't even have time to duck.

And she didn't even try to when he swung the sword back again.

'It doesn't work here,' she said, as he stared at it in astonishment. 'The blade doesn't *exist* here. There's no *Death* here!'

She slapped him across the face.

'Hi!' she said brightly. 'I'm the inner baby-sitter!'

She didn't punch. She just thrust out an arm, palm first, catching him under the chin and lifting him backwards over the rail.

He somersaulted. She never knew how. He somehow managed to gain purchase on clear air.

His free arm grabbed at hers, her feet came off the ground, and she was over the rail. She caught it with her other hand – although later she wondered if the rail hadn't managed to catch her instead.

Teatime swung from her arm, staring upwards with a thoughtful expression. She saw him grip the sword hilt in his teeth and reach down to his belt –

The question 'Is this person mad enough to try to kill someone holding him?' was asked and answered very, very fast . . . She kicked down and hit him on the ear.

The cloth of her sleeve began to tear. Teatime tried to get another grip. She kicked again and the dress ripped. For an instant he held on to nothing and then, still wearing the expression of someone trying to solve a complex problem, he fell away, spinning, getting smaller . . .

He hit the pile of teeth, sending them splashing across the marble. He jerked for a moment . . .

And vanished.

A hand like a bunch of bananas pulled Susan back over the rail.

'You can get into trouble, hittin' girls,' said Banjo. 'No playin' with girls.'

There was a click behind them.

The doors had swung open. Cold white mist rolled out across the floor.

'Our mam –' said Banjo, trying to work things out. 'Our mam was here –'

'Yes,' said Susan.

'But it *weren't* our mam, 'cos they *buried* our mam –'

'Yes.'

'We watched 'em fill in the grave and everything.'

'Yes,' said Susan, and added to herself, *I bet you did.*

'And where's our Davey gone?'

'Er . . . somewhere else, Banjo.'

'Somewhere nice?' said the huge man hesitantly.

Susan grasped with relief the opportunity to tell the truth, or at least not definitely lie.

'It could be,' she said.

'Better'n here?'

'You never know. Some people would say the odds are in favour.'

Banjo turned his pink piggy eyes on her. For a moment a thirty-five-year-old man looked out through the pink clouds of a five-year-old face.

'That's good,' he said. 'He'll be able to see our mam again.'

This much conversation seemed to exhaust him. He sagged.

'I wanna go home,' he said.

She stared at his big, stained face, shrugged hopelessly, pulled a handkerchief out of her pocket and held it up to his mouth.

'Spit,' she commanded. He obeyed.

She dabbed the handkerchief over the worst parts and then tucked it into his hand.

'Have a good blow,' she suggested, and then carefully leaned out of range until the echoes of the blast had died away.

'You can keep the hanky. Please,' she added, meaning it wholeheartedly. 'Now tuck your shirt in.'

'Yes, miss.'

'Now, go downstairs and sweep all the teeth out of the circle. Can you do that?'

Banjo nodded.

'What can you do?' Susan prompted.

Banjo concentrated. 'Sweep all the teeth out of the circle, miss.'

'Good. Off you go.'

Susan watched him plod off, and then looked at the white doorway. She was *sure* the wizard had only got as far as the sixth lock.

The room beyond the door was entirely white, and the mist that swirled at knee level deadened even the sound of her footsteps.

All there was was a bed. It was a large four-poster, old and dusty.

She thought it was unoccupied and then she saw the figure, lying among the mounds of pillows. It looked very much like a frail old lady in a mob cap.

The old woman turned her head and smiled at Susan.

'Hello, my dear.'

Susan couldn't remember a grandmother. Her father's mother had died when she was young, and the other side of the family ... well, she'd never had a grandmother. But this was the sort she'd have wanted.

The kind, the nasty realistic side of her mind said, that hardly ever existed.

Susan thought she heard a child laugh. And another one. Somewhere almost out of hearing, children were at play. It was always a pleasant, lulling sound.

Always provided, of course, you couldn't hear the actual words.

'No,' said Susan.

'Sorry, dear?' said the old lady.

'You're not the Tooth Fairy.' Oh, no ... there was even a damn patchwork quilt ...

'Oh, I *am*, dear.'

'Oh, Grandma, what big teeth you have ... Good grief, you've even got a shawl, oh dear.'

'I don't understand, lovey –'

'You forgot the rocking chair,' said Susan. 'I always thought there'd be a rocking chair ...'

There was a pop behind her, and then a dying creak-creak. She didn't even turn round.

'If you've included a kitten playing with a ball of wool it'll go very hard with you,' she said sternly, and picked up the candlestick by the bed. It seemed heavy enough.

'I don't think you're real,' she said levelly. 'There's not a little old woman in a shawl running this place. You're out of my head. That's how you defend yourself ... You poke around in people's heads and find the things that work –'

She swung the candlestick. It passed through the figure in the bed.

'See?' she said. 'You're not even *real*.'

'Oh, *I* am real, dear,' said the old woman, as her outline changed. 'The candlestick wasn't.'

Susan looked down at the new shape.

'Nope,' she said. 'It's horrible, but it doesn't frighten me. No, nor does that.' It changed again, and again. 'No, nor does my father. Good grief, you're scraping the bottom of the barrel, aren't you? I *like* spiders. Snakes don't worry me. Dogs? No. Rats are fine, I like rats. Sorry, is *anyone* frightened of *that*?'

She grabbed at the thing and this time the shape stayed. It looked like a small, wizened monkey, but with big deep eyes under a brow overhanging like a balcony. Its hair was grey and lank. It struggled weakly in her grasp, and wheezed.

'I don't frighten easily,' said Susan, 'but you'd be amazed at how angry I can become.'

The creature hung limp.

'I ... I ...' it muttered.

She let it down again.

'You're a bogeyman, aren't you?' she said.

It collapsed in a heap when she took her hand away.

'... Not *a* ... *The* ...' it said.

'What do you mean, *the*?' said Susan.

'*The* bogeyman,' said the bogeyman. And she saw how rangy it was, how white and grey streaked its hair, how the skin was stretched over the bones ...

'The *first* bogeyman?'

'I . . . there were . . . I do remember when the land was different. Ice. Many times of . . . ice. And the . . . what do you call them?' The creature wheezed. '. . . The lands, the big lands . . . all different . . .'

Susan sat down on the bed.

'You mean continents?'

'. . . all different.' The black sunken eyes glinted at her and suddenly the thing reared up, bony arms waving. 'I was the dark in the cave! I was the shadow in the trees! You've heard about . . . the primal scream? That was . . . at *me*! I was . . .' It folded up and started coughing. 'And then . . . that thing, you know, that thing . . . all light and bright . . . lightning you could carry, hot, little sunshine, and then there was no more dark, just shadows, and then you made axes, axes in the forest, and then . . . and then . . .'

Susan sat down on the bed. 'There's still plenty of bogeymen,' she said.

'Hiding under beds! Lurking in cupboards! But,' it fought for breath, 'if you had seen me . . . in the old days . . . when they came down into the deep caves to draw their hunting pictures . . . I could roar in their heads . . . so that their stomachs dropped out of their bottoms . . .'

'All the old skills are dying out,' said Susan gravely.

'. . . Oh, others came later . . . They never knew that first fine terror. All they knew,' even whispering, the bogeyman managed to get a sneer in its voice, 'was dark corners. I had *been* the dark! I was the . . . first! And now I was no better than them . . . frightening maids, curdling cream . . . hiding in shadows at the stub of the year . . . and then one night, I thought . . . why?'

Susan nodded. Bogeymen weren't bright. The moment of existential uncertainty probably took a lot longer in heads where the brain cells bounced so very slowly from one side of the skull to the other. But . . . Granddad had thought like that. You hung around with humans long enough and you stopped being what they imagined you to be and wanted to become something of your own. Umbrellas and silver hairbrushes . . .

'You thought: what was the point of it all?' she said.

'. . . frightening children . . . lurking . . . and then I started to watch them. Didn't really used to be children back in the ice times . . . just big humans, little humans, not *children* . . . and . . . and there was a different world in their heads . . . In their heads, that's where the old days *were* now. The old days. When it was all young.'

'You came out from under the bed . . .'

'I watched over them . . . kept 'em safe . . .'

Susan tried not to shudder.

'And the teeth?'

'I . . . oh, you can't leave teeth around, *anyone* might get them, do terrible things. I liked them, I didn't want anyone to hurt them . . .' it bubbled. 'I never wanted to hurt them, I just used to watch, I kept the teeth all safe . . . and, and, and sometimes I just sit here listening to them . . .'

It mumbled on. Susan listened in embarrassed amazement, not knowing whether to take pity on the thing or, and this was a developing option, to tread on it.

'. . . and the teeth . . . they remember . . .'

It started to shake.

'The money?' Susan prompted. 'I don't see many rich bogeymen around.'

'. . . money everywhere . . . buried in holes . . . old treasure . . . back of sofas . . . it adds up . . . investments . . . money for the tooth, very important, part of the magic, makes it safe, makes it proper, otherwise it's *thieving* . . . and I labelled 'em all, and kept 'em safe, and . . . and then I was old, but I found people . . .' The Tooth Fairy sniggered, and for a moment Susan felt sorry for the men in the ancient caves. 'They don't ask questions, do they?' it bubbled. '. . . You give 'em money and they all do their jobs and they don't ask questions . . .'

'It's more than their job's worth,' said Susan.

'. . . and then *they* came . . . stealing . . .'

Susan gave in. Old gods do new jobs.

'You look terrible.'

'. . . thank you very much . . .'

'I mean ill.'

'. . . very old . . . all those men, too much effort . . .'

The bogeyman groaned.

'. . . you . . . don't die here,' it panted. 'Just get old, listening to the laughter . . .'

Susan nodded. It was in the air. She couldn't hear words, just a distant chatter, as if it was at the other end of a long corridor.

'. . . and this place . . . it grew up round me . . .'

'The trees,' said Susan. 'And the sky. Out of their heads . . .'

'. . . dying . . . the little children . . . you've got to . . .'

The figure faded.

Susan sat for a while, listening to the distant chatter.

Worlds of belief, she thought. Just like oysters. A little piece of shit gets in and then a pearl grows up around it.

She got up and went downstairs.

Banjo had found a broom and mop somewhere. The circle was empty and, with surprising initiative, the man was carefully washing the chalk away.

'Banjo?'

'Yes, miss.'

'You like it here?'

'There's trees, miss.'

That probably counts as a 'yes', Susan decided.

'The sky doesn't worry you?'

He looked at her in puzzlement.

'No, miss?'

'Can you count, Banjo?'

He looked smug.

'Yes, miss. On m'fingers, miss.'

'So you can count up to . . .?' Susan prompted.

'Thirteen, miss,' said Banjo proudly.

She looked at his big hands.

'Good grief.'

Well, she thought, and why not? He's big and trustworthy and what other kind of life has he got?

'I think it would be a good idea if you did the Tooth Fairy's job, Banjo.'

'Will that be all right, miss? Won't the Tooth Fairy mind?'

'You . . . do it until she comes back.'

'All right, miss.'

'I'll . . . er . . . get people to keep an eye on you, until you get settled in. I think food comes in on the cart. You're not to let people cheat you.' She looked at his hands and then up and up the lower slopes until she saw the peak of Mount Banjo, and added, 'Not that I think they'll try, mind you.'

'Yes, miss. I will keep things tidy, miss. Er . . .'

The big pink face looked at her.

'Yes, Banjo?'

'Can I have a puppy, miss? I had a kitten once, miss, but our mam drownded it 'cos it was dirty.'

Susan's memory threw up a name.

'A puppy called Spot?'

'Yes, miss. Spot, miss.'

'I think it'll turn up quite soon, Banjo.'

He seemed to take this entirely on trust.

'Thank you, miss.'

'And now I've got to go.'

'Right, miss.'

She looked back up the tower. Death's land might be dark, but when you were there you never thought anything bad was going to happen to you. You were beyond the places where it could. But here –

When you were grown up you only feared, well, logical things. Poverty. Illness. Being found out. At least you weren't mad with terror because of something under the stairs. The world wasn't full of arbitrary light and shade. The wonderful world of childhood? Well, it wasn't a cut-down version of the adult one, that was certain. It was more like the adult one written in big heavy letters. Everything was ... *more*. More *everything*.

She left Banjo to his sweeping and stepped out into the perpetually sunlit world.

Bilious and Violet hurried towards her. Bilious was waving a branch like a club.

'You don't need that,' said Susan. She wanted some sleep.

'We talked about it and we thought we ought to come back and help,' said Bilious.

'Ah. Democratic courage,' said Susan. 'Well, they're all gone. To wherever they go.'

Bilious lowered the branch thankfully.

'It wasn't that –' he began.

'Look, you two can make yourselves useful,' said Susan. 'There's a mess in there. Go and help Banjo.'

'Banjo?'

'He's ... more or less running the place now.'

Violet laughed.

'But he's –'

'He's in charge,' said Susan wearily.

'All right,' said Bilious. 'Anyway, I'm sure we can tell him what to do –'

'No! Too many people have told him what to do. He *knows* what to do. Just help him get started, all right? But ...'

If the Hogfather comes back now, you'll vanish, won't you? She didn't know how to phrase the question.

'I'm, er, giving up my old job,' said Bilious. 'Er ... I'm going to *go on* working as a holiday relief for the other gods.' He gave her a pleading look.

'Really?' Susan looked at Violet. Oh, well, maybe if she believes in him, at least . . . It might work. You never know.

'Good,' she said. 'Have fun. Now I'm going home. This is a hell of a way to spend Hogswatch.'

She found Binky waiting by the stream.

The Auditors fluttered anxiously. And, as always happens in their species when something goes radically wrong and needs fixing instantly, they settled down to try to work out who to blame.

One said, It was . . .

And then it stopped. The Auditors lived by consensus, which made picking scapegoats a little problematical. It brightened up. After all, if everyone was to blame, then it was no one's actual *fault*. That's what collective responsibility meant, after all. It was more like bad luck, or something.

Another said, Unfortunately, people might get the wrong idea. We may be asked questions.

One said, What about Death? He interfered, after all.

One said, Er . . . not exactly.

One said, Oh, come on. He got the girl involved.

One said, Er . . . no. She got herself involved.

One said, Yes, but he told her . . .

One said, No. He didn't. In fact he specifically did *not* tell –

It paused, and then said, Damn!

One said, On the other hand . . .

The robes turned towards it.

Yes?

One said, There's no actual *evidence*. Nothing written down. Some humans got excited and decided to attack the Tooth Fairy's country. This is unfortunate, but nothing to do with us. We are shocked, of course.

One said, There's still the Hogfather. Things are going to be noticed. Questions may be asked.

They hovered for a while, unspeaking.

Eventually one said, We may have to take . . .

It paused, loath even to *think* the word, but managed to continue.

. . . a risk.

Bed, thought Susan, as the mists rolled past her. And in the morning, decent human things like coffee and porridge. And *bed*. *Real* things –

Binky stopped. She stared at his ears for a moment, and then urged him forward. He whinnied, and didn't budge.

A skeletal hand had grabbed his bridle. Death materialized.

IT IS NOT OVER. MORE MUST BE DONE. THEY TORMENT HIM STILL.

Susan sagged. 'What is? Who are?'

MOVE FORWARD. I WILL STEER. Death climbed into the saddle and reached around her for the reins.

'Look, I went –' Susan began.

YES. I KNOW. THE CONTROL OF BELIEF, said Death, as the horse moved forward again. ONLY A VERY SIMPLE MIND COULD THINK OF THAT. MAGIC SO OLD IT'S HARDLY MAGIC. WHAT A SIMPLE WAY TO MAKE MILLIONS OF CHILDREN CEASE TO BELIEVE IN THE HOGFATHER.

'And what were *you* doing?' Susan demanded.

I TOO HAVE DONE WHAT I SET OUT TO DO. I HAVE KEPT A SPACE. A MILLION CARPETS WITH SOOTY BOOTMARKS, MILLIONS OF FILLED STOCKINGS, ALL THOSE ROOFS WITH RUNNER MARKS ON THEM... DISBELIEF WILL FIND IT HARD GOING IN THE FACE OF THAT. ALBERT SAYS HE NEVER WANTS TO DRINK ANOTHER SHERRY FOR *DAYS*. THE HOGFATHER WILL HAVE SOMETHING TO COME BACK TO, AT LEAST.

'What have I got to do now?'

YOU MUST *BRING* THE HOGFATHER BACK.

'Oh, must I? For peace and goodwill and the tinkling of fairy bells? Who *cares*? He's just some fat old clown who makes people feel smug at Hogswatch! I've been through all this for some old man who prowls around kids' bedrooms?'

NO. SO THAT THE SUN WILL RISE.

'What has astronomy got to do with the Hogfather?'

OLD GODS DO NEW JOBS.

The Senior Wrangler wasn't attending the Feast. He got one of the maids to bring a tray up to his rooms, where he was Entertaining and doing all those things a man does when he finds himself unexpectedly tête-à-tête with the opposite sex, like trying to shine his boots on his trousers and clean his fingernails with his other fingernails.

'A little more wine, Gwendoline? It's hardly *alcoholic*,' he said, leaning over her.

'I don't mind if I do, Mr Wrangler.'

'Oh, call me Horace, *please*. And perhaps a little something for your chicken?'

'I'm afraid she seems to have wandered off somewhere,' said the Cheerful Fairy. 'I'm afraid I'm, I'm, I'm rather dull company ...' She blew her nose noisily.

'Oh, I certainly wouldn't say that,' said the Senior Wrangler. He wished he'd had time to tidy up his rooms a bit, or at least get some of the more embarrassing bits of laundry off the stuffed rhinoceros.

'Everyone's been *so* kind,' said the Cheerful Fairy, dabbing at her streaming eyes. 'Who was the skinny one that kept making the funny faces for me?'

'That was the Bursar. Why don't you –'

'*He* seemed very cheerful, anyway.'

'It's the dried frog pills, he eats them by the handful,' said the Senior Wrangler dismissively. 'I say, why don't –'

'Oh dear. I hope they're not addictive.'

'I'm sure he wouldn't keep on eating them if they were addictive,' said the Senior Wrangler. 'Now, why don't you have another glass of wine, and then ... and then ...' a happy thought struck him '... and then ... and then perhaps I could show you Archchancellor Bowell's Remembrance? It's got a-a-a-a very interesting ceiling. My word, yes.'

'That would be very nice,' said the Cheerful Fairy. 'Would it cheer me up, do you think?'

'Oh, it would, it *would*,' said the Senior Wrangler. 'Definitely! Good! So I'll, er, I'll just go and ... just go and ... I'll ...' He pointed vaguely in the direction of his dressing room, while hopping from one foot to the other. 'I'll just go and, er ... go ... just ...'

He fled into the dressing room and slammed the door behind him. His wild eyes scanned the shelves and hangers.

'Clean robe,' he mumbled. 'Comb face, wash socks, fresh hair, where's that Insteadofshave lotion –'

From the other side of the door came the adorable sound of the Cheerful Fairy blowing her nose. From this side came the sound of the Senior Wrangler's muffled scream as, made careless by haste and a very poor sense of smell, he mistakenly splashed his face with the turpentine he used for treating his feet.

Somewhere overhead a very small plump child with a bow and arrow and ridiculously un-aerodynamic wings buzzed ineffectually against a shut window on which the frost was tracing the outline of a rather handsome Auriental lady. The other window already had an icy picture of a vase of sunflowers.

*

In the Great Hall one of the tables had already collapsed. It was one of the customs of the Feast that although there were many courses each wizard went at his own speed, a tradition instituted to prevent the slow ones holding everyone else up. And they could also have seconds if they wished, so that if a wizard was particularly attracted to soup he could go round and round for an hour before starting on the preliminary stages of the fish courses.

'How're you feeling now, old chap?' said the Dean, who was sitting next to the Bursar. 'Back on the dried frog pills?'

'I, er, I, er, no, I'm not too bad,' said the Bursar. 'It was, of course, rather a, rather a shock when –'

'That's a shame, because here's your Hogswatch present,' said the Dean, passing over a small box. It rattled. 'You can open it now if you like.'

'Oh, well, how nice –'

'It's from me,' said the Dean.

'What a lovely –'

'I bought it with my own money, you know,' said the Dean, waving a turkey leg airily.

'The wrapping paper is a very nice –'

'More than a dollar, I might add.'

'My goodness –'

The Bursar pulled off the last of the wrapping paper.

'It's a box for keeping dried frog pills in. See? It's got "Dried Frog Pills" on it, see?'

The Bursar shook it. 'Oh, how nice,' he said weakly. 'It's got some pills in it already. How thoughtful. They *will* come in handy.'

'Yes,' said the Dean. 'I took them off your dressing table. After all, I was down a dollar as it was.'

The Bursar nodded gratefully and put the little box neatly beside his plate. They'd actually allowed him knives this evening. They'd actually allowed him to eat other things than those things that could only be scraped up with a wooden spoon.

He eyed the nearest roast pig with nervous anticipation, and tucked his napkin firmly under his chin.

'Er, excuse me, Mr Stibbons,' he quavered. 'Would you be so good as to pass me the apple sauce tankard –'

There was a sound like coarse fabric ripping, somewhere in the air in front of the Bursar, and a crash as something landed on top of the roast pig. Roast potatoes and gravy filled the air. The apple that had been in the pig's mouth was violently expelled and hit the Bursar on the forehead.

He blinked, looked down, and found he was about to plunge his fork into a human head.

'Ahaha,' he murmured, as his eyes started to glaze.

The wizards heaved aside the overturned dishes and smashed crockery.

'He just fell out of the air!'

'Is he an Assassin? Not one of their student pranks, is it?'

'Why's he holding a sword without a sharp bit?'

'Is he dead?'

'I think so!'

'I didn't even *have* any of that salmon mousse! Will you look at it? His foot's in it! It's all over the place! Do you want yours?'

Ponder Stibbons fought his way through the throng. He knew his more senior fellows when they were feeling helpful. They were like a glass of water to a drowning man.

'Give him air!' he protested.

'How do we know if he needs any?' said the Dean.

Ponder put his ear to the fallen youth's chest.

'He's not breathing!'

'Breathing spell, breathing spell,' muttered the Chair of Indefinite Studies. 'Er . . . Spolt's Forthright Respirator, perhaps? I think I've got it written down somewhere –'

Ridcully reached through the wizards and pulled out the black-clad man by a leg. He held him upside down in his big hand and thumped him heavily on the back.

He met their astonished gaze. 'Used to do this on the farm,' he said. 'Works a treat on baby goats.'

'Oh, now, *really*,' said the Dean, 'I don't –'

The corpse made a noise somewhere between a choke and a cough.

'Make some space, you fellows!' the Archchancellor bellowed, clearing an area of table with one sweep of his spare arm.

'Hey, I hadn't had any of that Prawn Escoffé!' said the Lecturer in Recent Runes.

'I didn't even know we *had* any,' said the Chair of Indefinite Studies. 'Someone, and I name no names, Dean, shoved it behind the soft-shelled crabs so they could keep it for themselves. I call that cheap.'

Teatime opened his eyes. It said a lot for his constitution that it survived a very close-up view of Ridcully's nose, which filled the immediate universe like a big pink planet.

'Excuse me, excuse me,' said Ponder, leaning over with his

notebook open, 'but this is vitally important for the advancement of natural philosophy. Did you see any bright lights? Was there a shining tunnel? Did any deceased relatives attempt to speak to you? What word most describes the –'

Ridcully pulled him away.

'What's all this, Mr Stibbons?'

'I really should talk to him, sir. He's had a near-death experience!'

'We all have. It's called "living",' said the Archchancellor shortly. 'Pour the poor lad a glass of spirits and put that damn pencil away.'

'Uh . . . This must be Unseen University?' said Teatime. 'And you are all wizards?'

'Now, just you lie still,' said Ridcully. But Teatime had already risen on his elbows.

'There was a sword,' he muttered.

'Oh, it's fallen on the floor,' said the Dean, reaching down. 'But it looks as though it's – Did I do that?'

The wizards looked at the large curved slice of table falling away. Something had cut through everything – wood, cloth, plates, cutlery, food. The Dean swore that a candle flame that had been in the path of the unseen blade was only half a flame for a moment, until the wick realized that this was no way to behave.

The Dean raised his hand. The other wizards scattered.

'Looks like a thin blue line in the air,' he said, wonderingly.

'Excuse me, sir,' said Teatime, taking it from him. 'I really must be off.'

He ran from the hall.

'He won't get far,' said the Lecturer in Recent Runes. 'The main doors are locked in accordance with Archchancellor Spode's Rules.'

'Won't get far while holding a sword that appears to be able to cut through anything,' said Ridcully, to the sound of falling wood.

'I wonder what all that was about?' said the Chair of Indefinite Studies, and then turned his attention to the remains of the Feast. 'Anyway, at least this joint's been nicely carved . . .'

'Bu-bu-bu –'

They all turned. The Bursar was holding his hand in front of him. The cut surface of a fork gleamed at the wizards.

'Nice to know his new present will come in handy,' said the Dean. 'It's the thought that counts.'

Under the table the Blue Hen of Happiness relieved itself on the Bursar's foot.

*

THERE ARE ... ENEMIES, said Death, as Binky galloped through icy mountains.

'They're all dead –'

OTHER ENEMIES. YOU MAY AS WELL KNOW THIS. DOWN IN THE DEEPEST KINGDOMS OF THE SEA, WHERE THERE IS NO LIGHT, THERE LIVES A TYPE OF CREATURE WITH NO BRAIN AND NO EYES AND NO MOUTH. IT DOES NOTHING BUT LIVE AND PUT FORTH PETALS OF PERFECT CRIMSON WHERE NONE ARE THERE TO SEE. IT IS NOTHING EXCEPT A TINY *YES* IN THE NIGHT. AND YET ... AND YET ... IT HAS ENEMIES THAT BEAR ON IT A VICIOUS, UNBENDING MALICE, WHO WISH NOT ONLY FOR ITS TINY LIFE TO BE OVER BUT ALSO THAT IT HAD NEVER EXISTED. ARE YOU WITH ME SO FAR?

'Well, yes, but –'

GOOD. NOW, *IMAGINE WHAT THEY THINK OF HUMANITY.*

Susan was shocked. She had never heard her grandfather speak in anything other than calm tones. Now there was a cutting edge in his words.

'What are they?' she said.

WE MUST HURRY. THERE IS NOT MUCH TIME.

'I thought you always had time. I mean ... whatever it is you want to stop, you can go back in time and –'

AND MEDDLE?

'You've done it before ...'

THIS TIME IT IS OTHERS WHO ARE DOING IT. AND *THEY* HAVE NO RIGHT.

'What others?'

THEY HAVE NO NAME. CALL THEM THE AUDITORS. THEY RUN THE UNIVERSE. THEY SEE TO IT THAT GRAVITY WORKS AND THE ATOMS SPIN, OR WHATEVER IT IS ATOMS DO. AND THEY HATE LIFE.

'Why?'

IT IS ... IRREGULAR. IT WAS NEVER SUPPOSED TO HAPPEN. THEY LIKE STONES, MOVING IN CURVES. AND THEY HATE HUMANS MOST OF ALL. Death sighed. IN MANY WAYS, THEY LACK A SENSE OF HUMOUR.

'Why the Hog–'

IT IS THE THINGS YOU BELIEVE WHICH MAKE YOU HUMAN. GOOD THINGS AND BAD THINGS, IT'S ALL THE SAME.

The mists parted. Sharp peaks were around them, lit by the glow off the snow.

'These look like the mountains where the Castle of Bones was,' she said.

THEY ARE, said Death. IN A SENSE. HE HAS GONE BACK TO A PLACE HE KNOWS. AN EARLY PLACE ...

Binky cantered low over the snow.

'And what are we looking for?' said Susan.

You will know when you see it.

'Snow? Trees? I mean, could I have a clue? What are we here for?'

I told you. To ensure that the sun comes up.

'Of *course* the sun will come up!'

No.

'There's no magic that'll stop the sun coming up!'

I wish I was as clever as you.

Susan stared down out of sheer annoyance, and saw something below.

Small dark shapes moved across the whiteness, running as if they were in pursuit of something.

'There's . . . some sort of chase . . .' she conceded. 'I can see some sort of animals but I can't see what they're after –'

Then she saw movement in the snow, a blurred, dark shape dodging and skidding and never clear. Binky dropped until his hooves grazed the tops of the pine trees, which bent in his wake. A rumble followed him across the forest, dragging broken branches and a smoke of snow behind it.

Now they were lower she could see the hunters clearly. They were large dogs. Their quarry was indistinct, dodging among snowdrifts, keeping to the cover of snow-laden bushes –

A drift exploded. Something big and long and blue-black rose through the flying snow like a sounding whale.

'It's a pig!'

A boar. They drive it towards the cliff. They're desperate now.

She could hear the panting of the creature. The dogs made no sound at all.

Blood streamed on to the snow from the wounds they had already managed to inflict.

'This . . . boar,' said Susan. '. . . It's . . .'

Yes.

'They want to *kill* the Hogf–'

Not kill. He knows how to die. Oh, yes . . . in this shape, he knows how to die. He's had a lot of experience. No, they want to take away his real life, take away his soul, take away everything. They must not be allowed to bring him down.

'Well, stop them!'

You must. This is a human thing.

The dogs moved oddly. They weren't running but flowing, crossing the snow faster than the mere movement of their legs would suggest.

'They don't look like real dogs . . .'

No.

'What *can* I do?'

Death nodded his head towards the boar. Binky was keeping level with it now, barely a few feet away.

Realization dawned.

'I can't *ride* that!' said Susan.

WHY NOT? YOU HAVE HAD AN EDUCATION.

'Enough to know that pigs don't let people ride them!'

MERE ACCUMULATION OF OBSERVATIONAL EVIDENCE IS NOT PROOF.

Susan glanced ahead. The snowfield had a cut-off look.

YOU MUST, said her grandfather's voice in her head. WHEN HE REACHES THE EDGE THERE HE WILL STAND AT BAY. HE MUST NOT. UNDERSTAND? THESE ARE NOT REAL DOGS. IF THEY CATCH HIM HE WON'T JUST DIE, HE WILL ... NEVER BE ...

Susan leapt. For a moment she floated through the air, dress streaming behind her, arms outstretched ...

Landing on the animal's back was like hitting a very, very firm chair. It stumbled for a moment and then righted itself.

Susan's arms clung to its neck and her face was buried in its sharp bristles. She could feel the heat under her. It was like riding a furnace. And it stank of sweat, and blood, and pig. A lot of pig.

There was a lack of landscape in front of her.

The boar ploughed into the snow on the edge of the drop, almost flinging her off, and turned to face the hounds.

There were a lot of them. Susan was familiar with dogs. They'd had them at home like other houses had rugs. And these weren't that big floppy sort.

She rammed her heels in and grabbed a pig's ear in each hand. It was like holding a pair of hairy shovels.

'Turn left!' she screamed, and hauled.

She put everything into the command. It promised tears before bedtime if disobeyed.

To her amazement the boar grunted, pranced on the lip of the precipice and scrambled away, the hounds floundering as they turned to follow.

This was a plateau. From here it seemed to be all edge, with no way down except the very simple and terminal one.

The dogs were flying at the boar's heels again.

Susan looked around in the grey, lightless air. There had to be somewhere, some way ...

There was.

It was a shoulder of rock, a giant knife-edge connecting this plain to the hills beyond. It was sharp and narrow, a thin line of snow with chilly depths on either side.

It was better than nothing. It was nothing with snow on it.

The boar reached the edge and hesitated. Susan put her head down and dug her heels in again.

Snout down, legs moving like pistons, the beast plunged out on to the ridge. Snow sprayed up as its trotters sought for purchase. It made up for lack of grace by sheer manic effort, legs moving like a tap dancer climbing a moving staircase that was heading down.

'That's right, that's right, that's –'

A trotter slipped. For a moment the boar seemed to stand on two, the others scrabbling at icy rock. Susan flung herself the other way, clinging to the neck, and felt the dragging abyss under her feet.

There was nothing there.

She told herself, *He'll catch me if I fall, he'll catch me if I fall, he'll catch me if I fall . . .*

Powdered ice made her eyes sting. A flailing trotter almost slammed against her head.

An older voice said, *No, he won't. If I fall now I don't deserve to be caught.*

The creature's eye was inches away. And then she knew . . .

. . . Out of the depths of eyes of all but the most unusual of animals comes an echo. Out of the dark eye in front of her, someone looked back . . .

A foot caught the rock and she concentrated her whole being on it, kicking herself upward in one last effort. Pig and woman rocked for a moment and then a trotter caught a footing and the boar plunged forward along the ridge.

Susan risked a look behind.

The dogs still moved oddly. There was a slight jerkiness about their movements, as if they flowed from position to position rather than moved by ordinary muscles.

Not dogs, she thought. Dog shapes.

There was another shock underfoot. Snow flew up. The world tilted. She felt the shape of the boar change when its muscles bunched and sent it soaring as a slab of ice and rock came away and began the long slide into darkness.

Susan was thrown off when the creature landed, and tumbled into deep snow. She flailed around madly, expecting at any minute to begin sliding.

Instead her hand found a snow-encrusted branch. A few feet away the boar lay on its side, steaming and panting.

She pulled herself upright. The spur here had widened out into a hill, with a few frosted trees on it.

The dogs had reached the gap and were milling round, struggling to prevent themselves slipping.

They could easily clear the distance, she could see. Even the boar had managed it with her on its back. She put both hands around the branch and heaved; it came away with a crack, like a broken icicle, and she waved it like a club.

'Come on,' she said. 'Jump! Just you try it! Come *on*!'

One did. The branch caught it as it landed, and then Susan spun and brought the branch around on the upswing, lifted the dazed animal off its feet and out over the edge.

For a moment the shape wavered and then, howling, it dropped out of sight.

She danced a few steps of rage and triumph.

'Yes! Yes! Who wants some? Anyone else?'

The other dogs looked her in the eye, decided that no one did, and that there wasn't. Finally, after one or two nervous attempts, they managed to turn, still sliding, and tried to make it back to the plateau.

A figure barred their way.

It hadn't been there a moment ago but it looked permanent now. It seemed to have been made of snow, three balls of snow piled on one another. It had black dots for eyes. A semi-circle of more dots formed the semblance of a mouth. There was a carrot for the nose.

And, for the arms, two twigs.

At this distance, anyway.

One of them was holding a curved stick.

A raven wearing a damp piece of red paper landed on one arm.

'Bob bob bob?' it suggested. 'Merry Solstice? Tweetie tweet? What are you waiting for? Hogswatch?'

The dogs backed away.

The snow broke off the snowman in chunks, revealing a gaunt figure in a flapping black robe.

Death spat out the carrot.

Ho. Ho. Ho.

The grey bodies smeared and rippled as the hounds sought desperately to change their shape.

YOU COULDN'T RESIST IT? IN THE END? A MISTAKE, I FANCY.

He touched the scythe. There was a click as the blade flashed into life.

IT GETS UNDER YOUR SKIN, LIFE, said Death, stepping forward.

Speaking metaphorically, of course. It's a habit that's hard to give up. One puff of breath is never enough. You'll find you want to take another.

A dog started to slip on the snow and scrabbled desperately to save itself from the long, cold drop.

And, you see, the more you struggle for every moment, the more alive you stay ... which is where I come in, as a matter of fact.

The leading dog managed, for a moment, to become a grey cowled figure before being dragged back into shape.

Fear, too, is an anchor, said Death. All those senses, wide open to every fragment of the world. That beating heart. That rush of blood. Can you not feel it, dragging you back?

Once again the Auditor managed to retain a shape for a few seconds, and managed to say: you cannot do this, there are rules!

Yes. There are rules. But you broke them. How dare you? *How dare you?*

The scythe blade was a thin blue outline in the grey light.

Death raised a thin finger to where his lips might have been, and suddenly looked thoughtful.

And now there remains only one final question, he said.

He raised his hands, and seemed to grow. Light flared in his eye sockets. When he spoke next, avalanches fell in the mountains.

Have you been naughty ... or nice?

Ho. Ho. Ho.

Susan heard the wails die away.

The boar lay in white snow that was now red with blood. She knelt down and tried to lift its head.

It was dead. One eye stared at nothing. The tongue lolled.

Sobs welled up inside her. The tiny part of Susan that watched, the inner baby-sitter, said it was just exhaustion and excitement and the backwash of adrenalin. She couldn't be crying over a dead pig.

The rest of her drummed on its flank with both fists.

'No, you can't! We *saved* you! Dying isn't how it's supposed to go!'

A breeze blew up.

Something stirred in the landscape, something under the snow. The branches on the ancient trees shook gently, dislodging little needles of ice.

The sun rose.

The light streamed over Susan like a silent gale. It was dazzling. She crouched back, raising her forearm to cover her eyes. The great red ball turned frost to fire along the winter branches.

Gold light slammed into the mountain peaks, making every one a blinding, silent volcano. It rolled onward, gushing into the valleys and thundering up the slopes, unstoppable ...

There was a groan.

A man lay in the snow where the boar had been.

He was naked except for an animal skin loincloth. His hair was long and had been woven into a thick plait down his back, so matted with blood and grease that it looked like felt. And he was bleeding everywhere the hounds had caught him.

Susan watched for a moment, and then, thinking with something other than her head, methodically tore some strips from her petticoat to bandage the more unpleasant wounds.

Capability, said the small part of her mind. A rational head in emergencies.

Rational something, anyway.

It's probably some kind of character flaw.

The man was tattooed. Blue whorls and spirals haunted his skin, under the blood.

He opened his eyes and stared at the sky.

'Can you get up?'

His gaze flicked to her. He tried moving and then fell back.

Eventually she managed to pull the man up into a sitting position. He swayed as she put one of his arms across her shoulders and then heaved him to his feet. She did her best to ignore the stink, which had an almost physical force.

Downhill seemed the best option. Even if his brain wasn't working yet, his feet seemed to get the idea.

They lurched down through the freezing woods, the snow glowing orange in the risen sun. Cold blue gloom lurked in hollows like little cups of winter.

Beside her, the tattooed man made a gurgling sound. He slipped out of her grasp and landed on his knees in the snow, clutching at his throat and choking. His breath sounded like a saw.

'What *now*? What's the matter? What's the matter?'

He rolled his eyes at her and pawed at his throat again.

'Something stuck?' She slapped him as hard as she could on the back, but now he was on his hands and knees, fighting for breath.

She put her hands under his shoulders and pulled him upright, and put her arms around his waist. Oh, gods, how was it supposed to go, she'd gone to *classes* about it, now, didn't you have to bunch up one fist and then put the other hand around it and then pull *up* and *in* like *this* –

The man coughed and something bounced off a tree and landed in the snow.

She knelt down to have a look.

It was a small black bean.

A bird trilled, high on a branch. She looked up. A wren bobbed at her and fluttered to another twig.

When she looked back, the man was different. He had clothes now, heavy furs, with a fur hood and fur boots. He was supporting himself on a stone-tipped spear, and looked a lot stronger.

Something hurried through the wood, barely visible except by its shadow. For a moment she glimpsed a white hare before it sprang away on a new path.

She looked back. Now the furs had gone and the man looked older, although he had the same eyes. He was wearing thick white robes, and looked very much like a priest.

When a bird called again she didn't look away. And she realized that she'd been mistaken in thinking that the man changed like the turning of pages. All the images were there at once, and many others too. What you saw depended on how you looked.

Yes. It's a good job I'm cool and totally used to this sort of thing, she thought. Otherwise I'd be rather worried . . .

Now they were at the edge of the forest.

A little way off, four huge boars stood and steamed, in front of a sledge that looked as if it had been put together out of crudely trimmed trees. There were faces in the blackened wood, possibly carved by stone, possibly carved by rain and wind.

The Hogfather climbed aboard and sat down. He'd put on weight in the last few yards and now it was almost impossible to see anything other than the huge, red-robed man, ice crystals settling here and there on the cloth. Only in the occasional sparkle of frost was there a hint of hair or tusk.

He shifted on the seat and then reached down to extricate a false beard, which he held up questioningly.

SORRY, said a voice behind Susan. THAT WAS MINE.

The Hogfather nodded at Death, as one craftsman to another, and then at Susan. She wasn't sure if she was being thanked – it was more a gesture of recognition, of acknowledgement that something that needed doing had indeed been done. But it wasn't thanks.

Then he shook the reins and clicked his teeth and the sledge slid away.

They watched it go.

'I remember hearing,' said Susan distantly, 'that the idea of the Hogfather wearing a red and white outfit was invented quite recently.'

NO. IT WAS REMEMBERED.

Now the Hogfather was a red dot on the other side of the valley.

'Well, that about wraps it up for *this* dress,' said Susan. 'I'd just like to ask, just out of academic interest ... you were sure I was going to survive, were you?'

I WAS QUITE CONFIDENT.

'Oh, *good*.'

I WILL GIVE YOU A LIFT BACK, said Death, after a while.

'Thank you. Now ... tell me ...'

WHAT WOULD HAVE HAPPENED IF YOU HADN'T SAVED HIM?

'Yes! The sun would have risen just the same, yes?'

NO.

'Oh, come *on*. You can't expect me to believe *that*. It's an astronomical *fact*.'

THE SUN WOULD NOT HAVE RISEN.

She turned on him.

'It's been a long night, Grandfather! I'm tired and I need a bath! I don't need silliness!'

THE SUN WOULD NOT HAVE RISEN.

'Really? Then what would have happened, pray?'

A MERE BALL OF FLAMING GAS WOULD HAVE ILLUMINATED THE WORLD.

They walked in silence for a moment.

'Ah,' said Susan dully. 'Trickery with words. I would have thought you'd have been more literal-minded than that.'

I AM NOTHING IF NOT LITERAL-MINDED. TRICKERY WITH WORDS IS WHERE HUMANS LIVE.

'All right,' said Susan. 'I'm not stupid. You're saying humans need ... *fantasies* to make life bearable.'

REALLY? AS IF IT WAS SOME KIND OF PINK PILL? NO. HUMANS NEED FANTASY TO BE HUMAN. TO BE THE PLACE WHERE THE FALLING ANGEL MEETS THE RISING APE.

'Tooth fairies? Hogfathers? Little –'

YES. AS PRACTICE. YOU HAVE TO START OUT LEARNING TO BELIEVE THE LITTLE LIES.

'So we can believe the big ones?'

YES. JUSTICE. MERCY. DUTY. THAT SORT OF THING.

'They're not the same at all!'

YOU THINK SO? THEN TAKE THE UNIVERSE AND GRIND IT DOWN TO THE FINEST POWDER AND SIEVE IT THROUGH THE FINEST SIEVE AND THEN *SHOW*

ME ONE ATOM OF JUSTICE, ONE MOLECULE OF MERCY. AND YET – Death waved a hand. AND YET YOU ACT AS IF THERE IS SOME IDEAL ORDER IN THE WORLD, AS IF THERE IS SOME ... SOME *RIGHTNESS* IN THE UNIVERSE BY WHICH IT MAY BE JUDGED.

'Yes, but people have *got* to believe that, or what's the *point* –'
MY POINT EXACTLY.

She tried to assemble her thoughts.

THERE IS A PLACE WHERE TWO GALAXIES HAVE BEEN COLLIDING FOR A MILLION YEARS, said Death, apropos of nothing. DON'T TRY TO TELL *ME* THAT'S RIGHT.

'Yes, but people don't think about that,' said Susan. Somewhere there was a bed ...

CORRECT. STARS EXPLODE, WORLDS COLLIDE, THERE'S HARDLY ANYWHERE IN THE UNIVERSE WHERE HUMANS CAN LIVE WITHOUT BEING FROZEN OR FRIED, AND YET YOU BELIEVE THAT A ... A BED IS A NORMAL THING. IT IS THE MOST AMAZING TALENT.

'Talent?'

OH, YES. A VERY SPECIAL KIND OF STUPIDITY. YOU THINK THE WHOLE UNIVERSE IS INSIDE YOUR HEADS.

'You make us sound mad,' said Susan. A nice warm bed ...

NO. YOU NEED TO BELIEVE IN THINGS THAT AREN'T TRUE. HOW ELSE CAN THEY *BECOME*? said Death, helping her up on to Binky.

'These mountains,' said Susan, as the horse rose. 'Are they *real* mountains, or some sort of shadows?'

YES.

Susan knew that was all she was going to get.

'Er ... I lost the sword. It's somewhere in the Tooth Fairy's country.'

Death shrugged. I CAN MAKE ANOTHER.

'Can you?'

OH, YES. IT WILL GIVE ME SOMETHING TO DO. DON'T WORRY ABOUT IT.

The Senior Wrangler hummed cheerfully to himself as he ran a comb through his beard for the second time and liberally sprinkled it with what would turn out to be a preparation of weasel extract for demon removal rather than, as he had assumed, a pleasant masculine scent.* Then he stepped out into his study.

'Sorry for the delay, but –' he began.

There was no one there. Only, very far off, the sound of someone

---

* It was, in fact, a pleasant masculine scent. But only to female weasels.

blowing their nose mingling with the *glingleglingleglingle* of fading magic.

The light was already gilding the top of the Tower of Art when Binky trotted to a standstill on the air beside the nursery balcony. Susan climbed down on to the fresh snow and stood uncertainly for a moment. When someone has gone out of their way to drop you home it's only courteous to ask them in. On the other hand . . .

WOULD YOU LIKE TO VISIT FOR HOGSWATCH DINNER? said Death. He sounded hopeful. ALBERT IS FRYING A PUDDING.

'*Frying* a pudding?'

ALBERT UNDERSTANDS FRYING. AND I BELIEVE HE'S MAKING JAM. HE CERTAINLY KEPT TALKING ABOUT IT.

'I . . . er . . . they're really expecting me here,' said Susan. 'The Gaiters do a lot of entertaining. His business friends. Probably the whole day will be . . . I'll more or less have to look after the children . . .'

SOMEONE SHOULD.

'Er . . . would you like a drink before you go?' said Susan, giving in.

A CUP OF COCOA WOULD BE APPROPRIATE IN THE CIRCUMSTANCES.

'Right. There's biscuits in the tin on the mantelpiece.'

Susan headed with relief into the tiny kitchen.

Death sat down in the creaking wicker chair, buried his feet in the rug and looked around with interest. He heard the clatter of cups, and then a sound like indrawn breath, and then silence.

Death helped himself to a biscuit from the tin. There were two full stockings hanging from the mantelpiece. He prodded them with professional satisfaction, and then sat down again and observed the nursery wallpaper. It seemed to be pictures of rabbits in waistcoats, among other fauna. He was not surprised. Death occasionally turned up in person even for rabbits, simply to see that the whole process was working properly. He'd never seen one wearing a waistcoat. He wouldn't have expected waistcoats. At least, he wouldn't have expected waistcoats if he hadn't had some experience of the way humans portrayed the universe. As it was, it was only a blessing they hadn't been given gold watches and top hats as well.

Humans liked dancing pigs, too. And lambs in hats. As far as Death was aware, the sole reason for any human association with pigs and lambs was as a prelude to chops and sausages. Quite why they should dress up for children's wallpaper as well was a mystery. Hello, little folk, this is what you're going to eat . . . He felt that if only he could find the key to it, he'd know a lot more about human beings.

His gaze travelled to the door. Susan's governess coat and hat were hanging on it. The coat was grey, and so was the hat. Grey and round and dull. Death didn't know many things about the human psyche, but he did know protective coloration when he saw it.

Dullness. Only humans could have invented it. What imaginations they had.

The door opened.

To his horror, Death saw a small child of unidentifiable sex come out of the bedroom, amble sleepily across the floor and unhook the stockings from the mantelpiece. It was halfway back before it noticed him and then it simply stopped and regarded him thoughtfully.

He knew that young children could see him because they hadn't yet developed that convenient and selective blindness that comes with the intimation of personal mortality. He felt a little embarrassed.

'Susan's gotta poker, you know,' it said, as if anxious to be helpful.

WELL, WELL. INDEED. MY GOODNESS ME.

'I fort – *thought* all of you knew that now. Larst – *last* week she picked a bogey up by its nose.'

Death tried to imagine this. He felt sure he'd heard the sentence wrong, but it didn't sound a whole lot better however he rearranged the words.

'I'll give Gawain his stocking and then I'll come an' watch,' said the child. It padded out.

ER ... SUSAN? Death said, calling in reinforcements.

Susan backed out of the kitchen, a black kettle in her hand.

There was a figure behind her. In the half-light the sword gleamed blue along its blade. Its glitter reflected off one glass eye.

'Well, *well*,' said Teatime, quietly, glancing at Death. 'Now this *is* unexpected. A family affair?'

The sword hummed back and forth.

'I wonder,' said Teatime, 'is it *possible* to kill Death? This must be a very special sword and it certainly works *here* . . .' He raised a hand to his mouth for a moment and gave a little chuckle. 'And of course it might well not be regarded as murder. Possibly it is a civic act. It would be, as they say, The Big One. Stand up, sir. You may have some personal knowledge about your vulnerability but I'm pretty certain that Susan here would quite *definitely* die, so I'd rather you didn't try any last-minute stuff.'

I AM LAST-MINUTE STUFF, said Death, standing up.

Teatime circled around carefully, the sword's tip making little curves in the air.

From the next room came the sound of someone trying to blow a whistle quietly.

Susan glanced at her grandfather.

'I don't remember them asking for anything that made a noise,' she said.

OH, THERE HAS TO BE SOMETHING IN THE STOCKING THAT MAKES A NOISE, said Death. OTHERWISE WHAT IS 4.30 AM *FOR*?

'There are children?' said Teatime. 'Oh yes, of course. Call them.'

'Certainly not!'

'It will be instructive,' said Teatime. 'Educational. And when your adversary is Death, you cannot help but be the good guy.'

He pointed the sword at Susan.

'I *said* call them.'

Susan glanced hopefully at her grandfather. He nodded. For a moment she thought she saw the glow in one eye socket flicker off and on, Death's equivalent of a wink. *He's got a plan. He can stop time. He can do anything. He's got a plan.*

'Gawain? Twyla?'

The muffled noises stopped in the next room. There was a padding of feet and two solemn faces appeared round the door.

'Ah, come in, come *in*, curly-haired tots,' said Teatime genially.

Gawain gave him a steely stare.

His next mistake, thought Susan. If he'd called them little bastards he'd have them bang on his side. But they know when you're sending them up.

'I've caught this bogeyman,' said Teatime. 'What shall we do with him, eh?'

The two faces turned to Death. Twyla put her thumb in her mouth.

'It's only a skeleton,' said Gawain critically.

Susan opened her mouth, and the sword swung towards her. She shut it again.

'Yes, a nasty, creepy, horrible skeleton,' said Teatime. 'Scary, eh?'

There was a very faint 'pop' as Twyla took her thumb out of her mouth.

'He's eating a bittit,' she said.

'Biscuit,' Susan corrected automatically. She started to swing the kettle in an absent-minded way.

'A creepy bony man in a black robe!' said Teatime, aware that things weren't going in quite the right direction.

He spun round to face Susan. 'You're fidgeting with that kettle,' he said. 'So I expect you're thinking of doing something creative. Put it down, please. Slowly.'

Susan knelt down gently and put the kettle on the hearth.

'Huh, that's not very creepy, it's just bones,' said Gawain dismissively. 'And anyway Willie the groom down at the stables has promised me a real horse skull. And anyway I'm going to make a hat out of it like General Tacticus had when he wanted to frighten people. And anyway it's just standing there. It's not even making woo-woo noises. And anyway *you're* creepy. Your eye's weird.'

'Really? Then let's see how creepy I can be,' said Teatime. Blue fire crackled along the sword as he raised it.

Susan closed her hand over the poker.

Teatime saw her start to turn. He stepped behind Death, sword raised ...

Susan threw the poker overarm. It made a ripping noise as it shot through the air, and trailed sparks.

It hit Death's robe and vanished.

He blinked.

Teatime smiled at Susan.

He turned and peered dreamily at the sword in his hand.

It fell out of his fingers.

Death turned and caught it by the handle as it tumbled, and turned its fall into an upward curve.

Teatime looked down at the poker in his chest as he folded up.

'Oh, no,' he said. 'It couldn't have gone through you. There are so many ribs and things!'

There was another 'pop' as Twyla extracted her thumb and said, 'It only kills monsters.'

'Stop time *now*,' commanded Susan.

Death snapped his fingers. The room took on the greyish purple of stationary time. The clock paused its ticking.

'You *winked* at me! I thought you had a *plan*!'

INDEED. OH, YES. I PLANNED TO SEE WHAT YOU WOULD DO.

'Just *that*?'

YOU ARE VERY RESOURCEFUL. AND OF COURSE YOU HAVE HAD AN EDUCATION.

'What?'

I did add the sparkly stars and the noise, though. I thought they would be appropriate.

'And if I *hadn't* done anything?'

I daresay I would have thought of something. At the last minute.

'That *was* the last minute!'

There is always time for another last minute.

'The children had to watch that!'

Educational. The world will teach them about monsters soon enough. Let them remember there's always the poker.

'But they saw he's human –'

I think they had a very good idea of what he was.

Death prodded the fallen Teatime with his foot.

Stop playing dead, Mister Teh-ah-tim-eh.

The ghost of the Assassin sprang up like a jack-in-the-box, all slightly crazed smiles.

'You got it right!'

Of course.

Teatime began to fade.

I'll take the body, said Death. That will prevent inconvenient questions.

'What did he do it all for?' said Susan. 'I mean, why? Money? Power?'

Some people will do anything for the sheer fascination of doing it, said Death. Or for fame. Or because they shouldn't.

Death picked up the corpse and slung it over his shoulder. There was a sound of something bouncing on the hearth. He turned, and hesitated.

Er ... you did *know* the poker would go through me?

Susan realized she was shaking.

'Of course. In this room it's pretty powerful.'

You were never in any doubt?

Susan hesitated, and then smiled.

'I was quite confident,' she said.

Ah. Her grandfather stared at her for a moment and she thought she detected just the tiniest flicker of uncertainty. Of course. Of course. Tell me, are you likely to take up teaching on a larger scale?

'I hadn't planned to.'

Death turned towards the balcony, and then seemed to remember something else. He fumbled inside his robe.

I have made this for you.

She reached out and took a square of damp cardboard. Water dripped off the bottom. Somewhere in the middle, a few brown feathers seemed to have been glued on.

'Thank you. Er . . . what is it?'

ALBERT SAID THERE OUGHT TO BE SNOW ON IT, BUT IT APPEARS TO HAVE MELTED, said Death. IT IS, OF COURSE, A HOGSWATCH CARD.

'Oh . . .'

THERE SHOULD HAVE BEEN A ROBIN ON IT AS WELL, BUT I HAD CONSIDERABLE DIFFICULTY IN GETTING IT TO STAY ON.

'Ah . . .'

IT WAS NOT AT ALL CO-OPERATIVE.

'Really . . .?'

IT DID NOT SEEM TO GET INTO THE HOGSWATCH SPIRIT AT ALL.

'Oh. Er. Good. Granddad?'

YES?

'Why? I mean, why did you do all this?'

He stood quite still for a moment, as if he was trying out sentences in his mind.

I THINK IT'S SOMETHING TO DO WITH HARVESTS, he said at last. YES. THAT'S RIGHT. AND BECAUSE HUMANS ARE SO INTERESTING THAT THEY HAVE EVEN INVENTED DULLNESS. QUITE ASTONISHING.

'Oh.'

WELL, THEN . . . HAPPY HOGSWATCH.

'Yes. Happy Hogswatch.'

Death paused again, at the window.

AND GOODNIGHT, CHILDREN . . . EVERYWHERE.

The raven fluttered down on to a log covered in snow. Its prosthetic red breast had been torn and fluttered uselessly behind it.

'Not so much as a lift home,' it muttered. 'Look at this, willya? Snow and frozen wastes, everywhere. I couldn't fly another damn inch. I could starve to death here, you know? Hah! People're going on about recycling the whole time, but you just try a bit of practical ecology and they just . . . don't . . . want . . . to . . . know. Hah! I bet a *robin*'d have a lift home. Oh *yes*.'

SQUEAK, said the Death of Rats sympathetically, and sniffed.

The raven watched the small hooded figure scrabble at the snow.

'So I'll just freeze to death here, shall I?' it said gloomily. 'A pathetic bundle of feathers with my little feet curled up with the cold. It's not even as if I'm gonna make anyone a good meal, and let me tell you it's a disgrace to die thin in my spec–'

It became aware that under the snow was a rather grubbier whiteness. Further scraping by the rat exposed something that could very possibly have been an ear.

The raven stared. 'It's a *sheep!*' it said.

The Death of Rats nodded.

'A *whole* sheep!'*

Squeak.

'Oh, wow!' said the raven, hopping forward with its eyes spinning. 'Hey, it's barely cool!'

The Death of Rats patted it happily on a wing.

Squeak-eek. Eek-squeak ...

'Why, thanks. And the same to you ...'

Far, far away and a long, long time ago, a shop door opened. The little toymaker bustled in from the workshop in the rear, and then stopped, with amazing foresight, dead.

You have a big wooden rocking horse in the window, said the new customer.

'Ah, yes, yes, yes.' The shopkeeper fiddled nervously with his square-rimmed spectacles. He hadn't heard the bell, and this was worrying him. 'But I'm afraid that's just for show, that is a special order for Lord –'

No. I will buy it.

'No, because, you see –'

There are other toys?

'Yes, indeed, but –'

Then I will take the horse. How much would this Lordship have paid you?

'Er, we'd agreed twelve dollars but –'

I will give you fifty, said the customer.

The little shopkeeper stopped in mid-remonstrate and started up in mid-greed. There *were* other toys, he told himself quickly. And this customer, he thought with considerable prescience, looked like someone who did not take no for an answer and seldom even bothered to ask the question. Lord Selachii would be angry, but Lord Selachii wasn't here. The stranger, on the other hand, was here. Incredibly here.

'Er ... well, in the circumstances ... er ... shall I wrap it up for you?'

---

* Which had died in its sleep. Of natural causes. At a great age. After a long and happy life, insofar as a sheep can be happy. And would probably be quite pleased to know that it could help somebody as it passed away ...

No. I will take it as it is. Thank you. I will leave via the back way, if it's all the same to you.

'Er... how did you get *in*?' said the shopkeeper, pulling the horse out of the window.

Through the wall. So much more convenient than chimneys, don't you think?

The apparition dropped a small clinking bag on the counter and lifted the horse easily. The shopkeeper wasn't in a position to hold on to anything. Even yesterday's dinner was threatening to leave him.

The figure looked at the other shelves.

You make good toys.

'Er... thank you.'

Incidentally, said the customer, as he left, there is a small boy out there with his nose frozen to the window. Some warm water should do the trick.

Death walked out to where Binky was waiting in the snow and tied the toy horse behind the saddle.

Albert will be very pleased. I can't wait to see his face. Ho. Ho. Ho.

As the light of Hogswatch slid down the towers of Unseen University, the Librarian slipped into the Great Hall with some sheet music clenched firmly in his feet.

As the light of Hogswatch lit the towers of Unseen University, the Archchancellor sat down with a sigh in his study and pulled off his boots.

It had been a damn long night, no doubt about it. Lots of strange things. First time he'd ever seen the Senior Wrangler burst into tears, for one thing.

Ridcully glanced at the door to the new bathroom. Well, he'd sorted out the teething troubles, and a nice warm shower would *be very refreshing. And then he could go along to the organ recital all nice and clean.*

He removed his hat, and someone fell out of it with a tinkling sound. A small gnome rolled across the floor.

'Oh, another one. I thought we'd got rid of you fellows,' said Ridcully. 'And what are you?'

The gnome looked at him nervously.

'Er... you know whenever there was another magical appearance you heard the sound of, er, bells?' it said. Its expression suggested it was owning up to something it just knew was going to get it a smack.

'Yes?'

The gnome held up some rather small handbells and waved them nervously. They went **glingleglingleglingle**, *in a very sad way.*

'Good, eh? That was me. I'm the Glingleglingleglingle Fairy.'

'Get out.'

'I also do sparkly fairy dust effects that go twing too, if you like ...'

'Go away!'

'How about "The Bells of St Ungulant's"?' said the gnome desperately. 'Very seasonal. Very nice. Why not join in? It goes: "The bells [clong] of St [clang] ..."'

Ridcully scored a direct hit with the rubber duck, and the gnome escaped through the bath overflow. Cursing and spontaneous handbell ringing echoed away down the pipes.

In perfect peace at last, the Archchancellor pulled off his robe.

The organ's storage tanks were wheezing at the rivets by the time the Librarian had finished pumping. Satisfied, he knuckled his way up to the seat and paused to survey, with great satisfaction, the keyboards in front of him.

Bloody Stupid Johnson's approach to music was similar to his approach in every field that was caressed by his genius in the same way that a potato field is touched by a late frost. Make it loud, he said. Make it wide. Make it all-embracing. And thus the Great Organ of Unseen University was the only one in the world where you could play an entire symphony scored for thunderstorm and squashed toad noises.

Warm water cascaded off Mustrum Ridcully's pointy bathing cap.

Mr Johnson had, surely not on purpose, designed a perfect bathroom – at least, perfect for singing in. Echoes and resonating pipeways smoothed out all those little imperfections and gave even the weediest singer a rolling, dark brown voice.

And so Ridcully sang.

'– as I walked out one dadadadada for to something or other and to take the dadada, I did espy a fair pretty may-ay-den I think it was, and I –'

The organ pipes hummed with pent-up energy. The Librarian cracked his knuckles. This took some time. Then he pulled the pressure release valve.

The hum became an urgent thrumming.

Very carefully, he let in the clutch.

Ridcully stopped singing as the tones of the organ came through the wall.

Bathtime music, eh? he thought. Just the job.

It was a shame it was muffled by all the bathroom fixtures, though.

It was at this point he espied a small lever marked 'Musical pipes'.

Ridcully, never being a man to wonder what any kind of switch did when it was so much easier and quicker to find out by pulling it, did so. But instead of the music he was expecting he was rewarded simply with several large panels sliding silently aside, revealing row upon row of brass nozzles.

The Librarian was lost now, dreaming on the wings of music. His hands and feet danced over the keyboards, picking their way towards the crescendo which ended the first movement of Bubbla's Catastrophe Suite.

One foot kicked the 'Afterburner' lever and the other spun the valve of the nitrous oxide cylinder.

Ridcully tapped the nozzles.

Nothing happened. He looked at the controls again, and realized that he'd never pulled the little brass lever marked 'Organ Interlock'.

He did so. This did not cause a torrent of pleasant bathtime accompaniment, however. There was merely a thud and a distant gurgling, which grew in volume.

He gave up, and went back to soaping his chest.

'*– running of the deer, the playing of . . . huh? What –*'

Later that day he had the bathroom nailed up again and a notice placed on the door, on which was written:

'Not to be used in any circumstances. This is IMPORTANT.'

However, when Modo nailed the door up he didn't hammer the nails in all the way but left just a bit sticking up so that his pliers would grip later on, when he was told to remove them. He never presumed and he never complained, he just had a good working knowledge of the wizardly mind.

They never did find the soap.

*

Ponder and his fellow students watched Hex carefully.

'It can't just, you know, *stop*,' said Adrian 'Mad Drongo' Turnipseed.

'The ants are just standing still,' said Ponder. He sighed. 'All right, put the wretched thing back.'

Adrian carefully replaced the small fluffy teddy bear above Hex's keyboard. Things immediately began to whirr. The ants started to trot again. The mouse squeaked.

They'd tried this three times.

Ponder looked again at the single sentence Hex had written.

+++ Mine! Waaaah! +++

'I don't actually think,' he said, gloomily, 'that I want to tell the Archchancellor that this machine stops working if we take its fluffy teddy bear away. I just don't think I want to live in that kind of world.'

'Er,' said Mad Drongo, 'you could always, you know, sort of say it needs to work with the FTB enabled . . .?'

'You think that's better?' said Ponder, reluctantly. It wasn't as if it was even a very realistic interpretation of a bear.

'You mean, better than "fluffy teddy bear"?'

Ponder nodded. 'It's better,' he said.

Of all the presents *he* got from the Hogfather, Gawain told Susan, the best of all was the marble.

And she'd said, what marble?

And he'd said, the glass marble I found in the fireplace. It wins all the games. It seems to move in a different way.

The beggars walked their erratic and occasionally backward walk along the city streets, while fresh morning snow began to fall.

Occasionally one of them belched happily. They all wore paper hats, except for Foul Ole Ron, who'd eaten his.

A tin can was passed from hand to hand. It contained a mixture of fine wines and spirits and something in a can that Arnold Sideways had stolen from behind a paint factory in Phedre Road.

'The goose was good,' said the Duck Man, picking his teeth.

'I'm surprised you et it, what with that duck on your head,' said Coffin Henry, picking his nose.

'What duck?' said the Duck Man.

'What were that greasy stuff?' said Arnold Sideways.

'That, my dear fellow, was *pâté de foie gras*. All the way from Genua, I'll wager. And very good, too.'

'Dun'arf make you fart, don't it?'

'Ah, the world of haute cuisine,' said the Duck Man happily.

They reached, by fits and starts, the back door of their favourite restaurant. The Duck Man looked at it dreamily, eyes filmy with recollection.

'I used to dine here almost every night,' he said.

'Why'd you stop?' said Coffin Henry.

'I . . . I don't really know,' said the Duck Man. 'It's . . . rather a blur, I'm afraid. Back in the days when I . . . think I was someone else. But still,' he said, patting Arnold's head, 'as they say, "Better a meal of old boots where friendship is, than a stalled ox and hatred therewith." Forward, please, Ron.'

They positioned Foul Ole Ron in front of the back door and then knocked on it. When a waiter opened it Foul Ole Ron grinned at him, exposing what remained of his teeth and his famous halitosis, which was still all there.

'Millennium hand and shrimp!' he said, touching his forelock.

'"Compliments of the season",' the Duck Man translated.

The man went to shut the door but Arnold Sideways was ready for him and had wedged his boot in the crack.*

'We thought you might like us to come round at lunchtime and sing a merry Hogswatch glee for your customers,' said the Duck Man. Beside him, Coffin Henry began one of his volcanic bouts of coughing, which even *sounded* green. 'No charge, of course.'

'It being Hogswatch,' said Arnold.

The beggars, despite being too disreputable even to belong to the Beggars' Guild, lived quite well by their own low standards. This was generally by careful application of the Certainty Principle. People would give them all sorts of things if they were certain to go away.

A few minutes later they wandered off again, pushing a happy Arnold who was surrounded by hastily wrapped packages.

'People can be so kind,' said the Duck Man.

'Millennium hand and shrimp.'

Arnold started to investigate the charitable donations as they manoeuvred his trolley through the slush and drifts.

'Tastes . . . sort of familiar,' he said.

'Familiar like what?'

'Like mud and old boots.'

'Garn! That's *posh* grub, that is.'

'Yeah, yeah . . .' Arnold chewed for a while. 'You don't think we've become posh all of a sudden?'

'Dunno. You posh, Ron?'

'Buggrit.'

---

* Arnold had no legs but, since there were many occasions when a boot was handy on the streets, Coffin Henry had affixed one to the end of a pole for him. He was deadly with it, and any muggers hard-pressed enough to try to rob the beggars often found themselves kicked on the top of the head by a man three feet high.

'Yep. Sounds posh to me.'
The snow began to settle gently on the River Ankh.
'Still . . . Happy New Year, Arnold.'
'Happy New Year, Duck Man. And your duck.'
'What duck?'
'Happy New Year, Henry.'
'Happy New Year, Ron.'
'Buggrem!'
'And god bless us, every one,' said Arnold Sideways.
The curtain of snow hid them from view.
'Which god?'
'Dunno. What've you got?'
'Duck Man?'
'Yes, Henry?'
'You know that stalled ox you mentioned?'
'Yes, Henry?'
'How come it'd stalled? Run out of grass, or something?'
'Ah . . . it was more a figure of speech, Henry.'
'Not an ox?'
'Not *exactly*. What I *meant* was –'
And then there was only the snow.
After a while, it began to melt in the sun.